DANGEROUS WAYS
Selected Mysteries

DANGEROUS WAYS

Selected Mysteries

JACK VANCE

*Edited by Terry Dowling
and Jonathan Strahan*

Subterranean Press 2011

First Edition

ISBN
978-1-59606-359-4

Subterranean Press
PO Box 190106
Burton, MI 48519

www.subterraneanpress.com

To the grandchildren,
Alison, Glen and Jack

Table of Contents

INTRODUCTION

"There is mystery here; I confess that I am tantalized."
—Ifness, *The Asutra*

JACK Vance has always been a mystery writer at heart. Even while ranging the starways and arcane dimensions under the name we best know him by, taking us to alien worlds, strange climes and fabulous yonders, this acclaimed F&SF Grand Master and world-builder par excellence also used his given name of John Holbrook Vance (plus a few selected aliases) to turn out novels of intrigue and suspense set on *this* world, dealing with people almost like you and me.

Whether featuring exotic locales such as Morocco and the Marquesas, forgotten corners of his beloved California, or even more modest, mundane settings like downtown San Francisco and Oakland, these beguiling, often hard-hitting tales explore the same depths of greed, obsession and depravity that mark his highly praised Demon Princes novels, feature the same resourceful, some-times remote, often fraught protagonists as travel Tschai, Durdane or Cadwal, show the same canny insights into the workings of

9

human nature, the familiar trademark wit, the same fabulous gift for language and creating a living, breathing sense of place.

More to the point, the stories being told and the mechanics of narrative being employed, despite the genre trappings, aren't all that different. The private investigator relentlessly tracking down the members of the crime syndicate who kidnapped and murdered his family and friends just happens to be SF adventurer Kirth Gersen; the reclusive crime bosses are the Demon Princes. The young police officer investigating first a missing person case, then a murder, finally uncovering a large-scale immigration rort in a vast nature preserve is none other than Glawen Clattuc; the preserve is the Conservancy on the planet Cadwal. So too the interstellar effectuators Miro Hetzel and Magnus Ridolph may be closer to the Sherlock Holmes style of sleuth than the Sam Spade or Travis McGee variety, but the sort of game that's afoot is inevitably the same: uncovering inheritance scams, solving murders, putting an end to dark and nefarious schemes involving trade, religion, even social custom and the exploitation of native peoples.

Vance's many faithful readers will be interested to learn that these days (just as it has been for the past twenty years) Jack listens almost exclusively to novels by his favorite mystery writers, using his audio-book player to pursue his great enjoyment of the form. At the top of his list are such notables as John D. MacDonald and Arthur Upfield (author of the Bony novels set evocatively in Outback Australia; in Jack's words "a great writer" and, incidentally, the same author and series that helped lead Tony Hillerman to create his celebrated Joe Leaphorn and Jim Chee tales). There's Patricia Wentworth, Elizabeth George, Marion Chesney writing as M.C. Beaton, Lawrence Sanders ("one of the best writers there is") and Philip R. Craig ("a guy I really like").

And often it's the sense of place Jack loves as much as the featured mystery—Beaton's use of the English countryside and the Scottish highlands, MacDonald's and Sanders' Florida, Craig's vacation getaway of Martha's Vineyard—reminding us that in his long career Jack too has spent much of his time serving up intrigue and mystery in exotic locales, searching for elusive villains, uncovering hidden identities and amazing secrets in one remote location after another, often at the end of fascinating planetary and inter-planetary journeys.

But at a practical level, as Giuseppe Pontiggia points out in his essay on Borges, "Nothing is less mysterious than the solution of a mystery. Thus the strong point of any thriller is also its biggest weakness." Or, as Andrew Rilstone put it so aptly in a recent issue of *SciFi Now*, giving the truism a far more positive spin, "A good mystery is more fun than the best solution," reminding us that there has to be more on hand than just a mystery and a solution, that other things need to be in play. As MacDonald, Upfield, Beaton, Hillerman et al repeatedly demonstrate, we need the *right* setting, the *right* people, the *right* mood and flavor.

As ever, Vance is adept at delivering such things. Our present volume serves up three of the master's richest, most diverse offerings from the fertile early to middle period of his long and productive career: the Edgar Award-winning *The Man in the Cage*, the unforgettable hider-in-the-house thriller *Bad Ronald*, and the exotic South Seas murderfest *The Deadly Isles*, all originally published under the byline of John Holbrook Vance.

The Man in the Cage (working title: *No-One Knows Where He Went*) appeared from Random House in 1960 and won the Edgar for Best First Novel from the Mystery Writers of America the following year. In terms of setting, it draws on Jack's experiences while traveling with his wife Norma in Morocco in 1957, a part of the world they both loved. Jack and Norma actually stayed at the hotel in Erfoud visited by Jack's protagonist Darrell Hutson, a lavish, nearly abandoned resort built by French railway developers to accommodate the tourists who never materialised. The resulting story was filmed for television as Episode 18 of Boris Karloff's *Thriller* series, screened in the US on 17 January 1961.

Bad Ronald was first published in 1973 by Ballantine Books and made into an acceptable if rather pedestrian television movie the following year. It belongs to an ever-growing thriller sub-genre of what can usefully be called 'hider in the house' mysteries, a canon that includes the classic Arthur Conan Doyle Sherlock Holmes adventure *The Norwood Builder*, and even more Gothic fare like Charlotte Bronte's *Jane Eyre*. It's a theme visited, often with mixed results, in films such as the 1989 Gary Busey thriller of that name, *Hider in the House*, in *The People Under the Stairs* and *Fear No Evil*.

Jack is very fond of *Bad Ronald* and, in delivering his simple yet effective tale of the young "hider" of the title, took great pains to make us feel compassion for Ronald's plight. Moreover Ronald Wilby is a familiar character type in the Vance oeuvre, the overly sensitive, obsessive, self-absorbed loner who feels both blessed by destiny and yet bafflingly misunderstood, thwarted and under-appreciated. We find him in Howard Hardoah (aka Howard Alan Treesong) in *The Book of Dreams*, even the slightest hint of him in Chickweed in *The View from Chickweed's Window* (tellingly, all three characters possess a "book of dreams"), detect traces in the secretive Paul Gunther in *The House on Lily Street*, catch a definite touch of him in Viole Falushe in *The Palace of Love*, can trace echoes in Ramus Ymph in *Maske: Thaery* and even in the gifted surgeon Faurence Dacre in "Freitzke's Turn." And just as a certain poignancy attends the fates of nearly all these characters, so it elevates Ronald's sorry predicament into something memorable.

The Deadly Isles was published by Bobbs-Merrill in 1969 and reflects the author's lifelong love of sea-travel, drawing on his experiences both in the Merchant Marine and from subsequent post-War travels with his family. Jack long held the dream of sailing the Pacific in a vessel of his own and for many years captained a 45-foot ketch, the *Hinano*. While the voyage itself never eventuated, the romance and intrigue of such an adventure is vividly captured in Luke Royce's ocean crossings to French Tahiti and the Marquesas.

Interestingly, in all three novels on offer here the explanations for the mysteries are largely known to us—Noel Hutson's fate, Ronald Wilby's presence in the house at 572 Orchard Street, the identity of Ben Easley and the intention (if not the underlying details) behind his deadly actions against the Royce family. These novels are more *why*- and *how*-dunnits than whodunnits, novels of suspense rather than mystery per se, but it's the combination of those others things mentioned: the setting, the people, the right mood and flavor that makes them into tales that deliver the magic and are worth prizing.

INTRODUCTION

And just as Jack spends countless hours with his audio book enjoying this favorite form of storytelling, *Dangerous Ways* does the same for us, presenting three of the master's self-penned works in the *other* popular genre he has always loved so dearly.

—Terry Dowling & Jonathan Strahan,
Sydney & Perth, October 2010

The DEADLY ISLES

Chapter I

FROM the social news of the *San Francisco Chronicle*, November 20, 1967:

LIA WINTERSEA ANNOUNCES TROTH
TO YACHTSMAN BRADY ROYCE

At a Saint Francis Hotel luncheon Lia Wintersea told six close friends of her engagement to popular socialite and yachtsman Brady Royce. Lia is daughter of the talented oboeist Paul Wintersea, who plays with the San Francisco Symphony, and Maude Ridlow Wintersea, an accomplished pianist in her own right. Lia's sister Jean is a flautist of professional caliber who instead of a career in music has chosen the field of industrial psychology to make her mark.

The wedding will take place in the late spring at Golconda, the fabled Royce town house, and will be followed by a cruise aboard Brady's schooner *Dorado IV* to remote and romantic islands in the South Seas.

Present at the luncheon were Lia's sister Jean, Kelsey McClure, Mrs. Christian deBrouf (Peggy Satterlee)…

From the *San Francisco Examiner*, January 26, 1968:

DANCER TORTURED, STRANGLED; APARTMENT RIFLED

Inez Gallegos, 23, a specialty dancer employed by the Martinique, 619 Ellis Street, this morning was found dead in her apartment at 1526 Powell Street. She had been strangled with a stocking. On her face, neck, legs and body were numerous burns, inflicted with a cigar, according to Detective Inspector William Reinhold.

The body was discovered at 11:10 A.M. by Richard B. Cody, 34, a bartender at the Polka Dot Bar, 320 O'Farrell Street, who had come to take Miss Gallegos to breakfast.

The apartment had been ransacked; Miss Gallegos' purse and belongings had been rifled but she apparently had not been subjected to sexual assault.

Cody states that a metal document box containing Miss Gallegos' birth certificate, car ownership certificate and other papers is missing.

Chapter II

BRADY Royce, at forty-eight, was heavy-shouldered, a trifle ungainly, with overlarge features, a heavy jaw and mouth, coarse dark hair thinning across the scalp: not a handsome or even a distinguished-appearing man; but, in the words of his friend Dorothy McClure: "With money like Brady's got, who needs looks?" Brady's humor was broad and sometimes unkind, but generally his bark was worse than his bite and his friends liked him in spite of his faults. His enemies thought him obstinate, domineering, peevish, narrow-minded, unsympathetic.

Brady's engagement to Lia Wintersea gave rise to predictable sniffs: "Dear Brady. Who'd ever think he'd go all senile, gamboling with pretty young things and all?" When such remarks were brought to Brady's attention he only smiled with grim complacence. Lia was as extravagantly beautiful as Brady was wealthy, and if the marriage derived from considerations other than mutual rapture, each party seemed satisfied with the contract.

Lia, while she looked a year or two younger than her twenty-two years, was a woman of poise, charm and dignity. She was deliciously shaped, supple and slender, with an ease of motion that was almost musical. From a Spanish grandmother came rich black hair, Castilian complexion, a look of latent Spanish passion; a Welsh grandfather gave her eyes of magic grey. Lia was casual and low-key;

she never preened nor wore exhibitionistic clothes, and achieved an effortless elegance. Brady's friends scrutinized her with care. Some commended her lack of vanity, others suspected reverse arrogance; Lia would have recognized herself in neither point of view. She was herself, just as she had been all her life, with her unique and particular problems. She had no delusions regarding the marriage, though she rather liked Brady and thought him virile and masterful. She might have liked him even had he not been wealthy.

By the San Francisco time-scale the Royces were an old family, having arrived shortly after the Gold Rush.

In 1859 at Bodie, Nevada, a hobo named Ham Royce filled an inside straight and won three demonstrably worthless mining claims near Virginia City (although a man named Comstock thought he had detected silver nearby). Of the two hundred and twenty million dollars yielded by the Comstock Lode, Ham Royce took thirty million.

Easy come, easy go, but not for Ham Royce. He invested in farmlands, cattle, railroad stock, real estate. Money came so easily that by 1880 the zest was gone. Ham Royce, one-time hobo, traveled to Europe. At Fiesole he admired the Villa Portinari, which, so it happened, was not for sale. Ham Royce tapped a pencil against his yellow old teeth, drew a set of sketches in his notebook, despatched a shipload of Carrara marble, rugs, candelabra, tapestries, Hellenistic urns, Spanish armour, early Italian paintings, antique oak beams and walnut paneling to San Francisco, where, on Pacific Heights, with a clear view from the Golden Gate to Yerba Buena Island, he built Golconda.

In 1890 he acquired the first *Dorado*, a sea-going yawl, which he sailed to the Aleutians for the purpose of hunting Kodiak bear.

Ham's only son was William. At the age of twenty William drank too much champagne and married a chorus girl. The experience had much to recommend it; a week later William drank more champagne and married another chorus girl. Ham Royce declared both marriages null and void and sent William off to Japan on the *Dorado*.

Ham Royce now gave serious thought to the future. The episode had cost relatively little: a hundred thousand to each of the girls, another twenty or thirty thousand in incidental expenses—but William was not a satisfactory son. He had never worked a day in his life; he condescended toward his father; he could not hold his liquor. Ham walked gloomily around Golconda, wondering what would become of his wonderful Italian palace when William was able to drink all the champagne he liked. Ham, a man predisposed toward extreme solutions, acted immediately. He paid the totality of his wealth into a trust fund dedicated to the maintenance of Golconda and its various adjuncts, such as the *Dorado*. The administrator he stipulated to be that legally sane, legitimately born Royce in the line of succession as established by the English common law schedule of primogeniture. A spouse would qualify as 'resident administrator' only when consanguinity to the third degree had been exhausted. For personal expenses the 'resident administrator' drew upon the income of the fund, but was subject to a set of provisions which made his remuneration precisely equal to his expenses. Legally the administrator was a pauper; practically he was a millionaire. William could drink champagne, he could marry chorus girls as he chose, at their own risk. When it came time to sue, William could truthfully assert that he was allowed no funds for any such contingencies. By this means Ham hoped to protect William against himself and to preserve Golconda against sequestration and folly.

William's two sons were Philip and Lemuel. Philip, upon becoming administrator, urged that Lemuel continue to make his home at Golconda. Lemuel refused and sued for a share of the estate, claiming that the Golconda Fund constituted an illegal entail. The courts decided otherwise. Lemuel moved south to La Jolla and never returned to San Francisco. His son Luke, less inflexible, was a frequent visitor to Golconda during his undergraduate years at the University of California and crewed aboard both *Dorado III* and *Dorado IV*.

Philip's only son Brady began his career as a typical Royce. He married Hortense Lejeune, a French cinema star, by whom he bred a son, Carson, then, at a scandalous trial, divorced her for flagrant adultery. Hortense haughtily returned to France, leaving Carson, the future administrator, in Brady's custody.

For a dozen years Brady reigned as San Francisco's most eligible bachelor. Then, at the home of his friend Malcolm McClure, Kelsey McClure introduced him to Lia Wintersea.

———•———

THE MARRIAGE OF BRADY Royce to Lia Wintersea on May 10, 1968, was the grandest event of the season. The guest list defined San Francisco quality; and those who felt that they should have been, but were not, invited found compelling reasons why they could not be on hand: excursions to Europe, conferences in Washington, in one instance a canoe trip down the Athabasca River to the Great Slave Lake.

The ceremony took place in the ballroom at Golconda. The reception was lavish beyond the experience of anyone present: like his great-grandfather Ham, when Brady Royce did something, he did it right. The honeymoon would be in the same scale: a week at Brady's lodge in the Sawtooth Mountains, then an extended cruise aboard the *Dorado IV*, touching at Honolulu, the Marquesas Islands, Tahiti, and wherever else the winds blew: Rarotonga? Samoa? Bali? The Philippines? One was as likely as the other, declared Brady.

Aboard the *Dorado IV* would be a number of guests: Carson, now nineteen; Jim and Nancy Crothers; Malcolm and Dorothy McClure; their daughter Kelsey, who had introduced Lia to Brady; Don Peppergold, a young attorney to whom Brady had taken a fancy. At Honolulu Jim and Nancy Crothers would leave the party, while Lia's sister Jean would come aboard, as would Brady's cousin Luke at Tahiti.

———•———

THE WEDDING PROCEEDED WITH the pomp and pageantry of a coronation; the bride by general agreement was the most beautiful woman ever to become a Royce. Malcolm McClure was Brady's best man; the single bridesmaid was Jean Wintersea, who appeared pinched and colorless beside her white jade, rose and jet sister.

The reception followed; Lia cut an enormous cake, then she and Jean slipped away to change clothes.

Lia seemed listless and wan—even dejected. Jean, two years older than Lia, and well-acquainted with her sister's temperament, felt completely baffled.

After the maids carried off the wedding gown Lia dropped upon a couch to stare out the window. Jean watched a careful moment, then seated herself beside her sister. "What on earth is the matter? You act as if you're headed for a concentration camp!"

Lia grimaced, gave her hands a nervous little shake. "Don't be silly."

"Better show a little more enthusiasm when you're with Brady," warned Jean, "or he'll think you don't like him."

Lia drew a deep breath. "I like him well enough. It's not that. In fact, he's very considerate." She put her chin in her hands. "The truth is shocking. I'm three months pregnant. Now you know."

"Good heavens," breathed Jean. "By Brady, I hope?"

Lia gave a bitter laugh. "That's the tragic part... It's that wretched you-know-who."

Jean considered a long moment, watching her sister sidelong. Then she said, "I thought that was all over long ago."

"I thought so too," said Lia in a dreary voice. "It wasn't my idea."

"But *why?*" demanded Jean. "It's incredible! It's insane!"

Lia gave another bitter little laugh. "I couldn't help it. He made me. I guess I don't have much will-power."

"I still don't understand. How could he make you? Do you mean force?"

Lia considered a moment. "No. Not exactly. I don't want to talk about it. Really."

"Poor little Lia." Jean gave her sister a slow frowning inspection, while Lia, chewing at her lip, stared out the window.

Lia said, "If Brady found out—after a six months' engagement—he'd be very upset. He'd be worse than upset. Do you know," she spoke in hushed wonder, "he's actually quite strait-laced!"

"You'll have to get rid of it," said Jean flatly.

"I know," said Lia. "But where? Aboard the *Dorado*? With a belaying pin? Or a boat-hook? Whatever they're called."

"Why didn't you have it done before?"

"I wasn't sure till a couple weeks ago. I missed the second month. After that—well, I didn't have time. There was so much to do."

"It doesn't show. You'll be in Honolulu in two or three weeks. Have it done there."

"Yes," said Lia. "I suppose I'll have to... You could telephone me that Mother was sick, and I'd fly back to San Francisco for a few days."

"He'd want to come with you: dutiful new husband and all."

"I suppose he would... Oh, heavens, how do I ever get in such messes?"

"I know how," said Jean with a grim smile. "But it wouldn't do any good to tell you."

———•———

ON MAY 30TH JEAN received a letter from Lia, postmarked May 29th, at Honolulu:

> Well, we arrived. Intact. The ship is beautiful; all are very nice, though puzzled. I blame everything on seasickness. Carson is a brat, and very cynical. He won't keep his hands off Kelsey, who is bored with him. I've made a few discreet inquiries, but I can't find anything except some Chinese herb doctors. If nothing this afternoon I may have to fly back to San Francisco. Brady is visiting Kona for a few days, to look at a coffee plantation somebody wants to sell him. I told him I wanted to do some shopping and recover from my seasickness, so I'll be staying at the Royal Hawaiian.

Kelsey is visiting friends and will not get to Kona either. I wouldn't be surprised if she suspects things. She looks at me with a funny half-grin. If I could only find a you-know-what! In San Francisco there wouldn't be any trouble. I wonder how long I'd be sick? Maybe I could fly over and fly right back. Well, we shall see. I'll go to the beauty salon; they always know about these things. *Important!* Brady has set departure date for June 6. He's very stern about such matters; he thinks he's a sea-captain or something. Anyway, plan to be here by the 5th or earlier. Try the Royal Hawaiian first, then the Kamehameha Yacht Club.

Love,
Lia

Sard's was situated south of Market at 69 Homan Street, half-way along a disreputable alley, between the Embarcadero and the railroad yards: not a fashionable district, but then Sard's clientele was, by and large, not a fashionable crowd. The façade was self-consciously smart: heavy squares of earth-colored Mexican tile set in rough black grout. There was a door of iron-bound oak, and SARD's spelled out in small black back-lit letters.

Within all was different—or perhaps the same? The bar, the tables, the chairs, the walls—all were rude and rough, as if the proprietor had sought to reproduce an old cow-town saloon. The effect was accentuated by carefully dramatic lighting, and the room seemed more like a stage-set than a tavern.

The patrons were almost exclusively young men, some with low side-burns, others with drooping mustaches, others with heads shaved bald. Excessively tight trousers with heavy leather belts were much in evidence, and two persons wore boots with spurs. Almost everyone drank straight Scotch and stood at the bar, thumbs hooked in belts, legs splayed. One wall was vivid with bullfight posters; at the back of the bar was a human skull in a Reichswehr helmet, a red rose clenched between the teeth.

At nine o'clock on the night of Sunday, June 2nd, a strange-looking woman came into Sard's bar. Her face was unnaturally white; her hair was pulled tightly back under a black scarf. She wore a long black coat, large dark glasses; her mouth was a black smear of lipstick. Just inside the entrance she paused to look along the bar. Failing to find whom she sought she went to a table at the back wall. Only two other women were present: a pair of thin nervous blondes with bushes of teased hair. They sat at a table with two young bucks in black turtleneck sweaters, and all took turns telling dirty jokes.

The men standing along the bar turned appraising looks at the woman in the black coat, then shrugged and gave her no further attention.

She sat an hour sipping gin and tonic. Patrons departed, others swaggered in. Voices rose; there was much boisterous laughter.

At twenty minutes to eleven the woman in black leaned quickly forward. The man who had just entered was tall, broad of shoulder, lean of hip; he wore tight beige trousers, a black cap, black shoes, a tight black sport shirt, open at the neck. He was an extremely handsome man, with dark hair, a splendid jaw and chin, a high-bridged nose. His cheek-bones were perhaps a trifle dull; his eyes, which were a remarkable black, were perhaps over-bright and somewhat too close together; but these flaws, if such they were, detracted little from the overall effect. He was as dramatic as his setting; he carried himself like a character in a silent movie, a synthesis of Douglas Fairbanks, John Gilbert, Ramon Navarro.

The woman in black signaled to him. He stared, then crossed the room with an incredulous expression on his face. "Good God, the disguise! I didn't recognize you."

"I didn't want to be recognized."

"No risk! What's on your mind?"

"One thing and another. How are your finances?"

The black opal eyes narrowed. "As usual, which means bad. Why? Are you distributing loot?"

"Not exactly. But sit down."

"Wait till I get a drink. What's yours?"

"Gin and tonic."

The man returned with a pair of drinks, threw a leg over the back of the chair, eased down into the seat. "Something of a surprise seeing you. I thought you were far away."

The woman in black sipped the gin and tonic. "You've been reading the society section."

"When something interesting happens."

"What about the front page?"

"I look at the headlines."

"I see where poor Inez Gallegos died."

The man raised his eyebrows in perplexity—whether real or feigned, the woman, who was now looking toward the ceiling, made no attempt to distinguish. She asked, "How would you like to make a lovely trip through the South Pacific?"

"I'd like. Who do I have to sleep with? Don't tell me. I'll go regardless."

"Be serious," said the woman. "This is a very serious situation… Very, very serious… "

Chapter III

LUKE Royce worked out of a native-style cottage in Teahupoo, on the western shore of Tahiti Iti, the small end of the Tahiti hourglass. The location was remote; the surroundings were picturesque in the extreme. Luke's front porch stood on stilts above a white beach, with his outrigger canoe drawn up above high water. Papayas, bananas, mangos and a small tart red fruit known locally as 'dragon's-eye' grew in his back yard. Cocoanut palms slanted up at all angles around the periphery of a small cove, created by a projecting point of land on one side, a cliff of volcanic rock on the other.

During the fifteen months of his residence Luke had hooked, netted and trapped thousands of fish. To the tuna, albacore and swordfish he pinned stainless steel tabs and turned them back into the sea, to the wonder of Armand Tefaatau, his assistant. A very few of these fish carried tabs affixed by other stations, and when Luke found one of these he immediately reported the circumstance to La Jolla.

Luke, twenty-eight years old, bore little resemblance to his cousin Brady, except, perhaps, for the square Royce forehead and something of the outward splay of jaw-bone which gave Brady's face a heavy Cro-Magnon cast. Luke was of medium height, good if unobtrusive physique. His disposition was even; his style of conduct tended toward understatement; the expression of his face was wry, as if everywhere he looked he found amusing contradictions. Nothing about Luke caught the eye or attracted attention except his remarkable beard: a shapeless brown scurf which owed its existence, not to ideology, but to a lost razor. The Tahitian girls found the beard fascinating. The little ones liked to tie it full of hibiscus and frangipani, and sometimes the older ones as well.

On the afternoon of Saturday, June 8, Luke started his Vespa, bumped up the rutted track to the road, turned left toward Papeete, thirty miles distant: a weekly routine. The road led along the shore, through enchanting scenery: dense forests of *mape*, ironwood, breadfruit, pandanus, cocoanut palms leaning across beaches; dark grottoes framed by ferns and big-leaved plants; and always flowers: banks and bowers of scarlet, orange, indigo, mauve, pale blue. One by one Luke passed through the various districts, each named for the ancient tribe which had controlled it: Papeari, Mataiea, Papara, Paea, into increasing traffic; through Punaauia and Faaa, beside the new air-terminal, at last into the outskirts of Papeete. Luke turned off Broom Road, swung down to the Quai Bir Hakeim, parked across from the post office. Here was the central node of the South Seas. To right and left boats were moored: ketches, schooners, sloops, yawls, several trimarans; boats from San Francisco, Los Angeles, Auckland, Sydney, Acapulco, New York, Boston, Monaco, London: all drawn to Longitude 149° 33' W, Latitude 17° 33' S, by the glamour of the word 'Tahiti'. Tied up to the dock not a hundred feet from where Luke had parked was the *Rahiria*, a big inter-island trading schooner. In about a month Luke's cousin Brady would arrive at Papeete in his own schooner, about the same size as the *Rahiria*, but inexpressibly more comfortable.

Luke crossed the street to the big new glass and concrete post office. He entered the side annex in which was his box, No. 421.

On a bench beside the window-wall a dark-haired man in white shorts sat reading a newspaper. Luke might never have heeded him except for a French lady in a gaudy pareu, her small boy and her poodle. Sidling around the group, Luke met the intent gaze of a pair of glittering black eyes. Surprised, Luke looked back. The man was absorbed in his newspaper.

Luke opened his box. The glass front of the box to the side reflected a somewhat distorted image of the man in white shorts, again watching Luke with a peculiar fixity.

When Luke turned Black-eyes was engrossed in his reading. Strange, thought Luke. To the best of his knowledge he had never seen the man before in his life... He went outside, looked through his letters, two of which were important. The first announced termination of the fish-migration study. Luke was instructed to close down his operations. This was a notice he had been expecting for three months, and it could not have come at a better time.

The second letter, from his cousin Brady, had been mailed at Honolulu on June 5. It read:

Dear Luke:

We're making departure tomorrow. Weather cooperating, we'll raise Nuku Hiva in the Marquesas about June 24. If you can break away from your job why not join us there? There is plenty of room—comparatively speaking that is; you'll have to share a stateroom with Carson. I don't think you know anyone else aboard, except old Bill Sarvis, who is still Chief Engineer. But I assure you that it is a jolly crew.

I propose to explore Nuku Hiva for a week, more or less, then make for Hiva Oa, which I understand to be spectacular. Everybody is in the best of spirits. If you ever marry, this is undoubtedly the proper honeymoon, although Lia had a rocky trip over from San Francisco. She is feeling much better now, much more enthusiastic, and no doubt will be taking to the nautical life like a real Royce. Her sister Jean is also with us, having come aboard yesterday. Well, I will knock this off and take care of some last minute details. We hope to see you either at Nuku Hiva or at Hiva Oa. Our first stop will be the port of entry at Taio Hae Bay, as I say about June 24. If you are not waiting for us I will leave word with the officials as to our anchorage, and also leave a letter for you.

Regards, and see you at Papeete in any case.

Brady

Luke re-read the letter, tugging absently at his unsightly beard... He could close down his job in two hours. And there was the *Rahiria*, conveniently at hand. Luke walked up the street to the Vaima, the popular sidewalk café. Under gaudy parasols the tables were crowded: tourists from a Swedish cruise ship and from the hotels; Foreign Legionnaires in white caps; local French and Tahitians. The visitors watched the girls, the locals watched the tourists, each deriving amusement from the other. Luke found a seat and ordered beer. The waitress presently brought him a bottle with the familiar Hinano label: a girl caressing a flower. Automatically Luke turned the bottle around, studied the label from the reverse side, whereupon a lewd scene became evident, or so his Tahitian friends assured him. Luke had never been able to see it. A clean mind, no doubt. Perhaps stupidity...

Luke sat back, thrust out his legs. Pleasant to sit at the Vaima and watch the life of Papeete flow past. Many before him had found it so. Pleasant especially to watch the girls, some of whom were very appealing.

The time had come when he must leave Tahiti. Luke felt mingled anticipation and sadness. Out in Teahupoo the world was far away, isolated by a quality far more elemental than miles. Never again would he live so close to water and air and sunlight; his friends—the Tefaataus, the Vaita'ahuas, the Himeas, their cousins and aunts and uncles—would gradually forget him; gradually he would forget the songs and his few words of Tahitian. At Teahupoo the days passed slowly—but the months slid by with disturbing ease. A man tended to lose contact with the world. The real world? Perhaps, perhaps not: Luke wasn't sure. Still, more and more of late he had known small pangs of guilt. Perhaps someday he might return, but more likely not. The risk of anticlimax would be too great... Luke suddenly became aware that, without conscious deliberation, he had decided to meet the *Dorado* in the Marquesas. Armand could look after his belongings until he returned to Papeete.

Luke sat up in his seat, consulted his watch, looked down the street toward the blue façade of Etablissements Donald, agents for the *Rahiria*. They were now closed; Luke would have to wait until

Monday before booking passage. If he were lucky he might still find a berth available. If not, he'd go deck class, like the Polynesians.

Luke drank a second bottle of beer, re-read his mail, then considered how he would spend the rest of the day. He had intended to dine at Chez Chapiteau or perhaps the Bougainville, which was quieter and cheaper and more pleasantly situated among the trees to the back of town... On the other hand, a delay meant riding the Vespa home after dark, which in the unpredictable traffic was hard on the nerves. Then there was Armand, who might be difficult to find on a Saturday night... Suddenly anxious to be on his way, Luke rose to his feet, walked up the Quai Bir Hakeim, toward his motor-scooter.

Across the street, sauntering idly in the same direction, was the man with the black eyes. The post office was a queer place to read a newspaper, thought Luke. Perhaps the fellow had been waiting for someone. The man, turning his back, paused to inspect a very ordinary boat moored to the wharf. Crossing the street Luke approached the *Rahiria* and in execrable French called up to a Tahitian deck-hand: *"Quand partit le bateau?"*

"Mardi, m'sieu."

"Peut-être je vais aussi."

"Bien. C'est un voyage agréable."

"Vous allez aux îles Marquises, n'est-ce pas?"

"Oui, m'sieu. D'abord les îles Tuamotus: puis les Marquises. Très belles, m'sieu!"

"Bien. Merci beaucoup."

Luke turned away. He glanced back along the waterfront. Black-eyes was nowhere to be seen. Odd. From the side of his eye Luke saw a flicker of white. The man had been standing nearby, behind the trunk of an enormous flamboyant. But he had only been getting into his car, an old Citroën 2 CV. A rented car, thought Luke. Only a Frenchman would deign to own such a Citroën and the man did not look French.

Luke went to his Vespa, cranked it into action, swung out on the street. He drove past the fabled old Grand Hotel, now occupied by the French Army, then turned up to the highway and so departed town.

Once over the hill between Papeete and Faaa traffic thinned out and Luke sputtered along at a good clip. The afternoon sun was dropping upon the bizarre silhouette of Moorea. The kilometer posts fell behind. To the right, behind a fringe of cocoanut palms was the lagoon, with surf crashing soundlessly over the reef, half a mile offshore. Lagoon, reef, coral: Luke knew them well indeed, and all their inhabitants: sea urchins, cowries, *bêches de mer;* the brilliant little fish; the groupers which hid under the coral; the bizarre pipe-fish. Other creatures were less pleasant: the stone-fish, the moray eel; the *hue-hue* or puffer, deadly poisonous if carelessly cleaned and eaten; the occasional shark. The Tahitians insisted that any shark inside the lagoon was harmless. A smart slap on the surface was said to frighten them away: *"Voilà!"* (the slap on the water) *"Ils courent!"* ("They run!") Luke, nonetheless, gave the sharks right of way, and the Tahitians, so he observed, had a healthy respect for these sharks encountered beyond the reef. Luke had seen many of these: white shark, mako, hammerheads, gray nurses: and he considered them the most frightening creatures alive.

He passed Paea, its handsome white church and fine new school, the Chinese grocery, the cheerful homes of his friends M. Omer Tefaatau, and M. Philibert Tefau, the district sub-chief and brother-in-law to M. Omer... Some of Luke's fondest memories were of Tahitian parties, with endless music and song and drinking of Hinano. And the *tamure*... Ah! the *tamure!* which was to the hula as whiskey to milk... Out past Paea into Papara, through cocoanut groves; past thatched huts surrounded by papaya and banana, hibiscus, tiare, ginger, frangipani. After Papara the houses were less frequent and traffic dwindled to nothing. An old Citroën bounced along about three hundred yards behind Luke, but made no effort to overtake him... Mataiea and Papeari, where Gauguin had lived. At the Taravao peninsula Luke turned off the main highway toward Teahupoo, which seemed also to be the destination of the old Citroën. Old Citroëns were common... Luke's mind was on Brady and his invitation. He knew the *Dorado* well; five years before he had crewed aboard the boat on a trip down the coast of Mexico. Luke had never warmed to Brady; their relationship had always been cordial but never intimate. Perhaps a twinge of envy, Luke was frank to admit. Also, Brady carried his good fortune without humility, as if it were the natural consequence of cosmic law... Then there was Brady's new wife. A San Francisco friend had written, perhaps effusively: "Lia, the most delectable collection of female fluff since Deirdre. Strong men roll up their eyes, women weep; small boys point and say, 'Daddy, buy me one of those' and Daddy mutters, 'If I could afford it, I'd buy one for myself'. A love match? Maybe on Brady's side. Lia, being composed of whipped cream and sandalwood, has no soul." Luke wondered what Lia's sister was like. Beautiful girls rarely came two to a family. "Well, we shall see," said Luke.

Armand lived at the edge of Vairao District, in a strange old wooden house of two stories, built long ago by a French eccentric whose ghost yet prowled the premises. As Armand told the tale, the Frenchman had quarreled with the *tahua* Airo-Tane, the district's most respected witch-doctor. The *marae* of Airo-Tane's ancestors was situated on the Frenchman's property; Airo-Tane considered it his right to trespass. One day, in an angry effort to end the incursions, the Frenchman toppled the basalt necroliths. Airo-Tane came and looked, and quietly took himself away, to a secret grove at the head of Teahupoo Valley. The next day the Frenchman became violently ill. He foamed at the mouth, thrashed, and kicked, screaming that devils gnawed at his spine, and presently died. A few days later old Airo-Tane, as mild and affable as ever, returned to his home.

"And what of the Frenchman's ghost?" Luke asked Armand, only half-facetiously. "Does he give trouble?"

Armand made a deprecatory gesture. "Only on nights of the full moon. Not always then."

At the moment Armand was fishing, so Luke learned from the oldest of Armand's sisters. Luke decided not to wait, and again set forth along the road. Behind came an old Citroën: the same or another similar. The road deteriorated to potholes and ruts and ran close beside the edge of the cliff; the sun was low to the horizon and Luke drove with care.

There below: his private cove, his house, his dock and boat, from which he was departing, never to return! The thought was unsettling; he barred it from his mind.

He turned down the driveway, wound through a clump of *mape*, the Tahitian chestnut, then a darker patch of banana trees. He coasted to a halt, turned off the engine. Home—at least for a day or two longer. He climbed the steps to his front porch where he ruminated a moment, tugging at the obnoxious beard, which he definitely would shave off tomorrow, if he could find his razor. As for now, after making arrangements with Armand, it might be well to ride back to the Taravao isthmus for dinner at the hotel or perhaps the Restaurant Atchoun... An old Citroën returned east along the ridge of the cliff, heading toward Papeete. Luke hardly noticed. He showered, dressed in fresh clothes, started his Vespa and rode back up to the ridge. The sun was just now dipping into the water, casting a blaze all the way to the surging water at the base of the cliff. A beautiful sight, but dazzling; Luke needed his vision for the road. Ahead loomed a car—a Citroën, black against the sunset sky. The same Citroën? The driver was coming recklessly fast, hugging the wrong side of the road. Was he drunk? Luke swung wildly left. The Citroën moved likewise, struck the Vespa just under the seat, sent it bounding. For the briefest flicker of time Luke looked into the face of the man behind the wheel: a calm intent face burnished by the dying sunlight.

Before he could so much as wonder why, Luke sailed cleanly off the edge of the cliff, riding the Vespa out over the sharp rocks.

Chapter IV

IN the middle of the air, alone except for the motor-scooter, Luke saw everything at once: the sunset sky, the cocoanut palms, the surf and sharp rocks below.

He and the motor-scooter started to tip forward, as if they were riding down the trajectory. Luke kicked hard at the Vespa, thrust it back toward the cliff. The impetus sent the Vespa hurtling in at the rocks and pushed Luke seaward. Luke fell into shallow water, fortuitously augmented by an incoming surge. He struck the shingle with force enough to stun him and was only feebly aware of being swept up toward the base of the cliff. But here he clung and when the surge drained back, Luke remained.

He lay collecting his wits… There was furtive movement on the rocks above. Luke lay limp, watching through half-closed eyes. A human shape stood silhouetted on the bronze-gray sky, in a pose consciously or unconsciously dramatic: legs apart, shoulders back, head broodingly turned down, with eyes fixed on Luke. A new surge of water swept in, lifted Luke, carried him a foot or two forward, floated him back about the same distance. Luke let himself loll, limbs loose.

The dark shape remained watching for another minute, then departed. Luke waited. Over the sound of the surf he heard the vibration of an engine, a transmission in low gear.

The Citroën had departed.

Luke waited five minutes, then crawled up the shore to a broken cocoanut bole, where he seated himself, hunched and shuddering. He tested his limbs. There seemed to be no broken bones, no serious sprains. Impact with the water and the bottom had dealt him a tremendous blow, enough to daze him, and even now there was a ringing in his ears. He felt as if he might like to vomit... Luke drew a deep breath. No point feeling sorry for himself. He rose to his feet, staggered around the base of the cliff to the beach and plodded home. Divesting himself of his wet clothes he pondered the amazing fact that someone had tried to kill him.

Why? A question of enormous fascination. The *who*, at least, was known, or, rather, half-known.

Luke considered all the circumstances. Black-eyes had waited at the post office. This argued that Black-eyes knew only his address: the number of his post office box. So Black-eyes had sat with his newspaper until Luke came to claim his mail, then, following Luke home, had tried to kill him, and now no doubt felt certain that he had succeeded.

Imagining the look of his own corpse, Luke shuddered. The situation was weird. Luke could conceive no motivation for the act. Two other events had been coincidental: the closing down of Teahupoo project and the invitation to join the *Dorado* at Nuku Hiva. Was either event connected with the third? Absurd.

Perhaps the attempted murder was no more than a ridiculous accident: an Englishman holding to the wrong side of the road. Luke rejected the idea. More probably the attack stemmed from a case of mistaken identity, the renter of Box 420 or 422 being the intended victim. Again Luke shook his head. Black-eyes would be on his guard against so basic an error.

Luke went into his kitchen, poured rum and canned guava juice into a glass and watched dusk settle over the ocean. Presently Luke became angry, more angry than he had ever been in his life. He poured more rum and decided that money must be the root of the affair: Royce money. But why attack Luke, whose connection with the estate was remote? It would be instructive to discuss the matter with Brady, and learn his opinions. More definitely than ever Luke resolved to be aboard the *Rahiria* on Tuesday.

Meanwhile, he would have a reckoning with Black-eyes. If he could find him.

Chapter V

ABOARD the *Dorado* the course was southeast 136° on the gyrocompass, with the last of the northeast trades on the port beam; a course which, extended, struck the coast of South America somewhere near Valparaiso. Lia innocently inquired why they did not sail directly to their destination instead of zig-zagging here and there across the ocean; before she could change her mind Brady brought out *Ocean Passages* and explained the wind systems of the world. "We sail east now," said Brady in conclusion, "so that when we meet the southeast trades, we can reach into Nuku Hiva instead of fighting head-winds."

Lia nodded. "That's interesting."

"Yes," said Brady, "it is. I do believe there's a Bowditch aboard; you'd probably like to look through it."

Lia glanced down the deck to where Kelsey and Jean were basking in deck-chairs. "I really would, Brady—"

One of the paid hands approached, apparently with a problem. Brady said, "Excuse me a minute," and Lia went quickly off to join Jean and Kelsey.

With all sails set the *Dorado* cut a bubbling furrow through the water. Cumulus clouds stood dreaming above the horizon but never edged in close enough to obscure the sun. Who could ask more from life? Brady demanded of himself. Never before had he been fully sentient! Lia's indisposition was a thing of the past—another source of gratification—though now and again a pensive mood came over her. Oh well, shrugged Brady: a minor matter. He professed no insight into the mysteries of womanhood. Male and Female were as incommensurable as cats and crows; Lia's quirks only corroborated this point of view. She probably wasn't accustomed to idleness and needed something to do. A good job to teach her navigation: make her a true sea-going Royce!

By and large the cruise was a success. Carson as usual had been something of a trial: a situation now rectified, and Brady gave a grim chuckle. In Honolulu, the night before departure, Carson had gone off wenching. At sailing time, with Carson nowhere in evidence, Brady had slung his bag to the dock and put to sea, leaving Carson marooned. No one seemed to miss him.

Malcolm and Dorothy McClure who owned a boat of their own were in their element and vigorously savored each instant. Kelsey's attitude was more complicated: no surprise, since she was far more complicated than her father and mother, a situation comparable to the evolution of a Corvette convertible from a pair of pre-war Buicks. Kelsey was dark, vivacious, on the smallish side, with an inexhaustible capacity for mischief. Brady considered her an unpredictable little minx and was careful to maintain absolutely correct relations. With nothing better to do, Kelsey teased and agonized Don Peppergold, a pugnacious crew-cut young man with a homely bull-terrier face. But the more he excited himself, the more haughty and flip she became, while Jean Wintersea looked on from the side, trying to calculate Kelsey's technique. When Jean managed to isolate Don and engage him in small talk, he became orderly and polite.

Brady discussed the situation with Lia. "I suppose I should have evened the party out more carefully. I'd planned on Carson, of course—although Jean isn't exactly Carson's type." Especially, Brady reflected, with Carson's father married to Jean's younger sister.

Lia had a trick of listening with eyebrows raised and eyes widened, as if in a state of intense concentration. She now agreed with Brady's analysis. "Jean has never been terribly interested in men. I suppose what with her music she's never had the time. Perhaps," she mused artlessly, "I should have studied harder at the piano myself."

Brady could not decide what she meant and the whole subject was dropped.

The *Dorado* proceeded into the southeast, through glorious blue and gold weather. During the late morning and early afternoon Brady, Malcolm McClure and Don Peppergold each stood a two-hour wheel-watch, relieving the paid hands, although with gyro-steering there was little to do except glance from time to time at the compass, occasionally trim or free a sheet. Brady navigated with assistance from and much boisterous argument with Malcolm McClure, who considered himself a navigational genius. McClure usually made the evening fix, using the 'McClure Calculated Zenith Principle'.

"Absolutely barbarous!" scoffed Brady. "Only a person predisposed against order and justice could contrive such a boondoggle!"

"Not at all, not at all!" exclaimed McClure. "To the contrary, I've organized chaos."

"You expect me to believe that? What could be simpler than shooting three stars, then—after a few trivial calculations, of course—laying down the position?"

"My system. It's simpler by far."

"Please, Mal! This isn't a cocktail party. You're talking to a man of the sea."

"I've noticed the barnacles between your ears. My system is utterly logical. Imagine the celestial surface and the earth as concentric globes. It's clear, is it not, that fixing the globes at any two points establishes their relationship? This is the basis of the system. Two star altitudes relate one sphere to the other. Calculation gives me the declination of the zenith, and with a time correction, the right ascension. I transpose coordinates to latitude and longitude and there we are. What could be simpler? I don't even need to draw lines of position. I put a dot on the chart and say: 'Right here!'"

"Unconvincing. Very very questionable. In fact, it sounds like the old Lamont system which is not only tedious but—"

"No, no, no!" The muscles in McClure's gaunt face twitched in indignation. "I can work the whole routine on a spherical trig slide-rule."

"Thereby introducing a new source of error."

"Okay," said McClure. "That's it." He slapped his palm upon the roof of the after dog-house. "We'll do this. Lia can be judge and timekeeper."

"Oh heavens," said Lia half-laughing, "don't involve me! I don't even know what you're talking about."

"You can read a watch, can't you?" Brady asked, with just a trace of tartness in his voice.

"Oh yes, if that's all you want me to do."

"That's all," said McClure. "You say: 'Get ready—get set—go.' Then Brady, you shoot your stars and plot your position; I'll shoot my stars and plot my position. We'll see who lays down a point first, then we'll recheck and see which of us is forty miles off."

"I'm too old for antics like that," Brady declared bluffly. "Too old and too smart. A pity Carson isn't here. He'd be a good match for you. As a matter of fact, Carson is a pretty fair navigator," Brady told Lia. "I've taught him quite a bit. I'll start with you too. Something everyone should know: celestial navigation."

"Oh Brady. I'd be impossible. Things with knobs and scales just confuse me."

"You'll catch on, don't worry. Mal, why don't you sit in and maybe pick up a few shortcuts?"

"Shortcuts? What's faster than no time at all?"

"How do you propose to fix a position in no time at all? I admit I'd like to learn."

"I'm designing a computer to perform all the horse-work instantly: the McClure Navigator."

"There's been a dozen of them," said Brady. "None were practical."

"None made use of modern electronics," stated McClure. "That's the difference. Nowadays with loran and consolan and satellites, the emphasis is away from a purely navigational computer. Mine would fill a need."

Lia had been thinking: Jean is a musician, Kelsey is a vamp. I'll learn navigation and show them all. She asked brightly: "How does it work?"

"It's a big wooden box," Brady told her. "Inside sits a navigator with a sextant, a chronometer, a nautical almanac. Mal punches a button, the navigator writes the position on a slip of paper and pushes it out a slot."

McClure nodded with placid good humor. "Something like that. Only the box is nine inches on the side, with three controls: an on-off switch, a selector for any of fifty major stars, an adjustment to correct for height above horizon. There are three read-out windows. The first is a clock, indicating the exact time—the instrument hears the time-tick and makes its own correction. The other two windows show longitude and latitude."

"Oh?" sneered Brady. "And how do you use this miraculous device?"

"Simple. You select a star, say Arcturus."

Lia interposed a question. "But how can you tell one star from another? This is something which has always puzzled me."

"You learn the constellations," said Brady. "It's just like learning the streets of a city."

"But they all look alike!"

"It's just a matter of familiarity," said Brady. "You'll soon learn to recognize them."

"Or else," murmured Kelsey, lounging in a deck-chair twenty feet away.

"Well then," said McClure, "back to my miraculous device. Looking through a sighting device you bring Arcturus into the field of vision. That's all—no cross-hairs, no bubble, no finagling, no nothing. The instrument automatically centers itself on the star, once the star is brought into the circle of sensitivity. The instrument includes an artificial horizon, and can be used at any time of day or night. The artificial horizon is a mirror floating in mercury, with a pendant gyroscope."

"That kind of set-up isn't practical," stated Brady. "It's been tried."

"No one has ever damped the surface electrostatically, using the earth's magnetic field as a stable reference. I won't go into the electronics of the thing. So: you turn the optics in the general direction of Arcturus, press a button. Then you do the same with another star, say Vega. Instantly your fix appears in the read-out windows. Any questions?"

"No questions," said Brady. "If the Ouija board works, anything will work."

"Don't pay any attention to Brady," Lia told McClure. "He only wants to get you excited."

"I realize this," said McClure. "Too bad, Brady. I'm not the excitable type."

Jean, also sitting nearby in a deck-chair, gave a brittle laugh. "I'm not either, luckily for Brady. Last night he asked me to play the harmonica."

"You should have brought your flute," declared Brady. "Mal dances a mean horn-pipe."

"At high school Lia used to tap dance," said Kelsey McClure.

"Kelsey!" protested Lia. "You're telling all my secrets!"

"Not all of them," said Kelsey, with a wicked grin. "But don't worry, I won't."

Dorothy McClure had been listening with half-closed eyes. She was pert and wholesome, with a clever straightforward face, curly reddish-gray hair, a complexion ruined by overmuch exposure to the sun. Now she opened her eyes and sat up. "Time goes by so fast! I remember that little skit so well; it seems only yesterday."

"What little skit?" asked Brady.

"When Lia did that tap-dance routine."

"Oh please, Dorothy! don't bring that up. I was so clumsy."

"You were nothing of the sort. Who was the other girl? Inez something or other."

"Inez Gallegos," said Kelsey. "She's dead."

"Dead? How could she be? Was it an accident?"

"She might have been accidentally murdered."

"But how shocking! I met her downtown just a few months ago; she was with a young man. She didn't introduce him, so it wouldn't have been her husband."

"She never married," said Kelsey.

"Of course she did!" Lia declared. "I'm sure she was married."

Kelsey shrugged. "If she had a husband the police couldn't locate him."

"Maybe for professional reasons she wanted to keep her marriage secret," suggested Jean.

Having no share in the conversation Don Peppergold became impatient. "Secrets, secrets!" he sang out. "Everybody has secrets."

Lia sighed. "I wish someone would tell me Brady's secrets. Does anyone know?"

"Yes indeed," said Brady. "There's two of us. God is one, I'm the other. We're both keeping quiet."

McClure said in a tone of mild complaint: "If you or your colleague would ordain a few hatfuls of wind we might log a decent daily run for a change. The current's taking us west faster than we can sail east."

"Are you in a hurry?" Brady demanded.

Dorothy McClure gave Brady an affectionate pat on the knee. "Of course not. I hope we *never* get home. I feel like I'm on a honeymoon myself."

"Life in the old dog yet, eh?" said Brady, with an appraising glance toward McClure.

The voyage proceeded. The ocean was an unbelievable bright blue, the swells were long and lazy: great low dunes of water ruffled by cat's-paws.

On the morning of June 10 a succession of rain-squalls appeared from nowhere. Gusts of wind caused the *Dorado* first to heel, then to skirl away to the west, to the annoyance of Brady and Malcolm McClure, who were more than ever anxious for easting. On the same evening a spectacular thunderstorm moved in from the northwest. Great leaden clouds burnt purple when the lightning flashed. The sound of the thunder was almost inaudible and presently the storm moved to the northeast. By ten o'clock only dancing wires of lightning could be seen which by midnight had glimmered away completely.

Chapter VI

LUKE drained his glass, set it down with a thud. He went into the house, packed a suitcase, threw it into the old Fiat pickup which seemed to belong to Armand. He drove up to the highway and turned left toward Papeete. Parked at the spot where he went over the edge was the black Peugeot sedan of the Taravao Gendarmerie.

Luke stopped, slowly alighted from the pickup. At the foot of the cliff a pair of gendarmes were turning flashlights this way and that across the rocks... Luke pulled at his beard. How had they learned of the accident so quickly? Only one other person besides himself had known... Luke returned to the Fiat, drove on.

Along the Papeete waterfront were a number of inexpensive hotels rarely if ever patronized by tourists. One of these, a few doors from the Vaima, was the Hôtel du Sud. For 200 francs Luke rented a second-floor room with a private verandah overlooking the waterfront: a vantage remarkably picturesque.

At the Vaima he bought a ham sandwich which he took up to his verandah. Here he sat until midnight formulating and rejecting schemes and plans. The gendarmes? He could put forward no evidence other than an identification made in a tenth of a second with the setting sun in his eyes. A waste of time. Finally he went to bed and presently fell asleep.

In the morning Luke borrowed a pair of scissors from the manageress of the hotel. He slashed off his beard, then shaved with the razor he had found in his suitcase. He scowled at the strange naked face in the mirror: how ingenuous, how foolishly cheerful he looked, even while scowling! Partly responsible was his unruly overlong hair. He needed a haircut. Without halting even for breakfast, Luke went to the barber shop off Rue Général de Gaulle and there was shorn. Returning to the waterfront he bought a copy of the local newspaper, took an outside table at the Vaima and ordered breakfast... An item caught his attention. The headline, translated from French, read: *American Scientist Suffers Fatal Disaster.* It appeared that M. Luke Royce, engaged in oceanographic research near Teahupoo, had been killed when his motorbike skidded from the road and plunged into the sea. The gendarmes, notified of the accident by a horrified passerby, had rushed to the scene but to no avail. The body undoubtedly had been swept out through the reef, the current running with great force at the time.

Luke sat brooding. The gendarmes would be disturbed if Luke did not report himself alive. Still, he need not have seen the item in the newspaper. If Black-eyes considered him dead, herein lay some small advantage for Luke... The object of Luke's reflections came sauntering along the sidewalk: Black-eyes himself. Today with his white shorts he wore a black polo shirt, black socks and sandals.

Luke raised the newspaper across his face. The man took a seat about twenty feet distant, facing toward the harbor. Luke lowered the newspaper, studied the side of the sleek dark head. There he sat, comfortable and placid, with no pang whatever for the condition of poor Luke Royce. The next step, thought Luke, was to engage the man at closer quarters, to learn his identity, hopefully to bring him to grief.

Kill him? Why not?

Luke's stomach gave a small jerk of distaste.

In spite of haircut and shave Luke felt vulnerable. A few steps away, where Rue Bréa entered Quai Bir Hakeim, was a souvenir shop. Luke went in, bought a green and black Tahitian shirt, a pair of dark glasses, a jaunty coco-fiber hat. He looked in a mirror. The transformation was complete. He had changed to where he no longer could recognize himself.

Luke returned to the Vaima. He stopped short in disgust. His enemy had departed.

Chapter VII

THE *Dorado* had entered the doldrums. The winds had fled, leaving a glassy calm. Up and down a few slow inches eased the ocean, in near-invisible heaves. The *Dorado* floated motionless, all sails loose. Brady put out a shark-watch: two crewmen with snorkels and face-masks at bow and stern, and now his guests enjoyed a mid-ocean swim. They plunged from the rail into the transparent blue water, swam under the hull, floated on the surface, splashed and sported.

Neither Brady nor Lia joined the fun. Lia, in her bathing suit, sat somewhat self-consciously in a deck-chair; Brady rowed around the edge of the group in a dinghy. Swimming with four watery miles below gave him the shudders. Suppose he were to lose his buoyancy and sink? How dark and cold and lonely would be the four miles! On rare occasions—this was not one of them—he forced himself to join the more confident swimmers, whereupon he kept his eyes tightly closed under water, to avoid seeing the sunlit blue fading through indigo into blue-black murk.

Most of the others felt no such inhibitions. Rather enviously Brady watched them playing in the water. Don Peppergold swam two hundred yards directly north. In mid-ocean sharks were no great threat, but the creatures were notoriously unpredictable. Not impossibly some pelagic monster might come cruising past, with dire results.

Brady rowed out to where Don Peppergold loafed on his back, looking up at the sky. Brady communicated his fears. "Nothing is as wicked as a shark. If one caught you out here you'd be done. Better head back to the ship."

"Okay, skipper." Don clipped back toward the ship. Brady paused to admire the *Dorado:* the rake to the bow, the generous hull, the expanse of the white sails. An excellent thing to be Brady Royce, master of the *Dorado!* Everything was going well. Lia seemed to be enjoying herself, although Brady thought to detect occasional cryptic moods. Depression? Boredom? Hard to believe. Brady gave his head a thoughtful shake. His plans to teach Lia navigation had come to nothing, Lia showing no penchant for the subject. She held the sextant as if it were a dead animal, and turned the pages of the almanac with an air of quiet desperation. Brady felt he had no cause for complaint. Lia had tried; she clearly had done her best. Some people simply did not have navigational minds. Lia had other qualities—beauty, charm, amiability—which more than made up for her inability to lay down lines of position; in fact, if Brady had been pressed to criticize his beautiful new wife he would have specified only her baffling and sometimes irritating reticence. Perhaps she felt constrained by the presence of her sister. The two shared no obvious affection and from time to time bickered in low voices, stopping short only when someone came within earshot. Brady did not know what to make of Jean. She was attractive, even fascinating, in an odd over-civilized way. In a science-fiction movie she might, without makeup, have played the part of the Martian woman. At times Brady had to admit that she intrigued him. Lia was beautiful, but just a trifle listless. Jean, though pale and withdrawn, looked anything but listless, and seemed to be continually roiling with unorthodox impulses.

No one was perfect, reflected Brady, not even himself. He took it for granted that his guests, if only subconsciously, resented him— for his wealth, and for the authority that, as master of the *Dorado,* he exerted over them. In his turn he felt impelled to play the role: the bluff, half-benevolent, half-irascible tyrant. But he really wasn't like that at all. Brady gave a despondent grunt. There were worse things than being poor; at least you knew who your friends were.

When you married a beautiful young wife, you knew for sure what she thought of you, and everyone else knew for sure too.

Brady gave a grim chuckle. If he were poor, with no wealth, no *Dorado*, no Golconda, he might have no friends and no beautiful young wife either. Best to accept things as they were. Who the hell cared what people thought in the first place? Be damned to everybody!

Brady rowed back to the *Dorado*. Lia, Jean and Kelsey McClure stood together on the deck. Lia's bathing suit was old rose, Jean's was white, Kelsey's was baby blue. A highly palatable picture, thought Brady. Lia of course was the most beautiful. Jean was more intense and, well, yes, more intelligent. She was not so supple, so well filled-out as Lia; she was built like a fashion model, though she probably would have resented the comparison. Kelsey was smaller than either of them, with a slender energetic body. Kelsey also was a rather puzzling young woman. Watching her toy with Don Peppergold, Brady wondered if she might not have something of a malicious streak. Lia displayed only a vague absent-minded vanity that offended not even other women. Jean seemed unaware of her own peculiar appeal. Kelsey was aware of everything. She knew how men felt; she knew how to make them feel even more so. Brady had heard rumors that during her adolescence she had been something of a problem.

The swimmers all climbed back aboard the ship; Brady and the shark-watch followed; the dinghy was hoisted aboard. William Sarvis, Chief Engineer aboard the *Dorado III* and now the *Dorado IV*, came to consult Brady. "We won't have more wind today. Might be a good idea to give the diesels a spin. They could stand a bit of exercise."

Brady considered the sky. It was blank of clouds except for a few nubbins of cumulus far over the eastern horizon. He gave a curt nod. "Start 'em up."

Sarvis turned away. The engines coughed, the exhaust gargled and bubbled. Five minutes later that spot where the ship had paused, where the passengers had swum, was a half-mile astern, indistinguishable from any other spot on the face of the ocean.

Chapter VIII

LUKE considered himself the most reasonable and tolerant man alive. But here was a special situation. It was bitter frustration to find that his quarry had taken cover. "Still," Luke told himself, in order to put his emotion on a rational basis, "no one has ever tried to kill me before."

He searched north and south along the waterfront. Black-eyes might have sauntered off in any of four or five directions. Where, on this placid Sunday morning, would so restless a man be apt to go? To his hotel? To the rented Citroën, for a ride in the country? To church? Not bloody likely.

Luke walked to the Quai du Commerce, examined the decks of the *Godesund,* a Swedish cruise ship tied up to the wharf. No sign of his enemy.

Luke returned along the waterfront, beside the moored yachts, past the *Rahiria,* searching in all directions. Black-eyes was nowhere to be seen. Luke crossed to the Vaima, flung himself into a chair and prepared to wait. Sooner or later Black-eyes must return along the Quai Bir Hakeim, and so come into his range of vision.

Luke waited two hours, drinking coffee, while the folk of the town passed along the sidewalk. A large group from the Swedish cruise ship appeared, walking in a stately herd. All were dewed with perspiration; all appeared vaguely uneasy as if they felt inadequate to the legends. Some were glum, some muttered and nudged each other, some contrived a thin gayety. It was difficult to be a Swede, reflected Luke.

Time passed. Luke looked at his watch. Two o'clock. Black-eyes undoubtedly had returned to his hotel for lunch, and now sat out on the terrace with a tall rum punch. Luke called a cab. He visited each of the large hotels in turn, looking through lobby, bar and terrace, scrutinizing those who lay on the beaches. He dared not inquire at the desks; the clerks might mention him to Black-eyes. Everywhere the result was negative. Luke returned through the lavender dusk to the Vaima. Here he himself drank a couple of rum punches.

The events of the previous evening began to recede. They were too grotesque for credibility. Luke blinked and shook his head. Without a focus, his first rapture of rage was hard to maintain. Luke began to reason with himself. Might the episode simply be coincidence? An ordinary run-of-the-mill accident? Luke grimaced. This was carrying dispassionate analysis too far. The circumstances were all too real. The bruises along Luke's ribs ached with a real ache. Once again Luke became angry. So then, what of the future? Assuming that he had not located, identified and punished Black-eyes by Tuesday, as seemed more than likely, should he sail aboard the *Rahiria* anyway? Or should he remain in Papeete? Luke inclined first one way, then the other. Meanwhile lights appeared up and down the waterfront. Quinn's, a block up the street, showed its ancient festoon of olive-green bulbs.

At eight o'clock Luke gave up his vigil. At the Chez Chapiteau on the Rue des Ecoles he dined on steak, *pommes frites*, a bottle of claret. Returning to the waterfront, he passed Quinn's, and for lack of better entertainment, looked in through the open doors. The orchestra: three guitars, drums, a string bass, saxophone, was rendering *Rose of San Antone*, with Polynesian whoops and hoots. The cavernous interior was already crowded. The dance-floor pulsed to the vehemence of the dancers, two-thirds of which were Tahitians wearing garlands of flowers, totally indifferent to the fact that a hundred ladies and gentlemen from the Swedish cruise ship, sitting at an isolated section of tables reserved for them, had traveled halfway around the world to inspect them. French soldiers, sailors, a contingent of Foreign Legionnaires in white undress caps, stood at the bar or danced with the girls: the notorious, somewhat unkempt and completely unrestrained 'Quinn's Girls'.

Elsewhere, crowded in booths, knee to knee around tables, were tourists from the hotels, sun-burned young men from the yachts, Frenchmen and Frenchwomen in garish clothes from the holiday camp on Moorea. There was too much color, too much din, too much movement to be encompassed. The Swedes in particular seemed dazed. Pushing to the bar, Luke fortuitously found a vacant stool and ordered a bottle of beer. Immediately he saw the man whom he had been seeking all afternoon. Black-eyes sat at a table near the wall with a young Tahitian woman in a very tight red and blue pareu. On her head, somewhat askew, was a crown of ginger blossoms. Tonight Black-eyes wore gray slacks, white shoes, a light-weight turtle-neck shirt striped black, grey and white. A rather vulgar outfit, thought Luke with a trace of disappointment. He would have preferred a gentleman for his murderer. Black-eyes was something of a puzzle. He had the arrogance of a lord; he was undoubtedly handsome, if speciously so; he looked deft and competent. A professional killer? Luke's spine tingled. He watched in fascination. Black-eyes sat back in a relaxation close to boredom, a long thin cigar smouldering in his fingers. The girl performed her most trusted exertions: pouting, hunching her shoulders, wrinkling her pug nose, tilting the ginger lei even more precariously over her forehead. Black-eyes watched in noncommittal amusement. The girl was not altogether to his taste, and Luke would have agreed that she looked blowsy and well-used, at the dangerous verge of portliness.

The music came to a thudding halt, like a stampede stopping short at the edge of a cliff. The musicians stood back to catch their breath, the dancers moved off the floor. Voices, laughter, the clink of glassware were suddenly audible. Only temporarily. The musicians shifted position, the guitarists stepping forward, the saxophonist taking up a baritone ukulele, the drummer tucking a leather-topped drum between his knees. A pause, an expectancy: then four quiet chords on the ukulele; four quick chords from the guitars: the *tamure!* Ignoring all protests, the girl pulled Black-eyes out on the dance-floor. Luke craned his neck, but they were lost in the seethe.

Luke turned his glass this way and that, watching the lights twinkle and distort around the islands of foam. He had found Black-eyes: what now? Luke had no clear idea. It occurred to him that he had failed to define his objectives. What did he want to do?

Most urgently Luke wanted to know *why*, so he decided. Revenge, legal or otherwise, could follow. Investigation therefore was in order. Luke leaned back against the bar, watching the dancers convulse, writhe and jerk. The music halted. The dancers gave a great sigh, then shuffled from the dance-floor. Twisting in his seat Luke fleetingly met the gaze of Black-eyes, but let his eyes slide past. When he looked back Black-eyes was signaling the waitress. Evidently he intended no immediate departure.

A second girl came to sit at his table: a friend of the woman in the red and blue pareu. The newcomer was younger and more supple, with a fresh smiling face. Black-eyes sat up straighter in his chair. The woman in red and blue scowled across the dance-floor.

Luke thoughtfully drank the last of his beer. The music began once more: an old island tune derived perhaps from a missionary hymn. Luke gave a sigh for his easy old life; the time had come when he must commit himself. He stepped down from the bar stool, gave his shoulders a shake, crossed the room to Black-eyes' table, halted in front of the girl in the red and blue pareu. *"Voulez-vous danser?"*

She looked up, gave Luke a dispassionate scrutiny. Then, glancing toward Black-eyes and the girl who had just joined the table, she shrugged. *"Oui, m'sieu."*

Luke steered her across the floor, shuffling dispiritedly to the music. The girl smelled of ginger blossom, perfume, sweat; her body felt bulky; her hair rasped against his cheek.

Presently she pushed slightly back, to look up with a gap-toothed grin. "You American, *oui?*"

"Right," said Luke. *"Et vous?* What about you?"

"Moi? j'suis Tahitienne!" And she gave Luke a look of amused wonder. "You like Papeete? Nice place, eh?"

"Very nice indeed."

"That's good. Lots of pretty *vahines*. Where you stay?"

"I'm at the Blue Lagoon," lied Luke.

"Nice place. *Très cher.* Costs too much money, eh?"

"Right. Far too much."

"You like pretty *vahine* for girl friend? Maybe you like take nice girl back to States?"

"I'm afraid that's out of the question. By the way, that man over there at the table: what is his name?"

The girl gave a complicated shrug and grimace. She tugged at Luke's arm. "Come on, we sit down; you not a very good dancer. But you buy me a drink."

"With pleasure."

They returned to the table. The girl dropped into her seat and Luke, pulling up a chair, essayed a friendly grin toward Black-eyes. "Mind if I join the group?"

"Help yourself."

"I'm Jim Harrison." And Luke smiled expectantly toward Black-eyes.

"How-de-do." Luke was favored with a glance so cursory as to be insulting. Then prompted perhaps by a sudden subconscious admonition Black-eyes looked back with a glitter of puzzled interest.

Luke hastily signaled the waitress. "What's everybody drinking? Rum punches for the girls? What's yours? Er, what's your name?"

"Scotch and soda."

"A bottle of beer for me." Luke turned once more to Black-eyes, considering subjects which might make acceptable small talk. As he thought, there was a shuffle and bump and someone else joined the group: a massive heavy-shouldered woman with a slab-sided face, a wild bush of coarse black hair under a palm-frond hat, a festoon of *pikake*. She gave Luke an enormous grin, squeezed herself and a chair up to the table.

"*Voilà Odette,*" said the girl with whom Luke had danced, in a subdued voice.

"*Bonsoir, tout le monde!*" called Odette in a hoarse voice. She nudged Luke with her elbow. "What you think, cowboy? How you like?"

"Everything is fine," said Luke. "Odette, let me introduce you to—" he looked toward Black-eyes. "Sorry, I didn't catch your name?"

"Ben Easley."

"Odette, meet Ben Easley."

"How-de-do."

"Hi, cowboy." Odette pushed closer to the table, appraised the bottles and glasses. She spoke in Tahitian to the other girls, provoking them to mirth.

"What in the world are they saying?" inquired Ben Easley, mildly curious, addressing no one in particular.

"They're dividing us up," said Luke. "That's my guess."

Easley raised his glass. "I hope the big one likes you."

"She's a formidable woman," Luke agreed. "Your first time at Quinn's?"

"Yeah."

"You can't have been in Papeete very long."

"Not too long."

Straining to maintain his amiable grin, Luke said, "I've been around a couple of months. Long enough, actually. Time to move on."

"Two months? You must be loaded. It costs a fortune to live here." Easley had a characteristic mode of speech, a clipped sardonic rasp.

"Too right," said Luke. "I cut every corner I can. Where are you staying?"

"Big place up the road." Easley glanced across the table toward Odette and her two friends. "The local population isn't all it's cracked up to be. Where are the dollies in cellophane skirts?"

"Here, there, around the island. They exist."

"You know some of them?" For the first time Easley regarded Luke with interest.

"A few."

"What are they like? Real friendly?"

Luke pursed his lips. "About like girls everywhere, I'd say— maybe just a little bit more so."

Easley leaned back in his chair and lit a new cigar. Odette put her elbows on the table, looked from Easley to Luke, back to Easley, each movement wafting an opulent odor of rose talcum powder toward Luke. "One of you fellows going to buy me a drink?"

"Not me," murmured Easley.

Odette swung around upon Luke. "Hey, cowboy, buy me a drink, eh?"

"Oh well," said Luke uneasily, "why not?" He signaled the waitress.

"You pretty good guy. That guy—" Odette jerked her thumb toward Easley "—he cheap *popaa*."

Easley paid no heed.

Odette shoved Luke with her elbow. "You know me? Odette."

"Yes, we've met," said Luke.

"That one's Aiinea, that one's Ellie. She's my daughter." Ellie, the pretty one, grinned: a wide, bashful, rather appealing grin. "Eh? What you say?" bellowed Odette. "I'm pretty good mama, eh? I drink, you drink. You got *popaa*, I got *popaa*."

"Is she saying 'papa'?" Easley asked, mildly curious.

"No," said Luke. "*Popaa* is 'white man'. Sounds like she's hinting for a double date. She's interested in you, I believe."

"I'm not her type," said Easley.

The music started. Easley quickly rose to his feet, walked around the table to Ellie, led her out on the dance-floor. Odette and Aiinea examined Luke, but he pretended not to notice.

Quinn's had filled to capacity. Faces flickered and glimmered among the lights and colored shadows; the music was secondary to laughter, whoops, shouted conversation. In one corner a fight started; with a dexterity approaching elegance a pair of bouncers flung the combatants into the street.

The music halted; Easley returned to the table, his arm around Ellie's waist. He called the waitress and ordered for himself and Ellie. Odette and Aiinea watched with undisguised disgust; but now they were distracted by a pair of lurching young Foreign Legionnaires.

Assuming his genial grin, Luke called down the table to Easley: "Do you plan to stay in Papeete long?"

The persistent affability at last appeared to arouse Easley's suspicion; he pierced Luke with a black-eyed stare. "What?"

Luke was sure he had heard. With the smile fixed and stiff on his lips, he repeated the question.

Easley's suspicion, if such it was, passed. "Not too long," he said gruffly. "I'm leaving Tuesday, going out to the boondocks."

Luke's grin slowly became unfastened; his jaw dropped. "'Boondocks'? The outer islands? Aboard the *Rahiria?*"

"Yeah."

"That's a coincidence. I'm going out on the *Rahiria* myself. At least I think I'm going on the *Rahiria*," Luke said in a thoughtful voice. The old schooner might be somewhat small should Easley discover his identity. And why should Easley be sailing on the *Rahiria* in the first place? Like Luke, to meet the *Dorado*? Luke's mind reeled. He shook his head in despairing perplexity. So many variables, so many imponderables!

Easley had noted Luke's bewilderment, and Luke felt the chill of the black eyes. But now Easley was diverted. A Foreign Legionnaire approached the table, to lean over Ellie. Easley lifted his eyebrows in disapproval. The Foreign Legionnaire, a blond German with a fine yellow mustache, paid no heed. The music started. Easley rose purposefully but before he could act the German had hoisted the girl and with a brisk Teutonic gesticulation swept her out on the dance-floor.

Easley returned to his seat, to sit staring into his drink. Luke watched with eery fascination. This might be Easley planning his own murder. Luke winced. Perhaps it was time to be leaving. He had achieved his minimum objectives. The man's name was Ben Easley; on Tuesday he would be sailing aboard the *Rahiria*. But Luke's stubborn streak objected. What was the quotation about alcohol and a loose tongue? *In vino veritas?* If he poured enough liquor into Easley he might learn something more. There was the equal possibility of disaster. He could hardly pour liquor into Easley without taking a drink himself; the evening might end with the two babbling their secrets into each other's ears... Luke saw something which stiffened him in his seat: his cousin Carson, somewhat drunk.

Chapter IX

CARSON sat half-slouched, an elbow on the bar. He had not yet seen Luke through the dim lights and surging shadows. Additionally Carson did not seem particularly alert. Through Luke's mind flickered a terrible conjecture, that Carson and Ben Easley were associates, together planning his death... Insane!

Another possibility: suppose Carson saw him and bawled "Hey Luke!" This would make for embarrassment. Luke half-rose to leave, then slowly settled back. Carson was not about to recognize anyone. Other questions suggested themselves. Why and how was Carson here? Surely the *Dorado* was not in port! Warily Luke studied Carson. In many ways, he was like his father—a loose, untidy, less definite and younger Brady Royce. His hair was dark and lank; he displayed Brady's heavy cheek-bones; his mouth, somewhat over-full, hung in a petulant droop. But Carson was not all bad. His wilfulness and brazen indolence were tempered by a rather charming gayety, an easy generosity.

The theory of Carson conspiring with Ben Easley was absurd. But the puzzle of Carson's presence in Papeete remained. To resolve the mystery was simplicity itself; he need only ask Carson.

But first: were Easley and Carson known to each other? Luke furtively watched Easley, who could not have avoided seeing Carson, only ten yards distant, in the full illumination of the yellow lights above the bar. Easley sat brooding across the dance-floor. Easley was becoming drunk, thought Luke. His black eyes were almost wetly brilliant; he moved with studied control. He showed no interest whatever in Carson.

Spotlights shone upon a platform high against the back wall. A girl in a grass skirt appeared; she gyrated, heaved and oscillated. Easley gave her the whole of his attention. Luke arose, walked to the bar, touched Carson's shoulder. Carson gave a raucous cry. "I was looking for you!"

"Quiet," said Luke. "Come around to the other side of the bar."

"What's wrong with this side?" asked Carson. "I'm watching those calisthenics. It's like a woman with no hands trying to get out of a corset."

"Never mind that just now," said Luke, glancing toward Easley. "Come around over here."

Carson followed him around the bar. "Why all the mystery? Are you trying to dodge somebody?"

"Not exactly. What are you doing in Papeete?"

"The same thing you're doing: waiting for the *Dorado*. The old man sailed from Honolulu without my permission, in fact I wasn't even aboard. So I flew down on the credit card. Now what's all the mystery? Who are we hiding from?"

Luke pointed out Easley. "The dark-haired fellow next to the girl in red and blue. Do you know him?"

"Never saw him before in my life."

"His name is Ben Easley."

"If his name was Jesus Christ I still wouldn't know him. Does he know me?"

"Apparently not. He's a bill collector, something of the sort. I told him my name is James Harrison, so don't recognize me. Above all, don't call me 'Luke'. Got that?"

"Nothing to it. 'James Harrison', yes; 'Luke Royce', no. What else?"

"Discretion. Does Brady know you're here?"

"I talked to him by radio. I guess he knows. I don't think he cares. His wife has him hypnotized."

"Oh? What's she like?"

"Hard to say. She once had a job modeling clothes, if that answers your question. I take it you're joining the cruise?"

Luke nodded. "I'm sailing up to the Marquesas, to go aboard there."

Carson blinked, lurched, drained his glass. "When do you leave? I'll come with you."

"Tuesday. On the *Rahiria*. It's a schooner, not too comfortable. No stewards, no lap robes, no shuffleboard."

"Who cares? I'm in revolt against civilization. We're all too soft, too careful, too tidy. I plan to devote myself to the elementals. Food, drink, TV, females. If I were you, Luke—"

"Not 'Luke'! 'Jim Harrison'! Remember, you don't know me! We're strangers!"

"Luke, you amaze me!"

"I'll explain some other time. But for now—incidentally, where are you staying?"

"Hotel Tahiti, in a little thatch hut, with artificial lizards on the ceiling."

"I suspect they're real. If I were you I'd go back to the hotel. You've got a snootful."

"I know, Luke—"

"Jim Harrison!"

"Okay, okay. But this is exactly what I mean. Look at you now. Respectable, clean-cut, sober—and so ashamed that you call yourself Jim Harrison. Look at me. Drunk, raggedy-ass, but proud! I call myself Carson Royce! See the difference?"

"Yes, yes, the 'elementals'. Goodby, goodnight. Go back to your hotel. I'll see you tomorrow."

"Much too cautious, Luke. It's a pity."

"Perhaps so." Luke patted Carson on the shoulder, gave a final gesture of admonition, and returned through the press of shoulders, torsos and hips, to the table.

Easley was to the stage where even Aiinea looked good; he had committed himself to the extent of listening to her remarks and making an occasional humorous grimace. Odette had given up and taken herself elsewhere.

Luke licked his lips and once more brought forth his genial smile. "Place is getting crowded," he told Easley.

Easley agreed. "It's a madhouse. All these soldiers yet. Do they expect an invasion?"

Luke signaled the waitress, ordered Easley a double Scotch on the rocks, a bottle of Hinano beer for himself.

"I won't ask why all the largesse," said Easley. "I'd rather not know." He lifted his glass. "Cheers. Two more like this and I'll recite a poem by Longfellow."

"Cheers," said Luke. "What poem did you have in mind?"

But Easley's attention was diverted by Aiinea, who giggled and nudged him with her elbow.

Luke looked to where she pointed, to see Carson dancing a clownish contemporary jig in the company of the monstrous Odette. Luke rolled his eyes toward the ceiling, then looked at Easley, who exhibited only contemptuous amusement.

The music halted; with fiendish perversity Odette brought Carson back to the table. "Sit down, cowboy, sit down. You dance very hard, you poor tired drunk cowboy. Maybe one more drink, eh?"

"Sure. One more drink for all." Carson called the waitress. "Set 'em up!" He turned a leer of dreadful intimacy upon Luke. "What's yours, cowboy?"

"A bottle of beer," said Luke in a strained voice.

"Everybody spends their money on me," marveled Easley. "Scotch on the rocks, so long as the dream goes on."

"Rum punch," ordered Aiinea. "Scotch and coca-cola," ordered Odette.

Carson looked from face to face. He waved his finger toward Luke and Easley. "I recognize both of you. Captain Kangaroo and Batman."

"Wrong," stated Luke in a trembling voice. "Still—close enough. I think we'd all better go. This place closes at midnight. Another ten minutes."

"That's ridiculous!"

"Complain to the management."

The music started: the final *tamure* of the evening. Over the table loomed the German soldier with the handsome blond mustache. Apparently he had misplaced Ellie and was seeking a replacement. He addressed himself to Aiinea. *"Voulez-vous danser, mademoiselle?"*

Aiinea grinned and shuffled her feet. Easley glared up in outrage. "Get lost. *Heraus,* you stupid kraut."

The German raised his blond eyebrows. "You speak to me?"

Aiinea held up her hands in alarm. "You two be nice boys. Sit down, we all drink."

The German bowed stiffly. *"Alors, nous dansons; c'est mieux."* He gave Easley the briefest and most wooden of side-glances.

The German reached to assist Aiinea to her feet. Easley arose. "The lady, so it happens, is with me."

The German seemed not to hear. Easley pushed his hand away; the German shoved Easley back into his chair, which tilted backwards, toppling Easley to the floor.

Aiinea and Odette yelped in excitement; Carson gave a caw of laughter. Easley jumped to his feet. The German cuffed him smartly on the ear. Easley stood back glaring, then came forward, a creature of the utmost menace. Before he could strike, the bouncers arrived. The German assumed a posture of innocence and forbearance; Easley was seized and hustled swearing and stamping out the door.

The German gave his head a jerk of approval; glancing incuriously toward Luke, he escorted Aiinea out upon the dance-floor. Odette seized Carson and led him away; they disappeared into the crowd. Luke waited until midnight but saw no more of Carson.

The next day, calling at Hotel Tahiti, he was told that Carson was not in.

Chapter X

BRADY sat in the shadow of the mainsail, pretending to doze. The afternoon was warm; the wind was capricious; overhead vast constructions of cumulus reared into the upper air.

Brady slouched with his white cap tilted over his nose, watching the game Jean Wintersea and Kelsey played with Don Peppergold. Jean had become interested in Don; Kelsey, previously lukewarm, was now stimulated to exert herself. Still, neither wanted to commit herself too openly for fear that Don should conspicuously prefer the other; hence Don was treated to a bewildering campaign of ploys and plots, enigmatic half-smiles and equally perplexing snubs. Brady looked toward Lia, where she lounged on a cushion, gazing out across the ocean. What in the world was she thinking? Now she frowned a trifle, now she gnawed at her lower lip. Brady knew that if he asked for an explanation, her only response would be a wide-eyed stare. A phrase rose unbidden into Brady's mind, from some back chamber of his subconscious: "A woman without a soul." Brady scowled, adjusted his cap, heaved himself erect. He looked at his watch, surprised to find that the time had gone so fast. In fact— He glanced at the sails, at the water, at the wake, at the sky; he performed a mental calculation. Now was as good a time as any.

He touched a button. Hector the Filipino steward appeared. Brady gave him a nod. "Now."

Hector went below and a moment later reappeared with a tray of champagne glasses and an ice-bucket with four dark green bottles.

Corks popped; Hector poured and served.

"What's the occasion?" asked Don Peppergold.

Brady pointed back the way they had come. "There's the Northern Hemisphere." He pointed ahead. "There's the Southern Hemisphere. At this instant we are crossing the equator."

Chapter XI

ONE o'clock Tuesday afternoon, an hour before sailing time: the *Rahiria* seethed with activity.

Passengers, friends, relatives crowded the deck, passed up and down the gangplank, in a blaze of flower crowns and coronas, vivid shirts and pareus. All were excited, some were drunk. Luke came aboard, paused to get his bearings. The *Rahiria* was a hundred and ten feet long, a husky, German-built ship, devoid of brightwork, unknown to varnish, the timbers and decks scarred by forty years of weather and hard knocks.

There were two cargo hatches and two deck-houses. The hatches were situated forward of each mast, the houses aft. In the forward house were the crew's quarters and the galley; in the after house were the saloon, four small cabins for the passengers—these to port and starboard—cabins for the captain, the super-cargo and the engineer. The sails were stout oatmeal-colored canvas, the hull was rusty black, the deck-houses a nondescript gray. The hatches were now burdened with deck passengers and their multitudinous belongings.

Luke approached a chubby man wearing shorts, a white and blue shirt, a dark blue nautical cap, who, at a guess, might be Polynesian mingled with Portuguese and Chinese. "Are you the supercargo?"

"*C'est ça!* That's me!"

Luke tendered his ticket; the supercargo took him to a cabin on the starboard side of the after deck-house. It contained upper and lower bunks, a pair of lockers, a low stool, a rectangle of gray carpet on the deck. Luke's room-mate sat on the lower bunk: a middle-aged Chinaman wearing a shiny black suit.

Luke and the Chinaman bowed, smiled, shook hands.

"My name," said Luke, "is Jim Harrison."

"I am Ching Piao; you call me Ching. I sleep downstairs below, okay?"

Luke understood Ching to be referring to the lower bunk. "Wherever you like."

"Good. I get seasick very much. Too bad."

"Too bad, indeed," agreed Luke. The cabin was somewhat warm. Luke pushed open a porthole, looked out upon the dock. He observed Ben Easley, sauntering toward the gangplank, a thin black cigar clenched between his teeth.

Luke's stomach muscles constricted; he felt a sudden reluctance toward going out on deck—could it be fear? Yes, it was fear. Luke smiled, amused and annoyed by his qualms. Deliberately he strode out upon the deck.

Easley, mounting the gangplank, halted at the rail, glanced casually around the deck, paying Luke the gratuitous insult of non-recognition. He spoke briefly with the supercargo and was conducted to his cabin.

Luke thought that he seemed fretful and preoccupied.

Other passengers came aboard—a middle-aged couple, in near-identical suits of cloud-grey seersucker. Both were thin as whippets, fair, with scrubbed pale pink complexions and ash-blond hair. Eyes averted, they edged through the Tahitians, mounted the gangplank: cool, humorously aloof in the manner of veteran globetrotters. They spoke to the supercargo; Luke heard the clipped consonants and plangent vowels of far-away England. With a final wry glance toward the Tahitians the two went to their cabin.

Next aboard was a man Luke knew well by sight and by reputation: a certain Rolf Clute, originally of Norway. Clute, a man of many enterprises, lived at the edge of the Mataiea district, in a *fare* of his own construction, with a Tahitian wife and half-a-dozen beautiful daughters. Luke had heard him described, without rancor, as a rascal, a beachcomber and, less precisely, a drunken Swede. Today Rolf Clute was sober and well turned-out, in suntan trousers, a white shirt stylishly half-unbuttoned, pointed red-brown shoes. Luke hoped that Clute would not recognize him; if so, the fat was in the fire.

But Rolf Clute, affable and waggish, merely gave Luke a wave of the hand, and went to chat with the supercargo, with whom he seemed to be on intimate terms. Turning from the supercargo, he called out in Tahitian to one of the deck passengers, and took his suitcase around the port side of the deck-house.

Sailing time was close at hand; never had Luke seen such a frenzy of confusion. Up and down the gangplank streamed the deck passengers, their friends and their relatives, carrying paper bags, jugs, stalks of bananas, cardboard cartons, guitars, suitcases. Two motorbikes, a wheelbarrow, a crate of live chickens were brought aboard. In spite of the supercargo's protests a pig was placed in the port lifeboat. The farewells became fervent, tears fell; underfoot was a litter of empty Hinano bottles. Those departing staggered under heaps of flower leis; everyone embraced repeatedly.

A deck-hand went to stand by the gangplank; the supercargo went forward, urging all visitors ashore. In line with the genial unpredictability of everything Tahitian, the *Rahiria* was about to sail precisely on time, if not sooner. Luke searched the pier, praying that Carson had forgotten all about his plan to make the trip north. Aboard the *Rahiria* Carson could only be a source of uneasiness—though his presence might well catalyze new information in regard to Ben Easley. But, in the long run, it would be far better if Carson neglected to show up before sailing time.

Unfortunately this was not to be the case. Idling half-heartedly along the pier, dragging one foot in front of the other, came Carson.

Luke shook his head in vexation and disapproval. Carson looked a mess. His clothes were rumpled; his eyes were red-rimmed; his mouth hung in a dyspeptic droop. With a scowl for the Tahitians he slouched up the gangplank, then looked wildly around the deck as if half of a mind to debark immediately. Carson was evidently suffering the pangs of a titanic hangover.

The supercargo came forward; Carson made a sullen exposition of his purposes. The supercargo flashed a typical Tahitian gap-toothed grin, pointed to the No. 2 hatch. Carson stared in astonishment. "You must be kidding! Get me a place to sleep!"

"Cabins all gone, boy. Too bad. Sleep on deck. Maybe you catch a flying fish."

Carson turned a glare of outrage toward the hatch. Among the passengers was a girl in a black and orange pareu, innocently beautiful, who found Carson's predicament amusing, and Carson encountered her delighted grin.

Carson hesitated. He scowled, he rubbed the back of his neck, he jammed his hands in his pockets and seemed to be talking to himself. Perhaps he interpreted the grin as admiration, perhaps he was infuriated to the point of defiance. Perhaps he wanted to get on board the *Dorado*. Perhaps, conjectured Luke, he was fleeing something, or someone, in Papeete. At any rate he turned away from the gangplank.

His eyes fell on Luke. "Hey, L—" he scowled, bemused by Luke's instant gesticulations. Luke came forward. "Don't forget! The name is Jim Harrison!"

Carson's mouth sagged in disgust. "For Christ sake. Aren't you done with that nonsense?"

"Not yet. In fact—I don't suppose you'd take some excellent advice?"

"I've been ducking advice for years, my boy."

"You're coming aboard deck-class?"

"Sure. Why not?"

"First of all—rain. Lots of it."

Carson shrugged. "I'll move in with you."

"Not on your life. Don't even speculate along those lines."

"The Tahitians don't look worried—especially that cute one."

"Deck-class food isn't too good."

"So what? It's probably no good cabin-class."

"Be that as it may—my advice to you is stay here in Tahiti."

Carson gave Luke a glance of jaundiced suspicion. "What for?"

"Never mind what for."

"Forget it; I'm going. Deck-class and all."

Luke compressed his lips. He had played his cards wrong. To ensure that Carson remain in Papeete, he should have implored him to sail deck-passage aboard the *Rahiria*. "Well then: will you do me a favor?"

"Hell no."

"I'm serious. I want you to call yourself Bob Smith, something of the sort, until we get aboard the *Dorado*."

Carson stared in wonder, then asked, in the voice of one reasoning with a lunatic: "Now why should I call myself Bob Smith?"

Luke looked right and left. "I can't give you the details now. That fellow Easley tried to kill me, deliberately."

"Come, come, Luke. This is the twentieth century."

"Who says otherwise? You asked why; I'm telling you."

Carson heaved a sigh. "Easley tried to kill you. You retaliate by calling yourself Jim Harrison. It seems a subtle revenge. Perhaps I'm stupid—"

Around the deck-house came a dark shape; Luke moved hastily away, to Carson's vulgar amusement. The man was Rolf Clute, swinging and swaggering like an old-time zoot-suiter, his mop of grizzled red hair glinting proudly in the sunlight. He came to lean on the rail between Carson and Luke, and spat through his teeth down at the dock. "Well, looks like we got a good trip. Good wind, good weather. Nice."

"I hope you're right," said Carson. "I'm in no mood for emergencies."

"Don't worry!" declared Rolf Clute. "Nothing to worry about." He pointed across the dock. "See that old woman down there? That's her nephew with her; he's coming aboard. She told him, 'Go ahead, sail on *Rahiria!*' That's all I need to know. She's a witch-woman. Lives out in Papeari."

Carson's interest was stirred. "A witch-woman?"

"Yep. That big lady in the green dress, with the big fat face." The woman looked up at the *Rahiria;* Clute shouted something raffish in Tahitian; she gave him a good-natured salute.

"I get along good with her," said Clute. "She's not one of them bad witches, not unless you get in her way. Then she's pretty bad."

"How do you mean 'bad'?" asked Carson.

But Clute only grinned and shook his head. He peered sidelong at Luke. "Seems like I seen you before. Out by—"

"My name is Jim Harrison," stated Luke.

Carson snorted derisively. Luke gave him a frown.

As if struck by a sudden thought Clute ran down the gangplank, and presently returned with three huge bottles of Hinano. He snapped off the covers, handed one to Carson, one to Luke. *"Skoal."*

"Skoal." Carson tilted the bottle. Bubbles vibrated up behind the sunstruck brown glass. He brought down the bottle. "Ahh!" Bubbles still rose in Rolf Clute's bottle. They continued to rise. Carson watched in respect.

Rolf Clute finally lowered the bottle. He wiped his mouth with the back of his hand, looked shrewdly from Luke to Carson. "You fellers from the States, eh? I got two daughters in the States. The guy in my cabin he's from the States too. You know him?"

"No," said Carson. "I don't know anybody. Not even 'Jim Harrison' here."

"Here he comes now." Clute beckoned to Ben Easley. "Hey, come over here. What's your name again?"

"Ben Easley."

"This is—what's your name?"

"Jim Harrison."

"I'm Carson Royce."

Easley's face twitched, then became unnaturally bland and blank. Or so it seemed to Luke. "Welcome aboard," said Easley in an offhand voice.

Luke turned away, unable to look into Easley's face. One thing was certain—or almost certain: Carson and Ben Easley had no prior acquaintance.

From below decks came the thump-thump-chuff-chuff of the diesel; a bell clanged. The supercargo bawled orders, herded the last of the visitors ashore.

On the dock the farewells became fervent. The last leis were thrown; the last bottle tilted. The captain came out on deck, a lean Frenchman with a gray complexion and an uneven gray mustache. He gave a jerk of his head; the gangplank was pulled to the dock even while the last passengers were scrambling aboard. Lines were thrown off. The *Rahiria* eased away from the dock, swung slowly out past the breakwater. Winches rattled; the sails went aloft and bellied to the breeze. The diesel gave a final roar, then quieted; the *Rahiria* heaved quietly northward through the blue swells, with Moorea astern and Tahiti bulking green and golden to the starboard.

Carson's excesses of the past few days caught up with him; he became wretchedly seasick. Clute watched with a brisk but sympathetic shake of the head. Ben Easley moved away in distaste. Presently he retired to his cabin, and Luke suspected that perhaps he too felt unsettled.

On the foredeck the guitars had been brought out. There was singing and gayety. Rolf Clute went forward and joined the fun.

So passed the bright afternoon. Tahiti became a gray blur astern and presently, toward sunset, disappeared.

Supper was served to the cabin passengers in the saloon: beef stew, rice, sliced raw onions in oil and vinegar, bread, raw red Algerian wine. The deck passengers, filing past the galley, were served on tin plates. Carson, huddled against the No. 1 hatch, ignored the meal and Luke thought better of offering him encouragement. "The experience will be good for Carson's character," Luke told himself.

At the meal Luke made the acquaintance of the two middle-aged Britishers, Derek and Fiona Orsham, and two German students who completed the passenger list. Derek and Fiona conducted wonderfully airy dialogues in clipped well-bred accents: "The salt, dear, if you please." "Oh! Sorry. Of course. Here you are!" And: "Please may I try the sauce, dear, meat's a bit heavy." "Oh! Of course! Here we come, full speed on."

The Germans spoke no English and very little French. They muttered only briefly to each other and seemed intent on finishing the meal as expeditiously as possible. Luke's cabinmate, Ching Piao, appeared only briefly, still wearing his black suit. He smiled a brief pasty grin at the others, dished himself a small bowl of rice and gravy which he took from the saloon, presumably to the cabin. Derek and Fiona were amused. "Well, really! Do our habits offend him?" "The inscrutable Orient; something we've got to adapt to." "Yes, I know; twilight of the Empire and all that."

Rolf Clute drank largely of the wine and described the marriage of his oldest daughter to a Seattle physician. Derek and Fiona gave their eyebrows brisk twitches and murmured: "Really?" and "How interesting!" Rolf Clute, not at all abashed, poured himself another glass of wine and spoke of the marriage of his second daughter to a wealthy Las Vegas real estate broker.

"How marvellous!" and "You must be very proud of your daughters!" said Derek and Fiona.

Luke took a mug of tea, excused himself and went out on deck. Carson, sitting on the hatch, looked at him accusingly. "What a fiasco! No hammocks, no bunks, no nothing! Where am I supposed to sleep?"

"I guess you just pick a spot," said Luke.

"I never thought it was going to be like this," complained Carson. "That Chinaman in your cabin, I wonder if he'd sell his berth. How much money do you have on you? I'm a bit short."

"I've got a couple hundred," said Luke. "Take it, if it'll do you any good, which I doubt."

Rolf Clute, leaning on the rail with the breeze ruffling his curly top-knot, laughed in vast amusement. "That Chinaman, you know something? He owns the boat."

Carson threw up his hands in disgust. His attention was distracted by the pretty girl he had noticed before. Instantly his condition improved. He went to sit by her and tried to talk pidgin English. The young Polynesian buck squatting nearby grunted and stalked ostentatiously forward.

Dusk drifted out of the east, the ocean became vague. Presently the moon rose, to lay a smoky yellow trail across the water. From the foredeck came the throb of guitars, the muffled chant of Polynesian voices. Luke leaned back on his elbows. The voyage would be pleasant indeed were it not for his worries and fears and perplexities.

As if to emphasize Luke's reservations, Ben Easley emerged from the deck-house, paused a moment, then seated himself at the far end of the hatch.

"Hey Luke," called Carson. "Come over here, translate for me! This young bonbon don't take me seriously."

Luke grimaced. "Er—Clute! Carson's calling you."

"Eh? Who?"

"Carson wants you to help him out with that girl," Luke explained. Easley seemed engrossed in his own thoughts.

"Not me." Clute pointed a crooked finger. "That was Leon Teofu who walked away. He's a good fighter and he's pretty mean. I don't want him mad at me."

"That's his girl friend?"

"Leon thinks so. Carson better look out."

Derek and Fiona joined the group, and the air at once was full of verbal shuttlecocks: "What an enchanting evening." "Never like this in dear old Blighty." "Oh my aunt no." "Exactly where are we, dear?" "Hard to say. A bit north of Tahiti, or so I'd reckon it."

Fiona searched the moon-silvered horizons. "Nothing in sight. Where is our first landfall?"

"Somewhere in the Tuamotus," said Derek. "Ask Mr. Clute; he's a knowing sort."

"I think we land on Kaukura first," said Rolf Clute. "Then Apataki. Then Arutua. Then Rangiroa, and that's where I leave the ship."

"Indeed?" inquired Fiona brightly. "You're not a tourist like the rest of us?"

Clute chuckled. "My touring days are over. I'm a businessman. I got property on Rangiroa. Now I go out to look."

"How nice."

"Nice when they don't steal my copra. Some people are pretty grabby. I'm taking out a boy to watch things for me." Clute leaned forward, peered up the deck. "That's him in the white shirt, playing the guitar."

Luke looked. "That's the witch-lady's nephew."

"'Witch-lady'?" inquired Fiona. Derek asked, "Did I hear correctly?"

Rolf Clute glanced sidewise to discover if possibly the Orshams might be indulging in facetiousness. But both were entirely in earnest. "Yeah, the big fat lady in the green dress that was sitting on the gasoline can. I've known her a long time. She witched me once on Rangiroa. I told her I knew what she was doing. I told her she'd better stop or I'd cut her throat." Rolf Clute nodded in grim recollection of the event. "She stopped the curse, just like that. We get along good now. She knows I'm not scared of her. I can take care of anything along those lines."

"My word," breathed Derek, raising his eyes to the heavens. "Witches!" Fiona gave her breathless little laugh. "One travels for new experiences, and now, my dear, you've met a witch." "Not precisely met! Sheerest, most glancing contact. We're not even acquainted."

Rolf Clute said in a deprecatory tone, "She's no real strong witch. There's some on the outer islands: *tahuas* they call 'em. They get mad at a man, they lay on a real strong curse. Then the man goes to another *tahua* to take off the curse. Otherwise he dies like a mad dog."

"Poison, most likely," was Derek's opinion. "I suppose that poison is available?"

Clute snorted. "Nothing to it. In the old days they'd just cook up a dish of *hue-hue*—that's puffer fish—or they take the poison from a puffer fish and mix it into good fish. But that was just for the common people. The *tahuas* would use a curse, or send out ghosts—*tupaupaus*, they call 'em."

"'Ghosts'? Oh really now. You're joshing us."

Rolf Clute shook his head as if at knowledge too vast to communicate. He looked up toward the No. 1 hatch. "Go up there; ask for Ari'aitere or just yell 'Jono': that's his French name."

"'Jono'?" asked Fiona doubtfully. "French?"

Rolf Clute continued. "He's from one of the oldest families; ask him about the *tupaupau* that walks around behind his house. Go over to Raiatea. Some American guy built a house on the Vaitate family tomb. He's dead, his son is dead, his uncle is dead. The house is empty. Sit on the porch the night of the full moon. You'll see all the ghosts you want."

"You've seen these ghosts?"

"Sure I've seen 'em. Dozens."

"Well, well!" "I suppose we can't dispute eye-witness testimony!"

Ben Easley came across the hatch and seated himself beside Rolf Clute. "They must have had some pretty fierce times out here."

"You betcha. Nobody gets as mad as a Polynesian. Look at 'em now, laughing, singing—you'd think they was the gentlest people in the world. Wait till they get mad. Then they go crazy." Rolf Clute jerked his thumb forward to where Carson sat with the girl. "Chances are nothing will happen. Leon Teofu will sulk and go off with some other girl. Unless he sulks too hard and gets mad. Then Carson might get a beating, or maybe cut with a knife. That's the way it goes."

"Oh my," exclaimed Fiona. "Shouldn't someone warn him?"

Rolf Clute shrugged. "I'll pass him a word." He rose to his feet, stretched his wiry arms, let them flap against his hips. "He can't get in trouble tonight. Not unless he's a pretty good man, better than I give him credit for."

Rolf Clute departed for his bunk. Easley strolled forward to the bow, where he could be vaguely seen, silhouetted against the jib. Derek and Fiona Orsham yawned and rose to their feet. "Time for shut-eye." "But it *is* so lovely out here!" "Worth all the tawdry gimcrack of Papeete." "I think I could sail on like this forever." "Yes, but we mustn't be greedy. There'll be more tomorrow." "Of course. Goodnight all." "All, goodnight!"

The Orshams departed. Ben Easley strolled down the port side of the deck, passed behind the deck-house, and presumably went into his cabin. The two Germans had retired a half-hour before. Ching was nowhere to be seen. Of the cabin passengers only Luke was yet on deck. The time was perhaps eleven o'clock.

Carson came to sit on the hatch beside Luke.

"Two things I want to emphasize," said Luke. "First: you'd better lay off that girl. Her boy friend is a pretty tough customer."

"Who? Leon? Meek as a lamb. Besides, he's not her boy friend. Titi laughs at him."

"'Titi'? Is that her name?"

"So she tells me. Why should she lie?"

"No reason whatever. How do you exchange your little love secrets?"

"She talks French. I had French in high school. Funny how fast it comes back. Never thought I'd have any use for it."

"You don't think Leon is a threat?"

"Hell no."

"Clute says he's a tough cooky and mean as sin. If I were you, I'd lay off."

"Well, you're not me. If Leon looks at me sidewise I'll lay a karate chop on him. So much for Point Number One. What's Number Two?"

"Be careful of Easley. Really careful."

"What an odd world you live in! First Leon, now Easley."

Luke spoke in a measured voice: "I'll tell you exactly what happened. You can draw your own conclusions." He described his experiences. "The next day I shaved off my beard; I became Jim Harrison. I'm naturally interested in learning the reason for all this."

Carson seemed to be impressed. "I agree that Easley is a sinister type. Still, why should he pick on me?"

"My name is Royce, your name is Royce."

"You've never seen him before?"

"Never."

"Nor I." Carson pondered a moment. "It seems remarkable that he's headed for the Marquesas along with us. Is he planning to meet the *Dorado?*"

"Your guess is as good as mine. Exactly who is aboard the *Dorado?*"

Carson's voice took on a trace of zest. "First, the old man and his child bride. Do you watch old movies on TV?"

"I don't even watch new movies."

"Lia is like Hedy Lamarr at her best: dark hair, pale skin, a mysterious expression, not quite so slinky. She's a hard woman to figure out. Still, nothing like her sister Jean, who you wouldn't believe. She plays the flute. I patted her fanny one night and I don't think she knew what I meant; she said 'Excuse me' and moved out of the way. There's another cutie aboard, more my type: a certain Kelsey McClure, who knew Lia in high school—in fact, she introduced Lia to Brady. Then there's a junior executive known as Don Peppergold, two older McClures, and that's the lot. Some people name of Crothers made the trip to Honolulu, but they're not aboard now. By and large, a clean-cut bunch. Could it be that you're just a wee bit imaginative?"

"Call me anything you like. But don't take chances until you're aboard the *Dorado.*"

"Just as you say. I can't avoid being killed in my sleep, however. Speaking of sleep, fetch me a pillow and some blankets. Do you have a spare set of pajamas? I don't suppose you'd part with your mattress?"

"And sleep on the springs? Not much. Why didn't you bring aboard a bedroll?"

Carson managed a haughty stare. "Naturally I thought I could promote a cabin."

"I'll give you a blanket and maybe a pillow. Let me check and see what's available."

Luke went to his cabin. In the bottom bunk Ching snored softly. Luke pulled the blanket from his bunk but decided against the pillow. Carson would have to make do with his suitcase, or his shoes.

Chapter XII

IN the morning a brisk wind ranged out of the southeast, from the empty trade-wind spaces below Easter Island. The schooner wallowed and heeled; water rushed past the hull; the old timbers creaked and squeaked and made a hundred other less definite noises. One of these, a subdued dreary moaning, was almost human in its overtones. Luke, awakened by the multifarious noises shortly after dawn, watched the disk of sunlight admitted by the porthole sliding up and down the bulkhead. He presently traced the source of the near-human moaning to Ching in the lower berth. The cabin smelled of vomit. Luke's own stomach gave a jerk. He wasted no time going out on deck to breathe fresh air and steady himself against the horizon.

The ocean raced and rolled; whitecaps fell down the face of the blue-black waves. Luke drew several deep breaths and felt better.

The deck passengers were already at their breakfasts: coffee, bread and jam. Carson gave Luke a glance of bitter reproach, as if all his discomforts were the result of Luke's neglect. Luke returned a cheerful wave and went into the saloon. Derek and Fiona Orsham were breakfasting. Rolf Clute sat opposite smoking a cigarette.

"Good morning," said Luke.

"Good morning!" "A rough good morning it is!" "So windy!"

"Just trade-winds," said Clute. "Good sailing weather. We're going about nine knots. Maybe ten."

Ben Easley came in, wearing white shorts, his white and black sport-shirt, sun-glasses. He gave the company a reserved "Good morning", poured himself a mug of coffee. Luke studied him covertly. Amazing how a single human being could generate so dark an influence! Luke looked here and there; did the others feel the same oppression? Clute stubbed out his cigarette, raised his cup with a somewhat excessive action of arm. Derek ordered his tableware precisely in front of him. Fiona's voice became almost imperceptibly higher.

Derek rubbed his face and wondered whether he should shave. "After all, we're miles at sea." "Derek, you mustn't go slack. What would you think if I came to the table in a ghastly great bush?"

"Quite right, dear—but ladies aren't gentlemen. And, as the French say, *'Vive la différence!'* My feelings exactly."

"Beards are really so vulgar," said Fiona. "I simply can't imagine any of you wearing a beard." She looked from face to face. Luke excused himself and left the saloon. He went to his cabin, found his razor and shaved with care.

He came out and sat on the hatch. Carson joined him. "Speaking of Easley—have you done any investigating?"

Luke raised his eyebrows. "Such as what?"

"Oh—just general detective work."

"I don't know what you mean. Whatever it is—I haven't done any."

"Seems as if that would be the first order of business."

"Maybe so—but what should I do?"

"Search his luggage."

Luke grunted. "You make it sound so easy. Any other ideas?"

"Well—you might tell him you're Luke Royce. Confront him with the facts. Watch his reactions."

"Hmm. Then what?"

Carson shrugged. "It's a start. You asked for some ideas."

"And those are the best you can come up with?"

"Can you do any better?" snapped Carson.

"No. Which is why I haven't tried any detective work."

During the afternoon Rolf Clute brought out a pack of cards and enticed Carson and Easley into a poker game. Luke watched for a few minutes, then went out to sit on the hatch.

Carson's recommendations, he was forced to admit, made a certain degree of sense.

Luke grimaced. He strolled to the saloon, glanced in at the game. No one heeded him. He sauntered around to the port side of the deck-house. Here he hesitated. Embarrassing to be caught rummaging through Easley's belongings! Still—nothing ventured, nothing gained. Gritting his teeth, palms sweating, Luke opened the door, stepped into the cabin.

A new leather suitcase lay under the lower bunk—obviously the property of Easley. Luke slid it forth, puzzled a moment over the clasp, raised the lid.

Clothes, shoes, shaving gear, a case containing drugs and salves. A bottle of cologne. No papers, no letters, no documents. No passport.

Luke hastily closed the suitcase, shoved it back under the bunk. He slipped out of the cabin just as Easley came around the corner of the deck-house. Easley stopped short. "Were you in my cabin?"

"Is that your cabin?" Luke stuttered. "I thought it was somebody else's. I wanted a pillow—for Carson."

"A pillow for Carson, eh?"

"Well, he came aboard without a pillow. No blankets."

"And you were helping him out. Off my bed? It's kind of strange."

"Somebody said there was extra bedding..."

Easley gave Luke a sardonic glance, stepped into his cabin.

Luke went to sit on the hatch. Carson came to join him. "Well? What did you find out?"

"Shut up," said Luke.

"'Shut up'? What for? Didn't you go through Easley's gear?"

"He just about caught me in the act."

"Woof! What did you tell him?"

"I said I was looking for a pillow. I told him it was for you."

Carson raised his hands in horror. "Don't involve me! I'm playing all this straight."

Luke stared glumly out to sea. After a moment Carson asked: "Did you learn anything?"

"Nothing of consequence. Easley takes pills. He's got everything from aspirin to zinc oxide."

"Prescription pills?"

"I didn't check. I just saw a medicine case full of bottles."

"If you looked at the labels you might have learned his doctor's name and his home town."

"I was nervous. With good reason."

Carson gave a dour grunt. "I suggest that next time—"

"'Next time'! What are you saying! My career as a detective has come and gone. *You* go look for pillows in Easley's cabin."

"Not me."

Up on the foredeck Titi went to lean on the rail. She glanced back toward Carson, who at once jumped to his feet. "Time for my French lesson."

"You don't show very good sense, Carson."

"If I had good sense I'd be aboard the *Dorado*. Since I'm stupid I might as well enjoy it."

Luke remained on the hatch. Easley came back around the deckhouse. For a long minute he stood looking at Luke, then went into the saloon. A few minutes later Fiona came hurriedly forth. She turned a furtive glance toward Luke, went into her cabin, emerged with her big leather handbag which, with another glance toward Luke, she took with her into the saloon.

Carson, finding Titi in a bad humor, returned aft and wandered into the saloon. Presently he came forth and joined Luke on the hatch. "They're talking about personable crooks who make their living on trans-Atlantic liners."

"I'll remember this trip a long time," said Luke.

"Why are you complaining?" said Carson. "You at least have a bed."

"I also have a sick Chinaman," said Luke.

Easley sauntered from the saloon. He halted in front of Luke, a twitching half-smile on his face. Then, without words, he strolled forward, leaving Luke in a seethe of fury and frustration.

———•———

THE DAY PASSED AND another: hours of sunlight, cloud and wind, blue seas and flying fish; moonlight and starlight, singing and music and earnest discourse. The Orshams treated Luke with reserve. Ching occasionally appeared on deck, his face the color of old newspaper, wearing slippers, black pants and a white dress shirt. The German students after being snubbed by the Orshams held themselves aloof. Ben Easley had time for no one but Rolf Clute; hour after hour they discussed the strange and unusual. Luke eavesdropped when opportunity offered, but Easley said nothing of himself or his past. Rolf Clute described encounters with sharks, eels, eccentric tourists. He told of cannibals and missionaries, shipwrecks and lonely atolls, prescient birds and sacred trees. He commented upon the Chinese and Polynesians, Americans and French; he discussed the mad priest of Mangareva and the evil king of Hana Hana. He spoke of taboos, forbidden islands, lepers, poisons from the sea, the upoa bird whose call foretold the death of Tahitian royalty.

Ben Easley listened with deference, smoking his long thin cigars and nodding gravely.

On the morning after the third night Rolf Clute pointed ahead: "Niau."

"Where?" cried Fiona. Derek squinted. "I can't see a thing."

"Nothing to see," said Clute with his foxy grin. "We're thirty miles out. Keep watching."

Presently a blue-gray mark appeared on the northern horizon, which gradually metamorphosed through increments of solidity and detail into a beach shaded by cocoanut palms a hundred yards behind a low reef. The *Rahiria* skirted the island, with near-naked children running along the beach keeping pace. At last on the north shore a village appeared: a cluster of thatched huts, a few spindly piers running out into the water. The *Rahiria* nosed delicately close in to the reef; sails rattled down the mast; the anchor splashed into fifty feet of water so clear that every detail of the bottom was apparent. The *Rahiria* swung slowly about with the current. A motor launch put out from the village, loaded with sacks of copra, followed by a dozen outrigger canoes, each almost awash under sacks of copra fore and aft. They negotiated an almost non-existent channel through the reef, came up alongside the *Rahiria*.

Stores, supplies, crates, were brought up from the hold; the copra was heaved aboard and stowed, the supplies were transferred to the motor launch, together with a pouch of mail.

With no further ceremony sails were hoisted; the anchor raised. The *Rahiria* sheered off to sea. Niau dwindled astern.

"A very dull visit," Fiona commented sadly. "I was hoping for a feast on the beach."

"Not many people on Niau," Rolf Clute told her. "Not much copra. Ahead is Kaukura. Look, you can see it. We'll anchor in the lagoon tonight and you can go ashore. But no feast. Not any more, unless you pay for it yourself."

Kaukura, an almost imperceptible dark line between sea and sky, in due course became a chain of islets each with a top-knot of palms. In mid-afternoon the *Rahiria* gingerly negotiated a pass through the reef, and with a man at the masthead watching for coral heads crossed to the village. A dilapidated wharf thrust out from the beach. The *Rahiria* ghosted alongside; lines were thrown ashore and made fast.

The *Rahiria* would not depart until morning; the passengers were free to go ashore.

Carson drew Titi aside and spoke to her earnestly. She grinned and shook her head, and went off with her relatives.

With a glittering stare for Carson, Leon Teofu followed.

"At least she didn't act outraged," Carson told Luke. "That's a positive factor. I'll make the grade yet."

Luke gave a disgusted grunt. "How come you can't take a hint?"

"This is a free ocean. All she needs to do is say no."

"She just said it."

"The way she said it was strictly 'yes'. The girl is mad for me!"

"Leon Teofu is getting very upset."

"So what? He's just a guy that hangs around. Let's go for a swim. Hey, Clute, how are the sharks around here?"

"Go ahead, swim. No sharks in Kaukura lagoon. At Apataki, the same kind of lagoon, sharks everywhere. Nobody swims."

Fiona and Derek came briskly past, wearing white shorts, sneakers and floppy white hats. Fiona clutched her brown bag under her arm. They ignored Luke. "We're off to the beach, for shells! Mr. Clute, do come along, you're so knowledgeable!"

"No, no, not me," said Clute. "I got business ashore, with a man that does pearl-diving. He owes me money; maybe I collect in pearls."

"How marvellous!" "Hope you come up with another Black Mogul!"

The Orshams were off to the beach.

Ching went to the Chinese grocery store and disappeared into one of the dim back rooms.

The Germans tramped dutifully around the island.

Carson wandered through the village, hoping to find Titi, or someone equally agreeable.

Ben Easley went into the store, bought a package of Gauloise cigarettes, came out to the front, sat on a bench.

Rolf Clute returned along the lane which ran through the banana trees behind the store. He wore a disgruntled expression. Sitting down beside Easley he gave a voluble explanation of his difficulties. Then he made a sly sign, and ducked into the store, to emerge with a pair of beer bottles, containing an unidentifiable liquid. He gave one to Easley, who tasted, glanced speculatively at the contents, tasted again without enthusiasm.

Luke wandered aimlessly up the beach, perhaps a quarter-mile, then returned by way of the lane which ran through the village, and went to stand in the shade of a breadfruit tree near the dock. Easley and Clute still sat on the bench in front of the store. For lack of anything better to do, Luke cut open a green cocoanut and drank the milk. Surreptitiously he watched Easley. Familiarity—if contact with Easley's brooding presence could be so described—had done nothing to dissolve the macabre aura about his person.

As Luke watched, quivering in the intensity of his loathing, Ben Easley set aside his bottle and spoke to Rolf Clute: putting a proposition or perhaps making a request.

Clute assented without fervor. The two went aboard the *Rahiria*, and presently returned ashore. Clute carried a spear-gun, Easley had a towel slung over his shoulder.

They went into the grocery store and came out with a pair of face-masks and another spear-gun, either rented or borrowed. Then they set out along the road which paralleled the lagoon.

Luke watched them disappear behind a copse of mango trees. After a moment's hesitation he sauntered after them.

Two hundred yards down the road a strip of white beach sloped into the water. Luke watched from a distance as the two men prepared to swim. Easley had donned black swimming-trunks; Clute wore merely a sagging pair of jockey shorts. They waded out until the water was waist-high, adjusted their face-masks, cocked the spear-guns and began to swim.

Luke continued slowly along the road. From behind a clump of pandanus trees he surveyed the beach. Easley would hardly carry his passport into the water; it must be with his clothes, where he had left them on the bole of a fallen cocoanut tree.

Luke waited until the swimmers were well out in the lagoon, diving down among the coral heads. Then, as inconspicuously as possible, he approached the clothes. Easley and Clute were almost invisible: two small specks. Now one ducked under, now the other. Luke reached for Easley's trousers.

No wallet, no passport, no money. Luke looked in Easley's shoes. Nothing.

Odd, thought Luke. Had Easley left his papers aboard ship?

It seemed unlikely.

What would Easley do with such objects? Entrust them to the captain, or perhaps the Chinaman in the grocery store?

Again unlikely. Easley trusted no one.

Easley would hide his papers. Luke scrutinized the beach. He lifted a cocoanut frond, looked under the fallen trunk.

Nothing.

Easley's shoes had been set down very neatly, very accurately. Luke carefully moved them, felt in the sand below.

A wallet, a passport.

Luke took them back into the foliage.

He opened the passport. Ben Easley looked out at him, the eyes wide, as if angry; the mouth drooping. The name on the passport was Benjamin Eiselhardt.

The address was 2690 Cecily Street, Apartment E, San Francisco.

The passport was new, issued at San Francisco on June 10. There was a visa only for French Polynesia, granted by the French Consul at San Francisco.

Luke looked into the wallet. The name on the driver's license was Benjamin Eiselhardt, 1615 Golden Gate Avenue, San Francisco. There were no credit cards, no photographs. The money compartment contained twelve one-hundred-dollar bills, several thousand Polynesian francs. Luke reflected a moment, smiling grimly. His Vespa had been worth three hundred dollars, more or less. His hand hung for a moment over the money. Regretfully he drew it back. In all probability he would never have another chance to collect damages from Easley, or Eiselhardt—whatever the man's name—but confiscating the sum in such a fashion seemed beneath his dignity.

Luke checked the small compartments. He found several cards. The first was imprinted: Sard's Club, with the address, 69 Homan Alley, beside a black Doric column to the side. On the back was penciled a telephone number: 659-6090.

The second was imprinted: The Martinique, 619 Ellis Street, San Francisco, with a conventionalized drawing of a Latin-American couple dancing the samba.

There were three cards from modeling agencies, all with San Francisco addresses. Very likely Easley's occupation, thought Luke. He could not imagine Easley working with either his hands or his mind in any productive capacity. The only other item was a claim ticket upon the Romeo Cleaners, on Geary Street, San Francisco.

Luke whistled through his teeth. The character and background of Ben Easley, as he chose to call himself, were somewhat less vague. Still: no enlightenment, no revelations. But what could he expect?

Luke glanced across the lagoon. Rolf Clute had speared a fish; he and Easley stood on a coral head while Clute cut at it with his knife.

After a moment Clute threw the fish into the lagoon. Luke wondered what they were up to. Far down the beach he spied Derek and Fiona returning from their shell-gathering. Hastily he applied himself to the business at hand. He copied names and addresses, replaced cards in the wallet, made a final inspection of the passport, buried everything as he had found it, and returned to the *Rahiria*.

Fiona and Derek were not far behind him. They laid out their prizes on the hatch. "Nothing very much. A few lovely textiles." "Don't forget my nice little cowries!" "Naturally not, dear. Look at this one. It's an orange helmet, or so I believe."

Sometime later Rolf Clute returned, in a state of expansive good humor. He had found the man who owed him money; the two had discussed their business over a bottle. Clute looked around the deck. "Where's that guy Easley? Isn't he back yet? When I left him he was digging around the beach, looking for his stuff."

Half an hour later Easley came aboard, face like a thundercloud. He crossed the deck to confront Luke. "How come you moved my shoes?"

Luke looked up with a sinking feeling. He was too proud to lie; on the other hand... He temporized. "Why should I move your shoes?"

"For the same reason you frisked my room!"

Luke looked up into the clamped face wondering what to say. Fiona had overheard. "Did you say 'shoes'? I took them up the beach, safe and sound from the tide. Couldn't you find them?"

Easley turned slowly away. Luke drew a deep breath. "Yes, I found them," said Easley in a carefully toneless voice. "Thank you—a great deal."

Chapter XIII

FIVE degrees below the equator a series of squalls time after time sent the *Dorado* reeling over on its rail. A cloud, dense and black as an ink-blot, would appear, with a scurry of white foam on the ocean below, and then the wind would be upon the boat: a howling, whooping bluster, usually with a pelt of rain. The helmsman would instantly bring the bow into the wind, while the crew dropped the flogging mainsail and reefed the foresail. After five or ten minutes the fury of wind and driving wetness would pass and the fitful airs of doldrums would return.

In five days the *Dorado* logged only two hundred miles, and this in the wrong direction: to the southwest rather than the southeast. On a single day six separate squalls came boiling across the water. Brady finally ordered all canvas down except a pair of steadying staysails and fired up the diesels, to the approval of gruff old Sarvis. "After all, man, you've got fifteen hundred horsepower lying idle. Folly not to get the use of it. Your guests will like it better, as well."

To which Brady made a peevish reply: "Dammit, this is a sailing vessel, not a cocktail lounge. The guests can damn well take the good with the bad. It's been all cream so far."

Sarvis shrugged and went off to start the engines, which seemed to discourage the squalls; there was but one other relatively feeble display.

Brady, now stubborn, kept the engines running through perfect weather, to make sure of gaining back his easting, although he found every minute of running under power a trial.

There were other exasperations, each trivial in itself, but combining to build up in Brady a formless dissatisfaction, and his disposition had become testy. Lia was the principal source of his irritation. He had expected no transports of adoration from his young bride (except perhaps in his heart of hearts) and he had found none. Brady could find no fault in what Lia did, but what she didn't do left a void which he could neither define nor reasonably complain about. A question began to gnaw at his mind: had he, after all, made a mistake? Not in choosing a bride so much younger than himself, but in choosing Lia: a woman so withdrawn as to seem a stranger.

A stranger! Brady chewed on the word. It was not too strong. After two months of marriage he knew no more of Lia than he did on the day he married her.

Now Jean was another case. Brady had become increasingly aware of Jean: a girl somewhat angular, with an odd awkward grace, a face which mirrored a hundred subtle emotions. Jean did not have Lia's even disposition; she was now sullen, now vexed, now exhilarated, now downright malicious. It would be less ornamental but probably more fun being married to Jean, thought Brady.

And somehow he conceived that he had been given to understand that she did not find him totally unattractive... The drift of Brady's thoughts surprised him. He hauled himself up short. "Enough of this peevishness, old man! It doesn't become you. You'll make yourself ridiculous!"

For on a long ocean voyage no mood or trait could be concealed; everyone else was too watchful. Unobtrusiveness became not only a virtue but an advantage. Here Lia excelled, reflected Brady, for all her remarkable appearance. She irritated no one, except possibly himself. The obverse to this quality was a certain bland opacity, or, in Lia's case (as Brady preferred to think), a dreamy distrait quality which held an element of charm. Kelsey and Jean apparently took the uncharitable point of view and patronized Lia in a manner which put Brady's teeth on edge. Here must lie the reason for Lia's fits of brooding!

One afternoon, bantering with Jean, Brady worked the conversation around to Lia. "She puzzles me! Sometimes I'm sure there's something on her mind. Between the two of us: what's wrong? Or is it my imagination?"

Jean gave her brittle laugh. "Lia's always been moody, dear child."

"Moody about what? People aren't moody over nothing!"

"I can't imagine."

With Jean offering no enlightenment, Brady sought out Kelsey, where she sat curled like a kitten in a deck-chair. Brady came bluntly to the point. "Lia's been moping and won't tell me why. Do you know?"

Kelsey grinned. "You do ask awkward questions."

"So you know."

"I didn't say that. Anyway, even if I did know, I'd have to deny it, and I do deny it."

Brady was not in the mood for flippancy. "Suppose she had a cancer, or was going blind: you wouldn't tell me?"

Like Jean, Kelsey laughed. "No fear. Lia's healthy. If you're worried, why not ask Lia?"

"I have. She just gives me a funny look."

Don Peppergold approached. "Who wants to join the super grand spectacular landfall pool? Biggest event of the trip!"

"Not me," said Kelsey. "I don't have any money." In the competition with Jean she long ago had won. Don was her serf and now Kelsey's main concern was keeping him in his place.

"Only a dollar per pick," said Don and explained the rules of the game.

Brady sat back and watched Kelsey macerate Don's enthusiasm. Don's big problem, thought Brady, was his wholesomeness. He was by no means a fool, but he acted like a man who drank milk with his meals.

Kelsey rose to her feet. "I've got letters to write. 'Scuse me." She skipped off. Don stared slack-chinned after her.

"Adorable little cuss," said Brady kindly. "But I pity the man she marries. She'll give him a run!"

Don ran his fingers across his blond crew-cut and wandered off in search of Jean. Brady went down to the master's stateroom. He found Lia stretched out on the bed, watching reflections on the overhead.

Brady sat down beside her. "Well, sweet, what's on your mind?"

"Nothing really. I'm just lying here resting."

Brady had the tactless habit of challenging all unreasonable statements. He spoke almost explosively. "'Resting'? For Christ sake, there's nothing to do aboard ship but rest!"

He instantly would have recalled his words, but Lia only looked at him meekly. He started to apologize, but Lia raised herself to a sitting position. "I'm sorry, Brady. I'm not really antisocial. I was just, well, thinking about things. How nice everything is, really."

Brady was touched. He patted Lia's head. "Of course, sweet. Has anyone been hurting your feelings?"

"Oh no."

"If you have troubles—of any sort—I hope you'll come to me with them."

Lia rose to her feet and went to look out the porthole. "I'm always amazed how blue the water is."

Chapter XIV

THE *Rahiria* departed Kaukura at eight in the morning, when the tides were slack and the current through the pass at its least.

At noon the ship entered blue and green Apataki lagoon, and, finding no cargo, immediately moved on to Arutua, nine miles west, to anchor directly in front of the village. The transfer of goods, in four peculiar boats built of planks and corrugated roofing, proceeded slowly, and at dusk was still underway. The captain elected to remain at anchor overnight.

Dinner, more or less as usual, was rice, canned beef and fried bananas. Rolf Clute thumped a bottle of brandy down upon the saloon table. "Tomorrow we put into Rangiroa; I leave the ship."

"What a pity!" cried Fiona. "We'll miss you!"

Derek exclaimed, "We were hoping you'd be aboard the whole trip! You're so full of information!"

Rolf Clute shook his head. "Can't be done. But you'll see me again. I'll catch the *Taporo* on its way into Papeete. When you get back I'll tell my wife to fix up a real Tahitian meal like you never see in the hotels. My daughters are real good dancers; very pretty girls."

"How wonderful!" "Are you serious?"

"I'm serious!"

"We'll be sure to come!" "But you must give us your exact address."

"Just go out the highway to the store in Papeari, at fifty-two kilometers. Ask for Clute. They know me. Everybody come!"

"Oh, we will!" "Trust us to be on hand for a meal!"

Luke went out on deck. The night was warm and dark, with clouds covering the moon. The village showed a few yellow lights; guitar music and singing drifted across the lagoon. Luke looked around for Carson, but failed to find him. He checked forward, among the deck passengers, without success. He went aft to the quarterdeck. No Carson. Luke frowned, pulled at his chin. He looked into the head, the saloon, then his own bunk, where Carson occasionally napped.

No sign of Carson.

Luke went forward once more, looked among the deck passengers. Titi was nowhere to be seen.

Aha, thought Luke. The situation was clarified.

He went to sit on the No. 2 hatch. But he became restless and uneasy. Exactly *where* was Carson? Luke rose indecisively to his feet. Carson would not take kindly to an intrusion; still, on the other hand... Luke walked aft, glanced into the port life-boat, to find only the pig and a terrible stench. He walked forward, around the other side of the deck-house, glanced into the starboard life-boat. Empty.

The captain's cabin? The crew's quarters? The hold? Aloft? Somewhat unlikely. Certainly not the roof of the forward deck-house. The roof of the after deck-house was more secluded.

Luke hesitated. Carson might be outraged. Luke went to the ladder, climbed three rungs, looked along the roof. "Oh! Sorry," said Luke, and jumped quickly back to the deck. He doubted if either had heard him.

Luke went forward. Leon Teofu sat with a friend. Both had guitars. The friend was teaching Leon chords to a tune Leon did not know. Leon sat absorbed, scowling in concentration as he placed his fingers, grinning in delight when the chords came right. He and his friend began to sing.

They finished the song. Leon looked around the deck. He craned his neck, looked more carefully. He put the guitar down, rose to his feet. Luke wondered what to do before the situation got out of hand. But now Titi came quietly along the deck, looking neither right nor left. She went to where her mother sat shelling and eating peanuts. She sat down in the shadows. Presently she ate a peanut.

Carson appeared from behind the after deck-house, a bland expression on his face. He looked toward Leon Teofu, then went back to the No. 2 hatch.

Leon Teofu sat muttering to his friend, who shrugged and began to play the guitar. Leon made a furious movement, raising and lowering his elbows, then, squatting, turned his back on Carson.

Luke exhaled with vast relief. He went to sit beside Carson. "I was looking for you."

"Oh? I was in the can. What's on your mind?"

"Clute is leaving the ship tomorrow. There'll be a vacant bunk."

Carson nodded with easy superiority. "It's already taken care of."

"I see. Well, that's all. Except..."

"Except what?"

"Nothing. Only..."

"Yes?"

"Forget it." Luke got to his feet, returned to the saloon. In his present mood, Carson would give only insufferable condescension to sound advice.

"I hope Teofu punches his head," said Luke to himself.

In the saloon Rolf Clute's brandy was having its effect. Clute was explaining how to capture a turtle. "They're old! They're pretty smart. They know things we don't know. If you bother them, they want to kill you. And what they try to do is catch you with their tail. Then they sink."

"Oh come now!" chortled Fiona. "Not really their tails!"

"That's the truth," declared Rolf Clute. "If they get you with their tail you're a dead man. You sit on the shell, you get a grip and hold their head up in the air and you can ride old grandpa for miles."

"Have you ever ridden a turtle?" Derek asked.

"Sure! In my younger days. I don't do it no more. I'm an old man now."

"Oh come, come," teased Fiona. "A person is as old as he feels. I saw you swimming after fish yesterday, with Mr. Easley."

"Oh well, that's different," said Clute modestly.

"I've always wanted to try my hand at it," remarked Derek. "Must be gorgeous, down among the coral. Pity you're leaving; I'd have you take me out."

"Nothing to it," said Clute. "Just don't put your hand in any holes. An eel might take off your fingers, or maybe your whole hand."

Fiona gave a muted cry of distress. "It's really disheartening! Everything lovely down here has a dreadful aspect just out of sight! As if the most beautiful flowers had poisonous scents!"

Clute shrugged. "That's the way it goes. This is a pretty savage part of the world. In the old days it was worse. Now if you just watch out for the stone-fish and the sting-rays and the poison shells and the *hue-hue*—"

"Don't forget the ghosts!" Derek inserted facetiously. "The *tupaupaus!*"

Fiona jumped to her feet. "I'll have nightmares if I listen another instant. So I'll take my constitutional twice around the deck, and then it's beddy-bye. Goodnight all!"

— • —

RANGIROA, THE LARGEST ATOLL of the Tuamotus, lay ahead. The outline of the reef was marked by narrow wooded islands; two villages were situated along the northern shore.

With diesel chugging the *Rahiria* pushed through a pass in the reef, crossed the lagoon to a weather-beaten concrete jetty. Behind lay Avatoru village: a mission school and a church, a small hospital built of coral-blocks, a Chinese grocery, a clapboard office-building, a number of thatched huts, all shaded under flamboyants, mangos, cocoanuts.

The *Rahiria* tied up to the pier. Rolf Clute, freshly shaven, glossy with talcum, in clean sun-tans and a new shirt, shook hands all around. "See everybody back at Tahiti! Don't forget!"

"Small chance of that," cried Fiona, and Derek called: "We'll be there, with bells on!"

Rolf Clute swaggered down the gangplank. About half of the deck passengers also disembarked, not including Titi and her relatives, nor Leon Teofu. Luke was disappointed.

Rolf Clute called up from the dock: "Don't swim in the lagoon: lots of sharks around here!" With a jaunty wave of the hand he went off into the village.

Stores were discharged, copra loaded. Avatoru, a straggling disorganized line of thatched huts, had small diversion to offer other than the grocery store and the ever-present church. The passengers stayed close to the ship. Early in the afternoon the *Rahiria* pulled aboard its lines, backed away from the pier and departed the way it had come.

Tikehau, the last port to be visited in the Tuamotus, lay eighteen miles west. A brisk breeze bellied the sails; the schooner plunged and rolled and left a fine bubbling wake. With the sun setting, the ship entered the pass into the lagoon and immediately anchored.

Without Rolf Clute the saloon was quiet and decorous, even though Carson had formally joined the group. Easley, never talkative, had become taciturn and preoccupied. What a fantastic position! thought Luke. A murderer customarily knew the identity of his unsuspecting victim. Here the situation was reversed: the murderer sat unaware that the victim watched him from across the table with a crawling skin.

During the evening Titi was carefully attended by her mother. Carson played gin rummy with the Orshams.

In the morning the *Rahiria* hoisted anchor and proceeded across the lagoon to Hirua village. There was no wharf at Hirua; the copra was brought out on a platform laid across two canoes.

The *Rahiria* would not depart until early afternoon, when the currents in the pass were favorable. The passengers went ashore in pirogues to explore the island. According to the natives there was no shark danger, and the Orshams went for a swim, as did the German students. Ben Easley borrowed the supercargo's spear-gun and mask and went off alone, ostensibly to fish.

Noon approached and passed; the passengers returned aboard: all but Easley. At one o'clock the *Rahiria* would sail, with Easley aboard or not. Luke borrowed the Orshams' binoculars, looked across the lagoon, but saw nothing. "Maybe he's been eaten by a shark," suggested Derek Orsham in a gentle voice.

Luke made a noncommittal sound and returned the binoculars.

At ten minutes to one Easley came sauntering along the beach. Without haste he engaged a native boy to paddle him to the ship and climbed the ladder just as the captain ordered up the anchor.

The ship put to sea, and headed northeast, with the wind on the starboard beam. The Tuamotus were astern. Ahead, across six hundred miles of empty ocean, lay the Marquesas.

Chapter XV

THE time was an hour before dawn. Brady stood on deck with his sextant watching the sky take on color. The constellations had not yet faded from sight; Brady picked his stars and waited for the horizon to take an edge.

The wind was cool and gentle; the *Dorado* moved quietly over the dark water. This was the time of day when Brady felt most at peace. Guests, relatives, friends: all very well, no doubt, but their idiosyncrasies tended to grate on the nerves. If through some trick of fate he ever found himself single again, he might just chuck it all for a life of solitary voyaging. Unlikely that events would proceed so far, nor would he want them to do so... Brady found himself thinking about Jean Wintersea. Several times during the last few days he had surprised her watching him with fascinated attention: a circumstance which puzzled Brady. His sex appeal? Hmmf, said Brady to himself. High time that he was taking his sights. He stepped into the chart-room, started his stop-watch by the chronometer, went back out on deck and took an angle on Achernar.

Half an hour later he transferred his fix to the general chart, considered it a moment, then swept the forward horizon with his binoculars. Nothing in sight. He descended to the saloon where Hector served him coffee and orange juice. He was presently joined by Malcolm McClure. "Nine o'clock," said Brady. "To be absolutely precise, let's say eight forty-five."

"I'll be watching."

At ten minutes to nine the dimmest of shadows appeared on the southern horizon. Malcolm McClure was the first to see it, and gave a great halloo. "Nuku Hiva! Right on the nose! Everybody up! Marquesas landfall!"

"That's what I call precise navigating," said Brady.

"Pretty lucky," said McClure.

One by one the passengers came to peer and marvel, as if never had they seen land before.

The shadow rose into the sky and presently became a succession of great promontories, each the size of a mountain, receding one behind the other into the haze of distance. At noon the *Dorado* rounded Cape Martin and proceeded along the south coast with McClure comparing the chart with the landscape. "See that ledge? With the surf bashing over the top? That's called Teohote Kea... Look through there! That's Comptroller Bay. There ahead: Sentinel Rocks. We go between into Taio Hae Bay, our port of entry."

Flying the quarantine flag, the *Dorado* slid past Sentinel Rocks into the shelter of the bay. To all sides rose the incredible peaks and spires of Nuku Hiva.

Down rattled the sails. The *Dorado* lost way. The anchor splashed into clear cool water. The schooner, for the first time since leaving Honolulu, was at rest.

Ten minutes later a launch brought out port officials. They made a perfunctory examination of passports, the ship's log, and without further formality granted pratique.

———•———

COCOANUT TODDY HAD BEEN brought aboard the *Rahiria* at Tikehau. On the first evening out the deck passengers became extremely merry. The guitars generated an urgent emotion; there was laughter, hand-clapping, singing, the *tamure*.

The saloon passengers came forward to enjoy the fun, bringing what tipple they had available: the Orshams a bottle of Scotch; the Germans a jug of red wine; Luke, Carson and Easley, Hinano beer purchased from the supercargo.

Carson edged close to Titi, who pretended to ignore him. Leon Teofu, red-eyed from an excess of toddy, was not inclined to do so and began to stagger to his feet. Luke recognized the incipient stages of Polynesian rage. He quickly took Carson's arm and pulled him away.

"What's the matter with you?" demanded Carson peevishly. "I wasn't doing anything out of line."

"Leon thought you were."

Carson made a sour noise. "Bah. I can take care of myself. Do you think I'm a damn fool?"

"You know I do. Take my advice and leave that girl alone."

"I can't see what harm I'm doing. She doesn't object, her mother doesn't object—not too much. I don't object."

"But Leon objects. Do you intend to marry the girl?"

"Heaven forbid."

"Maybe Leon does. For heaven's sake, control yourself. You can't go waylaying every girl you see."

"It's worked out pretty well so far," growled Carson. "Now if you don't mind…"

Luke held up his hands. "I'm finished. You're on your own. If you get your teeth knocked out, don't come to me for sympathy."

"Don't worry," muttered Carson, and strode off in a huff.

But for the remainder of the evening he sulked by himself on the edge of the hatch, as discreet as even Luke could have wished: to such an extent that Titi began to turn teasing glances toward him.

The toddy ran short; the revellers began to fall asleep: the music dwindled to plaintive chords and single plangent notes. The Orshams bade everyone goodnight and took their Scotch back to their cabin, followed by the Germans and Ben Easley.

Luke rose to his feet. He looked expectantly toward Carson, who reluctantly came aft.

During the night Ching had a nightmare and called out hysterically in Chinese.

Luke leaned over his bunk. "Ching! Wake up! Ching! Hey!"

Ching's outburst ended in a gasp of sheer terror, then he lay back on the pillow breathing heavily.

"Ching! Are you all right?"

Ching made a sleepy inarticulate sound; somewhat reassured Luke lay back down in his bunk and adjusted himself once more to the slow heave of the ship.

AT BREAKFAST CARSON HAD little to say, and brooded sullenly over his bread and coffee. Luke divined that Carson resented the restrictions Luke and Leon Teofu had imposed upon his love life.

Luke left him to stew in his own juice and went out on deck with a book he had borrowed from the Orshams.

Ten minutes later Carson appeared on deck. He stood a moment by the rail, glowering at the hillocks of blue water, then he turned and swaggered forward.

Titi lay on the forward hatch, face down, basking. Her hair was tumbled artlessly to one side of her neck; she wore a faded old cotton dress, covering her brown legs to the backs of her knees.

Carson sat down beside her, arms clasping his own knees. He looked somberly out to sea. Now that he was here, now that he had defied Luke and Leon Teofu, he could think of nothing further he cared to accomplish at the moment.

Titi watched through her lashes, thinking her own thoughts, none very profound. She rather liked Carson. Leon was also good enough in his way.

Carson began a conversation in halting French. Leon Teofu, playing cards with three cronies, kept an attentive eye on the situation. One of his comrades made a joke. Leon scowled, then uttered a short bark of a laugh. Then he relaxed and laughed more easily. Then he scowled once more. Leon Teofu was examining all sides of the situation.

For the moment he decided to continue with the card game.

Easley came out on deck, looked briefly this way and that, went aft to the quarterdeck, sprawled in a deck-chair.

Titi raised up on her elbows, and kicking her legs up in the air, began to take an interest in the conversation. She laughed at Carson's drollery.

Carson glanced aft, speculated a moment, licked his lips. He turned, muttered to Titi, who gave her head a vigorous shake.

Carson spoke again; Titi's response was not so emphatic, and was followed by a glance toward her mother.

Carson spoke once more, then jumped to his feet, sauntered casually aft and into his cabin.

He waited. A moment passed. Were those angry words out on deck? He listened, but heard nothing more. Probably only the timbers of the old ship.

Quiet footsteps sounded outside. There was a tap at the door. Carson threw it open.

A terrible mistake! Leon Teofu, not Titi, stood looking at him.

Leon punched Carson's face, to send him hopping back into the cabin. Then Leon called Carson names in Tahitian, and shook his fist.

Carson sprang forward in rage, but Leon Teofu had already turned away. Carson wiped his mouth with the back of his hand and went off in pursuit. Leon turned. Carson was on him with a wild flurry of blows. Leon grinned, pushed his left fist into Carson's face. Carson tottered back, then once again rushed forward. He managed to hit Leon once or twice; then, in backing away, Leon tripped on a pad-eye and fell. Carson stood over him like a lord. "And there's plenty more where that came from!" shouted Carson furiously.

Leon Teofu picked himself up, but before he could make any new move the captain appeared, and peremptorily ordered Leon back. Then he turned a stinging spatter of French upon Carson and shook his finger under Carson's nose.

Carson went to sit on the hatch. Leon Teofu conducted an angry conversation with his friends, glaring from time to time toward Carson, who glowered back.

Luke, lounging in a deck-chair with his book, pretended not to notice the episode.

The afternoon passed. Dinner was as usual: canned beef with rice and fried sweet potatoes, together with grilled dorado, caught on a trolling line by the supercargo.

Tonight guitar music was absent from the foredeck. Clouds hung over the *Rahiria* and the deck passengers were worried about rain, which so far had been limited to one or two brief swishes. The sky seemed heavy and the air humid. In the west lightning crackled.

But the rain held off. One by one the deck passengers crawled into their bedrolls.

The Orshams and Luke sat in the saloon until almost midnight, sipping the Orshams' Scotch by the light of the kerosene lamp.

All finally turned in. There was little wind, and this came in panting damp little gusts, which barely gave the schooner headway.

———•———

LUKE WAS AWAKENED BY a sound. He listened. What had he heard? He could not recall.

He raised up on his elbow, strained his ears, his heart beating as if he were a little boy awakening from a nightmare.

Silence, except for the surge of water and the sigh of wind. From the bunk below came the sound of Ching's breathing.

A door closed.

Luke lay staring into the dark, wondering why he felt awed and terrified.

The ship surged on, heaving up, easing down over unseen hills and vales of water. Luke fell into a troubled slumber.

———•———

FIRST TO BREAKFAST WAS Ching, then the Orshams, then Luke and the Germans.

Ben Easley came late to the saloon. Fiona remarked saucily that he and Carson were slug-a-beds and deserved to miss their breakfasts.

Easley laughed. He seemed in an excellent good mood. "Me, yes. Carson, no. He's been up for hours."

"Ha ha! He must be out on deck, mooning over that little trollop—if one may so refer to undisciplined Polynesians."

But Carson was not on deck. In fact Carson was nowhere aboard the *Rahiria*.

Carson was gone.

"When a man disappears from a ship," said Derek, "there's only one place for him to go."

— · —

THE CAPTAIN, UTTERING STACCATO French oaths through a down-clenched mouth, ordered the *Rahiria* back on its course. He put one man at the masthead, another at the bow, while he himself stood on the forward deck-house with binoculars. The search obviously was a forlorn hope; among the great surges, reaching from horizon to horizon, how could such a small entity, even one so warm and desperate as a swimming man, be seen?

But the search was made.

All morning long the *Rahiria* roved back the way it had come, with everybody aboard standing by the rail, scanning every slope of water, every sudden view along a trough.

At noon the captain flung up his hands in a Gallic gesture, and ordered the ship back on course. Everyone looked at him reproachfully, though everyone knew that he had no remedy for the situation.

Titi lay weeping on the hatch while her mother clucked beside her. Leon Teofu sat gray-faced to the side, aware that all the ship's company were giving him glances of surreptitious speculation.

All except Luke. He watched Ben Easley, who lounged on the quarterdeck in a deck-chair. Easley wore dark glasses, white shorts, a white shirt. He held a long thin cigar. From time to time he puffed, then emitted a small stream of smoke through his pursed lips to be whisked away by the wind.

Luke could not bear to look at him, for the acrid lump of fury which rose in his throat. He had never thought it possible to hate a man as much as he hated Ben Easley.

First Luke Royce, then Carson Royce. And Ben Easley was on his way to meet the *Dorado*, on which rode Brady Royce.

The situation was significant, thought Luke. First Luke and Carson, then Brady, whereupon there would be no further Royces to administer the Golconda Fund.

Lia Wintersea Royce would be named administratrix.

From Ben Easley's point of view, the situation was proceeding with facility. Two-thirds of his work was done. Carson's appearance at Papeete, his presence aboard the *Rahiria*, his difficulties with Leon Teofu: these must have seemed the dispensation of an amiable if bloodthirsty god.

There was a single fatal flaw in the scheme. Eventually Ben Easley must face up to a staggering fact: he had not, after all, killed Luke Royce.

And once Luke had a chance to speak two words to Brady, the whole scheme would evaporate in a flash.

Luke thought of something else. If Brady were dead, he, Luke, would become administrator: lord of Golconda, master of the *Dorado*, with unlimited wealth at his disposal... Luke smiled: a small harsh smile. He felt soiled by the thought, yet why should he blame himself? The idea was one which loomed into the mind.

◆

LEON TEOFU WAS UNDER suspicion. The captain and the supercargo spoke together at length; then the captain called first Titi, then Ben Easley, into his cabin and questioned each in turn: had Titi seen Carson during the night? Had she observed anyone from among the deck passengers, specifically Leon Teofu, heading aft?

Titi had slept soundly. She had seen nothing, heard nothing.

Ben Easley said the same. He had gone to his bunk, he had slept. In the morning the top bunk was empty. He knew no more.

No sounds, no outcries, no scuffle?

Easley could not help.

One by one the other passengers were questioned. All declared that they had heard and seen nothing.

Leon Teofu burst into a furious tirade. He knew that everyone suspected him of a foul deed. He was innocent! He was not a man of the night; he went to his enemies by day and confronted them face to face! Whoever declared otherwise: let the slanderer beware!

The captain shrugged. "*Eh bien*. We will turn the matter over to the authorities. They will know how to deal with the matter." He would proceed directly to Taio Hae Bay on Nuku Hiva, instead of putting into Hiva Oa, as had been his schedule.

Chapter XVI

THE wind died to a whisper. Overhead hung a huge bank of black and grey clouds, ordinarily the signal for a thrashing rain-squall. But the air barely moved, as if the sky were holding its breath. What with the circumstances aboard the *Rahiria*, the effect was one of awful portentousness.

Luke wondered if Easley felt the oppression. If so, Easley gave no sign. He sat aft in the deck-chair, smoking his thin cigar. When he looked astern, what did he see?

There was a belated lunch. The Orshams picked despondently at their food. Luke ate a banana and drank two cups of tea. Easley lunched as usual, with a thoughtful pause from time to time. Luke could not bring himself to look into Easley's face. Easley, as a rule indifferent, seemed to sense Luke's emotion, and from time to time turned him a curious glance.

Luke thought: he wonders if I know something no one else knows. He wonders what I have seen or heard. He is casting back, reviewing the events, trying to calculate just how much I know, if anything.

Easley heaved a small sigh, once more addressed himself to his plate.

ON SATURDAY MORNING THE black peaks of Nuku Hiva appeared over the horizon. At midmorning the *Rahiria* sailed into Taio Hae Bay.

Borrowing the Orshams' binoculars Luke scanned the reach of dark water. In various quarters four yachts were at anchor. None was the *Dorado*.

Luke put down the binoculars. The *Dorado* had certainly arrived at the Marquesas. Brady would naturally prefer not to anchor at Taio Hae, the most frequented port of the islands. He would seek out an isolated cove, under great black crags, near one of the famous Marquesan cataracts.

A letter or a message of some kind presumably awaited Luke, with instructions as to how to join the ship.

The water of the bay was like a dark green mirror. The *Rahiria* eased with hardly a ripple up to the pier at the head of the bay. The sails came down; mooring lines were made fast to the dock.

"Everyone must remain aboard the ship," said the captain. "I will consult with the authorities."

THE PORT COMMISSIONER AND the commandant of the gendarmerie returned aboard the *Rahiria* with the captain: the commissioner a plump Frenchman with a gray toothbrush mustache, the commandant a massive white-haired Marquesan with a face carved from teak. They closeted themselves with the captain for twenty minutes, then called in the passengers, one by one. Ching Piao was first. He was dismissed almost immediately and went ashore. Next the Germans were called; they too were allowed to disembark. Easley was next. Luke paced back and forth, wondering what Easley would say, but more immediately concerned by the dilemma in which he found himself. Was he 'Jim Harrison' or was he 'Luke Royce'? In either case he faced a potential embarrassment.

Luke paced and pondered. 'Easley'—actually Benjamin Eiselhardt—was in something of the same fix. But Easley sauntered from the cabin, showing no sign of embarrassment. Luke turned sharply away. Easley went ashore.

The Orshams were questioned next: first Fiona, then Derek. Finally Luke was summoned into the cabin. The commissioner looked hot and rumpled and disgusted with the whole proceeding. The commandant sat to the side, stolid as a stump. He fixed his eyes upon Luke's face and never moved them, with unnerving effect.

Luke's dilemma was resolved at once. "Passport, please."

Luke heaved a sigh, pushed it across the table.

"Hmm. Luke Royce." The commissioner raised his eyebrows. "You are related to the lost man?"

"We are cousins."

"Indeed. Well, then, what can you tell me regarding the tragic circumstances?"

"Nothing. I went to bed; when I awoke Carson was gone."

"I see." The commissioner glanced at a sheet of paper. "Who then is 'Jim Harrison'?"

This was the question Luke had been hoping to avoid. "In Papeete there was a person I wanted to avoid—someone from the States. I called myself 'Jim Harrison' because I was afraid she might follow me aboard the *Rahiria*."

The commissioner gave a soft snort of derision, but did not pursue the subject. "How do you account for your cousin's disappearance?"

"I have no idea. As you probably know, he had a quarrel with one of the deck passengers, but I can't believe that the man would push Carson overboard on that account. It's totally unreasonable."

The commissioner gave a noncommittal jerk of the head. "What of suicide? Was your cousin in poor spirits?"

"No, I wouldn't say so. I can't imagine him killing himself."

The commissioner grunted, and spoke in French to the commandant, who returned a few gruff words.

The commissioner turned back to Luke. "Can you tell us anything more?"

"I wish I could." For a moment Luke was tempted to blurt out everything: all his suspicions, all his inferences. He restrained himself. He could prove nothing; to act hastily would startle his quarry. His first and urgent task was to locate Brady Royce. "Has the schooner *Dorado* arrived from Honolulu?"

"Several days ago, perhaps a week."

"Where is it anchored now?"

The commissioner gave a shrug and rustled his papers. "I do not know."

"Did the captain leave a letter in your care for me?"

"No." He pursed his lips, pulled at his mustache. "The subject was mentioned. I suggested that the post office offered a convenient service."

"I see. Where is the post office?"

"Next to the Englishman's store. But it will be closed by now, or so I suspect, since it is Saturday afternoon. Perhaps if you hurry, you will find the postmaster on the premises."

Luke left the cabin in haste. He ran down the gangplank, to stand looking this way and that. Two heavy-faced women in limp white dresses and palm-frond hats turned to stare at Luke, then continued on their way chuckling. Luke realized that he must cut a ridiculous figure. But no matter! Where was the post office?

A hundred yards north, tall trees shaded a row of frame buildings with rusty corrugated metal roofs. Luke set off up the road at a half-trot. Easley stood at the end of the dock inspecting a trimaran moored by fore and aft lines: a ketch-rigged craft perhaps thirty-five feet long, with an intriguing little stern-cabin. An Australian flag drooped from the stays.

As Luke passed, Easley looked around, then with insulting deliberacy turned back to his contemplation of the boat.

Luke gritted his teeth. Easley recognized his detestation, but clearly couldn't care less.

Luke stopped in front of a store with a faded sign reading: McDERMOT, MERCHANDISER. A half-dozen Marquesans of various ages sat on benches outside or squatted, smoking and talking. Taking note of Luke, they became quiet, turning their heads to watch him. A different people from the amiable Tahitians, thought Luke: these were a brooding, heavy-minded folk, oppressed by their tragic history.

Next to the store was a small frame building: the post office.

Luke tried the door. It was locked. He gave the door-knob a rattle, stood back in disgust. The Marquesans watched with faint smiles for Luke's discomfiture. A young man with peculiarly red hair curled tightly against his head murmured, *"Fermée."*

Luke gave a curt nod, and went to sit on a bench at the end of the porch. What to do next? Around Nuku Hiva's shoreline were a dozen delightful coves and bays where the *Dorado* might be anchored. A pair of other islands were little more than an hour's sail away: Ua Huka to the east, Ua Pu to the south. Brady might have taken the *Dorado* across to Hiva Oa, the largest and most beautiful island of the group. In the absence of information there were no decisions to be made. It might be instructive, thought Luke, to watch Ben Easley and learn something of his plans.

But first, a try at the Marquesans. He crossed the porch: as before they halted their conversation, to look at him with faintly hostile indifference.

Luke spoke in his halting French: *"Connaissez-vous la grande goélette* Dorado?"

The young man with the red hair said, *"Oui, monsieur. La goélette* Dorado, *je connais."*

"Où est-elle, savez-vous?"

"Elle est partie. Maintenant—je ne sais pas. Peut-être Hiva Oa. Peut-être Tahiti."

"Merci, monsieur." Luke walked back down the road toward the dock, more slowly than he had come. The trimaran had set sail, he noted, and was skimming easily over the smooth bay. Easley no longer stood on the dock.

Apprehension stabbed Luke. He ran back down the road, stopping short as the Orshams came past. "Where is Easley?"

Derek Orsham facetiously raised his eyebrows at Luke's brusqueness. He pointed to the trimaran. Luke's worst fears were confirmed. "He picked up a letter at the post office—something about a boat he expected to meet. Then he dickered for a ride with the trimaran fellows and off they went."

Luke stared after the dwindling sails. He asked: "How did he get a letter? The post office is closed."

"I fancy it was open when he went ashore. Must have closed shortly after."

Luke turned and raced back to the store. He approached the red-haired man. *"Où est la maison du maître de poste, connaissez-vous?"*

"Oui, monsieur." The man made an indifferent gesture up the valley. *"Là-haut."*

"Montrez-moi, s'il vous plaît. Je vous paie cinq cents francs."

"Cinq cents francs?" The Marquesan considered. He looked sidelong at his fellows. They gave him no signal. He temporized: *"Voulez-vous y aller maintenant?"*

"Oui, monsieur, tout de suite. C'est très important."

The young man rose languidly to his feet, shook his head to his companions in wry derogation. *"Bon, allons-y."*

He led the way up the road toward the head of the bay. In and out of the dank shade they walked, through the glaring contrasts of sunlight and gloom which distinguished the Marquesas Islands from Tahiti, where the air was open, the light even. The red-haired man turned aside into a lane angling up toward a cleft in the black crags. They walked in a melancholy hush punctuated by bird calls; foliage pressed in on them: tree ferns, breadfruit, *mape*, an occasional banana palm, ti plants with broad heart-shaped leaves. At irregular intervals paths led to thatched huts, each on its ancient stone *paepae*.

The red-headed man turned up one of those paths, jumped aside as a raw-boned cur leapt out to the end of its chain. With fangs gnashing the air only inches from their legs, Luke and his guide sidled past the dog and approached a thatch hut differing from the others only in the motor-scooter parked on the *paepae*. A girl of fourteen or fifteen came to the door, gnawing at a chunk of cold breadfruit. The red-haired man spoke in the Marquesan dialect; she glanced sullenly at Luke, shrugged, uttered a few words, then took another bite of breadfruit as the red-haired man turned to Luke. *"Pas ici."*

"Où est-il? C'est très important que je le voie."

The red-haired man spoke again to the girl. She nodded toward Luke and spoke at somewhat greater length.

The red-haired man turned to Luke once again. *"Vous n'êtes pas français, n'est-ce pas?"*

"Non, non! Je suis américain."

A new colloquy with the girl: this time she gave grudging directions. The two men returned to the lane.

The red-haired man spoke over his shoulder: *"Le maître de poste, il visite ses amis."* He made a motion as of drinking, and looked furtively up the lane. *"Les Français—"* he made a gesture indicating contemptuous disapproval, and Luke nodded in comprehension. Cocoanut toddy, the illicit brew derived from the flowing sap of the cocoanut palm, was far more potent than it tasted, and likewise went untaxed, as did orange beer.

The red-haired man led the way along a dark path which ran beside a patch of vanilla vines, crossed a meadow where a half-dozen brown Marquesan ponies grazed, then up the mountainside. Muffled through the foliage Luke heard the throb of a rather out-of-tune guitar, then a murmur of voices. Presently they came to a large *paepae* with a ramshackle hut at the back from which came smoke, the reek of frying fish and garlic. On the ancient stones sat two dozen men and women drinking toddy and orange beer: the first milky pale, the second the color of diluted orange juice. To the side lounged a dozen young bucks with pomaded hair, who laughed and joked but did no drinking. Luke wondered at their restraint.

At the sight of Luke the group immediately became rigid. Scowls appeared; someone uttered a gruff challenge. The red-haired man called out; there was an exchange of conversation; Luke heard the word *Rahiria*. Then a portly man in gray trousers and a gray shirt rose to his feet, came unsteadily down from the *paepae*.

To Luke's gratification he spoke English with a furry, half-French, half-Marquesan accent. "Yes sir. I am the master of the post. You want to find me, eh?"

"Yes. My name is Luke Royce. I think you have a letter for me at the post office."

"A letter is there. For Mr. Luke Royce. The post office is closed. I close it myself. On Monday I open it myself."

"The letter is very important," said Luke. "I'll pay you, say, a thousand francs to open up and give me the letter."

"No. That is against the rule. The French are very—how you say, *pointilleux*."

The red-haired man had quietly accepted a glass of toddy, and now he took another which he handed to Luke. The postmaster climbed with sodden dignity back up to the *paepae*, where he sat pointedly ignoring Luke.

"Attendez un petit peu," whispered the red-haired man. *"Il boit beaucoup. Après—peut-être qu'il vous donnera votre lettre. Buvez avec lui. Il pensera que vous êtes son cher ami."*

The advice, that Luke should drink with the postmaster until that official in an excess of camaraderie should totter to the post office and give Luke his letter, seemed far-fetched. But Luke had no better plan in mind. He climbed up on the *paepae* and seated himself on a bench. The toddy tasted like acrid cocoanut milk, not at all unpleasant. Luke sipped it cautiously. Not so the Marquesans, who drank enormous competitive gulps, as if each hoped to become more thoroughly drunk than his fellow. In the cook-house older women were working, without pleasure; from time to time a spate of angry words could be heard. Presently two girls carried forth platters heaped with what appeared to be fish balls and offered them among the celebrants. Luke took the smallest on the platter and found it to be more garlic than fish. The postmaster ate hugely and drank orange beer to match. As yet he showed no tendency to regard Luke as an old drinking buddy, and Luke began to wonder if, when totally drunk, his opinion would change.

Luke became restless. He drank the toddy, looked at his watch, studied the postmaster, who now had removed his gray shirt to reveal a perspiration-stained undershirt and huge brown arms.

Luke's impatience became overpowering. The *Dorado* might already have departed for Hiva Oa, the *Rahiria*'s next port of call. But no; in this case Ben Easley would hardly have sailed off in the trimaran. The *Dorado* must be relatively close at hand.

Luke could no longer contain himself. He jumped to his feet, approached the postmaster, and ingenuously put his request, as if it were a sudden new idea.

The postmaster blinked glassy eyes, barely comprehending. Luke added an inducement: "I'll buy you a bottle of whiskey!"

"Letter comes Monday. You bring bottle of whiskey Monday."

Luke made a gesture of despair, jumped down from the *paepae*. The red-haired man showed no disposition to leave. Luke paid over five hundred francs and set off alone down the dank path. Only the young men with the oiled hair took note of his departure. Then once more they watched the drinkers, waiting until one or another of the women would stumble into the undergrowth to relieve herself.

Seething with frustration Luke returned down the lane to Taio Hae village. He looked along the wharf: the trimaran had not returned. Luke cursed under his breath. He halted in front of the post office, peered through the dusty windows, hoping against hope to find an assistant or underling working overtime. The office was empty save for a dozen large wasps. Luke returned to the *Rahiria*. The cargo had been discharged; sacks of copra were being loaded aboard.

The Orshams had been taking photographs of the copra-loading. "Have a nice jaunt?" Fiona asked brightly. "Boat's about ready to leave," said Derek. "We feared that you'd be left ashore."

"Mr. Easley went for a sail," said Fiona, "and he's nowhere in view. I'm sure he'll miss departure."

"I'm staying here as well," said Luke.

"What?" cried Fiona. "Our little group is breaking up so soon?"

"I'm meeting some friends on a yacht," Luke explained. "I'd better get off my luggage. What have the police been doing?"

"Interviewing deck passengers and the crew," said Derek. "No one admits to a thing, though everyone blames that surly Leon Teofu."

"Yes, he's a bit of a beast, isn't he?" Fiona remarked.

"Still—he claims innocence," Derek pointed out. "The girl gives him an alibi."

"Declares that they were sleeping together, sly little basket!"

"Hmmf," said Luke. "Under the circumstances there's not much to be done. It's hard to investigate when there's no evidence, no witnesses, nothing."

"Not even a corpse," murmured Derek.

"Poor Carson!" cried Fiona. "A shame, a dreadful shame!"

Chapter XVII

THE *Rahiria* had sailed from Taio Hae Bay. Already the events aboard were diminishing. The faces seemed vague, the sounds remote, Carson's disappearance an unlikely nightmare.

At the rooming house annexed to the Englishman's store, Luke was taken to a room at the back overlooking the chicken-yard. He put his suitcase on the bed and went to the front porch. There was a sail on the bay. Luke recognized the trimaran *Banshee*.

He ran down the road to the wharf, and stood waiting. The wind was slight; the trimaran eased toward the dock with maddening deliberation. Two figures sat in the cockpit. Neither was Ben Easley.

Fifty yards offshore the man at the tiller flung out the anchor, paying off line as the trimaran slid up to the wharf. The second man stood on the foredeck with a coil of line. He called to Luke: "Hey, matey, lend a hand, there's a good chap." He tossed over the line. "Just make fast to the bollard."

Luke hitched the line as directed. He spoke to the man on the foredeck, now lowering the mainsail. "Did you just take a man to the *Dorado?*"

"Couldn't be righter," said the seaman. "Friend of yours?"

"In a way. Where did you take him?"

"Round the coast, place called Tai Oa Bay. Regular little Garden of Eden."

"Even got some nymphs," said the Australian aft. "Saw a couple aboard the *Dorado*. Queer feeling; I'd almost forgotten what a white girl looks like."

"Will you take me to the *Dorado?*" asked Luke. "I'll pay the going rate."

"It's the Banshee Bloody Ferry Service we are," groused the man forward. "But if you pays the money, you gets the ride. Right, Bob?"

"Right. Morning will suit, no doubt?"

"I want to go now."

"Can't be done, bucko. There's no wind out yonder."

"Don't you have an engine?" demanded Luke. "I've got to get to the *Dorado* as soon as possible."

"We've got a ruddy fine engine," said Bob. "One thing wrong: no fuel."

"Two things wrong. The bugger won't start."

Luke looked out across the bay. He pointed to a cat's-paw. "Surely there's wind enough! It can't be more than a few miles."

"Seven miles by the chart. But notice, old chum, it's close to sundown. Hard on Tai Oa inlet is a rock, long as Sydney Bridge, ugly as the opera house. What chance do we have in the dark? Hey, Mike?"

"With that current? A farthing's worth."

"In the morning, matey. Right now it's time for a bottle of beer, providing the Englishman got in his cargo."

Luke returned to the rooming house. Two girls were tending the store: the Englishman's gold-toothed daughter and a Chinese girl. Luke leaned on the counter. "How can I get to Tai Oa Bay? Is there a road?"

The girls giggled as if Luke had propounded the riddle of the Sphinx. "No road, sir," said the daughter in quaintly accented English. "Only the path up the valley, then back down into Tai Oa Valley. You'd never get a horse this time of day. If you walked you'd be sure to lose yourself; it's all of ten miles just up and down the crags."

"Give me a bottle of beer," said Luke through gritted teeth. He noticed the Australians trudging up the road toward the store. "Make it three bottles."

126

The Australians entered the store, to stand back in gratified shock when Luke handed each a bottle of Hinano beer. "This makes the day!" declared Mike, a round-faced young man with a fringe of ginger-colored hair encircling his face.

"An absolute stroke of luck! Don't happen often enough!" stated Bob, who was tough and stocky, with a corded ugly face, a stubble of yellow hair.

"Cheers!" "Cheers!"

"Cheers," said Luke. "Let's sit down on the bench. Something I want to ask you."

"Ask away, we've got nothing to hide!"

"You took Easley directly to the *Dorado?*"

"Correct!"

"He went aboard?"

"Correct!"

"Did he speak to anyone? Did anyone call him by name?"

"Didn't hardly notice, I was so busy with the bevy of beauties. Seems to me it was the captain who piped the man aboard. What do you say, Mike?"

"Well, it was something different. Easley—that's the bloke's name?—he was standing by the mast, looking toward the boat. One of the women saw him—it was almost like she was watching for him. She went to talk to the captain. He came to the accommodation ladder and Easley went aboard."

"I see. Which woman was it?"

"I don't know any of 'em by name, matey. Wish I did. All was really smashers."

"Well, what did she look like?"

"Bang-up. A bit of all right, as the saying goes. How do you call 'em in the States? A real pip."

"Thought old Mike's eyes would bulge clear out," said Bob.

"Did you hear anybody speak to Easley?"

"No, can't say as I did."

"There was some talk," said Bob, "but it didn't register. The usual type chatter, man coming aboard ship and all. 'How de do' and 'Welcome aboard' and 'What a surprise to see you' and that sort of thing."

"Who said it was a surprise?"

"One of the ladies; but it wasn't the one that ran to the captain."

"Anything else that you noticed?"

"No. We sheered right off and came back to Taio Hae. We still lack clearance from Papeete; probably won't get the word until Monday morning."

"Yeah, the Frenchies give everybody a clean bill of health before they let 'em in. Don't want no agitators or unsavory types."

"Our goose is cooked right there," said Mike. "What did you say your name was?"

"I'm Luke Royce."

"Pleased to meet you. I'm Mike Hannigan; there's Bob Higgins... Come to think of it, the captain on the *Dorado* mentioned a Luke. He says to Easley: 'You're just in from Papeete?' And Easley says, 'Right ho.' And the captain says, 'Was Luke on the boat?' And Easley says, 'Never heard of no Luke!' Words to that effect."

Luke groaned in dismay.

"Speaking of women," said Bob, "did you notice the dollies in the store? Maybe we'll have a party after all."

"A bit young, my boy. Still showing their milk teeth."

"You're right, of course. Well, you sit out here and yarn with Luke. I want to do a bit of shopping."

"Not so fast. Which one do you favor?"

"I rather fancy her in the pink dress with the gold tooth."

"In the best of taste. A real smasher. I'll settle for the other. A jolly little soul, no doubt. Just my type."

"Where does that leave poor Luke?"

"Luke can carry the picnic basket. Let's go give it a whirl."

The two went into the store. Mike said, "Think we'll make a large purchase: three more bottles of beer, and what would you ladies like to drink?"

"Nothing, sir, nothing at all."

"Oh come now. Surely you wouldn't want to hurt our feelings? Do you like beer?"

"Oh no!"

"Never touch the stuff, eh? Well, you're right. Bob here has swilled the stuff all his days. Look what a wreck it's made of him."

"He doesn't look so bad!"

"No matter how he looks, he's still kind to his mother. Incidentally, this is Saturday night. What goes on in the way of social activity?"

"Nothing. Just a dance at the Mormon mission."

"Wonderful! Maybe you girls would take us over. Always wanted to meet a Mormon."

"Susy can't go," said the Englishman's daughter. "Chinese people are very strict."

"Worse than the Mormons?"

"I don't know about that."

"Does Susy speak English?"

"No. Just French."

"Ask her if she can leave the house by the back door."

"Oh no! Her father would beat her."

"Well, Bob," said Mike, "I fear you'll have to watch the store with Susy... Unless—what's your name?"

"I'm Angel."

"Unless Angel has another beautiful friend. What about it, Angel?"

"There'll be girls at the mission."

———◆———

WITH NOTHING BETTER TO do, Luke also went to the dance, and stood for an hour or so watching the couples dancing prim foxtrots to records. The affair was strictly chaperoned. On the grounds of the mission sat several dozen young men in glistening white shirts, drinking wine and calling out to the girls, to the intense disapproval of the missionaries. Mike and Bob behaved far better than Luke had expected, dancing with propriety and arousing little suspicion from the missionaries.

Luke left early and he had no knowledge of how the evening ended.

Returning to the rooming house he looked out on a weirdly beautiful sight. The night was dark; the crags loomed black against the stars. Out on the bay drifted dozens of pirogues, each with a flickering torch held over the water. Luke went to his room, undressed, stretched out on the bed. Last night he had slept aboard the *Rahiria:* a time already an aeon distant.

He awoke early, to crowing and cackling from the chicken-yard. Mist clung to the lower slopes of the crags; a cool mother-of-pearl light seemed to rise from the bay.

The surface of the water was dead calm. Luke went back to bed, and dozed another hour or two.

———•———

THE ENGLISHMAN'S WIFE SERVED a hearty breakfast: canned bacon, eggs, fried bananas, a huge hemisphere of Polynesian grapefruit, Marquesan coffee. Luke ate without appetite, and was presently joined by Mike and Bob who seemed a trifle subdued.

Luke inquired when they could leave for Tai Oa.

"Anytime," replied Mike. "There's not much breeze but once we reach the ocean we'll catch a wind."

The wind was ample for the feather-light trimaran. It skimmed out of the bay on a single tack, veered between the Sentinels and turned west with the wind dead astern.

The crags and peaks of Nuku Hiva shifted past. Mike pointed ahead to a set of vertical pinnacles. "That's the entrance to Tai Oa Bay. Here." He passed Luke the binoculars. "Look below."

Luke saw a long half-submerged ledge half across the opening upon which the ocean swells seethed and swirled. Mike and Bob were vindicated. A sail through the dark into Tai Oa Bay with little or no wind would have been foolhardy.

The *Banshee* sailed past the entrance, jibed, slid deftly through the entrance. Luke went to stand on the foredeck. The bay was split into a pair of coves. Heavy dark green foliage came down to white sand beaches; from crags to right and left hung the famous Marquesan cataracts. Two yachts lay at anchor. Neither was the *Dorado*.

"That's odd," said Mike. "She seems to have disappeared."

"Not disappeared, old man: simply sailed away."

Luke spoke in a carefully controlled voice. "Naturally you're sure that this is the right place?"

"Heavens yes. She was hooked over yonder, near that blue yawl."

Luke gave a deep sigh. No mystery what had happened. Brady, informed that Luke had not been aboard the *Rahiria*, had hoisted anchor and set sail for Tahiti.

They approached the spot where the *Dorado* had lain at anchor, in thirty feet of water as clear as air, with white sand and occasional growths of orange and blue and purple coral below. The yawl was the *Viviane* out of Santa Monica; on the deck sat a young man and a woman.

Mike came about, made a slow approach into the wind. Luke stood on the foredeck and called across the water: "Hello aboard the *Viviane*. When did the *Dorado* leave?"

"Late yesterday: three or four o'clock."

The trimaran edged slowly closer, and drifted as Mike eased the sheets. Luke asked, "Any idea where they were bound for?"

"Hiva Oa, according to the skipper. Then Tahiti."

"Would you know what particular place on Hiva Oa?"

"We just came up from Hana Menu: that's a bay on the north coast: very beautiful! I mentioned it to the people on the *Dorado*; I think they might be putting in there."

"Thank you!"

Luke turned to the Australians. "How much to sail me to Hiva Oa?"

"Well, let's consider," said Mike. "That's about sixty miles, give or take a bit. It's on the way to Tahiti. Bob, have you had enough of Nuku Hiva?"

"I'm ready for Hiva Oa."

"Right. Well, then: say thirty dollars. Why so cheap? We're lonesome and crave company. Also we're short of funds."

⸺ ⋅ ⸺

THE *BANSHEE* PUT OUT of Tai Oa Bay, tacking into the southeast trades which suddenly had come to life. Hiva Oa lay dead southeast, and unless the wind shifted the trip would be a thrash into head-winds.

The seas began to mount. The Australians furled the mainsail and continued under jib and mizzen with some small diminution of speed and a far easier motion.

During the afternoon Hiva Oa became visible: a long black outline marked by the twin mountains Heani and Ootua.

The wind lessened, and it became apparent that the trimaran would not reach Hiva Oa by nightfall. The breeze became fitful; clouds began to gather in the east; a squall was imminent. At sunset, with the sky a weird muddle of hurrying clouds, the Australians hove to under the mizzen. With the first gust of wind and rain, all went below.

In the cabin there was quiet except for the gentle surge of water against the hull. The boat moved easily, rolling not at all, rising and falling with a gentler motion than Luke had experienced on the *Rahiria*. When he slid back the hatch and raised his head to see what was going on topside, the wind whistled past his ears, raindrops stung his face. He quickly returned below. "Are we moving ahead or astern?"

"About holding our own, I fancy," Mike told him. "Maybe we'll be blown back five miles or so. Maybe we'll draw ahead a little. Nothing to fear." He glanced at the chart. "Ua Pu is thirty miles west, ample under the circumstances. We're right as rain."

Dinner was soup, bread, fruit, canned meat stewed with potatoes and onions: much the same fare Luke had enjoyed on the *Rahiria*.

After the meal, Bob went up on deck, Mike washed dishes, Luke sat brooding on the settee. Bob returned below with cheerful news. "Weather's breaking up; she'll be calm the rest of the night. Might as well all turn in."

Mike and Bob slept in the wing bunks; Luke spent what he believed to be a fitful night on the settee, but before he knew it the light of dawn was flooding the cabin. He roused himself, pulled on his shoes, went out on deck. The day was clear; the wind gentle, but still from the southeast. Ahead lay Hiva Oa, at about the same distance as on the previous evening.

Mike came on deck, raised jib and mainsail, set the wind-vane which automatically steered the boat. Bob made coffee and boiled oatmeal. "If conditions keep like this," said Mike, "we'll make Hiva

Oa by noon. A beastly trip, of course. With anything like a fair wind we'd do sixty miles in three or four hours."

The sun rose into a sky of the purest blue; the wind lessened, the trimaran lazed through clear blue water.

Luke went to sit on the forward part of the cabin with binoculars, peering toward Hiva Oa, in dread lest he spy the *Dorado* with all sails set faring to the south. It was a wonderful morning. He thought with regret how much he might have enjoyed such a sail had circumstances been different...

The morning wore on. The *Banshee* moved at a leisurely pace toward the island. The peaks lifted into the sky; the terminal capes extended across the horizon; the blacks and grays began to reveal shades of green.

After consulting the chart, Mike set a course directly toward Mount Heani, and presently the two juts of rock enclosing Hana Menu became visible.

Beyond, dividing the bay into an eastern and western cove, stood an enormous tower of rock, which Bob announced to be seven hundred feet high.

Exactly at noon the *Banshee* entered Hana Menu. In the eastern bight were two vessels. The first was the *Rahiria*, tied up at a dock; the second, to Luke's inexpressible relief, was the *Dorado*, at anchor two hundred yards off a fine white beach, and almost in the shadow of the great tower.

"Well, matey, looks like you're in luck," said Mike. "There's your boat at last."

"There she is indeed," said Luke. "Put me alongside, if you will."

"Ten dollars if you please: fare from Taio Hae to Tai Oa. Another thirty, passage from Tai Oa to Hana Menu."

Luke found his traveler's checks, signed his name. "Here's fifty. Buy a beer when you reach Papeete."

"That we will, and much obliged."

"Much obliged to you."

The trimaran approached the *Dorado*. Mike said, "There's nobody aboard. Looks to me like they're all ashore."

Luke took the binoculars, and indeed the *Dorado* appeared to be deserted. Where was everybody? He scanned the shore. At the end of the bay was a village, picturesque under cocoanut palms. Some sort of celebration seemed to be in progress. Smoke from a number of fires drifted up through the trees; light-colored garments flickered in the shade.

Bob studied the scene through the binoculars. "Looks like a big *tamaraa*. Maybe we should stay over."

"We're not invited, Bob my boy. It's Papeete for us."

"You're making a mistake, Hannigan. Remember those gorgeous dollies aboard the *Dorado*?"

"I also saw a couple of hard-looking Yanks, not to mention that chap we ferried aboard. Seems to me he got the glad-eye from one of them."

"You're right," said Bob. "Noticed it myself. The one who was on the lookout for him."

Luke was immediately interested. "Which one was that?"

"Hard to describe, matey. They had a great deal in common."

"Careful, Mike! Maybe one was Luke's sister?"

"No," said Luke. "Nothing like that... Well, put me ashore, if you will. That's where everybody seems to be."

"Just as you say."

The trimaran slid up to the dock; Luke jumped ashore and Mike handed up his suitcase. On the beach appeared a girl in white shorts and a pale blue halter. Bob snatched up the binoculars. "Oh, you beauty! You wonderful specimen!"

"Here! Let me look." Mike seized the binoculars, but the girl had already turned back under the trees.

"Who was it?" asked Luke anxiously. "The one who gave the 'glad-eye' to Easley?"

"Can't be all that certain; she was walking away from me. The other had her hair in a tuft, or so I recollect. I'd wanter see more of her than just her backside."

Mike snorted. "Never satisfied, that's Bob Higgins for you."

"I said I couldn't make no good identification of just her backside!"

"Nothing wrong with that either."

"Well then. Kick us off, Luke, we'll be putting to sea."

Luke obliged. The sails bellied, the *Banshee* leaned upon its lee float and slid away toward the ocean.

Luke took his suitcase and set off down the dock, past the *Rahiria*, then along the road beside the bay. Ironwood trees, an occasional mango, the ever-present cocoanut palms overhung the road. Thatch huts stood a few yards back in the shade.

Luke pondered as he walked. If Brady was attending a feast on the beach, he could not know that Carson was dead. Luke made his plans. By one means or another he would signal Brady away from the party, break the bad news and reveal what he knew about Easley. The identity of Easley's accomplice—Lia? Jean Wintersea? Kelsey McClure?—could not be concealed. The whole sorry mess must be illuminated, for better or worse.

Luke passed through the little village with its inevitable church and Chinese grocery, and approached the *tamaraa:* a feast obviously commissioned by Brady. Food was heaped on four tables: steamed pork and chicken; crayfish, raw fish in lime juice, *langouste*, fried fish, fish balls in cocoanut cream, three kinds of poi, rice, bananas, papaya, avocados, minced clams in fermented cocoanut curd, heart of palm, octopus stewed in its own ink, a custard of canned milk flavored with vanilla bean and coffee.

It appeared that the company from the *Dorado* had already eaten. Now they sat drinking wine and watching dancers from the village. Halting back in the shadows, Luke studied the people present. Brady was invisible; Easley was nowhere to be seen; no one fit his mental picture of Lia. With the exception of Bill Sarvis, the *Dorado*'s Chief Engineer, the persons at the *tamaraa* were strangers.

Sarvis, now sixty years old, was a man not too tall, pale for a seaman, with a face all bone and cartilage. Luke tossed a pebble at Sarvis, who looked around. Luke signaled. Sarvis rose to his feet, ambled across the clearing. "Hello, Luke. Thought we were to meet you in Nuku Hiva."

"That was my idea too. I was delayed. By the time I found out where the *Dorado* was anchored, you'd already set sail."

Sarvis scowled, rubbed his chin. "Strange. The skipper got word that you weren't aboard the schooner."

"For reasons I can't explain right now, I used another name: Jim Harrison. Does Brady know that Carson drowned?"

"What? You don't mean it?"

"I certainly do. On the way up from Tahiti."

"My lord no. What a terrible thing! Poor Brady! He left the kid in Honolulu. Well, I guess you know about that. How did it happen?"

"Something of a mystery. Where is Brady?"

"He took sick, ate something which didn't agree with him. He and the missus went back aboard the *Dorado*."

Luke stared at Sarvis, then at the loaded tables, then out toward the *Dorado*. "What made him sick?"

Sarvis shrugged. "Hard to say. Whatever it was he didn't like it."

Luke drew a long deep breath. Had Easley been at work so swiftly?

He heard a footfall, and there, as if summoned by Luke's conjectures, stood Easley. "Hi, there, Harrison," said Easley, without enthusiasm. "What brings you here?"

"I might ask the same of you."

Easley waited a moment before replying, an insulting pause, as if Luke's question deserved no instant response. "I'm a guest aboard the *Dorado*." He jerked his head toward the *Rahiria*. "You'd better get aboard or you'll be marooned. They're about ready to cast off."

Luke opened his mouth, then shut it. Let Easley think he had arrived aboard the *Rahiria*.

"How come you didn't tell Mr. Royce that his son was drowned?"

"Who? Carson?" Easley wore an expression of surprise. "Was he Royce's son? I don't believe I ever heard his last name."

Luke turned to Sarvis. "Take me out to the *Dorado*. I'll have to tell Mr. Royce what's happened."

Easley looked toward the *Rahiria*, which indeed was on the verge of departure, then shrugged and walked away.

Luke said, "That man is the reason I'm calling myself Jim Harrison."

"I've been wondering," said Sarvis.

"Well, it's my name until I tell you otherwise. Let's go out and give Brady the news."

"Come along then. The launch is this way."

A few minutes later they nosed in under the *Dorado*'s accommodation ladder. Luke climbed aboard. The decks were vacant. He looked into the main saloon, to find a Filipino steward wiping down the brass work.

"Where's Mr. Royce?"

"He's in his stateroom. Pretty sick."

"Mrs. Royce is with him?"

"Yes sir."

"Go ask if I can speak to him."

The steward went aft. A moment later a dark-haired young woman with a pale olive skin appeared in the saloon. She wore white shorts, a pullover blouse of beige cotton, and Luke was forced to admit that Lia Wintersea Royce was far and away the most beautiful creature he had ever seen face to face. At the moment she appeared nervous and on the verge of tears. "Yes? What do you want?" Her voice was gentle; her brusqueness was not intended to give offense.

"I'd like to see Mr. Royce."

Lia jerked out her hands. "I don't see how you can just now. He's terribly sick."

"How sick?"

"Well, he's vomiting. He has stomach cramps and—he's really not himself."

"You've called for a doctor?"

"Of course. There's a hospital down the shore; the doctor should be here at once. Who are you?"

Luke evaded the question. "Does Mr. Royce know that his son Carson is dead?"

Lia blinked, drew back and became ghostly pale. "Carson? Dead?"

Luke nodded grimly. If Lia was acting, her performance was superb.

"He drowned on the way up from Tahiti. Apparently he fell overboard."

"How perfectly awful," whispered Lia to herself. She looked uncertainly down the passageway. "I can't tell Brady. I simply can't tell him now. He's so miserable..."

"May I see him a moment or two?"

Lia searched his face with as much concentration as she seemed able to summon. "You're a friend of his?"

"That's about it."

"I really don't think you should. Not right now. I should be with him... Thank God! Here's the doctor!"

A young man in white trousers and a white shirt came into the saloon, carrying a professional black bag. He asked questions in barely accented English, and Lia, ignoring Luke, took him aft to the stateroom.

Luke turned to Sarvis. "Well, that's that."

"What's going on, if you don't mind my asking?" Sarvis asked.

"I don't mind. I believe that Easley knocked Carson on the head and threw him overboard. In Tahiti he tried to kill me. I was wearing a beard then; now he doesn't recognize me. He's a murderer—but I can't prove it. I tried to get here, to talk to Brady, but it looks like I'm late."

Sarvis' eyes jerked open wide. "You don't mean—"

"I don't know. It's strange that no one else is sick. Just Brady."

"Strange for a fact." Sarvis rubbed his chin, producing a grating noise.

Luke went out on deck and looked toward shore. The sound of music and singing drifted across the water; the *tamaraa* was a great success. The *Rahiria* had departed, the *Dorado* was the only yacht in the bay.

Fifteen minutes passed. Luke returned to the saloon. Sarvis sat brooding.

Luke paced back and forth.

The doctor appeared, followed by Lia, who was biting her lips.

Luke asked, "How is he?"

The doctor set his bag on the table. "Frankly, he's not well." He spoke in a precise voice. "I believe that he has eaten poison fish. There are many kinds of poison fish. Some become toxic from the waters where they live, the food they eat. A parrot fish caught here is safe, a parrot fish caught ten kilometers around the island is toxic... But these are not so dangerous. A person may become very sick. But usually he recovers. If Mr. Royce has eaten what the natives call *hue-hue*—that is to say, puffer fish—then the situation is more critical."

"I see. Well—what do you think?"

"I can't be sure. The symptoms are in many cases the same: vomiting, diarrhea, convulsions, loss of sensation in the extremities. I've done what I can for him. We can only hope for the best. Additionally,

Mr. Royce seems to have a history of liver trouble which complicates matters." He picked up his bag. "No one else is sick?"

Sarvis replied, "No one that we know of."

"Strange... The natives won't catch *hue-hue*; they're afraid of it. Although if the gland is removed it's quite safe." He shrugged, turned to Lia. "I must go ashore, but I'll be back in two hours."

"Shouldn't we move him to the hospital?" quavered Lia.

"It would do no good. I can't do anything there I can't do here. In Papeete they might do better. If you wish I'll radio for the seaplane. Naturally there is expense."

"Don't mind the expense! Radio for the seaplane!"

"Very well. In the meantime, see that he's quiet. Let him rest as much as possible." The doctor departed; a moment later his launch surged past and away toward shore.

Luke flung himself down on the settee and stared at the carpet. Lia went back along the passageway. Sarvis came to stand in front of Luke. "You think Easley is responsible for this?"

"I know he is."

"Why?" asked Sarvis evenly. "What for? For whose benefit?"

"Figure it out for yourself."

"The way things stand, you'd be the only one to benefit."

Luke raised his head, met Sarvis' cool grey gaze. "Easley tried to kill me first. He thought he had succeeded. I was riding a motor-scooter; he drove me over a cliff. He thinks I'm dead."

"If he had known you were alive, he might not have killed Carson. If, in fact, he did so."

"That's true," said Luke. "But I knew nothing of his intentions. If he's responsible for this—" Luke nodded toward the aft stateroom "—then things start to take shape."

Sarvis grunted. "If Brady dies, it's your word against his."

"Just one matter," said Luke. "How am I supposed to have poisoned Brady?"

"You had as much chance as Easley had. The *Rahiria* has been in port since last night."

Luke grinned. "I see. Well, Sarvis, you suspect whomever you like. But for now—until things straighten out—I'm Jim Harrison. Remember that!"

"Whatever you say. I think I'd better pick up the folk ashore."

"Bring my suitcase over, will you? I left it near where we were talking."

"Right."

Sarvis presently returned with a load of subdued guests. Sarvis tersely introduced Luke as 'Mr. Harrison', which seemed to suffice for the moment. Easley, coming into the saloon, stared thoughtfully at Luke, then went off to his stateroom.

Lia emerged. In a hushed voice she reported the doctor's diagnosis, and then she began to sob. Luke watched her carefully, and the other two young women as well. If Lia was acting, thought Luke, her technique was beyond reproach.

The other two? He was able to form no immediate opinion. Both were formally sympathetic; neither gave evidence of deep concern. Jean was cool and didactic: her emotions were carefully intellectualized. Kelsey, saucy, spoiled, effervescent with mischief, clearly intended to waste no concern on troubles not her own. A fascinating little creature, thought Luke—more vital and self-aware than Lia, more feminine than Jean, and already appraising Luke, the new man aboard. Luke refused to respond. She was quite possibly a murderess—more properly, a murderer's accomplice, but why boggle at the distinction? The word almost certainly fitted one of the three young women aboard the *Dorado*.

Which?

Simple inspection yielded no information.

The other guests Luke dismissed with a cursory inspection. Don Peppergold seemed a straightforward young man if somewhat bumptious. The older McClures could not possibly be anything but what they seemed to be: a prosperous middle-aged couple, civilized, intelligent, decent by long habit rather than conscious doctrine. Easley was alien to the group: at least to the older McClures and to Don Peppergold. Luke heard Kelsey call him "Ben" and Jean for a period sat with him in the corner of the saloon.

The doctor returned and without words went into the stateroom. Lia came into the saloon, to stand troubled and alone.

Conversation halted. The steward brought tea, which was sipped in near-silence. Everyone ignored Luke.

140

The doctor appeared briefly. "I radioed for the seaplane," he told Lia. "It is probably the best we can do for Mr. Royce, to get him to Papeete. They have new techniques and drugs which so far are not available to us."

"When will the seaplane arrive?"

"I can't be sure. Certainly within an hour or two. There will be trained attendants aboard; I have seen to that."

"Thank you very much."

The doctor returned to the aft stateroom. Lia sat down and listlessly sipped the tea which Mrs. McClure forced upon her. Whatever her thoughts, she kept them to herself, with only jerks and twitches of her mouth to indicate that she was thinking at all.

Luke leaned back on the settee, watching everyone through half-closed eyes. No one seemed to heed him except possibly Easley, who from time to time turned him a brooding glance of speculation.

The doctor emerged from the stateroom. He looked haggard, dismayed, a trifle bewildered, as if he too found the events confusing. Without preamble, without so much as clearing his throat he announced: "Mr. Royce has passed away."

Silence held the air. Lia gave a little moan and fell to sobbing against Mrs. McClure. Easley reached for a cigar but thought better of it. Luke watched to see with whom, if anyone, he would exchange a glance of triumph.

Jean sat with her mouth pinched, her forehead creased, as if she were worried. Kelsey watched Lia with an unreadable expression.

Luke met the gaze of William Sarvis. He knew what Sarvis was thinking: the obvious; what else? He, Luke Royce, was now administrator of the Golconda Fund, a *de facto* millionaire, master of enormous wealth. The *Dorado*, which heaved on the easy swells of Hana Menu, was his. Beautiful women, as beautiful as Lia, were at his command. He was now a powerful man. Luke gave a wry grimace, trying to drive the thoughts from his mind. For a fact, they held no pleasure. The only reality was here in the saloon of the *Dorado*. The murderer was known; who was the murderess? Luke looked from face to face: from Lia to Jean to Kelsey. The doctor was talking in tense hurried tones to Lia, who listened numbly, nodding from time to time, her beautiful eyes glinting with tears. Jean watched with a detached frowning interest. Now she darted a quick glance toward Easley. So far as Luke could determine it seemed exploratory, questioning, rather than communicative. Easley was making bored O's with his mouth, smoking a non-existent cigar. Kelsey? She appeared resentful, as if Brady's death were a tiresome and inconsiderate act.

Lia? Jean? Kelsey? One must be guilty; one of these had brought Easley to the *Dorado;* either Lia or Jean or Kelsey had plotted with Easley to kill three men.

Two were dead; one remained alive. Easley and someone unnamed were about to receive a terrible shock.

Luke looked again toward Sarvis. The cold gray eyes no longer probed him. Instead they were fixed upon Ben Easley. By some unconscious device, Luke had convinced William Sarvis of his innocence.

Luke pulled himself upright on the settee. It was a time for plans. Easley and his accomplice would not casually reveal themselves. Their guilt had to be demonstrated. At the moment Luke could invent no method to compel such a demonstration.

Chapter XVIII

THE seaplane arrived at seven o'clock, skimming low across the dusky bay, settling in a fan of spray.

The district gendarme had already been aboard and had conferred with the doctor. He manifestly felt out of his depth; he stated that he would investigate the circumstances at the *tamaraa* and report to the Papeete authorities, which would be to the convenience of all, since the *Dorado* was bound there in any case.

Brady's body was transferred to the seaplane.

Lia declared her intention of accompanying the body to Papeete. The McClures argued against this course, pointing out that she could effect nothing meaningful at Papeete, that for the time she was better off aboard the *Dorado* in the company of her friends.

Lia listened dubiously. "But I should get in touch with Luke Royce—after all, he's the new administrator of the estate."

Jean joined the conversation. "Send him a radio message. A few days won't mean anything to him."

Lia turned to Sarvis. "What do you think?"

"We'll be in Papeete inside of four days, if we hoist anchor right now. We can certainly send a radiogram to Luke Royce at his Papeete address."

"Very well then," said Lia in a wan voice. "Can we sail right now?"

"Certainly, ma'am."

Lia turned wearily away. As she passed Easley he stopped her, muttered a sentence or two. Lia turned a puzzled gaze toward Luke, and hesitated. Then she turned back. "I'm sorry, but I don't quite understand why you're aboard."

Luke had been expecting some such challenge; indeed for the last few minutes he had been receiving dubious glances from everyone in the saloon.

He responded carefully, aware that everyone was watching and listening. "I came up from Tahiti aboard the *Rahiria*, as perhaps Mr. Easley has told you."

"'Easley'?" Lia looked around in puzzlement. "You mean Ben? His name isn't Easley." She looked toward Ben Eiselhardt, who merely grinned and fished in his pocket for a cigar.

"Whatever he chooses to call himself," said Luke, "he and I and Carson were all aboard the *Rahiria*. I came aboard the *Dorado* to speak to Brady Royce, and while I was here the *Rahiria* sailed."

Ben Eiselhardt spoke in an offhand voice. "And now the *Dorado* is about to sail. It's time you were going ashore."

Luke paid him no heed, and continued to address Lia. "I hoped to presume upon your good nature for transportation back to Tahiti."

Lia gazed at him numbly, not wanting a stranger aboard, but unwilling to seem ungracious. She looked helplessly toward Malcolm McClure, who cleared his throat. "I think, sir, that under these tragic conditions—"

Luke rose to his feet. He addressed Lia. "May I speak to you privately?"

Lia took him out on deck. "Well?"

Luke sighed. To reveal his identity even to one of his suspects was a pity—but now a necessity. Lia had been on the point of ordering him off the ship.

Luke looked around to make sure that he could not be overheard. "You've never met me. I'm Luke Royce."

"You're Luke Royce!" Lia raised her hand to her neck, peered at him. "I thought your name was Harrison, or something of the sort!"

"For reasons I won't go into now, I called myself Harrison. But I'm Luke Royce. Bill Sarvis knows me well. If you don't believe me, ask him. Or I can show you my passport."

"I believe you—but why… There's so much I don't understand."

"There's a great deal I don't understand either. I came aboard hoping to discuss the situation with Brady. But—as you know—"

"Yes. I know. Well—I can't very well order you from the boat. It's actually your boat."

"I'd like you not to tell anyone who I am. I want to—"

"No," cried Lia, in a strange desperate voice. "I won't have any more mystery! I can't stand any more! Come back into the saloon. Naturally you can stay aboard. But everyone must know who you are."

"Oh very well," said Luke. "It doesn't make that much of a difference."

Lia marched back into the saloon, with Luke coming behind, feeling a trifle sheepish.

Lia spoke in a voice so sharp as almost to be strident: "This man's name is not Harrison. He tells me that he is Luke Royce. He owns the boat. We are all his guests, not the other way around."

Luke was desperately trying to watch three faces at once, those of Easley, Jean Wintersea, Kelsey McClure. All three faces changed. Easley's face suddenly lost its cool bravado, and for a stricken instant became the face of a little boy. His eyes glistened—with tears? He turned abruptly away, went to look out a porthole. Luke could understand his frustration. The totality of his hopes, the entire cast of his plans, lay in ruins. What he had striven to achieve was totally lost; he had strained and worked and killed for nothing.

Jean's face altered by no twitch of a muscle. But an internal change occurred, or perhaps this was Luke's imagination. Her head seemed to be all skull, with the finest membrane of skin stretched over bare bone, with hollow pits for eyes. Kelsey's surprise was less controlled. Her jaw dropped; her eyes seemed to bulge and where Jean had grown pale, Kelsey suddenly flushed.

Reactions there were, beyond dispute. But how to interpret them? And what of Lia? He had spoken to her in the semi-darkness, he had not been able to study her as closely as he might have wished. She had evinced natural surprise, together with a trace of equally normal resentment. Still, if Lia were in fact Ben Eiselhardt's accomplice, she already had demonstrated an ability to dissemble far beyond the ordinary. Luke looked back to Easley—he must start thinking of him as Eiselhardt—hoping to observe an exchange of glances with someone, when he finally turned away from the porthole.

The silence persisted a moment or two, with everybody uncertain how to meet the new situation. Malcolm McClure said at last, in a stifled voice, "I won't pretend that I understand any of this, but I suppose the least we can do—" he changed to a tone of facetious irony "—is make you welcome to the group."

"What are your orders, Mr. Royce?" Bill Sarvis asked in a quiet voice.

"Just as before. We'll proceed to Papeete."

Don Peppergold had been standing back, head skeptically cocked, giving Luke a careful inspection. "Just for the record," he said, "may I look at your passport?"

"Certainly." Luke produced the document. Don Peppergold studied it. Malcolm McClure came to look over his shoulder; Ben Eiselhardt made a similar move, then checked himself. He looked toward Luke, and for an instant Luke met his gaze. It was so full of dreadful meaning that Luke felt sick. Ben Eiselhardt's first attempt on his life had been a casual act upon which Eiselhardt had spent no emotion. Eiselhardt would try again, as an act of passion. Emotion bloated him, distended his mouth, affected the pitch of his voice. Never in his life had Ben Eiselhardt been so frustrated.

Don Peppergold returned the passport with a faint shrug. Lia had been watching with poorly disguised hope. Her face sagged. She turned to Luke. "I'll move out of the owner's stateroom; you can move in."

"Of course not," said Luke. "Don't inconvenience yourself in any way. I'll be happy anywhere. Just carry on as before."

Lia thought a moment. Then she said, "Jean will move in with me, and you can have her cabin."

"That suits me very well," said Luke.

Sarvis caught his eye. "Shall we heave anchor?"

Luke nodded. "I don't imagine any of us wants to prolong the cruise. At Papeete whoever wishes can fly back to the States."

Sarvis departed; others in the group went off to their staterooms, Jean to move her belongings, others to change clothes. McClure and Peppergold muttered together, and presently both approached Luke.

"Sorry to be persistent, Mr. Royce," said McClure, "but Don and I are profoundly disturbed by the situation. First Carson dies, then Brady. You are the obvious beneficiary. Mind you, we make no accusations; we merely want to bring the situation out into the open."

"Quite all right," said Luke. "I understand your doubts. There'll be an investigation as soon as we reach Papeete. I'm sure that the facts of the case will emerge."

Peppergold thrust his face pugnaciously forward, stimulating himself into a state of artificial and unconvincing zeal. "You don't intend to explain why you used a false name?"

"No, I don't," said Luke. "I had a good reason."

"I'm afraid I can't be satisfied with that."

"Let's not jump to conclusions," said McClure in a reasonable voice. "As Mr. Royce points out, there's sure to be an investigation at Papeete. Mr. Royce doesn't appear to worry about this, so I think we ought to defer judgment."

Peppergold shook his head, turned away and left the saloon. "He's an attorney," McClure told Luke. "He wants everything in black and white, cut and dried. An impatient fellow, perhaps a trifle bull-headed. I've no doubt that he'll be a great success."

"And what about you? How do you feel?"

McClure smiled. "I'm uncommitted—for now. I think I can guess what's at the back of your mind. If I'm correct, you naturally don't want to tip your hand."

"Close enough," said Luke. "Well, I'd better have a word with Sarvis. I've crewed aboard this ship, but I'm no navigator. If we steer southwest for about three days, and don't run aground in the Tuamotus, I imagine we can home into Papeete by radio direction-finder."

"As good a system as any," said McClure. "As a matter of fact, I'm a navigator. If you'll allow me, I'll take charge of that end of it."

"Please do."

Chapter XIX

THE next morning found the *Dorado* cruising across a sparkling blue sea, flying fish skipping away to either side.

Lia and Jean appeared for breakfast, both reserved and thoughtful. Lia made a wan effort to be gracious; Jean brooded through the entire meal, her face a mask.

Luke found the company's mood even chillier than on the previous evening, as if, after reflection, all had decided Luke to be an unfeeling interloper—if nothing worse. Luke ate his breakfast with equanimity. From the corner of his eye he saw Easley studying him, a wistful droop to his mouth.

After breakfast Luke found Sarvis and took him aft to the taffrail. "Well, Bill," said Luke, "you've slept on the situation. What do you make of it now?"

"I think what I thought yesterday," said Sarvis. "There's something dreadful going on."

"I'll tell you the rest of the story." Luke described his initial encounter with Ben Eiselhardt. "If everything had worked out as planned, Mrs. Royce would now be sole administrator to the Fund. This must be the motivating force behind the affair."

"What would she gain?" demanded Sarvis. "Brady gave her everything she wanted. Why risk any of it?"

"People do strange things," said Luke. "But perhaps she's not responsible at all. It might be Jean Wintersea or Kelsey. How would one of these profit? She'd have to know that she could control Lia; Eiselhardt would also have to be certain. He wouldn't work for nothing... Here's Lia now, she's got something on her mind."

Lia came slowly aft. "May I join you?"

"Certainly," said Luke. "In fact, there's a question I want to ask you."

Lia instantly became wary, and looked as if she wished she had stayed away.

"Sarvis and I are wondering how Mr. Eiselhardt comes to be aboard the *Dorado*. Was he a friend of Brady's?"

"Oh no, nothing like that." Lia compressed her lips and looked aft down the line of wake. "I knew him long ago—when I was in high school in fact. In Nuku Hiva he heard the *Dorado* was nearby and came to visit. I was naturally surprised, and invited him aboard. It's as simple as that."

"Brady didn't object?"

Lia shrugged. "I don't think he cared much, one way or the other."

"They were strangers?"

"Oh yes. But Brady was very generous. Why are you asking these questions?"

"Curiosity," said Luke. "They are questions the police are sure to ask."

Lia nodded slowly. "That's what I came to talk to you about: the police. Do you think there will be an investigation?"

"I'm sure of it."

"I've been wondering—well, why can't it be avoided? Brady's death was a tragic accident—but certainly an accident. Wouldn't it be best to minimize the situation? People can be so cruel."

"Whose idea is this?" asked Sarvis. "Your own? Or have you been advised by others?"

Lia flushed. "It's partly my own idea. I've naturally discussed the matter with other people."

"Who, for instance?"

"My sister, for one."

Luke shook his head. "We can't avoid a police inquiry, even if we wanted to. The circumstances are very strange, to say the least."

"I suppose you're right." Lia turned away, but halted. "We couldn't just—well, sail directly back to California?"

"I don't think it would be wise, Mrs. Royce."

Lia sighed and once more turned away.

Luke called after her. "One more question, Mrs. Royce. Was your sister previously acquainted with Mr. Eiselhardt?"

"Yes, I suppose so. She was two years ahead of me, in the same class with Ben."

"What about Miss McClure?"

"She was in my class. She knew Ben too, at least by sight. But why are you asking these questions?"

"As before, curiosity. And I'd just as soon you kept our conversation to yourself."

"Oh, certainly. I wouldn't want to disturb anyone." She smiled politely and went forward.

"It's hard to imagine Mrs. Royce guilty of anything—on her own hook," remarked Sarvis.

"No. She seems malleable—but not vicious. Can we get in radio contact with the States?"

"We should be able to raise Honolulu without any trouble. San Francisco if the atmosphere is right."

"I want to send a message right away."

⁕

A DAY PASSED AND a second day, with the *Dorado* sliding closer to Papeete on fair winds. The passengers sat in clusters, talking together with furtive glances up and down the deck. Luke wandered here and there. When he approached one of the groups, voices dwindled away. Meals were even more uncomfortable, with conversation confined to brief unreal spatters, like the dialogue in an amateur theatrical. Lia haunted her cabin, appearing on deck or in the saloon with a wan face and eyes red-rimmed behind dark glasses.

Tension gripped the *Dorado:* knuckle-gnawing stomach-griping anxiety. Luke could feel it, but could not trace its source. Eiselhardt, who should be on tenterhooks, seemed unconcerned. Lia, Jean, Kelsey: all showed signs of edginess. One of the three, by Luke's theories, should feel an almost unbearable foreboding. Nothing of the sort was evident. Luke wondered why. Were the guilty pair so nerveless, so confident of their invulnerability? Or was there some new grimness in the offing? Luke winced and looked over his shoulder. The tension and anxiety quite possibly derived from himself. For instance, if he were to disappear from the ship, if a scrawled note, purportedly in his handwriting, were to be found, the French authorities would not be likely to look farther for a solution. Luke walked with care, looking and listening. He found and took possession of Brady's .38 revolver which seemed to be the only fire-arm aboard.

The *Dorado* entered the Tuamotus. Twice atolls appeared on the horizon like mirages, to move astern and disappear. Luke pondered and watched and wondered. From time to time he became aware of Ben Eiselhardt's puzzled inspection, as if he were wondering who was the bearded man who had been forced over the Teahupoo cliff?

Lia remained numb. She refused to speak to Luke or even look at him. Jean's coolness verged upon hostility. Kelsey's moods were more complex, ranging from an insouciance which annoyed her parents to a bored indifference which provoked and frustrated Don Peppergold. On the afternoon of the third day she came from the saloon and as Don loped forward to meet her she smartly accelerated her pace, dropped into a deck-chair beside Luke. Don glared for a moment, then swung away.

Luke sat in silence, though acutely aware of the shapely brown legs, the turn of hip in the tight white shorts. Kelsey, he suspected, was equally aware of the circumstances.

A minute or two passed, and Kelsey at last spoke. "What a strange man you are!"

"Come now," said Luke. "You know better than that."

"*I* know? How should *I* know?"

"Female instinct."

"That's one way," Kelsey admitted. "But it's not infallible. My mother, for instance, is afraid that an era has passed. You don't impress her as being a true Royce. Not spectacular enough."

"Well—I've never really set my mind to it. What would she think if I marooned her on that atoll out there?"

Kelsey laughed and stretched out her legs. "She'd be outraged. But she'd never again accuse you of being meek and unobtrusive."

"'Meek and unobtrusive', eh?" Luke glanced sardonically side-wise at Kelsey, who sat with her lips pursed. "Oh well, I guess it's better than being called 'rude and obtrusive'."

"Unfortunately," said Kelsey, "you've aroused criticism along these lines too."

"I never considered myself perfect," said Luke. "Well then— what's your opinion?"

"I'm not saying."

"You knew Brady a long time?"

Kelsey reacted to the change of subject by giving her feet an irritated twitch. "As long as I remember."

"And Lia?"

"Since high school. We were both on rally committee. Pom-pom girls, if you must know the truth. Jean played in the orchestra. Not the marching band. She was a serious-minded teenager."

"And she's changed?"

"She's no longer a teenager, if that's what you mean."

"I don't mean anything in particular. But it's strange to find three beautiful girls being chums."

Kelsey wrinkled her nose. "'Chums' isn't quite the word. Close enough, I suppose. They lived in a very odd household, very musical, very intense. Lia upset everyone, being tone-deaf, and I used to fear for her morale."

"What about Eiselhardt?"

"There he is. He exists."

"You knew him in high school too?"

"I knew who he was. We moved in different circles."

Don Peppergold could restrain himself no longer. He sauntered past, halted as if in surprise. "Hi there, girl. How about a game of cribbage to break the monotony?"

"No thanks."

"But it's three o'clock!"

"Go try Mother. She's a lot better player than I am."

Don Peppergold departed. Five minutes later Dorothy McClure emerged from the saloon and called Kelsey in a faintly scandalized voice. "Don is such a tattle-tale," said Kelsey. "Oh well..." She hoisted herself to her feet and strolled off to the saloon. With tremendous effort Luke restrained himself from looking after her. From the corner of his eye he noticed that as Kelsey swung down the companionway she flashed a glance toward him over her shoulder.

The voyage proceeded. Luke's suspicions inclined first this way, then that. In the strictest sense, Dorothy McClure should also be considered a suspect, Luke told himself. She was slender and small and almost as well-shaped as her daughter, though here the similarity ended... Luke brought his imagination under control. The idea of Dorothy McClure as the accomplice of Ben Eiselhardt was too weird to be entertained. Still, stranger things had happened.

———◆———

THE TUAMOTUS LAY ASTERN. At sunset of the fourth day clouds piled up in the west: towers of gold looking westward over a vermilion skyscape: sheer exaltation. Dinner this particular evening was a strange affair, with everyone in a state of hyperaesthesia, so that the most minute signals took on extravagant meanings. The situation had reached a stage where a touch, a jolt, a word, might easily set off someone's screaming hysteria. Sarvis alone seemed steady, a rock of normalcy.

"Tomorrow, about noon," said Malcolm McClure, "we should have landfall, and be into port by two or three."

"What a relief," murmured Dorothy McClure. "With Brady dead, it's been such a desolate ship."

Malcolm McClure gave a noncommittal grunt. "A pleasure, certainly, to put all this behind us."

Lia asked gingerly, "And there will really be an investigation? By the police?"

"I should imagine so," said Malcolm McClure curtly.

"There'll be an investigation," said Luke.

"But—" Lia started to speak then became silent.

Dorothy McClure said somewhat nervously: "Surely they'll understand that the whole thing was a ghastly accident, a mistake on somebody's part."

"Unfortunately," said Sarvis, "the circumstances suggest something worse. Not an accident. Not a mistake."

"But that would be—murder!"

The word had a peculiar resonance. To Luke's knowledge no one had used it before.

"Yes," said Sarvis. "Murder."

Dorothy McClure made a sound—a girlish titter—which was quite out of character. "I suppose I've lived a sheltered life. Of course, there was that other girl, what was her name?"

"Inez," said Jean flatly. "Inez Gallegos."

"Yes, of course. She seemed so pleasant. Why would anyone want to do such a wicked thing?"

Lia screamed. Everyone looked at her startled. The scene was like an unkind flashlight photograph: Lia leaning back, eyes bulging, mouth open, tongue displayed. She screamed again. "Why do you all torture me?" She fell awkwardly to the deck, picked herself up and half-ran and half-limped from the saloon.

Jean followed her. The sound of muffled sobbing came from the after stateroom.

THE NIGHT WAS DARK. The *Dorado* hissed through the water. Luke sat on his bunk, fully dressed.

There came a scratching on the panel of his door. The knob turned, the door strained against the lock.

Luke rose to his feet, went to the door. "Who's there?"

A husky female voice said, "Let me in. I want to talk to you."

Luke strained to hear. "Who is it?"

"Open the door, before someone sees me."

"But who is it?"

"Quick! Open the door and you'll see."

"Just a minute." Luke backed away, took up Brady's revolver, cocked it. He went slowly to the door. His hand was trembling. He backed away, sweating. He was afraid to open the door, afraid of what he might see.

There was a stir from somewhere: a door opening, hasty footsteps. Cursing himself for his hesitation, Luke threw open the door, revolver extended toward the opening.

He saw nothing.

Along the passageway, bound for the head, came Malcolm McClure. Luke put the revolver behind his back. McClure nodded, gave a grunt, walked by. Luke said, "I thought I heard someone in the passage. Did you see anyone?"

"One of the girls coming back from the head."

"Oh. Which one?"

"Didn't notice." McClure's eyes glinted as he surveyed Luke head to toe. "Why do you ask?"

"Just general vigilance. This is a nervous ship."

"I'll agree to that." McClure continued down the passage. Luke stood with his door open a crack, waiting, listening. McClure returned to his cabin. Luke eased the door close as he passed and opened it a crack once more, to stand looking out into the passageway.

Water rushed under the hull: a soothing rustle. From somewhere above came the creak of rigging. Otherwise the ship was quiet. But somewhere, two persons lay sweating. Eiselhardt shared a cabin with Don Peppergold, which would handicap Eiselhardt to some extent. Jean and Lia were together; Kelsey was alone.

Luke stood half an hour, but no one returned into the passageway. Who had come to his door? The voice had been a barely audible murmur; it could have been anyone. And why? There seemed three possibilities: to dally, to talk, to kill. The first seemed remote, as did the second. Anyone who wanted to talk could do so by daylight. Luke grimaced and tightened his grip on the revolver. Another ten minutes passed. The *Dorado* was silent. In the saloon the ship's clock sounded eight bells: midnight. There were distant footsteps as the watch changed.

Luke considered going up into the saloon. A dozen eventualities he had not considered: for instance, suppose Eiselhardt... A dreadful thought came to Luke. Caution forgotten he pushed out into the passageway, ran forward to Sarvis' cabin. He knocked. No response. He knocked again, then tried the door, thrust it open. He switched on the light, fearful of what he might see. No Sarvis.

Luke went to McClure's door, rapped. "Open up, McClure; it's Royce."

McClure appeared, belting his dressing gown. "What's the trouble?"

"I don't know. Probably nothing. But come with me please; I need your help."

McClure stepped out into the passage. At the sight of the revolver he scowled. "Why the artillery?"

"Do I have to draw you a picture?" demanded Luke. "Right now I want to find Sarvis; his cabin's empty. I don't want to look alone for fear of someone jumping on my back."

"Very well. But I don't know what you're worried about."

They looked into the saloon. No Sarvis. Luke called out to the man at the wheel. "Anyone out on deck besides you?"

"No, sir."

"Let's try the engine room," said Luke.

The engine room was locked. Luke pounded. "Anyone inside?"

Sarvis' voice came from within. "Who is it?"

"Royce and McClure."

"Are you there, McClure?" asked Sarvis.

"Yes," grumbled McClure. "I'm here."

The door opened, to reveal the grizzled face of the chief engineer.

"I'm not suspicious," said Sarvis. "I just don't believe in taking chances."

"Perhaps I'm a dunce," said McClure, "but why all this to-do?"

"The sea-cocks," said Sarvis. "They're down here in the engine room. Someone might prefer taking his chances in the boats."

"What a dreadful idea," said McClure dubiously.

"I don't like the prospect either," said Sarvis. "That's why I'm here."

Chapter XX

T**HE** familiar harbor opened in front of the *Dorado:* the sheds and warehouses of the Quai du Commerce to the left; the old buildings at the back of storied Quai Bir Hakeim ahead; the new post office, and the tall flamboyants and ironwood trees to the right. The customs launch crossed the harbor; the usual set of officials came aboard and with them a brisk young man in a light gray suit, fresh-faced and limpidly blue of eye who, in flawless English, introduced himself as Inspector Charles Duhamel, of the Provincial Gendarmerie. "And who is captain?"

Luke stepped forward. "Since the death of Mr. Brady Royce I have been acting in that capacity."

"I see. You are—?"

"Luke Royce."

Duhamel examined Luke more closely. "You are a former resident of Tahiti?"

"Yes."

"And was there not a circumstance perhaps a month ago—"

"Yes."

Duhamel nodded sagely. "No doubt we will presently find an explanation. I have been in radio communication with the authorities at both Nuku Hiva and Hiva Oa. The circumstances are such that we may not avoid a close investigation. I am sure that you all see the necessity of this." He looked from face to face. "Naturally, no one may leave the island until we are satisfied that all is in order. We will work with speed, but inconvenience cannot be avoided. Now, may I ask your names? And please allow me to glance at your passports. You, sir?"

"I am Malcolm McClure. Here is my passport."

"Thank you, sir." Duhamel made a note of the name. "And you, madame?"

"I am Dorothy McClure."

Duhamel proceeded through the entire group. "Now, may I ask, where you intend to reside during your stay?"

McClure said in a somewhat ponderous voice, "I think that under the circumstances we—myself, my wife and daughter—will stay in a hotel."

Lia looked at Jean. "We will too."

"I'm definitely going ashore," said Don Peppergold.

"Ashore," said Ben Eiselhardt.

"I'll stay aboard," said Luke.

"Very good. All then is decided. The crew no doubt will stay with the ship." Duhamel tapped his teeth with his pencil and looked off across the harbor. "The yacht must of course be moored, and I think that during this time we will begin our inquiries. Mr. McClure, if you please, I will speak with you first. The saloon will be convenient."

Duhamel spoke fifteen minutes with McClure. He spent half an hour with Lia. The *Dorado* meanwhile had backed into the dock, with an anchor holding the bow into the harbor.

Luke was summoned into the saloon next. Duhamel rose to his feet, bowed as Luke entered. "Mr. Royce, please take a seat."

Luke sat down.

"You are the cousin of Mr. Brady Royce?"

"Yes."

"I understand that you traveled to the Marquesas Islands aboard the *Rahiria* and there met the *Dorado*."

"That's correct."

"Aboard the *Rahiria* was the son of Mr. Royce, who was lost overboard?"

"Yes."

"How do you account for this?"

"I have no certain knowledge of what happened."

"I see. Well, Mr. Royce, let us be frank. I am sure that you realize that we must investigate this matter very carefully."

Luke grinned. "Certainly. I, the apparent beneficiary of the two deaths, am necessarily the prime suspect."

"Naturally!" Duhamel arranged his notebook and pen carefully in front of him, then glanced up sharply at Luke. "What then do you know of the tragic circumstances?"

Luke considered. "I know, or, let us say, I suspect a great deal. I can prove very little. I think that before I tell you what I know and what I suspect—which would take a great deal of time—I would prefer that you interview the other passengers. And then—"

"Ah. But you have definite suspicions?"

"I do. There are one or two matters I want to verify—"

Duhamel held his hand. "Please, Mr. Royce! Allow me to do the investigation. Tell me your suspicions frankly; I will verify or disprove them."

"Just as you say."

"I ask this, you understand, as a formality—are you responsible for these deaths?"

"No."

"I see. And what of your own accident—I now recall some of the circumstances. Were you not reported killed in an accident?"

"This may be the case," said Luke. "The affair occurred just before I left Papeete on the *Rahiria*."

"Why did you not clarify the situation? Your friends must have been distressed."

Luke smiled. "At the time I preferred to be thought dead."

"For a reason connected with our present case?"

"I know now that there is a connection. I didn't then."

Duhamel leaned sharply forward, started to speak, then changed his mind. "Why do you suggest that I interview the others before you describe your suspicions to me?"

"Very simple. I'd like you to acquaint yourself with the persons involved."

"Perhaps this is reasonable. You plan to stay aboard the ship?"

"I'd like to visit the post office."

"I have no objection to this. I think that you had better leave your passport with me."

"I need it to get my mail."

"Yes, of course. A problem. Let me think. There are no airplanes departing until tonight. You may hold your passport. Please return without delay."

Luke nodded. "Thank you."

LUKE WENT ASHORE, THE collective gaze of his erstwhile guests pressing against his back.

The pavement felt strange to his feet: a curious solidity which after days aboard first the *Rahiria,* then the *Dorado,* felt unfamiliar and strange.

He walked along the waterfront toward the post office and almost at once discovered a familiar object: the trimaran *Banshee.* Luke halted, but the decks were empty, the hatches were closed. Mike and Bob were ashore.

Luke continued to the post office, asked for and received his mail. A few personal letters he thrust into his pocket. There was one post-marked the day previously at Papeete. This Luke opened and read:

> Dear Mr. Royce:
>
> According to your instructions I am at the Hotel Tahiti with what material it was possible to accumulate in the time available to me. I fear it will be of no great value.
>
> I await your further instructions,
>
> Sincerely,
> Andrew Dell.

Luke crossed the street to the taxi rank, and attracted the attention of a driver.

"*Allez au Hotel Tahiti, trouvez M. Andrew Dell; le portez au* yacht Dorado, *voilà! Comprenez-vous?*"

"*Oui, monsieur.*"

"*Dépêchez-vous, s'il vous plaît.*"

"*Oui, monsieur.*"

Luke summoned another driver. "*Connaissez-vous Rolf Clute, qui demeure à Papeari?*"

"*Rolf Clute? Oui, monsieur. Tout le monde le connaît.*"

"*Allez chez Rolf Clute; disez que c'est nécessaire qu'il vient avec vous au yacht* Dorado *tout de suite. Comprenez-vous? Le* Dorado *c'est la grande goélette là.*"

"*Oui, monsieur.*"

Luke walked slowly back to the *Dorado.*

Something was wrong. He saw it in the faces of those aboard as he climbed the gangplank. All studied him with a curious detachment. To the rear stood Inspector Charles Duhamel, who once more bowed courteously. "A word with you, Mr. Royce, if you please."

McClure mumbled to Duhamel, "May we go now? There's no further point in our remaining."

"Another small moment or two, sir. Just possibly another item of information will be needed." He signaled Luke into the saloon. Luke entered, slowly took a seat. "What's going on?"

Duhamel stood with his knuckles pressed against the table-top. "Mr. Royce, I regret that I must bring a serious charge against you."

Luke leaned back in the chair, surveyed Duhamel with a grim smile. "On what basis?"

"On the day of Mr. Brady's death, your actions were observed by three independent witnesses. You came from the *Rahiria,* along the beach, to the outskirts of the *tamaraa.* There you quietly signaled Mr. Brady Royce, in a manner to suggest secrecy. You took him aside. Mr. Royce came back and said, 'I can't understand Luke. He is demented. He insists that I do not recognize him, that I do not tell anyone that he is here on the *Rahiria,* and then he makes me take a drink of wine. It is very strange.'

"Mr. Brady Royce repeated this statement to several persons. Immediately after, he became ill. The conclusions are unavoidable. What do you have to say to this, Mr. Royce?"

Luke laughed. "I'm delighted. You can't imagine how pleased I am."

Duhamel seemed hurt. "You are delighted? I fail to understand."

"You are convinced by the accusation?"

"It is verified by several persons."

"You have not yet heard what I have to tell you."

"No, of course not. You desired it so."

"Well then, bring everyone into the saloon. Everyone can listen."

"If you like." Duhamel went to the door. "Please, everyone into the saloon."

The passengers filed in from the afterdeck.

"I am sorry to inconvenience you," said Duhamel. "But Mr. Royce has a statement to make, which he feels will interest everyone."

McClure growled under his breath; Don Peppergold glared; Eiselhardt coolly lit a cigar.

"Proceed then, Mr. Royce."

"On Saturday, June 8—this I believe was the date—I rode into Papeete on my motor-scooter. I went into the post office to get my mail. A man I then did not know but who I now know as Mr. Eiselhardt was waiting there, watching the post office boxes. The inference is that he knew my box number, but not where I lived. Later, when I had a chance to examine his passport I noticed that he had entered Papeete on June 5. I assume that he had been waiting in the post office every day. Inspector, this is a matter for you to verify. I am sure you'll be able to locate witnesses. Mr. Eiselhardt is a conspicuous man.

"He followed me from the post office..." Luke described the events of the day, his fall into the ocean, his bewilderment, his return to Papeete. "As I say, I was totally surprised. I could not understand why a stranger would want to kill me. This is why I did not report the affair to the police. The attempted murder would probably be dismissed as an accident; the murderer would be put on his guard. I shaved my beard, changed my clothes, and became James Harrison."

Luke started to describe his meeting with Carson, but was interrupted by the arrival aboard the *Dorado* of a tall lean man in a gray suit with a green turtle-neck shirt.

"Excuse me a moment," said Luke. He went out on deck, and the group inside the saloon saw him shake hands with the newcomer, exchange a few words, point up the waterfront. The man in the gray suit nodded, once more left the *Dorado*. Luke returned into the saloon. Charles Duhamel sat stiffly, his face frigid. The confrontation was proceeding along lines different from those he had envisioned. Eiselhardt sat relaxed, apparently indifferent, blowing small puffs of smoke into the air.

Luke watched Eiselhardt a moment, then continued. "There's not much I can tell you about Carson. He came aboard the *Rahiria* and Eiselhardt couldn't believe his good fortune—especially when Carson involved himself in a quarrel over a girl. Over the side went Carson. No witnesses, no clues, no proof, nothing. Nothing, that is except a negative kind of proof. Eiselhardt and Carson shared a cabin. The ship was so crowded that any kind of a scuffle must have attracted attention. Only Eiselhardt had privacy enough to deal with Carson. I imagine he hit him over the head when Carson came into the cabin, waited until the coast was clear and slid him over the side. By morning, Carson was fifty miles astern.

"Now to Nuku Hiva. Eiselhardt leaves the *Rahiria,* goes to the post office. Someone has left a letter for him. Who? A mystery. Eiselhardt has an accomplice—someone who perhaps has planned the entire scheme.

"In fact, before we proceed any farther, perhaps we should consider the motivation behind these acts. Brady Royce was administrator of the Golconda Fund. Carson was next in line. Then me. If Carson and I were both dead, and lacking a male heir, Mrs. Lia Wintersea Royce would become administratrix.

"It would seem as if this were the plan: but perhaps I'm anticipating matters."

Luke looked out to the dock. "Well, look who's here. Some old friends, Mike Hannigan and Bob Higgins from the trimaran *Banshee*. Quite a gathering." Luke went to the door, called across to the dock. "Come on in, join the fun."

The Australians filed into the saloon, followed by the tall man in gray. Luke performed introductions. "Mike Hannigan,

Bob Higgins, and this is my attorney Andrew Dell who has only just arrived from the United States. Gentlemen, we are discussing the murder of Brady Royce, and all of us are now pondering the identity of Ben Eiselhardt's accomplice. But again, perhaps I anticipate.

"At Hana Menu, the most beautiful bay of Hiva Oa, Brady commissioned a *tamaraa* for his guests. Everyone began eating. Ben Eiselhardt and two other witnesses state that I came over from the *Rahiria* and gave Brady a dose of poison."

"This is the case," said Eiselhardt in an even voice.

"In any event Brady was poisoned. He went aboard the *Dorado* and presently died. The doctor in attendance diagnosed fish poisoning, probably the toxic serum found in the *hue-hue*, or puffer fish."

Luke paused, rose to his feet, looked out along the waterfront. A taxi turned out of one of the side-streets, approached. Luke said, "I think that in a minute or so we'll have some expert testimony."

The taxi halted in front of the *Dorado;* Rolf Clute alighted. He saw Luke, gave a large wave of his hand. "Who's paying this taxi?"

"Tell him to wait. Come aboard. I need your help."

"Sure. What for?"

"A long story."

Rolf Clute came slowly up the gangplank, peered in surprise at the group in the saloon. "That's Duhamel in there. He's the gendarme!"

"Right. Some bad things have been happening." Luke led the way into the saloon. "This is Rolf Clute, who was aboard the *Rahiria* as far as Rangiroa. Rolf, you and Ben Eiselhardt went fishing in the Rangiroa lagoon, did you not?"

"Ben who? You mean Ben Easley? Him?" Rolf Clute pointed a long knobby finger.

"Yes. Did you go fishing with him?"

"Sure! Why not?"

"What did you catch?"

"Nothing much. Now that you mention it, he was interested in the *hue-hue*."

"Did you spear any?"

"Yeah, we got two."

"Then what?"

Rolf Clute licked his satyr's mouth, ran his hand through his shock of red hair. "Well, Ben asked me to show him the poison sac. I cut them up, pulled out the gland. Rest of the fish is good eating."

"Did Eiselhardt keep the sacs?"

"Eiselhardt—you mean Ben Easley again?"

"That's the name he was going by on the *Rahiria*."

"Well, Eiselhardt, Easley—whatever his name—I don't know what he did."

Luke addressed Duhamel. "For your information, Eiselhardt went spear-fishing by himself in the Tikehau lagoon. Perhaps he wanted to make sure that he had ample poison. Once at the *tamaraa* it was a simple matter to doctor Brady's plate, or perhaps pour a few drops of poison into a glass of toddy."

Eiselhardt spoke again, in the same even voice: "You lack all proof of this—just as you lack proof of your other accusations. Ask your lawyer, he'll tell you. So far it's guess-work."

"You and two others saw me come over from the *Rahiria*—that's better evidence?"

"Certainly."

"I see. Well, on Nuku Hiva I hired Mike and Bob to take me to Tai Oa Bay. The *Dorado* had departed; I was too late to save Brady's life. Along the way they told me that when they had ferried you to the *Dorado* that you had made a signal to one of the women aboard. They weren't sure which one; they saw nothing but her back. Right, Mike? Right, Bob?"

"Right." "Right."

"But she wore her hair in a tuft, eh?"

"Right again, all the way."

"Like one of the women in this room?"

"So right. Like her." Mike pointed.

"Yep. That's her," said Bob. "So far as I can prove from frontwards."

Luke turned to Charles Duhamel. "This is one of the witnesses who saw me approach Brady?"

"That is correct." Duhamel gnawed furiously at his mustache.

"I should mention," said Luke in an offhand voice, "that Mike and Bob took me to Hiva Oa aboard their trimaran. We arrived after the *tamaraa* was in progress, sometime after noon. Right, fellows?"

"Right." "Just so, matey."

"It becomes evident that Eiselhardt and his two witnesses gave the police false evidence. Mrs. Lia Royce of course was blackmailed; they had her totally in their power; they told her what to say. Is that correct, Lia?"

Lia, pale as milk, could only stare numbly. Her beauty was no longer real; it had vanished, giving way to a brittle white face.

"Just for the record: Mrs. McClure, do you ever wear your hair in a 'tuft'—a pony tail, that is?"

"Of course not," gasped Dorothy McClure.

"Kelsey—what about you?"

"Hah! With hair two inches long? No."

"Only Jean, then, wears her hair in a pony tail?"

"That's true," said Kelsey, examining Jean with sudden wonder.

Luke turned to Charles Duhamel. "There you have it: two murderers. They plotted to kill me. Eiselhardt drowned Carson, one or the other poisoned Brady. With Lia administrating the Golconda Fund, they were set for life." Luke paused to grin. "When I introduced myself as Luke Royce, this was the worst shock in their lives. Because they had failed. Never could they get the estate back to Lia. If I died, it would work its way through my branch of the family. They had lost—completely. All they could do was try to pin the killings on me and hope that a court would transfer the trusteeship back to Lia. Any questions, Inspector?"

"Yes, of course. Mrs. Royce, please tell me—is all this substantially true?"

"Yes," whispered Lia.

"Be quiet, you little fool!" shrieked Jean.

"What's the difference?" whispered Lia. "I've done nothing wrong—except lie for you to the police officer. You killed Brady—and poor Carson. I hope you hang."

"They had some kind of hold on you?" asked Duhamel.

"Yes. But nothing really disgraceful—just foolishness. In high school I became infatuated with Ben. He wanted me to live with him. I said no unless we were married. So he married me. It lasted two months. I wanted a divorce. He told me to forget it, that we never had been married to begin with, that he had been married to a girl named Inez Gallegos and had never got a divorce.

"A while later I became engaged to Brady. Inez was killed. I know what happened. Ben went to her for the marriage certificate. She wouldn't give it to him. He killed her and took the marriage certificate. Then I couldn't prove that we had not been married—that we were not still married. He began to humiliate me. He forced me to do things. Sleep with him. I even became pregnant. I didn't dare tell Brady, and I wanted to marry him. I know I should have been braver—but I'm not a brave woman."

Jean jumped to her feet, eyes staring, fingers clenched and bony. "Lia! Don't you dare say another word! Do you realize what you're doing?"

Lia nodded. "I'm just telling the truth."

Jean slowly sank back down in her chair.

"Lia was caught," said Luke. "Eiselhardt could demonstrate that he was married to her, that they had never been divorced. With Inez Gallegos dead and the marriage certificate in Eiselhardt's possession there was no way of proving otherwise—without going to an impossible amount of trouble. So anytime Eiselhardt wanted to do so he could invalidate Lia's marriage to Brady. Lia, I fear, lacked the fortitude to defy him, to tell Brady."

"I'm a coward," said Lia in a dreary voice. "I know it... There's nothing much more to tell," said Lia. "At Nuku Hiva, Jean told me that Ben was coming aboard, that I was to make it right with Brady. Which I did." She lowered her face into her hands. "I wish I had died along with him. I wish I were dead."

Luke spoke to Duhamel: "I asked Mr. Dell to get together what information he could and meet me here. I don't know what he has; I haven't had a chance to talk with him yet."

"In the main, corroboratory material," said Dell briskly. "It seems that Eiselhardt derived much of his income from pornographic movies. It's possible..." his eyes strayed toward Lia, then he looked away. "I suppose that aspect of the affair need not be pursued."

Duhamel rose to his feet. "Miss Wintersea, Mr. Eiselhardt: you have heard the accusation. What do you have to say?"

"Nothing, of course," said Ben Eiselhardt.

Luke said to Duhamel, "He waited for me in the post office three or four days. Find someone to identify him. He rented a Citroën; it must have been returned with a dent. Perhaps some of the natives at Tikehau saw him spearing *hue-hue*."

"Yes, yes," said Charles Duhamel in a haughty voice. "We are quite able to handle the details of our affairs. Miss Wintersea, Mr. Eiselhardt, you are under arrest."

Eiselhardt put a new cigar in his mouth, brought forth a large metal lighter.

"Look out," yelled McClure.

The lighter belched fire; a slug sang past Luke's ear.

Eiselhardt shook his head sadly. Don Peppergold sprang forward but Eiselhardt ignored him. He held the mechanism to his head. Once again there was an explosion and Ben Eiselhardt fell to the floor with a hole in his forehead.

Chapter XXI

T𝐇𝐄 *Dorado* was quiet. The police had departed with Jean and the body of Ben Eiselhardt. Lia, the McClures and Don Peppergold had gone off to a hotel. Of the crew, only the stewards were aboard, packing Brady's personal effects for shipment to San Francisco.

Luke sat in the empty saloon watching twilight drift down upon the harbor. In spite of the events of the day, the saloon seemed peaceful and mellow. Luke felt at peace.

There was no immediate urgency for anything. Sooner or later he must return to San Francisco, but at the moment he felt disinclined to do anything but laze, to dawdle, to swim in cool blue lagoons, to explore remote white beaches.

No reason why he should not, of course. Here was the *Dorado,* ready to hand. Out across the Pacific were the Cook Islands, the seldom-visited Ellice group...

Steps sounded on the gangplank; female steps, brisk, light, yet somehow tentative.

Luke went to the door. It was Kelsey. "Oh, hello."

"Hello, Luke. I left my vanity case aboard."

"I suppose it's in your cabin."

"Yes. I suppose so..." She looked tentatively into the saloon. "You're sitting here all by yourself?"

"It's peaceful... Er, how about a glass of sherry?"

Kelsey gave a lame little laugh. "All right. In fact, that's why I came here."

"For sherry?"

"No. To talk a bit."

Luke poured sherry, handed a glass to Kelsey. "Sit down."

She sank upon one of the settees. "I want to apologize. Really I do. We were frightful to you—even when we knew you were guilty of nothing whatever."

"I understand. Say no more. Herd instinct: drive out the interloper."

"Partly that. And in my case, because I'm perverse and malicious. I know it. I deceive other people, like my mother and father and Don, but I don't deceive myself."

"All right. You're no good. I believe you."

"I came here to beguile you. I know I can do that too."

"All right. I'm beguiled. It's pleasant for a change. I like it. But why?"

"Shall I be utterly candid?"

"You won't offend me."

Kelsey slid a foot closer along the settee. "I don't want to go home. I don't intend to go. Mother and Father are flying out as soon as the police take their depositions. Don—I don't know. There may be a scene. Still, if he can't find me he can't argue or bluster... What will you do?"

Luke gave a small dry chuckle. "I'm taking a vacation—aboard the *Dorado*. I'm sailing out into the middle of the Pacific."

Kelsey sipped her sherry, cocked her head sidewise. "I rather thought you might... Can I come along?"

Luke looked up at the ceiling. "I don't know whether I want company or not. Or what kind of company."

Kelsey moved several inches closer.

"I wouldn't be in the way," she said earnestly. "And think: shuffleboard. Wouldn't you rather play shuffleboard with me than old Sarvis?"

"Sarvis comes in a poor second. No question about it."

"Luke—do you consider me extremely forward?"

"Well, yes. I do."

"For a very good reason. I am that. May I have more sherry?"

"Of course. Pour for me too, if you will."

"With pleasure. You see, I can do things, like pouring sherry."

Luke watched her. Fetching, beyond doubt: charming, provocative. Perhaps too much so. Luke again considered the ceiling.

Kelsey clinked glasses. "To set matters perfectly straight," she said softly, "I am not a cold-blooded opportunist. Certainly not cold-blooded, at any rate."

They sat in silence for a moment or two, watching the lights twinkle into existence across old Papeete.

"It's been dreadful," whispered Kelsey. "But I wouldn't have missed it for the world."

"You knew Eiselhardt in high school?"

"I never could tolerate him. Only weak-minded girls like Lia and Inez liked Ben. He was so obviously twisted and cruel... But let's not talk about the past. Can I come with you?"

Luke drew a deep sigh. "You catch me at a weak moment. I want someone to soothe me, to stroke my head, to pour me sherry from time to time."

"And Sarvis doesn't do it the right way?"

"He doesn't know the first thing about it."

Kelsey touched a finger to his forehead. "It feels like it might be nice to stroke. I'll be ever so careful."

"I don't want any scenes with your family. I don't want to fight Don Peppergold."

"I'll handle everything. That's included in the soothing part. All you have to do is play the ukulele and pay for running the boat."

"Oddly enough," said Luke, "I can do both. Well, then, another glass of sherry and after that—"

"After that," said Kelsey, "I will be going ashore. Otherwise you'd think I was worse than I really am. And I'm really not bad at all. Not too bad. I just want to visit those far-away islands."

"I hope I'm not called to San Francisco on an important matter," said Luke. "Then you'd have to start all over again, beguiling Sarvis."

"Sarvis is really an old dear," said Kelsey. "Perhaps he might like to be petted and soothed too."

"Please, not on the same ship." Luke rose to his feet. "Are you hungry?"

"Starving."

"Way out around the island, at Taravao, there's a restaurant. It's called the Atchoun. Shall we go there for dinner?"

"I'd love to."

———•———

CANDLES FLICKERED TO THE airs drifting in from hibiscus bushes. Looking across the table, Luke thought, I wonder what I'm getting into? Whatever it is, it can't be all bad.

Kelsey spoke. "Luke."

"Yes."

"You're thinking of something."

"I realize that."

"And I know what it is. Never, never, never, would I marry you."

"'Never' is a long time," said Luke.

"Never, never, never is even longer. Do you know why I wouldn't?"

"First of all, I haven't asked you."

"No. It's nothing like that. It's because of this. Right now you're in a stage of nervous reaction. After a while, you'd start thinking. You never could trust me. Not really. You'd never forget how I acted when you were all alone and everyone was against you. Would you?" She searched his face.

Luke reviewed a dozen answers, found pitfalls everywhere. He said at last, "People are dead. Others are miserable. Don Peppergold is angry. But for me, and perhaps for you—everything is pleasant. So why should I complain?"

Kelsey smiled and looked into the candles. "You didn't answer my question."

"No."

"Perhaps it's just as well."

THE MAN IN THE CAGE

Chapter I

AT noon on March ninth, a dump-truck loaded with coarse gray gravel bumped south through a haze of dust and sunlight. The road, narrow and pot-holed, seemed to cut the visible universe into halves: life on one hand, death on the other. To the right were vistas, areas and masses of verdure, in a thousand sunlit shades of green: feather-green date palms, sea-green tamarisk, truck gardens, plots of emerald alfalfa. To the left spread the desert, hot and dreary, sprinkled with black flints.

Noel Hutson drove the truck, a fair-skinned young man with mouse-brown hair, a rather dandified mustache, a tolerant happy-go-lucky expression. Beside him, leaning forward on the edge of the seat, sat Habdid el Kazim, square-faced, narrow-eyed, thick-set and powerful. A curious thin beak of a nose protruded from otherwise flat features; black stubble blurred the lower half of his face. He wore a homespun brown djellaba with the hood thrown back, and at his hip hung a dagger, with a silver-inlaid handle in a silver scabbard shaped like a fish-hook.

The two men had been riding together for fourteen hours, accepting each other's presence with neither hostility nor cordiality. Habdid el Kazim spoke a hundred words of English; Noel Hutson knew a single word of Arabic: *la*, which meant 'no'. Neither knew the other's name.

The road presently swung into the palm grove. After a mile Habdid el Kazim jerked up his hand: "Slow." He looked up and down the road: no vehicles in sight. He pointed. "Turn through there."

Noel twisted the steering wheel. The truck lurched into the shallow roadside ditch, groaned up the hummock opposite, scraped between a pair of palm trees. El Kazim indicated a track leading off across a carpet of rank salt grass. In low gear they rumbled through the grove, past irrigation ditches, low walls of adobe brick, thickets of tamarisk. Palms of random size and character rose over them, some tall and lordly, others squat, with great unruly heads; most erect, a few twisted and leaning.

El Kazim sat rigid on the edge of the seat. Once, when the wheels slid in mud, Noel gunned the motor: el Kazim made an urgent motion. "The French." His face split in a nervous grin, showing a row of gold teeth. He pointed through the trees. "Two kilometers, no more. Soldiers."

Noel thereafter drove as quietly as possible. The trees thinned; ahead appeared a typical kasbah of the region, a village behind walls thirty feet high, with corner watchtowers, a heavy timber gate. El Kazim motioned Noel to a halt and jumped to the ground. Beside the track stood a sentry; the two conferred. The sentry spoke into an army-type field telephone, listened, gave a signal to proceed. El Kazim climbed back into the cab, jabbed his forefinger toward the kasbah. "We must go fast."

Noel worked the balky gearshift: compound-low, low, second; the Diesel roared and chattered. El Kazim fluttered his fingers nervously. "Fast, fast." Noel thrust his foot down on the accelerator; the truck roared along the road. The timber gate opened, the truck entered a large compound, the gate swung shut.

Noel brought the truck to a smart halt, switched off the engine. He opened the door, stepped out on the running-board. Sunlight stung his damp skin. Three- and four-story mud dwellings, similar to the pueblos of Arizona, surrounded the courtyard—masses of rectangular blocks and planes, penetrated by tunnel-like passages. A caravan had either just arrived or was about to leave: across the courtyard stood a dozen camels, with nearby a heap of saddles, panniers, ropes and straps. An odor of urine, decay, wet straw and smoke of smouldering fires filled the courtyard. Noel pursed his lips in distaste, eased back into the shade of the cab.

A number of men and boys wearing ragged smocks approached to stare in fascination. Noel grinned, gave them a debonair salute. They stared as before, making no response. Noel climbed up into the driver's seat, and ignored them.

Habdid el Kazim, crossing the courtyard, had curtly embraced a hard-faced man wearing a smart gray djellaba and a red fez: urban clothes, as incongruous to the kasbah as Noel's sun-tans. The man in the gray djellaba was slender and fine-boned, taller than the stocky Habdid, but with the same curious thin wedge of a nose, like a parrot's beak. Another man, short, fat, wearing a nondescript uniform, joined them; the three spoke earnestly. The short fat man jerked his head toward one of the larger buildings, discussing someone not in evidence. Both Habdid el Kazim and the man in the gray djellaba shook their heads decisively, and the short fat man nodded in vindication, as if his side of an argument had been upheld.

Noel watched without interest. Habdid el Kazim hardly seemed a romantic figure; the kasbah was no more than a smelly little village. Thirteen more trips—unless Arthur Upshaw rented another truck, or hired another driver. Unlikely, thought Noel. If it weren't for the money... He slumped back against the leatherette cushion, drummed his fingers on the black rim of the steering wheel. Not too much money, in view of what Upshaw would be making. Well, he had had the experience, and that was what counted.

Across the courtyard the three men had reached a decision. The fat little soldier marched forward. He barked orders, clapped his hands. Men and boys swarmed up into the bed of the truck. Noel descended to the ground, leaned against the hot front fender to watch. The gravel was brushed aside; wooden cases strapped with metal bands were tilted up on end, slid to the ground. At once they were attacked and broken open. The little officer bellowed in anger, herded his crew back to work.

The truck was presently free of its cargo. There were ten crates containing two thousand Mauser pistols, each in a cardboard box complete with trilingual instruction booklet, flask of oil and bristle brush; twenty-four crates of submachine guns, sealed in transparent plastic sacks, six to the crate; thirty cases of nine-millimeter ammunition.

Now, in spite of the officer's expostulations, the group fell on the crates like wolves tearing at a carcass. Noel's interest became revulsion. He shifted his gaze, reassuring himself with reasonable and well-tried assertions. If I don't earn the easy money, someone else will. If the French have a right to weapons, so do the Algerians. He leaned nonchalantly on the fender, cleaning his fingernails with a straw.

The tribesmen swarmed around the crates. They waved aloft the pistols, shouting and calling to each other, tucking one and sometimes two into their ragged garments. The fat man in the army uniform stalked forward and back, calling futile orders which no one heeded. Noel watched the scene with amused detachment: none of his business, he merely drove the truck. He examined his fingernails, which were now clean. His detachment wore thin. He darted a frowning glance across the courtyard. In Tangier a truckload of weapons was a romantic abstraction, symbolic of adventure and excitement. Some day, in circles far removed, he could hark idly back to "the time I worked running guns out of Tangier. Drove south through Morocco, back of the Atlas, out to a little desert fort on the Algerian border..." But now the guns were visible, ugly and black, ready to be discharged into the bodies of young Frenchmen. Noel turned away. Thirteen more loads? Not for me. He climbed sourly back into the cab, displeased with himself, anxious to depart.

Something had changed. The babble in the courtyard quieted. Noel looked around. A tall old man in a white djellaba had appeared. He wore a white turban; a jeweled dagger hung at his waist. His eyes were bright gray, his features lean and austere. He gazed at the plundered crates, called out wrathfully. The babble in the courtyard died completely. The sheikh—such he evidently was—spoke again, holding up his clenched fist. Sullenly, with foot-dragging reluctance, the tribesmen sidled close to the crates. Furtive hands went into garments, came out holding pistols. The short man in the uniform busily stowed the guns back into the crates; the men and boys of the kasbah backed away, glum with disappointment.

The patriarch watched grimly. He gave another order; Habdid el Kazim and the man in the gray djellaba turned about sharply. The little soldier stared in new annoyance.

The patriarch was obeyed. Men went into the building, brought forth four cardboard cartons, which they carried to the rear of the truck. The round-faced man in uniform ran forward, protesting. The patriarch made a small gesture; the soldier's voice broke off in mid-sentence. Two men climbed up into the bed of the truck; the cartons were handed up.

Noel jumped out of the cab, stepped up on the frame, looked back into the bed. The cartons, according to the red and blue label, contained soap powder. Soap? Disconcerting. Awkward. Highly awkward. Noel called across the courtyard to the sheikh. "What's this? I don't know anything about this stuff."

No one heeded him. Habdid el Kazim and the man in the gray djellaba both were voicing vehement objections. The sheikh listened impassively. When they had finished he spoke a curt sentence. The discussion was closed. Habdid el Kazim and the man in the gray djellaba abruptly turned away, walked out into the courtyard. They spoke together for several minutes, glowering toward the sheikh. Habdid el Kazim threw up his hands in fatalistic acceptance of the situation. He patted the man in the gray djellaba on the cheek, strode across the courtyard to the truck. He climbed in the cab. "We go now, back to Tangier."

Noel jerked his head toward the rear of the cab. "What are we carrying?"

Habdid el Kazim turned his head, inspected Noel as if seeing him for the first time. Noel forced himself to meet the glitter of the eyes. Habdid el Kazim settled himself in the seat, made a circling motion with his hand. "Turn the truck."

Grumbling under his breath Noel started the motor, backed up with a jerk, cut the truck around in vicious swerves that expressed his frustration. He was anxious to leave the hot and foul-smelling kasbah. But the four cases of—soap?

The gate swung open; Habdid el Kazim thrust his forefinger ahead. "We go. Fast."

Noel hesitated. It had to be now. Now or never... But what could he do? He raced the motor, let it idle, looked angrily sidewise at Habdid el Kazim. "I don't drive unless I know what I'm driving."

Habdid el Kazim looked at him in surly surprise.

"I'm working for Arthur Upshaw," declared Noel. "He said nothing about a return load."

Habdid el Kazim pointed ahead. "We take to Arthur Upshaw. Fast now, until to the trees. The French are close."

Noel irresolutely shifted into low, engaged the clutch. "Faster, faster!" grated el Kazim. From inside his djellaba he pulled one of the Mauser pistols. Out the gate the truck rolled, bouncing and rattling across the open space. El Kazim snapped out the magazine, charged it with cartridges.

They gained the shelter of the palms; el Kazim waved his hand to the sentry, motioned Noel to proceed. "Now, back to Tangier."

Noel shook his head sulkily. "I've been driving all night, I'm tired."

"We must go to Tangier. It is necessary."

Noel jammed down the accelerator; the truck careened through the palms. El Kazim braced himself in the seat, half-grinning, half-scowling, the gold teeth shining through his lips.

Fifty yards short of the intersection el Kazim ordered a halt. He went ahead to look up and down the road. Noel stepped out on the running-board, climbed up on the frame, studied the four cartons. If they were what he thought they were—but what else could they be? Contraband for the Algerian rebels normally traveled by caravan, safe from French interception; these cartons of 'soap', originating in Egypt, were probably still warm from the camel's back. And, if they were what he thought they were, they represented a great deal of money. El Kazim whistled. Noel looked around. El Kazim beckoned him forward. Noel swung into the cab, shifted into low gear. The truck lurched forward. El Kazim swung aboard; they turned out into the road.

For an hour they drove north. Neither man spoke. The road ran beside the palm groves, then slanted up among red sandstone bluffs, to strike out across the desert. Noel's eyes drooped with fatigue. He blinked resentfully. After driving all night and most of the day, another fourteen hours on the road was out of the question! And the four cartons of 'soap'! They stuck in his mind, pressed on his nerves. Certain things just weren't done. Noel considered himself an adventurer, a man of gallantry and savoir-faire. Smuggling, gun-running—such affairs carried a cachet of glamour and dash; he collected escapades of this sort as a high-school girl strings ornaments on her charm bracelet. The cartons labeled 'soap' represented something else again, something sordid and disreputable. Involvement would befoul Noel's ego-image, the blurred synthesis of Errol Flynn and Cary Grant he had worked so carefully to build.

A few miles ahead lay Erfoud, a town with a good hotel. It was only reasonable that they should stop to rest. He would telephone to Arthur Upshaw at Tangier, who could come drive his own blasted truck. Noel cleared his throat. "We're stopping in Erfoud, at the Gîte d'Etape. I've driven enough for one day."

"No, no," said el Kazim shortly. "We must go to Tangier."

"What's the rush?" Noel asked peevishly.

"There is a mistake. The sheikh is old man, he's afraid the French will come. He says we must take the boxes to Tangier. It is a mistake, but now we must do."

"There's not all that rush," Noel grumbled. "I'm too tired to drive. And I don't know about taking those packages. What's in them?"

Habdid el Kazim squinted sidewise at him. "It goes to Tangier."

"I'm not driving to Tangier today," said Noel, looking ahead down the road to avoid meeting el Kazim's angry stare. "I'm in charge of this rig, and I'm not trucking any cargo until I know what I've got." The idea, so expressed, infuriated him. They took him for a simple-minded truck driver, an underling! He jammed on the brakes; el Kazim made a hoarse exclamation of annoyance.

"No, we must not stop! The French will come."

"What's in the cartons?"

"It is not for you!" cried el Kazim. "Go on!"

———•———

IT WAS A MISTAKE, a misunderstanding. Sobbing and gasping, Noel stared down at the blood-smeared face. It had happened so fast, with such dreadful finality—why had el Kazim brandished the gun? Noel had struck down his arm; with frantic suddenness they were fighting. Noel had thrust his shoulder under el Kazim's chin, banged the sun-darkened temple against the door frame. He twisted at the gun, saw el Kazim's thumb working at the safety, his forefinger squeezing at the trigger. Noel wrenched the barrel down against el Kazim's wrist; el Kazim's fingers loosened, the gun dangled, then dropped to the seat. Grunting, el Kazim clawed for his dagger; steel whirred free. Before it had been a scuffle; now the issue was life or death.

Noel ground his forearm into el Kazim's neck, held him back against the door, seized the wrist with the dagger. El Kazim rasped through his constricted throat; Noel fought with hysterical strength, too intent to feel fear. El Kazim doubled up his knees, buffeted Noel back. Noel had el Kazim's wrist under his arm; the effect of the kick jerked el Kazim around, down off the seat, where he thrashed arms and legs to recover himself. He lunged, the dagger slashed an inch past Noel's throat. Noel seized the gun by the barrel, beat him on the forehead. Blood squirted down the dark face, between the eyes, down each side of the nose, an awful sight. Noel screamed, struck again and again. He saw el Kazim's eyes staring; they seemed accusing and stern. Noel cried out in agony, struck as hard as he could, to drive away the ghastly sight. The skull broke, the metal sank into something yielding. The head twisted, the mouth wrenched and gaped.

Noel groped open the door, tottered out on the road. He looked down at the bloody gun, at his bloody hands. He flung the gun desperately away, thrust his hands into the sand at the side of the road, rubbed and scrubbed till only a dark dirty stain remained.

Beside him the Diesel engine throbbed and ticked. A car appeared down the road, approached, passed; dark eyes under a white hood flashed incuriously. The car was gone in a pillar of rising brown dust.

Noel took deep breaths. If never before, he must think sensibly. This was adventure, and he didn't like it.

First he must dispose of the corpse. But not here. There was no concealment; it would be found quickly and the UAR, or FLN—whatever they called themselves—would come for him. He climbed up into the cab. Gingerly moving the sprawled shape out of the way, he shifted into low. The truck moved forward.

Ten minutes later the road zigzagged down through sandstone bluffs toward the floor of the valley. Noel stopped beside a deep gulch, opened the door, pulled the body out. It slid and tumbled through the dust, djellaba flapping, until half-way down it caught against a straggling bush. Noel backed down the slope, thrust with his foot; it rolled almost to the bottom. He kicked fragments of rusty sandstone after, and now it was almost invisible. The sound of a motor in the distance? Noel clawed his way back up to the road, jumped into the cab, drove hurriedly away.

A mile farther on he stopped, scooped sand into the cab, scrubbed and swept until the blood stains were one with the rust and grease of years.

He drove slowly north through the palm grove, fretting over a dozen unsatisfactory plans of action. Police? Flight? Tangier? Casablanca? The cartons gnawed at his nerves; what a relief if he could pitch them off into a ditch. But other considerations intervened: those of his personal safety. He had stumbled into this frightening mess; now he must contrive to evade the consequences.

Through the palms appeared a high biscuit-colored wall which marked the outskirts of Erfoud. He drove beside the wall until he reached a crossroads. He paused, looked first one direction, then the other. The main road to Meknes and Tangier stretched ahead. To the right, through a tall Moorish arch, a street led into the French settlement and business district. A side road to the left wound through the palms toward an imposing building on a hill a half-mile distant. This was the Gîte d'Etape, a regional staging hotel built in preparation for tourists who so far had avoided this remote corner of Morocco.

Noel rubbed his face. If he tried to drive through to Tangier he'd kill himself. And the cartons. Why should he do Arthur Upshaw's dirty work? At the hotel he would telephone Tangier. Arthur Upshaw could drive south, or Duff. It was their mess, let them take care of it. Noel wrenched the steering wheel, sent the truck lumbering through the palm grove to the hotel.

He parked in a graveled area near the front entrance, took his jacket and zipper bag from behind the seat, descended to the ground.

A page in a red uniform opened plate-glass doors with ceremony. Noel entered a marble lobby of astonishing amplitude. The floor glowed with Berber rugs; leather armchairs surrounded embossed copper cocktail tables. The far corner of the lobby was given to a bar; here a white-coated bartender polished glassware. The desk clerk stood poised behind the marble registration counter. The three men, all apparently French, watched Noel silently. The lobby was otherwise empty.

Noel went to the desk, produced his passport and was assigned a room. With the guidance of the page, he garaged the truck, then went to his room, showered, changed into fresh clothes.

He lay on the bed, dozed, drifted off into uneasy sleep.

The telephone, ringing in short sharp jingles, awakened him. "Yes?" he muttered.

"Do you want dinner, sir?" inquired a heavily accented voice. It was not the desk clerk, who spoke careful, if pedantic, English.

"Yes," said Noel thickly. "Just a minute." He looked at his watch. Seven-thirty. Arthur Upshaw might be at his apartment by now. "I want to make a call to Tangier."

"Very well, sir. What number?"

Noel gave the number. The line hummed, buzzed; ghost-voices whispered. A man spoke: "Hotel Balmoral."

The long-distance operator turned the line over to Noel. "Is Mr. Upshaw in?" Noel asked.

"No, sir."

"Do you know where I can call him?"

"No, sir. Will you leave a message?"

"No," said Noel shortly, and hung up.

He went down to the lobby, which still was empty. Crossing to the bar, he ordered a highball, took it to one of the deep leather chairs, and sat looking across the expanse of barbaric rugs.

Presently he rose to his feet, went to the desk. The clerk, now back on duty, was chewing a toothpick which he hastily discarded. "I want to make a call to Tangier."

"Yes, sir," said the clerk. "Will you take it here?"

Noel looked about him. "Is there a booth?"

"No, sir. Only this desk telephone."

"It'll do." Noel consulted his address book, read a number to the clerk, who went to the switchboard, put the call through.

The clerk watched with covert interest. American, hence rich, yet he drives up in a truck and wears rough workman's clothes. Bizarre! Certainly not a tourist... There was a wait. A far bell rang again and again. The clerk shook his head. "There is no answer, sir."

"Confound it," muttered Noel. He pondered, flipped to another page in his address book. "Try this number." He read the number to the desk clerk.

The connection was made. The desk clerk shuffled papers with ostentatious disregard for the conversation.

"Hello? This is Noel Hutson. Is Arthur Upshaw available?"

There was a pause.

"Or I'll speak to Duff, if he happens to be there."

Another pause. Noel waited impatiently.

"Damn. Do you know where they are?... Well, give Arthur this message, will you? It's urgent, so make sure he gets it. Okay?... Good. Tell him I'm resigning. Tell him his friends gave me a shipment I don't plan to haul, for him or for anybody else. Tell him if he wants it to come for it himself."

Pause, while Noel listened.

"I don't like to say, not over the phone. Arthur will know. It's business I don't plan to get involved in."

Bizarre and more bizarre, thought the desk clerk.

Noel was describing his whereabouts to the person at the other end of the wire. "...at the Gîte d'Etape. If I don't hear from him I'll throw the stuff in a ditch, and come back to Tangier on the bus."

Pause.

"Right. Also, if you don't see Arthur, will you make sure that Aktouf gets the message? Thanks very much."

Noel hung up the receiver. So much for that. The issues were now resolved. He felt rather pleased with himself.

He sauntered into the dining room. Chandeliers twinkled; glass and silver glittered on crisp table linen. Noel was the solitary diner. Two waiters and a bus boy served him while the head waiter stood a little apart, hands clasped behind his back. Noel seemed to be the only guest in the hotel.

Returning to the lobby he bought an air-letter form at the desk, took it to a chair, and using a late copy of *London Illustrated News* for a pad, wrote:

> Dear Dad:
>
> Trouble has caught up with me and I've got to yell for help. It's a long story which I won't go into, except to admit that, as the family has long maintained, I'm a prize dunce, and half a rascal. But only half. I had to back out. There are some things I can't bring myself to do. I've just now put a message through to my boss, told him I'm quitting. More than anything in the world I want to come back home and start a civilized life—anything, so long as it's peaceful and dull. I need a thousand dollars, to settle a few bills and buy a ticket home. I promise you'll never have to worry about me again. Wire the money care of the Lombard Bank at Tangier. I'll collect if and when I get there.

Noel paused in his writing, chewed on the end of his fountain pen. He rose, went to the desk. "What time does the morning bus leave for Tangier?"

"There's nothing direct, sir, you'd have to change at Meknes. The early bus for Meknes leaves at eight."

Noel nodded. "I want to be called at six."

"Very good, sir. Six o'clock."

Noel returned to the chair, resumed his letter.

THE MAN IN THE CAGE

I just figured a way to copper my bets, and I'm safe as far as Tangier. I may have to do some fast talking—but I won't go into that. I'll see you in a week or so, and give you the whole story.

Noel stopped, thought a moment, then, with a brave flourish of his pen, continued:

Love to Mother, Molly, Darrell and yourself. See you all soon—I hope.
Noel

He folded the letter, sealed and addressed it to: R. M. Hutson, 625 Berry Farm Road, Everton, Pennsylvania. He took it to the desk, dropped it in the mailbox.

He went to his room, locked the door, undressed and went to bed.

His mind raced; sleep was slow in coming. A picture returned again and again to his mind: a stubble-bearded face, the eyes stern and bewildered, blood streaming in a black net over the nose. Then the final crushing blow, the eyes slowly closing, the mouth loose and askew.

Noel moaned softly, covered his head with his hands. "It wasn't my fault," he told himself, "I only did what was right!"

Finally he went to sleep.

◆

AT SIX O'CLOCK IN the morning the telephone rang. Noel, already awake and staring at the ceiling, acknowledged the call. With a mumble of glum curses, he swung himself out of bed.

He looked out the window. The morning sunlight was golden and clear; the palms trembled and swayed in the morning air. All serene.

Noel dressed, assuring himself that the situation, though delicate, was still not critical. A day or two must elapse before the FLN—whoever they were—could know that Habdid el Kazim was missing. In the meantime Noel would have returned to Tangier, have made forwarding arrangements with the Lombard Bank, and be safely out of reach in Málaga or Lisbon.

Nevertheless, descending the broad marble stairs, Noel went furtively, and scrutinized the lobby before showing himself.

The clerk who had been on duty the previous evening bade Noel a punctilious good morning. "Will you have breakfast, sir?"

Noel hesitated. By this time Arthur Upshaw should have received his message. Why had he not called back?

The hell with Arthur Upshaw. "No breakfast; I'm rather in a hurry. May I have my bill?"

The page was not yet on duty; the clerk left his desk to unlock the garage.

The cartons of 'soap' were as Noel had left them. He started the truck, backed out and around, set off down the neat black-top driveway.

The clerk watched the truck disappear through the palms, shaking his head and smiling, then went back into the cool lobby.

Not long afterward his switchboard flashed and buzzed to an incoming call.

The clerk responded. *"Le Gîte d'Etape d'Erfoud."*

"Je veux parler avec Monsieur Noel Hutson," said a voice. "Mr. Hutson—is he there?"

"I'm sorry, sir," said the clerk. "Mr. Hutson has already checked out, not twenty minutes ago."

There was a brief silence. Then the voice said, "Thank you very much," and rang off.

Chapter II

AT noon on Wednesday, April ninth, Darrell Hutson, wearing light-gray flannels and carrying an old leather suitcase, stepped out of the airport waiting room. He signaled; a Fiat *petit-taxi*, hardly larger than a wheelbarrow, darted up. The door swung open, Darrell Hutson climbed in.

The driver twisted around. "Where you going? The El Minzah?"

"You speak English? Good. Calle Erasmus, 20. The Hotel de los Dos Continentes."

With a whir of minuscule motor, the cab turned out onto the highway. Darrell Hutson settled back in the seat. He was two years older than Noel, not quite so tall, more compact, and showed nothing of Noel's flair and dash. His hair was black, cropped short; his expression thoughtful, wary; his mouth compressed, almost grim.

A twenty-minute drive took them into Tangier. With no warning the road burst out upon a magnificent view over the sun-drenched crescent of city, with the Strait of Gibraltar and the mountains of Spain beyond. They angled down the hill, past stucco villas flaming with purple and pink bougainvillea, along streets shaded under eucalyptus, acacia and pepper trees; finally came out into the Place de France. A policeman in white helmet and jacket signaled them to a halt. Pedestrians surged in front of them: tourists from Europe, Australia, North and South America; Turks, Egyptians, Persians,

Berbers from the Rif. Jews, Sephardim and Ashkenazi; East Asians; Moroccans proud of their wax-pale skins; Indian merchants with bovine eyes and soft mouths; Negroes from France, the United States, Central Africa; native Tangerines.

The taxi driver, a Spaniard who claimed to have lived ten years in New York, gestured toward the crowd. "The town is dead. Not like old times." Darrell would hear the remark frequently during the next few days. "The stores, they go broke. Before, people come here to buy; now there's Moroccan duty. Prices is high. People come to change money, then they go to Gibraltar to spend."

"I understand there's no more smuggling either."

"Nothing." The taxi driver's voice was disgusted. "Why you think I drive a cab? For my health? When I make some money, I leave." He snapped his fingers over his head.

The policeman signaled with hands and baton; the taxi drove along Boulevard Pasteur, Tangier's commercial center, crowded with banks and booths of money changers. They turned sharply downhill toward the harbor. The buildings became meaner and dingier as they descended: second-class apartment houses, café-bars, shops.

A block above the water-front the driver turned into Calle Erasmus. He drove slowly, searching along the house fronts, stopped with a jerk. "Number 20. Hotel de los Dos Continentes."

The hotel, by no means as impressive as its name, was a narrow three-story building, freshly whitewashed, with red-tiled steps and window boxes bright with geraniums. Darrell alighted, paid off the cab. The door being locked, he rang the bell. A sturdy button-nosed woman of thirty-five appeared, her face pink with exertion. At the sight of Darrell and his suitcase, she tucked lank strings of blonde hair behind her ears. "Yes, come in, please."

Darrell entered a narrow hall, furnished with a plywood registration desk, a bench, a mirror and a calendar. He put down his suitcase. "Noel Hutson lives here, I believe?"

"Yes, yes," said the landlady, already behind the registration desk.

"Is he in now?"

She shook her head; the strings of hair fell loose, she automatically tucked them back in place. "No, he is not here. One month I have not seen him."

Darrell's voice came more sharply than he intended. "A month? An entire month?"

"Yes. One month."

"Do you know where he is?"

"No. He tells me nothing. I do not ask his business."

Darrell took an envelope from his pocket, extracted a crumpled blue air letter. The postmark was smeared and undecipherable. It had been received three weeks ago. Allowing a week in transit—the times corresponded closely enough.

"I'm his brother," said Darrell. "I've just arrived from the United States, and I'm anxious to find him. Do you know where I could look, or whom I could ask?"

The round pink face became stupid and blank. "He worked on a boat. That is all I know."

Darrell turned away, puzzled and annoyed. "May I see his room?" he asked at last. "There might be something there. A note, perhaps."

"There is nothing. But you may see." The landlady took a key, led him up narrow steep stairs. She turned down the hall, stopped by a door. "Number five." She opened the door, motioned Darrell to enter.

The room was clean and sunny, though by no means luxurious. A double bed, covered with a white counterpane, occupied the center of the room. There was an enormous Spanish wardrobe to the right, a marble-topped table to the left. The table was graced by a bedraggled bouquet of acacia blossoms in a pale blue vase, and under the vase were a number of letters. Mrs. Ritterman—so she had introduced herself—murmured an apology, took up the vase of flowers and left the room. Darrell examined the letters. There were two from his father, the contents of which he knew well; two envelopes, one lavender, one green, addressed in two different feminine handwritings; three commercial letters—bills or notices. Neither the lavender nor the green envelope bore a return address; one was postmarked Málaga, the other Casablanca; both were dated toward the end of March.

Mrs. Ritterman returned; Darrell replaced the letters, looked around the room. There seemed to be no clue whatever to Noel's whereabouts. He half-heartedly opened a drawer: he saw socks, handkerchiefs, half a carton of cigarettes, several matchbooks, one of which he brought out. On one face it advertised the Masquerade Bar, Calle Miranda 37; on the other, the Balmoral Hotel, of the same address.

"The Balmoral," asked Darrell, "is it a good hotel?"

Mrs. Ritterman shrugged. "Very dear. Here it is much less, with all comfort. Do you want a room?"

"I don't think so. I haven't made my plans yet. Is Noel's rent paid?"

"He is two weeks overdue."

Darrell brought forth his wallet. "How much does he owe?"

"Two thousand four hundred francs."

Darrell extracted a five-thousand franc note. "Does that cover a month?"

"Ah! Yes! I will give you a receipt."

Darrell opened the wardrobe, looked at Noel's clothes: a gray-green Glen plaid, a blue worsted of a color richer than Darrell would have chosen for himself, two sport coats, several pairs of slacks.

Darrell felt the pockets. "What are you looking for?" Mrs. Ritterman inquired in a voice which had become a trifle brittle.

"Nothing in particular," said Darrell, closing the wardrobe. "Anything to give me a hint as to where he is."

"You should try at the yacht club; that is where he works. He is sometimes gone for several days before."

"But never so long as a month."

"No, never so long as a month."

They left the room. Mrs. Ritterman spoke over her shoulder as they descended the stairs: "One friend of his came to ask." Mrs. Ritterman shook her head tersely at the recollection. "He was angry that I did not know. How should I know? I have my work. I do not follow the lodgers. Let him be angry. He was not nice."

Darrell made a sound of polite commiseration. In the little downstairs lobby he asked, "If Noel comes, will you tell him I've been here?"

"Yes, of course. Where are you staying?"

"I think I'll try the Balmoral—for a night or two, at least. If I change I'll let you know."

"Very well!" said Mrs. Ritterman, annoyed that Darrell should prefer the Balmoral Hotel, sight unseen, to the Hotel de los Dos Continentes. She bustled forward, opened the door. Darrell took his suitcase, started back up the hill. No cabs came past; he walked all the way to the Boulevard Pasteur. Here, while catching his breath, he noticed the front of the Lombard Bank a short distance up the street.

He picked up his suitcase, pushed through the ornate black iron and glass door, went to a counter where a placard read:

INFORMATION

MAN SPRICHT DEUTSCH
On parle français
Si parla italiano
Se habla español
English spoken
Svenska talas

A handsome gray-haired woman came forward. "I'm the brother of Noel Hutson, who has an account with you," said Darrell.

"Yes?" The woman, brisk and noncommittal, spoke with a clipped British intonation.

"A month ago my father paid a thousand dollars into Noel's account, but we've received no acknowledgment. He's not at his hotel, and we're disturbed. I'd like to know if he's been in, if he's made any withdrawals in the last month?"

The gray-haired woman seemed doubtful. "Noel Hutson—isn't he a very fair young man, with a mustache, dusty-brown hair?"

"Yes, that's Noel."

The woman inspected Darrell's black crew cut, his flat cheeks, his wide thin mouth. "You don't resemble him very much."

"No, we're quite different types."

"I wish I had his complexion. But I haven't seen him for some time. Just a minute." She went behind the wicket, consulted the files, then returned. "His account hasn't moved for over two months. Except for your father's deposit, that is to say."

"I see. Thank you very much. If he happens to show himself, will you mention that I've been in?"

"Yes. Where are you staying?"

"The Balmoral—or so I hope."

"The Balmoral? I don't think you'll get in. It's more of a residential hotel. Most tourists, especially Americans, go to the El Minzah."

"Hmm." Darrell considered a moment. "Well, I've already given the Balmoral address to Noel's landlady, so I'd better go there."

"Good luck in your search."

Darrell returned to the street. He hailed a cab and was taken to the Balmoral Hotel: along Boulevard Pasteur to the Place de France, around and up the hill, left into Calle Miranda, to a stop in front of a marble-paneled vestibule with a bronze and glass door. Discreet bronze letters spelled: BALMORAL HOTEL. Darrell glimpsed an extravagantly large chandelier, wide mirrors, elegant furniture. In the same building, a few yards up the street, a façade of dark brown boards rose behind a border of blue-green century plants. Green neon tubing, not at all discreet, announced:

MASQUERADE BAR

Darrell alighted from the cab, paid the driver.

A bellboy came smartly forth to take Darrell's suitcase. He entered the lobby, and found the atmosphere even more luxurious than it had appeared from the street. The carpet, buttermilk-color, was thick and resilient; the walls were divided between golden-beige marble and plate-glass mirrors, in which the chandelier generated a thousand glittering simulacra of itself. The furniture, confections of gilt and red plush, could loosely be called Louis Quinze. The registration desk, a flight of marble steps, an elevator occupied the far end of the room. A glass door with a gilded grille led into the Masquerade Bar.

Darrell approached the desk. The clerk was a thin young man with well-brushed black hair, a pencil-line mustache. Darrell requested a room with a bath. The clerk, putting his hands behind his back, smiled quietly. "Sorry, sir. There are only suites and apartments here. Now we are full. Across the street is the Hotel Miranda."

"I see. Are you acquainted with Mr. Noel Hutson?"

"I don't know anyone of that name, sir. But I have been here only two weeks; he may have lived here before."

Darrell nodded, turned away. He crossed the street to the Hotel Miranda, and booked a room. Returning to the Balmoral he left his name and address in the event of a message, then walked down the hill, ate a thoughtful lunch in a café on the Place de France.

Noel was missing—this was the basic situation. His landlady had not seen him for a month. Where to look for him? Darrell had small information. Noel had worked on a boat at the yacht harbor; at some time he had visited the Masquerade Bar (since apparently he was not known at the Balmoral Hotel). Darrell unfolded the air letter and reread it. The sinister hints might mean much or nothing; from an early age Noel had enjoyed the trappings of derring-do. In letters home he had maintained the fiction of work on an excursion boat, but Darrell knew that the excursions were stealthy trips through the night to Sicily, the Balearics, the long Spanish coastline, with cargoes of contraband cigarettes. During the past year, with Moroccan customs effective in Tangier, smuggling had dwindled. How had Noel made his living? Judging by the Hotel de los Dos Continentes, he had enjoyed no particular prosperity, but these were questions of no immediate concern. Where was Noel now?

Speculation was pointless till he had more information. Darrell hailed a cab, asked to be taken to the yacht harbor.

The cab descended the hill in zigzags, turned out into an avenue paralleling the beach, presently discharged him at the white concrete office of the Tangier Yacht Club.

Darrell looked along the line of boats. There were all sizes, both sail and power. Many berths were empty and he saw a number of "For Sale" signs. He entered the gear and paint shop at the end of the pier. A bearded man in a nautical cap turned toward him.

Darrell asked, "Do you speak English?"

The bearded man nodded dourly. "I was born in Belfast and given no choice."

"I'm looking for Noel Hutson. Are you acquainted with him by any chance?"

"I know who he is. You're interested in his boat?"

"Does Noel own a boat?"

"Call it a boat. It floats, it's pointed at the foreparts, there's a motor to push it."

"I don't suppose you've seen him lately?"

"I'd like to. The boat's taking water. Either I pump it out or I let it sink. Berth 108, if you're interested, down along the dock."

"Can you tell me someone who might know his whereabouts? I'm his brother; I've just arrived from the States and I can't seem to run him down."

The bearded man grunted without interest. "You might make inquiry of Arthur Upshaw. Seems to me Hutson did a bit of work aboard the *Deirdre*."

"Where can I find Mr. Upshaw?"

"That I don't know, my friend." The man seemed disposed to speak further, but only said, "There's Upshaw's *Deirdre* out there; the big teak job."

Five minutes later Darrell stood looking down at Noel's boat. The bearded man had dealt with it unkindly; nevertheless it was little enough to look at: a stubby hull with a cabin like a telephone booth. Rust streaked the paint; deck seams were open; a pool of oily water glistened in the cockpit. A card tacked to the cabin offered the boat for sale: "Call N. Hutson, Hotel de los Dos Continentes, or harbor master."

Darrell descended a rickety ladder to the float, peered into the cabin. He could see nothing in particular: a pair of unkempt bunks, a Primus, a bucket, the bulky outline of an engine.

Darrell straightened up, stood thinking. The ugly little hulk was not the craft he would have expected Noel to own. Noel selected his possessions for the effect they would produce. Unless—and Darrell smiled cynically. One of Noel's redeeming traits was a stubborn honesty. Without a boat, he could never speak of the "days in Tangier when I did a bit of smuggling—owned my own boat, in fact. Not much to look at, but with a little luck and a following wind I could take a cargo across to Spain…"

The mystery of the boat was solved. Darrell turned away and met the gaze of a Moroccan youth on the dock, a gaze which instantly shifted to the flight of a distant seagull. The youth was beautiful—a faun. Black hair curled over his olive forehead, he had large hazel eyes, a short straight nose, a curving tender mouth. He wore baggy gray slacks, a green and white pull-over, pointed white Moroccan slippers.

Darrell climbed back up on the dock, stood looking down at the boat. The youth approached, smiling winsomely. He was older than Darrell had first supposed—perhaps seventeen or eighteen.

"You want to buy boat?"

Darrell shook his head. "I think not."

"It's a good boat, runs good. Maybe you like to look inside?"

"No," said Darrell. "Not today. I'm looking for the owner."

"You his friend, huh?"

"I'm his brother."

"You his brother?" The youth's voice rose in glad excitement.

Darrell made a cool appraisal of the eager countenance. "Do you know him?"

"Sure! He's my good friend. I try to help him. I sell boat for him."

Darrell continued to search the affable face. The hazel eyes met his own without a flicker. "So you're a friend of my brother."

"Sure!"

"Where is he now?"

The youth made a vague gesture, looked off and away. "He's somewhere. I guess you see him pretty soon, huh?"

"I suppose so."

"I go tell him you here. You want?"

"I certainly do."

The Moroccan lad poised himself. "I go tell him. Where?"

"Where what?"

"Where is Mr. Hutson? I go tell him."

Darrell grinned sadly. "You don't know either. But you'd like to. Does he owe you money?"

The lad's face was blank; apparently he failed to understand.

"Thanks anyway," said Darrell. He sauntered down the dock. A few steps behind came the Moroccan youth.

Darrell found his way to the *Deirdre*, a far cry from Noel's dingy little craft. It was fifty feet long with a powerful black hull, varnished teak decks and cabin.

"That's Mr. Upshaw's yacht," said the Moroccan youth by Darrell's shoulder. "The 'Derder'—that's how they call him. Nice, huh?"

"Yes. Very nice."

"You like to buy?"

"No. Not especially."

"For sale cheap. I like to buy," he told Darrell with a look of confiding candor. "But I don't have money."

Darrell nodded without interest. From aboard the *Deirdre* came sounds of activity.

Darrell asked, "Is Mr. Upshaw aboard now?"

The youth shrugged. "Maybe so. He wants to sell. Mr. Upshaw he's got no more money. He's broke." He giggled playfully. "Noel—he's got lots of money, huh?"

"Noel? Lots of money?" Darrell stared at the youth in surprise. "What makes you say that?"

"He make lots of money. Noel's smart guy. I like to see him." His voice took on a wheedling note. "You tell me where Noel is. I like to see him."

Darrell looked back to the *Deirdre*. "I'd like to see him too."

A young man in tan shorts and striped yellow and white shirt appeared on deck, carrying an aqualung harness with two tanks. He had long legs, burly shoulders, a face rather pale and set, with brooding eyes, a sensitive mouth drooping disdainfully.

Darrell turned to the Moroccan lad. "Is that Mr. Upshaw?"

"Him? That Mr. Duff Mekkinisser. Mr. Upshaw is uncle of him."

Duff climbed up from the float to the dock, shot Darrell a quick cold stare.

"Hello," said Darrell. "You're Mr. Duff Mekkin—Mek-k—"

"McKinstry."

"Oh. McKinstry. I'm looking for Noel Hutson."

Duff laughed bitterly. "You too? What's he done you out of?"

"Nothing, during the last year or two. As a matter of fact I'm his brother."

"His brother, eh?" Duff McKinstry spoke in the rounded accents of the upper-class English. He put down the aqualung equipment, stared fixedly at the young Moroccan, whose smile became glassy. Duff looked back to Darrell. "Then you don't know where Noel is camped out?"

"No," said Darrell. "I've come here looking for him. We had a letter, and it seems to be the last anyone knows of him."

Duff cocked his head in quick interest. "You had a letter?" He swung on the Moroccan youth, spoke in a rush of guttural Arabic, waved his hand. The Moroccan youth, a smile pasted inaccurately over his mouth, sidled away.

Meeting Darrell's puzzled glance, Duff said sharply, "That's Slip-Slip. He's a bad lot. Sneak-thief and worse. Don't get mixed up with him. Let me see the letter," he said gruffly. "There might be something in it which concerns me."

"I think not," Darrell replied politely. "It's a personal letter."

Duff opened his mouth to speak, closed it again. He turned his head at the sound of an automobile approaching along the dock. A black Mercedes-Benz convertible darted close beside them, halted. A girl of eighteen or nineteen, wearing a black turtle-neck sweater, a gray tweed skirt, sat behind the wheel. She was pale, pretty, with a look of wild undisciplined intelligence, and noticeably resembled Duff. But where Duff's eyebrows rose in an arrogant arch, hers were skeptical and supercilious. Duff's mouth drooped in something like petulance; the girl's mouth was wry and reckless.

Duff hoisted the aqualung equipment into the car, jerked his head toward Darrell. "Another Hutson. He's looking for Noel."

"Who isn't?" said the girl without interest.

Duff jumped into the car; she shifted into low. Duff made the briefest of salutes. The motor roared, they were gone.

Darrell stood looking in puzzlement after the diminishing car. The two McKinstrys—the girl was evidently Duff's sister—had been antagonistic, as if Noel had inflicted some serious harm upon them. "What's he done you out of?" Duff had asked. The situation evidently was complicated, but Darrell could not see Noel in the role of a thief or a swindler. Noel was addicted to the flamboyant, the picaresque; he was sometimes irresolute, sometimes irrational, a braggart, a spendthrift, a woman-chaser. But Noel had never been devious, never a thief. Cigarette smuggling, yes, this was a crime which entailed no loss of face. Theft or swindling, no. Noel was very sensitive as to the figure he cut.

But Noel was also missing. If Arthur Upshaw and the McKinstrys were ignorant of Noel's whereabouts, what had happened? Just what was going on? Darrell could envisage a number of possibilities, all dire: illness, death, flight, detention. Another theory could be derived from Noel's notorious weakness for pretty girls: he might be holed up at some nearby resort, heedless of the trouble he was causing.

Darrell set off down the dock. Slip-Slip followed at a discreet distance. Darrell swung around. "What do you want?"

The smile was genial, the face beatific. "You like a guide? I take you through the medina. I show you girls."

"No, thanks."

Slip-Slip became even more affable. "Anything you like, I fix."

"No, thank you." Darrell turned to go then hesitated. "Why are they angry with Noel? What's he done?"

Slip-Slip shook his head. "I don't know." And he added thoughtfully, "Mr. Duff, he's always mad at something."

Once again Darrell turned away. Slip-Slip tugged at his sleeve. "You want to find where Noel is?"

"Naturally."

"You know where is the Masquerade?"

"Yes."

"Many times Noel goes to the Masquerade. Phil—that's his good friend. Maybe he knows."

"Phil?"

"That's right."

Darrell nodded. "If I see him I'll ask." He walked out to the street, hailed a cab, gave the address of his hotel. Slip-Slip stood on the dock, looking after him.

Chapter III

CALLE Miranda was dim with twilight, at that indistinct time between the color of day and the chiaroscuro of night. The tubing which spelled MASQUERADE shone pallid green, but had not yet become charged with the poisonous crackling brilliance it would assume at midnight.

Darrell went into the Hotel Miranda, obtained a telephone guide. He opened to the U's, ran his finger down the page—*Upshaw, Arthur. Miranda 37. 29-66-42.*

Miranda 37, no problem there. Miranda 37 was the address of the Hotel Balmoral.

Darrell stepped out into the dusk, crossed the street, and for the third time that day entered the marble, gold and red-plush lobby. In one of the straight-backed chairs sat a raw-boned young man wearing reddish-brown slacks and a brown tweed jacket. His face was sunburned to the same color as his trousers, except where a white streak above his ears indicated a recent haircut. He sat cracking his knuckles and tapping the floor, either nervously or impatiently.

The desk clerk with the bony jaw and rat-tail mustache nodded with remote courtesy at Darrell's approach. Darrell said, "I want to speak to Mr. Arthur Upshaw, who lives here, so I understand."

The clerk's manner altered. "Mr. Upshaw is the owner, sir. He is not in. I'll be glad to take a message."

"Mr. Upshaw owns the hotel?"

"Yes, sir. The entire building."

"Well, well," said Darrell thoughtfully. "I'm at the Miranda across the street, as I told you. Will you have him give me a call?"

"With pleasure, sir." The clerk wrote on a pad of forms.

"Perhaps you know where I can get in touch with him now?"

"I believe he's at the old family home on Calle Costanza. If it's an important matter you can call him there."

Darrell nodded. "Where's the telephone?"

"In the booth, sir. I'll put you through."

Darrell entered the booth, heard the whir of a ringing bell, a click. A voice said, "Hallo. Duff McKinstry here."

"This is Darrell Hutson. I'd like to speak to Mr. Upshaw, if it's convenient."

Duff's voice was cool. "I'm afraid it's not really convenient. He's at his accounts and I assume he'll be occupied all evening."

"If he finds that he has a minute to spare, will you ask him to call me? I'm at the Hotel Miranda. It's about my brother—"

"You've had word from Noel?"

"No. I hoped Mr. Upshaw could give me some idea where to look for him."

Duff laughed harshly. "You're barking up the wrong tree, old man. If Arthur knew where to find Noel, he'd be there and so would I."

"I'd still like to talk to Mr. Upshaw."

"I'll give him your message. You say you're at the Miranda?"

"That's right."

"Hmm. Isn't that a bit thick? Just a wee bit?"

"Why?"

"Don't be naïve, old man. We're in a very difficult position, and you don't help, turning up like this. It's just a bit suggestive. We can't afford it."

"I don't know what you're talking about. I'd still like to speak to Mr. Upshaw."

"I'll give him your message."

Darrell hung up and stood fuming. It was unlikely, he thought, that he and Duff McKinstry would ever become close friends.

Arthur Upshaw he had never met. Arthur Upshaw might be more reasonable.

Darrell's reflections were disturbed by a girl descending the marble stairs. She was of medium height, supple and loose-limbed, wearing an oyster-white linen suit another woman might have considered a trifle too tight. Silky chestnut hair hung to her shoulders, her pink mouth was twisted up at the corners into an insolent little crook. She looked merry, happy-go-lucky, marvelously beautiful, and Darrell had the puzzling feeling that he had seen her before. The girl joined the bony-faced young man in the sorrel slacks. They left the lobby, she laughing and impulsive, he tongue-tied.

Darrell went to the registration desk. The clerk, divining by professional insight that Darrell had suffered a rebuff, had resumed his austere pose.

Darrell asked, "Who is the young lady who just went out?"

The clerk looked at Darrell from under lofty eyebrows. "One of our residents, sir."

"What is her name?"

"I'm sorry, sir. I'm under strict orders not to—"

But Darrell had already departed, and was pushing through the bronze and glass doors. At the edge of his vision was a swift and furtive motion. Darrell stopped short, peered through the dusk.

Street lights shining through foliage were no aid to the eyesight. They served only to camouflage anyone who might choose to stand in a doorway.

Darrell shrugged. Tangier's reputation as a city of intrigue possibly had warmed his imagination. Possibly. He went to the Masquerade Bar entrance a few yards up the street, walked in.

The interior of the Masquerade Bar was rich with color. Heavy beams supported a rattan-covered ceiling; the walls displayed brass and copper plates, up to a yard in diameter, stamped with intricate arabesques. From the beams hung three large globes—brass lighting fixtures, studded with coin-size lenses of blue, green and red glass. Booths upholstered in red, yellow and green goatskin skirted the front and far side of the room. The bar ran across the rear, with a kitchen behind.

Darrell had come in at a quiet time. Only three of the booths were occupied, only three people sat at the bar—a portly little man in a snuff-brown corduroy suit and two carefully dressed young women: one dark and sleek as a wet otter, with gold rings five inches in diameter hanging from her ears; the other blonde, a trifle over-weight, her breasts constricted into the shape of a pair of large Dutch wooden shoes. The three animatedly chaffed and chatted in quick British accents with the bartender.

Darrell took a stool a few places down the bar. The portly little man stared at him critically, then looked away. "American," he said in a voice of mild disappointment. The dark girl puffed a cigarette with lips carefully pursed; the blonde girl arranged her fundament more evenly over the stool.

The bartender came to serve Darrell. No ordinary bartender, he wore a beautiful gray Shetland sport coat, olive-drab flannel slacks. He was tall and sunburned, with a loose dry thatch of silver-blond hair, a long droll mouth, a long chin, eyes the color of quicksilver—unquestionably American. "What'll it be, sir?" he asked.

"A martini, please."

"You've come to the right place," said the bartender. "Right here is martini capital of the world." He occupied himself behind the bar.

"I like Phil because he's so modest," said the blonde girl, voice more than a trifle slurred.

"I'm full of old-fashioned virtues," said Phil the bartender. "A real complex mess."

"I like Phil too," said the dark girl. "He gave me a tip on a horse race once. I lost my chemise, of course. Phil made a pot on a different horse."

"Phil's a deep one," said the portly little man. "There's a bit from Gilbert and Sullivan that deals with men like Phil. What is it now? Something, something...?"

"'A loaf of bread, a jug of wine,'" sang the blonde girl, who appeared befuddled by drink.

"That fits," said the bartender. "At the end of the week, after paying my bills, that's about what I got left." He set the martini before Darrell, the glass frosted, the liquid sparkling and swimming with light. "Try that, and if you don't like it, we'll just throw it out."

"Oh, don't do that, just pass it down here," said the portly little man. "You can test several before you decide."

"I'm trying to earn an honest living," Phil told Darrell, "but Mr. Burdette wants to turn me out to my creditors."

"You've taken enough of my money to buy the place," said Mr. Burdette.

"I'm proud to have you for a customer, Mr. Burdette. I wish I had more like you." He turned back to Darrell. "How's the martini?"

"Fine... I've been told that you're acquainted with Noel Hutson."

"Sure, I know Noel. Haven't seen him around for some time. I guess he ducked over to Spain to taper off the mad pace."

"Do you know for sure he's gone to Spain?"

Phil looked at him curiously. "Heavens no. I don't know nothing for sure, except water runs downhill and I gotta pay my rent. Rent. That's a bad word." He poured himself a small half-finger of whiskey, added a splash of soda, drank the mixture in a gulp. "How'd you like to be my landlord, Mr. Burdette? Good hotel going cheap."

"No, thanks."

"How about you girls? Tangier's a boom town—so they say."

"Boom is right," said Mr. Burdette. "Flat on its face."

Phil grinned at Darrell. "Mr. Burdette is a seller of high-grade automobiles, in case you need another Rolls or a couple Porsches to run on a leash."

Darrell shook his head. "Not just now. I'm only in town long enough to locate my brother."

"Your brother? Who's he? You mean Noel Hutson's your brother? Well, well, well. Glad to meet you. I'm Phil Beresford."

"Who is Noel Hutson?" asked Mr. Burdette without interest.

"You've seen him a dozen times," said Phil. "Tall nice-looking lad, wears one of them musketeer mustaches."

"Yes, I know who you mean. What's he done?"

"That's a rude question, Mr. Burdette."

"Sorry."

"He's disappeared into thin air," said Darrell. "I've checked everywhere, with everyone. No one knows a thing."

"Well, that's Tangier for you. Wicked city."

"Where everything shuts up at ten o'clock," sniffed the blonde girl. "You call that wicked?"

"It stands to reason," Phil told her. "You can't be wicked with the doors open. At least I can't."

"I'll be wicked any time I want," said the blonde girl carefully and with emphasis.

Darrell somberly drank his martini. Mr. Burdette and the dark girl presently took their leave. The blonde girl remained. She looked toward Darrell, who avoided her gaze. She let herself carefully down off the stool, walked toward the restrooms.

"She's absolutely tanked," remarked Phil admiringly. "You'd hardly know it. Wonderful capacity."

"I'll have another martini," said Darrell. "How about yourself?"

"I never refuse."

Darrell watched while Phil Beresford mixed the drinks. "You know Noel fairly well?"

"From across the bar. Nice lad, never made trouble."

"He wrote a letter home a month ago. It doesn't say much, except that he's in trouble. It must have been about the time he disappeared. What do you suppose happened to him?"

Phil ran a hand through his silver-blond hair, shook his head. "I couldn't say. This place is always full of emergency."

"There must be talk."

"That's where I bow out," said Phil. "I gotta live here."

The blonde girl returned from the restroom. She hoisted herself back up on the bar stool, stared at Darrell with steady intensity.

"She's harmless," muttered Phil, "but don't buy her a drink, unless you want to carry her out."

A middle-aged couple entered, the man in a tweed jacket and knickers, the woman in a tailored suit. They ordered brandy, turned frozen stares first at Darrell, then at the blonde girl.

Phil came back to stand in front of Darrell. "Have you talked to Arthur Upshaw?"

"No. Just Duff McKinstry."

"Duff can't tell you anything. You won't get much more from Upshaw."

"Just what goes on?"

"Oh, high finance, excursions and alarms, just the general run of things." He looked up as the outside door burst open. Into the bar ran the girl in the cream-colored linen suit. Behind her, more sedately, came the raw-boned young man in the red-brown slacks.

Phil saluted the girl with enthusiasm. "Here's T-Bone and her latest beau. Gracious, how you do get around, T-Bone!"

T-Bone came to the bar, took the stool beside Darrell. The young man stood at her shoulder, fidgeting and restless.

The blonde English girl said loudly, "Who left the door open?"

Phil leaned over the bar and stared deep into T-Bone's clear blue eyes. "T-Bone, what did I tell you when I hypnotized you last night?"

T-Bone frowned, pursed her lips. "I forget."

"I said that whenever I snapped my fingers you'd feel the irresistible urge to throw your arms around my neck and kiss me."

"I don't remember that!"

"That's the beauty of hypnotism," said Phil. "Next, when I snapped my fingers twice—"

From the kitchen came a short thick woman in a black dress, walking with a peculiar long slow stride. "Psst," said T-Bone. "Mrs. Phil!"

Looking neither right nor left Mrs. Phil walked quietly along behind the bar. She poured out a bucket of ice cubes, looked over the counter. T-Bone wrinkled her nose. Mrs. Phil walked quietly back the way she had come.

T-Bone jumped down off the stool, flounced over to one of the booths with her young man. Phil Beresford heaved a deep sigh. "You've just witnessed the cross I bear through life," he told Darrell. "T-Bone."

"I have a feeling I've seen her before," Darrell said reflectively. "Where, I don't seem to remember..."

Phil shook his head. "You'd remember."

"As a matter of fact—" Darrell twirled his glass, looked down into the pale vortex. Occasionally Noel, in his letters home, had enclosed photographs. "Is she friendly with Noel?"

"Oh, about like the catnip is friendly with the cat."

"I'm almost sure that Noel sent home a photograph of her and himself on the beach."

"I've seen the picture," said Phil. "In fact I took it. T-Bone modestly wearing a couple of lace handkerchiefs. She drove me near crazy."

A waiter was bending over the booth. T-Bone ordered with expressive gesticulations of hand and wrist.

The blonde called out, "Phil, ducky, serve me a drink, there's a boy."

"Sure! What do you want?"

"A nice Pimms cup, the way I like it."

"We're out of that just now. How about a beer?"

"I'll have a pink gin."

Phil poured grenadine into a dollop of gin, added three maraschino cherries. "There. How's that?"

"Lovely."

Phil sidled back down the bar. "It's the cherries that does it," he told Darrell. "Whenever a fancy drink comes up I invent a new recipe. So long as I'm lavish with cherries, there's no kicks. I even get compliments."

The waiter was serving T-Bone and her escort. Phil watched with a marveling shake of the head. "The way I see it, when the Creator made T-Bone he had one idea in mind, and that was the nicest most alluring piece of female humanity he could think up."

Darrell admitted the felicity of the plan.

"Kinda have to suspect the good Lord of our own human failings," Phil reflected. "'Scuse me if that's blasphemy, I don't mean no offense."

He looked over Darrell's shoulder; his manner changed; he began to wipe the bar with a damp cloth.

Darrell turned to see Duff McKinstry's sister, still wearing her gray skirt, her black turtle-neck sweater, her expression of precocious wisdom and recklessness.

"Hello, Ellen," said Phil diffidently.

Ellen nodded. She looked at Darrell. "You called the house tonight."

"Yes."

"Mr. Upshaw was busy at the time, but he'd like to see you now."

Darrell swiveled around on the stool, sat collecting his thoughts. His mind was fuzzy: three martinis, no dinner. "Very well. Where is he?"

"He's not here. He sent me to pick you up."

Darrell stepped down from the stool. "Let's go."

"Hey!" Phil Beresford called after him. "You was buying me that drink; I wasn't buying for you."

"Oh," said Darrell. "Excuse me." He hurriedly paid his bill.

"That's the margin between profit and loss right there," Phil explained to his customers, as Darrell followed Ellen McKinstry from the bar.

The Mercedes-Benz was parked a few yards down the street. Ellen jumped in; Darrell followed more carefully, and his caution seemed to irritate Ellen. She waited with pointed patience as if he were a person of advanced years who might be startled or injured by too sudden a start. At last he was settled; she flicked the starter, switched on the headlights. White light reached down the street, picked out a figure leaning against a tree. The face was no more than a pale blur, but the clothes showed distinctly: baggy gray trousers, a green and white pull-over.

The Mercedes-Benz throbbed, swept forward; the figure slipped back out of sight. Darrell looked at Ellen; if she had noticed she said nothing.

Chapter IV

AT the bottom of Calle Miranda the Mercedes-Benz swung to the left, rushed up the hill. Darrell braced himself. He asked, "Have you ever killed anybody driving this thing?"

"Not yet." Ellen's voice was flat.

The car swooped over the crest of the hill, veered around a corner. Ellen lifted her foot from the accelerator, fed power half-way through the turn. Darrell gripped the door. White villas fled astern like wisps of cloud behind an airplane.

Darrell slumped into the seat. Ellen seemed bored and lax. Darrell asked, "Do you always drive this way?"

"What way?"

"Idiotically fast."

"Fast?" She made a sound of contempt. "I can do a hundred and thirty in this job."

"I understand why your Uncle Arthur wanted me to come to him. He's ridden with you before."

"No," she said in a voice even chillier than before. "He doesn't dare."

An odd thing to say, thought Darrell. Ellen made no explanation.

They swept along Calle Costanza, a narrow lane cut into the steep hillside and overhung by great masses of foliage, made a hairpin turn that sent gravel flying.

A moment later Ellen said, "You can relax your grip, we're there." She bore down on the wheel; the convertible swerved through a stone archway, spraying up another wake of gravel. Two quick twists, application of brakes, the convertible stood at rest under a stucco portico. Ellen switched off the ignition, jumped to the ground. "This way," she said crisply. "Mind the flower pots. Or kick them over if you care to, it's all the same to me."

Darrell came to life. He opened the door, alighted. Ellen ran up the steps to the porch, turned and waited. Darrell searched her face for any hint of amusement, but found only unconcern. "That was quite an experience," he said thoughtfully.

Ellen opened the door. "This way, please." She led him through a living room, furnished in dark oak and rust-colored leather, into an old-fashioned study. Bookcases occupied two walls; the other two walls were paneled in walnut. The ceiling was white plaster, heavily beamed. Logs blazed in a fireplace, a table supported a lamp with green glass shade. The head of a massive lion, mounted as a trophy, hung over the fireplace.

Back to the fire stood Arthur Upshaw, a man of about fifty, wearing a suit of conservative gray twill. He was tall, heavy-boned, gray-haired, gray-eyed, heavily handsome. He nodded, but made no move to come forward and shake hands. "Mr. Hutson? I'm Arthur Upshaw. Sit down, if you please."

Darrell lowered himself into the corner of a leather couch. Ellen sprawled into a chair nearby, thrust her legs toward the fire, fixed her eyes on Darrell's face.

"A glass of sherry?" asked Upshaw.

"No, thanks."

Upshaw clasped his hands behind his back. "You arrived in Tangier this morning, so I understand."

"That's correct."

The pewter gaze roved Darrell's face. "My nephew tells me that you want to help us locate Noel Hutson."

Darrell started to reply, then checked himself. He said after a moment, "I want to find Noel, certainly. I had hoped that you might know, in a general way at least, where he might be."

"You are his brother, eh?"

THE MAN IN THE CAGE

"I'm his brother."

"You'll consider this an impertinence, but may I see your passport?"

Darrell handed over the green booklet. Upshaw flipped through one or two pages, returned it. "Thank you. Damned imposition, I know. But I like to be sure with whom I am dealing. Good plan, don't you think?"

"I assume the worst to begin with."

Ellen made a small sound. Arthur Upshaw's eyes widened an eighth of an inch.

"I understand," he said, "that you come in response to a letter from Noel." Elaborately casual, he probed at the fire. Ellen maintained her fixed scrutiny of Darrell's face.

Apparently, thought Darrell, they believe the letter to be of relatively recent date. He saw no reason to disabuse them. "Yes," said Darrell. "Quite true. As a matter of fact, parts of this letter puzzle me." He started to reach into his breast pocket, then checked the motion.

Arthur Upshaw's eyes followed his every move. "Perhaps I'll be able to clear it up."

"Possibly. Of course I'm mainly concerned in finding Noel. Could you tell me the circumstances under which he disappeared? In complete confidence, naturally."

Arthur Upshaw teetered up and down on his toes. "A month ago he set out to perform a certain bit of business for me. He never returned. That's the essence of the situation. This letter of his, do you have it with you?"

Darrell ignored the question. "What I'm getting at, exactly where did Noel disappear? He must have left some sort of trail."

Arthur Upshaw nodded. "We'll get around to that, but I think the letter might possibly be helpful. I wonder if I might see it?"

"It's a personal letter, Mr. Upshaw. I doubt if it would tell you any more than it has me."

From the corner of his eye Darrell became aware that Ellen was grinning, faintly but unmistakably.

Arthur Upshaw poked at the fire. "It's very important that I locate Noel. I don't mind saying that a considerable amount of money is involved. A very considerable amount."

"I understand your concern."

"It seems to me that our interests coincide. I think it's to your advantage to help me as much as possible."

Darrell looked into the fire a moment. "I'm not so sure that our interests coincide. They touch here and there. You want to recover your money. I want to find my brother."

Upshaw made a small impatient gesture; Ellen's grin became wider. Darrell could not decide whether her malice was directed against her uncle or himself. "It's a distinction without a difference," declared Arthur Upshaw. He jabbed at the fire.

"Perhaps I haven't expressed myself well," said Darrell. "I suspect that my brother is in trouble. I'm anxious that we cooperate, but I don't want to rescue your money and leave Noel in the soup."

Arthur Upshaw's eyes were once more riveted on Darrell's face. "You pose a hypothetical and complicated situation. Isn't it easier—"

"It's not complicated," said Darrell. "If you'll answer my questions, I'll show you the letter. It's as simple as that."

Upshaw considered. "What sort of questions?"

"Where did Noel go when he disappeared? Is there a possibility of foul play? Who saw Noel last? Have the police been notified?"

Upshaw selected the last question. "The police have not been notified, for a very good reason. Our conversation is confidential, of course?"

"Certainly."

Upshaw nodded placidly. "I don't mind admitting that upon occasion, like other good people of Tangier, I've helped facilitate trade across artificial international barriers. In short, I am a smuggler. Still a gentleman, I hope."

"I thought smuggling out of Tangier had come to an end."

"To a large extent. Smuggling today is not only unprofitable, it's illegal. Therefore I can hardly take my problems to the Tangier police."

"I can, however."

Upshaw shrugged. "That naturally is at your option."

"Noel was working for you when he disappeared?"

"Yes. I can't take care of the donkey work, nor would I care to."

"But, if smuggling is unprofitable—"

Upshaw held up his hand. "Certain types of operation—regrettably those most flagrantly illegal—still offer opportunities. I won't expatiate for obvious reasons."

"Apparently then, Noel was engaged in a smuggling operation when he disappeared."

"I won't contradict you. Through the incredible stupidity of a certain person, Noel was entrusted with responsibilities far beyond his scope. I am afraid," said Upshaw pompously, "that Noel was tempted by the opportunity."

Darrell ignored the implied accusation. "Where did the operation take Noel?"

Upshaw turned to poke again at the fire. "Isn't that information contained in his letter?"

"Where you sent him and where he wrote this letter might be two different places."

Upshaw turned the full stare of his gray eyes on Darrell. "From where did he send the letter?"

"I don't know. He isn't specific."

Upshaw's shoulders sagged a trifle. "I see."

Ellen asked, "What about the postmark?"

"It's a smear."

Upshaw walked back and forth across the hearth. "This letter—does it mention any landmark, anything which might give a hint as to his whereabouts? I say, Mr. Hutson, wouldn't it be simpler to show me the letter?"

"Simpler for you, Mr. Upshaw."

"If the letter is so innocent, why won't you show it to me?"

"Because it's all I have to bargain with."

Upshaw made an impatient gesture. "Does he make even the slightest reference to his surroundings? I know Morocco well. I might be able to identify an allusion which escapes you."

"It's possible, but there's no such allusion. Where in Morocco did you send him?"

Arthur Upshaw realized that he had allowed himself to reveal a fragment of definite information, and his voice raised in pitch. "Actually, Mr. Hutson, your question is immaterial. He certainly is no longer at this particular place. Under the circumstances I consider it only your duty to show me the letter you received from Noel."

Ellen said in a neutral voice, "It's clear he doesn't intend to, Arthur, so why not change the subject?"

Upshaw turned Darrell so cold a stare that Darrell tensed to duck, should his host decide to swing the poker.

"Damn it," muttered Upshaw, "there's a large sum of money involved. I don't know whether Hutson is alive or dead. I don't really care, if only—"

Darrell nodded. "I mentioned that our interests aren't identical. I want Noel; you want your money."

"The money is enough! I'm severely compromised! You ignore the damages I've sustained. Do you intend to make good your brother's obligations?"

"Perhaps you have grounds for a suit?"

"Naturally not. I'm a smuggler; I've relinquished my claims to legal protection. But there's still a point of honor involved."

"I can't see how it affects me."

"You have a letter from the man who ran off with my property. I want to see it. I have every right to see it."

"I'm not convinced that Noel ran off with your property," said Darrell. "And that changes the whole picture. I know Noel pretty well. For all his faults, he isn't a thief."

Upshaw snorted cynically, "My property and your brother disappeared in very close conjunction. He was a free agent up to the moment of his disappearance. I claim, and any reasonable man would agree, that Noel stole my property!"

"Consider me unreasonable, if you like," said Darrell.

Upshaw shrugged in defeat; Ellen stared at Darrell in something like fascination.

"Exactly what is this missing property?" Darrell asked.

"That's beside the point. You should feel an obligation to show me that letter."

"I don't believe it would help you, Mr. Upshaw. That's my honest opinion. Why can't you do things my way? We'd both profit if I knew where to start looking for Noel."

Upshaw slowly shook his head, as if straining for patience. "My nephew and I have made exhaustive inquiries. During the last month we have traveled everywhere in Morocco; we have hired agents in Casablanca and in Spain. Do you think you can succeed where we have failed?"

"I don't know till I try."

"Do you speak French?"

"Very little."

"We do. Do you speak Arabic?"

"None whatever."

"We are both quite fluent. Do you know the details of this business, the people involved, the Moorish mentality, the officials who have been bribed, those who have not?"

"Naturally not. But I've got to look; it's my duty. The rest of my life I'd never feel easy if I made no attempt to find Noel, and you seem to be the logical man to come to for information."

Ellen, her face a mask of absolute boredom, rose to her feet, sauntered from the room.

"You have offended Ellen," said Arthur Upshaw gravely.

"I have?"

Arthur Upshaw held up his hand. "Please don't apologize; I do the same thing continually. She is disgusted by any reference to honor, faith or duty; she experiences physical nausea at the mention of altruism, chivalry—virtue of any kind, in fact. She is not yet twenty years old, but she affects the cynical wisdom of a strip-tease dancer." And he prodded viciously at the fire.

Darrell watched him with curiosity; he spoke with a deeper and more bitter emotion than the topic seemed to merit. Upshaw, as if reaching a decision, put down the poker, turned, clasped his hands behind his back, gazed pontifically at the ceiling. "There seems no point continuing the discussion. You state that this letter is of a personal nature. I am forced to take you at your word. Indeed, if it were otherwise, you would not be here, but out seeking Noel at whatever address he might have mentioned."

Darrell rose to his feet. "Please don't bother to call Ellen. I prefer walking."

Upshaw started to speak, then rubbed his chin. "Just as you please, Mr. Hutson." He conducted Darrell to the front door, bade him good night.

Darrell walked down the driveway, out into Calle Costanza. Before him spread the twinkling lights of the city. He turned east, sauntered downhill along the winding street.

The evening had yielded no information to speak of. Nothing from the Masquerade Bar, very little more from Arthur Upshaw. The two sources on which he had been counting, both barren. Upshaw seemed to fear that if the brothers got together they would make common cause and flee with the booty; a suspicion undoubtedly reinforced by Darrell's refusal to show the letter.

Darrell rounded the hairpin bend, and a moment or so later passed back below the McKinstry villa. He looked up through heavy shrubbery overhanging the road, toward the back of the house. A single dim light showed, from an upstairs window.

Behind him appeared headlights; the Mercedes-Benz swerved to a stop. Ellen looked out at him with sullen hostility. "Jump in."

Darrell smiled and shook his head. "It's very decent of you—" here Ellen snorted "—but I prefer to walk. You English people live under such a strain, you drive yourselves and your cars at such a nerve-racking pace—"

"Oh dry up," muttered Ellen. "Are you getting in or not? And I'm not English, I'm Scottish."

"If you'll keep all four wheels on the ground. Perhaps you'd like me to drive."

"No, thanks. Please get in."

Darrell opened the door, gingerly settled himself. She started off with a roar, with a sly sidelong look at Darrell, but thereafter drove at a fairly conservative speed.

"Where do you want to go?"

"My hotel, I suppose. The Miranda."

There was a moment of awkward silence. Once or twice Ellen half started to speak. Finally she said, "By the way, if you're thinking of going to the police, I wouldn't."

"Ah!" said Darrell. "I understand now."

"You understand what?"

"Your altruism in coming after me. Uncle Arthur thought of something he'd neglected to tell me."

She drove several blocks in silence. "In any event, the police are not likely to be of any help."

"Why not? What are they paid for?"

"Use your brain. Noel is missing."

"That's what everybody tells me."

"Why are persons usually missing?"

"For various reasons."

"Reasons connected with loot. To be quite blunt, Noel has hopped the twig."

"I don't think so."

"Oh you don't?" Her voice trembled with scorn. "So Noel is . virtuous and forbearing. Pious and good."

"Noel is a retarded adolescent, but not a thief."

Ellen laughed mockingly. "These windy assertions—what do they prove?" She swung the car to the curb in front of the Hotel Miranda. "Of course he's a crook! Why else did he duck out?"

"He might have run into trouble. An accident, perhaps."

"If there was an accident, he could have telephoned. No, he just saw a good thing and helped himself. But don't think the police can help you, because they can't. And wouldn't if they could."

"This is all far over my head. I can't quite believe that—"

Ellen made a furious gesture. "Very well, listen! I'll tell you what everybody knows anyway. Smuggling is a thing of the past around here. But there's money in gun-running."

"Gun-running? To whom? The Algerian rebels? The FLN, whatever they call it?"

"Yes, naturally. It's dangerous, because the French still maintain troops in Morocco. But if you're willing to take risks, it's worth your while."

"It seems rather a roundabout route to Algeria."

"Not at all. It's one of the most direct. Don't forget, the French patrol the Mediterranean. Every few months they stop a ship and seize the cargo. But with proper organization, other cargoes get through, and Uncle Arthur—" she spoke the name with a flat intonation "—bought such a cargo."

"Isn't this all rather casual? Presumably the French have agents in Tangier."

"The streets are thick with them. The operation naturally is supposed to be secret. Thanks to your precious Noel the whole town is laughing at Arthur."

"But how could Noel—"

Ellen interrupted impatiently. "The Algerians paid for the whole shipment, but they received less than a tenth of what they paid for. The manufacturer's agent won't release the balance of the weapons until he's paid. And Noel has the loot. So now you know why Noel is not exactly popular around Tangier."

"Yes," said Darrell. "It becomes clear."

"In any event you'll gain nothing from the police. They know the trade is going on. They're Moslems, they're sympathetic to the FLN. They don't care how many guns get through, the more the better. If you complain about Noel, you're talking about something they don't want to hear. You might even find yourself ejected as an undesirable."

Darrell opened the door, descended to the ground. Ellen watched him with raised eyebrows. She said in a pleasant voice, "If I were you, I'd clear out and leave Noel to stew in his own juice."

Darrell stood looking down at her. "That's a peculiar thing to say."

"Why peculiar?"

"I just arrived. You don't expect me to leave just like that."

"You might be wiser."

"I've been wise all my life. Noel's been foolish and he's had all the fun."

"He's not having fun now," said Ellen. "Wherever he is." She snatched at the gearbox; the engine growled; the convertible sprang down the street. Darrell watched it around the corner. He sighed, shook his head, went into the hotel.

The desk clerk handed him an envelope printed with his name. It contained a newspaper clipping. The headline read:

TORTURE VICTIM

FOUND IN FIELD

Darrell turned to the clerk. "Who brought this?"

"A boy."

"You don't know him?"

"No, sir."

Darrell read the clipping through:

TANGIER, March 28—The mutilated body of Mohammed Ali Aktouf, 58, was found last night by a farm laborer in a field 20 kilometers south of Tangier, a few meters off the road connecting Sidi Boussen with the Tangier-Rabat highway. He was victim to one of the most sadistic assaults of recent years.

Aktouf's ankles and wrists were bound with copper wire. His body had been badly burnt, apparently with a petrol blowtorch. The cause of death is presumed to be heart failure, since Aktouf had a medical history of heart disease.

Officers of the Sûreté Nationale are investigating the crime but state that they have no clues as to either the identity of the torturers or their motive.

Aktouf, employed at a local hotel, a man of modest means, had no criminal record and was not known to be involved in political activity. There is speculation that the crime was a gruesome case of mistaken identity or possibly the work of Pan-Arab terrorists.

Aktouf's employer, Mr. Arthur Upshaw, Calle Miranda 37, has reported his accounts to be in good order, with no shortage of funds and no thefts reported at the hotel.

Darrell crossed the street to the Masquerade Bar.

Chapter V

THE Masquerade Bar was noisy and gay. The booths were crowded; two white-coated waiters ran back and forth. Phil Beresford, assisted by a second bartender, mixed drinks, chaffed the customers, rang the cash register, greeted newcomers, consoled the departing. Mr. Burdette emerged from the kitchen chewing and patting his mouth with plump little fingers; Phil feigned astonishment. Mr. Burdette gave a nonchalant wave of the hand, walked into the Balmoral lobby.

Darrell seated himself at the far end of the bar. Phil Beresford came to serve him. "I see you're back in one piece."

"Just barely. Can I get something to eat?"

"You certainly can. All we serve is food, nothing fancy. The steaks sometimes are pretty good." He squinted around the room. "I can't put you in a booth; do you want to eat right here?"

Darrell nodded. "A steak sounds fine, medium, and a bottle of beer."

"Right." Phil called the order into the kitchen, spread a napkin on the bar, set out a knife and fork. "How did you get along with Arthur Upshaw?"

"I don't know much more now than I did before. Except that Upshaw doesn't like to be fooled with."

223

"I could've told you that," said Phil. He poured a bottle of beer, went to serve another customer. Ten minutes later he brought the steak. "Ketchup? Worcestershire?"

"No, thanks. Take a look at this." He pushed the clipping across the bar.

Phil read, wrinkled his long nose in distaste. "A mess. I guess they never found out anything more. Poor old Aktouf. He worked right here in the Balmoral. I guess you knew that."

Darrell nodded, returned the clipping to the envelope. "It came tonight by messenger."

"Somebody thinks you need advice."

"It might even be considered a gentle hint."

"Could be."

Phil sprang down the bar to attend to the wants of a thirsty patron. Presently he returned. "Everything okay?"

"Fine."

Phil looked over his shoulder down the bar. There was a lull; the other bartender was handling the business. Phil ducked under the counter, pulled over a stool. "Funny things happen in this town. I'm just a newcomer—I've been here eight years—but the tales I've heard..." He looked sidewise at Darrell. "What did Upshaw tell you?"

"Nothing very much. What he did tell me he labeled confidential."

"All these secrets." Phil drummed his fingers on the bar. "Upshaw is about to lose his shirt."

"That bad, eh?"

"Worse. His shirt and most of his underpants. He worked up this big deal, he sank every cent he could raise into it. He put the hotel up the spout, he got Duff to take a loan on the house, borrowed on the *Deirdre*. Instead of a bonanza, a fiasco. That's why I'm sweating. I got the most miserable lease in the world."

Darrell ordered a second bottle of beer. "How about you?"

"I never refuse."

The bartender brought Phil a highball. Phil cradled the glass in his fingers, considered the motion of the bubbles. "Upshaw is like one of the old-time maharajahs. When he dies the whole palace brigade throws themselves into the grave. When Upshaw goes, we all go—me, Ellen, Duff, the whole caboodle, wailing and screaming."

"Why Duff and Ellen? Don't they have a father and mother?"

"Dead." Phil swallowed two-thirds of the highball. "They're one of the old families, go back to the last century. Ben Upshaw, the grandfather, got run out of Scotland and came here. Arthur is his son." He finished the highball, looked reflectively at the ice. Darrell signaled the bartender.

"I never refuse," said Phil. "Well, to make a long story short, Peggy, Ben Upshaw's daughter and Arthur's sister, married Scotty McKinstry. Arthur and Scotty worked together; they bought the first *Deirdre* and made good money. When Grandpa Upshaw died he left the house to Scotty and Peggy, this building here to Arthur. Times was good; Arthur put his money into the hotel. Scotty blew his on this and that. Peggy died, and just after I arrived Scotty stopped a Spanish bullet off Alicante. Duff and Ellen got the house, a little income, not much. Duff worked with Arthur on the new *Deirdre* and they did pretty good until things closed up. Then Arthur hatched this other big deal. Duff was all for it but Ellen, out of sheer cussedness, wouldn't let 'em mortgage the house until they gave her a down payment on that big black widow-maker she drives. I guess they hoped she'd kill herself." Phil ducked back under the bar, prepared to go to work. "Well, that's how the story goes. They had a sure thing, then something happened. And now they're all bollixed up."

There was a rustle of movement beside Darrell, a smell of violets, a swish of silky chestnut hair. "It's T-Bone the war correspondent," exclaimed Phil, "and her handsome young millionaire. Where have you been?"

"We've had dinner out at Cape Spartel," said T-Bone. "It was lovely! First lobster in coral sauce, and then some little partridges and then chateaubriand. Harvey ordered three bottles of champagne. Isn't he nice?" She patted the arm of her raw-boned young escort, who beamed proudly.

"You eat like that you'll ruin your lovely figure," said Phil.

"I eat every chance I get. I never know when will be my next meal."

Phil shook his head. "Never worry, T-Bone. Not while there's millionaires like Harvey to take starving young women under their wings."

"Harvey isn't a millionaire!"

"Right now ah'm just a private fust-class," said Harvey, "but ah'm from Texas, and they's still hope if ah scratch around a little. Ah'll make sahgeant too. Ain't you gonna bring us nothin' to drink?"

"Sure I'm going to bring you something to drink! That's my business. You call it, I bring it."

"I want a crème-de-menthe frappé," said T-Bone.

"Bonzo. Make that two, whatevah it is."

"With cherries, Phil."

Phil sighed, shook his head. "T-Bone, you're making an old man of me. When are you going back to Paris?"

"I don't know. I don't have any money."

"T-Bone's on the lam," Phil told Darrell. "She's committed a little peccadillo on the Champs-Elysées—debrained an old man with an axe, or something similar. They chased her to Rome, in and out of St. Tropez, but she ducked 'em at Majorca. She's waiting here till the indignation dies down."

"Phil! I never did any such thing!"

"Don't apologize, T-Bone. He was probably making a pest of himself."

Harvey descended from the stool, took T-Bone's drink. "C'mon honey-pup. I see a booth, let's join the humans."

T-Bone allowed herself to be led to a vacant booth. Phil and Darrell watched her cross the floor.

"Is she English?" Darrell asked. "She has some kind of accent."

"French and English. Her father's professor of archaeology at the Sorbonne, believe it or not. Contrary to rumor, it's T-Bone's father who pays her rent. Costs him half what he makes, no doubt."

"What is she doing here?"

"Heaven only knows. Maybe she just likes the place. T-Bone's a woman of mystery. She's also bird dog to a couple of newspapermen around town. Don't tell her anything you're ashamed of; you'll have your secrets all over the front pages."

"I can see how Noel would be interested."

Phil nodded. "She wouldn't play. Not very hard. T-Bone is highly moral. She wants holy wedlock. It's gotta wear pants, carry a big bank-roll, and use an American passport. She hasn't had much luck around here. The Americans have all been raggedy-ass fugitives like me and Harvey; the rich blokes have big bellies and wives. Duff's the one who's got it bad. If he comes in, look for trouble."

"What kind of trouble?"

"He kinda drew a line around T-Bone." Phil shook his head ruefully. "One time I had to give him a real serious talking to. I said, 'Duff, you swing on me, you'll be minus a bowel. I don't like this brawling. I'm delicate.'" A customer signaled and Phil moved off down the bar.

Darrell sat drinking his beer and musing. Ideas passed through his mind like pedestrians hurrying through the rain—images, half-formed speculations, fleeting tail ends of recollections: the fact of Noel's disappearance, the letter which occasioned so much interest... Blank-eyed Arthur Upshaw, truculent Duff McKinstry. Ellen... The clipping describing the death of Mohammed Ali Aktouf, the desk clerk at the Balmoral Hotel... Mrs. Ritterman, with the hair hanging down her face like seaweed over a rock... Noel's pathetic excuse for a boat... Across the room in a booth, T-Bone...

Phil Beresford's voice came from close beside his shoulder. "Watching T-Bone gets to be a kind of disease. I'm saving my cigarette money; as soon as I get a million, I'm gonna propose."

"I thought you were married."

Phil made an airy gesture. "The work of a minute. This is a Moslem country. All I gotta do is say 'I renounce thee' three times and bingo! That's it. I already said it twice." Phil's gaze focused on the door. He clapped his hand to the side of his head. "Oh oh. Here it comes."

Duff stalked in, swung up on a bar stool, turned a brief cool stare at Darrell.

"Hello, Duff," said Phil heartily. "Where you been this time of night?"

"Down on the boat. Weeds a yard long, deck going to hell."

"Put on fiberglass, like I told you. You'll get a better price."

"Over the teak? Good lord! You Yanks are barbarians." He seemed to see T-Bone for the first time, and groaned. "Where did she locate that specimen? What is it?"

"A resident of the great state of Texas, now employed by the United States Army."

"That's the absolute limit." Duff winced.

"It seems reasonable to me," said Phil. "She got hungry and Harvey fed her. I don't think the attraction goes much further. Although Harvey plans to be a millionaire."

Duff swung around with a sardonic twist to his mouth. "She told me she was staying in. Little dickens."

"A hungry woman don't stay in, that's well known." Phil moved off to attend to a customer. Duff looked into the mirror behind the bar, then turned to Darrell. "So now what'll you do?"

"I don't know. According to Mr. Upshaw you and he already went to look for Noel."

"We did that."

"And you found nothing? No leads? Nothing?"

"Nothing."

"Where did you go to look?"

Duff laughed. "A professional secret, old boy."

"I'm not in the profession. Why not cooperate?"

"Don't care for any, thank you. Do your own dirty work."

"But if there's any chance—"

"There isn't. Noel has taken to the tall grass. My guess is Casablanca." He looked over his shoulder. Harvey was holding T-Bone's fingers in his big red fists. Duff snorted in disgust. He stepped down off the stool, walked across the bar.

"Here it comes," groaned Phil. "Some day, some day..."

Duff bent over T-Bone, remonstrating. Harvey stared at Duff, morosely attacked his green drink. T-Bone smiled, made her prettiest excuses. Duff argued. Harvey slowly raised his head, squinting up at Duff. He spoke with cold Texas formality. Duff made a cool retort, turned his shoulder. Harvey brooded for a few seconds, his face red. He put his hands on the table. He spoke: an ultimatum. Duff glanced at him disdainfully. Harvey hoisted himself to his feet.

With a rapidity almost magic Phil stood beside the booth. "First settle the bill, then outside."

Harvey tossed a pair of dollar bills on the table. He and Duff marched to the door, followed by a string of curiosity seekers.

Phil returned behind the bar. "Every week, once a week, it happens."

"Duff doesn't show any scars," observed Darrell.

"He's pretty good by now. He's quick and mean; he don't get excited."

T-Bone flounced across the room, stood fuming beside the bar. "That Duff! I wish he'd leave me alone!"

"Don't encourage him."

"But I don't!"

"Sure you do. You can't help it."

"I'm never, never, never going to talk to him again."

From outside came sounds of conflict: cries, blows, curses. Phil listened with a critical ear. "Harvey seems to be holding his own."

"I wish he'd *kill* Duff."

"No such luck."

There were whistles, sharp commands, a sudden cessation of movement, then measured official voices. "The gendarmes," said Phil. "A short walk up from the corner."

"I'm going to bed," said T-Bone. She walked swiftly through the connecting door into the lobby of the Balmoral. Customers filed back into the bar. Duff marched in, arms swinging wide, eyes glowing. Harvey followed, slouching angrily. He was disheveled; his cheek was bruised; he looked as if he had fallen. He searched around the room. "Where'd she go?" he asked in a thick voice.

"She said to thank you for a pleasant evening," said Phil, "and ran off to bed."

Harvey hesitated, looked at Duff, who leaned against the bar. Harvey slowly turned away, evidently aching to demolish the entire interior, then walked with slow steps to the door. Here he turned a last look toward Duff, who made no move. Harvey departed.

Duff rubbed his knuckles. "Nothing like a little sport to liven a dull evening." He turned a level glance toward Darrell, who made no comment.

Five minutes later Arthur Upshaw strode smartly in from the Balmoral lobby. At the sight of Darrell he stopped short, then came over to the bar. "I still hope to see that letter, Mr. Hutson."

"That's a forlorn hope, Mr. Upshaw."

"We may still come to an understanding." He nodded to Phil. "Plain whiskey and soda." Signaling to Duff he crossed the room, settled into the booth vacated by Harvey and T-Bone. Duff joined him; they conversed earnestly.

Darrell paid his bill. He pushed through the door, stepped out on the sidewalk. The time was eleven o'clock, Calle Miranda was quiet. Street lamps shone through the acacia trees; century plants made a jungle of sharp wild shadows behind him; cars crouched in the gutter like the hulks of dead beetles.

A figure left the dark blot of a doorway, stood waiting. Green light from the MASQUERADE sign shone on his face: Slip-Slip the Moroccan.

"Good night, Mr. Hutson," he called softly. "Good night, how are you?"

"I'm well. How are you?"

"Good." The hazel eyes glittered in the green light. "You looking for your brother Noel?"

"Yes."

"You want to find him?"

"Yes. Do you know where he is?"

"Maybe I know a man who knows where is Mr. Noel. You want to come see?"

"Tonight? No."

"No, not tonight. Maybe tomorrow. First I find out. But you come, eh?"

"That all depends."

"Sure. I know. Maybe I see you tomorrow. Then you go talk to the man. Good, eh?"

"Good, maybe. Where is this man?"

"That's what is maybe. Tonight what you do?"

"I go to bed."

"You want something?"

"No, thanks."

"You like to look at some girls? Maybe just look, maybe you like."

"No, I don't think so."

"You like anything else?"

"No. Just bed."

Darrell started away, looked back. Slip-Slip stood watching him, lonesome and wistful.

THE MAN IN THE CAGE

Darrell went up to his room. From his suitcase he took the letter Noel had written home. He looked at it a moment, weighed it in his hand. He left the room, returned downstairs. At the desk he requested an envelope, bought a stamp. He addressed the envelope to himself, care of American Express, Tangier. He tucked Noel's letter within, dropped it into the mailbox. Then he climbed the steps to his room, locked the door, went to bed.

Chapter VI

DARRELL sat at a sidewalk café looking across the Place de France. The population of Tangier passed in front of him: ragged Berbers, sleek Spaniards, tourists of every description. There were men in fez and djellaba with European shoes; men in slacks and sport coat with fez and white Moroccan slippers. There were women in tweed suits, women in California sportswear, women veiled to the eyes with white robes sweeping the sidewalk. Vendors of silk scarfs, bright-colored skull-caps, toy balloons, jewelry, gewgaws and oddments prowled the sidewalk eyeing the café customers. The sun shone brightly, the air was heavy with the scent of acacia. Darrell sipped mint tea from a thick glass, considered his visit to the American consulate.

The interview had been unrewarding—predictably so, Darrell recognized. He had been received with promptness, heard with courtesy. He had detailed as many circumstances as he thought necessary; the consul had been sympathetic but uncooperative. "You have consulted the police? I presume not, since your brother was involved in illegal activity."

"It's been suggested," said Darrell, "that the police look the other way in these matters."

The consul shrugged. "I can't make any official comment as to that. However, times being as they are... Cigarette?"

"No, thanks."

The consul leaned back in his chair, looked reflectively out the window. "It's a difficult situation for you."

"Yes," said Darrell. "I feel rather helpless. Unofficially, what do you think happened to him?"

"A month ago he left Tangier with a load of guns and hasn't been heard from? My guess is that he's dead. The French take a dim view of gun-running. In the second place, other groups—rival groups, you might say—work out of both Tangier and Casablanca. Violence, hijacking, murder—they've all occurred in the past. Perhaps you read of the launches which were blown up in the harbor? No? There was considerable publicity."

He put his hands briskly on the table; the interview was over. Darrell stood up. "Thank you for your time, at least."

"Not at all. I can only make the obvious suggestion: go to the police. If and when they locate him, if and when they place him under arrest, I'll see that he has the help he's entitled to."

Darrell sipped the mint tea. He had expected no more from the consul, but it was a step he felt bound to take. An urchin approached, took a large rubber tarantula from a basket, set it on the table. The legs moved, the thing gave a jump. "How much, mister? How much you give?"

"No, thank you. I'm not interested."

"Very cheap. Look." The rubber insect leapt forward.

"I don't want it."

"How much? Six hundred francs? That's a good price."

"No, thanks."

"Look at this." He produced a rubber figure which, on manipulation of a pneumatic bulb, kicked out its legs and arms. "You like better? I give you a good price."

"I don't care for either one of the things."

"Both for eight hundred francs. Very good. You won't get no cheaper anywhere. You look, you try. This is cheap price."

"I'm not in the market."

"How much you give? How much?"

"Nothing."

"I give to you for seven hundred."

"No."

"Just today, six hundred."

"No."

"Okay, mister, okay. Don't get sore." He departed to place his tarantula in front of two elderly ladies eating ice cream. Darrell continued his contemplation. So far as he could determine, he had reached a dead end. Slip-Slip had offered mysterious hints, which probably would come to nothing except requests for money. Still they supplied a pretext for further consultation with Arthur Upshaw, during which he might glean one or two fragments of information. He had nothing better to do, in any event. He paid the waiter, rose from his table, walked up the hill to the Hotel Balmoral.

Arthur Upshaw was not in. The desk clerk professed ignorance as to where he could be found.

Darrell returned to the street. He hailed a cab, gave the address of the McKinstry house on Calle Costanza.

Arriving, he found the Mercedes-Benz parked in the driveway. When he rang the bell, Ellen opened the door. Standing with the shadows of the house behind her, wearing threadbare blue jeans and a dark blue cotton T-shirt, she had for a moment the look of dreaming adolescence. She stared at Darrell from dispassionate gray eyes. "Hello. What do you want?"

"I'd like to talk to your uncle, if he's available at the moment."

"He's not here."

"Do you expect him?"

"No. This isn't his home. I don't invite him; he merely comes." Her voice had taken on a faint ring, like a cymbal brushed with a coat sleeve.

"Do you know where I can find him?"

Ellen eyed him with suspicion. "Why all the urgency?"

"I hope I can persuade him Noel isn't as guilty as he thinks."

Ellen laughed grimly. "You'll find that Arthur is immune to your charm, Mr. Hutson."

"I wasn't aware that you'd noticed it."

Ellen swept him with an icy glance.

"Excuse me," said Darrell.

"Come along," she muttered ungraciously, "I'll take you to Arthur."

"That's not necessary," said Darrell. "Just tell me where he is; I've got a cab waiting."

"I'm not sure myself. I've nothing better to do anyway."

She jumped down from the porch, into the Mercedes-Benz with an artless disregard for dignity that Darrell suddenly found ingratiating. No matter how provoking her arrogance it was hard to dislike her.

He paid off his cab, seated himself beside her. With a roar and gnash of tires they were away. Trees and houses flashed past; they tracked along the road like a bobsled down a run. Darrell put his hand on the ignition key. "Must you drive so fast?"

Ellen darted him a malicious glance, reduced her speed. At a relatively moderate pace they reached the main part of town, crossed the Boulevard Pasteur, swung on down the hill. At a dingy yellow stucco building Ellen stopped the car, jumped to the sidewalk. The door bore letters in flaking gold leaf which read:

OSCAR VENTRISS
General Agent

Ellen opened the door, walked inside; after a moment's hesitation Darrell followed.

A fat man in a brown suit and a broad-brimmed brown homburg looked up. He took the cigar from his wet pink mouth. "Well?"

"Is Mr. Upshaw here?"

Ventriss shook his head, replaced the cigar in his mouth, stared from small black eyes. "He comes, he goes."

"Where did he go?"

Ventriss popped his eyes, waved a fat pink hand. "How would I know?" He jerked his thumb at Darrell. "Who is this gentleman?"

"This is Noel Hutson's brother."

Ventriss chuckled—a doleful gurgle, like a bilge pump sucking air. "You are sure?"

"I really don't care, one way or the other."

Ventriss shook his head in disapproval. "Now they come. From all directions. Like flies." He turned back to his desk, sliding the cigar to the other side of his mouth.

Ellen motioned to Darrell. "Let's go."

They returned to the car. "Now where?" asked Darrell.

"There's another place he might be." She turned up the hill.

Darrell asked, "Does Ventriss have something to do with Noel?"

"Not directly."

"General Agent—he represents the weapons manufacturer. Am I right?"

"What difference does it make?" Ellen asked in utter boredom. "Unless you plan to place an order of your own. It's cash on the nail. No credit."

"He's the man to see? The importer, so to speak?"

She turned an appraising glance at him. "You're very interested, aren't you?"

"No. Not really. As you say, what difference does it make?"

The conversation languished. Back up the hill they drove, bearing westward toward the ancient fortress—the kasbah which dominated the medina. Darrell asked politely, "Where are we going now?"

"Tracking down Arthur. It's certain that Ventriss refused to release any more merchandise without payment, so Arthur will automatically try to squeeze the other end of the business."

"The FLN?"

"Call it that if you like."

"What do you call it?"

"Egypt. UAR. Pan-Arabia. The Moslem Empire. FLN is only a front—the people that do the fighting. In another ten years...well, there may still be a few Europeans alive in North Africa."

The street opened into an enormous square, clotted with the stalls of flower vendors. At the far end rose the minaret of a mosque.

Ellen parked the Mercedes-Benz. "Come along."

"Where are we going?"

"Down to Soco Chico."

"Who may that be?"

She gave him a glance of contemptuous amusement. "This square is the Soco Grande. Soco Chico is another square further down. It's easier to walk than to drive."

She led the way into a street lined with money changers' booths, and the shops of Indian merchants. The crowd was almost wholly

Moroccan, the men wearing fezzes, turbans, multicolored skull-caps; the women nondescript behind veils. Minute donkeys overloaded with hides, vegetables, fodder, staggered down the middle of the street.

Two or three hundred yards from Soco Grande they broke into Soco Chico, narrow and shadowed under five-story buildings with decaying woodwork and weathered brown paint. "You wait here," said Ellen. "I'll be gone only a minute."

Darrell watched the slender, rather taut figure in blue jeans disappear into a side street. The minute stretched into two; Darrell stepped over to a nearby café, took a seat at a sidewalk table and watched the passers-by. A waiter approached; Darrell ordered a bottle of beer.

Five minutes later Ellen returned, coming across the dingy picturesque little square, threading through the Moroccans with a jaunty elastic stride. Her gaze was focused on nothing, her expression was something between indifference and disdain. It came to Darrell with a faint sense of surprise that Ellen was a pretty girl. Her tawny hair was clean and fine; she had admirable clear eyes, square shoulders and slim hips—the figure of a tennis player. She felt Darrell's gaze; her mouth took on a sardonic twist. "They've gone. I can't find anyone."

"Sit down," said Darrell. "Have a drink."

She looked at him quizzically. "A social invitation?"

"Yes, I suppose that's what it amounts to."

Ellen compressed her mouth until the lips were almost invisible and little creases, like smile marks, appeared at the corners. "Perhaps you'll tell me why you wanted to see Arthur?"

"If you'll tell me one or two things in return."

"Maybe." She lowered herself into a chair. The waiter approached. Ellen spoke three words in Arabic; the waiter bowed, retreated. Ellen looked sidewise at Darrell with curiosity and calculation. "Well? Why all the rush to find Arthur?"

"To tell the complete truth," said Darrell, "I had to do something, and talking to Mr. Upshaw was as good as anything."

Ellen nodded, mouth twisted more sardonically than ever. "And I drive you all over town merely because you feel restless."

"Not quite. A couple things have happened."

The waiter returned with a small cup of black coffee, set it before Ellen.

"I hoped," said Darrell, "that I could trade information with Mr. Upshaw."

"Hmf. That's a useless hope. What's happened?"

"I've been approached by a Moroccan, who said he could give me information. That was last night. I didn't see him this morning, but no doubt he'll show up. I suppose money will change hands."

"You'll be sold a pup."

Darrell shrugged. "Perhaps. There's a chance—"

"No chance whatever. If anyone wanted to sell information they'd have gone to Arthur long ago."

"True. Unless—"

"Unless what?"

"Nothing really. There are a hundred possibilities. Suppose the Moroccan came direct from Noel?"

She laughed. "Much more likely that our friend Noel saw a good thing, and took it."

Darrell shook his head. "I know Noel too well."

"He'd turn down four hundred thousand pounds? Over a million dollars?"

Darrell looked off across the square. "The figure has a certain glamour... The glamour might tempt Noel...but I still don't believe it. The whole thing is ridiculous. Who'd be fool enough to hand that much money over to him?"

"Who said anything about money?"

Darrell raised his eyebrows. "You did. Four hundred thousand pounds."

"Four hundred thousand pounds' worth of heroin."

Something inside Darrell took a queer lurch, the skin of his face contracted. He sat back in his chair and contemplated Ellen with fascination. She watched him with a cool half-grin. Darrell's convictions regarding Noel returned with greater intensity than ever. He felt excited and feverish, and the awareness of his emotion made him angrier than ever. "Beyond any possible doubt, you're wrong," he finally said. "It's just possible that Noel might steal a million dollars. But he'd never touch a dime's worth of heroin."

"It's gone and Noel's gone with it." Ellen was grinning openly. "Why are you so upset?"

"I had no idea you were in the dope business." Darrell was surprised to hear himself say this. Ellen seemed surprised too. The grin faded, her face became cold.

"I'm not—if it makes any difference. Arthur and Duff aren't either. They buy and sell commodities and arrange for their transportation. They serve a function, they don't make judgments."

"That's pretty glib. Do you tell yourself that often?"

"I never think of it. As a matter of fact, I don't work with Duff and Arthur. I detest Arthur and quarrel with Duff."

"You have an odd set of moral principles."

Ellen sat back, stretched out her fine slim legs. "I don't have any moral principles—except the principle of self-interest. Precisely like everyone else, though other people profess noble ideals. I profess to nothing."

"Do you enjoy injuring other people?"

"Not at all. I'm free from sadism, masochism and any other ism—or so I believe."

"Still, you must know what dope addiction does to people."

"Certainly. Almost as much damage as cigarette smoking." She raised herself energetically in her seat. "Don't preach to me about narcotic rings. Nobody passes any laws about the tobacco industry. Compared with them, narcotics peddling is kid stuff."

"You make a very convincing point; in fact, you press it rather heatedly—"

"Not at all; I merely want to drive it home."

"In which case, why don't you show the same indignation about narcotics?"

"My dear young man, I'm not at all indignant. I merely observe that many socially accepted enterprises profit from potential harm done to their fellow men. The presidents of the tobacco companies aren't indicted for murder. So when you sit here wringing your hands over the narcotic traffic, I merely wonder whether you are a hypocrite or a fool, or something of both."

Darrell grimly set about the task of collecting his wits. "Have you come to any decision?"

"It's not important."

"You feel then that because some people are scoundrels, you can be a scoundrel too."

"I really don't care," said Ellen flippantly. "Haven't I told you I have no moral sense? None whatever. I observe the minimum number of social conventions, and if I'm neither a cigarette nor a narcotic salesman it's for no reasons of morality. But I'm running low on funds and soon I'll have to turn my hand to something. There is only one logical move."

"Rather an untidy business."

"Not if the price is right."

"How much do you plan to charge?"

She looked at him sidelong. "Oh—a hundred, perhaps. As much as the traffic will bear."

Darrell counted out some change. "There's a hundred and fifty."

She looked at it with raised eyebrows. "In francs? That's hardly flattering. I was thinking in terms of pounds."

"A hundred pounds. That's rather high."

"Not so high. I'll make it interesting."

"No doubt. How about fifty?"

"Let's see your money. Or is this just talk?"

"Just talk. Fifty pounds is a hundred and forty dollars."

Ellen got to her feet. "If we don't find Noel fairly soon, I'll cut prices. Are you coming?"

"Wait. I'd like to show you something."

She sat down again. "What?"

Darrell gave her the clipping he had received. "What do you make of this?"

She read the clipping, returned it. "What about it?"

"It came in an envelope addressed to me."

"If I were you, I'd go home."

"That seems to be the message. Does your immorality extend to torture?"

She darted him a swift glance. "No. Not through lack of immorality. Lack of nerve and enterprise. Hmm. It never occurred to me that Aktouf might know anything. I can't imagine why anyone should think he did."

"I don't suppose, then, that you sent me this clipping?"

She shook her head. "As I've told you I have no personal concern with this business."

"I thought your money was tied up in it."

"Like a fool I let Duff mortgage the house and realize our capital. Unless Noel shows up it's gone. I'll lose the car; Duff will owe me twenty thousand pounds which of course I'll never see. To that extent I'm anxious to see Noel."

Darrell crumpled the clipping, tossed it into the gutter. "It's a good guess that Aktouf was tortured for information."

"If you're wondering who did it," said Ellen coldly, "the answer is, I don't know. I did not. Duff could not do it alone; he has no real will of his own. Arthur is capable of any cruelty. I owe my present clear-sighted outlook on life to Arthur." She jumped to her feet, turned her head away with a jerk that sent her blonde-brown hair flying. "Let's go," she said in a muffled voice.

Chapter VII

DARRELL lunched in a quiet restaurant off the Place de France. Ellen had sneered at his suggestion that she join him, had jumped in her car and roared off across the Soco Grande scattering pedestrians like chickens.

As he ate he pondered Ellen. Pretty girls were seldom misanthropes. The usual run of anti-social rebels—the anarchists, existentialists, bop mystics, beatniks, Trotskyites, nihilists, pacifists, outsiders, angry young men, Platonic aristocrats—huddled in careful cliques, fearing nothing more than the absence of social order. Ellen walked alone. She admitted to at least indirect involvement in the narcotics trade; she had offered herself for fifty pounds, she had jeered when he balked at the price. She drove like a madwoman, contemptuous of life and limb. She proudly claimed immorality for a creed. Misfit, thought Darrell, was something of an understatement. The word depravity came to mind but it failed to ring true. Ellen looked anything but depraved; depravity was moral collapse. Ellen was too stubborn and bitter and intelligent for collapse. Peculiar, thought Darrell.

As an exercise in incongruity he transposed Ellen to his home environment; he pictured her shopping in a supermarket, sunning herself beside the back-yard swimming pool, pelting along the freeway in her Mercedes-Benz. And strangely the pictures weren't grotesque at all; Ellen looked bright and happy. Darrell roused himself.

He paid his check, left the restaurant in a mood of depression. He walked to the telephone office, put a call through to the United States, reached his father without difficulty. He reported what he had learned, added one or two of his speculations.

"Apparently Noel's been traveling with a rough crowd," came his father's voice.

"Yes, it looks that way."

"Well, don't take any risks. I don't want you in trouble on Noel's account."

"We're agreed there. Well, I'll keep plugging. Maybe something will turn up. I'll call back in a day or two."

"Right. Take care of yourself."

"I'll be careful. Good-by."

"Good-by."

Darrell walked down the hill to Calle Erasmus and the Hotel de los Dos Continentes. He found Mrs. Ritterman on her knees scrubbing the front steps. At the sight of Darrell, she raised up on her knees, wiped her nose with her forearm. "Now what is it?"

Darrell said politely, "I suppose you've had no news of Noel."

Mrs. Ritterman said suspiciously, "I think something wrong goes on. You are his brother?"

"Yes, of course I'm his brother."

"That is what you say."

Darrell brought out his passport. "Check on this. Here's my name: Darrell Hutson."

Mrs. Ritterman hauled herself to her feet with a grunt. "It is very strange. A boy comes this morning who wants Noel's letters. He says Noel has told him to come."

"Did you give them to him?"

Mrs. Ritterman laughed indignantly. "You think I don't know my business? I tell him, bring a letter from Noel, that he wants to give these things to you. And he says yes, he will get the letter."

"How long ago was this?"

"This morning."

"And he said he was coming back today?"

"Yes. Look!" She took his elbow in one of her hands, pointed with the other. "It is him! That one!"

Darrell turned, observed Slip-Slip coming along the street. At the sight of Darrell, Slip-Slip halted, then came forward with a pleased smile. "Hello, Mr. Hutson. I'm glad to see you."

"I imagine you are. What do you want with Noel's letters?"

"Letters, Mr. Hutson?"

Darrell reached, took the paper the youth carried. He unfolded it. Careful round handwriting read:

Manager,
Hotel de los Dos Continentes:
Please give Suliman my post.
Mr. Noel Hutson

Darrell handed the letter to Mrs. Ritterman. She read without amusement, turned with her arm raised. Slip-Slip ducked back. "You think I am stupid? You think I get in trouble for nothing? Wait. I call the police."

Slip-Slip sidled away. "I was bringing the letters to you, Mr. Hutson. I think you want them."

"Thanks," said Darrell dryly.

"You want to know about your brother?"

"Naturally."

"I been trying to find out. Maybe tomorrow I come see you." He departed, looking back over his shoulder.

"That one is no good," declared Mrs. Ritterman. She pulled at her skirt preparing to resume work.

Darrell smoothed his voice into the accents of persuasion. "Would you let me see the letters?"

Mrs. Ritterman's face became determined; Darrell saw that he had been tactless. "No. I keep them. When Noel comes, I give him his post. No one else."

Argument was useless; Mrs. Ritterman was clearly an obstinate woman. Darrell asked politely, "Will you put the letters away, lock them up somewhere to keep them safe?"

"I lock them up. No one gets them."

DARRELL WALKED TO THE Masquerade Bar, which at four-thirty was almost deserted. Phil Beresford stood writing in a canvas-bound ledger, heavy horn-rimmed glasses on his nose. T-Bone sat in front of him wearing a short-sleeved black frock, drinking a Tom Collins in which floated a dozen maraschino cherries.

"Good afternoon," said Phil. "I'm trying to balance my books, but T-Bone keeps breathing on me and frosting my glasses."

"You asked me to sit here," said T-Bone.

"You promised to behave. That means no breathing." He snapped shut the ledger. "I can't make these books balance and the reason is simple." He looked owlishly at Darrell. "I spend twice as much as I earn. What'll you have, Mr. Hutson?"

Darrell ordered a martini. T-Bone looked at him with knitted brows. "Noel's name was Hutson, too," she told Phil in wonder.

"That's how the system works," said Phil. "Brothers use the same last names."

"But I didn't know he was Noel's brother. Is he? Really?"

"Certainly he is. Doesn't he look like Noel?"

T-Bone laughed in sudden gayety. "Is he the one who makes so much money building highways?"

"Here we go," groaned Phil.

T-Bone turned so that she sat facing Darrell. She fished one of the cherries from the glass, nibbled at it. "You are older than Noel?"

"Two years."

"And you are not married?"

"I saw him first," said Phil. "Lay off."

T-Bone laughed in quiet superiority. "You're already married."

"I'm not planning bigamy," Phil explained. "I merely want to sell him a bar."

"Lord no," said Darrell.

"A fine going concern. Elite clientele, good stock, Arthur Upshaw for a landlord. Name a figure, any figure." He snapped his fingers. "I'll sell like that. Just so it's enough to get me and Flounce here to Honolulu. T-Bone, I tell you, it's wonderful. I got a little shack on the Kailua beach; what with you, me and the badger game, we'll do all right. The finest of fish, home brew, okulehao—"

"Sh," said T-Bone. "Mrs. Phil."

"So what? She knows, she's just waiting." But he looked over his shoulder. He turned back. "You little devil, trying to scare me like that."

"No, here she comes," said T-Bone.

Mrs. Phil came walking with her long slow strut from the kitchen. "You're wanted on the phone," she said gruffly. "It's Grandin, about the invoice."

"Okay, Mama, I'll take it here. 'Scuse me, folks." He ducked under the bar, crossed to the phone booth. Mrs. Phil, with the merest flicker of a glance toward T-Bone, strode back to the kitchen.

"Brrr," said T-Bone, pretending to shiver. "Like an ice cube." She glanced archly sidewise at Darrell. "Why are you looking at me like that?"

"I was wondering."

"About me?"

"Noel sent home a photograph of you and him on a beach."

T-Bone nodded without enthusiasm. She turned away from Darrell, as if the subject bored her.

Phil returned. "I'm gonna get that phone moved out of the kitchen for sure. It scares the customers to have Mama come sneaking in like that, and it scares me."

"She wants to see what's going on," said T-Bone sagely.

"She just likes to parade back and forth," said Phil. "When Mr. Burdette bit at her hook, she got to thinking of herself as a goddess."

T-Bone wrinkled her nose, and ate a cherry.

The glass and iron door from the Balmoral swung open; Arthur Upshaw and Duff came in. Upshaw signaled to Phil; they went to the far end of the bar and conferred earnestly. Duff planted himself beside T-Bone, with a scowling side-glance for Darrell. "Are you ready?"

"Yes," sighed T-Bone. "Where are we going?"

"To Graham's house for a drink."

T-Bone rubbed the tip of her finger in a spot of water on the bar, traced a wet circle.

"You act like you don't want to go," suggested Duff.

"I don't like Graham. He tells dirty jokes."

"We don't need to stay long."

T-Bone slid off the stool. "I've got such a headache, Duff. Really, I can't go anywhere."

"But I've already—"

"Good night, Duff." She turned a wistful smile toward Darrell. "Good night, Mr. Hutson."

"Good night."

T-Bone departed. As she passed into the lobby of the Balmoral, her pace quickened and she ran up the stairs.

Duff swung on his heel and left the bar.

Darrell sat watching Arthur Upshaw and Phil. Upshaw spoke forcefully; he slapped the bar with the tips of his fingers. Phil's face was long and doleful. He argued, protested.

Upshaw made a terse remark, turned away. He strode along the bar to Darrell. "Come over here, Mr. Hutson, if you will. I want to talk to you."

He motioned Darrell into a booth, sat down opposite. "You've been talking to my niece."

"Yes."

"I suppose that she's told you a great deal."

"Just the background of this business."

Upshaw bared his teeth in a swift grimace, fast as the flick of a camera shutter. "She'd do anything to spite me. Do you realize that this whole mess could have been avoided? If she had only come to me when Noel telephoned her."

"Noel telephoned her?"

Upshaw looked at Darrell sharply. "She did not mention this telephone call to you?"

"No."

"What did she tell you?"

"Enough that I understand what's going on."

Upshaw grunted. "I hardly need tell you that I don't want this information shared with French intelligence agents."

"I don't know any French intelligence agents."

"You've just been talking to one."

"Who? Phil?"

"No."

"You don't mean T-Bone?"

Upshaw held up his hand. "She's no undercover agent, but she has friends who are. They explain what they want to know, suggest persons to ask, and pay her if she's successful. I tell you this so that you'll be on your guard."

"But Duff—"

"Exactly. Why else do you think she tolerates him? I've explained this to Duff. His vanity resists the idea; nevertheless, he takes care to hold his tongue."

"Hmm."

"I also urge you not to confide in Beresford. He's careless, he drinks heavily and talks too much. If you make a call from the telephone booth, either he or his wife listens on the kitchen extension. They know more about my business than I do."

Darrell said nothing. Upshaw watched him with impassive eyes.

"There is considerable money at stake in this matter, as you now realize. One man, my former desk clerk, has already died—a futile death, since I'm sure he knew nothing. It might happen again. I suggest that you go home, and leave your brother to fend for himself."

"You hardly expect me to do that, Mr. Upshaw."

Upshaw said in a heavy voice of absolute conviction: "Noel has stolen a valuable consignment. So much is fact. At the worst he'll get only what he deserves."

Darrell restrained his first retort and said simply, "Noel wouldn't touch dope. He just wouldn't do it."

"The fact remains that he did do it. Otherwise, where is he? The French don't have him, nor the Moroccans. There's no one else. He's run off. Decamped."

"An accident—"

"We'd have found the truck. Don't forget, Mr. Hutson, a million dollars can sweeten a man's revulsion for most anything. In this regard, you personally are in a precarious position."

"That's ridiculous. I—"

Upshaw ignored the interruption. "Your brother disappears with a million dollars, is presumably waiting his chance to win free. At this juncture you appear. Personally I believe that you know nothing of Noel's whereabouts, but there are others who don't. I advise you to give me this ridiculous letter and get on home."

"I'll show you the letter—when you tell me what I want to know. Where to look for Noel, what kind of truck he was driving, who he was supposed to meet, who he actually did meet, who knew where and when he was going."

Upshaw swung away without a word. Darrell returned to his seat at the bar, ordered another martini.

Phil served him, his silver-blond hair ruffled, his tie askew. He turned a waspish glance toward Upshaw. "You know this pecking order the chickens work up, where they all got someone lower than themselves they can peck? Well, I'm that poor wild bird at the bottom of the list. They all come flying when they get irritated. Arthur just now says he's raising the rent."

"Raising the rent? I thought he was losing the building."

"He's been haggling with the bank, trying to work something out. In the meantime he's broke and wants me to pay his way. He drives a big Chrysler, Ellen runs that insane black mowing machine. Me, I got a beat-up MG and Arthur thinks I should economize. It's a funny family, I'll tell you that much." He shot a glowering glance across the room.

"Tell me something," said Darrell. "Why does Ellen go around with a chip on her shoulder?"

"Search me. She's been queer ever since Scotty McKinstry got his off Alicante. That was eight years ago, when I first came here. She was a real pretty kid with big eyes and long hair; one of them Alice-in-Wonderland types. They sent her all over to school: England, Switzerland, France. She'd get kicked out just as fast as they enrolled her."

Customers entered; Phil became busy. Mr. Burdette came in with a chesty young matron who spoke in a hoarse growling voice. Arthur Upshaw ordered and ate dinner, interrupted once by Mrs. Phil, who summoned him to the telephone. Then he strode into the Balmoral lobby, looking neither right nor left.

Darrell presently left the Masquerade. He strolled the length of Boulevard Pasteur, dined in a cafeteria, bought a magazine and returned up Calle Miranda. He went up to his room, read for an hour, then tossed away the magazine and lay staring up at the ceiling. Light from the crackling green MASQUERADE shone through the window, enticing him almost against his will.

He went back downstairs, crossed the street, took his usual place at the bar. A few minutes later T-Bone peered cautiously in from the lobby of the Balmoral. Phil beckoned to her. "T-Bone! I thought you was in bed. Where you been?"

T-Bone sauntered over to the bar. "I'm going to bed now. A nice Swedish man telephoned, a Mr. Sverdlup. Do you know him?"

"Can't say as I have that honor."

"He took me to dinner, and I'm so tired. Good evening, Mr. Hutson."

"Good evening."

"Better not let your boy friend catch you out of your pajamas," said Phil. "His feelings might be hurt."

"Oh, that Duff!" T-Bone compressed her sweet mouth. "He's the worst nuisance. Absolutely impossible."

"That's the hazard of your profession."

"My profession?"

"Your main profession. Being beautiful for a living. We're all in love with you. Duff, me, Mr. Burdette, Mr. Hutson, everybody. All of us snapping and snarling and warning each other off."

T-Bone looked pertly at Darrell. "Mr. Hutson isn't in love with me. Are you, Mr. Hutson?"

Phil laughed gleefully. "What can he say? If he says no, he's a liar; if he says yes, he's got to feed you."

T-Bone said with quiet dignity, "He can take me to dinner even if he doesn't love me."

Phil clapped his hand to his forehead. "When will I learn? T-Bone, please don't marry Darrell. He's a civil engineer. He roams the wilderness, with no champagne for miles around. He eats hard-boiled eggs and soda crackers. He sleeps in a tent, usually with a big grizzly bear just outside. His blankets are all too short, and icicles hang from his toes. Right, Darrell?"

"More or less."

"See?" said Phil. "You stick with me, don't go marrying strangers."

JACK VANCE — *DANGEROUS WAYS*

"You're ridiculous, Phil. Darrell asked me to dinner, not to marry him."

Phil looked at Darrell. "Which was it? I don't seem to remember."

"I guess it was just dinner."

Phil nodded. "That was it. I remember now. I'm going to write a book: The Care and Feeding of T-Bone. The first chapter starts: 'To keep her pelt glossy and smooth, take a gallon of the finest cream'—"

"Phil! You clown!"

Phil looked across the room. "Brace yourselves."

Duff came into the bar, wearing flannel slacks, an old tweed hacking coat. His face was mottled, his eyes were round and hard and bright. He ignored Phil and Darrell. "Hello, T-Bone."

"Hello, Duff. I'm just going to bed."

"I thought you were going to bed hours ago."

"I was—but after I took the aspirin I felt better, so I went out."

"Oh? Where did you go?"

"Out to dinner. I was hungry. And now I'm going to bed."

"You could have called me. You had a date with me, remember?"

"But I had the headache! That's why I couldn't go!"

"So you had the headache. So you took the aspirin. So you went out. Why, then—"

"Duff, you get things so mixed up."

"Ha ha. We'll go tomorrow night instead. And—"

"I'm sorry, Duff. I can't. I'm going to dinner with Mr. Hutson."

"What? That be damned. I'm taking you to dinner."

"I've promised, Duff."

"You promised me last night for tonight."

"No, Duff." T-Bone was indignant. "I did no such thing! I said that—"

"Oh, never mind what you said. That's past and done. I'm talking about tomorrow night. Here's Hutson, you can break the date right now."

"Sh, Duff! Don't make a scene."

Phil said, "Duff, if you can't keep your voice down in here, you'd better leave."

"I'm not talking to you, Phil."

"I know you're not, but I hear you. These rows is getting to be an awful drag."

Duff lowered his voice. "All right. I'm talking quietly. But I mean what I say. You can break this engagement with Hutson. I'm sick of Hutson. Everywhere I look, there's Hutson."

"Duff, behave yourself."

"Will you do as I ask?"

"That's not a nice attitude to take," said T-Bone.

"Do you hear me, Hutson? You keep yourself clear. That means anything to do with this young lady."

Phil said, "Be sensible, Duff. Calm down."

"I will after I get this thing settled."

"It's something you can't settle. If T-Bone wants to go out with you, she'll go. If she doesn't want to, you can't bully her into it."

Duff stared at him cold-eyed. "I'll do without your advice. You can mind your own damned business if you please."

"I'm trying to."

Duff looked at Darrell. "Will you be good enough to tell T-Bone you're not taking her to dinner tomorrow night?"

Phil said, "Duff, I'd be careful if I were you. These quiet ones—"

Duff ignored him. "You heard what I said, Hutson. Tell her, if you will."

Darrell heaved a deep sigh. "Let's forget all this. It's like a bad dream. I'm in no mood to play."

Duff viciously sucked in his breath, edged forward. "That's of no matter to me."

"Outside!" cried Phil. "Outside!"

Duff started to the door, turned and waited. "Are you coming, Hutson?"

"Yes. Why not?"

They were followed by the usual crowd of sports-minded tipplers. Phil slipped out from under the bar. "I've got to watch this one myself."

T-Bone remained seated, her head drooping wistfully. Through the open door came sounds of conflict: hisses, grunts, the scuff of shoes on pavement. A muffled thud, louder than the others, then a drier more resonant sound. A brief period of silence. The thuds, bumps, hisses commenced again, somewhat slower in tempo. Then came a bass-drum thump, followed by a crisp wood-block effect. Again the silence. The noises recommenced, now rather deliberate. *Thump! Click! Bump!* Silence, quite profound.

Phil returned inside the bar. Shaking his head, he ducked under the counter. "I warned him. He sure got warned."

The tipplers returned to their stations; the Masquerade Bar sounded again: inconsequential chatter, the cheerful clink of bottle against glass. Darrell came unobtrusively back to his place. "I had a rather irritating day, I guess I took it out on Duff."

"Don't mention it. It's not your fault. Hell, it's not even Duff's fault. It's Miss Sizzlebritches here. She's been using Duff like a yo-yo, until the poor jerk is walking backwards."

"Phil, stop being so foolish. I'm going to bed. Really, this time." T-Bone gave her silky chestnut hair an indignant toss. She paused, turned rather hesitantly to Darrell. "Do you really want to take me to dinner?"

Behind the bar Phil croaked derisively. Darrell said, "Oh, yes. Certainly."

"About eight then?"

"Very well, eight o'clock."

T-Bone smiled briefly, departed into the lobby of the Balmoral. They heard her heels clicking up the marble steps.

"That's how it's done," said Phil. "That girl will never go hungry."

"Does she have any income at all?"

Phil wiped the bar industriously. "That's a matter of conjecture. I guess there's money seeping from somewhere: alimony, back taxes, blackmail. She makes a dollar here, a dollar there... She got one of her boy friends to buy a Jaguar; Mr. Burdette gave her a salesman's commission. Once in a while she sells a little dirt to her newspaper cronies. She models clothes once or twice a week. One way or another she makes out."

Darrell heaved a deep sigh. "Well, I'm off to bed too. Tomorrow..."

"Tomorrow what?"

"I don't know. I've come to a dead halt."

But as Darrell left the bar a familiar figure moved out of a shadowed doorway. "Mr. Hutson!"

"Well?"

"I saw you fight Mr. Mekkinesser. You pretty good fighter." Slip-Slip performed a series of rather inept feints and jabs. "Please don't never fight me."

Darrell turned to continue across the street but Slip-Slip protested. "Mr. Hutson, wait! Don't you want to know about Noel?"

"Have you found out anything?"

Slip-Slip nodded with solemn emphasis. "I talk to a man. Tomorrow morning he come to see you. Okay?"

"Okay," said Darrell. "Who is this man?"

"He's a good man. Maybe he knows something."

Darrell felt no large optimism. "Very well. I'll talk to him tomorrow."

"How much money you give?"

Darrell looked at him without friendliness. "How much money for what?"

"I work for you, I talk to this man."

"If I get any news of Noel you'll be paid. Well paid. You come see me later."

Slip-Slip smiled impishly. "Maybe better you give me money now."

"No. You see me tomorrow."

"You think I lie? You think the man don't come?"

"If I learn anything about Noel, you'll be paid."

Slip-Slip's grin faded slowly, like an afterglow.

Darrell asked, "What time does the man come?"

"In the morning. Early. Nine o'clock."

"Why haven't you told Mr. Upshaw about this man?"

"I don't understand, Mr. Hutson."

Darrell repeated the question.

Slip-Slip's face showed dubious comprehension. "They don't like me. They chase me off the boat. They think I'm bad guy. I'm not bad guy. I'm good guy. I work for you."

"That remains to be seen," said Darrell. "Well—at nine o'clock tomorrow."

"That's right. The man come to see you."

AT NINE THE NEXT morning the man came indeed: a thin Moroccan in a gray gabardine djellaba, a man with a shrewd tight face, a curious thin wedge of a nose. He looked into the lobby, saw Darrell, beckoned.

Darrell went out into the street. It was a beautiful morning, clear and cool, with sunlight pouring through the acacia trees. Darrell went to where the man stood beside the sun-burnt stucco wall of the hotel, watching with hard clever brown eyes. "Your name is Darrell Hutson?" He spoke English with the hard quick local accent.

"Yes."

"You looking for Noel Hutson?"

"Yes."

"You come with me." The Moroccan made a quick motion, started to walk away.

"Just a minute. Come back here."

The Moroccan stopped, motioned; then returned.

"We can talk here," said Darrell.

"No." The Moroccan shook his head decisively. "We go to Fez."

"To Fez! What for?"

"To see Jilali."

"Who is Jilali?"

"He is very important man. I take you to see him."

"Does Jilali know what's happened to Noel?"

"I take you, you ask him."

Darrell thought of Mohammed Ali Aktouf and his unpleasant death. Still, why should this happen to him? He had no irons in the fire; he knew nothing of guns or narcotics; he had no enemies among the Moroccans. On the other hand, what could Jilali tell him in Fez that could not be told here? Also, if someone had knowledge of Noel, why had they not taken it to Arthur Upshaw, who would pay at least as handsomely as Darrell?

There might be sensible answers to the questions, but Darrell could think of none. Which, of course, did not mean that answers did not exist. The essence of the matter was, that if he accompanied this hard-faced Moroccan to Fez, he was submitting himself to circumstances beyond his control, a process at which his instincts rebelled. Still, there it was; the only remaining possibility of learning something about Noel's disappearance. Take it or leave it.

He could take it—but also take precautions. He approached the Moroccan. "Let me see your identity card."

The man stared at him in silence, then brought out his card. The photograph was correct, the name read: Abd Allah el Kazim.

Darrell copied the name and the number of the card on the back of an envelope. "How are we going?"

Abd Allah el Kazim beckoned him to a small dusty Citroën. He entered, motioned Darrell toward the opposite side. "Just a minute," said Darrell. He made a note of the license number, returned to the hotel.

He went to the desk clerk, displayed the envelope. "See this number? It's the license of a car, a Citroën. I'm going to Fez with this man, Abd Allah el Kazim. This is the number of his identity card. If I'm not back here tomorrow take this to the police. Do you understand?"

The clerk dubiously accepted the envelope. Darrell made sure that his instructions were understood, and returned outside, half-expecting the Citroën to be gone.

But it had not moved. Darrell climbed in; el Kazim wordlessly started the motor. They rolled down Calle Miranda, turned up the hill, joined the coast highway, and presently left Tangier behind.

Chapter VIII

ABD Allah el Kazim drove hunched forward, chin almost resting on the wheel. Hostility was implicit in his silence. Evidence of baneful intent? Or the opposite? If he and Jilali meant harm, would they not take greater pains to hide their animosity? So Darrell reasoned, without conviction. Now that he was underway, he thought of a dozen precautions he should have taken: a visit to the police station, the company of a third party, insistence on learning more details before leaving Tangier. Well, the die was cast. Confound that cursed Noel.

Between Tangier and Fez lay three hundred kilometers, one hundred and ninety miles. El Kazim drove with the speedometer needle wavering between 80 and 90 kilometers per hour. They should arrive in Fez during the early afternoon.

They passed across a landscape of rolling hills, green with spring grass, patched with flowers. Here and there Moroccans cultivated fields using camels teamed with donkeys: a strange sight. Occasionally they passed a dingy village consisting of a gas pump, a fruit stand, a French-owned café, a huddle of mud huts.

El Kazim finally broke the silence. "You have never been to Fez?"

"No. This is my first visit to Morocco."

"Fez is a very old city, a holy city. Very interesting."

"So I should imagine."

They passed through another squalid village; el Kazim gestured toward the mud hovels. "You think the people are poor?"

"They seem to be."

"That is the fault of the French. They own everything in Morocco. They are everywhere, like ants, and carry everything away."

Darrell made no comment.

"There is much wealth in Morocco," said el Kazim, "but the people are poor. I tell you something very few Americans know; some day North Africa is rich!"

"I hope so," said Darrell. "I dislike poverty."

"But you do nothing to help us! You give the French money to buy guns; you help them kill the Moslems."

"That's not the intention," said Darrell. "We've also sent aid to Morocco."

"Do you know what the Russians will do for us? They are planning to help us, like brothers. They will make good water from the sea and build a great pipeline to take it into the middle of the Sahara. There will be a great lake, everything will be changed!"

Darrell laughed. "You don't believe that, do you? The project isn't possible."

El Kazim smiled thinly. "You would naturally say that."

"Yes. Because I'm a civil engineer. The plan is not practical. There's no basin for a Sahara lake in the first place. In the second no one knows how to remove salt from sea-water in the quantity necessary for such a lake."

El Kazim sniffed. Presently he asked, "What do Americans think of the Pan-Arab Union?"

"I suppose we feel it's the business of the countries involved," said Darrell.

"Then why do you help the French?"

Darrell laughed. "The French ask, 'Why do you help the Arabs?' It's like most human problems, rights and wrongs on both sides. I don't know the solution."

"When the French are pushed into the sea: that is the solution," said el Kazim grimly.

"If you can make it stick."

"The French can't resist the Moslem people. All North Africa will be Pan-Arab soon. Much sooner than you think. Nasser will do this. He is a great man! He is our George Washington!"

From the Moslem point of view, the analogy was by no means absurd, thought Darrell.

"What do you think?" challenged el Kazim. "Do you believe the French should own Algeria, that they should be rich while we are poor?"

Darrell hesitated. "Eventually I suppose all the states of the world will be organized into great territorial federations; I suppose in principle I'm in favor of the Pan-Arab Union. Although I can't say I care much for Nasser."

"Because he is a Moslem who spits in the Westerner's face."

"It's an unpleasant habit," Darrell remarked.

El Kazim made no reply; the conversation languished. The countryside became dry and harsh, the hills bleak. Eucalyptus occasionally lined the road; spiky white asphodel grew thick on the rocky slopes. They came to a junction: Rabat and Casablanca to the right, Meknes and Fez to the left. Without hesitation el Kazim swung left. The kilometer markers fell behind, the road looped up and over the low hills. Shortly after noon they reached Meknes, but passed through seeing no more than the main street of the French town. Leaving Meknes the road turned sharply northeast, and seemed to rise on a long slow slant. Far ahead a gray mass loomed along the horizon, the Atlas. They passed a kilometer marker, FEZ *60*. Darrell calculated. Sixty kilometers, thirty-seven miles. An hour's drive.

The landscape was dull and ugly, the engine buzzed hypnotically, the hour passed swiftly. They entered the outskirts of Fez—small wind-softened houses of mud, commercial buildings of brick and corrugated metal. The road branched; el Kazim bore to the left, and the road became an alley, winding and bumping around the hillside, which appeared to be a great disheveled cemetery. To his right Darrell glimpsed the city, dust-colored, intricate as the cross section of a beehive, then a mud wall cut off his view. The road widened into a square, thronging with men, women, children, in djellabas rich and ragged, of white, off-white, drab, brown and gray; donkeys staggering under cruel loads; gaunt dogs. The square ended at a forty-foot wall pierced by an arched portal; here sat a row of beggars. El Kazim parked the car, jumped nimbly out. Darrell followed more slowly. "Where do we go now?"

"This is Bab Boujeloud. Bab means gate. It is the entrance to the medina. You come with me."

They passed through Bab Boujeloud into a narrow street. The crowd paid them no attention. The passage was paved with cobblestones, slippery where water trickled across, constricted by tall mudbrick walls. It wound, forked, joined, jerked aside in erratic doglegs, widened, narrowed, ducked under beamed archways. El Kazim turned right, left, right, left, left, left, right, apparently at random. They passed heavy doors of carved wood, blue-tiled fountains, small dark workshops. An irregular bar of blue sky followed overhead, and sometimes there was a glimpse of the sun. Occasionally the passage became a dark tunnel, thirty, forty or fifty feet long. Darrell became lost at once; the city was without pattern or form. Then, after twisting along a runway hardly wide enough for two persons to pass abreast, they emerged into a broad avenue. El Kazim turned through a gate; they stood in a large public garden planted with cypress, orange and lemon trees, rose bushes in full flower, privet hedges, banks of heliotrope and verbena, violets and pansies. A large colonnaded building of buff sandstone surrounded the garden on three sides. Moslems, as well as men and women in European clothes, strolled through the garden, passing into the rooms behind the colonnade.

Darrell looked about in puzzlement. "What are we doing here?"

"This is the Dar Batha. It is an old palace, now it is a museum. Come. I show you some interesting things."

Darrell asked, "Is this where we meet your friend?"

"He is not here. It is not time to see him. We go to the museum."

Darrell turned away, looked across the garden. Nothing, he thought, makes a person appear more foolish than helpless anger; to express his exasperation would only prompt el Kazim to amusement. "Very well," said Darrell with formal politeness. "If you wish to look at the museum, we shall do so."

"It is not for me," said el Kazim sharply. "It is for you!"

Darrell made a courteous gesture, implying that el Kazim should feel free to enjoy himself at his leisure. El Kazim's mouth compressed, his eyes shone. "Come," he said. "I show you some things."

In one of the halls hung an exhibition of contemporary Moroccan oil painting. Darrell, who had no particular interest in such matters, glanced around with perfunctory attention. So far as he could judge, the paintings seemed competently executed, after one or another of the conventional modern fashions.

El Kazim, however, was more enthusiastic. He walked here and there, looking from the paintings to Darrell, with eyes shining. "What do you think?" he demanded. "Are these not good?"

"They certainly seem to be," said Darrell.

"You see, we know these things as well as you," said el Kazim. "We are not ignorant natives!"

"I never imagined that you were," said Darrell.

"We look at other things," said el Kazim. He led the way through an armory displaying hundreds of Berber muskets, with short curved stocks and freakish long barrels. Another rack held daggers, stilettos, poniards, cutlasses—rows of shining steel blades, murderous points, symbols of hate and death.

El Kazim led Darrell into another chamber, this hung with ancient rugs and the brocaded robes of long-dead grandees. The center of the room was occupied by a cage, about three feet on a side, framed with heavy timbers, grilled with iron bars three-quarters of an inch in diameter. El Kazim seemed to find the cage interesting. He walked around it, peering into the cramped interior. "Look!" He pointed to a card. "Read!"

Darrell confessed his inability. "It's in French."

"It says that the cage was used in 1909 by the Sultan. He put a rebel inside until he died. Not nice, yes?"

"No. Not at all nice."

El Kazim laughed shortly, nodded in profound thought. He led Darrell into a room housing a collection of nondescript pottery. Darrell made not even the pretense of inspecting it.

El Kazim turned him a series of quick sardonic glances, then said, "Let's go see Jilali."

Once again they plunged into the fantastic complexity of the medina. They walked for twenty minutes, el Kazim never faltering, never pausing at a turning. It seemed impossible that he could know where he was going. Each corner was like every other; every passage and alley seemed identical to the one they had left. They passed through the spice market: a row of shops displaying in shallow bins heaps of paprika, nutmeg, saffron, cumin, pepper, turmeric. The colors burnt rich as paint pigments: ocher, vermilion, raw sienna, umber, cadmium orange, chrome yellow.

El Kazim struck off into a warren of dark winding passages smelling of carrion and ammonia, unpopulated except for anonymous huddles of rags, bone and gristle. He stopped beside a particularly scabrous wall, pounded on a heavy timber door.

The door was opened; an old woman peered out. El Kazim motioned, Darrell stepped into a small garden. Lemon trees clipped into perfect globes circled a fountain which sent up a dozen thin jets of water. Four identical cypresses marked the corners of a square, each cypress surrounded by a bed of violets. Pomegranates grew against the wall, roses climbed the columns of an arcade at the back of the garden.

The old woman retreated to the arcade, backed through a door. El Kazim motioned Darrell to follow. They entered a hall paved with elaborately patterned tiles. A door opened; a pale handsome man with striking black eyebrows, wearing a neat dark blue suit, bowed, moved politely back.

Darrell obeyed the implicit invitation, entered the room. El Kazim came behind him.

"This is Moulay Aziz ben Jilali," said el Kazim. "This is Mr. Hutson. Be seated, please."

Darrell looked from one man to the other. In Jilali's house, did el Kazim issue the orders? He settled himself gingerly on a low divan. A handsome red rug covered the floor; on the wall opposite hung a portrait of Gamal Abdel Nasser.

Jilali and el Kazim established themselves on a divan across the room. No one spoke. There was a long moment of silence.

Darrell stirred impatiently. "Mr. Jilali, I understand that you can give me news of my brother Noel."

Jilali made an uninterested gesture. "We will talk business soon. There is time. Did you enjoy your ride?"

"Very much. Morocco is an interesting country."

"Morocco is a great country," said Jilali.

The old woman hobbled in with a teapot, a bowl of sugar and three cups on a brass tray. There was further delay while the tea was poured. Through a window Darrell could look out over the garden. There was no sound but the splash of the fountain.

Jilali spoke in a mild almost apologetic voice. "There are many such gardens in Fez. A man walking through the streets never knows what is behind the walls. Here in his house a man is truly a king."

Darrell drank his tea thoughtfully. An ominous hint? He had committed no offense against these people; they had no reason to wish him harm. And was not the Moslem code of hospitality extremely rigid, especially if the guest had broken bread? Still—they had served no bread.

"Fez is the oldest of the imperial cities," said Jilali. "It is one of the holy cities of Islam; students from everywhere come to study the Koran. Did el Kazim show you a *medersa*? A *medersa* is a college."

"No. We looked at other things."

Jilali nodded languidly. "Perhaps you will have another chance." He put down his cup. "It is good of you to come here."

"I am anxious to find my brother."

El Kazim spoke in Arabic; Jilali lazily put his hands behind his head, leaned back on the divan. "Good, we will talk."

"This is what we can tell you," said el Kazim rapidly. "Noel Hutson drove a truck with guns to a supply center for the Algerian National Army. It was the first of fourteen deliveries. By mistake he was given payment for the entire shipment, over forty tons of weapons. Returning to Tangier he met a group of French soldiers. Noel drove away from them. He feared capture, and hid the payment for the guns. But he was captured soon after. The French are cruel when they suspect that someone works to help make Algeria free. They beat Noel. He told them nothing. They put him in a cage— like the one you saw at the Dar Batha."

Darrell raised his eyebrows. "Strange that I should see just such a cage today."

El Kazim continued in a flat voice. "There is a man among the French who we pay. He told us they have Noel. We said, make him loose! No, he can not do that; it is a great risk. Not unless we pay much money. Too bad! We do not have the money. All our money is gone. If we find where Noel hid the payment, then we have much money, and Noel would go free."

Darrell leaned back, smiling bitterly. "You don't credit me with much intelligence."

El Kazim looked a trifle puzzled.

Jilali made a lazy remark in Arabic, and el Kazim turned back to Darrell. "You understand?" he asked sharply. "First we find the payment, then Noel is free from the French."

Either they take me for a fool, thought Darrell, or they think they're showing me the escape hatch, a way to save face. "I find it hard to believe that the French put Noel in a cage."

"No, no," said el Kazim vehemently. "They are cruel! It is never said in the newspapers what the French do."

Jilali sat up. He reached in his pocket, brought forth a photograph which he thrust at Darrell.

"This is the picture our friend made," said el Kazim in a formal voice. "It shows Noel in the cage."

Darrell studied the photograph. It undoubtedly depicted a man crouched within a cage, and the man's head was certainly that of Noel. Darrell examined the picture so carefully that Jilali became impatient and held out his hand. Darrell returned the picture. "I'm afraid your friend is deceiving you."

"What do you say?" asked el Kazim in a sharp voice.

"The picture is a fake."

Jilali and el Kazim stared at him: Jilali in reproach, el Kazim in waspish irritation.

"It is a photograph," said Jilali. "Is it not Noel?"

"Oh, it's Noel all right. And that's certainly a cage. But notice the shadows on the left side of Noel's face. The cage was photographed by flash from the front. Noel's face shows through the bars. Are they made of glass? Why is Noel smiling so happily? Because he feels secure?"

Jilali frowned down at the picture. El Kazim looked at Darrell with a hard smile. "Sometimes it is wrong to be too clever. The picture is not important. What you must do is tell us how to find the narcotic. Where is it?"

"I have no idea."

"You had a letter from your brother. This is our information. He must have told you."

"He told me nothing of the sort."

"It is very serious, Mr. Hutson. You realize?"

"Gentlemen, let's be reasonable." Darrell hitched himself forward on the divan. "I know you want to see the letter that Noel wrote home. I'm willing to show it to you in exchange for some information; in fact, that's the only reason I came to Fez, to make this exchange with you."

Jilali nodded thoughtfully and started to speak, but el Kazim thrust his arm out sharply. "So that you can help Noel escape with the narcotic!"

"No," said Darrell patiently. "Definitely not. I want nothing to do with it." He looked from el Kazim to Jilali. "Now—all this talk about cages aside—can you tell me anything about Noel? Is he alive or is he dead?"

El Kazim waited until Darrell had finished, the hostility now shining frankly and unpleasantly from his face. "We must ask about this letter. You have it with you?"

"No. It doesn't mention your heroin. If it did, I'd have turned it over to the police."

"Ah! Ah! Ah!" El Kazim leaned forward triumphantly. "Then you are against us!"

"I'm neither against you nor for you. I'm against traffic in narcotics."

"Then why have you and Noel made arrangement to sell the heroin?"

Darrell sighed, barely able to restrain his disgust. "You make everything so complicated. Believe me, I know nothing, care nothing for your business. If you can give me news of my brother, please do so; otherwise, I'd like to go back to Tangier."

Jilali spoke in Arabic, el Kazim nodded. He turned back to Darrell. "You are right, there is no need to be angry. Show us this letter, and we will take you to Tangier."

"If you'll tell me what you know of Noel."

"He has disappeared with our property; that is all we know. We wish to find him."

"But where did he disappear from? Who saw him last? Did he leave any message?"

El Kazim shook his head. "We can not tell these things. Perhaps you will tell the French..."

"No. I only want to find Noel and return to the States."

"Impossible. And now—"

Darrell struggled to keep his voice even. "You've brought me down here for nothing!"

"And now—the letter, please."

"I don't have it here. In any event it's a personal letter; it contains nothing to help you."

"I'm sorry, Mr. Hutson, we can not take your word for this. Will you stand up? I will search your pockets."

Darrell felt his muscles turn to stone.

El Kazim's voice came smoothly. "Please do not make trouble, Mr. Hutson. Please stand up. I do not want to call the servants. It is much easier if you help."

Darrell looked from one to the other. Jilali raised his fine black eyebrows in deprecation; el Kazim, grinning like a fox, stepped forward.

Burning with humiliation, furious with himself, but unwilling to make an issue of an inconsequentiality, Darrell rose to his feet. El Kazim patted his pockets, extracted his wallet, his passport, a few miscellaneous odds and ends. Jilali watched, mouth drooping in annoyance.

"Where is the letter?" asked el Kazim. "In your hotel?"

"No."

Jilali uttered a terse sentence in Arabic; el Kazim sat back. "I must explain this carefully, so you will see exactly how important is this letter. Please sit down."

Darrell resumed his seat on the divan.

"There is a large shipment of weapons at Tangier. It is ours. We sent the heroin to pay for it. No, do not look in disgust. The heroin will be sold in Paris. Is that not justice? That the French who try to make slaves of us should pay for our guns? No matter. We do not care for right or wrong. We have one truckload of the weapons.

We cannot have the others until we pay for them. But this is now impossible. The heroin comes across the desert from Egypt, a long way, very dangerous, very expensive. A million dollars, it is worth so much. I am what you call the purchase agent; the heroin is in my charge, and they say it is my blame. I do not want the blame. So you help us, and there is no blame. Even if you do not want to help us, you must. I have explained that this is very serious. Do you understand?"

"Yes. I understand."

"Where is the letter?"

"It is in the mail."

"The post office? You put it in the post?"

"Yes."

Jilali spoke in Arabic; el Kazim responded, then turned back to Darrell. "Where did you send this letter?"

Darrell weighed his answer. It would be simple to tell them an untruth; they could not disprove it. He thought of Aktouf, the desk clerk. Let them have the letter, which after all could tell them nothing. It was folly to make himself trouble merely because he resented coercion.

El Kazim and Jilali watched him keenly.

"I mailed the letter to myself," said Darrell. "Care of American Express."

"In Tangier?"

"Yes, in Tangier."

"Good," said el Kazim. Jilali clapped his hands; a sour-faced Negro servant appeared. Jilali gave orders.

"You will write to American Express," said el Kazim. "You must tell them to give your letter to the man who brings your passport. Then you must wait here till I get the letter."

Darrell sat still. The request followed from what had gone before; but enough was enough. Too much. He rose to his feet, leaned forward, took the passport. "I'll show you the letter. But I'll keep my own passport."

Jilali's raven-wing eyebrows rose, his mouth drooped in distress. El Kazim, however, smiled. "Please, Mr. Hutson, do not make trouble. This will be done as we think best."

"You take me back to Tangier; tomorrow I'll get you the letter. You have my word on that. I don't see any reason why I should stay here."

Jilali spoke in Arabic, apparently a counsel of moderation; el Kazim remonstrated, gesticulating with his fingers. Jilali shrugged.

"I am sorry," said el Kazim. "Perhaps you will change your mind. It is better that you write the letter."

Darrell turned, walked from the room, started down the hall. Behind him came el Kazim's voice, "If you go into the garden I will shoot you."

Darrell stopped short, looked back. El Kazim held an automatic pistol aimed at his middle. He spoke through a tight smile. "Come back, please."

Darrell slowly returned, feeling rather more comfortable. The situation was less damaging to his self-respect; he was submitting not to browbeating, but to the universal language of the bullet. El Kazim, by the same token, had become angry; he had enjoyed humiliating the American; he had relished the understated menaces and silken hints. Now he had become secondary to the gun.

He motioned Darrell back toward the divan. Jilali had not moved, and watched with resignation as el Kazim prodded Darrell with the gun. "Please sit." He thrust forward paper and a ball-point pen. "Write: 'Please give all my letters to the man who shows you my passport.' Sign it."

Darrell wrote. El Kazim took the letter, scrutinized it carefully. "Your passport."

Darrell wordlessly handed it over.

"Thank you. Now, please stand up."

Jilali spoke in Arabic; el Kazim responded emphatically. Darrell looked from one to the other. Jilali seemed to have nominal authority, but el Kazim, exerting greater energy, set the mood of the situation. El Kazim had the last word; Jilali gave a sour-faced shrug. El Kazim waved the gun. "Go to the door, turn to the right, walk to the far end of the hall."

Darrell did as instructed, walking until a door of heavy planks barred the way.

"Open the door."

Darrell pushed the door open.

"Go in."

Darrell entered a large dim room smelling of straw and damp wood, evidently at one time a stable. Massive plank doors on iron hinges hung on the wall opposite; a pair of high windows admitted late-afternoon light through panes clouded with dust and spider webs.

The room now served other purposes than the shelter of donkeys. In the center of the straw-littered floor was a cage, almost identical to the one Darrell had seen in the museum.

He stared at it. At his back el Kazim said in a voice which had regained its fluency, "We have no nice way to keep you safe. So we will put you in the cage for tonight. Tomorrow, if all goes well, you will be allowed to go free."

Darrell slowly turned, stared into el Kazim's hard brown eyes. In the gloating, the triumph, the unreasoning malice, he saw the new face of the East; he knew that he was making atonement for centuries of enforced obsequiousness. "You force me to take sides," said Darrell. "I'm sure now that I don't care for the Pan-Arab Union."

"What you care makes no difference. We will cleanse Africa; we will drive you into the sea. You think you are better than we are, with your pink bellies and painted women. You are rich and fat and weak; we are poor and strong. We shall see who wins. Into the cage."

Darrell looked at the cage. It was no larger than a dog kennel. The top was hinged back; el Kazim evidently intended that he should step inside and crouch. El Kazim then would slam down the lid.

El Kazim said, "If you don't enter the cage—" he reached to the floor, picked up a loose coil of rope "—I will call the servant and he will tie you. Hurry!"

"This is simply fantastic," muttered Darrell. "Do you think you can—"

"Into the cage! Or do you prefer the rope!"

Darrell stifled the useless words which rose to his tongue, along with his pride. He went sideways to the cage, hoping that el Kazim would offer him a chance to seize the gun. But el Kazim stood well away.

He raised a leg, straddled the side of the cage. El Kazim came a step closer. Darrell slowly drew his other leg over.

"Down," rasped el Kazim throatily.

Darrell slowly lowered himself. El Kazim's expression sickened him. It would mean real danger to thwart him in his present excitement. He squatted on his haunches. El Kazim approached with long elastic strides, slammed down the lid to the cage. Darrell ducked. The impact vibrated the bars, rang through his head. The padlock clicked. El Kazim backed away, tucking the gun into his pocket.

"You thought the picture of your brother in the cage was false? So it was. If he were in the cage he would not be smiling."

"Where is Noel?" asked Darrell, as if the question had only just occurred to him.

El Kazim grinned. "I do not know. But we will find him. Do you know something? He killed my brother; it is right that you should suffer something. Be thankful that I do not shoot you. Be thankful that the cage is all you suffer!"

Darrell said nothing. El Kazim watched him another ten seconds, then went to the door. He turned for one last look, then departed. The door slammed shut; Darrell was alone, hunched in the cage, arms across his knees. He blew out his breath in enormous annoyance. "This is incredible... Noel, wherever you are, I'd be very happy if you were here instead of me."

He changed his position, leaned back against the bars, knees spraddled to the side. He looked at his watch. Six o'clock. When Noel learned of this, he would laugh with vast merriment. Everyone else would laugh too. Noel calls for succor, Darrell comes gallantly to the rescue, and is clapped into a cage... Where the devil was Noel? Paris? The Riviera? Capri? Darrell's assurance wavered. Everyone else might be right and he wrong. Perhaps Noel indeed had fled with the loot. And meanwhile Darrell crouched in a cage... He looked at his watch again. One minute after six. It would be a long night.

Chapter IX

DARRELL shifted his position several times. For the twentieth time he looked at his watch. Seventeen minutes had passed. Fury rose up in him, choking in his throat, like vomit. He gave a faint hoarse cry of passion, then, instantly ashamed, crouched back against the bars. Was there no way he could free himself from this damnable cage?

He pulled at one of the bars. It was soft wrought iron, about three-quarters of an inch in diameter, and gave a fraction of an inch under the strain. He pulled with every ounce he could muster, but the bar, fixed at top and bottom in the timber frame, only quivered. Darrell relaxed. Nineteen minutes had passed.

Perhaps el Kazim would sleep in Fez tonight, and not make the journey to Tangier until tomorrow, which meant an additional twelve hours in the cage. Darrell's detestation for Abd Allah el Kazim surpassed any emotion he had previously felt. He took hold of a bar once more, tugged till his throat corded. He doubled himself up, pushed with his feet. The bar gave slightly, until its tensile strength resisted further bending.

He examined the timber above and below. It was weathered and old and possibly a little rotten, but proof against any exertion of his muscles. He thought of the tools accessible at home: hydraulic jacks, air chisels, bolt cutters, oxyacetylene torches. Even with a hacksaw, a keyhole saw, any variety of saw, he could work himself free. In the dusty light seeping through the windows he searched the room. Since el Kazim and Jilali were not fools, they would leave no useful implement within his reach. As he expected, the stable offered him no assistance. A heap of firewood occupied one corner; rotting straps, blankets and donkey harness hung from pegs. A few odds and ends were visible—bottles, boxes, a threadbare automobile tire, the coil of rope with which el Kazim had offered to tie him, a stack of cracked dishes. Darrell's eyes fixed on the rope. A resourceful man could accomplish marvels with a length of rope. But he could not reach across the twenty feet intervening.

Darrell considered. He could tear his shirt into strips, knot the strips together, tie his shoe to the end, cast and drag the rope to him. Feasible, but perhaps there was another method which would spare him his shirt. He tried to rock the cage. It was very heavy; with his utmost exertion he could do little more than jar it. He rearranged himself within the cage, worked his foot through the hole in the floor. He put his back under the top of the cage. Heave, thrust. The cage raised, slid an inch; the edge of the hole banged against his ankle. Heave, thrust. Two inches... Ten minutes later Darrell obtained possession of the rope. The light was fading fast, and Darrell worked with all haste. He made a loop, cast it at the pile of firewood, and after several attempts managed to drag over a stout stick something over a foot long. "Now we shall see," thought Darrell. An engineering degree, plus six years of hard work and a certain amount of ordinary horse sense, should prove of some advantage.

But he hesitated, looking toward the door. Suppose el Kazim came to inspect him before leaving for Fez? Suppose the servant brought food? They would notice that the cage had been moved; they would investigate and take away the rope. Cursing and sweating, Darrell worked his foot through the hole, humped the cage inch by inch back across the floor to its original position.

He rested, easing the strain in his back, massaging his bruised ankle. He listened: no sound. He could wait until dark or try now... He lacked the patience to wait; it would have to be now.

He selected a bar on one side of the cage. He took the end of the rope around it, back through and across the cage, around three bars opposite, then back across, around the original bar, making a triangular circuit. He repeated the process four times, drew the rope tight, tied a knot. He inserted the stick into the triangle, between the two sets of strands, began to twist. Around and around. The ropes tightened; turning became hard. The bar bent, pulled inward. Darrell unwound the rope, took in the slack, and for greater margin of strength, added two more circuits. He started winding again. The bar bent, the timber creaked. The winding became difficult. Darrell loosened, took in the slack, began twisting again. The tension became very great; Darrell turned slowly, cautiously. There was a sharp snap of splitting wood, the twisting came suddenly easy; he had pulled the top end of the bar through the timber.

"One down," said Darrell. "Two, or possibly three to go."

Hurriedly he untied his rope, repeated the process on the next bar; this came more easily, for the timber had been split. A third bar and a fourth; and now by dint of twisting, bending, pulling, he made a gap large enough to crawl through.

He rose to his feet, stretched his cramped muscles. So much for the cage. Now to leave the house. He went to the doors which communicated with the street; they were barred, solid as the walls. In the gray dusk he could see a pair of enormous iron locks. He went to the door through which he had entered. This was also locked, but seemed less substantial than the outer doors.

He put his ear to the keyhole and seemed to hear a faint murmur of voices. He could not force the door without attracting attention.

He looked up at the windows. No great problem here. He dragged the cage under the window. It made a soft scraping sound which Darrell hoped could not be heard outside the room. Then boxes: two small ones side by side, a larger one on top. Darrell gingerly climbed on top, explored for the window hardware. It was nonexistent; the windows were set solidly into the wall.

He jumped down, folded an old blanket, tossed it to the top of his makeshift ladder. He tied one end of the rope to the cage, clambered back up, carried the coil to the wide mud windowsill.

Now he was ready. He peered through the window, unsuccessfully trying to look down into the street. There was no reason to hesitate. He raised the folded blanket, held it against the pane, struck it with his fist. Glass tinkled, clattered below.

Darrell removed the blanket, put his head out. He looked into a passage only fifty feet long, quite deserted. He pushed the rest of the glass into the street, laid the blanket over the sash, threw out the rope. Then, crawling after the rope, he lowered himself to the street.

He stretched his arms, laughing in exultation. His ankle throbbed, his back ached, but these were minor considerations. He was free. Now, to find his way out of the maze. He had not the remotest notion of his location, or the distance to the nearest gate. On his way in he had seen nothing like a main street or thoroughfare, nothing but the incredible capillary system of passages and alleys.

He felt in his pockets and found about a thousand francs in loose change. Enough to hire a guide. El Kazim had mentioned the name of the gate by which they had entered: Bab Bou—something. Bab meant gate, which might be enough.

He set forth along passages now dimly illuminated with bare bulbs. Few people were abroad, and these looked at him suspiciously. Somewhere he had read that Christians were unwelcome in Moslem cities after sunset. If this were true, it could not be helped, and he was quite willing to leave. He passed a thin-faced boy of sixteen, stopped him, pointed to himself, then away. "Bab? You take me to bab?" He reached in his pocket, brought out two hundred francs. "I want to go to the bab."

The boy backed away, rubbing his nose in puzzlement.

"Bab." Darrell pointed in various directions. "Bab?"

The boy smiled with the easy superiority of the metropolitan for the rustic. He pointed. "Bab Ftouh." He pointed in another direction. "Bab Boujeloud."

Darrell nodded. "Bab Boujeloud." He took the boy's arm. "Come. Bab Boujeloud. You show me. Two hundred francs."

The boy at last comprehended the nature of Darrell's requirements, and became full of an excited officiousness, running ahead, gesturing. Darrell saw that he had selected a half-wit for his guide. "The blind leading the blind," he told himself. "Lead on, I'm not proud, so long as we arrive."

With the boy prancing and skipping ahead, Darrell plodded back through the warren of the Fez medina. The boy was not content merely to lead; he felt it necessary to assure Darrell that they were approaching their destination, beckoning, pointing, hopping backwards. When they came to the more populous streets Darrell began to feel conspicuous. The boy felt only pride in his occupation. Darrell doggedly marched after him, and at last was rewarded by the sight of the massive wall, the tall pointed-arch gate.

The boy led him to the opening, took the two hundred francs and departed. Darrell walked out into the open area, past the spot where el Kazim had parked the Citroën. The place was now vacant. Evidently el Kazim was on his way to Tangier.

Fifty yards beyond he found a taxi stand. He went to the first in line. *"Taxi, monsieur?"* called the driver.

"Yes," said Darrell. "I want to go to Tangier."

"Tangier?" the driver asked in mingled doubt and suspicion. *"Beaucoup d'argent, monsieur."*

"I expect so," said Darrell. He opened the door, flung himself wearily into the seat. "Nevertheless—Tangier."

The driver scrutinized him over the back of the seat. An American, hence a millionaire, either mad or drunk. "Tangier, *monsieur?"*

"Tangier."

The driver shrugged: a fare was a fare. He got out of the cab, spoke to one of his fellows, then returned. He started the motor, swung around and set forth.

———•———

SOMETIME AFTER MIDNIGHT THE cab swung over the hill and down into the bright amphitheater of Tangier. Darrell roused himself, directed the driver to the Masquerade Bar.

Here the night was young. A babble of conversation and laughter issued through the door, the brass globes spattered color against the windows. Darrell motioned the driver to follow him inside. Booths and bar were crowded. Mr. Burdette occupied his favorite stool near the end of the bar, drinking with the chesty young matron, who called him "Dolling" in an abominable froglike croak. Behind the bar Phil Beresford worked, talked, laughed, drank, exchanged quips with old friends, welcomed newcomers, wished Godspeed to those departing, took orders, mixed drinks, collected funds, punched the cash register, opened bottles, cracked ice. Tonight he wore a mint-green sport coat, dark green gabardine slacks, a dark green silk tie. Darrell attracted his attention. "Good evening, kind sir," called Phil. "Where you been? T-Bone thought famine had struck when you failed to show up."

"T-Bone? I forgot all about her." He drew Phil to the side. "I lost my wallet. Will you pay the cab for me? A loan until tomorrow."

"Delighted. This the man? How much?"

"I don't know. I don't speak his language. All the way from Fez."

Phil's eyebrows rose. "From Fez by taxi? That's like coming down from London on the Royal Barge. Well, well, well." He settled with the driver, returned to Darrell. "Fifteen thousand francs. About thirty bucks. Not too bad."

"Give him an extra thousand and a drink if he wants one."

The driver declined the drink, took the money, departed.

Darrell found an empty stool, seated himself. "Is the kitchen still open? I'm starving."

"From two in the afternoon till two at night."

"I want a steak the size of a suitcase. I haven't eaten since breakfast."

"Sure thing. Here, come down to this end of the bar, next to Mr. Burdette, where it's a little handier. Something to drink?"

"I'll have a highball. One for you?"

"As usual."

Mrs. Phil presently sailed in from the kitchen with the steak, her face placid and remote. She strutted past Phil as if he were nonexistent, put down the plate, departed.

Mr. Burdette addressed Darrell in a voice loud enough for Phil to hear. "Notice Phil's new outfit? Pretty gay, what?"

Phil regarded Mr. Burdette in hurt amazement. "Sure it's gay. Why not?"

"Business must be picking up," Mr. Burdette told Darrell. "I saw Mrs. Phil pricing a mink coat today."

"Mink fertilizer for the African violets, more likely."

Mr. Burdette winked at Darrell. "African violets! What a lovely hobby!"

"After the first acre it gets old," grumbled Phil. "I'm willing to quit right now."

"Marriage is give and take, Phil."

"Don't get me wrong! I don't mind a plant here and there. But you can't let it get to be a mania. One day I had to pull apart the leaves at the window to see if the sun was shining. I told her, 'This is it! Get rid of this jungle or I'm gonna hack me a clearing with my machete!' So she crammed the whole works into her room. I don't know where she sleeps."

"I often wonder why and how you got married," mused Mr. Burdette.

"That's something I don't like to talk about," said Phil. "Still— since you're courtin' Mama—I guess you got a right to know. Just don't pass it on. We both come from the same town, Atlanta, Georgia. Mama got herself put on the draft board. One day she told me, 'You know something? Tomorrow we call in a new selection, all the single men whose initials is P.R.B.' My middle name being Roger, I took the hint. Sometimes I think I'd been better off in the paratroops."

Mr. Burdette loomed around the bar. "Speaking of Mama, where is lovely young T-Bone tonight?"

"Last I seen of her," said Phil, "she was out sitting on the curb, waiting for Darrell. How that girl loves to eat. I used to bait her once in awhile. But the last sandwich I ordered for her, Mama put in a long black hair."

"Aha! Jealousy!"

Phil shook his head. "Mama's not jealous. She's got her African violets. She just don't like T-Bone."

"Telephone," said Mrs. Phil, from a point two feet behind Phil. "For Mr. Burdette."

"Oh yes, of course." Mr. Burdette slid down from his stool, in the manner of a seal leaving an ice floe. "Excuse me." He trotted around behind the bar and into the kitchen.

Phil watched him with a knowing grin. "T-Bone, bah! Mr. Burdette's wooing Mama. He's the only man she allows in the kitchen, including me. And he always comes out chewing."

Mr. Burdette presently emerged, popping a last morsel into his mouth. The chesty young matron bellowed, "Dolling, dolling!" Mr.

Burdette looked around. "Come along, dolling. We're all going. If you want to come, that is."

"Oh yes," called Mr. Burdette reedily. "Don't leave me here." He departed.

Phil came down the bar to Darrell. "See what I mean about the kitchen? He fascinates Mama with his African violet lore, and while she's daydreaming he fries himself a steak."

"What's he do for a living?"

"Automobile agency. He sold Ellen McKinstry that black engine of wrath. All he's got to do now is collect his money. How's the chow?"

"Only half enough. Otherwise fine."

"Want more? I hate to see a man go hungry. How about some pie?"

"I better settle for the pie."

Phil brought the pie himself. "You eat like you had an eventful day."

"I talked to some men in Fez."

"Learn anything?"

"Nothing much."

Darrell finished the pie, hoisted himself wearily to his feet. "I'm going to bed. I'll settle my bill tomorrow. Or as soon as I get a wire from home."

"Your credit's good."

Darrell went to the door. He looked up and down the street. The night was quiet. Wind rustled the acacia leaves; street lights blinked and flickered through the foliage. A few forlorn shop windows glowed on empty sidewalks; a dozen cars stood desolate along the curb.

Darrell crossed the street, entered the hotel. At the desk he left a call for eight o'clock, climbed the stairs to his room. He took a hot shower, went to bed.

For a long time he lay staring into the dark. If he had not been able to reach the rope! At this moment he would be sitting in the cage, hunched, cramped, aching... They must know by now that he got away; Jilali or a servant would have brought in food and drink. They might or might not have been able to inform el Kazim; el Kazim might or might not show himself in the morning.

The American Express office opened at nine. Darrell would be there. He hoped that el Kazim would be there too. He smiled in the dark, and presently fell asleep.

Chapter X

THE morning was fresh and clear; Tangier sparkled like a bowl of crushed ice. The streets sounded to the squeal of tires, voices in a dozen languages. Tourists and Tangerines mingled along the Boulevard Pasteur, each marveling at the whimsies of the other.

At twenty minutes to nine Darrell posted himself in a doorway across the street from the American Express office. Not the optimum situation, but if el Kazim presented himself at the crack of nine, there would be no time for Darrell to enter, explain matters to the company officials. El Kazim might look in the doorway, see Darrell and depart, taking the passport with him.

Minutes passed; the hour of nine arrived. A man in a brown suit—clearly a company official—stopped by the door, put a key in the lock, entered. Darrell stood looking up and down the street, watching for the flash of gray gabardine.

At four minutes after nine Abd Allah el Kazim appeared, striding briskly from the direction of the Arab Quarter. Beside him, to Darrell's surprise, walked Jilali, dapper and handsome in his neat black suit.

They approached the door with assurance. Darrell, observing their calm faces, burned with fury. Sauntering at their ease, they believed him in Fez, crouched in the cage.

Jilali opened the door; el Kazim marched in looking neither right nor left, with Jilali at his heels.

Darrell crossed the street, went to the door, looked into the office. The man in the brown suit was coming forward from the rear. El Kazim tendered him the note Darrell had written.

Someone came up behind Darrell—a clerk arriving for work. He gave Darrell a curious glance, opened the door, entered. Jilali looked around at the clerk, turned back. Darrell stepped in before the door closed.

The man in the brown suit was reading the letter, scratching his cheek with a thoughtful finger. He spoke; el Kazim tossed the passport down on the counter.

Darrell stepped forward. El Kazim turned his head; the hard round brown eyes stared. He turned swiftly, reached for the passport. Darrell clutched his wrist, ground his fingers into the bones, took the passport.

The man in the brown suit stood back in alarm. "What is this, what is this?"

Darrell said, "I decided to come for my own mail. I am Darrell Hutson. This is my passport." He turned to el Kazim. "Give me my wallet."

El Kazim turned and started for the door; Darrell caught the hood of the gabardine djellaba, jerked him back. El Kazim wheeled, stood glaring like a hawk. "My wallet," said Darrell. "Or I'll call the police."

Jilali, without loss of dignity, reached into the breast pocket of his black coat, brought forth Darrell's wallet. "We do not rob you," he said in an injured voice.

Darrell looked inside the wallet; so far as he could judge his money was secure. The Moroccans started from the office. "Just a minute," said Darrell. "We've got a few things to talk about."

Jilali paused uncertainly by the door. El Kazim whirled himself furiously out into the street.

The official in the brown suit had been first leaning forward in agitation, then standing back in frozen-faced disapproval. "Is this a police matter? Do they rob you, sir? I will call the police!"

"No," said Darrell. "It is a mistake. Please see if I have any mail."

The man indecisively went to the mailbox, brought out a single letter. "Darrell Hutson."

"Yes, that's right. Thank you."

He went outside, followed by Jilali. El Kazim glowered from a hundred feet away.

Darrell spoke in a brittle voice. "Do you know why I haven't brought the police? There's only one reason. I want to find my brother. Do you understand?"

Jilali raised his handsome black eyebrows in reproach.

"I'll make a bargain with you. The same I went to Fez to make. You answer my questions and I'll show you this letter."

"What questions?" Jilali asked guardedly. "What do you want to know?"

"Only things that will help me find Noel."

El Kazim, fascinated against his will, returned step by reluctant step.

"Well, do you agree?" asked Darrell. "If not, I'll call the police."

Jilali looked toward el Kazim, jerked his head. The two spoke in Arabic. El Kazim looked sidewise at Darrell. "Come with us."

Darrell laughed in bitter amusement. "Not much chance of that."

Jilali said, "It is wrong to talk like this. We meant only to keep you safe. We want to win our great war. One man, two men—it is nothing."

"Will you answer my questions?"

"You must ask the questions. Perhaps I will answer."

"If you don't answer, I won't show you the letter, and I'll turn you over to the police. Come over here." Darrell led them a few yards up the side street.

El Kazim held out his hand. "You must show us the letter first."

"You talk like a fool," said Darrell contemptuously.

Jilali restrained el Kazim's retort with an impatient gesture. "Ask the questions."

"Noel left Tangier on the night of March ninth with a truckload of guns. Where did he go?"

El Kazim said harshly, "We cannot tell you these things."

"What is the difference?" asked Jilali. "The French know that guns come to somewhere near Taouz."

"Taouz? Where is Taouz?"

"It is a village in the Tafilelt near the Algerian border—a caravan station."

"Noel brought the truck to Taouz. Then what?"

"The arms were unloaded. Then there was a mistake. We had brought the payment across the desert from Egypt. But the sheikh at Taouz was afraid the French would come, and sent it with Noel and Habdid el Kazim to Tangier. On the road they fought. Noel killed Habdid el Kazim."

Abd Allah el Kazim thrust himself forward. "He threw him from the truck like a piece of refuse! Your brother did this to my brother!"

Darrell ignored him. "Go on," he said to Jilali.

"Noel drove to Erfoud. He went to the hotel there. The French call it the Gîte d'Etape. He stayed there over the night. He wrote a letter and he made two telephone calls to Tangier. The next morning a telephone call came to him. But already he had left the Gîte and no one knows where he went, or where is the payment for the guns."

"And that's all you know of Noel?"

"That is all we know."

"He made two telephone calls, you say?"

"That is our information."

"Who did he call?"

"We do not know. We have made questions at Erfoud. Noel asked for Arthur Upshaw, and spoke to someone who answered the call."

Darrell looked sidewise at el Kazim. "That man might have been Aktouf, the desk clerk at the Balmoral."

"We thought so," said Jilali in a neutral voice.

"You don't think so now."

"No."

"You tortured him to death to find out."

El Kazim could not restrain himself. "He was the most detestable of all swine. He was an Arab who hated his people, an Arab who loved the French. He was filth, he was unclean, with my two hands—" he showed Darrell a pair of quivering hands "—I would tear the throat of all these French-loving curs!"

"This matter does not concern you or your brother," said Jilali shortly.

"Did you send me a newspaper clipping describing Aktouf's death?"

Jilali and el Kazim both looked puzzled. "You were sent this clipping? By whom?"

"I don't know."

Jilali shrugged. "Do you have any more questions?"

"No." He handed Jilali the letter. El Kazim snatched it, ripped it open, held it to the light. They read laboriously, then reread, looked up with eyes that were puzzled and hurt, as if Darrell had deceived them. "But there is nothing here," said Jilali.

"I told you there was nothing."

"Then why did you conceal it? Why did you put it into the mail?"

"Because the people who wanted to read it would tell me nothing in return."

The two Moroccans read the letter once more. "What is 'copper my bets'?"

"I won't tell you. That's half an inch past the edge of the bargain. I wouldn't give you a quarter-inch. You put me in a cage, remember? For no reason whatever."

"Your brother killed a good Moslem! My brother!" grated el Kazim.

Jilali signaled him to quiet. "I wish to copy this."

"Go ahead."

Jilali made a careful copy on the back of an envelope, then returned the letter. The two Moroccans looked at each other, listless with disappointment.

"One more thing," said Darrell. "You took me on a wild goose chase to Fez."

"A—what you say?"

"You took me on a useless journey to Fez. You owe me fifteen thousand francs for my taxi fare back to Tangier."

El Kazim blew scornfully between his teeth. "That is your fault. Your letter told us nothing. It was not worth the trouble of speaking to you."

"You had no need to drive me to Fez. You could have spoken to me here. But you took me to Fez, and I had to spend fifteen thousand francs to get back. I want it returned."

"You will not get it from us." They turned and without further ceremony set off down the street.

Darrell looked at Noel's letter. "Copper my bets"—what the devil did he mean? The letter hinted much, told little... There was a tugging at his sleeve. Darrell swung around. Slip-Slip jerked back with great agility. He slowly approached, smiling archly.

"I'm glad to see you, Mr. Hutson. Maybe now you give me the money."

"Money? For what?"

"I say the man come at nine o'clock. You don't believe me. I work to bring the man."

"You brought him all right. He cost me fifteen thousand francs. Not to mention one or two other items. Get lost."

Slip-Slip shook his head dolefully. "I work for you. Now you don't pay!"

Darrell started back up the Boulevard Pasteur. Slip-Slip came after him. "What you want me to do, Mr. Hutson? I do what you want."

A sign attracted Darrell's attention: OFFICIAL MOROCCAN TOURIST BUREAU. He crossed the street, entered the building so designated, to emerge a few minutes later with a dozen maps and folders.

Slip-Slip was waiting for him. "You want to go for a ride? I know where is a good car. Cheap. Good car."

"No, thanks."

"I'm good guide."

"I don't need a guide." Darrell walked up the Boulevard Pasteur, leaving Slip-Slip staring disconsolately after him. In the Place de France he took a seat at a sidewalk café, ordered coffee. Shoe-shine boys converged like sharks on bloody meat. Darrell rebuffed them, waved away the nasturtium-colored silk scarfs, the rubber tarantulas, the jewelry, wrist watches and skull-caps, refused to inspect lewd photographs, and presently was allowed to sip his coffee in peace.

He unfolded a map, located Erfoud. It lay across the Middle Atlas, on the brink of the Sahara. The road led past Erfoud to a smaller village, Rissani. Another road, hardly more than a track, led to Taouz, almost against the Algerian border. The road by which Noel must have returned from Erfoud led to a town called Ksar-es-Souk. Here he could have turned either southwest toward Ouarzazate, and eventually Marrakech and Casablanca, or north toward Meknes and Tangier. Somewhere he must have halted for fuel. By now the trail would be cold, but there was a bare chance that someone would remember Noel. Or even the truck, especially if it had some distinguishing feature.

Darrell tried to deduce Noel's probable halting-places. The truck undoubtedly had left Tangier with a full tank of gas, and more than likely Noel had filled up again at Meknes. Returning from Erfoud he would refuel at Ksar-es-Souk, if facilities were available. Much depended on the fuel capacity of the truck. Arthur Upshaw could furnish this information, should he choose to do so. Darrell thought this highly unlikely. It would be equally futile to expect cooperation from Duff. Ellen could hardly be expected to know the cruising range of the truck, but she possibly could tell him its make and where it had been bought, what it looked like.

Darrell considered. To telephone Ellen carried the risk of an embarrassing rebuff. Nevertheless... Why not? He telephoned from a nearby drug store.

Ellen showed the least possible cordiality when he identified himself. "Are you very busy?" he asked.

"Why?"

"I want to talk to you."

"About Noel, I suppose."

"Yes, I'm afraid so."

"I'm not interested. I'm busy packing, as well."

"Packing? Why?"

"The house is no longer ours."

"Oh. I should think then you'd want to help me find Noel." Darrell felt an immediate pang of guilt, for he seemed to imply that she, Duff and Arthur Upshaw were entitled to a million dollars' worth of heroin. Through familiarity, the shipment was losing its flavor of evil.

"I'm sick of the name Noel," said Ellen. "I'm sick of the name Hutson."

"Well, answer a question or two for me. I've learned that Noel left Tangier in a truck."

"A lorry."

"A lorry, then. What make of lorry? What color?"

"I don't know what make. Why do you want to know?"

"I'm going to Erfoud to make inquiries. I want to know what to inquire for."

"So you found out about Erfoud." Ellen's voice became thoughtful. "How?"

"That's a long story."

There was a pause. Then she asked, "Where are you now?"

"The Place de France."

"I'll be down in five minutes."

"Make it ten. I'd rather you didn't kill yourself."

"Oh you would, would you?" Ellen's voice was neutral. "I won't be long, in any case."

Darrell hung up the telephone, went out to stand on the sidewalk.

Eight minutes passed, then up the street prowled the drooping snout of the Mercedes-Benz, with Ellen's tawny head behind the windscreen. She stopped, Darrell jumped in beside her. The motor throbbed and they were away.

"Where are we going?" he asked.

"Nowhere particular." On this warm sunny day Ellen wore a pair of white tennis shorts, a white blouse, old white sneakers. Darrell averted his eyes from the slender sun-polished legs. Ellen's hair blew in the wind, and he noticed a faint sprinkle of freckles across the bridge of her nose.

"When you've stared as long as necessary," she said without turning her head, "you can tell me why you wanted to talk to me."

Darrell grinned. Ellen was not in her friendliest mood. "You're the only one in the family who *will* talk. I'm staring at you because every time I see you, you look prettier."

Ellen made a scornful sound.

"Let's go somewhere and have lunch," Darrell suggested.

"No, thank you."

"Aren't you hungry? It's after one."

"You can eat if you like. I'll wait in the car."

"At least we can have a drink somewhere."

She nodded distantly, swung downhill toward the water-front.

"What about that truck? Or lorry, rather?" Darrell asked.

"It was light gray with a dump bed. Rather a large lorry."

"Large light-gray dump-truck," said Darrell. "Anything peculiar or noticeable characteristics that might attract attention?"

"Of course not," said Ellen. "What kind of a fool do you take Arthur for?"

"No fool whatever. It was just a forlorn hope."

"I suppose you have something ingenious in mind?"

"I want to ask at service stations where Noel might have refueled."

"You'll get nowhere. There's hundreds of similar lorries on the road. They're used by the road-menders. That's why Arthur bought it, to deceive the French."

"I see." They swung out on the Avenida de España, drove to the right, paralleling the fine wide beach.

"How did you learn about Erfoud?" asked Ellen. "Arthur certainly never told you, nor Duff."

"Nor you."

"You never asked me."

"Would you have told me?"

"Certainly. Why not?"

"I wish I'd asked you. I got my information the hard way. From a Moroccan, Moulay something ben Jilali. Do you know him?"

"I've heard the name. He's contact in Fez for the Algerian rebels—bigwig politician of some kind."

"Do you know Abd Allah el Kazim?"

"No. Who is he?"

"In the same line of business. Not a friendly chap. He insists that Noel killed his brother."

Ellen laughed in great good humor. "If he's an old-fashioned Moslem he'll want to kill you."

"You seem pleased."

"I'd like to see cemeteries full of Hutsons." But there was more gloom than sting in her voice. She stamped suddenly down on the accelerator, as if surprised to find herself driving at so modest a speed. The road ahead was comparatively clear; Darrell held his tongue.

"Where did you meet these Moroccans?" Ellen asked presently.

"They met me. They knew I had a letter from Noel. Slip-Slip apparently told them; he heard me talking to Duff the first day I arrived."

Ellen nodded. "Slip-Slip's been watching the docks—just in case Noel should try to cut out for Spain. I'd hate to be in Noel's shoes when they catch him." She turned Darrell a quick malicious side-glance. "You'll be in hot water too, if anyone decides for certain that you and Noel are working together."

"The idea's ridiculous."

"Not so ridiculous. It's occurred to everyone."

She swung into the parking area of a shore-side restaurant, ran a comb through her wind-blown hair, jumped to the ground. Darrell followed her across the parking area, out on a terrace overlooking the sea, to a table under a large orange and green parasol. Ellen flung herself into a chair, insolently crossed her legs, exchanged stares with the other patrons.

A waiter came, Darrell ordered. Ellen watched him with sardonic disinterest. "Does Arthur realize that you plan to go to Erfoud?"

"I haven't told him."

"I advise you not to. He doesn't approve of your investigation."

"He's unreasonable."

"You forget that Arthur is very upset. He put his money on a sure thing, but instead he finds himself destitute. I and Duff like-wise, of course. The house is up for sale; we're to be out by the end of the week. The car is mine only until that odious Mr. Burdette catches me. The *Deirdre* is gone, or will be in a few days."

Darrell looked uncomfortably out to sea. "Where are you moving to?" he asked.

"I don't know. I'm sick of Tangier, and everything else I can think of." The waiter brought the drinks, Ellen picked up her glass, tilted it, clinking the ice back and forth. "What will you do if you find the heroin? Not that it's likely."

"Throw the stuff in the ocean, I suppose. What would you do if you found it?"

She drank, set the glass down with airy nonchalance. "Sell it to Ventriss and clear out. Before Arthur did me in."

"You really believe Arthur would do you in?"

"I know he would, with pleasure. I'd kill him with even more."

"You're a savage little beast."

"I have my reasons. I suppose you're acquainted with *Hamlet?*"

"A few of us in the States have learned to read."

"Hmmf. Where did you go to school?"

"Massachusetts Institute of Technology."

"Is that one of your Ivy League colleges?"

"Hardly."

"Massachusetts is somewhere in the east, I believe. Or is it in the Bible Belt?"

Darrell understood that she was mocking him. "Since you're leaving Tangier, you should visit the States and see for yourself."

"A hundred eighty million Phil Beresfords? No, thanks. How are you going to Erfoud?"

"I'll rent a car."

"I'll drive you—for ten thousand francs. You'll have to buy the petrol."

Darrell looked at her in surprise. "It's a long way."

"I know where Erfoud is."

"We'd have to spend the night."

"Not necessarily together."

"Not necessarily. I presume there'd be a surcharge if we did."

"Since you'll be saving money on the car, you might be able to afford it."

"Not at a hundred and forty dollars—or whatever your price is. But I've no objection if you want to drive me, purely as a business arrangement. Ten thousand francs and expenses. Correct?"

"Correct."

"One other matter which we had better settle now. If by some chance we find this heroin, I don't plan to turn it over to you."

Ellen's eyes glinted. "Perhaps you'll give me half. Half for me, half for you."

Darrell wondered if she were still mocking. "No. I won't give you half, or any."

"Qualms of morality?"

"Call it what you like. That much heroin can wreck a hundred lives. Perhaps a thousand, or ten thousand, for all I know."

"That's where you're wrong, my muddle-headed friend. The heroin wrecks no lives. The lives are already wrecked. The heroin is the symptom, not the cause. I'll tell you a secret, Mr. Hutson."

She sat up, put her elbows on the table. "This is not the best of all possible worlds. In fact it's an evil world."

"It's just a world, neither good nor evil."

"Human beings are the world, and human beings live by evil. Evil is like air, so basic and pervading that you don't notice it."

"I can't admit that."

"No? Look. Look there on the street."

Darrell turned his head, to see a man in a dirty and ragged djellaba, a small overloaded donkey. The man carried a short sharp stick, which he repeatedly thrust into the donkey's haunch, with a twisting vicious pressure. Occasionally he made a target of an open sore. The donkey, dazed and dull, either refused or was unable to move more quickly, and only jerked his head.

"Look," said Ellen. "Look at these people around us. Are they excited or indignant? They pay no attention. You would not have looked either. You pretend the evil doesn't exist. The man tortures the donkey. The Russians torture the Hungarians. Americans torture Negroes. Evil is everywhere. You're so excited about the heroin; why don't you do something about the man who tortures his donkey?"

Darrell looked at her sullenly. "What could I do?"

"Jab him with his own stick. Explain that the donkey feels exactly the same sensation. You'd also have to buy the donkey, or the man would have his revenge later."

Darrell sat silently looking across the sea.

"Well," said Ellen gently. "You're not plunging to the donkey's rescue. Why not? You're afraid to make a scene. And you know that this one little viciousness is just a drop in an ocean of evil. Since you tolerate an active evil, you are passively evil, because by your intervention you could stop it. Presently you'll go home and resume your old life, selling sausages or whatever you do, and go along quite placidly. You'll buy a new car every year, complain at the price of ice cream and steak, you'll get fat and even more pompous, and continue to maintain that the world is sweet and good."

"Hey!" Darrell protested. "I'm not quite as bad as all that."

Ellen paid no attention to him. "I think I detest the passive evil more than the active evil. The Russians smothered the Hungarian rebellion. It was a vile act. All over the world people coughed and averted their eyes. Sometimes they called names like fox terriers barking from behind a fence. That nauseating Nehru denied that anything happened. There's a certain grandeur in the evil of the Russians. The people who look on are merely despicable."

Darrell recalled his visit to the house of Jilali in Fez. Without resistance he had submitted to search. A rational submission. Dishonorable? He did not know. Certainly it had been humiliating, and he burned at the recollection. He said, almost savagely, "I make compromises, I won't deny it. But I neither torture donkeys nor sell narcotics. And I don't recall that you ran out to protect that donkey."

"No. I admit I'm evil. I know it. I'm evil and callous and cowardly. I make no other pretense."

Darrell was surprised to see tears glistening in her eyes. He looked guiltily away.

For a space they sat in a not uncompanionable silence, sipping their drinks, looking across the bright water.

"Over-reaction," said Darrell in a meditative voice.

"What about it?"

"Just a thought. About you. Anyone so preoccupied with ethics can't be bad. You're much more virtuous and idealistic than I am."

Ellen rose to her feet. "First you make me listen to your platitudes, then you smear me all over with sentimentality. Furthermore, if we find that heroin—which I doubt—please don't attempt any gallant gestures on behalf of society."

"I'm not looking for heroin," said Darrell. "I'm looking for Noel. If just by chance I did locate the heroin, I plan to do something drastic to it. Arthur, Duff, the FLN, and yourself notwithstanding."

"Bah," sneered Ellen. "You and your windy heroics."

They returned to the car. Ellen said shortly, "We'd better start early. It's a long drive."

"You still want to go?"

"Certainly. Do you think your attitude surprises me?"

"I suppose not. Well, what time is early? Six o'clock? Eight o'clock?"

"About seven. I'll fill up with petrol tonight. You'll have to give me my money now, also five thousand francs for petrol."

"Good heavens," said Darrell, "are you that short?"

"Short? I'm broke. Why do you think I'm hiring out as a chauffeur?"

"I don't know. I don't want to take advantage of you. Ten thousand francs isn't very much, really. Maintenance, tires, depreciation—things like that—"

"Mr. Burdette's loss, not mine."

Darrell gave her fifteen thousand francs. "Seven o'clock in the morning, then."

———————

LATE THAT EVENING DARRELL wandered into the Masquerade for a nightcap. He bought Phil Beresford a drink and settled his debt.

T-Bone came in from the Balmoral lobby. At the sight of Darrell she stopped short, then turned and quickly went back through the glass and iron door.

"Duff doesn't need to worry about me," Darrell told Phil. "I'm far down T-Bone's list."

Phil was puzzled. "Because of breaking a dinner date? That's easy to fix. Just ask her again."

Darrell shook his head. "Yesterday in Fez I saw a photograph of Noel—a fake photograph. His face came from that picture with T-Bone on the beach."

"Odd," remarked Phil. "Odd indeed. And so?"

"Well, I happened to meet her this afternoon, down in the Place de France, and I asked her about it. Just idle curiosity—did she have a copy, had she lost one recently? Did she know this Abd Allah el Kazim? T-Bone denied everything with considerable indignation."

"The problem is solved," said Phil. "You tweaked her most mysterious secret. T-Bone's practicing to be an undercover agent."

Darrell was shocked. "Upshaw told me she carried tales to the French. She can't work for the Arabs at the same time?"

"It's just one of T-Bone's fantasies," said Phil. "Just now she considers herself a double agent. She'll take on as many customers as she can get. Why don't you set her after Noel? She'd ferret him out."

"If I don't make some headway pretty soon, I might do just that."

"Have you got any leads, if you don't mind my asking?"

"Nothing everybody else hasn't got. Tomorrow night at this time things might be different. I'm going out to where he disappeared."

Chapter XI

DARRELL awoke at six o'clock to a call from the desk. For a moment he lay drowsily, collecting his thoughts. Today, Erfoud. Ellen McKinstry was coming by to pick him up. Darrell threw off the covers, swung out of bed.

He showered, shaved, dressed, descended to the lobby, where rolls and coffee awaited him. It was another miraculous spring day, with strands of golden sunlight sifting through the acacia branches.

At seven Darrell went out to stand in the street. Ten after seven, seven-fifteen. Then, preceded by the now-familiar throb, the Mercedes-Benz rounded the corner, slid up the hill.

Darrell stepped forward; the car stopped. Ellen looked out at him, face clear, mouth relaxed. Darrell found it hard to control a smile. Ellen's gaze narrowed. "What's funny?"

"Nothing whatever," Darrell apologized. "Just high spirits."

"Jump in before Arthur looks down from his window and sees us."

Darrell seated himself. "What if he does?"

"A good point. We're of one mind there." She shifted into low. "What if he does?" The car roared up the hill. "We're off and it's a beautiful day."

This time Darrell held a straight face. He swung around in the seat and looked her over. She wore her turtle-neck sweater, a gray tweed skirt, moccasins, a beret which more or less successfully constrained her hair. "Have you had breakfast?" Darrell asked.

"Just tea."

"Are you hungry?"

"No."

Conversation languished. The Mercedes-Benz found the open road. The speedometer needle swung up, across the dial. Then they met a patch of heavier traffic—trucks, a bus packed full with white-robed passengers—and were forced to slacken speed.

"We don't go to Fez today," said Darrell.

"No. Straight on through from Meknes."

"I was in Fez two days ago, to see this Jilali person."

"Fools rush in, and so forth."

Darrell smiled faintly. "I had to get information somewhere."

"Did you enjoy Fez?" she asked politely.

"Not really. I was concerned with other matters. But the shops, or bazaars, whatever they're called—"

"The *souks.*"

"They looked interesting, what I saw of them, which wasn't much."

Ellen thrust down on the accelerator; the Mercedes-Benz lunged ahead, around a truck. They pulled up behind a big yellow bus. Ellen swept around, avoiding an oncoming oil truck by half a second. Darrell glimpsed a startled face in the passing cab. Ahead a pair of camels walked beside the road. One of them turned its neck out, started to amble across to the other side. Ellen swerved; they passed under its neck. The mournful eyes looked down at Darrell.

"Ellen," said Darrell, "Ellen!"

"Yes?"

"Slow down, please."

"Too bad you're so nervy; we'd get there sooner."

"We've got all day."

"Now that we've shaken off the car that was following us."

Darrell whirled in the seat. The road was clear. He turned slowly back.

There was another period of silence. Ellen relaxed. In the rush of wind Darrell could not be sure, but it seemed as if Ellen were humming to herself.

Darrell kept watch on the road behind, but saw nothing suspicious. Finally he asked, "Was there really a car following us?"

"It left Tangier the same time we did, and stayed about the same distance behind; an old Renault or Fiat, something of the sort."

"Who would be interested in where we're going?"

She looked at him incredulously. "You can't be that naïve. You're Arthur's only hope. He's sure you're in touch with Noel. The Moroccans probably have the same idea. You're the focus of many eyes."

"That's ridiculous."

"Four hundred thousand pounds isn't ridiculous."

Darrell looked over his shoulder at the road behind. He saw a faint swirl of dust, retreating ranks of eucalyptus trees, a truck moving toward Tangier, with speed exaggerated by their own motion. He turned back. "I don't care much for this sort of adventure."

"You should have made this clear to your brother."

"I've made things clear to Noel from the first minute he could understand me. The more I talked, the worse he got. Two years ago I stopped talking."

"You have a sister too?"

"Yes. She's about your age."

"Undoubtedly much nicer than I am."

"In some ways. She's not as pretty as you are."

Her face became disdainful. "Pretty. What an insipid word."

"Handsome. Lovely. Attractive. Beautiful. Striking. Magnificent. Exquisite."

"Sex-mad, like all Americans."

Darrell said no more, but gave his attention to the passing landscape: groves of hag-ridden cork-oaks, dusty vineyards, rocky hillocks clumped with rosemary, spurge, asphodel.

Miles slid past, up hill, down dale; the Mercedes-Benz coursing as smooth as the electricity in the wires beside the road. The sun mounted, glaring white in the dusty blue sky.

At eleven they entered Meknes, where they stopped to refuel. Together they put the top up against the combined brilliance of sun and sky. Darrell offered to drive; Ellen curtly refused.

Studying the willful profile, Darrell wondered what went on behind the wind-blown thatch of hair.

They departed Meknes through the French town, seeing nothing of the old city except a glimpse of great mud ramparts to the north.

Ahead rose the Middle Atlas. The road became narrow, dusty, high-crowned, the sort of road which anywhere in the world leads to the back of beyond. Sun-burned foothills rose on either side, crusted with olive trees frangible as dry foam. The traffic became more various, more primitive: camels lurching and swaying; donkey caravans bringing shredded bark, hides and faggots out of the hills; goats herded by Berber women dressed in orange and lavender and black.

The road swung up the valleys, across the round ridges. The olive groves fell below, fresher, brighter vegetation appeared beside the road. The air became cool, sliding in a silent wind down the ravines. They came out on an upland savannah, open to the sky, with the mass of the mountains ahead, spattered with forest, streaked with snow.

At noon they came to Azrou, a lonely little French settlement. A Berber village of adobe houses occupied a nearby hillside: ten thousand rectangular shapes and shadows, a cubist construction painted in colors ground from sand, mud and lamp-black. Darrell suggested lunch; Ellen agreed without enthusiasm. She parked the car and alighted with the air of one reluctantly conferring a favor.

They ate in the dining room of a small French hotel. Ellen had nothing to say, and Darrell reminded himself that her moody preoccupation, whatever its cause, was no concern of his. The meal proceeded in silence and at last came to an end. Darrell called for the check; Ellen, opening her purse, brought out a thousand francs, which she tossed across the table. "What's this for?" asked Darrell.

"My lunch, obviously."

"Just as you like," said Darrell. "However, the arrangement was that I should pay expenses."

"Ostentation is not an endearing trait, Mr. Hutson."

"But, confound it, I'm not being ostentatious! I'm only—" Darrell stopped short. He took the money, and after paying the bill, returned her change.

They left the hotel. "Would you like me to drive?" asked Darrell with elaborate politeness.

"No, thank you." Ellen serenely seated herself behind the wheel. "I'm all on edge when anyone else drives." She started the motor, shifted into low. The Mercedes-Benz sprang down the road. Telephone poles began to snap to the rear.

Darrell said patiently, "You couldn't be as exasperating as this by accident. You must have a good reason for wanting me to hate you."

"None whatever. Haven't you discovered? I'm perverse."

"You'll discover yourself walking unless you slow down."

Ellen curled her lips in lofty contempt. "We won't reach Erfoud before evening."

"At least we'll get there."

The road began to climb, twisting, turning, bending back on itself in tight hairpins. Stands of cedar trees appeared; patches of snow lay in the shade. Half an hour after leaving Azrou they breasted up onto a high plateau. Snow lay deep to either side of the road, distorted black peaks jutted up on all sides.

Ellen glanced sidewise toward Darrell. "Unless you prefer to sit there glowering, I'll let you drive."

"I'll be glad to drive, if you want a rest."

Ellen considered. Darrell watched her frowning and debating and was rather surprised when without a word she stopped the car. They both jumped out, both circled the car. Meeting at the front, they almost bumped into each other. Darrell put his hands on her shoulders; they stared into each other's face. Ellen raised her eyebrows in frosty inquiry; slowly with great dignity she shook Darrell's hands from her shoulders. Raging inwardly, Darrell seated himself behind the wheel. Ellen picked a small white crocus growing beside the road, which she brought into the car with her.

Darrell told himself, she's either a lunatic, or a great actress. Distinctly a puzzling creature... If she wants me to hate her, she's not succeeding. The more I hate her, the more I want to kiss her. That's out, naturally. I wouldn't take advantage of her... So reflecting he adjusted the seat, gingerly shifted into low.

"Be careful not to oversteer," said Ellen. "When you turn the wheel, the car turns too."

Darrell touched the accelerator; the car slipped forward.

"You can do a hundred and forty on the flat," said Ellen. "Please don't try here."

After a few miles Darrell gained confidence. Ellen relaxed, curling sideways on the seat. Darrell once again felt a near-irresistible impulse to smile. He was certain his face did not move, but Ellen looked at him sharply. "Are you laughing at me?"

Darrell shook his head. "It's the wrong frame of mind for this particular project."

"Are you very fond of Noel?" asked Ellen.

Darrell shrugged. "We've never been close. He thinks I'm dull, I think he's foolish."

"Foolish? You're over-generous. Noel's an ass. Bumptious, noisy, bustling here and there, bursting with over-enthusiastic boyishness."

"Noel, like yourself, is a romantic."

"I romantic?" cried Ellen in astonishment. "What rot."

"Certainly you're a romantic."

She shook her tawny head. "Definitely not. Romanticism is a rosy veil across the eyes."

"The veil isn't necessarily rose-colored. But it exists."

"Aren't you being rather presumptuous?" said Ellen haughtily.

"Everyone has a right to his opinions. As a matter of fact, when I first met you I thought you were half-mad."

Ellen smiled with grim satisfaction. "And now?"

"I wouldn't like to say. You'd be annoyed and call me names."

"Perhaps. But tell me anyway."

"Well, there're three sections. First, you're a precocious brat."

"Hmm."

"Secondly, you're a romantic. You don't belong to this age. Where you do fit, I'm sure I don't know. Thirdly—I can't put it into words very clearly."

"Try."

"No. And this time I'll be firm."

They drove on in silence, across a rock-strewn moonscape, through a quiet winter-dull Berber town, Midelt, then entered a great down-slanting gap that yawned forward a vast distance, finally spreading apart into empty air. The snow vanished, the rocks were harsh and bare. They passed a half-dozen Berber villages: cubicles of mud and stone built wall to wall. The inhabitants watched them without animation; the men somber and weather-beaten, the women rather more spirited, in black-, white- and blue-striped robes, faces tattooed with blue designs.

They came to another town, Rich, with a French hotel, a few French shops, and now the Atlas lay behind. Ahead, still invisible behind a dwindling series of lesser hills, lay the Sahara.

Shortly after Rich they saw the first palms. The road now followed the Oued Ziz, a gray-green river, sluggish and shallow, with little cultivated plots along the banks. The palms began to appear in greater numbers, in clumps of two or three, then by the sixes and tens, then in a continuous green ribbon along the river.

With the sun hanging in the west they came to tomato-red Ksar-es-Souk, where they filled up with gas at a large modern service station. At Ksar-es-Souk the road divided. The principal fork led southwest, behind the Atlas, linking the kasbahs, or fortress villages, of the desert's edge to Ouarzazate and Marrakech. The lesser fork continued south to Erfoud and out in the desert to Taouz, this latter a caravan terminus.

Turning south to Erfoud, they passed a Land Rover parked beside the road. Four soldiers stood drinking coffee in tin cups from a Thermos on the fender. Ellen looked back over her shoulder. "French road patrol."

"Is there any chance the French captured Noel?"

"Very slight. The Moroccans would be sure to know."

The road now stretched across a dead desolation covered with innumerable millions of round black stones. In the distance a dark spot appeared, trailing dust like a comet. It grew, approached, passed: a big blue bus packed to capacity with crates, suitcases, bicycles, furniture, sacks and bundles. The dust settled slowly; again there was nothing to be seen but desert, flat as a griddle out to a far pair of cinnamon-colored buttes.

But the flatness was an illusion; suddenly the road dipped, slanted abruptly through bluffs of red sandstone, into the valley of the Ziz. Now the palms were more beautiful than ever; feathery and soft-looking, of various heights and various suave greens, leaning over gardens of fruit and grass and vegetables. The river swung wide to the right; the road climbed back to the desert floor, the fertile ribbon disappeared from view.

Kilometers passed, the sun hung low; the time was almost six o'clock. "Further than I had expected," Darrell remarked.

"Seven hundred kilometers," said Ellen colorlessly.

As the sun was sinking they came to a heavy crenelated wall among the palms: Erfoud. A side road turned off to the right, with a sign indicating the Gîte d'Etape. Darrell stopped the car. "Is that the hotel where Noel stayed?"

"So I understand."

"Unless you have objections we'll spend the night here."

"No objections whatever. This is your venture, not mine."

"Very well. I suppose they'll be able to feed us and give us beds."

"I imagine so."

The driveway wound through the palms; the Gîte d'Etape appeared silhouetted on the sunset. "Good heavens," said Darrell. "A hotel or a castle?"

"It's a hotel, waiting for tourists which so far haven't arrived."

"And this is where Noel telephoned to Tangier?"

"Yes."

"And when he left here—"

"He disappeared."

The road curved up, ended in a graveled parking area. Darrell switched off the ignition, opened the door for Ellen, followed her out. He looked around the landscape. "What a beautiful spot."

"Very romantic."

Darrell took her arm. "I refuse to be enemies with you. We'll wash up; we'll have a drink and dinner and pretend that we're friends."

"You're paying the piper, you can call the tune." She pulled her arm free. "But I don't care to dance."

A page pushed open plate-glass doors; they climbed carpeted steps to the great bright lobby.

Darrell went to the registration desk. The clerk, a man thin and precise, wearing horn-rimmed glasses, bowed. He showed no surprise when Darrell requested two rooms.

"If you will leave your passports, please." He spoke English with only a trace of accent. "Do you wish dinner?"

"Later in the evening."

"And your car, you wish it garaged?"

"Please."

The page conducted them to their rooms, which gave on a balcony circling the lobby. Darrell said to Ellen, "After I wash up, I'm going down to talk to the clerk. So I'll meet you in the lobby."

"Do you prefer to talk to the clerk alone?" asked Ellen in her most colorless voice.

"Not at all. If you like, I'll wait for you."

"I won't be long."

When Darrell came down the stairs, Ellen sat perched on the arm of a chair. In deep leather chairs nearby sat a middle-aged couple, the only other guests visible.

"Would you like a drink first?" Darrell asked.

"Whatever you please."

"It might help with the inquiry."

They crossed the lobby to the bar. Darrell ordered highballs, then looked around the lobby. "One month ago Noel sat here. He'd just killed a man—el Kazim's brother. Undoubtedly he came to the bar, undoubtedly he had a few drinks." He looked speculatively at the bartender, who, he had discovered while ordering the highballs, spoke only French. "Ask him if he remembers Noel."

Ellen spoke in French. The bartender listened, appeared to think, replied.

"He remembers Noel," said Ellen, "but did not talk to him. Noel had three or four drinks, he thinks."

"Does he remember anything else?"

The answer was an uninterested *"Non, madame."*

"Not too illuminating," said Darrell. "Well, shall we tackle the clerk?"

"Whenever you're ready."

They crossed the lobby. The clerk put his hands correctly and precisely on the plate glass. "Yes, sir?"

"My name is Darrell Hutson, as you already know."

"Yes, sir."

"A month ago my brother stayed here. Noel Hutson."

"Yes. I remember. Other gentlemen have made inquiries. I hope there is no trouble."

"None, except that I haven't been able to find him."

The clerk shook his head. "I'm sorry to hear that, sir. But I know nothing. He left no address."

"It is very puzzling," said Darrell. "I understand that he telephoned to Tangier?"

"Yes. I've discussed this with the other gentlemen. He telephoned to Tangier, and left a message for a man named Arthur. I could not help overhearing, and of course I have been asked several times about it."

"Do you remember the message?"

"Not distinctly. I paid no attention after Mr. Hutson finally reached his party. It was something like, 'Send somebody down here. I do not care to drive to Tangier with this load.' And then he said, 'Yes, at the Gîte.' I don't think he said much more."

"He asked only for Arthur? No one else?"

"In the second call I believe he did mention another person."

"Duff?"

"Yes, Duff. That is the name. But he left the message to be given to Arthur."

Darrell turned to Ellen. "Arthur never got the message?"

"He says not."

"I don't suppose you answered the phone."

"No," said Ellen. "It was not I. Arthur's mind has been exploring the same channels. It wasn't Aktouf, so it must be I. But I wasn't home."

Darrell rubbed his chin. "There was something else I wanted to ask. Oh yes." He turned to the clerk. "You said he *finally* reached his party. He made more than one call?"

"Two calls. He failed to reach his party on the first call. And on the second call he left the message."

Darrell ran his fingers through his hair. He looked at Ellen dubiously. "Strange."

"Why strange?"

"He made two calls. It stands to reason that he would first have called the Balmoral. Then he would have tried your house, where he might have expected to find Duff if Upshaw weren't there."

"Very well, I agree to that. As does everyone else."

"But on Noel's first call he made no connection. So he must have called your house first, and then the hotel. But this doesn't make sense, for two reasons. Because he asked for Duff and because Aktouf never took the message—so I've been assured." He turned back to the clerk. "These were the only calls he made? Just these two?"

"Two are all he made, sir. I have told the other gentlemen the same."

"I suppose you're sure of this?"

"Yes, sir. He came down from his room and made only two calls. It will be evident from his bill." He opened a drawer, flipped back through a sparse set of papers, withdrew a statement. "Two calls, as I have—" He peered. "No, there are three." He looked up in puzzlement. "But I am sure he called only twice. Perhaps he used his room telephone while I was at my dinner. That, of course, is possible. The manager would have made the connection." He looked at Darrell in concern. "Is this an important matter? I told the other gentlemen—"

"It's of no significance," said Darrell. "The numbers are not noted on his bill?"

"No, sir."

"I see. And the other gentlemen who asked are not aware that Mr. Hutson made three calls?"

"No, sir."

"These three were the only calls he made?"

"They are all. Of course he received a call in the morning."

"So I understand. Were you on duty?"

The clerk nodded with a kind of terse pride. "We do not have many guests, and consequently a minimum staff. I am on duty mornings and evenings. The manager relieves me during the afternoon and during my meals."

"Do you remember what time Mr. Hutson left?"

"I think about seven o'clock. He took no breakfast, as I recall."

"And what time did the call come through?"

"I don't remember exactly, sir. Just after Mr. Hutson had left."

"Did the person who called identify himself?"

"No, sir."

"I assume it was a man who called?" From the corner of his eye Darrell saw Ellen stiffen.

"I believe so, sir. I hardly remember."

"There was no message?"

"No."

"Is there anything else you remember about Noel? Any detail? Did he speak to anyone?"

"No, sir. We had no other guests that night. In fact, Mr. Hutson was our only guest during four days." He smiled. "It makes it easier to remember when there are so few guests. He posted a letter, of course."

"Did you notice the address?"

"A letter to the United States, I believe."

"Anything else?"

"That's all I remember, sir."

"Did anyone else speak to him? The manager?"

"I don't believe so. The other gentlemen inquired, but I am sure the manager told them nothing."

Darrell looked at Ellen. "Can you think of anything to ask?"

"No."

Darrell turned back to the clerk. "May we speak to the manager?"

"He is not here, sir. He is at a conference in Casablanca."

"Oh, I see. Thanks very much for your help." He laid a thousand francs on the counter.

"Thank you, sir."

Darrell took Ellen's arm, led her back toward the bar. Half-way across the lobby she became conscious of his grasp, and disengaged herself.

"Young hellion," said Darrell mildly.

"I hired out to drive you. If you want to exercise your gallantry, you'll have to pay more."

"I'll keep to myself. I know your rates."

"They've gone up. I've decided you're a bore."

With exaggerated formality Darrell seated her in one of the deep leather chairs, ordered another round of highballs from the bar.

"Do you know anything now you didn't know before?" asked Ellen in her coolest and most flippant manner.

"I know that Noel made three telephone calls instead of two."

"Is that significant? He never did speak to Arthur, and the message never was delivered."

"So Arthur claims."

"You don't believe him?"

"Arthur could be playing a deep game."

Ellen shook her head. "Not that deep. Noel made three calls instead of two. What else?"

"The telephone call in the morning came after Noel had left."

"Is that all?"

"That's all."

"It seems to me you've had your trouble for nothing."

"Perhaps. We're not finished yet."

"No?"

"The call that came in the morning intrigues me. Who called him? Certainly no girl friend."

"What difference does it make? Noel was already on his way."

"Why should anyone call him? Who knew he was here?"

"It's immaterial. He'd already decided to scuttle. He was well on his way to Casablanca."

Darrell shook his head. "If that's what he intended, why bother to call Arthur?"

Ellen looked at him, her lip curling in impatience. "Because he changed his mind! Because four hundred thousand pounds is a great deal of money to think about all night!"

"I know Noel better than that. He might talk himself into delivering a load of guns, but Noel wouldn't touch narcotics. It would violate his whole picture of himself, destroy his self-respect. He was probably more concerned with how to get rid of the stuff."

Ellen snorted. "In that case, why not fling it in the ditch?"

"Perhaps out of loyalty to Arthur, even though he despised the whole business."

"What rot."

"Not at all. He'd feel bound to declare himself. That's exactly what he did. He says so in his letter to me. Although I still don't understand what he meant by coppering his bets—"

"Coppering his bets?"

Darrell reached in his pocket. "You haven't seen the letter."

Ellen read it with interest. "It doesn't sound as if Noel planned to decamp. Still, he might have changed his mind."

"Barely possible. But 'coppering his bets'—how? He must have had the FLN in mind. If they learned that he had killed el Kazim's brother, he'd get short shrift. He wanted to make sure of reaching Tangier, or Casablanca—wherever he was headed for. Shall we have dinner?"

"If you like."

Darrell rose to his feet, held out his hand. She ignored it, jumped up, sauntered ahead of him to the dining room.

The head waiter, wearing tails and a glistening shirt, ushered them across the echoing dining room. Fifty tables glittered with silver and sparkled with crystal under three massive chandeliers. Darrell and Ellen were seated beside one of the tall plate-glass windows overlooking the palm grove. Across the room the elderly couple were already eating, attended by two waiters. The dining room otherwise was empty.

Hors d'oeuvres were served, wine was uncorked and poured. An enormous apricot moon rose behind the far pinnacles. Darrell thought, if I make a comment Ellen will sneer about American sentimentalism; hence I'll say nothing. He pretended to ignore the moon and from the corner of his eye watched Ellen. She looked at the moon, turned him a searching glance, then looked back across the moonlit palm grove.

Darrell could contain himself no longer. "Even if we don't find Noel, I'm glad I came."

"It's pleasant here," Ellen agreed grudgingly.

"You've never been here before?"

"Is this your idea of how to grill a suspect?"

"An idle question, pure and simple."

"I've never been to Erfoud before."

They ate in silence. The elderly couple finished, rose and stalked from the room. The moon floated high over the hills, the palm grove was like a growth of dark crystals.

Dinner came to an end. Darrell and Ellen returned to the lobby, where they stood uncertainly, neither meeting the other's eyes.

"Would you like to go for a walk?"

"A walk in the moonlight?" said Ellen indifferently. "All right, if you like."

The page ran ahead to open the plate-glass doors; they wandered out into the wan white glare. The palm grove lay before them, black net and cloth-of-silver; they turned off along a path. The moonlight illuminated the landscape to the finest detail; each clod of earth threw an India-ink shadow; each lead-foil blade of grass, each platinum cat-whisker maintained a fragile distinction from every other. From the direction of the kasbah came the sounds of life: the barking of a dog, frogs croaking, the dry whistle of crickets.

They wandered on: Darrell took Ellen's hand; after ten seconds she snatched it away. "Excuse me," said Darrell with dignity.

They came to an open area, spiked here and there with two-foot stones. "A graveyard," said Ellen. "They just dig down a few feet, put in the body, cover it with a stone at the head and feet."

They turned back into the grove. Darrell said, "I've been very annoyed with Noel, but if it hadn't been for his letter I'd never be here. Your company is at least stimulating... I'm beginning to fear the worst."

"About what?"

"About Noel. If he were alive—"

"Noel, Noel, Noel," said Ellen crossly. "Is that all you think about?"

Darrell heaved a deep sigh. "You're a complete puzzle. When I take your hand, you vault away as if I were a leper. When I'm properly respectful, you find fault again."

Ellen stooped, picked a blade of grass. "Yes," she said thoughtfully. "I'm inconsistent and perverse..." She faced him, put her hands on his shoulders. "Kiss me."

"Free?"

"Yes. Free."

Darrell kissed her... A peculiar kiss, he realized with the disengaged fraction of his mind: warm, pliant, earnest—but somewhere behind lay another quality, cool careful attention. Darrell kissed her forehead. Ellen stood quietly. Darrell looked down into her face. Am I insane? Am I imagining things? Why is she watching so closely? Does she want me to make love to her? Is she teasing, blowing hot and cold?... He relaxed his grip. Ellen and her motives were beyond his understanding.

She stood soberly looking up at the moon. Her mouth relaxed, her eyes were clear; she looked young and innocent and full of dreams. Darrell once again put her into the context of his life at home. He saw her frying eggs at a counter-top stove, sprawled out reading the Sunday newspapers, excitedly planning a new house... Good heavens, thought Darrell, where are my thoughts taking me?

"What are you thinking?" she asked.

Darrell focused on her face. She was watching him intently. He took her hands; they lay warm, subtly responsive in his. "I was thinking of you, naturally."

"What kind of thoughts?"

Darrell shook his head. "I'm confused, like a neurotic rat in a laboratory. I don't know which button to push. You hate me and despise me, and then when I kiss you it's like a mixture of whiskey and electricity."

She started to speak, then caught herself. "Kiss me."

"No," said Darrell sadly. "Much as I'd like to."

"Are you afraid?"

"No... Yes... This is like hitting myself with a hammer... I made an arrangement with you. I've already violated the spirit of it. By kissing you."

"But I asked you to. That releases you from the agreement." Ellen's voice was soft as the moonlight, silky and wan.

"That's true—in a way. It releases me from my agreement with you, but not from my agreement with me. It's not that I don't want to. But something tells me, no, Darrell. Don't cave in so easily. I don't know why... Good lord," he said in disgust. "How I'm babbling."

Ellen picked another blade of grass, chewed on it. "Very revealing."

He picked a blade of grass for himself. "It's not that I'm not willing. When we get back to Tangier, we'll go somewhere—come back here if you like—and stay a week. Do you like that idea?"

"Whether I do or not, now is now, and now is different."

"That's exactly the trouble! Now is different! I made that damned bargain. It's a contract and I can't quit just because the going gets rough. You wouldn't want me to."

"But I do."

Darrell put his hands on her shoulders, looked into her moonlit face. "You want me to break this contract made with you and with myself?" Suddenly it seemed he was approaching some glimmer of understanding, some hint—vague, fragmentary—of the truth. It was bigger than he ever had imagined.

"Yes, if you like."

Darrell stared at her eyes; some trick of the moonlight gave them a weird shine; her mouth smiled at a strange angle.

"But I won't do it, naturally." He dropped his hands, turned away. Astonishing. Five minutes before he had been thinking fatuous thoughts about this girl, picturing her as a part of his life. Now they were separated by a gulf far darker than the distance to the moon.

She asked in a measured voice, "Why are you looking at me like that?"

"I'm trying to understand you."

"Are you succeeding?"

"I'm groping. It's hard going. I'm not used to these situations."

"What have you arrived at so far?"

"You encouraged me to lose my head, to break my promise—in short to make a fool of myself."

"Why yes. So I did."

"I understand that—but why?"

"I have my reasons." She spoke airily, but she turned her head away, switched at her leg with the blade of grass.

"Are they secret?"

"Yes. But I'll tell you." She threw down the blade of grass. "Perhaps you wonder why I came out here like this, put myself in this position."

"Not after we made our arrangement."

She made an angry gesture. "I came out here because I wanted to hate you. I've been anxious for a chance to hate you. You haven't given me any opportunity. You've frustrated everything. And I hate you for that!"

Darrell said in an astonished voice, "But why? Why do you want to hate me?"

"I hate all men," said Ellen. "I hate men like poison." She turned and walked rapidly back toward the hotel.

Darrell seated himself on the bank of a convenient irrigation ditch. Ellen. He spoke the name aloud, hoping that some inner reflex would give him a clue to his emotions. His subconscious was no help.

He rose to his feet, returned to the hotel. The lobby was bare of guests. Ellen had gone to her room. Darrell sat at the bar, ordered a highball, drank it; ordered another, took it to one of the deep leather chairs.

The dining room was dark, the clerk stood idly behind the desk, the bartender read a magazine. Darrell studied the Berber rugs. He counted them; there were seventeen. The patterns were barbaric, the colors even more so, dissonance which sophisticated minds would never think to employ: ocher with salmon pink; lavender, saffron and peacock blue; black, white, lemon yellow, pumpkin orange... A step. Ellen, pale but composed, seated herself beside him. "May I have a drink?"

"Immediately." He ordered a highball for her and another for himself.

She leaned back, scrutinized him impassively. Darrell returned the inspection, trying to recapture the insight he had felt in the palm grove: not to reinforce the unpleasant impression, but to prove or disprove its validity. No avail. Ellen was a composed if pale young woman with a sullen reckless expression. Darrell finished his second highball, started on his third. He was tired and unsettled; the Scotch had a soothing effect. Ellen made short work of her own highball. "Another?" asked Darrell. She nodded; Darrell signaled the bartender.

He thrust his legs out, leaned back in the chair. "Something I'm not clear on. You hate men—all men. May I ask why?"

"Yes, you may ask," said Ellen, "and I'll tell you. It's something I've only told one other person, and he's dead." She took a long sip of her highball, continued in a flat voice: "When I was younger—fourteen, to be exact—I had a very unpleasant experience."

"Oh?"

"Yes. Through the instrumentality of—let us say—a close acquaintance."

Darrell could think of nothing to say.

"I told my father. He was furious. The same night he was killed."

There was a period of silence. Darrell fought to subdue a sense of unreality. "You don't mean—Arthur."

"I mean Arthur."

"But you're his niece."

"You and your fat round little set of rules! What difference does that make? He's a man!"

Darrell paused to collect his wits. "Then you think that your father spoke to him, that they had an argument, a fight, and Arthur shot your father."

"I'm sure of it. I've planned to kill Arthur ever since. I've tried at least twenty times. I can't do it. I went so far as to point a gun at him once. I couldn't pull the trigger."

"Does Arthur know this?"

"Of course he knows."

"Does Duff know?"

"Duff? He doesn't care."

Darrell reached out for her hand. She jerked violently away. "Don't touch me."

"I'm only trying to console you. Clumsily, no doubt."

"I don't want your sympathy. I don't need it."

"Certainly you do. Why brood? You're young—"

"I'm old and wise and evil as a witch."

They sat in silence. "Another highball?" Darrell asked.

"All right."

Darrell signaled for another round, his head already a trifle light. "We'll both be drunk in another ten minutes."

"Afraid?" asked Ellen.

Darrell shook his head. "No. But returning to this hate business: you hate Arthur, well and good. Why herd me in with him? This project of yours—coming down here to hate me—is it quite fair?"

Ellen said in an uninterested voice, "I warned you that I was unmoral."

"I didn't believe you. I still don't."

"I've tried to prove it to you."

Darrell shook his head. "You can't deny that you're honest. I haven't suspected you of lying to me."

"Please, Mr. Hutson, don't inflict me with a code of morals I've insisted on denying. Besides," she added irrelevantly, "you're hardly the one to preach of fairness."

"So?" Darrell was surprised and disturbed. "I'm not conscious of unfairness."

"Because you're a stupid egotist, much like Duff."

Darrell winced, grinning ruefully. "Explain."

"You make me a magnanimous offer—a sordid week in a hotel. Do you expect me to clap my hands in excitement?"

Darrell fidgeted with his highball. "It does sound sordid now. Then it didn't."

Ellen snorted. "You preen yourself on your faithfulness to the terms of a contract. Integrity? Dedication? No. You're afraid to break your so-called arrangement. You're a moral weakling. You don't have the courage to adapt to a changed situation. You're afraid of guilt. It's not the act itself you want to avoid—in fact you hopefully propose a week of the same—but only after you break the taboo by touching home base at Tangier. Isn't that the act of a prig?"

Darrell listened in wry discomfort. "Well, you've done it."

"Done what?"

"You've figured out a way to hate me. And you couldn't rest till you came down to tell me about it."

Ellen sat bolt upright, stiff as the back of a chair. Then she relaxed, fell limply back. "Very well. And I've told you."

"You certainly have. There's enough truth in what you say to make me hate myself. I'm afraid of guilt. I admit it. Fear of guilt is a poor guide to the conduct of one's life. Better than none, of course. Well—that's that. You hate me; I'm disillusioned with you and myself both. The pattern of our relationship is set. Which is for the best. When I leave Tangier there'll be no pangs for either of us."

Ellen stood up. "None whatever. I'm going to bed."

"Good night."

She made no answer. He watched the slender figure crossing the lobby, the jaunty stride now just a trifle listless.

Darrell sat with his head whirling, feeling the alcohol with his body, thinking with a mind which had never seemed more clear. He looked at himself from a dispassionate height. Ellen was bitingly right. He had prided himself on his conservatism; he was no more than a coward. He had conducted himself according to precepts, and found that he set greater store by the precepts than by the honor they represented. He yearned for Ellen, but feared to venture anything for her. He had pictured a week in a hotel room but had blocked out of his mind the larger vision. She had a right to despise him. The problem suggested its own solution. He made a decision. So much for that.

There was Noel to consider. But where was the problem? The situation seemed crystal-clear. Astonishing, that he should have felt a momentary puzzlement! Arthur Upshaw, the Moroccans—were they so stupid, so dense? But no. He did them an injustice. They were ignorant of two key facts. First, Noel would never use a shipment of heroin for his own financial gain. Second, there had been three telephone calls instead of two.

Darrell rose unsteadily to his feet. The clerk had departed, the lobby was almost dark. Darrell nodded good night to the bartender, who put down his magazine with relief.

Darrell went up to his room, removed his clothes. The hotel was silent. Through the open window came the sound of frogs and crickets. He thought of Ellen, only a few feet down the hall, listening to the same sounds. He wanted to go to her, to tell her everything: of his decisions, his deductions, the probable whereabout of Noel. But his head was swimming; he felt limp and wrung dry of energy. She would misunderstand; it would be a mess. Darrell heaved a sigh, composed himself to sleep.

Chapter XII

EARLY sunlight streaming through the window aroused Darrell. Half-awake he raised his arm, focused on his watch. Seven o'clock.

After a few minutes he propped himself up, threw his legs over the side of the bed. His head felt thick. He staggered into the bathroom. There was no hot water. Cursing and hissing between clenched teeth, he stepped under the cold shower.

Fifteen minutes later he was shaved and dressed, ready for the day. He went to Ellen's door, knocked. There was no response.

He knocked again. Still no answer.

Darrell descended the stairs. The lobby was dim and empty, the dining room locked. He went to the front door, looked out over the parking area. No sign of Ellen. Darrell stood deep in reflection. At the far wall a glass door opened out upon a balcony. Darrell crossed the lobby with swift steps. Ellen stood by the rail, looking thoughtfully over the bright landscape.

Darrell joined her. "Good morning."

"Good morning." Ellen looked fresh and crisp.

"I pounded on your door. When you didn't answer I thought you'd left for home."

"It didn't occur to me."

Darrell leaned on the rail. The palm grove had no secrets in the morning sunlight; the previous evening seemed unreal.

"What do you intend to do today?" Ellen asked indifferently.

"Throw out a line for Noel. I have a theory I'd like to test; it came to me last night after you'd gone to bed."

Ellen glanced at him with aversion.

"Not immediately after you'd left, of course," said Darrell hurriedly. "I sat drinking and worrying and fretting, wondering about things. Then this idea about Noel came to me. I turned it over a few times, and there it was. I've figured the whole thing out."

"An exercise in pure reason?"

Darrell nodded. "It's not particularly difficult."

"Your theory can't be very sound. Arthur has been cudgeling his brain an entire month, and Arthur isn't stupid."

"Arthur has been working under two handicaps. The idea that Noel would refuse to steal a million dollars is beyond his imagination. Then he only knew of two calls to Tangier. The first presumably to your house, the second to the Balmoral. Since Aktouf took no message, Arthur wonders who did."

"He thinks it was the other way around. The first call to the Balmoral, the second to the house. He thinks I answered the phone and then never gave him the message."

"Well, either way it makes no difference. We know that Noel made three calls: the first from his room, almost surely to the hotel; the second to your house; the third, where? Someone answered, call him X. Noel gives X a message for Arthur, to the effect that if Arthur wants his heroin hauled, Arthur had better come to Erfoud and haul it himself."

"Yes. I follow you there."

"Noel sits here in the lobby, jumping at every sound. He's just killed a man, his nerves are in poor shape. There's no word from Arthur, so in the morning he leaves—about seven. A few minutes later someone telephones, asks for him. Who? Arthur?"

Ellen shook her head. "Arthur insists that he received no message from Noel."

"Probably not," said Darrell. "More likely Mr. X. Now think. Noel called Tangier at seven or eight o'clock in the evening. The call came the next morning at about seven-thirty. A lapse of approximately twelve hours. Right?"

"Right."

"We left Tangier yesterday at seven-thirty in the morning; we drove at a fairly good pace, arrived here at seven. A lapse of eleven and a half hours. Very close to the same interval."

"Right again."

"Suppose whoever took Noel's call in Tangier—Mr. X—decided to collect a million dollars worth of narcotics. A risky business, but not too risky. Suppose Mr. X jumped into his car, drove all night, then telephoned Noel from somewhere in the neighborhood."

"The times apparently match."

"Now I've got to make one or two suppositions. I put myself in Mr. X's place. Would I drive all the way to Erfoud before calling? I'd be anxious and nervous. I'd wonder whether Noel were still at the hotel, whether I were making the drive for nothing. I'd call from Ksar-es-Souk—to learn Noel's plans, to make whatever arrangements with Noel I had worked up during the night."

"That's reasonable enough."

"What would Mr. X do when he learned that Noel had left the hotel? The suppositions take on a sinister color. If Mr. X were determined to take the heroin, he'd start down the road from Ksar-es-Souk and pick a spot to wait for Noel."

"I see. Granting all this, what do you propose to do?"

"We go to Ksar-es-Souk, inquire at likely spots if anyone made a phone call to Erfoud at seven-thirty or eight in—" He stopped short. Ellen stood stiffly, her eyes fixed on something across the palm grove. He followed the direction of her gaze. "What are you looking at?"

She pointed. "See between those two tall clumps? That's the main road. A dark car just went by, a small dark car."

Darrell watched the gap through the palms for a few moments. A Moroccan rode by on a bicycle, djellaba flapping behind. "All the cars out here are small and dark," said Darrell.

Ellen turned him a sarcastic glance, but restrained whatever response had occurred to her.

Darrell asked politely, "Are you ready for breakfast?"

"Yes."

The austere elderly couple were already in the dining room, with toast and orange juice in front of them, an elaborate silver coffee urn on a service cart beside their table.

A waiter in a starched white jacket seated Ellen with a click of the heels, presented menus.

Darrell said, "You can have bacon and eggs, ham and eggs, omelettes of all kinds, herring, cheese, mixed grill—"

"Just tea, please."

"Tea? You'll starve."

Ellen shrugged, looked off out the window. Darrell hesitated, then ordered orange juice, toast, bacon and eggs for them both, with tea for Ellen, coffee for himself.

Jugs of orange juice in basins of crushed ice were set before them, a coffee urn and a china teapot wheeled up on a service cart. Covered dishes were carried in, served, the covers whisked off.

Ellen poured herself a cup of tea, sat sipping, looking out the window.

Darrell helped himself to toast, began to eat. Presently he asked, "Who's the moral coward now?"

Ellen said in a measured voice, "I'm not hungry."

Darrell nodded in profound understanding. "In that case, I apologize. You're not a moral coward."

Ellen wrenched her gaze away from the window. "Darn it," she muttered. "I am hungry. And now I've got to eat."

Darrell consoled her. "You won't feel quite so edgy."

Ellen savagely attacked the bacon and eggs. Ten minutes later she looked up from her empty plate. "There. You talked me into eating. A rather petty triumph. Are you pleased with it?"

"I'm glad you had your breakfast." He finished his coffee. Ellen again was looking stonily out the window. Darrell sighed. "I suppose we'd better think about leaving."

"Whenever you wish."

Half an hour later they drove away from the hotel—out to the main road, north beside the palm grove, up through a group of red sandstone pinnacles, out across the flint-covered desert.

Darrell said, "There can't be too many places in Ksar-es-Souk from which a person could telephone at seven-thirty in the morning. The obvious place would be the service station where we filled up last night. Mr. X's car would need gas too."

Ellen nodded distantly.

"We'll fill up again in Ksar-es-Souk, and ask questions at the same time."

Ksar-es-Souk appeared in the distance, a line of low tomato-red blocks against the dun background of the Atlas. At the outskirts of town, near the fork in the road, was the service station.

Darrell slowed the car. "Here's where we test my theories. Mr. X comes driving down from the mountains. It's seven-thirty in the morning; he's later than he wants to be, and he's anxious—perhaps Noel has already left Erfoud. He's also low on gas and here's a service station." He pulled into the station, stopped beside the pumps. From the office the attendant emerged, limping on a crippled leg; a short heavy-shouldered man, with black hair combed in a mid-Victorian swirl down over his forehead. He had careful inquisitive eyes in a bland face. *"Oui, monsieur?"*

"The language barrier again," said Darrell in disgust. He turned to Ellen. "You'll have to translate. Better have him fill the tank."

Ellen gave the necessary instructions; the attendant hobbled to the pumps. Ellen jumped out of the car, Darrell followed. She addressed a question to the attendant. Darrell watched his expression. He raised his eyebrows, looked rather queerly at Ellen, at Darrell, shrugged, shook his head, replied. Darrell could not decide whether his answer were positive or negative.

Ellen translated. "He says a clever man remembers only to count his change after his patrons leave; and so avoids getting into trouble."

Darrell took a five-thousand franc note from his wallet. "This may stimulate his memory."

The attendant took the note, pursing his lips reverently, appeared to concentrate. He spoke at length.

Ellen said grudgingly, "Your theories seem to be correct. A car stopped here early in the morning a month ago; the driver made a telephone call. This man was busy under the lubrication rack; his assistant took care of the car. He paid no particular attention and only remembers because of the telephone call to Erfoud, which as you supposed is not a usual occurrence."

"Well, we're on the right track," said Darrell. "Where is the assistant?"

Ellen inquired; the attendant, screwing the cap back on the gas tank, made a vague gesture, replied.

"He's not here," Ellen told Darrell. "He quit two weeks ago, and apparently went to Rabat."

"Confound it! Can this man describe the driver?"

Ellen asked, listened to the response. "He says he paid very little attention. He thinks there were two in the car, a man and a woman."

"A man *and* a woman?"

"That's what he says."

"Young or old?"

Ellen asked, received the response. "He doesn't know. He paid no attention."

"How about the car?"

There was the sequence of question and reply. Ellen hesitated, looked doubtfully at Darrell.

"Well?"

"He says it was a car like this one. He says he thought it was the same car when we drove up. He thought we were the same people."

"Well, obviously we're not. Damn! So near and yet so far. Isn't there anything else he remembers?"

Ellen inquired. The answer came; she translated. "He says he thinks the car drove off toward Erfoud."

"And that's all he knows?"

"Apparently."

"Does he know where we can locate the mechanic who quit?"

"I already asked him. He says no, the man was on his way back to France."

Darrell paid for the gas. "What a let-down. If only he had noticed *something*! Was the man big? Little? Fat? Thin?"

Ellen asked; the attendant shrugged, spoke.

"He says the man seemed about average size. He never saw his face, in fact paid no attention to him or the car."

Darrell started the car. "Well, that's that." He left the station, drove slowly back down the road toward Erfoud. "While I think of it, Duff drives this car, doesn't he?"

"Not often. I discourage it."

"Did he borrow it a month ago?"

"I don't think so. Are we going back to Erfoud?"

"No more than half-way, because the X's and Noel would have met before then."

"And what happened when they met—since you're theorizing?"

"Let's pretend we're the X's. We've been driving all night. We're planning to hijack a load of heroin. We're nervous. We want the money, but we don't want to be caught."

"We wouldn't stay here, on the flat area," said Ellen. "We'd go down the road farther—where we could see traffic coming from both directions."

"Right. We drive till we find a good spot. Noel may or may not expect us... No, he wouldn't know we're here. He thinks Mr. X gave the message to Arthur. He'll be looking in his rear-view mirror, watching for the FLN."

They returned back over the barren area. "Every minute, every kilometer we're more tense," said Darrell, "because we're not sure where we'll meet Noel. If he sees us, the game blows up; he's no fool; he knows we have no business here."

Ellen said woodenly, "If that's how we feel, then we've already decided to kill Noel. Because we can't have tales carried back to Tangier."

Darrell nodded. "That's undoubtedly what we've decided. Ambush."

The road dipped briefly into the valley, rose back to the desert, crossed a mile of barrens, then dropped again, winding in hairpin switch-backs through red sandstone bluffs down to the fertile green ribbon. Darrell jammed on the brakes. "Look. From here you can see the road behind, before it takes that dip. There's a car turning down now. Ahead you can see the road, not quite as well, but far enough for two or three minutes warning. Look, way down there—a bus. See it?"

"Yes."

Darrell parked at the side of the road, alighted. The sun, already intense, beat into his face. To the right was the valley; to the left a ledge of rusty sandstone, a wind-tormented crag, a wide area of flint-covered desert. Ahead the road curved sharply down to the valley floor. Ellen came to stand beside him. They heard the bus approach, wheezing and grinding up the slope.

"Here comes the truck," said Darrell. "We're waiting for it. We're ready. It's coming slowly, pulling up the hill in low."

The bus nosed around the turn; a row of curious dark faces looked down at them; then the bus was past, roaring off toward Ksar-es-Souk.

"So," said Darrell. "I stopped the truck. I jumped on the running-board, or maybe I stood here and shot. Noel's foot would slide off the accelerator. One way or another we've got the truck. We've got to work fast. I throw out the heroin. You pile it in the car—in the rear compartment, behind the seat, on the floor, anywhere. We're in a frenzy. There's traffic along here, we can't loiter. We're exultant too. A million dollars! But now, here's the truck, and a body. How to hide the horrid deed? We don't want to be discovered. So—" he looked off to the left "—we drive it off the road, out across the rocks." He walked out, scanning the landscape. Ellen followed.

"We could drive it out here, if we didn't care about tires— and of course we don't. We'd head out behind that big jut of rock. Nobody would have a reason to come out here. A truck could rest fifty years..."

They climbed over the ledge of sandstone, walked behind the crag. The sun glared on their heads; rocks rolled and twisted underfoot. Nothing grew except little green balls of lichen, dry and spongy.

"No truck," said Ellen. "The theory isn't working so well."

Darrell looked around the barren waste. "No. Apparently not. Unless—" he pointed. "There's a gully over here."

They walked across the desert. The gully opened abruptly before them, a harsh steep-sided watercourse, now dry, draining into the river valley. Below them a gray dump-truck lay on its side, battered and crumpled.

"You wait up here," said Darrell.

Ellen waited. Darrell clambered down to the truck, looked into the cab, jerked his head back. He walked around the truck, then struggled back up the slope. Ellen waited silently.

"Noel's in there. What's left of him." They stood looking down at the truck, the heat of the sunshine tingling against their skin. The truck lay asprawl and clumsy like a dead dinosaur. And in the cab, the withered brain of the dead beast, Noel.

"Well, we've found him," said Darrell.

"I'm sorry," said Ellen. She hesitated, then reached over and took his hand. "I'm really sorry."

"It's no surprise, no great shock. I'm sorry too—but it was the chance he took."

Ellen stiffened. "Listen." Darrell had also heard the faint sound of rock touching rock. He looked around. From the direction of the road came three men. One wore a rough brown djellaba. The second wore baggy trousers and a green pull-over: Slip-Slip. The third, in smart gray gabardine and a red fez, was Abd Allah el Kazim.

Chapter XIII

THE Moroccans came to look over the edge of the gully. Abd Allah el Kazim gestured; Slip-Slip scrambled down to the truck. El Kazim turned to Darrell. "We meet again."

Darrell agreed guardedly. He glanced toward the road; the crag and the low sandstone ridge hid it from view. "So you knew the truck was here all the time."

El Kazim shook his head, teeth glistening. "No. We did not know. But we knew that you would lead us to it. Ever since you first arrived in Tangier, we have watched you. Because we knew that you would bring us here."

"I didn't bring you to much," said Darrell. "Just Noel."

"Where is the heroin?" El Kazim asked the question casually, as if he were inquiring the time of day.

"I suppose that whoever killed Noel took it. I don't know, I really don't care."

El Kazim turned him a quick glance, lips drawn back in his feral grin. "You don't care to know who killed your brother?"

"Noel played with fire. He got burned. He knew it was hot."

"But he was your brother, the son of your father, your own blood!" His glance went to Ellen, returned to Darrell.

"I'm sick of the whole business," said Darrell. "I've found Noel. He's beyond any help I'm able to give him."

El Kazim laughed politely. "A good Moslem could never rest until he had dealt with the man who did such a foul deed." His glance once again rested on Ellen.

"That may be," said Darrell shortly. "Let's go, Ellen."

El Kazim held up his hand. "Just one moment, before you go. I am curious."

"About what?"

"How did you know the truck was here? Did Miss McKinstry tell you?"

"No, of course not."

"Then how did you know? In all the great desert, you found this place."

"It seemed reasonable that someone had stopped Noel along this road. I picked the first likely spot."

El Kazim nodded, eyes traveling back and forth between Darrell and Ellen. "You are clever. But, you see, we are as clever as you. Never forget that."

Slip-Slip clambered back up out of the gully. He reported in guttural Arabic, spat disgustedly into the dirt. El Kazim replied softly, almost jocularly. All three turned to look at Darrell and Ellen.

"We're going," said Darrell.

"A moment, please do not go yet. One or two things I wish to ask you."

"Well?" Darrell waited half-turned away, with Ellen pressed against his back.

"Who did Noel call from Erfoud?"

"I don't know."

"But you lie, American," said el Kazim, grinning. "You lie."

"I'm telling you the truth."

"But you stopped at the service station in Ksar-es-Souk. We watched you, and we stopped too. You paid five thousand francs, we paid five thousand francs. A month ago a man and a woman came from Tangier in a black sports car. In Miss McKinstry's car. If you are not lying, then you are stupid."

"I don't understand you," said Darrell coldly. Ellen's body felt tense and tight; her breath came fast.

El Kazim nodded toward Ellen. "She understands well enough. Noel telephoned her. He made two telephone calls from Erfoud. Is it not clear? He called the Balmoral Hotel. Aktouf assured us that he took no message. We have suspected Miss McKinstry for some time. She took the message, she came in her car, with someone else. They killed Noel, took the heroin."

Darrell laughed. "It sounds well, but it just doesn't make sense. In the first place Noel made three calls, not two."

"No, Mr. Hutson. We also have consulted the clerk. He tells us Noel made only two calls."

"You ask him now, and he'll tell you differently."

El Kazim shook his head. "Let us be sensible. There is no need for further waste of time. I will ask Miss McKinstry, pleasantly and politely, where she has taken the heroin. I am sure she will tell me, because she remembers the difficulties poor Mr. Aktouf discovered... I will ask. Where is the heroin, Miss McKinstry? Don't answer hastily. Think well. There is ample time, and we are quite alone; no one will overhear."

Ellen said nothing.

"Where is the heroin, Miss McKinstry?"

"I haven't any idea," said Ellen.

"Who came with you to Ksar-es-Souk a month ago?"

"No one. Because I didn't come."

"Please think hard, Miss McKinstry." El Kazim turned, looked here and there over the desert. He spoke in Arabic; Slip-Slip trotted away. The other reached into his pouch, brought forth an automatic pistol, ostentatiously snapped a shell into the firing chamber.

"Are you thinking, Miss McKinstry? Think quickly. My friend is getting certain helps for us from the car."

"I don't know anything," said Ellen. "If you hope to frighten me with that ridiculous gun, you're mistaken." She turned, walked toward the road.

"Stop!" called el Kazim hoarsely. "Stop. Or you will be shot."

Ellen made no answer, continued.

El Kazim muttered over his shoulder; his aide raised the gun, aiming high on Ellen's thigh. "Ellen!" cried Darrell.

Ellen looked over her shoulder. She saw the leveled gun, threw herself to the ground. At the same instant the Moroccan fired.

Something peculiar happened to Darrell. The world became a different world, and he was a new creature. He threw himself at the Moroccan. His goal was the throat; his hands hooked to claw through flesh. At contact with the burly body, other reflexes came into play. The Moroccan flailed with the gun; Darrell struck a terrible blow with his right fist, half-jumping off the ground with the thrust of his leg. The Moroccan's head rolled askew, he tottered backwards. The gun dropped. Darrell lurched for it, looked behind, recovered himself. Abd Allah el Kazim came dancing forward like a crow, pulling out his own gun. Darrell rushed with head down, almost on all fours, running to keep from falling on his face. He struck el Kazim with a charging football block; el Kazim toppled back over the edge of the gully, rolled, tumbled, thrashed to the bottom. Darrell turned to the Moroccan, now crawling on hands and knees to the gun. Darrell ran forward, kicked him under the jaw, bent for the gun.

He heard Ellen's scream. A shadow loomed over him: Slip-Slip. Darrell glimpsed steel; he dropped to the ground, rolled. Slip-Slip spit and hissed, dancing over the rocks with a fluttering of the djellaba, leaning forward with his knife. Darrell rolled away, jumped to his feet, picking up lumps of rock in each hand. He threw with all his power; the rock, grape-fruit size, struck Slip-Slip in the chest. From a different angle came another rock, which missed, but which distracted Slip-Slip's attention. Ellen had returned. Darrell threw his second rock; Slip-Slip dodged, backed away.

Darrell picked up the gun; Slip-Slip took to his heels. The older Moroccan lay on his face, hands clenching and unclenching. Ellen stood uncertainly a few yards away, carrying stones in her hands. She smiled at Darrell—a ghostly smile of encouragement. Darrell made a meaningless gesture, went to look over the side of the gully. El Kazim, eyes wild and red as pomegranate kernels, was half-way up the slope, crawling with gun in hand, dragging one leg, blood streaming down his cheek. At the sight of Darrell he squealed, raised his arm, fired. Darrell jumped back; the shot whistled past his ear.

Darrell pushed a round black rock twice the size of his head over the edge of the gully. There was a rumble, a clatter, dying away in a diminishing rattle of small stones. Darrell glanced cautiously over the edge. El Kazim lay crumpled at the bottom of the gully. Unconscious or shamming? Darrell could not be certain.

"Best to shoot him," said Ellen huskily.

"I can't."

"When I think of what he wanted to do—"

"Let's go," said Darrell, but Ellen pulled at his arm.

"Look at his head!"

El Kazim's head hung far back, twisted so that he looked along his shoulder.

"If he's not dead he's awfully sick," said Darrell. There was motion to the side; the older Moroccan was tensed against the ground, staring at them.

Darrell took Ellen's arm. "Let's go."

They walked back across the rock-strewn desert. Around the side of the crag Slip-Slip watched them. The older man rose to his feet, hobbled to the edge of the gully, looked down. He beckoned; Slip-Slip went to him.

Darrell and Ellen returned to the road. Beside the Mercedes-Benz were el Kazim's Citroën and a small black Fiat.

Ellen looked sidewise at Darrell. "You were right," said Darrell. "You saw a small black car this morning."

"I thought I saw one," said Ellen. "It may not have been this one, of course."

"This one is close enough. Another thing—last night I made up my mind to ask you something, at the right time. Maybe this is the right time, maybe it isn't. But I'll ask anyway. Will you marry me?"

"It's the right time," said Ellen. "Almost any time would have been right."

"Then you will?"

"Of course. Why else would I try so hard to hate you?"

"That's illogical," said Darrell, "but I think I know what you mean." He lifted the Moroccan's automatic—a new Mauser—snapped the safety, put it in his pocket. "I'll keep this for a souvenir. It might come in handy, who knows?" They climbed into the car. Darrell started the engine, shifted, they were away.

Ellen kissed his cheek. "Thank you for protecting me."

Darrell grinned. "Thanks for drawing the fire."

"I was hysterical."

"But we're both alive, and with all our arms and legs, thank heaven!"

"Now what do we do?"

"Police, I suppose."

She sighed. "There'll be no end of trouble."

"Probably, but I can't leave Noel's body out there in the desert."

The road dwindled behind them; they passed Ksar-es-Souk, started up the approach to the Atlas.

"Darrell," Ellen said thoughtfully.

"Yes?"

"El Kazim thought I had killed Noel."

"So he said."

"It sounds reasonable, doesn't it?"

"In a way."

"Do you think I did?"

"I've considered the possibility."

"What if I had?"

"It would set me quite a problem. I don't think you did."

"Why not?"

"First, the three telephone calls. Second, you went to the service station with me, quite openly. If you were Mrs. X—I should say Miss X—you'd be afraid of recognition. So far as I could see, it never occurred to you."

"Well, it wasn't I, so you don't have the problem. And if it had been I, I'd tell you. Then I'd weep, and say I was sorry, that I only did it to spite Arthur, and you'd forgive me."

"Yes, I probably would."

They rolled back over the Atlas: past Rich, up over the Pass of the She-Camel to Midelt, down through the Col du Zad to Azrou, and the sun hung low over the great plain of the Maghreb.

In Meknes they ate dinner, refueled, turned the Mercedes-Benz north, and at midnight coasted down out of the hills into the bright crescent of Tangier. Ellen pressed close to Darrell.

"What's the trouble?"

"Coming back to Tangier. I feel tight inside, and hard and angry... Darrell, must I go home?"

"Of course not. You're coming with me. Now and always."

She sighed. "I don't want to go back to that house. For eight years I've planned to kill Arthur, and I can't get it out of my mind."

"Sh," said Darrell. "In a few days we'll be leaving, and it'll all be behind you."

They turned up Calle Miranda, parked. At the Miranda Hotel Darrell booked a room for Ellen, ignoring the bland manner of the clerk.

At her door she kissed him. "Give me time for a shower."

"Fifteen minutes?"

"Ten is enough. But I may still be wet."

Chapter XIV

T**HE** next morning Darrell went to the headquarters of the Sûreté Nationale, on the second floor of an airy white building at the bottom of Boulevard Pasteur. In the outer office a dozen men and women waited, while behind the counter an unhurried functionary examined, marked, stamped, approved, disapproved or rejected the forms they had filled out—applications for travel permits, exit visas, any of the other special documents required by citizens and aliens alike.

Darrell went to the far end of the room, signaled to a fat young man in sun-tans, who without troubling to rise from his chair pointed to the clerk. Reluctant to explain his business in front of a dozen bystanders, Darrell made a more peremptory gesture. The fat young man paused, glumly heaved himself from his chair, approached. "What do you want, sir?"

"I want to report a homicide. A death."

The fat young man looked at Darrell with increased interest. "You kill somebody?"

"No. I want to speak to the officer in charge of such matters."

"Please, one minute." He disappeared into a back room. A moment passed. He emerged, lumbered forward to open the gate in the counter. "Captain Goulidja," he hissed under his breath, "you will speak to him."

Behind a green metal desk sat a short thick man of Napoleonic mien. Ringlets of mingled black and gray clustered over his broad forehead. He wore an expression of mildly amused skepticism, as if to warn malefactors, actual or putative, that their guile had been foreseen and discounted. He held out his hand.

"Your passport, please."

Darrell handed over the green booklet. Captain Goulidja flicked it open with an expert hand, assimilated what information it contained with an air of faint astonishment, placed it carefully down on his desk. "What did you wish, please? You report a death?"

"My brother Noel has been missing for a month. I came to Tangier to find out what was wrong. I learned that he had been carrying guns to the Algerian rebels—"

"The FLN," interjected Captain Goulidja, without emphasis.

"He wrote me a letter from Erfoud."

"Ah yes, Erfoud."

"I went to Erfoud, I made some inquiries, which convinced me he had run into trouble. Yesterday I checked the road from Erfoud to Ksar-es-Souk, finally found my brother. He was dead, in a truck which had been driven into a ravine. I left him there, and last night returned to Tangier. If you will give me a map, I will show you where he is to be found."

Captain Goulidja nodded perfunctorily, leaned back in his chair. "I see. And your position is what?"

"My position?" asked Darrell in surprise. "I have no position. I came here to report the death of my brother."

Captain Goulidja shook his head in polite condolence. "He is an American citizen also?"

"Yes."

"And so you wish us to investigate this death?"

Darrell inspected the placid face in perplexity. Was the captain practicing a local variety of one-upmanship, or merely, in all innocence, seeking information? A third possibility occurred to him: Captain Goulidja might be collecting his thoughts. Darrell said in a formal voice, "The investigation is your concern. I suppose you have your regulations."

"Yes. We have regulations, just as in the United States. And why have you come to us? You wish us to find the killer of your brother?"

Darrell moved in his chair. "Does it make any difference what I want? My brother is dead—killed, murdered. I am reporting this death to you because I assume the law of Morocco requires me to do so."

"Yes," said Captain Goulidja. "That is right. Why did you not report to Erfoud?"

"Because I am staying here in Tangier, at the Miranda Hotel."

Captain Goulidja made a note. "You are carrying guns to Algeria too?" he asked casually.

"No. I arrived here recently. The date is in my passport. I came because my brother wrote me he was in trouble. This is the letter."

Captain Goulidja read the letter with amused incredulity—or so it seemed. He put the letter beside the passport, leaned back in his chair, looked up at the ceiling. "I will say that we have heard something of this case. We know many things, but in these times we must walk with care. There is much trouble in the world, is there not?"

"A great deal of trouble, I would say."

Captain Goulidja nodded. "What is right, what is wrong..." he held out his hands, raised his eyebrows, smiled. "It is for men wiser than I to say."

Darrell realized that Captain Goulidja was imparting information with great delicacy, talking around the circumference of his meaning, defining his theme without ever touching it.

"It is very sad for you," Captain Goulidja continued. "Such things happen, of course. As you know there is great international concern over Algeria. There are negotiations. The French are being asked to take their garrisons from Morocco. There is always much talk of arms traffic; it is a shame. The French stop ships, they force down airplanes. It is not legal, but what can we do?" He shook his head dolefully. "There is much trouble in North Africa now. We know many things. But we must be careful."

Darrell nodded briefly. "About Noel—"

"I will make the investigation. But perhaps it will be quiet. A non-political matter." He pounded the table lightly with his fist. "In

Morocco, there is law, just as in the United States. So we forget nothing, we make the full investigation. You are not leaving Tangier?"

"No. Not for a few days. I want to get my brother's body." Darrell stopped, an image of Noel, as he had been in his youth, coming before his eyes: feckless, lazy, good-humored, boundless in his fine conceits. This flamboyant, slightly ridiculous Noel was truly dead. "I want to ship him home."

Captain Goulidja stared out the window, out over the bright blue harbor. He turned back brusquely. "Very good. Wait one moment please." He took up his telephone, called a number, waited, spoke in Arabic. The conversation continued several minutes. At one point he turned to Darrell. "Where exactly is the truck?"

Darrell explained with as much precision as possible; Captain Goulidja returned to the telephone, the conversation continued. Finally he hung up, reached in his desk, brought out a pad of paper, took a fountain pen from his pocket. "Now. I must ask questions."

Two hours later Darrell returned to the hotel. As he arrived Ellen drove up in the Mercedes-Benz, three suitcases on the seat beside her. "I'm moved out," she said flatly. She seemed to be avoiding Darrell's eyes.

"What's the trouble?" he asked.

She got out of the car, wearing a dark green frock, with a white collar close around her neck. "I've just had an upsetting quarrel."

Darrell lifted her suitcases to the sidewalk. "With Arthur?"

"No. Just Duff. He called me all kinds of names."

"Because of me?"

"Yes, partly. He doesn't like you."

"It doesn't matter. How long does it take to get married?"

"Two days, I think."

"We'll start the process this afternoon. And we'll go to the consulate also, in case there's any red tape."

She shook her head. "It won't work, Darrell. I can't do it. You go home. I'm going to London and get a job."

"Good heavens. What brought this on?"

She looked sullenly up the street. "Good sense. I'm not in love with you, you're not in love with me."

"I see," said Darrell.

"It's been propinquity. The moon, the palm trees. Emotions, guns going off, more propinquity..."

Darrell considered a moment. "If we get married there'll be nothing but propinquity."

"I know."

"Do you object?"

"No." She spoke in a muffled voice. "But I can't come back with you, a bedraggled waif you picked up in Tangier."

"I won't go back without you."

"You won't?"

"Not unless you make it clear that you don't want to come."

She laughed. "That's asking a lot. I don't think I can do it."

Darrell heaved a deep sigh. "That's that, then. Has Duff been putting those ideas in your head?"

"Not altogether. They've been there."

"Are they gone now?"

"Yes, I suppose so."

"Good. I'll take these suitcases in, then we'll go for lunch. Some place cheerful."

Fifteen minutes later they were high on the top floor of the Hotel Velasquez, sitting by a window, with the wide blue, white and yellow panorama below. She reached across the table, squeezed his hand. "You're very calm and settling, Darrell. I feel much better."

"I don't feel calm. I'd like to punch Duff's nose."

"If you persist in marrying me, he'll be your brother-in-law."

"I'll have to take the bad with the good. After all, you don't know what you're getting into either."

"I'll take my chances. I'll be polite and ladylike and no one will suspect what a monster I really am... Tell me about the police."

"There's not much to tell. They're bringing in the body. I telephoned my father; he wants me to ship it home. I'll have to make arrangements."

Ellen twisted the stem of the wine-glass between her fingers. "Did they ask you many questions?"

"About what you'd expect."

She looked into her glass, at the satin disk of wine. "What did you tell them?"

"Everything I knew. Except about Noel's cargo being heroin. They'll have to find that out from someone else."

Ellen seemed on the point of speaking; she moved uncomfortably in her seat.

"What's the trouble?" Darrell asked.

"I'm wondering—suppose the police think I did it, or helped do it?"

"It's a possibility."

"That I did it?"

"That the police will suspect you."

Ellen laughed shakily. "Well, I didn't. I haven't even killed Arthur, whom I quite desperately want to kill." She sighed. "Darrell, you've changed my life. Since I can't convince you to be evil, I'll have to give up my wickedness and become a nice American housewife—or at least pretend to be—and spank our children for naughtiness I secretly approve of."

Darrell looked at his watch. "Before we can have children we've got to be married. Let's go get the license, or whatever it's called here."

"What time is it?"

"Two o'clock."

Ellen nodded. "Good. We've got time. I've got to go back to the house this afternoon. There's an auctioneer coming out to look at the furniture."

"Would you like me to come?"

She shook her head. "It's a dismal business. I'd much rather do it by myself."

"Whatever you'd like to keep, we'll ship home."

"Home?" She looked surprised for a moment. "Yes, I've got a home now, haven't I?" She reflected. "It would be nice to keep the grandfather clock. And the piano. And the books."

"Doesn't Duff have anything to say?"

She laughed shortly. "Duff owes me twenty thousand pounds. He has nothing to say."

They drove to the rambling old municipal building, roamed tall dark corridors, checked dozens of doors with triplicate inscriptions in French, Spanish and Arabic. They found the appropriate office, filled out appropriate forms, displayed documents, paid the fee and received the marriage license, likewise printed in three languages.

They returned to where they had parked the car. "I've got to see that damned auctioneer," said Ellen. "What are you going to do?"

"One thing and another. Perhaps I'll go down to the Hotel de los Dos Continentes and pick up Noel's belongings. A melancholy task, but it's got to be done. I'll meet you when you're finished with the auctioneer."

"Very well. Where?"

"The Masquerade?"

Ellen wrinkled her nose. "All right. The Masquerade. At six o'clock. Can I drop you down to Noel's hotel?"

"I'll take a cab."

Ellen said, "Let me see the marriage license once more. Just to be sure it's real."

"It's real. And I'm real."

"I know you're real." She kissed him. "I'm very lucky, Darrell. I promise you I'll try to be good, whether my heart's in it or not." She laughed. "I've never been so excited!"

"Until six," said Darrell grinning. "And don't get into any trouble."

He watched her walk to the car, slim and jaunty, her blonde-brown cap shining in the Tangier sunlight. She waved at him, then she was gone.

Darrell walked to the Boulevard Pasteur. He visited several shops, made a purchase in the last. The time was now almost five o'clock. The Hotel de los Dos Continentes and Noel's clothes could wait until tomorrow. He walked up to the Hotel Miranda. He showered, changed into his dark suit; at quarter to six he crossed the street to the Masquerade Bar.

Phil Beresford greeted him with a careless wave of the hand. Darrell slipped up on a bar stool; Phil shook his head. "That's Mr. Burdette's throne. He's out in the kitchen selling Mama a Rolls-Royce. Move over one."

Darrell ordered a highball; Phil flipped ice into a glass. "What's new? That brother of yours showed his guilty face yet?"

"His face wasn't guilty when I saw it."

Phil stopped dramatically with whiskey bottle in mid-air. "You found him?"

Darrell nodded. "Dead."

Phil mixed the highball with reverence. "Well, that's too bad. No particular surprise of course. Where did you locate him?"

"In a truck a hundred yards off the road, down toward the desert."

"Hijack, eh?" He set out the highball.

"I wouldn't know for sure."

"You tell the police?"

"This morning."

"Who did you talk to?"

"Captain Goulidja."

"I know him. Not a bad fellow. But he won't move on anything stronger than a wife-beating until he gets official policy. Do you mind if I tell a journalist friend of mine? A scoop's a scoop."

"Go ahead."

"By 'journalist friend', naturally I mean T-Bone." He ducked under the bar, looked into the Balmoral lobby. "Hey, Lucky! Call T-Bone, tell her I want to talk to her. A hot news story."

He ducked back under the bar. Mr. Burdette emerged from the kitchen, wiping his mouth. "Here, Mr. Burdette! Fingers in the cookie jar again!"

"Please, Phil," said Mr. Burdette, "let me enjoy your last few days."

Phil shook his head. "It's bad enough you plundering the larder; don't make me get sentimental about it."

"Are you leaving?" Darrell asked Phil.

Phil nodded. "I got my notice. New owner to the building wants to run the bar himself."

"That's too bad."

"I don't mind. I been here too long. The wild geese is flying south. I'm leaving Mama with Mr. Burdette. They'll make out fine. Me and T-Bone will be far away, dancing to the music of castanets and flutes."

"Have you told Mama about this?" asked Mr. Burdette.

"Mama don't need to be told. She *knows* these things."

Mrs. Phil said in a neutral voice, just under Phil's elbow, "You're wanted on the phone."

"Who, me? Yes sir. I mean, yes, ma'am. I'm coming."

Phil presently returned, pounding his temples with his fists. "That T-Bone. Tact and grace of a cow in mud. Sending Mama to fetch me to the phone." He turned to Darrell. "She'll be right down. She just wanted to know what's so all-fired important."

"You told her?"

"I gave her the bare outlines."

"Was she surprised?"

"You're asking me to read T-Bone's mind? That's like asking a blind ape to read Egyptian hieroglyphics, with no Rosetta Stone."

"She doesn't write these things herself, does she?"

Phil shook his head. "T-Bone's the roving reporter. She passes on the tip, and if it's any good they slip her a few thousand francs. It went pretty high when she found a certain Swede actress staying incognito in the Balmoral. Here she comes. Brace yourself."

T-Bone slipped in from the Balmoral wearing a tight black jersey blouse and a soft pleated skirt the color of old whiskey—almost a match for her shoulder-length hair.

"Darrell! You've found Noel! And he's dead!"

"My word," squeaked Mr. Burdette. "Is this true?"

Darrell assented politely. "I'm afraid so."

"We're very sorry," said T-Bone. "It was the Algerians who did it?"

"I don't know," said Darrell. "The police are investigating now."

T-Bone made careful notes on a paper napkin, using a ball-point pen lent her fatalistically by Phil. "Careful, T-Bone, don't lick the point. You'll get streaks all up and down your tongue."

Darrell glanced at his watch. Six-thirty. Where was Ellen? Late. Why should she be late? Something heavy slid down into his stomach. Why should Ellen be late? A dozen possible reasons—one of which terrified him.

Darrell jumped to his feet. "Phil, if Ellen McKinstry comes in, tell her I'll be right back."

"Okay, will do."

Darrell ran out into the street, looked for a cab. He started down toward the Place de France, halted, ran into the Hotel Miranda.

With maddening deliberation the clerk gave him his key. Darrell bounded up the steps to his room, pocketed the Mauser automatic he had brought back from Erfoud, ran downstairs. A cruising taxi came past; Darrell flagged it, gave the address of the McKinstry villa on Calle Costanza. "Fast," he said. "Hurry."

They raced up the hill, the little motor whirring like a power-saw. Darrell pointed out the house. "Wait for me."

He jumped from the cab. The Mercedes-Benz was parked in the driveway. At the curb was Arthur Upshaw's big pale blue Chrysler, across the street a dusty black Citroën.

Darrell stood looking at the house. Smoke was rising from the chimney. The evening was rather warm.

Time seemed to move slowly. Darrell drifted to the house. It loomed larger and larger before him, filling the sky as he mounted the front steps. He tried the door, it was locked. He went along the porch to a window, looked in, but the curtains were drawn. He listened, and seemed to hear a murmur of voices.

He put out his finger to ring the bell, stopped short. He jumped down off the porch, raced around to the back, climbed wooden steps to the service porch. The door was also locked. By standing on the rail, reaching to the side he could grasp the sill of an open window. He made an awkward leap, wriggled through the window, landing face down on the floor. He picked himself up, took the gun from his pocket, snapped off the safety, opened the door into the kitchen. Here he stopped to listen.

The voices were clearer but still inaudible. Darrell started forward, then hesitated, uncomfortably aware of his position. If conditions were all in order, he would appear ridiculous. He put his hand and the gun into his coat-pocket, eased open the swinging door, slowly entered the polished walnut and silver-gleaming dining room.

There was silence—a heavy cotton-wool silence. Then a sharp gasp. Then came Arthur Upshaw's voice, quiet and controlled. "She's fainted."

Conditions were not all in order.

Duff said, "Look here, Arthur, I don't think—"

"Shut up. Get some cold water."

Duff came out of the study. He saw Darrell, stopped stock-still. Darrell pointed the gun. "Back," he said in a guttural voice.

Duff backed into the study. Darrell followed. Arthur Upshaw looked up, stern and scowling. Jilali sat on the sofa, smoking a cigarette. The fire burnt cheerfully. Ellen sat in a kitchen chair, wrists lashed behind the back with cellophane tape. Heavy cord bound her waist, thighs and ankles to the chair. Her legs were bare, the skirt pulled high up over her knees. Arthur Upshaw held a poker, white-gray with heat, smoking gently. One of Ellen's knees showed a long red mark.

Darrell stood in the doorway, pointing the gun, unable to speak. No one moved. Smoke curled up from Jilali's cigarette. Ten seconds passed, twenty seconds. Arthur Upshaw gently straightened his back, stood erect, the poker hanging loosely in his grip.

Darrell finally spoke. "Listen carefully. I'll kill you if you don't do exactly what I say. There won't be a second chance. Do you understand? Answer me. Do you understand?"

Duff nodded dumbly.

"Answer me," said Darrell.

"I understand," said Duff.

"I understand," said Jilali equably.

Darrell looked at Arthur Upshaw.

Arthur Upshaw nodded, his mouth compressed into a length of white string.

Darrell said slowly, "Turn around, Upshaw."

Upshaw swung the poker a fraction of an inch. The gun pointed at his middle. He turned to face the fire. The firelight glowed, cast ruddy shadows on his face.

"Drop the poker."

The poker clattered on the bricks. He said contemptuously, "You're making a bloody damn fool of yourself."

"Duff, go to the wall, at the other side of the fireplace. Put your hands on the wall."

Duff obeyed.

"Jilali, put your hands in the air. Stand up. Turn around. Walk into the corner. Lean against the wall."

Jilali, cigarette in hand, went to the corner with an air of boredom.

"Upshaw—put your hands out and lean on the wall."

Arthur Upshaw obeyed without comment.

Darrell surveyed the three. "If any of you makes the slightest move—so much as turns a head, I'll shoot to kill. I'm aching for the excuse."

He listened at the door, concerned that there might be others in the house. The house was still.

Ellen was conscious; she smiled at him, a ghastly thin grin. Darrell asked her, "Are there any more?"

"No. Just those three."

Darrell went slowly to the desk, opened a drawer, never taking his eyes from the three men. A glance showed him a pair of scissors. He took it, walked slowly to Ellen, cautiously cut the tape. She brought her hands in front of her, rubbed her wrists.

Darrell gave her the scissors. "Cut yourself loose."

Feebly, hands trembling, she did so, rose swaying to her feet.

Darrell decided that Jilali was the one most likely to be carrying a gun. He said, "Jilali, hold your hands in the air. Walk backward, toward me... Don't move, Upshaw. Don't even quiver... Stop, Jilali. Sit down in the chair, put your arms behind you. Ellen, get that tape. Tie his wrists... Good. Now search him for a gun."

Ellen removed a small automatic from his coat-pocket. Darrell took it, examined it, snapped a shell into the firing chamber. "Can you use this?"

"Of course," said Ellen in a husky voice.

"It's cocked, ready to go off if you pull the trigger."

"I know."

"Keep it pointed at Upshaw... Duff, lie face down on the floor."

Darrell warily taped Duff's wrists, his ankles. "Now, Upshaw, face down on the floor."

"She killed your brother, you ruddy fool," said Upshaw savagely. "She's playing you for a goat!"

"Down on your face."

"What do you think you're up to with this monkey-business?"

Darrell came cautiously forward; Upshaw grudgingly lowered himself to the floor. He was taped, wrist and ankle.

Darrell stood looking at them. Ellen came to stand beside him. "How many times did they burn you?"

"Just once... What are you going to do?"

"I don't know. At first I planned to kill them."

Darrell picked up the poker, put it into the fire. The three men watched him with fascinated eyes. Duff raised his head, called out in a hoarse voice: "Help!"

Darrell balled a handkerchief, thrust it into Duff's mouth. Duff spat it out, tried to bite, thrashed on the floor. Darrell rapped him with the muzzle of the gun, tied the handkerchief in a haphazard gag.

The poker was hot. "You three are lucky that I came when I did. You only had time to burn her once... Perhaps I ought to do what you might have done..."

Ellen clutched his arm. "Don't touch them, Darrell. Don't burn them."

"No? Why not?"

"I don't know. I can't explain. They're too horrible to touch."

Darrell grinned. "A little reminder?"

"No. Please don't. It's not because I'm merciful. It's just that— I can't explain. I want to get out of here. I don't want to breathe the same air they breathe."

"Just as you say. Do you have everything you want?"

"Yes. Please, let's go."

Darrell inspected the three men. Duff glared, Upshaw watched coldly, Jilali looked at him with mild reproach, a hint of derision.

"Ellen knows nothing of your heroin, nor do I. Please leave us out of your future plans."

Upshaw opened his mouth, closed it with a snap.

"My information is different," said Jilali.

"Your information is that a man and a woman in a black sports car came into Ksar-es-Souk the morning Noel was killed. That's all the information you have."

"It's enough to work on," said Jilali.

"You work somewhere else from now on." He turned away, took Ellen's hand. "Does your knee hurt?"

"A little. Not badly."

Darrell put the gun in his pocket. He took a last look at the three men, then turned. They left the house. The taxi-driver looked up sleepily. Darrell paid him off.

He drove the Mercedes-Benz back down the hill. "Where do you want to go?"

"I don't care. I was so glad to see you, Darrell, you'll never realize." She started to cry, then angrily wiped her face with her arm.

"I suppose they wanted their blasted heroin."

She nodded. "Jilali told Arthur that I'd killed Noel."

"What his men told him yesterday."

"I told them I didn't, they wouldn't believe me."

Darrell patted her. "I can't imagine Duff being a party to that kind of thing. The others yes. But Duff... After all, he's your brother."

"He does what Arthur tells him," said Ellen. "He can't help himself. And I suppose he thought I'd taken his heroin."

Darrell parked on the Place de France, in front of a drug store. "Let me see your knee." He examined the angry red blister. "I'll get some salve and some gauze. I think that's about all we can do for it."

He returned with salve, gauze, adhesive tape, and made a neat bandage. "Thank you," Ellen said weakly.

He patted her face. "Now, I've got something nice for you. Hold out your hand."

"What is it?"

"It's in this box."

She opened the box, took out the ring—a single square diamond on a platinum band. "Darrell, when I think how wicked I've been to you..."

"Let's go somewhere quiet and romantic. We'll drink a bottle of champagne, and then if you're hungry—"

"Oh no," said Ellen. "I feel as if I never could eat again. But I'd like to drink and drink... No, on second thought I think not. I'm too tired. In fact—I'm going to be sick."

Leaning out of the car, oblivious to the stares of passers-by, she vomited into the gutter.

"Darn," muttered Darrell. "I wasted my handkerchief on Duff."

"Never mind," she said faintly. "Drive away from here. I feel an awful fool."

"I'm the fool," said Darrell. "I should have taken you to the hotel and put you in bed."

"I don't want to go to bed... I feel better now. What a thing to do. I'm ashamed of myself."

"You've been under a terrible strain."

She nodded listlessly. "I know."

They went to a dimly lit restaurant at the crest of the hill. A girl in a red and yellow Berber costume served Ellen a Tom Collins, Darrell a highball.

"And still the problem remains," said Ellen. "Who's got the heroin, but I don't care any more. I'll be so happy to leave here."

"Tomorrow we'll go to the consulate. Undoubtedly there's a dozen documents to fill out."

Ellen examined her ring with a fond expression. "What a fool I've been. I really don't deserve you, Darrell. I won't badger you about ethics and morals any more. It's clearly better to be good than bad."

"You've summed it up very well," said Darrell. "I nearly killed three men tonight. I suppose that's bad... I don't know what stopped me. Squeamishness, I suppose."

"Let's not talk of it. It's all strange and blurred, as if it never happened. And I'm hungry enough now."

There was a dining room adjacent to the bar, hung with Berber rugs, scimitars, and long fantastic rifles. They sat on cushions of bright goatskin and were served Moroccan food: barbecued lamb, couscous with slivers of chicken in a bright yellow sauce.

Returning down the hill, Darrell slowed two blocks from Calle Miranda, coasted to a halt. "What's the trouble?" asked Ellen.

"This business has me worried. They're loose by now. Upshaw's upset, Duff is peevish, Jilali has lost face. Suppose they're waiting for us in front of the hotel? It's dark under those trees."

"I don't think they'd bother tonight. They're probably sick of the whole thing themselves."

"I'm not going to take any chances." He drove another block, parked. "I'll reconnoiter."

He went to the corner, looked around. The sign MASQUERADE was cut into sizzling green dots and dashes by the foliage. A party of men and women in evening clothes left the bar amid noise and hilarity. Everything appeared innocent and above-board.

Darrell walked slowly down the street across from the hotel. The parked cars were empty, no one lurked in doorways. He returned to the Mercedes-Benz.

The seat was vacant.

From the shadows came Ellen's voice. "Here I am." She stepped forward.

"You gave me a scare," said Darrell. "For a moment I thought... Well, never mind. The coast is clear. Let's go."

Chapter XV

T**HE** next day began placidly and quietly. Darrell and Ellen visited the United States consul, filled out several forms, and were asked to return after they were married.

They left the consulate, walked to the car, which had been parked in the Soco Grande. Ellen stroked the front fender. "Poor Mr. Burdette. I should have returned his car long ago."

"We'll let him have it this afternoon," said Darrell.

Ellen crossed the sidewalk to a newspaper kiosk, read the face of one of Tangier's Spanish newspapers. "Here's news about Noel."

Darrell bought the newspaper. "What does it say?"

"Not too much. 'Noel Hutson, American citizen, resident of Tangier, yesterday was found dead near Erfoud, village in the Tafilelt, over the Atlas. He had been driving a truck, presumably carrying contraband arms to the Algerian rebels, and had been killed by a shot through the heart.'"

"What's this?" asked Darrell. "A shot through the heart?"

"That's what it says here. You didn't see?"

"No. I just glanced in the cab. Strange. Go on."

"'The cadaver was discovered in a truck concealed a short distance off the Ksar-es-Souk–Erfoud highway. The truck is registered to the Europe–Africa Transfer Society Anonymous '—that means corporation—' of Tangier.

"'Tangier officials, as well as important Rabat authorities, are investigating the death. It would be very disturbing to current sensitive French–Moroccan negotiations if a new contraband weapon-delivery system were found to be operating under the noses of the authorities. The French would undoubtedly harden their attitude toward King Mohammed's representations that French troops leave Moroccan soil.

"'Knowledgeable students of the situation will remember'—" Ellen stopped, looked down the column. "That's all there is. They go on about the French seizure of the *Slovenija* a while back. They don't mention us at all."

"I'm just as pleased." Darrell opened the door of the car for Ellen. "You drive, and I'll look at you."

"Darrell, you idiot. I'm not that nice to look at."

"Of course you are. Nicer. If we didn't have so many errands—"

"But we do." Ellen started the motor, drove to the police headquarters. Captain Goulidja informed Darrell that Noel's body had been brought to Tangier and now lay in the city morgue. He verified that Noel had been shot through the heart.

"That should simplify matters for you," mused Darrell.

"Why is this?"

"It means that whoever killed Noel did not shoot him from the road, or from the running-board—the bullet hole would be in Noel's head. Noel must have stopped the truck, come down from the cab. Under the circumstances he would have done so only for someone he trusted, someone he expected to see. Or someone he wasn't afraid of."

"Yes. That's quite possible." Captain Goulidja did not seem to consider the matter significant. "This afternoon, if you desire, we will release the body to your undertaker."

Darrell did so desire, and from the police headquarters went to the black marble office of an undertaker, where he made the necessary arrangements.

The time now was two o'clock. Darrell and Ellen ate a sandwich at an ice cream parlor, walked three blocks to the auctioneer's office and spent a lively period arguing with the auctioneer. He protested that the articles Ellen wished to withhold from sale were the only ones worth selling. Ellen retorted that the sale was not being arranged for the auctioneer's benefit; he in his turn pointed out that he had his own interests to consider, and that hawking a cupboardful of pots and pans, a few old tables and floor lamps was not his idea of a dignified livelihood. Eventually the contract was signed, and they went to the American Express to arrange for the packing and shipment of the articles Ellen had retained: a grand piano, a grandfather clock, books, silver, a few pieces of Chinese porcelain, two Persian rugs.

Ellen was taken aback at the shipping charges. "Darrell!" she whispered. "That's more than all the other things will sell for!"

"So what? We'll have a piano and a clock and some rugs. We'll build a house around them. What do you think of that?"

"It's very nice, but am I worth all this money?"

Darrell assured her that a pedigreed sheep, in good health, sometimes brought even more.

They returned to the car. "Where now?" Ellen asked.

"Anywhere you like."

Ellen drove aimlessly through the streets.

"I shouldn't feel so happy and carefree," said Darrell presently. "It's hardly decent with poor Noel lying in the morgue."

"And you're really not interested in who killed him?"

Darrell laughed hollowly. "Abd Allah el Kazim wondered about that too. Of course I'm interested. It's been on my mind ever since we found him. It must have been someone he considered harmless, otherwise he never would have stopped. Remember, he's carrying all this heroin. He's scared, anxious, suspicious. Last night he tried three times to call Arthur Upshaw, but only made contact with X— Mr. or Mrs. or Miss, as the case may be. X promised to deliver a message to Arthur Upshaw, but Upshaw never calls back. What is Noel thinking? He wonders, did Upshaw get my message? If not, why not? Suppose X failed to deliver it? But why should X not deliver the message? When Noel comes up that slope he's got X on his mind. Lo and behold! Here stands X flagging him down. Noel can either stop or drive on past like the wind. He stops. Why? It must either be someone he considers innocuous, or someone he thinks is entitled to the heroin. In either case Noel sees X with pleasure and relief. He's glad to get rid of the heroin, he's glad to have company back to Tangier. Unluckily X shoots him. This was a month ago.

The X's—Mr. X and Mrs., or Miss X—are sitting tight, waiting for the commotion to die before cashing in.

"I eliminate you from suspicion, for reasons already stated, also because I know you couldn't do such a thing. Arthur is the person for whom Noel would stop most readily. He seems perturbed and distressed—is he putting on an act? Duff, Ventriss, Jilali—all more or less possible. Perhaps some of them have alibis. If so the situation narrows even more. So that's it. What do you think?"

Ellen shook her head rather dismally. "I don't know. Your reasoning is certainly impressive. But there's still one matter you haven't accounted for."

"What?"

"Noel wrote you he was coppering his bets. How?"

"That I don't know," said Darrell. "No doubt we'll learn eventually."

They returned to the hotel. The clerk had a message for Darrell. "A lady has telephoned for you, Mr. Hutson. I told her you were not in."

"A lady? Did she leave her name?"

"No, sir. She said she would call again."

"I see."

Ellen went to her room; a few minutes later Darrell knocked at her door, and was admitted. She had changed into a pale blue suit; her tawny hair was brushed smooth and glistening.

"What about a drink before dinner?" Darrell proposed.

"I'll be ready in ten seconds."

"A lady has been telephoning me," said Darrell.

"Really? Who? Mrs. X?"

"I don't know. Perhaps someone from the undertaker's office. Shall we go across to the Masquerade, in case she calls back?"

Ellen hesitated. "We might see Duff and Arthur."

"If they have the nerve to show their faces, I have nerve enough to look at them."

Ellen laughed rather weakly. "When you put it that way, I do too."

Darrell stopped by the desk on their way out. "If the lady telephones again," he told the clerk, "I'll be over in the Masquerade."

"Very well, sir."

They crossed the street, pushed through the doors. Ellen stiffened. Arthur Upshaw and Duff sat in a booth. Upshaw watched them without expression, Duff scowled and ran his fingers through his already untidy hair.

Darrell stopped short, anger beginning to rise in him. Ellen took his arm, led him to the bar.

"Good evening, folks," said Phil Beresford. "What'll it be? Make it good, because there's just three more days."

Darrell ordered martinis. Mr. Burdette, sitting on his usual stool, waved a stern finger at Ellen. "Well, young lady. It's about time you were showing your face. I've got business to discuss with you."

"Yes, Mr. Burdette. It's parked outside. You can have it now." She offered him the keys.

Mr. Burdette held up his hands in plaintive dismay. "But I'm driving a demonstrator; what in the world will I do with two cars?"

"Would you like me to bring it in tomorrow morning?"

"Excellent. Please, please drive carefully tonight."

Phil served the drinks. "Incidentally, Mr. Hutson, the roving reporter wants to talk to you."

Darrell laughed uneasily, conscious of Ellen beside him. "She squeezed me dry last night."

"I'll call her down anyway. T-Bone makes things hum." He beckoned to his waiter. "Charley! Go call T-Bone, tell her that the place is in an uproar. Mr. Burdette's drunk and giving away big boxes of chocolate bonbons."

Mr. Burdette rubbed his plump face. "Saturday's your last night, Phil?"

"That's right, Mr. Burdette. Kinda hate to go."

"I assume that the house buys all day Saturday?"

"All day Sunday, and Monday too."

T-Bone appeared, halted at the sight of Ellen, then came forward. She looked at Mr. Burdette, then wrinkled her nose at Phil. "He's not giving away boxes of bonbons."

Mr. Burdette said, "I've got something else you can have."

"Quiet, Mr. Burdette," said Phil. "That kind of talk draws Mama out here. I'd hate to see you lose out on all those snacks."

T-Bone slid up on a stool beside Darrell. "Good evening, Mr. Hutson."

"Good evening, T-Bone."

"Is there anything new about Noel?"

"Nothing I know of."

"Do the police know who shot him?"

"If they do, they haven't told me."

"What a shame," said T-Bone. "Noel was such a nice boy. I was in love with him, wasn't I, Phil?"

Phil scratched his head. "I forget. Which day was it?"

"Aren't you ever serious, Phil?"

"You act on me like strong drink, T-Bone. Speaking of drink, since nobody's buying, I guess I'll pour one for myself." He mixed himself a highball. "Next time Mr. Burdette orders he'll only get half a jigger."

Mr. Burdette looked at him quizzically. "For a man who's being driven from business, you seem in the best of spirits."

"Laughing to keep from crying, Mr. Burdette."

T-Bone turned to Darrell. "What will you do with Noel's boat?"

"Nothing. Do you want it?"

T-Bone laughed delightedly. "Can I really have it?"

"Certainly."

"Shall I take it, Phil?"

"Take anything that's free."

"Will you help me paint it?"

"If you'll wear your bikini."

"This is a party I'd like to be in on," said Mr. Burdette.

Phil shook his head. "When T-Bone and I get busy painting we don't like to be disturbed." He looked over his shoulder, clapped his hand to his mouth.

Mrs. Phil came forward, looking neither right nor left. She muttered to Phil, turned, wheeled back into the kitchen. Phil turned to Darrell. "Telephone call. Take it in the booth."

Darrell told Ellen, "Must be the mysterious lady. Order us another drink." He slid off the stool, crossed the room, passing in front of Arthur Upshaw and Duff. They sat with heads averted.

He entered the booth, closed the door, picked up the receiver. "Darrell Hutson here."

"Hello. Mr. Hutson?"

"Yes, this is Mr. Hutson."

"This is Mrs. Ritterman from the hotel."

"Oh yes, Mrs. Ritterman."

"I saw in the newspapers about Noel. It is too bad. He was a nice boy. I am very sorry."

"Yes. I'm sorry too."

"He has his things here. His clothes."

"Will the clothes fit your husband? If they do—"

"Clothes from a dead man? No, never! And he has those two packages. He asked me to store them. These he said I must tell nobody. But now he is dead."

Darrell forced himself to speak casually. "What packages are these?"

"He sent me a letter about packages he is sending me to keep for him, in case he is not here. My husband has put them in the basement."

"How long ago was this?"

"After Noel left—a few days."

"I see. That's very interesting. Don't say anything about this to anyone else, please."

"Don't tell anyone?"

"No. There'll be somebody to pick them up tonight or tomorrow."

"Very well. I will wait."

"Thank you for calling, Mrs. Ritterman."

"I called because I saw in the papers about Noel. Terrible! The things they do!"

"Yes, it's a bad situation. Thanks again for calling."

Darrell hung up the receiver. He opened the door, stood looking across the room. Ellen watched curiously from the bar; Arthur Upshaw and Duff peered from under their eyebrows... Noel had coppered his bets. He had sent the heroin ahead as a precaution. His thoughts, his fears, his motives, his plans were all revealed. Sitting in the lonely lobby of the Gîte d'Etape he had evolved his scheme:

"...Wire the money care of the Lombard Bank at Tangier. I'll collect if and when I get there.

"I just figured a way to copper my bets, and I'm safe as far as Tangier. I may have to do some fast talking..."

So Noel had written. The next morning he had driven into Erfoud and mailed the heroin to Mrs. Ritterman.

He had coppered his bets—or so he believed.

Someone had given Noel no chance to do his fast talking, no chance to explain. Someone had killed Noel without asking.

Without asking? But Noel had been shot in the chest. Had someone asked, then fired the shot? Perplexity.

Ellen was watching him with growing puzzlement. Darrell started back across the room. Arthur Upshaw glanced up as he passed. Darrell stopped, looked down, skin crawling with detestation. In a strained metallic voice he said, "You two have a lot of gall showing your faces."

Arthur Upshaw sat impassively. Duff blurted, "She killed your brother, you stupid fool! She killed your brother, she ripped us up the back!"

"Ellen didn't take your heroin, Duff."

Duff laughed savagely. "She can talk sweet when she wants to. She's making a fool of you!"

Darrell shook his head, feeling the beginnings of a great content. "You saw me take a phone call? Ellen never had your heroin. I just found out where it is. In ten minutes I could put my hands on it."

"Where?" The word burst up out of Upshaw like a belch.

Darrell laughed. "Read about it in tomorrow's newspapers. Excuse me. I've got some thinking to do."

Darrell returned to his seat. Ellen asked, "Who was the lady?"

"Mrs. Ritterman from Noel's hotel. She wanted to know what to do with Noel's belongings." He squeezed her hand. "Excuse me a minute. I've got to think. I'm on the track of something."

"More theories?"

"Yes. Perhaps the right ones this time. My last were way off base." He sat looking into his glass. Noise flowed around him unheard—chatter and laughter, the clink of glass and ice, the jingle of the cash-register, the tapping of Ellen playing with her car keys.

Phil amiably bickered with Mr. Burdette: "You mean to say there's women more beautiful than T-Bone? You name one, I'll eat her. If I can catch her."

"Well, consider Helen of Troy."

"No comparison. They built 'em big and beefy in those days, not cute like T-Bone."

"What? The face that launched a thousand ships?"

"T-Bone's lunched with a thousand rips. That's not counting the dinners." He pinched her cheek.

"Phil! Be-*have* yourself! Psst, here's Mrs. Phil."

Mrs. Phil sailed past with a cold glare for T-Bone. "Telephone," she told Mr. Burdette gruffly, swung around, marched back the way she had come. Mr. Burdette slipped his round haunch off the bar-stool, vanished into the kitchen.

Phil shook his head. "It ain't right. I get a dirty look for checking T-Bone's tonsils, but Mama carries on like billy-o with Mr. Burdette in the kitchen. She claims it's the telephone, but she's feeding him lamb-chops with both hands. I'm gonna get that telephone moved out of the kitchen, so I'll know what's going on around here."

Someone tapped Darrell's shoulder. Darrell looked around, Arthur Upshaw loomed over him. "I want to talk with you. I've got a proposition you may be interested in."

"Forget your proposition, Mr. Upshaw."

"Don't make a fool of yourself, Hutson," said Arthur Upshaw in a menacing voice. "This matter is not your concern. Keep out of it."

"But it is. My brother was killed. And in about two minutes I'm going to call the police and tell them all about it."

"Tell them all about what?"

"Where they can find the heroin. Where they can come for the man who killed Noel."

"Tell me, tell me!" squealed T-Bone. "I want to know!"

Darrell twisted the stem of his glass. Five faces watched him. The group stood or sat at the end of the bar, out of earshot of the other patrons.

"Very well," said Darrell. "I'll tell you. I'll tell all of you. It's no mystery—now. Five minutes ago I learned that on the morning of the day Noel was killed, he mailed two packages to Tangier."

Arthur Upshaw and Duff leaned forward, their eyes burning down at Darrell. "Go on," Arthur Upshaw grated.

"Do I need to? Isn't it clear what happened? Somebody outside your organization killed Noel. Call him Mr. X. Neither you nor Duff nor anyone else associated with you would shoot Noel under these circumstances; you'd be too anxious to get your dope back again. But Mr. X went south in the middle of the night. He stopped Noel. There was nothing aboard the truck. No heroin. Mr. X shot Noel anyway, to keep tales from being carried back to Tangier." Darrell paused, sipped his highball. "So now the question: who is Mr. X?"

He looked around the group. Five pairs of eyes watched him.

"Go on," said Arthur Upshaw.

"Noel made three calls from Erfoud to Tangier."

"No," exclaimed Duff. "Two calls!"

"Three calls. The first to the Balmoral. Aktouf told him Mr. Upshaw was not in. Then Noel called the McKinstry house. No answer. On the third call he spoke to Mr. X. Noel was excited. He probably made it pretty clear what he was carrying—or refusing to carry. Mr. X drove south. He shot Noel. But no loot. Mr. X was furious. Also Mrs. X—or Miss X. There was a lady along too. All the work for nothing. The long drive, the killing, now the drive back. They must have been very disappointed. They drove the truck out in the desert, turned it down the gully, returned to Tangier."

"So much is clear," rasped Arthur Upshaw. "Who are these two people?"

"Where would Noel make a third call hoping to find you? Why not here, at the Masquerade Bar?"

Arthur Upshaw looked at Phil. Duff looked at Phil. Darrell looked at Phil. Phil drew back, looking from face to face. "Here, here, here. What's all this?"

"The call came to you," said Darrell. "Where else?"

"You're out of your mind!" cried Phil. "You think I ranted down there and shot Noel? You've lost your wits!"

364

"You own a sports car—an MG. No Mercedes-Benz, but something similar at a casual glance."

Phil leaned against the back counter, face twisted and wry. "Darrell, I give you credit for more sense. Look at me here in this bar. I haven't had a night off in a year. Anybody can tell you that. Ask Mr. Burdette. Ask T-Bone. You think I could leave here at two in the morning, half-gassed as I usually am, and make the trip to Erfoud? That's wild!"

Darrell hesitated. "You might have flown down."

"In my private airplane which I don't have? On a broomstick? Your reasoning is full of prunes. Take it from me, no such telephone call came here. If my word's not good enough, ask Mama. She takes all the telephone calls around here. She'll tell you. We'll settle this right now." He went to the door, looked into the kitchen. "Hey, Mama, come out here a minute. Hey, Mama!"

Phil leaned forward, went out into the kitchen. Duff walked quickly after him. They heard Phil's voice: "Mama!"

Phil came back, his face long and dubious. "Mama's gone goodbye. Mr. Burdette too. Unless they're eating somewhere on the sly."

Something popped inside Darrell's head. He felt as if ice water were trickling down his back. "Mama listens in on telephone calls?"

"I'm sorry to say she does."

"Then she heard Mrs. Ritterman call me."

"Ritterman!" bawled Duff. "That's the Hotel de los Dos Continentes. Noel's hotel. That's where the stuff is! Come on!"

"Call a cab!" bellowed Arthur.

Duff snatched the keys from Ellen's fingers. "We'll take the Mercedes!" They ran from the bar.

Phil stood holding his head with his hands. "This is wrong! This is one of T-Bone's fables. This can't be. Not nice Mr. Burdette and Mama. Somebody wake me from this bad dream."

"He's got a whole agency full of sports cars," said Ellen.

Phil came out from behind the bar. "We can't just stand here. Let's go! This is a gala event! It's so pathetic it's funny. Arthur and Duff chasing Mama and Mr. Burdette."

"What have they done?" cried T-Bone. "Won't somebody tell me?"

"I've got to call the police," said Darrell.

"I'll call them," said Ellen. "I can do it faster." She ran to the phone booth.

"If you're coming, come," cried Phil, ignoring the stares of his patrons. "They got a big head-start!"

T-Bone tugged at his arm. "I want to come too."

"You call your newspapers! There's a hundred thousand francs in it. This is big-time!"

T-Bone hesitated, then ran to the phone booth. She rattled the door. Ellen came out; T-Bone darted in, darted back out. "Phil! I don't have any money!"

"Get it out of the cash register! I can't wait!"

"But I don't know what to tell them! I don't know what's happened!"

"Tell 'em the unhappy truth: that Mama and Mr. Burdette massacred poor Noel Hutson!"

Darrell and Ellen piled into the MG; Phil started the motor, made a hard U-turn; they roared down the hill. From another direction came the sound of a siren. "We'll never catch them," groaned Phil. "To think I should see the day!"

"Well, I made a fool of myself," said Darrell dourly. "While I was theorizing, they were loading heroin into their car."

"You were pretty close at that," said Phil. "I don't blame you."

They crossed the Boulevard Pasteur, twisted left down the hill, bounced into the Calle Erasmus. Mrs. Ritterman stood in the doorway, looking up and down in bewilderment. She saw Darrell and asked hopefully, "You sent them for the packages, Mr. Hutson? It was right, yes?"

"Where did they go?" cried Phil.

"Down there." She pointed along the street. "Just one minute ago. And another car too. One minute ago!"

Behind came the sound of a siren, loud and shrill. The MG spun forward. "They must have turned down to the water-front. That's the only place this street takes you. Hang on! My, my! I'm really surprised. Mr. Burdette, so meek and quiet. Mama must have fed him awful strong meat."

They turned sharp right, bounded over a vacant lot. "Short-cut," Phil explained. "We gain two blocks on them."

They bumped across the sidewalk, swung out upon the waterfront highway.

A quarter-mile ahead appeared a small spark, a quick burst of poppy-colored flame.

Ellen gasped. Phil clicked his tongue against his teeth. "That looks bad."

The orange flame rolled and seethed, became a ball, heavy as honey, scrolled with black smoke. Phil pulled up to within two hundred feet, parked, jumped out. A gasoline truck lay twisted across the road. Underneath, revealed through fitful gaps in the flame, lay the smashed hulk of a sports car. Two dull black humps, anonymous as pillows, could be glimpsed.

A crowd had already gathered. Several cars had halted. Ahead was the Mercedes-Benz. Arthur Upshaw and Duff stood staring into the flames, Upshaw making little running movements forward, then drawing back. Behind, a police car screamed to a halt. Three white-uniformed troopers sprang out, ran toward the blaze, stopped helplessly.

Phil turned back to the car. "I can't watch any more of this."

They drove slowly away, great billows of orange light reflected in the windshield. Phil heaved a deep sigh. "I feel kinda sad. Poor Mama. Poor Mr. Burdette. The world has just come to an end for them… Gives a man a funny feeling."

Chapter XVI

PHIL parked in front of the Masquerade. The three alighted. T-Bone came running from the bar. "What happened, Phil? Where have you been?"

Phil put his arm limply around her shoulders. "We've been chasing Mama and Mr. Burdette, T-Bone. We chased and chased till the chase came to an end."

"But what happened? Where are they?"

"They're dead. Ran into a gasoline truck, probably doing eighty or ninety."

"Phil! Not really!"

"Really and truly. This very minute Mama's feeding Mr. Burdette ambrosia sandwiches. Or more likely, a brimstone milkshake."

T-Bone put her head against Phil's shoulder; he patted her hair. "Don't feel sorry, T-Bone—not for me. You know how things were."

"I know, but—"

He nodded. "It's a shock when things blow up so sudden. Come on, Darrell, Ellen. Let's go have a drink." He took T-Bone's arm, walked with her into the bar. Darrell and Ellen followed. Their glasses remained where they had left them; at Mr. Burdette's place a lonely highball waited, the last fragment of ice floating at the surface. Phil ducked behind the bar, snatched the glass, started to empty it, then halted. He went into the kitchen,

369

returned with an African violet blossom. He dropped it into the highball, set the little bouquet on top of the cash register. "In reverence to Mr. Burdette and Mama," said Phil. "Murderers and villains though they may be."

He looked around the room. It was the dinner hour, the bar was almost empty. A few faces looked back. Phil beckoned to the waiter. "Charley, go lock up. Bar is closed for the night. No more drinks."

Arthur Upshaw and Duff pushed in before Charley reached the door. Arthur Upshaw's skin was tight over his bones, his eyes blazed. He walked over to the bar, glared down at Darrell. "Do you understand the cost of your interference? Four hundred thousand pounds of my money!"

"A big shipment of heroin has been destroyed," said Darrell. "Isn't that what you mean?"

Upshaw abruptly swung toward Phil. "Give me a double whiskey."

"Bar is closed, Mr. Upshaw. I'm not serving tonight."

Arthur Upshaw strode into the Balmoral lobby. Duff hesitated, looked down at Ellen. "I'm sorry about yesterday. I'm really sorry, Ellen."

Ellen turned her head. Duff shrugged. He tossed the car keys upon the bar, followed Upshaw.

Phil set two bottles of whiskey on the bar. "Drinks is on the house. A shame Mr. Burdette can't be here to enjoy it. But that's the way things go."

"I don't understand any of this," T-Bone complained.

Phil, pouring highballs, shook his head. "I don't understand too much myself."

"But what happened, Phil?"

"Well, near as I can see it, Mr. Burdette and Mama thought they needed some extra money. They didn't quite make the grade and shot Noel Hutson out of vexation."

"But Mr. Burdette and Mama!"

"Yes, T-Bone, it's a shock." He swallowed two-thirds of his highball. "But one thing I've learned in my years on this earth: you never know what's going on in someone else's mind." He looked at her fixedly.

"Stop that, Phil!" T-Bone wriggled on the bar stool. "You make me feel all funny."

Phil finished his highball, set the glass down with a rap. "Yep. This is a funny business, this life thing. I haven't quite got it figured. Darrell, drink up. This is a momentous night. Chances are I'll get a little gassed. Ellen, drink up. It's a farewell party. For Noel and Mama and Mr. Burdette." He mixed himself another highball, raised the glass. "Hail and farewell." He signaled the waiter. "Charley. Start turning out the lights. Chase these people out of here."

Phil replenished glasses. "This is the right way to hold a wake, with a well-stocked saloon to roam around in. T-Bone, dip your beak. It's free."

"I don't like whiskey very much."

"Throw it out, I'll mix you a real drink. A French .75—champagne and cognac. There, how's that?"

"It's nice," said T-Bone. "But I don't have time to drink it." She looked toward the Balmoral lobby. "I've got to go dress."

"Dress? What for? You're dressed."

"I've got a date for dinner."

"That was before you became my new fiancée."

T-Bone laughed uneasily. "How can I be your fiancée, Phil?"

"It's got to be done, T-Bone. I can't smuggle you into the States unless I marry you." He shot a cautious glance over his shoulder toward the kitchen. "Confound it! I got myself into a mean habit."

"Phil, won't you ever be serious!"

"I'm utterly serious. I'm on my way to the States. If you want to come, you better start packing your trousseau."

T-Bone bent her head over her glass. "Where in the States?"

"New York. Beverly Hills. Honolulu. I don't know for sure."

"I have a friend in Hollywood," said T-Bone thoughtfully. "He promised me a screen test."

Phil put his knuckle under her chin, raised her head. "Does that mean yes or no?"

"Yes or no what?"

"Are you coming with me to the States?"

"Then you're really leaving?"

"Certainly I'm leaving. Do you think I want to stay here?" He poured himself a whiskey with a lavish hand. "We'll settle this matter now. T-Bone, look me in the eye. Repeat after me: 'I—'"

T-Bone jumped off the stool. "Phil, I can't stay another minute. Mr. Sverdlup will be here, and I haven't even had my bath." She patted his hand.

"T-Bone! Are you my fiancée or not?"

"I promised Mr. Sverdlup—"

"T-Bone! Yes or no?"

"Yes, but—"

"But what?"

"Nothing."

"Repeat after me: 'Mr. Sverdlup, go chase yourself.'"

"No, Phil, I couldn't do that. He's very nice and now—"

"T-Bone! Look me in the eye. Say, 'I love you madly.'"

"I love you madly."

"That's better. You've made me a happy man, T-Bone." He raised his glass. "To our new lives!"

They drank, and T-Bone departed for her dinner engagement.

Phil locked the door behind her. "If I got any brains I'll leave early tomorrow morning before T-Bone remembers she wants to go to Hollywood. I suppose I could always claim I was drunk." The bar was now almost empty. Phil poured out whiskey, soda, cognac, champagne indiscriminately. "Another toast. The memory of Noel, Mr. Burdette and Mama!"

Ellen laughed sadly. "That's a unique toast. The murderers and the victim in the same breath."

"Yeah," said Phil. "I guess it's not generally done." He went to the cash register, took the half-filled highball glass with the floating African violet, poured it slowly into the sink. "Farewell, Mama. Farewell, Mr. Burdette. In spite of your sins in life, I wish you luck."

He dropped the glass into the waste barrel.

Darrell and Ellen got down off the bar stools. "Come along, Phil," said Darrell. "Let's go get a bite to eat."

"Right," said Phil. "It's too sad hanging around here. I'll be with you, soon as I clean out the cash register."

"We'll wait in front."

They stood out under the green light of the sign. A click. The light died as the sign went out. The street seemed barren and colorless.

A few minutes later Phil joined them, and they walked down the hill toward the Place de France.

BAD RONALD

Chapter I

ELAINE Wilby seldom cooked elaborate meals; after eight hours behind a desk she felt no inclination for further toil in the kitchen, especially since she herself wasn't all that interested in food. It seemed ridiculous to invest two or three hours in some fancy concoction which tasted no better than a nice meat-loaf, and which was chewed, swallowed and digested by precisely the same processes. Ronald was not particularly fussy either, so long as he was allowed seconds and a nice dessert. Her former husband had been rather vulgar about food. He enjoyed dishes like pigs' feet with sauerkraut, and smelly cheeses, not to mention whiskey and beer, and cigars which permeated the house with the odor of dirty feet. A wonder the marriage had lasted as long as it did. Mrs. Wilby had been concerned principally for Ronald; a growing boy needed the guidance of his father, or so she had then believed. Now she knew better. Ronald was doing very well with no interference whatever from his father, and this was precisely the way Mrs. Wilby wanted it.

Tonight she had prepared a particularly nice Sunday dinner—a small rolled roast with peas and mashed potatoes, and for dessert the frozen banana-cream pie which Ronald liked so much. As Mrs. Wilby carved the roast, she reflected that this was a job Ronald should take over; carving was a skill which every gentleman should master. Of course Ronald was only sixteen, going on seventeen, and why push maturity upon the boy? He was growing up fast enough already, far too fast, in fact, for Mrs. Wilby's taste.

She watched him as he ate. Ronald had turned out well. His grades at school were better than average, and could be much improved if he'd only buckle down to his studies. A nice-looking boy, she thought, not handsome in the ordinary sense, but dignified and sensitive-looking. He could afford to lose fifteen or twenty pounds, but this was no cause for concern. Ronald had matured tardily; sooner or later he would convert all that baby fat to solid muscle. Ronald's hair was dark like his father's, and he had inherited his father's frame: heavy hips, shoulders perhaps a trifle too narrow, long legs and arms. The broad brow, the long straight nose, the full lips came straight from Elaine's side of the family, the Daskins, as did Ronald's courtesy, thoughtfulness and candor. Ronald shared her detestation of whiskey and cigars and had promised never to drink or smoke.

The thought excited a chain of recollections and she smiled grimly. Her subconscious must have been at work when she planned so festive a meal. She asked, "Do you know what day today is?"

"Of course. It's Sunday."

"What else?"

Ronald pursed his lips as he had seen his mother do. "It's not my birthday... That's next Saturday... March twentieth is your birthday... I don't think it's a holiday... I give up."

"You wouldn't remember. Ten years ago today your father and I decided to go our separate ways."

"Ten whole years! Do you miss him?"

"Not in the least."

"I don't either. But I wonder why he never comes to see us."

Ten years ago Mrs. Wilby had offered to waive child-support on condition that Armand Wilby give up part-time custody and visiting privileges, a proposition to which Armand, with his slick salesman's facility and eye for the main chance, had quickly agreed; and why trouble Ronald now with the sordid details? "He's probably just not interested," said Mrs. Wilby.

Ronald gave his head a shake of deprecation. "Well—I'm glad he lets us live in this house, even if it is an old monstrosity."

"The house is Victorian," said Mrs. Wilby evenly. "It's not a monstrosity, as you put it."

"That's what the kids at school call it."

"They don't know any better."

"I'll agree to that. They're a pretty common bunch. It's still nice of him, though."

Mrs. Wilby sniffed. Perhaps, after all, certain realities should be made clear to Ronald. "The situation isn't all that simple."

"Oh? Why not?"

"When a husband and wife are divorced," explained Mrs. Wilby, "the wife is entitled to a monthly payment called alimony, for all the trouble she's been subjected to. Instead of alimony, we are given the free use of this house."

Ronald gave an urbane nod. All was now clear. Remarkable, nonetheless, how anyone—Armand Wilby, the President of the United States, Jesus Christ himself—would dare cause his mother trouble of such magnitude! Elaine Wilby, a solid well-fleshed woman with a bun of ash-blonde hair, a pale complexion and cool blue eyes, was not a woman to be trifled with. At Central Valley Hardware, where she worked an accounting machine, her decisiveness had generated a whole cycle of office legends, and even Mr. Lang accorded her an uneasy deference.

Mrs. Wilby's great hope for Ronald was a medical career. Often she envisioned him proud and tall in a white coat performing miraculous cures. Ronald Wilby, M.D.! But whenever she mused along these lines a second thought clutched at her heart. In two short years Ronald would be going off to college, followed by medical school and internship. Every bit of fluff in sight would have her hooks out for him; no doubt he'd marry and start a life of his own, and what then for her? Going to work early and coming home late to a lonely old house, with only the television for company.

Ronald was aware of his mother's preoccupation. Sometimes when she refused him an extra helping of ice cream he would say,

"I'm lucky to have you worrying about me. I don't know how I'll manage when I'm off on my own." Whereupon Mrs. Wilby would say, "Well, I suppose it won't matter this once. But we've really got to put you on a firm diet."

"Heavens, Mother! I'm not fat! Just big!"

"You could easily lose twenty pounds, dear. It's not a healthy condition."

Ronald's bulk also attracted the attention of the football coach who wanted Ronald to try out for the team; Ronald said he'd think about it. He had no taste for hard knocks, and his mother would not care for the idea, he was certain. In matters regarding his health she took no chances. A sneeze meant hot-water bottles and layers of warm clothing; every scratch was bathed in alcohol, anointed with salve and dressed in an impressive bandage. Sports were vulgar, pointless and dangerous; how could people waste money at a football game when there was so much misery and devastation in the world crying out for attention? Ronald had come to share this point of view. Still, he could see that athletes enjoyed some very real advantages. There was a certain Laurel Hansen, for instance, who doted both on football and football players, but who evaded all Ronald's advances. Would she go to the movies? Sorry, she'd been asked to a slumber party. Would she like to drop by the House of Music to help pick out some records? Sorry, she had to wash her hair. What about Henry's Joint after school for a sundae? Sorry, she had a tennis date.

The situation gnawed at Ronald's self-esteem, even though he could readily perceive the intellectual limitations of such prognathous young louts as Jim Neale and Ervin Loder, both on good terms with Laurel Hansen. Ronald himself, of course, was a natural aristocrat, a gallant figure after the Byronic tradition, driven by a wild and tempestuous imagination. He had written several poems, among them *Ode to Dawn*, *The Gardens of My Mind*, *The World's an Illusion*, all of which his mother considered excellent. When he looked in the mirror and held his head just right, the heaviness at his cheeks and jaw fell away, and there, gazing back through heavy-lidded eyes, stood a dashing cavalier with a long noble nose and a dreamer's forehead, whom no girl could conceivably resist. If only he could induce Laurel off somewhere alone and enchant her with the splendor of his visions! For Ronald, a devotee of fantasy fiction, had contrived a wonderful land which lay behind the Mountain of the Seven Ghouls and across the Acriline Sea: Atranta. Ronald had spoken of Atranta and its inhabitants to his mother, but she seemed rather skeptical. On second thought, perhaps it was best not to confide in Laurel, not for a while anyway; he didn't want her thinking him a weirdo.

Chapter II

ON Ronald's birthday Mrs. Wilby always prepared a special dinner of Ronald's favorite dishes. This year the process would be less hectic than usual, since Ronald's seventeenth birthday fell on Saturday. For months Ronald had dreamed of impossible gifts: a motorcycle, a small color TV for his room, a three-day tour to Disneyland, a high-power telescope, a sailing kayak and also—this with a lewd private snicker—Laurel Hansen's underpants. He had dropped hints in regard to the motorcycle, to which his mother gave short shrift: motorcycles were simply invitations to injury, and the people who rode them were a seedy group indeed, and what was wrong with Ronald's fine three-speed bicycle of which he had been so proud only a few years before?

"Nothing's wrong with the bike," Ronald growled. "It's just that I'm old enough to drive; in fact I've been old enough for a whole year. I don't suppose you'd let me get a car."

"You suppose correctly. One car in the family is enough. Can you imagine what the insurance would cost?"

"Probably a lot."

Mrs. Wilby nodded curtly. "Still, it's time you learned to drive, just in case of emergencies. But put the extravagant notions about cars and motorcycles out of your head. A car would interfere with your grades, which aren't all that good for a person who intends to go on to university and medical school."

Ronald gave a disconsolate shrug. "Just as you say."

Saturday morning arrived, and Ronald found himself moderately pleased with his gifts. There was the stylish new 'Safari' jacket he had coveted; several books: *Lives of the Great Composers, How to Construct Your Own Telescope, Is There Life on Other Worlds?* by Poul Anderson, and the Tolkien *Lord of the Rings* trilogy. A greeting card from Aunt Margaret in Pennsylvania was given substance by the attached five-dollar bill; there was also a wallet of simulated alligator skin, with a certificate entitling Ronald Arden Wilby to ten lessons at the Delta Driving School. Ronald reflected that things might have gone far worse. The jacket fit perfectly; inspecting himself in the mirror Ronald thought that he cut quite a fine figure, and his mother agreed. "The color is very good on you, and the jacket is cut well: you really look quite trim."

Breakfast went according to Ronald's dictates: pineapple juice, Danish pastry with hot chocolate, followed by pork sausages and strawberry waffles with whipped cream. As Ronald ate he looked through his books. The *Lives of the Great Composers* he recognized as an attempt to interest him in 'good music', as distinguished from the 'din and rumpus' to which Ronald usually listened. For a fact, the book looked interesting, and he saw some rather rare episodes in the early life of Mozart which his mother certainly had not noticed.

He took up *How to Construct Your Own Telescope*. "Hmm," said Ronald, "this is interesting!... I didn't know that... They say grinding a mirror entails a great deal of painstaking work!"

"Nothing really worthwhile comes easy," said Mrs. Wilby.

"I'd just as soon work with a set of lenses," said Ronald. "They come in kits from Edmund Scientific, and there wouldn't be all that rubbing and polishing."

Mrs. Wilby made no further comment. Astronomy, whether by lens or by mirror, would make a wonderful hobby for Ronald, who spent far too much time daydreaming over heaven-knows-what. She cleared the table while Ronald considered the advantages of a telescope. His bedroom window commanded a view of the Murray house, about a hundred yards distant. One of the second-story windows opened into the bedroom of the Murray twins, Della and Sharon, and it might be interesting to see what transpired there of evenings. A really powerful telescope might resolve significant details even at the distance of Laurel Hansen's house, six blocks away. Unfortunately, a stand of eucalyptus trees obscured the view. Might it be possible to climb a eucalyptus tree carrying a telescope?... Something to think about, at any rate.

At three o'clock Mrs. Wilby served a birthday dinner of chicken-fried steak, mashed potatoes, and a big banana-cream cake from the bakery. Ronald extinguished the candles with a single blast, and elected to accompany his cake with a helping of vanilla ice cream.

After dinner Ronald wondered what Laurel might be up to and sauntered to the telephone. He started to dial, then hesitated. If he simply paid Laurel a visit, she wouldn't have a chance to say no. He'd be able to talk with her, and perhaps she'd recognize the glamour and scope of his personality, and who knows what might come of the episode?

He went to his room, combed his hair, sprayed himself with *Tahitian Prince* cologne. He donned his new 'Safari' jacket, glanced in the mirror, and gave the image a jaunty salute. He went downstairs. "I'm going out for a walk," he told his mother. "I'll be back after a bit."

Ronald marched along at a good pace, sternly erect, the better to set off his jacket. From Orchard Street he turned into Honeysuckle Lane, which skirted the rear of the old Hastings estate, walked down to Drury Way, turned right, and walked another two blocks to Laurel Hansen's home. Ralph Hansen, Laurel's father, operated the Sierra Lumber Company; the Hansens, by Oakmead standards, lived luxuriously in a large ranch-style house with a façade of used brick. White shutters flanked the windows; the shake roof was stained green. Mrs. Hansen was prominent in Oakmead society and also an assiduous gardener. Rose bushes lined the walk; chrysanthemums, asters, daisies and petunias bloomed around the edges of an immaculate lawn.

Ronald sauntered up the path, annoyed to find his heart beating faster than usual. There was no reason for nervousness, so he assured himself, none whatever. At the front door he settled his jacket, rang the bell, and waited. Perhaps Laurel was home alone; she'd look forth, wistful and lonely, and there would be Ronald.

So many wonderful things might happen... Laurel's mother opened the door—a slim, handsome woman of forty with a modish thatch of shining silver hair, sea-blue eyes like Laurel's, features delicate and brittle as porcelain. She had never met Ronald and looked him blankly up and down. "Yes?"

Ronald cleared his throat and spoke in his best voice. "Is Laurel home?"

Mrs. Hansen failed to notice Ronald's suave courtesy. "She's out in back."

"I wonder if I might see her."

Mrs. Hansen made an indifferent gesture. "Go right on through. You'll find her out at the pool."

Ronald marched stiffly into the house, where he paused, intending to chat a moment or two, but Mrs. Hansen had already gone off down the hall. A chilly woman, and rather proud of herself, thought Ronald. He looked around the room: Laurel's native habitat. The intimacy was thrilling. She breathed this air, she sat in these chairs, she looked at these pictures, she warmed herself at this fireplace! Ronald took a deep breath and expanded his soul, trying to absorb the environment: he felt he knew Laurel better already.

He heard light steps; Mrs. Hansen came back into the room with eyebrows slightly raised. She spoke in a bright clear voice, "Laurel's out in back."

"Oh yes," said Ronald hastily. "I was just admiring the room."

Mrs. Hansen seemed not to hear. "This way." She led Ronald across the living room, through a pair of sliding doors, and out upon the patio. "Laurel!" called Mrs. Hansen. "Someone to see you."

Laurel, splashing in the swimming pool with her friends, paid no heed.

Mrs. Hansen said to Ronald, "I imagine you can get her attention one way or another."

"Thank you very much," said Ronald. He advanced upon the pool. The situation was not at all to his liking; he felt hurt and angry with Laurel. She should have been home alone, moping and mournful, waiting for him to call. Instead, look at her: callously enjoying herself with her friends. There were two girls,

Wanda McPherson and Nancy Rucker; and two boys: Jim Neale, fullback on the football team, and Martin Woolley. Jim Neale's father owned Oakmead Liquors, which should have blasted Jim's social status: yet here he swam in the Hansen pool with complete aplomb! Not only that, Laurel was climbing up his back and diving from his shoulders, to Ronald's disgust and disapproval. Martin Woolley, the senior class president, lacked Jim Neale's physique; in fact, he seemed all arms, legs and ribs. His hair was a nondescript tangle; his nose hung like an icicle; his mouth drooped in a saturnine leer. Martin's popularity was a complete puzzle to Ronald, but there he sprawled beside the swimming pool with Wanda and Nancy hanging on his every word.

Ronald went to stand beside the pool. "Hello everybody."

Wanda, Nancy and Martin acknowledged his presence politely enough; Laurel gave her hand a casual flip; Jim, wallowing down in the water, ignored him. Ronald watched as he swam underwater, seized Laurel's ankles, put his head between her legs, raised up and tossed her screaming backwards into the water. Laurel wore a white bikini; Ronald watched in fascination as she paddled to the ladder and climbed out to stand dripping. Laurel was a blonde elf: slender, flawless, exquisite, enticing as a bowl of strawberries and ice cream. Never had Ronald seen anything so urgently beautiful. But how could her mother allow it? The bikini concealed nothing! She might as well have been nude!

Ronald sauntered around the pool. Laurel glanced at him sidewise and spoke in a voice almost without inflection. "Well, Ronald, how are you today?"

"Oh, fine. I was just wandering around and I thought I'd drop by and see what you were doing."

"I've been swimming."

"I see." Ronald hesitated, then asked, "Are you busy tonight? I mean, would you like to go to a show?"

Laurel shook her head. "I'm doing something else."

Ronald thrust his hands in his pockets and frowned out over the pool. "Well—what about tomorrow night?"

"We're having company."

"Oh... Well, maybe some other time."

Laurel said nothing. Jim Neale came floating past on his back; Laurel stepped forward, put her foot on his chest, and pushed him under. "That's for ducking me! Now we're even!"

Jim splashed up some water, and Ronald jumped back in indignation. "Hey! I'm up here too!"

"It's just water," said Jim. "It'll evaporate in an hour or so."

"Some people even drink it," said Martin.

Ronald forced an easy smile. "I don't object to water, but I'd just as soon it evaporated someplace else."

Laurel went to the diving board, poised herself, and dived. Ronald went to a deck chair and sat down, an elegant sophisticate amused by the happy play of children. He couldn't take his eyes off Laurel. The little patches of white cloth were more explicit than nothing whatever!

Ronald sat half an hour, no one paying him any attention. Mrs. Hansen came out to the pool. "Mrs. Rucker just called. They're starting up the charcoal. You'd better step lively if you want any steak."

The group went chattering off to the dressing rooms. Ronald remained in the deck chair.

He sat a half-minute. Then he rose to his feet and walked around the house, through a gate, and out upon the street.

Head lowered, shoulders hunched, he strode back up Drury Way. After a block he halted to gaze back toward the Hansen house. If emotion could be projected in a beam, if hate could be made hot, the house would roil up in a burst of flame, and all within would come dancing out, to roll and tumble across the lawn. Let them all die, the worthless futile creatures! He'd save none of them. Except Laurel. He'd take her to a far island, or a snowbound cabin, with nobody there but the two of them! How she'd regret her conduct! How she'd plead for forgiveness! He'd say, "Remember at your swimming party, how you went away and left me alone by the pool? I don't forget things like that!"

Unfortunately, such a requital was difficult to arrange.

Breathing hard through his nose, Ronald continued up Drury Way, with sunset light shining through the poplar trees of the Hastings estate. At Honeysuckle Lane he glanced back once more and saw the group come forth and climb into Jim Neale's old

Volkswagen. Ronald grimaced. He should have flattened the tires, or pulled a wire out of the distributor. Except that Jim Neale would guess the culprit's identity and that wouldn't be good.

After the barbecue Jim would no doubt take Laurel off in his car. Jim was bold; Laurel was feckless; Ronald knew what was going to happen. He felt curiously sick; his throat throbbed with woe and rage and mortification. No help for it, but sometime, somehow, he would get his own back!

He turned up Honeysuckle Lane, and the setting sun at his back projected a gigantic shadow ahead, which for fifty yards or so provided Ronald a gloomy diversion. How grotesquely the shadow reacted to his movements!

Toward him came Carol Mathews, riding her bicycle. Carol, eleven years old, as blonde as Laurel Hansen, lived around the corner on May Street. The sun shone into her face, illuminating her beautiful green eyes. She failed to see Ronald and rode directly into him. Ronald caught the handlebars and backing away brought the bicycle to a halt. The bicycle fell over; Ronald caught Carol before she fell to the ground and held her against his chest. "What do you think you're doing?" Ronald snarled.

"I'm sorry!" she gasped. "I didn't see you!"

Carol was already adolescent; Ronald could feel her breasts against his chest. He began to seethe with a complicated emotion. None of these blonde girls cared what they were doing; they thought they could get away with anything! He bent his head and kissed Carol's mouth. She stared up in amazement, then tried to squirm loose. "Let me go!"

"Just a minute," said Ronald. "You've got something coming."

"No I don't! Let me go!"

"Not so fast." Ronald's hand, seemingly of its own volition, groped under her skirt. Carol yelled in outrage. Ronald clapped his hand over her mouth. He glanced up and down the lane. Empty. He growled into Carol's ear, "Are you going to yell? Are you? You'd better not!"

Carol looked up with glazed green eyes and shook her head. Ronald took away his hand, and she gasped for breath. "Please don't, please let me go! I didn't do it on purpose…"

"I'm not thinking about that now." Clamping her mouth once more, Ronald dragged her, kicking and hopping, squirming and jerking, into the grounds at the back of the old Hastings Estate. Pulling her face free, Carol gasped, "I don't want to go in here!" She started to scream; Ronald thrust his hand over the wetness of her open mouth; she bit his palm, and received a slap in stern retribution.

Carol made frantic noises through his hand: she seemed to be saying, "I can't breathe! I can't breathe!"

Ronald eased his grip. "Don't you dare yell! Do you hear? Say yes!"

Carol obstinately said nothing and tried to pull away; Ronald cuffed her and dragged her back. He inspected the overgrown old garden. Carol whimpered, "What are you going to do?"

"You'll see."

"No!" Carol raised her voice once more; Ronald instantly closed off her mouth and thrust his face down to within six inches of hers. He spoke in measured ominous tones, "You'd better not bite me again, and you'd better not yell!"

Carol stared up like a hypnotized rabbit. Ronald withdrew his hand and Carol squeezed her eyes shut, as if by this means to obliterate the entire situation. Ronald thrust her to the ground under an old weeping willow tree.

"Relax," said Ronald. "This is going to be fun. Really it is."

Carol's mouth sagged and warped; tears began to stream down her cheeks. "Please don't! No! No, no, no!"

"Be quiet! And afterwards you'd better not tell!"

CAROL LAY SOBBING. LEAVES and grass had caught in her hair; she looked disheveled and distraught. This, thought Ronald, was what Laurel would look like under similar circumstances. That would have made it even better.

Ronald now decided to be nice. He stroked her hair. "There now. That was fun, wasn't it?"

"No."

"Of course it was! Let's do it again tomorrow."

"No!"

"Why not? I'll..." Ronald raised his head and listened through the dusk. Someone was calling. "Carol! Carol!" A woman's voice.

"That's my mother! I'm going home right now!" Carol started to sit up.

Ronald pushed her back down. "Just a minute. Are you going to tell?"

Carol compressed her lips and shook her head: a shake of resentment and obstinacy rather than a commitment to silence.

"Oh come on!" Ronald spoke in a bluff cajoling voice. "Wouldn't you like to do it again, maybe tomorrow?"

"No. And you won't either, because you'll be in jail." She pulled away from him, sobbing bitterly, and scrambled to her knees.

Ronald jerked her back. "Just a minute. You've got to promise to keep this a secret."

Twisting and pushing Carol tried to break away; she opened her mouth to scream. Ronald bore her to the ground, clasped her mouth; she bit his hand and, gasping, finally managed to emit a wild yell. Ronald seized her throat. "Be quiet!" he hissed. "Be quiet! Be quiet!"

Carol fought and thrashed and kicked, and Ronald squeezed her neck till she became quiet, and when he loosened his grip she lay limp.

"Carol," said Ronald, peering down into her face. "Carol?"

A weird cold sensation came over Ronald. He spoke in an urgent voice, "Carol! Are you just fooling?... I was just fooling, too. Let's be friends." And hopefully: "If you won't tell anyone, I won't."

Carol said nothing. Her eyes, half-open, reflected glints of gray twilight; her tongue lolled from her mouth.

"She's dead," muttered Ronald. "Oh my, oh my. She's dead."

He jumped to his feet and stood staring down through the shadows. "I mustn't lose my head," said Ronald. "I've got to think."

He stood listening through the twilight. Silence, except for the far hum of town traffic. Here, under the old weeping willow, all noises were hushed.

Ronald told himself, "I am different. I have always known I am different. I am superior to the ordinary person: stronger of purpose and more intelligent. Now I must prove this. Very well! I accept the challenge of fate!" He drew a deep breath, and exhaled. His nerves must be steel, his will strong as that of some unearthly supercreature! So then: first things first. The body must be concealed. He looked around the dim old garden and walked cautiously to a shed, where he found an ancient spade. Just the thing. He selected a spot to the side of the shed and began to dig, first removing his 'Safari' jacket so as not to soil it. Hark! a car coming down Honeysuckle Lane!

A squeal of brakes. The car halted. Ronald ran to the fence and peered out into the lane.

The car was a tan and white station wagon, which Ronald half-recognized. The headlights burned through the twilight to illuminate an object in the middle of the road: Carol's bicycle. Ronald's heart jumped up to fill his throat.

The driver alighted from the car and moved into the glare of the headlights: a big rawboned man with the face of an Apache chieftain. Ronald knew him for Donald Mathews, Carol's father. Could he be out searching for Carol? More likely he was just coming home from work. For a moment he stood looking down at the bicycle, clearly vexed by what he assumed to be Carol's carelessness; then he picked up the bicycle, loaded it into the back of the station wagon, and drove off.

There was no time to waste. Ronald thrust the body into the hole and spaded dirt upon the pale glimmer. One moment! Carol's torn underpants. Into the hole and buried with the rest. Ronald stamped the loam down firm and solid, then scattered leaves and twigs and rotten palm fronds on top. He replaced the spade in the shed after wiping it clean of fingerprints, then took one of the palm fronds and worked it over the ground wherever he had walked, hoping thereby to obliterate his footprints. Now he had better leave. He jumped the fence into Honeysuckle Lane and ran with long, fleet strides up to Orchard Street. Here he paused to catch his breath and take stock of the situation. The street was clear of traffic; Ronald continued at a more sedate pace, his mind full of veering thoughts. Certain notions he rejected as unworthy of consideration. The situation was at an end. A deplorable affair—an accident, really. He had carried it off very well. No doubt he should have moved the bicycle before Mr. Mathews found it, but a person couldn't think of everything. From now on, so far as he was concerned, the episode was finished—done with, null and void, nonexistent. He would put it clear out of his mind, as if it had never happened.

He climbed the steps to the front porch and paused once more. His mother was wonderfully keen; he must act normal at all costs. Light, easy, suave, nerveless: in short, his usual self.

He entered the house. His mother sat in the living room, watching a television travelogue. "Hello, Mother," said Ronald.

"Hello, dear. Where have you been?"

"Oh—here and there. At Laurel Hansen's house, mostly. I should have taken my swimsuit; everybody else was in the pool."

"Laurel Hansen? Isn't she the little blonde girl?"

Ronald twitched his lips. He didn't like the sound of the words "the little blonde girl." Carol really wasn't all that little; in fact—but this was a line of thought he absolutely intended not to pursue, now or ever.

"You look a little flushed, dear," said Mrs. Wilby. "And what's that in your hair?"

Ronald brushed at the object. "It's just a leaf." He laughed. "I guess I got a bit sunburnt out by the pool."

"It's too bad you didn't think to take your bathing suit. But there'll be other times. Where's your new jacket? You'd better hang it neatly on a hanger so it will keep its shape... What's the trouble?"

Ronald stood stiff and still.

Chapter III

"THE jacket—it's at the Hansen's. I got warm and took it off... I'll run back now and get it."

"Don't bother, dear, it's dark. I'm sure it will be safe until tomorrow."

"I'd just as soon run down and get it now. There's something I want to tell Laurel."

Mrs. Wilby darted an appraising glance at Ronald. It wasn't like him to be so energetic. But he was probably worried about his lovely new jacket. She returned to the affairs of the New Guinea headhunters.

Ronald ran back down Orchard Street, the pulse thumping in his throat. He turned into Honeysuckle Lane, and stopped short at the sight of headlights and a group of men at the back of the Hastings estate. Fascinated, Ronald stole a hundred feet closer. Two of the cars were police cars. Bright lights flickered around the grounds of the Hastings estate. Mr. Mathews had acted swiftly indeed.

Ronald turned and stumbled home. He opened the door, faltered into the living room, and slumped upon the couch. Mrs. Wilby looked at him in consternation. "Why, what's the trouble? Can't you find your jacket?"

Ronald found that he could not speak. Words stuck in his throat. He lifted his arms and beat the side of his head in frustration.

Mrs. Wilby flicked off the television. "What in the world is wrong? Ronald! Don't act that way! It can't be all that bad!"

"It's worse than bad," croaked Ronald. "It's the baddest thing that could be. I don't know how to tell you."

Mrs. Wilby said in a metallic voice, "Perhaps you'd better start at the beginning."

"I was coming home from the Hansen's," said Ronald. "In the lane I met a girl—Carol Mathews. She asked me to come with her into the old Hastings place to do something for her: to help her find her dog. I went in, and, well, she acted, well, fresh. Sexy, I guess you'd say. Anyway, she wanted me to do it with her, and, well, I did. Then she said she'd tell unless I gave her some money, and I said I wouldn't. She began to yell, and I tried to stop her, and, well, we had a big fight, and by accident... Well, she was dead."

There was a long silence.

"Ronald," breathed Mrs. Wilby. "Oh Ronald, how awful. How awful."

Ronald proceeded more rapidly. "I was afraid and scared. Horrified. It was all an accident, really Mother, I didn't mean to do it, it happened so fast, I couldn't help it."

"I understand that, Ronald... But what did you do then?"

"Well, I found a shovel and buried her. And then I came home. But I left my jacket. And when I went back just now the police were there. Mr. Mathews found her bicycle in the lane and I guess he figured that's where she was."

Elaine Wilby sat back in the chair, the structure of her life tumbling into ruins about her. And Ronald's life as well. There would be no mercy for Ronald. They'd take him and lock him up among criminals and degenerates.

Ronald said in a hollow voice, "I don't know what to do... I don't want to go to jail, and leave home, and leave you... What would they do to me?"

"I've got to think," said Mrs. Wilby.

After a moment Ronald said, "Nobody saw me. I covered all my tracks. There weren't any..." His voice drifted away. He had caught the handlebars of Carol's bicycle; he might have left his fingerprints on the metal.

Mrs. Wilby wearily shook her head. "They've got the jacket. The police will trace it to Gorman's by the label, and the girl will remember that I bought it. It was the last one in stock. Oh Ronald, how could you do such a thing?"

"I don't know, Mother, I really don't. I just lost my head. If she hadn't said she'd tell and wanted money and started to yell…"

"That makes no difference with the police. It'll be in all the papers. We're simply ruined! And the wonderful career we'd planned for you."

Ronald asked uncertainly, "Do you think I should go to the police and tell how it happened?"

Mrs. Wilby closed her eyes. This was a nightmare. How could such a thing happen to her? The circumstances were unreal! Unreasonable! Unjust! She didn't deserve them, nor did poor, foolish, scared Ronald who, after all, wasn't much more than a little boy, her own little boy, who trusted her to help him and protect him. But how?

"I really don't quite know what to do," she said in a passionless voice. "I don't have the money to send you away. Your Aunt Margaret… but she wouldn't involve herself in such a mess. Your father…" Mrs. Wilby became silent; the idea was too futile to verbalize.

"It was really an accident, Mother! I wish I'd never seen her!"

"Yes, dear, I understand this very well… You won't go to jail. We've got a day or two until they trace the jacket."

"But what can we do?"

"I don't really know."

"Oh how I wish this hadn't happened," moaned Ronald. "If I could only…"

"Ronald, be quiet. I've got to think."

Five minutes passed, with Ronald sniffling and fidgeting and making gurgling sounds in his throat to indicate his remorse and despair. Mrs. Wilby sat like a stone.

At last she stirred. Ronald looked at her hopefully. She gave her head a somber shake. "It's just a terrible mess. I really don't know what to do."

"Couldn't we both go away somewhere? Maybe to the mountains, or someplace where no one would look for us?"

Mrs. Wilby sniffed. "That's quite impractical, Ronald. I don't care to live the life of a fugitive. Even more to the point, I don't have any ready money in the house."

"I could go to work and support both of us," said Ronald hollowly.

Mrs. Wilby uttered a bark of sad laughter. "Quite honestly, I don't know what to do. Nothing seems feasible. I suppose I could send you away somewhere..."

"Oh Mother! I don't want to go off alone!"

Mrs. Wilby heaved a sigh. "I know, dear. I don't want you to leave. The least objectionable scheme is to hide you somewhere until I could get some money together. Then we'd move to the east coast or perhaps Florida, and start life all over again."

"That sounds as good as anything," said Ronald, blinking back tears for the old easy happy life, forever lost and gone. "I don't mind anything, so long as they don't take me away from you."

"That won't happen, dear. I'm just wondering where we could put you."

"There's the shed out in back. I could stay there."

Mrs. Wilby shook her head. "It's the first place the police would look."

"There's the attic. Remember the den I built up there when I was little?"

"They'll search the attic, very carefully, and any other obvious place. And the attic is a very long way to bring up your meals and then carry down the chamber pot, which would be the only possible method of sanitation. We'd want some place where you could live in decency and cleanliness, which means a bathroom... There's our own downstairs bathroom, of course."

"The downstairs bathroom? That doesn't seem too practical."

"To the contrary," said Mrs. Wilby. "It's quite practical indeed." She rose to her feet. "But we've got to work very hard."

———•———

THE FRONT DOOR TO the Wilby house opened into a hall. To the left lay the living room, to the right the dining room. Directly ahead, wide stairs rose to a landing, then reversed up to the second floor. Under these stairs was the bathroom: a combination cloakroom and lavatory, with a toilet at the far end under the landing. Only three months before Mrs. Wilby and Ronald had repapered both the front hall and the bathroom, to make them brighter and less old-fashioned. Now they took the door off the hinges, pried loose the molding and the doorjamb. To the studs, the header, and across the floor they nailed cleats, hammering as quietly as they could. Into the aperture they fitted a piece of plasterboard left over from the refinishing of Ronald's room. Before they nailed the plasterboard in place they brought a cot into the bathroom, several blankets, and an electric heater. The far wall of the bathroom adjoined the kitchen pantry. They cut away the lath and plaster of the bathroom wall, and low under the bottom shelf in the pantry sawed the plywood to make a secret little door, which Ronald used once or twice to demonstrate that he could get in and out. Then they nailed the plasterboard in place to fill the doorway, and carefully pasted wallpaper over the plasterboard.

The baseboard across the bottom of the doorway posed a problem, which they solved by prying a suitable length from an upstairs bedroom and fitting it into place.

The downstairs bathroom had now disappeared. The time was four o'clock in the morning.

Ronald from now on must not be seen. Taking a chance that Mrs. Schumacher, their rather inquisitive neighbor, was asleep at this hour, Mrs. Wilby carried the old door and the old moldings to the rubbish area behind the garage, where they made an inconspicuous addition to the material already there.

Ronald meantime brought into the lair his new birthday books, his radio with its ear-plug attachment, pajamas, bathrobe, slippers, a few other odds and ends.

Mrs. Wilby carefully cleaned the front hall and as a last refinement hung a picture across the old doorway. The illusion, in her opinion, was perfect; the lair was undetectable.

Dawn began to show gray in the east. "You'd better go in now," said Mrs. Wilby, "and remember! You must learn to be quiet! And never flush the toilet unless you're sure it's safe to do so!"

"One more thing," said Ronald rather importantly, "I want my Atranta notebooks; I might as well have something to work on. And I'm kind of hungry."

"Get your notebooks, and then go in. It's getting light outside."

Ronald brought the notebooks down from his room. "I guess that's about all I really need."

His mother hardly seemed to hear him. "From now on we just can't take any chances. Two knocks will be the danger signal! That means: no noise! Not a sound! When the coast is clear, I'll knock four times. Now go on in so you'll be safe. I'll fix your breakfast and pass it in to you."

Ronald looked sadly around the kitchen and into the dining room where he and his mother had enjoyed so many pleasant meals. Mrs. Wilby's emotions, which she had carefully held under control, almost got the better of her. He's saying goodby to all this, she thought, and for a fact it is goodby, because things can never be the same again, for either of us!

Ronald spoke in a hushed voice: "How long do you think it will be?"

"I just don't know. But we've got to be realistic, and I would guess several months at least."

Ronald looked glumly over his shoulder toward the secret door. "Several months?"

"At least. Perhaps as long as six months. I know it's difficult, for both of us, but it can't be helped."

"I don't mind, Mother, really I don't…I just hope it won't be too long."

"I hope so, too. As soon as we have enough money, and it's safe to do so, we'll leave. Meanwhile we'll have to be patient and very, very careful. The police will be on the lookout, and we can't do anything rash. That reminds me of something I'd better do. You go on into your den."

Ronald went into the pantry, slid open the secret door, crawled into his lair, and pushed the door shut behind him. Mrs. Wilby examined the pantry to make sure that the door was both inconspicuous and secure. She bent over. "Ronald! Can you hear me?"

"Yes." Ronald's voice was somewhat muffled.

"From now on, you're hiding! Don't call or knock or make any sound unless I give you the all-clear signal."

"What about some breakfast?"

"In just a few minutes."

Mrs. Wilby went up to Ronald's room and went to the box where he kept his savings. Twenty-two dollars. She took the money and left the box on his study table. She opened several of his drawers and rummaged up the contents, and left one of the drawers half-open. She lay down on her bed, in order to disarrange the spread and dent the pillows. The bed felt so soothing and she was so bone-weary she just wanted to lie there and rest, but she forced herself to her feet. There seemed to be nothing else to do at the moment. One great relief: today was Sunday and she need not worry about work.

Returning downstairs she fixed Ronald a good breakfast of oatmeal, bacon, eggs, toast and chocolate milk, and set it on a tray. She rapped four times on the secret door, pulled it aside and slid Ronald's breakfast through into the lair.

She washed dishes, made coffee for herself and sat down at the dining room table to wait.

Chapter IV

Ａ few minutes after ten o'clock the doorbell rang. Mrs. Wilby was still sitting at the table, a cup of lukewarm coffee in front of her. She rose to her feet. Now it starts. If ever she needed to keep her wits about her, it was now. Through the dining room window she glimpsed a man in a tan whipcord jacket sauntering past and into the back yard.

With slow, almost ponderous, steps, Mrs. Wilby went into the front hall where she gave two soft but definite raps on the wall. She listened. No sound from within. She opened the front door.

Two men stood on the porch: a stocky pink-faced man in a rumpled gray-brown suit, the other a taller younger man, hazel-eyed and quite handsome, in the uniform of a deputy sheriff.

"Mrs. Wilby?" asked the older man, and Mrs. Wilby thought she had never seen eyes so gray and hard.

"Yes. What do you want?"

"We're from the Sheriff's office. I'm Sergeant Lynch." He displayed credentials. "May we come in?"

Mrs. Wilby silently drew back, and the two men entered. They walked very lightly for such strong, heavy men, she thought.

She took them into the living room and pulled back the drapes, letting light into the room. "What do you want? Is it..." the words went heavy in her mouth. Both men were watching her with calm expressions; they seemed detached rather than unsympathetic.

Lynch said, "We're here on an unpleasant errand, Mrs. Wilby. Ronald Wilby is your son?"

Mrs. Wilby nodded. She had rehearsed this scene several times. "Why do you ask?"

"Will you please call him?"

Mrs. Wilby walked to the green plush armchair and sat down. "Why are you asking these questions?" And she forced herself to ask, "What has Ronald done?"

"Late yesterday a young girl was assaulted and killed. The evidence suggests that Ronald may know something about the business. This must come as shocking news to you, but the situation is as I've explained it, and now I'll have to ask you to call Ronald. It would also be wise for you to have a lawyer present while we're questioning him."

"Ronald isn't here," said Mrs. Wilby. "He left the house last night and hasn't come home."

For ten seconds the two policemen stared at her, and Mrs. Wilby wondered if guilty knowledge might be printed on her face. The deputy spoke for the first time. "What time did he come home yesterday afternoon?"

"I don't remember exactly. It must have been about six, or perhaps a bit later."

"Did he seem disturbed? Did he mention or even hint that he might have done something wrong?"

"Not in so many words."

"What do you mean by that?"

Mrs. Wilby spoke in a weary voice. "He didn't seem himself. I asked if anything were wrong and he said no. He'd been over to a friend's house, and I thought something might have happened that he didn't want to talk about, so I didn't press him."

"What friend had he visited?"

Mrs. Wilby sat dull and passive. The deputy repeated the question.

"He went to Laurel Hansen's house, on Drury Way."

"And he was disturbed when he came home. What did he say?"

Mrs. Wilby put her hand to her forehead. After a moment she said, "I can't believe Ronald would do such a thing. It's not like him. He's always been gentle."

"I certainly sympathize with you, Mrs. Wilby," said Lynch.

"How can you be sure Ronald did this?"

"We have several items of evidence," said Lynch. "His flight certainly isn't the act of an innocent person."

Mrs. Wilby sat silent.

"Do you have any idea where he might have gone?"

"No idea whatever."

Lynch glanced at the deputy, who rose to his feet. Lynch asked, "Do you mind if we have a look around? He just might be hiding—in the attic, or in a closet, or some such place."

Mrs. Wilby gave a weary shrug. "Look as much as you like."

The two men went upstairs. Mrs. Wilby leaned back in the chair and closed her eyes, listening to the footsteps as the men examined Ronald's room, his closet, the other three bedrooms, the bathroom and the attic. Returning downstairs, they passed through the dining room into the kitchen and out upon the back porch, where Lynch spoke to the man stationed in the back yard. A moment later Mrs. Wilby heard someone open the lattice door giving into the crawl-space under the house.

Lynch and the deputy returned to the living room. "Do you feel up to answering a few questions, Mrs. Wilby? I won't trouble you any more than necessary, I promise you."

"Ask your questions," said Mrs. Wilby in a cold voice. Nothing would arouse their suspicion so much as over-friendliness.

"You're divorced from Ronald's father?"

"Yes."

"Is Ronald friendly with his father?"

"He doesn't feel much one way or the other. He'd hardly be likely to seek him out, if that's what you're after."

"Where would Ronald be likely to go? Have you any ideas?"

"No. None at all."

"Don't forget, Mrs. Wilby," the deputy inserted, "it's to everyone's advantage to get this matter cleared up as soon as possible."

"Except Ronald's." Mrs. Wilby spoke bitterly.

"If Ronald committed this act, and it appears that he did, then he's got to be restrained before he does it again. I'm sure you'll agree to this."

"Of course. But he's my son, and I'm not convinced that he did what you say he did. Who was the girl?"

"Carol Mathews. She lived on May Street. About six o'clock she started home from a friend's house on her bicycle, apparently by way of Honeysuckle Lane, behind the Hastings place. Ronald would also have come by Honeysuckle Lane on his way home from Drury Way."

"That doesn't prove anything," declared Mrs. Wilby. "It might have been anyone. Perhaps Ronald saw what was going on, perhaps the real criminal threatened him, or frightened him in some way..."

"We found Ronald's jacket where the girl was buried. There was blood on the hem of the jacket. He left footprints on the grave and elsewhere, and they seem to match the basketball shoes we found in Ronald's room. We'll have to take them with us, of course. They're evidence. I don't have any doubt but what the soil in the treads will match the soil at the scene of the crime. And also—" he brought forth a sheet of paper "—this was in Ronald's room."

Mrs. Wilby took the paper. She knew what was there; she had dictated it herself and Ronald had written,

> Dear Mother:
> I've done something awful, and now I've got to leave and go somewhere far away. Please don't try to find me; I want to start a new life. If and when I can, I'll write you. I'm so very sorry to cause you unhappiness.
> All my love, your son,
> Ronald

Mrs. Wilby closed her eyes, half-convinced that Ronald had indeed written the note and had gone far away where she would never see him again. Oh, to be allowed to return twenty-four hours in time!

The two policemen remained politely silent until Mrs. Wilby opened her eyes. Lynch asked, "Has Ronald ever spoken of a place he particularly wanted to visit?"

"No," spoke Mrs. Wilby in a plangent, fateful voice. "Ronald is gone. If he did what you say he did..." She hesitated. The deed was unreal. The more they talked the more abstract it became. "I suppose the news will be in the papers, and all Ronald's friends will know?"

"I don't see how it can be avoided. You have my sympathy, Mrs. Wilby. Parents always suffer most—both sets of parents."

Mrs. Wilby had not yet considered the plight of the Mathews family. "I don't believe I know them." For some reason she could not bring herself to pronounce the name.

"Donald Mathews operates the Happy Valley Saloon on South Main Street. It's a very respectable place, incidentally. His son Duane used to be your paper boy."

Mrs. Wilby nodded without interest.

Lynch asked, "How much money would Ronald have with him?"

"I don't really know. Perhaps twenty or thirty dollars."

The policemen rose to their feet. "If Ronald communicates with you, we'll expect you to let us know at once."

Mrs. Wilby remained silent. She prided herself on her truthfulness and now found deceit very difficult indeed.

The police officers departed. A few minutes later Mrs. Wilby saw them next door, on Mrs. Schumacher's front porch, and presently they were admitted into the house. They'd get an earful there for sure! Mrs. Wilby thought of her job and the people with whom she worked. She thrust out her jaw. No help for it. If there were whispers and stares, she'd simply have to bear up and take no notice. As soon as possible, she and Ronald would quietly slip off to some far place and never think of Oakmead again. Until that day—well, at the very least she could dismiss her bleak fear of loneliness.

Mrs. Wilby felt upset to her stomach, almost queasy with tension and fatigue. She went around the house, wandering from room to room, looking out the windows. The police had departed. Almost certainly they'd maintain a watch on the house, and they'd probably keep her under surveillance as well. She'd have to be crafty and cunning, especially while shopping, since she'd still have to buy for two. And Mrs. Schumacher was always a threat. No doubt the police had asked her to keep her eyes peeled—as if Mrs. Schumacher needed any encouragement!

Mrs. Wilby at last went into the pantry and knelt down by the secret door. She rapped four times, and slid the door a few inches ajar. "Ronald?"

"Yes, Mother?"

"The police have been here."

"I heard them." Ronald's voice was peevish. "They don't sound too nice."

"They're only policemen doing their job. To them you're just like anyone else. We'll have to be very careful indeed."

"I realize that, Mother. I'm really sorry I'm making all this trouble. I just couldn't help it. It happened so quickly..."

"I know all about that. Push out your breakfast tray."

"I'd like my lunch. I'm really hungry. Is there any of that cake left?"

"I don't know what you'll do when I'm at work. But remember—under no circumstances come out! Mrs. Schumacher will be watching with her nose to the window, and the police will also be watching. If they see you, all our plans will go for nothing."

"I'll be careful. Can I flush the toilet now?"

"Just a minute. I'll go upstairs. When you hear the upstairs toilet, you flush yours. How is the air in there?"

"It's stuffy."

"Doesn't the fan over the toilet work?"

"It doesn't do much good. There's no place for air to come in."

"We'll have to figure something out. For now you'll just have to be uncomfortable. I'll go up and flush the toilet. Then I'll fix your lunch."

Chapter V

Ⱥ week passed, and two weeks. Mrs. Wilby went about her ordinary routines as placidly as she was able. At Central Valley Hardware she was admired for her dignity and fortitude: credit which she did not altogether deserve, for she had taken herself so deeply into her new existence that she was hardly aware of other people or their judgments. Two persons only were real: Ronald and herself. She worked toward a single goal: enough money to move away from California, perhaps to Canada, though how this could be achieved she was not quite sure.

At home Mrs. Wilby spent considerable time contriving economies. Ronald's requirements were now minimal except for food and whatever he needed to keep himself entertained. He wanted a small television with a set of earphones, which Mrs. Wilby refused to provide, citing the expense of such an instrument. Privately she felt that the television would provide far too much erotic stimulation for a person in his circumstances, and for which Ronald demonstrably had no need.

Mrs. Wilby had never squandered money on food, and now she spent less. Ronald made few complaints so long as he was served an ample dessert. Mrs. Wilby began to fear that Ronald might become seriously overweight, what with his inactivity and the rather starchy diet. She expressed her misgivings and recommended that Ronald not only eat less but undertake a regular regimen of exercise. Ronald rejected the suggestion out of hand. "It's too hard to exercise in here! There's not all that much room!"

"Nonsense, Ronald. You can do that running-in-place exercise, and all kinds of calisthenics. Certainly you don't want to become fat."

"Exercise just makes me hungry," Ronald grumbled. "I'd eat more."

"In that case, I'll have to cut down on your portions, and we'll forget about desserts. When we go east, we want you to be trim and healthy."

Ronald muttered something inaudible, but nonetheless began to exercise. Through some inexplicable quirk he became interested in the process, and Mrs. Wilby began to hear the regular thump of his feet as he ran in place. Indeed, she felt obliged to caution him. "When I'm not home, never run or jog, because the sound is quite noticeable, and there's also a vibration. The mailman might notice, or the man who reads the meter. Just do your push-ups and isometric exercises—anything that's absolutely quiet."

"When we have a new home, I'd like a room I could make into a gymnasium," said Ronald. "I might even take up weight lifting."

Mrs. Wilby had chanced upon a weight-lifting contest while turning the television dials, and had watched in fascinated disgust. "I don't know about that. Those people always look so grotesque. You just develop a good healthy body and never mind the weight lifting."

To Mrs. Wilby's relief, Ronald never expressed a desire to leave his lair, not even late at night when it might have been safe. Mrs. Wilby was afraid that if he left the lair even once, a precedent would be set, and Ronald would want to come forth at ever more frequent intervals, until by some freak of chance he would be noticed and his presence reported to the police. Better, far better, to play the game safely. They had worked so hard and sacrificed so much! Any relaxation would be sheer folly.

The issue never arose. Ronald felt comfortable and secure. The room was now adequately ventilated; he had broken a hole through the lath and plaster of the wall beside the toilet, which allowed a draught of air to enter from the attic, by way of the space between the studs. His meals were to his liking, if a trifle scant at times, but on the other hand he was no longer required to dry dishes. In fact, he had no responsibilities whatever, except to be utterly silent and to keep his weight down.

All, of course, was not a bed of roses. His mother's attitude did not altogether suit him. At times her tone of voice was just a bit peremptory and she tended to reiterate the most elementary instructions, as if she still considered him a child. That was just about the situation, thought Ronald wisely. His mother was competent in all things, but she had never reconciled herself to his growing up. The situation nonetheless had its compensations. Nothing too irksome was expected of him and if he coaxed long enough, he could usually get about what he wanted in the way of small treats. Matters could be a great deal worse, and if his mother wanted to baby him a bit, why spoil her pleasure? Ronald nodded sagely. This was generous and unselfish conduct on his part; he hoped his mother appreciated it. She enjoyed taking care of him, and until this unfortunate affair blew over she'd have ample opportunity to do so. Meanwhile, his little den was cozy and secure.

Ronald became obsessed with exercise. His mother drove into Stockton and bought some cheap exercising aids and a body-building manual, with which Ronald was very pleased. At his request she also supplied him a set of watercolors, a pad of good paper, ballpoint and felt-tip pens with various inks, as well as notebooks, a compass, a ruler and a dozen pencils. Ronald explained that he had long wanted to write and illustrate a history of the magic land Atranta and now seemed as good a time as any.

Mrs. Wilby gave only lukewarm encouragement to the project. She would have preferred that Ronald study biology and mathematics and anatomy, to prepare himself for the medical career to be undertaken after they had re-established themselves. Ronald agreed that the notion was sound, but when his mother brought him books on these subjects he showed little interest in them.

One Saturday about six weeks after his first visit Sergeant Lynch again dropped in on Mrs. Wilby. Hearing a car stop in front of the house, she looked out the window, then ran into the hall to rap sharply twice on the wall.

Lynch rang the bell; Mrs. Wilby opened the door and looked impassively forth.

"May I come in?" Lynch asked. "It's more comfortable than standing on the porch."

Mrs. Wilby silently took him into the living room. Lynch seated himself on the sofa.

Mrs. Wilby asked, "Have you been able to find Ronald?"

Lynch gave his head a slow sad shake. "Not a trace. Not even a whisper. It's as if he vanished into thin air, to coin a phrase. Have you heard from him, by any chance?"

Mrs. Wilby snorted almost derisively. "Wherever he is, I hope he lives a straight clean life, to make up for what happened here."

"I hope so, too, Mrs. Wilby. That would be practical rehabilitation, if it happened like that. Too often it doesn't, but we won't go into that."

Lynch leaned back and crossed his legs, apparently comfortable and in no hurry to leave. Mrs. Wilby sat tense and anxious, one ear straining for any sound that Ronald carelessly might make. What if he flushed the toilet now, for instance!

But silence prevailed. Lynch rose to his feet. "This is a real big house for just you to be rattling around in. Don't you get a little lonely?"

Mrs. Wilby managed a smile. "Believe it or not, after I work all day, I enjoy the quiet. I can do exactly what I want and when I want, which is worth a little loneliness."

"You might be right there. Well, I guess we haven't anything to tell each other, and I might as well be going. Don't forget to call me if you hear from Ronald."

Mrs. Wilby could not restrain a question. "Have you seen his father?"

Lynch nodded. "He was very disturbed, as you might imagine. But he knows nothing of Ronald's whereabouts, or so he claims." Lynch grinned. "Naturally we take the assertions of a parent with a grain of salt."

"I'm sure you know your business," said Mrs. Wilby, somewhat tartly.

"I'm not Sergeant Lynch for nothing. And if I don't produce results, I might be just plain Deputy Lynch again and in very short order. That's the way it goes. Goodby, Mrs. Wilby."

"Goodby." Mrs. Wilby watched through the window as Lynch got into his car and drove away. She walked around the house as before, looking out all the windows. The coast seemed to be clear. How she hated this conniving and working against the law! She who had never so much as incurred a traffic citation in her entire life! What a sorry mess! But if it meant having Ronald here with her instead of in some horrid jail full of sexual degenerates, any sacrifice was worthwhile. What was the phrase Sergeant Lynch had used? 'Practical rehabilitation'. Exactly what she was achieving. Ronald essentially was a dreamy, impractical boy who needed his mother to look after him, and probably would always do so. The idea gave Mrs. Wilby a flush of pleasure. It was nice to feel necessary in a world so cold and impersonal.

She went into the pantry and tapped four times on the door, which Ronald raised up. They had long since fitted hinges and a latch on the panel, and the secret door now functioned in a most convenient manner. "The police were just here," said Mrs. Wilby. "I think it was just a routine call, but once again it shows how careful we must be!"

"We're just too clever for them," declared Ronald. "You're really a wonderful actress!"

"I'm nothing of the sort," snapped Mrs. Wilby. This gloating jocularity was definitely not the tone she wanted Ronald to take. She wondered if he really appreciated the seriousness of the situation. He certainly evinced none of the restlessness and melancholy which would have made both their lives harder but which would have reassured her. To the contrary, he seemed quite happy eating, reading, sleeping, exercising and working on his imaginary history. She made up her mind to crack down on Ronald. She would insist that he study science and mathematics. But not just now; she was in no mood for argument. In the tension of Sergeant Lynch's visit she had forgotten to take her digestive tablet, and now she did so. Her stomach still felt twisted and queasy. The last thing she wanted was an ulcer!

She fixed dinner for herself and Ronald, and afterwards calculated how long it would be before they could consider leaving. Originally she had reckoned in terms of a few months, six months at the most, but money accumulated so slowly! They'd want at least two thousand dollars; she'd hate to leave with less. A year? By that time the furore and scandal would be forgotten. They could make an unobtrusive move and no one would be the wiser.

So—a target date of a year. A very long time, but the longer they remained in Oakmead, the better their chance for a successful new start in life. It was hard on Ronald of course. Poor dear Ronald! He had been such a cunning little chap. Who would have foreseen the terrible tragedy, which might have blighted his life had she not been able to help him! A year would go by very swiftly; she'd have the necessary two thousand dollars, or perhaps even three thousand—if she could cut down even more on expenses. For instance—life insurance premiums. They'd be taking new identities. What good was the old insurance? She'd cash it in at once. Ronald's health insurance was now a useless expenditure. She'd cancel that, and her own as well, and save another precious thirty-five dollars a month. Ronald's requirements for clothes, recreation and miscellaneous needs were now almost nil. Her own clothes were cheap and serviceable, and if she needed anything new, perhaps she'd try to sew for herself. After this month she'd stop the newspaper and renew no magazine subscriptions, and somewhere she'd heard that soybean meal made a cheap and nutritious meat extender. Well worth a trial, since meat was so high. The telephone? Mrs. Wilby deliberated, and decided against terminating service; sometimes she needed to call the office. But she could easily change to a party-line, limited-use basis. It all added up! Perhaps someday, when Ronald was rich and successful, they'd take a trip to Europe; she'd always wanted to visit Venice and Paris and the stately homes of England; and then perhaps they would be able to laugh at the dark times through which they were now passing. Or would either care to bring the subject up? Hmmf. Probably not.

Chapter VI

THE magic land of Atranta comprised six domains: Kastifax, Hangkill, Fognor, Dismark, Plume and Chult, each dominated by a wizard duke. Each duke lived in a grand castle, with turrets, towers and barbicans above and evil dungeons below. At the center of Atranta was wonderful Zulamber, the City of Blue-green Pearls, ruled by Fansetta, a beautiful pearl and gold princess. The wizard dukes conducted interminable wars, one against the other, using magic weapons, troops of weirds, ghouls and imps, and when not so occupied plotted against Princess Fansetta. An ancient legend prophesied that the man to win Fansetta's love would rule all Atranta; for this reason Fansetta's chastity, life and very soul were in constant danger.

Into Atranta from the far land Vordling has come Norbert, a fugitive from the tyrant of Vordling and himself a prince. By dint of craft and daring Norbert has defeated Urken, Wizard Duke of Kastifax and taken possession of his magic castle and all his wizardly spells.

Fansetta, Princess of Zulamber, the City of Blue-green Pearls, has seen Norbert in her magic lens and fallen in love with him, even though she thinks he is Urken...

413

RONALD HAD NOT YET developed the story beyond this stage; too many exciting possibilities existed. Furthermore, a great deal of preliminary work must be done: first, the detailed history of Atranta, with the genealogy of all the wizard duchies; the waxing and waning of their powers across the years; the ancient founding of the city Zulamber and the posting of the Guardians with their Seven Spells; the histories of all the various princesses who had come to power in Zulamber. All were fey, and their lives were not as delightful as one might expect, since Zulamber, the single great city of Atranta, was a hive of intrigue and derring-do. Secondly, the Grand Map of Atranta, which covered the wall across from Ronald's cot, was not yet complete, although Ronald had already lavished many hours of loving care upon the project. The scale was five miles to the inch; Ronald used pens of the finest nib and the most subtle gradations of color to depict every feature of the quaint and marvelous landscape: the rise and elevation of every hill, crag, knoll, ridge and cliff; the course of each river and rill; the extent of the Dismal Desert, the Windy Waste and the Fearful Fells. He plotted each road, lane and foot-path; he laid out each town and hamlet and indicated each landmark, monument, battleground, castle, fort, cave, sarsen, and megalith. As he worked, he compiled an index, listing places and coordinates. A work of enormous scope, but which afforded Ronald much satisfaction. After all, he was in no great hurry, and never before had so much spare time been available. Spare time? Ha! What with his exercises, the Grand Map, the History, his sketches of the castles of the Wizard Dukes, he barely had time to listen to the radio, much less study the dust-dry textbooks his mother brought him. Sometimes he wasn't even sure that he wanted to be a doctor. A pity his mother didn't make more money. Maybe his Aunt Margaret would die and leave them all her wealth. Unfortunately his cousins Earl and Agnes would get it all. Hmm, things might be different, Ronald reflected, if Earl and Agnes died before Aunt Margaret. But they lived far away in Pennsylvania. Earl and Agnes no doubt by now had heard of his 'wicked deed' and his 'disappearance'. If only they knew! Agnes was a rather pretty girl. Cousin or not, he wouldn't mind having her in to share his lair. She'd have to be quiet, of course, but they could have a fine time together. Even better would be that treacherous little bitch Laurel Hansen. How he hated her;

how he'd love to get his hands on her! Fansetta, the Pearl Princess, rather resembled Laurel, and no doubt she'd get her comeuppance somewhere in the story—probably at the hands of Gangrod, one of the most evil and sadistic of the Wizard Dukes. Norbert, of course, would rescue her, but Norbert might then be in love with Shallis, a dark-haired beggar girl, exquisitely pretty in spite of rags and dirt and certain sordid habits. Shallis looked a little bit like Laurel too, come to think of it. He seemed to have Laurel on the mind... Laurel, Laurel, that wicked little schemer! It was essentially her fault that he was here in his lair! No one would believe this if he explained it. Jeering feckless Laurel wouldn't believe it either, that was sure, and wouldn't care anyway. Some day she'd suffer, as much or more than he had suffered! Though for a fact his lair was quite snug and comfortable, and he had no responsibilities to distract him from the things he wanted to do. He'd like bigger helpings at meal-times, and more luscious desserts—he was getting just a bit tired of jello—but this was a minor complaint. His mother was right; he didn't want to become fat. Not too fat anyway. Despite everything he had gained a little weight. If he wanted to crawl out into the kitchen while his mother was gone, he could always find something to eat. But he didn't care to leave his lair; if once he left, it would somehow change things. The coziness would be gone. Also, his mother had strictly warned him against coming out; someone might see him. His mother knew best; he'd keep to his lair where he had his work, his exercise, his meals. Life was effortless; he was content.

Chapter VII

ONE Saturday afternoon in November, Mrs. Wilby went to do her week's shopping at the supermarket. At the pharmaceutical shelf she halted to look for a new digestive medicine she had seen advertised on television, for her old preparation was not giving the relief she expected. A thin nervous-looking woman of about her own age, with dark hair and expressive dark eyes, came down the aisle. At her side was a rather solemn lad perhaps a year older than Ronald, evidently her son. Seeing Mrs. Wilby he muttered something to his mother.

Finding the price of the medicine excessive, Mrs. Wilby turned to move on, and pushed her shopping cart into that of the other woman. She said, "Excuse me," and would have continued, but the other woman spoke to her in a quick anxious voice. "Aren't you Mrs. Wilby?"

"Why yes, I am," Mrs. Wilby could not quite place the woman. Perhaps Ronald had known her son, a medium-sized lad with an erect posture and a keen, rather bony face. For a fact, he looked familiar.

"I'm Mrs. Mathews. This is my son Duane, but I expect you already know him. He delivered your paper."

"Of course," said Mrs. Wilby, rather lamely. "I remember him very well." She felt hot and embarrassed; the last person in the world she wanted to chat with was Mrs. Mathews, even had her husband not been the owner of a saloon.

"I've often thought about calling you," said Mrs. Mathews in a rush of words. "I know how you must feel about that awful business. You must be suffering far more than we are, and I wanted you to know that you have our deepest sympathy."

Mrs. Wilby finally found words. "That's very kind of you, Mrs. Mathews, and you're right: we share the tragedy. I've decided that I simply can't brood, that I've got to go on living, and this is what I'm trying to do."

Mrs. Mathews' eyes glistened, and she took an impulsive step forward. Mrs. Wilby feared that she was either about to break into tears, or attempt an embrace, either of which would have embarrassed her dreadfully. But Mrs. Mathews controlled herself. She said simply, "The Lord has His reasons. He does nothing without cause, and it's presumptuous for us to question His wisdom."

"Yes, I suppose that's right."

"Still, for both our sakes, I can't help but wish that the Lord in His mercy had arranged things differently."

Mrs. Wilby bowed her head in agreement, wishing that Mrs. Mathews would get along with her shopping and allow her to do the same. Her cart was loaded with food: three pounds of hamburger, five pounds of rice, two chickens, two loaves of bread, a pound of margarine, two large cartons of chocolate milk, three heads of lettuce, which were on special, and it seemed that Duane Mathews was inspecting her purchases with something other than casual interest. "I'm so pleased to have spoken to you," said Mrs. Wilby and with a smile for Duane moved off down the aisle.

That evening she was unusually short with Ronald, who grumbled at his dessert. "Do we have to have jello every night? I thought you were going to get some ice cream."

For a fact, Mrs. Wilby had promised to do so, but after meeting Mrs. Mathews, she had come away without buying all she intended. "Please don't complain, Ronald. I do the best I can, and you don't help matters by being finicky." Implicit was the idea that any disappointment Ronald felt at the lack of ice cream derived from his own conduct.

Ronald said no more, but the evening was quite spoiled for him. After dinner, he lay sulkily listening to the radio. His mother needn't have been so sharp; after all, he had apologized for that wretched affair not once, but several times. She failed to appreciate him just like everyone else. As for Carol Mathews, in the final analysis, she was as much at fault as himself; if she hadn't been so defiant and revengeful things would have gone differently. Perhaps it wasn't logical to blame Laurel Hansen either; still, logic or not, that's what he felt, and perhaps someday... He heaved a deep sigh. No, he didn't want to get in any more trouble. When they moved to Florida he'd simply have to forget her.

For Thanksgiving Mrs. Wilby roasted a small turkey, and prepared sweet potatoes candied in pineapple syrup with marshmallows on top the way Ronald liked best. It would have been wonderful to pull all the drapes and bring Ronald out so that they might enjoy a real Thanksgiving dinner together—but better not. If Ronald were allowed out on one occasion, he might want to come out at every pretext, and sooner or later someone would learn their secret. So Ronald had his Thanksgiving dinner served on a tray, but he was allowed as much as he wanted of everything. Mrs. Wilby herself ate very little. Her ulcer, as she now diagnosed her difficulty, was causing her discomfort, and perhaps she'd better go see a doctor, though how she hated to spend the money! Christmas was coming up, which meant expense, no matter how she tried to avoid it: Christmas cards and postage, a gift for the office party, presents for Ronald, a tree—well, perhaps not a tree this year. In fact, she'd definitely do without a tree. And Ronald's presents would be absolutely minimal. There was not only the expense to be considered, but also the fact that when they departed Oakmead, they'd perforce go with the bare necessities. In fact, a month or so before the departure date, she might discreetly try to sell her furniture and appliances... On second thought, better not. Much too dangerous, if the police were still watching her. She had observed no evidence of surveillance, but it was hard to believe that they'd give up quite so easily. If they learned that she'd sold her furniture they'd know that she was planning to leave. Probably (so they'd think) to join Ronald, and they would keep a careful watch upon all her actions.

She explained to Ronald that Christmas this year must be very quiet and Ronald made no protest. For a fact, there was nothing he wanted except a small television set, and perhaps a subscription to *Playboy*—futile hopes, both.

"Don't get me anything at all," he insisted. "It's more important that we save the money. But I'd like you to get something for yourself, something that you want, so that I'd feel that you were having a nice Christmas."

Mrs. Wilby was touched. "We'll never have a nice Christmas until we're far away from Oakmead, where no one knows us. If you really want to make this a nice Christmas for me, you'll start studying. All this leisure could be put to good use, if you'd try."

Ronald said humbly, "I know you're right. After the holidays I'll really buckle down. There's no use neglecting my education."

"Of course not! I don't know how we'll get you back in school; usually they want transcripts. Perhaps we'll try a private academy where they won't be so involved in red tape."

———•———

CHRISTMAS WAS NOT ALTOGETHER drab. Mrs. Wilby bought a toy tree for Ronald's lair, and she roasted another small turkey, which was cheaper and went farther than steak or roast pork, which Ronald would have preferred. She couldn't bear to give Ronald no present whatever, and so bought him a bottle of *Wild Cossack* cologne, a book of crossword puzzles, and a very intricate jigsaw puzzle.

Ronald was profuse in his thanks. "I really didn't want anything, but these are all great! I hope you bought yourself something."

"Yes, dear, I did. I needed underwear very badly and I treated myself to some nice new things."

"Good! I'm glad! You should have gotten more!"

Mrs. Wilby's Christmas dinner was solitary and sad. How different from the old times, when she and Ronald had shared the joy of Christmas together! From sheer boredom she ate more than usual, and shortly after dinner felt an acute nausea, which persisted on and off throughout the evening.

The next day she decided that she could tolerate the pain in her abdomen no longer and went to the doctor.

LATE IN THE AFTERNOON Mrs. Wilby returned home. Through the thin plasterboard which covered the old doorway Ronald heard her footsteps as she mounted the outside steps. He heard the front door open and close, then there was silence. Evidently his mother was standing motionless in the front hall. Strange, thought Ronald, who had developed a peculiarly keen awareness of atmosphere and moods. An alarming idea came to him: was it really his mother who stood out there? He rose quickly to his feet, like a great stealthy cat, and put his ear to the plasterboard. After a moment or two the person in the hall walked into the dining room. Yes, it was his mother; the rhythm of her footsteps was unmistakable, though she sounded tired and dispirited.

Mrs. Wilby peered out all the windows as was her invariable habit, but then, rather than rapping four times on the wall, she took a seat at the dining-room table. Inside the lair Ronald listened with mounting uneasiness. But he dared not call out to ask what was wrong; he must wait until his mother rapped four times. He sat down on his cot. Something was not as it should be.

Presently his mother came into the pantry and tapped four times on the secret door; Ronald quickly pulled it open. "Is anything wrong?"

Mrs. Wilby replied in a steady and controlled voice. "Yes, to some extent. The doctor says I have something wrong with my gall bladder, and I've got to have an operation."

Ronald crouched silently while he considered implications. "You mean you'll have to go to the hospital?"

"Yes. For at least a week and probably longer."

Again Ronald reflected. "When will you go?"

"Next week, on Monday."

"Well, I hope it makes you feel better," said Ronald with hollow cheerfulness.

"Oh, I'll feel better. I'm not worried about that. It's the money. Such things are ruinously expensive, and we don't have health insurance anymore."

Ronald ruminated. "How much will it cost?"

"I don't know exactly. As much as seven or eight hundred dollars I should imagine."

"Hmm." Ronald could think of nothing to say. His mother spoke in a flat voice, "I'll get you a hot-plate and plenty of food. You'll just have to take care of yourself while I'm gone."

"Certainly. That's all right, Mother. There's nothing to worry about."

"Except money."

Ronald grimaced. He hated the word 'money'. "Well, the most important thing is your health, no matter what it costs."

"I realize that. We'll just have to do the best we can."

Chapter VIII

ON the following day Mrs. Wilby drove into Stockton, where the Canned Goods Discount Retailers sold packaged food products by the case at very reasonable prices. Mrs. Wilby was so impressed by the economies to be gained that she bought a case each of pork and beans, tamales, packaged macaroni and cheese dinners, and half-cases of peaches, pears and peas. She noticed ten-pound parcels of dry milk, which from now on Ronald must drink; chocolate milk was much too expensive and must be considered a luxury.

The store almost dazzled her with its array of bargains, and she resolved to return after her visit to the hospital. By dint of careful planning, she calculated that she could cut their food budget by perhaps a third even from its already low level. Ronald would hardly dare grumble, but to mollify him she bought an assortment of very reasonable soft drink powders and a dozen packages of devil's-food cupcakes. At a nearby hardware store she bought a cheap hot-plate, on which Ronald could cook his own meals, and then she returned home.

Here another problem presented itself: how to transport her carful of provisions into the house without exciting Mrs. Schumacher's curiosity?

Mrs. Wilby waited until dusk, when through the lighted windows she could see Mrs. Schumacher preparing dinner; then she hurried back and forth, from porch to automobile and in a very few minutes she had conveyed all her purchases inside.

As she expected, Ronald turned up his nose at the dry milk. Mrs. Wilby spoke sharply, "It's this or nothing! All the nutrition and minerals are there. It's the same except for water, which is a very expensive ingredient when you buy it in milk—or in any other food, for that matter."

Mrs. Wilby pushed the hot-plate and an ample supply of food through the secret door, and now her mind was easier. "Your meals won't be exciting, but at least you'll be able to feed yourself until I get back."

Ronald was suddenly apprehensive. "I hate to see you go for so long."

"It's unavoidable," said Mrs. Wilby crisply. "Please don't be difficult, Ronald. It's a case of either going to the hospital or becoming very ill indeed. I don't like it any more than you do."

———•———

On Monday morning Mrs. Wilby left for the hospital, after giving Ronald final instructions. "Now, dear, don't worry and don't fret. You have your books and your studies and your radio to keep you occupied. The time will go by very swiftly if you don't mope. Naturally, you won't leave the lair under any circumstances. For instance, I don't want you coming out to watch television or anything like that. Mrs. Schumacher is the busiest woman alive and she just might notice the light, or see you moving around. I've given you eight oranges, eight apples and eight nice raw carrots: eat one of each every day, and don't forget to take your vitamin pill. Don't neglect your exercises, and do get started on your studies. It's really very important if you ever want to make anything of yourself. Is everything clear now?"

Ronald said in a muffled voice, "Yes, Mother."

"All right then. I'll be going. And do behave yourself. Close down your secret door as soon as I'm gone."

BAD RONALD

Ronald made no reply. He heard his mother's steps: through the kitchen, the dining room, the hall. The front door opened, closed. She was gone. He was alone.

Ronald closed the secret door. He lay on his cot listening. The house was breathlessly quiet: a lonesome silence, very different from that during the days when his mother worked.

Ronald picked up one of the books his mother wanted him to study: *An Introduction to Algebra*. It looked difficult and very dull. Another book was *The Living World*, in which he found some interesting illustrations. The third book was *Men Against Death*, which described the lives of a dozen eminent doctors, medical experimenters and biologists. Ronald pursed his lips and put the volume aside. He didn't want to be a doctor. What did he want to be? He hadn't made up his mind yet.

The morning passed very slowly. For lunch, Ronald fixed himself peanut butter and jelly sandwiches, and for dessert ate two packages of cupcakes. He mixed a glass of dry milk and drank it without enthusiasm. So much for lunch.

He busied himself with Atranta. Each of the six wizard-castles was to be sketched and rendered in watercolor; the interior plans were also to be detailed, from dungeons and torture chambers to the garrets. Ronald also planned to draw views of the main hall in each castle, and a full-length portrait of each Wizard Duke. By dint of painstaking trial and error he had already produced pencil sketches of the wizard-castles which he thought very effective. With human figures and faces he was less successful. He simply must practice until he got the knack; every day he'd work to train his hand, copying figures in the newspaper fashion advertisements.

The afternoon dragged past. Ronald became restless. His usual occupations failed to interest him. He exercised without zest, examined the Great Map of Atranta, and for a few minutes busied himself tracing a path across Cloud-Shadow Moor.

Even though Ronald could not glimpse the outdoors from within his lair, he felt the special qualities of morning, afternoon, evening and night; some indefinable aspect of his lair altered as the day progressed; and when dusk had darkened around the house, Ronald was quite aware of the fact. Gingerly he raised the secret door and looked out into the pantry. The sense of vacancy was exceedingly strong. His presence did not make itself felt; he was like a ghost. Ronald shivered. He closed the secret door, and cooked dinner over the hotplate: tamales and beans, with bread and butter, a glass of the odious reconstructed milk, two more cupcakes and a banana.

Now it was night. Ronald wondered about his mother and whether the operation were over with. He knew she'd be thinking about him. He looked at the secret door again. His mother was really over-cautious. Certainly no harm could result from his leaving the lair, if he were careful. It was dark; no one could possibly see him. It would be fun to stretch his legs for a bit. Why not? His mother need never know.

He raised the secret door and started to crawl forth, when he noticed the glow of light reaching out ahead of him and into the pantry. Hastily he drew back and slammed the secret door. How careless could a person be? Probably no harm had been done; Mrs. Schumacher would have to be watching very intently to have noticed anything.

He extinguished his light, again raised the secret door, and crept out into the pantry. Slowly he hunched up on his hands and knees, and slowly rose to his feet. Hardly daring to breathe, he looked out into the kitchen. A streetlight about fifty yards down the street cast a pale illumination through the windows, somewhat less bright than moonlight, but exactly right for Ronald's mood. He stepped forth into the kitchen, thrilling with excitement. The Schumacher house was dark; perhaps they had gone out for the evening.

Ronald stole into the dining room: a place once so familiar and now like a strange and forbidden land. Ronald stood quivering with a peculiar excitement. He felt strange and strong and mysterious, like a supernatural being endowed with awful powers. No one knew of his existence; he could do as he wished; no one could stop him. He was beyond the control of any human agency!

On soft feet he slid into the living room. Through the front windows came slantwise shafts of pallid light. The submarine eye of the television stared at him from across the room. The sofa, the armchairs and escritoire stood in their appointed places: elemental entities, fixed and immutable.

I am alone, thought Ronald. I am unseen. I am a spirit of darkness, more than human! I have known more-than-human passion; I have done the forbidden deed! Human qualms no longer deter me, I know no human fears! And now an awesome enlightenment floated up from the depths of his mind: he was not sorry for what he had done to Carol Mathews. How could he be sorry for such wonderful fun! A pity only that he had blundered! Ronald drew and exhaled a deep breath. Moving closer to the windows, he peered out into the night. Somewhere out there was Laurel Hansen; probably in her house, but who knows? She might be coming home from some errand or a visit to a friend's house. Now there would be fun indeed! Oh Laurel, what anguish you have caused me! And Laurel, Laurel—what I would do to you if I could find you and take you somewhere alone!

But he dared not sally forth into the night. The streetlamp would shine upon his unmasked face; he might be seen and recognized, and then all the town would get up a hue and cry. He would be harried and chased and finally driven to bay... No, no, best not leave the house!

Fifteen minutes he stood in the living room, then he returned through the hall and into the dining room. He sat down at the table and breathed the odor of waxed wood and varnish and the sublimated essence of ten thousand dinners.

Ronald sat enjoying the silence. At last he arose, went back through the kitchen, with its own distinctive smell, into the pantry, down to the floor and back through the secret door into his lair. He closed the secret door; now he could turn on his light and return to human life! Here was the brain of the house, the pulsing node of intelligence and passion, here in this secret inner chamber, where he lived unseen and unknown!

He stretched out on his cot and lay staring up at the ceiling. It occurred to him that the secret room was complete except for one deficiency, which he would remedy as soon as possible—and keep secret even from his mother.

RONALD AWOKE EARLY TO a sense of excitement, for events whose imminence he could feel but not define.

He breakfasted on cereal and bananas, and meanwhile inspected the floor of his lair, which was covered with a checkerboard of yellow and white vinyl tile. After breakfast he deliberated a few minutes, then opened his secret door and looked warily forth. Sunlight streamed into the kitchen; a half-dozen flies buzzed against the window panes. Ronald crawled out into the pantry, across the kitchen, and out upon the back porch.

Over the years Mrs. Wilby had accumulated an assortment of household tools. Ronald selected a chisel, a hammer, a brace and bit, a keyhole saw and an ordinary crosscut saw. Moving on hands and knees, he conveyed these back across the kitchen, through the pantry, into his lair.

With the chisel he pried up a number of the floor tiles and scraped away the mastic to reveal the old tongue-and-groove floorboards. With the brace and bit he drilled several holes until he located a joist, then set to work with first the keyhole saw, then the regular saw. Both were rusty and dull; sawing was slow work, especially since he felt impelled to muffle the sound with a towel.

Ronald worked all morning, without haste. He dared not use hammer and nails; wherever necessary he used screws. When he was finished, he had constructed a trapdoor which permitted him access to the crawl-space below the house, and thence to the outside world through the lattice-work door beside the steps to the back porch.

Ronald carefully gathered all the shavings and splintered wood from the ground below the trapdoor. The trapdoor, so he determined, was difficult to detect unless a person were specifically looking for such a thing.

Ronald took the tools back to the porch, returned to his lair, and prepared a good lunch for himself. The trapdoor allowed him an extra dimension of flexibility, should the need arise. Today Ronald did not quite like to define what such a need might be, but it was always best to be ready for anything.

At about one o'clock Ronald crawled through the dining room into the hall, where he rose to his feet. Through the dining room window he watched Mrs. Schumacher come out of her house and change the sprinkler on her lawn. The Schumachers were very proud of their beautiful green lawn and constantly watered, mowed and clipped— always where they could look directly into the Wilby dining room. His mother had not exaggerated the need for vigilance.

He sidled into the living room and lying flat on the rug watched a football game on television, refreshing himself with orange-flavored drink and peanut butter sandwiches. The sound he kept down to the merest whisper.

When dusk came, he switched off the television for fear that the flicker might be noticed from the street. He returned on hands and knees to his lair and cooked a package of macaroni and cheese for his dinner. He mixed powdered chocolate into his reconstructed milk, vastly improving the flavor.

He lay on his cot, reflecting almost complacently upon the circumstances of his life. Things weren't all that bad. No school, no chores, plenty of time for relaxation. He thought about Carol Mathews and hissed through his teeth. He turned out his light, opened the secret door, and once more slid forth from the lair, to move like a ghost through the house. The new trapdoor augmented his might. He could be in and out, if he so chose, and no one would know of his weird comings and goings... He stood by the front window, looking out into the street. He wondered if there were a crawl-space under the Hansen house. He grimaced. The street-light was his enemy! Still, if he dressed in dark clothes and walked quickly north, away from the light, no one would ever notice. And even if he were seen, who would recognize him? For his hair had grown long, and he looked like a hippie.

But he simply lacked the courage to go forth from the house. Suppose that he found Laurel, or another girl, and, well, something happened and his mother found out about it, she'd be very annoyed. Ronald blew out his cheeks. She wouldn't tell the police, or anything like that, but she'd certainly punish him in some very unpleasant fashion—cut out his desserts for months on end.

Too much risk was involved. Perhaps he had never seriously planned to go forth in the first place. Although if a girl passed in front of the house—well, it might be worth the risk to dart out and make a capture. Ronald peered up and down the street.

Across the room the telephone jangled. Ronald jerked in terror. He took a quick step toward the phone, to take the receiver from the hook and stop the terrible noise. He drew back just in time. Let it ring! It was probably a wrong number, or someone who didn't know his mother was sick. Let it ring. This noise was no threat.

But how he hated that jangle! Somewhere someone waited with a receiver to his or her ear. Who could be calling? Ronald would never know. Somewhere someone decided that no one was home and hung up the receiver, and the phone at last became quiet. The house seemed more lonesome than ever, and somewhat dreary. Ronald went back to his lair, closed the secret door, turned on the light, and lay listening to his radio.

Chapter IX

MRS. Wilby finally came home from the hospital. Ronald heard the key in the lock and the creak of the door opening. He quickly closed his secret door and stood with his ear to the wall, to make sure that the entrant was his mother and not some stranger.

He recognized his mother's footsteps. They were slower and less crisp than before. Mrs. Wilby was still weak, and still dejected by the size of the bill.

She came directly into the pantry and rapped four times on the secret door. "Ronald, I'm home. Ronald?"

Ronald lifted the secret door. "I'm here. How are you?"

"Oh, well enough. I feel a bit weak, and I'm not supposed to work until next Monday at the earliest. How have you managed?"

"Very well. It's been lonely, but I guess it couldn't be helped."

"Definitely not." Mrs. Wilby's voice was dry. "I'm lucky I went in when I did. I had what is called 'cholelithiasis'—gall-stones, and the surgeon removed my gall bladder. The bill was appalling. The thought of it makes me sick all over again."

"Don't worry about it," Ronald advised. "The main thing is your health."

"I realize that. Still, the expense has set us back, and I want so desperately to leave this town, and start life over again. Have you been studying?"

Ronald pursed his lips. "Yes, quite a bit."

"Hmmf." Mrs. Wilby's tone was skeptical, but she did not pursue the subject. "I can't think of any way to get more money. We've got nothing to sell... We'll just have to grit our teeth and do everything we can to save."

"I suppose that means more dry milk?" Traces of petulance, self-pity, and even sarcasm could be heard in Ronald's voice.

"Yes," said Mrs. Wilby. "It means more dry milk, and anything else which might save us a few cents. You've got to do your part too, Ronald."

"You don't drink milk, so it doesn't mean anything to you," Ronald grumbled. "That stuff tastes like chalk."

"I'll give up coffee and tea, which aren't really necessary. The hardship will bear on us both. You've just got to face up to facts, Ronald. We've got to put aside every possible cent, and get out of here as soon as we can because this is the time you should be in school preparing for a career. You say that you've been studying?"

"Yes, of course."

"Have you done the exercises in the algebra book?"

"It's not all that necessary. I study the examples and make sure I understand them. There's no real reason to wade through all the routine."

"You start at the beginning of the book and do every single problem! Then you can pass the papers out to me, and I'll check them. You have all the time in the world. It's shameful that you don't use it to advantage!"

"I do the best I can," growled Ronald. "I've got my exercises and my art work and, well, other things that take up time."

Mrs. Wilby gave a grim laugh. "I suggest that you organize your time around your studies, rather than making them an afterthought. You've got to jack yourself up, Ronald. I realize that it's very tiresome for you, but you've got to keep up your morale! That means acting in such a way that you can take pride in yourself and I can be proud of you. Have you bathed since I've been gone?"

Ronald was supposed to take a sponge bath in the basin every day or so.

"I wash whenever I feel dirty," said Ronald. "It's not too comfortable, trying to wash in that little basin. I get all wet and clammy."

"Ronald, it's absolutely important that you don't let yourself go. Even in the tropics an English gentleman dresses for dinner. It's his pride in himself and his good breeding. Now I know that you're not an English gentleman, but you can certainly take the lesson to heart. I hate to say this, Ronald, but your lair doesn't smell all that well. You've got to tidy up. Put your head down where I can see you."

"What do you want to see my head for?"

"Don't argue, Ronald! Do as I say!"

Ronald grudgingly put his head into the aperture. Mrs. Wilby sniffed. "Just stay there till I get scissors."

"What are you going to do?"

"I'm going to cut your hair. Then I'm going to buy you a razor, and you can shave those straggling wisps around your mouth."

"Wait a minute! Long hair is in style now, and so are beards and mustaches!"

"You hardly need to concern yourself with 'style'."

Ronald said no more, and Mrs. Wilby chopped off a good pint of Ronald's lank curls. "Now," said Mrs. Wilby, "pass out all your bed things and all your dirty clothes and I'll give them a good wash. Meanwhile you mop the floor. I'll get you a bucket of soap and water and Clorox. Then I want you to give yourself a good scrubbing."

Sullenly Ronald cleaned the floor of his lair, and was somewhat surprised to see the water became opaque with dirt. Where did it all come from? A mystery.

He washed himself and dressed in clean pajamas. His mother brought him clean linen and he made up his cot. He more or less agreed that the room smelled fresher, and for a fact the clean pajamas felt crisp and smooth rather than limp and sticky, but what he objected to was his mother's attitude. She acted as if the whole thing were his fault. Well—perhaps it was, but that business was far in the past, and it wasn't fair to keep taking him to task about everything. Life was starting to seem bleak. Books, studying, poor food, this unreasonable emphasis upon everything being spic and span. And why all the haste to move to Canada or Maryland or Florida? Was it worth the trouble if they couldn't eat properly, or buy chocolate milk once in a while? He wasn't definitely set on becoming a doctor, and if not, all the effort of studying algebra and doing those tedious problems was just time down the drain. It didn't seem sensible to waste energy in preparation for a career which he might never pursue! But impossible to talk logic to his mother. Ronald sighed, and wondered whether she'd expect him to do the problems today. She was just home from the hospital! They should celebrate, forget about expense for a day or two!

"Mother," called Ronald softly.

Mrs. Wilby came into the pantry. "Ronald, you must never, *never* do that again! We don't have many visitors, but every once in a while someone is here. Never, never, never call out like that, even if you are sure we are alone—because you might be mistaken. Now what did you want?"

"I was thinking that it would be nice to celebrate your coming out of the hospital. Why don't we have a little party, or something of the sort? You can make a nice cake, and maybe cook barbecued spareribs and baked potatoes with butter..."

"Ronald," said Mrs. Wilby, "do you know what butter costs a pound? And what we'd have to pay for spareribs—which are all bone to begin with? Prices are just outrageous."

"Just for today we could forget about prices. I'm really awfully glad to have you home."

"It wouldn't be any celebration for me. I can't eat rich foods, or fats, or oils. The doctor put me on a strict diet. I'm really not all that well yet."

"Oh."

"I'm going to rest a bit now, and while it's quiet, you can get busy with your algebra. You've wasted quite enough time on your drawings. It's time to come back to earth. You can't make a career of dreams, you know. You've got to work with people, and serve people. It's hard work, and you might as well get at it right now."

A WEEK LATER MRS. Wilby made another visit to the Canned Goods Discount Retailers in Stockton and bought another carload of cheap food. Ronald loved peanut butter, a cheap and nutritious meat substitute; she bought three gallons of the substance, and also a gallon of catsup, a sack of beans, another case of macaroni and cheese dinners, twenty-five pounds of rice, a case of canned tuna, a case of canned frankfurters, and half-cases of various other items which she considered sound value, including two twenty-pound cartons of dry milk.

She drove home with a degree of wan satisfaction. She had spent a good deal of money, but she had secured a fine supply of wholesome food, enough to last several months, supplemented of course with hamburger and fresh vegetables... She recalled reading that a number of wild plants provided excellent spinach-like greens: the dandelion, wild mustard and alfalfa. She'd certainly have to check for the availability of these greens when growing weather began.

Once again she waited till dark to unload her supplies, and when everything had been carried into the house she felt exhausted. The illness had taken a great deal of her strength, and she wasn't growing any younger. But she couldn't relax, couldn't let down, couldn't give in an inch until they were comfortably resettled in Florida. So tomorrow: back to work. And Ronald must concentrate upon studies. She had tolerated his dillydallying long enough.

Chapter X

RONALD detested history; he despised biology; he loathed mathematics. Nevertheless every day except Sunday he was expected to produce evidence that he had completed what his mother considered a fair amount of work. She was an exacting taskmaster. Ronald must write résumés of the material he studied, in good writing, and in his own words. She allowed no vagueness or double-talk. If Ronald made a mistake in his mathematics, she gave him ten more problems of the same sort, and she insisted upon neatness. Ronald cursed and sulked and thought that school was never as hard as this.

His mother seemed to have changed. She was certainly less sympathetic with his wants and preferences, and sometimes even a bit sharp. Not that she loved him the less, of this he was sure, but she seemed preoccupied and worried, and almost overnight she looked ten years older. Her face had lost something of its solid blue-eyed imperturbability; her cheeks had become a trifle concave and her jaw seemed longer. Always Mrs. Wilby had been proud of her clear white complexion, and now her skin had become sallow and dull, with a muddy yellow undertone. Ronald knew that his mother worried far too much about money; she drove herself too hard and worked overtime whenever possible and sometimes late into the night, typing legal documents for one of her acquaintances who was a court-reporter. Ronald wished she'd ease up, relax just a bit.

It might take a few months longer before they were ready to move: what of it? He was quite comfortable and making no complaints— except at the food and the studies which often took up three or four hours.

One morning in early May, Ronald heard his mother descend the stairs more slowly than usual, and when she served his breakfast she gave him no instructions regarding his studies, which he thought odd. He lay flat on the floor and peered out through the secret door. "Mother?"

"Yes, Ronald."

"If you're tired, why don't you stay home today and rest?"

"I'd like to, dear, but the work is piled up on me, and I can't take the time off. If Mr. Lang thought I wasn't capable of doing the job, he might hire somebody else, and I'd be out in the street. I'll feel better tonight. I've picked up a bug of some kind, and it's made me a bit unsettled."

"You'd better see the doctor, Mother."

"No, it's nothing. I've taken my pills and I'll be good as new by noon."

A few minutes later she went off to work. Ronald heard the front door close and the diminishing steps as she crossed the porch and descended to the walk. A moment later he detected the grind of the starter, the hum of the engine, and then there was silence.

The day passed. Ronald exercised, worked out a set of the hated algebraic problems, forced himself to read a chapter in the biology text, and prepared the résumé which his mother required. He lunched on peanut butter and jelly sandwiches, reconstituted milk to which he was now inured, and a dish of lemon jello. During the afternoon he napped, then worked on full-length portraits of the six Wizard-Dukes. The costumes were picturesque indeed, each based upon the heraldic colors of the particular duchy. He became engrossed in his work and time went by swiftly; in fact, when he looked at his electric clock he discovered that five o'clock had come: time for his mother to be home, unless she were shopping or otherwise delayed.

At six o'clock he frowned and listened, but heard no sounds, nor did his mother return home at any time during the evening. Ronald sat hunched and worried until eleven o'clock, when in spite of his anxiety, he began to doze.

At nine o'clock the following morning, with no word from his mother, Ronald opened the secret door and after a period of rumination crawled forth.

The day was dark and dreary; rain fell in spasmodic gusts against the windows. Ronald crawled into the living room and hesitantly telephoned the office where his mother worked.

"Central Valley Hardware," said a brisk voice.

Ronald cleared his throat. "Mrs. Wilby, please."

"Mrs. Wilby isn't in today. Do you care to leave a message?"

"This is the pound. It's about her cat. I've called her home and she's not there."

"Mrs. Wilby is sick. She's in the hospital just now, and I don't know when you can get in touch with her."

"Thank you." Ronald hung up the telephone. So: his mother was sick. Again. He thought she had seemed somewhat peaked.

Ronald crawled back into the kitchen, where he sat on the linoleum floor and listened to the rain. The house seemed lonely and distant, not at all cozy. He went to the refrigerator and investigated its contents. Eight eggs, hamburger, half a pound of margarine, carrots, celery, two tomatoes in the crisper, a few oddments of this and that. Crouching out of Mrs. Schumacher's range of vision, Ronald fried the hamburger and four eggs, and sitting on the floor devoured the lot, along with four slices of bread, margarine and peanut butter, with a quart of milk to wash it all down. He had neglected the freezer! Here he discovered a carton half-full of vanilla ice cream which his mother doled out a spoonful or two at a time as a special treat. Ronald opened a can of peaches, which he poured into a bowl and scraped all the ice cream out on top, and this was his dessert. It was the best meal he'd had since his Christmas dinner. Gorged and torpid, Ronald crawled back into his lair, where he lay on his cot wondering how long his mother would be ill. There was little point in doing any algebra until she was on hand to correct the papers; she wouldn't want to come home to a lot of algebra problems. He'd just take a vacation from studies until she returned: certainly the most sensible program.

FOUR DAYS WENT BY and no word from his mother. Ronald began to dread her homecoming. She'd be sick with frustration over so much money spent on the hospital. It would mean rations even more spartan than before: beans, rice, dry milk, dandelion greens. No peanut butter, no juicy hamburgers, no ice cream, no cakes or pastry. A drab existence indeed. But he had no choice in the matter.

Ronald preferred to cook in his lair, where he could relax. To save himself trouble he moved in a quantity of those provisions he liked the most. The bread was all gone; he ate soda crackers until the package was empty.

On the morning of the sixth day, Ronald heard footsteps on the porch. He jumped up eagerly and put his ear to the plasterboard. The key rattled in the lock, the door opened. He heard a man's voice. "...those were my instructions from Mr. Wilby. He wants to sell as quickly as possible, and whatever furniture and oddments you don't want go to charity."

"I don't think I want a thing except some family photographs," said a woman's voice. "I've got all the furniture I need, and it wouldn't be worth shipping back to Pennsylvania anyway."

"You're right there. It doesn't appear that she had too much. What about the books?"

"I don't think I want them."

"China? Silver? That clock?"

"Yes, I'll take the old clock. It belonged to my father, and Elaine got it as a wedding present when she married Mr. Wilby."

"I'll put it aside. Is there anything else?"

"Let me just look into her room, in case I recognize any family jewelry. But I don't believe there's a thing I want except the photographs."

"Here's a picture. What about this?"

"My word, no. It's her son Ronald. I wouldn't want to be reminded of him an instant. Poor Elaine. She lived a tragic life."

"I'll agree to that. It was cancer, wasn't it?"

"No, it was something rather different. She'd had a gall bladder operation and evidently one of the stones slipped down into the bile duct, affecting the work of her liver."

"My word, think of that! I never knew gall-stones were so dangerous!"

"They are in a case like this, because the person thinks she's cured. Poor Elaine had a terrible attack at work, and before the doctors could help her she'd passed on."

"Far better than a lingering death."

"Yes indeed. I hope I go as fast."

"A pity. She was a comparatively young woman. Well, let's take a look in the bedrooms."

The two climbed the stairs; their footsteps sounded over Ronald's head where he lay stiff and terrified. His mother, his wonderful mother: she was dead! And he was alone, with no one to care for him! His dear mother, who loved him so! Tears sprang to Ronald's eyes; he wanted to wail out his grief; he wanted to pound his head with his fists, cover himself under his blankets. What would he do now? No one to talk to him, or cook his meals, or take care of him. Ronald bit the bedclothes to stifle his sobbing; the man and the woman—evidently his Aunt Margaret—were on their way downstairs.

The two stood in the front hall. The man said: "If that's all you want, you might as well take it now. Tomorrow I'll get the Goodwill truck out here and they can clean everything out."

"Such a funny old house," said Aunt Margaret. "Will anyone buy such a place?"

"You'd be surprised! With four big bedrooms, the big kitchen, dining room and living room? There's lots of people with families who'll find this just what they want."

"It's not my cup of tea. I like things a bit more modern. Oh, just one thing. I'll look at the silver, and maybe..." Ronald heard the dining room drawers being opened. "It's just plate," said Aunt Margaret. "Not worth the bother of carrying back to Pennsylvania."

"I can see your point. Well then, shall we go?"

"Yes. This place gives me the shivers."

The door opened and closed; Ronald heard them descending the front steps. He lay like a statue, his interior congealed and unresponsive. So now—what should he do? Where could he go? He had no money, no food... A truck would be coming tomorrow to take all the familiar old things, and he'd never see them again. Ronald crawled out his secret door and carried all the provisions his mother had bought in Stockton into his lair, and everything else edible he could find in the pantry. At least they couldn't take his food away.

What else would he want to keep? Up in his closet was his good suit and his best shoes. Ronald crawled forth and for the first time since his immurement went up to his room. It was just as he had left it, dear and friendly, but a place unthinkably far, like an old man's dream of his childhood. He examined his trinkets and mementos; they belonged to a world which had included his mother. That world had disappeared; the room had lost its meaning.

He packed a suitcase with clothes and one or two keepsakes he could not bear to leave behind: the Swiss Army knife which his mother had given him on his fourteenth birthday, the teddy bear which had been his first toy. He carried the suitcase and an armload of his favorite books down to his lair, closed the secret door and lay down on his cot to think. Sooner or later, when his food ran out, he'd have to leave. Ronald blinked back tears. The land was broad, the roads were long and led afar, to strange pitiless places Ronald really did not care to visit. He beat the pillow with his fist. "Oh my, oh my!" he half-whispered, half-wailed, "why can't things be like they were? I don't want to leave my home!"

Chapter XI

EARLY in the morning Ronald looked once more about the house for anything he wanted to keep. He considered the television set, but it was too large to fit through his secret door. He brought in all the light bulbs, toilet paper, and paper napkins he could find and a few kitchen implements. He also decided to retain the old toolbox; one never knew when tools might come in handy. There was no room in his lair, so he raised the trap door and took the toolbox down to the crawl-space and hid it in a dark corner.

He went up to his mother's room to look around and was almost trapped. He just happened to glance out the window and saw the Goodwill truck stopping in front of the house. He ran down the stairs, bounded on all fours across the dining room and kitchen and dived into his lair. Down went the secret door; he was secure.

A moment later the front door opened. Footsteps sounded in the front hall. The man who had come yesterday said, "Take every-thing. Clear the place out. One thing I want to ask you, or rather two things: be careful of the floors, they're in good shape now and I don't want to refinish them, and secondly, don't leave a mess. Clean up as you go."

"We'll do our best, but we're not going to haul off the trash, mister. We're not garbage movers."

"There's not a great deal of trash, if any. And if you can't cooperate with me, don't even start, because I can get somebody here who will."

"No need to get huffy, mister. I just want to state that we're here to move furniture, not tidy up the place."

"Take everything but the television. That's been spoken for elsewhere. I'm going now. Lock up when you're finished."

The real-estate agent planned to take the television for himself, thought Ronald.

The Goodwill men worked until noon. Ronald listened flint-eyed to their comings and goings. Finally the house was silent and Ronald came forth from his lair.

The house was stark and bleak: bare except for the television set. Now that his mother was gone Ronald actually preferred the house in its present condition. But what was he going to do with himself; what was he going to do?

Ronald looked over the television set with sabotage in mind, but the real-estate agent's car stopped in front of the house, and Ronald bounded back to his lair.

The man came and went. Ronald once more emerged; as he had expected the television set was gone.

Ronald sat down on the naked hardwood floor. Afternoon sunlight presently waned; twilight drifted in from the east. Ronald's mind was blank. He no longer felt anxious about the future; there was no future to feel anxious about. When his food ran out he would leave the house by night, hike ten miles to Mileta and hitchhike from there into Berkeley, where he would lose himself among all the other nameless waifs. Eventually—but there was no point probing that far into the mist. Right now he felt as sad and faded as the evening sky. He dozed and woke up in darkness with a shaft of light from the streetlamp glistening on the hardwood floor... Ronald lay quiet, not quite sure where he was. The house seemed very old and whispered with voices too dim to be heard. He was one with these voices; he need fear nothing... He felt stiff and cold and went to his lair.

THE NEXT MORNING RONALD awoke earlier than usual. He lay on his cot painfully conscious of the silence. Never again the brisk thud of his mother's footsteps descending the stairs, or the bustle in the kitchen as she cooked his meals. Ronald's eyes filled with tears.

After a good breakfast he felt better. Life must go on. He had ample paper and colored inks; with no vexing distractions like algebra and history and biology, he could work with far better concentration, and spend as much time as he liked on detail and elaboration.

First he performed his exercises: by now almost a compulsive act; he could not relax until his muscles had been stretched and twisted. Additionally, he had become a bit heavier than he wished to be.

About ten o'clock footsteps sounded on the front porch; the lock clicked and the door opened. Into the house came several people, and one of them was a woman.

Ronald heard a voice he recognized, that of the real-estate agent. "The living room is on your right. As you can see it's got good proportions and nice high ceilings. They didn't stint on space in the days when this house was built."

"Just when was that?" asked a man.

"I'd guess about the turn of the century. It's quite an old house, but absolutely solid and sound. They built well in those days."

"The floors are nice," said a woman. "Does the fireplace smoke?"

"I really couldn't say, Mrs. Putnam. I don't see why it should. The chimney's got a good long rise to get a draught going. We'll start a fire if you like."

"Oh no, don't bother."

"Now over here is the dining room, paneled very nicely in redwood—there's no wood that mellows more beautifully with age. Built-in sideboard, and a nice eastern outlook to catch the morning sunlight. A very cheerful room. If I owned this house I'd invest in a really good chandelier, and this would be a gracious room indeed."

"Yes, very nice," said Mrs. Putnam.

"Out here is the kitchen," said the agent. "Plenty space, lots of room to work, and a convenient pantry, again an item you don't find nowadays."

"The stove doesn't amount to much," said Mrs. Putnam, "and this refrigerator is absolutely antique."

"You'd probably want to modernize a bit," said the agent. "Quite understandable. I'd do so myself, and just between you and me, this is why the price is so attractive. The owner wants to sell. Out here is the utility porch."

"But no downstairs bathroom?"

"No downstairs bathroom. In those days, ha ha, indoor plumbing of any kind was a luxury."

"Well, I don't know about that," said Mr. Putnam. "It doesn't seem too convenient."

"Let's take a look upstairs," said the agent. "Four big bedrooms and a very nice large bathroom: just the house for a large family."

"I don't think we'll bother, Mr. Roscoe. We've only got our one boy, and already he's talking about the army. We'd just rattle around in a house this large."

"Very well. I just thought it might strike your fancy. We don't get these fine old houses on the market too often, and I decided I'd give you first look."

"Thanks very much, Mr. Roscoe, but I think we want something more modern: a ranch-style place with a nice patio."

"I've got some of those I can show you too, and in their price range they're good buys. Just how many..." The closing of the front door cut off Mr. Roscoe's question. Ronald heard them descend the front steps and presently it was quiet again.

Ronald sat scowling. He wanted no one moving into his house, annoying him with their noises, their comings and goings. Nothing he could do to prevent it, of course. Maybe the house wouldn't be sold.

Mr. Roscoe returned about three o'clock with another prospect: a young woman by the lilt of her voice. Ronald wondered what she looked like; she sounded pert and energetic and attractive, and Mr. Roscoe's gallant jocosities confirmed his suspicion. From the conversation Ronald gathered that her husband owned a service station, that she liked the house, but her children were very young, and she was afraid they might fall down the stairs. Mr. Roscoe pooh-poohed the notion, but the young woman was quite definite. Mr. Roscoe quickly took her elsewhere.

Ronald sat musing over the young woman's voice and her possible appearance. What his lair lacked was a vantage or one-way mirror which would allow him to see without being seen. He considered the walls. Perhaps something could be arranged. The built-in sideboard in the dining room backed up against his lair; at the rear of the central alcove was a rather cloudy mirror. Crawling into the dining room Ronald examined the mirror. Not a one-way mirror, of course. But still—well, it was worth a try. He brought his tools up from the crawl-space. First he measured, then broke into the wall of his lair behind the sideboard, removing lath and plaster until the heavy cardboard behind the sideboard mirror was laid bare. Once again he checked his measurements, then cut a hole through the cardboard, to reveal the gray coating at the back of the glass. With great care he scratched away a fragment of the silvering, to reveal clear glass. Aha! Ronald put his eye to the tiny window and was afforded a view across the dining room, very limited, to be sure, but better than no view whatever. The spot was so inconspicuous that Ronald felt justified in removing somewhat more of the silvering, to enlarge his field of vision. When the peephole was not in use, he would cover it with a bit of tinfoil and a cover to prevent any possible leakage of light from his lair, which of course could bring his whole secret world crashing down around his ears, if not worse.

The following day was quiet; Mr. Roscoe failed to appear. Ronald was of two minds about Mr. Roscoe's absence. He resented the intrusions; still and undeniably, the visitors made the day interesting.

The next day Mr. Roscoe made up for his poor showing and brought three different sets of prospects. Ronald, standing by his peephole, examined them as they walked past, but in no case did he approve of what he saw and heard.

On the next day Mr. Roscoe showed the house to a Mrs. Wood, a trim neatly dressed woman of about forty who approved the sheer old-fashioned spaciousness, and the four bedrooms which the size of her family made indispensable. She seemed a pleasant woman, although she vigorously bargained with Mr. Roscoe over the price of the house. Mr. Roscoe was smilingly firm. "I can't relax a dollar's worth. The owner gave me his first, last and final figure, and the only leeway I have is my commission, which naturally I want to keep. I assure you, the price is right. You won't get this much house anywhere. in Oakmead for the money, believe me. I know, I'm in the business."

"The house has possibilities," said Mrs. Wood, "and with my three girls I need the bedrooms... The kitchen is pretty bad, you'll admit. In fact, everything needs a good coat of paint. Still, the floors are beautiful, and I do like the feeling of space."

"They don't build them like this nowadays."

"Well, I'll talk to my husband. We've looked at five or six houses already and they're either too small or too expensive or both. The price here seems high to me, no matter what you say. The house isn't all that convenient and it needs redecoration."

Mr. Roscoe shrugged. "I'm sorry, Mrs. Wood. My hands are tied. I can't do a thing."

"Well, we'll just keep looking."

Two hours later Mr. Roscoe was back with a stout middle-aged couple whom he addressed as Mr. and Mrs. Florio. Mr. Florio, who was chubby and somewhat pompous, declared the house to be exactly what they were looking for. "A nice old-fashioned place, quiet neighborhood, low taxes—what more do we want? Look at that nice wood in the dining room."

"Yes, it's nice," said Mrs. Florio. "I like all the room, but there's lots of things wrong only a lady would see. The kitchen needs a new stove and a new sink. We could use our own refrigerator and give that old monster away. There's not good storage downstairs except for the pantry which is nice. And think of running up the stairs every time you wanted to go to the toilet."

"Oh well, maybe we could remodel that back porch, put in a little toilet out there. And there's nothing wrong with that stove. It heats up, don't it?"

"It doesn't suit me. Do you think I'd want to show my kitchen to Rosa and Mary and Mrs. Vargas with things in it like this?"

"Well, maybe we could fix it all up. What's money?"

"What's money, you say. Until I ask you to spend some."

"Well, listen, it wouldn't cost all that much, I'm telling you! Two, three thousand maybe."

"And you'd have a very nice house," said Mr. Roscoe approvingly. "Well, we'll talk about it," said Mrs. Florio, and there the matter rested.

The next prospect was a divorced lady, Mrs. Cindy Turpin, only recently arrived in Oakmead. "Do you know, I just love the look of this place! It's pure San Francisco: you've seen them, all those beautiful old white houses with the bay windows!"

"I know what you mean," said Mr. Roscoe. "They're very attractive."

"I was brought up in a house like this, on Russian Hill, and I know my little ones would love this place just as much. We're all folk-dancers and there'd be ever so much room just to swing and strut!"

"You have a very talented family! How old are the children?"

"Well, Jacob is fourteen, Cornelia is twelve, Todd is ten, and Guinevere is eight: all just two years apart. They're so cute in their costumes! I play the guitar, of course."

"It's a beautiful family. And there's plenty of room for them here."

"There certainly is! I'll have to bring Jeff—that's my ex-husband—here to see it. He's buying the place for me."

"You'd better hurry, because I've got several other people interested. There's not many old San Francisco-type houses like this on the market."

"Oh, I know! I'll call him tonight!"

They stood in the dining room; Ronald watched through the mirror. Mrs. Turpin was a nervously active woman, long-legged and long-armed, with a round big-featured face and large wet eyes. Ronald frowned. They'd be making a lot of noise and bothering him with their prancing around. Still—hmm. Ronald licked his lips; it might be interesting.

<hr />

ON THE NEXT THREE days, Mr. Roscoe brought five different parties, including a Negro family, which infected Ronald with a furious hatred toward Mr. Roscoe. Is this what he wanted to do with the house where a decent family had spent all their lives? He wondered if Mr. Roscoe would sell the house next to his own to Negroes!

The Negroes, Mr. and Mrs. Wayne, like most of the other prospective buyers, had a large family. Ronald by now was a keen judge of real-estate selling and sales resistance. He had decided that the more a person admired this and that, the less likely that person was to buy, inasmuch as enthusiasm could not help but firm the asking price, which everyone asserted to be unreasonable.

Abruptly the tours of the house came to an end. A week passed without a sign of either Mr. Roscoe or any of his prospects. Then one day a termite inspector appeared. He examined the periphery of the house, probed here and there with an ice pick, roamed the crawl-space conducting further investigations. Ronald wondered what the visit portended. Perhaps the house had been sold?

The same day Ronald made a careful survey of the living room. His peephole into the dining room had provided a good deal of edification; he wondered if possibly a similar arrangement could be effected through the opposite wall into the living room. At first glance the situation lacked promise. The stairs obstructed all but that section where the toilet was situated, and the wall in the living room lacked a mirror. However, six feet above the living room floor, an ornate plate rack, for the display of trinkets, plaques, dishes and bric-a-brac, encircled the room. Ronald calculated that by prying down the molding underneath the plate rack he could create a suitable crack. In the event that someone noticed the crack they would merely assume that the wood had shrunk, or a nail had given way.

Once more Ronald brought up his tools and presently produced so excellent a view that he crawled quickly around to the living room, spraddling like an enormous four-legged crab, in order to check the appearance of the crack. But all was in order: the crack, from this side, ran in the shadow of the overhanging ledge and was well camouflaged. To cover both of the peepholes when his light was on, Ronald contrived secure masks. A single lapse would spell disaster! He could afford no fit of absentmindedness!

On the following day a tall thin man with clear blue eyes, a mild good-natured face, grizzled brown hair worn in a rather scruffy crew cut, arrived at the house. Ronald inspected him through the living room peephole. The man's gray suit, blue-and-white striped shirt, and nondescript tie conveyed an indefinable sense of officialdom; Ronald thought that he must be a city employee, or a representative of the PG&E, come to check something about the house. A detective? Ronald's heart rose in his throat. Had someone seen him as he moved about the house? Ronald slowly relaxed. A man so vague and casual would hardly be a policeman.

The man paced slowly back and forth in the living room. Ten minutes passed, then another car drew up outside. The man went to the front door, threw it open, and in came three teenage girls, followed by the calm efficient woman Ronald remembered from a week or two previously. Mrs. Wood was her name; she was the lady who had haggled so insistently with Mr. Roscoe, and the man was evidently her husband.

"Well, here we are," Mrs. Wood said gaily. "Have you been waiting long?"

"Just a few minutes," said Mr. Wood. He asked the girls, "How do you like it?"

"Well—it's better than the other places," said the oldest girl. "But isn't it a bit dreary?" Ronald, watching through the peephole, put her age at about seventeen.

"I know what you mean!" said the second, who was about fifteen. "There's an atmosphere here!"

The youngest, aged about twelve or thirteen, wrinkled her nose. "It's not an atmosphere. It's just a funny smell, like old clothes, or something dead."

"That's just mustiness," said Mrs. Wood. "It'll go away as soon as we open the windows. Have you looked over the bedrooms?"

"Not yet." The girls ran up the stairs and Ronald heard them chattering as they prowled the upper floor. Bad smell indeed! That wasn't a nice thing to say. Smart-aleck girls, spoiled rotten all three of them. But he could hardly wait till they returned downstairs, because all three were extraordinarily pretty. Ronald moved back and forth between his peepholes, tense with excitement, while Mr. and Mrs. Wood wandered here and there, discussing various aspects of the house. Ronald gathered that Mr. Roscoe had telephoned the night before, announcing that the owner had reduced his price, and were they still interested?

The girls came back downstairs. "Well," said Mr. Wood, "what do you think?"

"It's okay," said the youngest, who was gay and cute and giddy. A real show-off! thought Ronald. "At least we'd all have bedrooms."

The oldest, who was quiet and mild and, like her father, rather vague, said: "We could paint the house, and make it a lot more cheerful."

"It's a challenge," said the middle girl, who seemed the most intense and perhaps the most intelligent. "No doubt about that."

Mrs. Wood said, "The place looks bleak just now. All empty houses do. Once we brought in our furniture and put down our rugs and hung up new drapes, there'd be a big difference."

"I wish we could get rid of that old stove. It's kind of icky," said the youngest girl, whose name seemed to be Babs or Bobby.

"We'll have to look at the budget and see how much it'll stand," said Mr. Wood. "But I think we could plan on a new stove and a new refrigerator."

"Then we're agreed," said Mrs. Wood, the most decisive. "We'll take the house."

"It's not a bad investment," said Mr. Wood. "If we redecorate and put in a lawn, we can always get our money back."

"Sometime we should convert that back porch to a bathroom," said Mrs. Wood briskly.

"Oh Daddy!" cried Althea, the second girl, "let's go down to the store right now and buy some paint and a stove and a new refrigerator!"

"Not so fast," said Mrs. Wood. "First we've got to make sure of the house. There'll be plenty to do, don't worry about that."

"Have you decided who gets which bedroom?" Mr. Wood asked the girls, half-smiling for their excitement and the fun they were having.

"No, not yet. We haven't talked about it."

"You can draw straws or something of the sort," Mrs. Wood suggested.

"Oh, we'll let Ellen have the front room," said Althea. "Babs can have whichever of the back rooms she wants. It makes no difference to me."

Mr. Wood held out his closed hands. "Whoever gets the hand with the penny gets the room to the right of the hall."

Babs touched her father's left hand and found the penny, and thus the bedrooms were allotted.

———•———

EVENING HAD COME. THE Woods had departed and the house was quiet. Ronald came forth from his lair and crawled into the living room. It was no longer the living room he knew so well; it was no longer the same house. The Woods now lived here: Mr. Benjamin Wood, Mrs. Marcia Wood, Ellen, Althea and Barbara Wood.

Ronald spent quite some time thinking about the girls. All were charming, each in her personal and distinctive way. Barbara was blonde and cute, with a snub nose, a pretty pink mouth. In every blonde girl Ronald looked for traces of Laurel Hansen, and in Barbara he thought to discern certain of Laurel's flirtatious habits. Barbara was extremely self-assured and full of merry pranks, as befitted the spoiled youngest daughter of the family.

Althea, the second daughter, was an inch taller than Barbara, and rather slender, with fine blonde-brown hair flowing to her shoulders; she seemed more moody and introspective, and perhaps more imaginative, than either Barbara or Ellen. Althea's cheeks were flat, her jaw was delicate; when she mused, her mouth drooped, and she seemed as forlorn as a wind-fairy. A girl of interesting attributes, thought Ronald.

Ellen, the oldest girl, was again a person unique and distinctive, although she lacked a definite style, like Babs' extravagant foolishness and Althea's dreamy-wry romantic quality. Ellen was merely beautiful. She exhibited a most curious quality of radiance. Her hair, fine brown-gold like Althea's, seemed to glow of itself; her eyes were transparent gray; her skin, golden from the sunlight, seemed to luminesce with health and cleanliness.

The three girls complemented each other. Each seemed to approve and enjoy the special qualities of the other two; each took pleasure in fulfilling her own role. Babs was the cute 'spoiled brat';

she was supposed to be reckless, saucy and flamboyant, though she was not really any of these; it was all an amusing, affectionate game, played with equal zest by all the sisters. Similarly, Althea was the poet, the dreamer, the source of odd ideas, while Ellen was the innocent impractical sister who overflowed with love and generosity.

THREE DAYS LATER THE Woods took up residence at 572 Orchard Street, and tranquility fled out the window. Turmoil was the new way of life as the Woods worked to alter the austere personality of the old house. Ronald's privacy became a thing of the past. Inconsequential conversations intruded upon his thoughts. He could no longer sleep, eat, or flush the toilet as he wished, but must wait upon the convenience of the newcomers.

Ronald was not only irritated; he was enthralled and fascinated. He could not get enough of the girls; they tantalized him with their comings and more with their goings, and their most interesting activities always occurred beyond his range of vision. If only he were able to open peepholes into their bedrooms!

In spite of his annoyance, Ronald became interested in the affairs of the Woods. He had no real choice; they surrounded him; their topics and concerns pervaded the air.

Ronald soon acquired background information regarding the Woods. Ben Wood worked for the telephone company, and had done so since leaving the army—a period of twenty years. He had been transferred to Oakmead from Los Gatos, a town halfway between San Francisco and Monterey. No one had wanted to make the move, but Ben Wood could not afford to pass up the promotion involved. Ellen and Althea would attend Oakmead High in the fall. Barbara would enter the ninth grade at junior high. No one in the family liked Oakmead very much, and they had bought the house at 572 Orchard only because it was cheap and roomy and could be made at least tolerable by dint of hard work and enthusiasm, which everyone was prepared to expend. Ronald became a passive participant in the project; again, he had no choice. The house and its refurbishing were almost the only topics of conversation. First there was cleaning, then scraping and painting, and likewise planting. Ben Wood blasted the family budget with a new stove, dishwasher, refrigerator, a washer and a dryer. He installed new kitchen cabinets, laid down new tile in the kitchen, removed the old washtubs from the back porch and wrecked the old shed at the back of the lot, and who should he hire to haul away the junk but Duane Mathews? He rented a cultivator, tilled the back yard. The girls set out a vegetable garden; Marcia Wood planted fruit trees and rose bushes; Ben Wood installed a new front lawn, which he declared would make the Schumacher lawn look sick, and the challenge somehow communicated itself to the Schumachers, who began to water and mow and clip more diligently than ever.

The outside of the house remained as before: chalk-white, the color of sun-bleached bone. Next year the Woods planned to repaint the house a dark green with white trim.

The work occupied the family most of the summer, but they did not lack for help. While hauling away the rubbish, Duane Mathews became acquainted with Ellen, and thereafter was almost a daily participant in the work. Various other boys came more or less regularly to lend their efforts. Mrs. Wood provided hamburgers and lemonade, and the girls wore shorts, which seemed sufficient inducement. "The more the merrier," said Ben Wood, "so long as they work."

"They work," said Marcia Wood. "The girls won't let them stop."

"Merciless little slave drivers."

IN SPITE OF HIMSELF Ronald became interested in the summer's work. With the assiduity of a scientist he kept watch at the peepholes. The girls aroused his special interest; their smooth brown legs and round little rumps were sources of sweet torment. Ronald, with his eye glued to the peephole, was never satiated. When one of the girls walked past his hands would grow moist, and he would make soft noises under his breath. He had no favorites, and appreciated the different quality of each girl. If he had been asked to make a choice he would have considered long before selecting, though he had formed quite definite opinions as to their special qualities. Barbara was the cutest and most seductive; Ellen was the most beautiful and perhaps the most passionate; while Althea's dreamy personality gave her a strange charm which Ronald found irresistible. For the boys who came to visit and perhaps to work he felt nothing but dislike and contempt, and most especially for Duane Mathews, who had fallen in love with Ellen.

One Sunday at lunchtime Duane mentioned horrid Ronald Wilby, the murderer. The Woods were shocked by the news. "I thought there was an evil atmosphere about this house!" said Althea in an awed voice. "I felt it when we first moved in. It was so strong you could almost smell it!"

"It's gone now, though," said Barbara. "Wickedness can't stand being painted."

"Don't be too sure!" Steve Mullins told her. "You've heard of evil influences? If they're strong enough they form into ghosts."

"Oh? And how do you know?" Ellen asked.

"Where else do you think ghosts come from?"

"I don't even know if there are such things."

"A lot of people swear they've seen them."

"A lot more swear they haven't."

"Even so," said Barbara, "the ghost wouldn't be here. It would haunt that old garden."

"Don't say that!" muttered Duane Mathews. "It was my little sister!"

"I'm sorry!" cried Barbara. "I didn't mean to say anything awful."

Duane managed a grim laugh. "That's all right. I shouldn't be all hung up on it. Maybe someday I'll find Ronald Wilby."

Seven feet away Ronald Wilby stood with his eye pressed to the peephole. More than anyone he knew he abhorred Duane Mathews, an ugly graceless fellow whose father was a bartender. How Ellen or anyone else could like a person so eaten up with malice exceeded Ronald's comprehension. Every aspect of Duane's appearance and personality repelled Ronald: his harsh bony features, his lanky body, all shoulders, arms and legs; his abrupt motions and terse, brusque voice. And most of all, his practicality and grim self-assurance, which in Ronald's mind were equivalent to arrogance and bloated egotism. Only a year or two older than Ronald, Duane had the presumption to act like a man! And in spite of all, the girls seemed to admire him. Only yesterday Ronald had heard them chattering about Duane in the usual half-foolish, half-mordant hyperboles which none but themselves could fully understand.

"He looks like an old-fashioned cowboy," Barbara had said. "From Texas, of course."

"He even acts old-fashioned," said Althea. "He's somebody out of an old movie."

"An old cowboy movie."

"Whatever you like. Tickets cost the same."

"His eyes are marvelous," sighed Ellen. "I wish I had sea-green eyes."

Snake's eyes, thought Ronald. Carol, so he recalled, also had odd green eyes.

"I'll have to look in my book of astral psychology and see what sea-green eyes mean," said Althea. "It might be something awful, and then we'd have to turn poor Duane away."

"Mom likes him, eyes and all," said Barbara. "That tells us more about who gets turned away around here than any old book with a purple cover."

"Then I'll look in my book on palmistry with the red cover."

"About Duane's eyes?"

"No, his hands."

"But he doesn't have green hands."

Althea liked to use a voice with a special cool twang when she propounded a paradox. "Duane has serious faults. He's too dependable and trustworthy. Around people like Duane a girl can relax and sometimes she falls asleep."

Ellen smiled sadly. "Only cads keep you awake?"

"Around cads I *stay* awake," said Althea. "But don't get me wrong. I'm not a bigot. Some of my best friends are cads." She thrust up her hands as Barbara started to speak. "Don't you dare say it."

Such had been the conversation of yesterday morning. Today Duane looked quizzical when Althea addressed him as "Tex", though, characteristically, he forebore to ask why the nickname.

After lunch the five went upstairs to paint the front bedroom: Ellen, Althea, Barbara, Duane, and Steve Mullins, who was one among the many enamored of Barbara and her outrageous antics. Ronald could hear their voices, and they seemed to be having a good time.

Ronald closed the peepholes, turned on his light, and went to sit on the cot. The conversation, specifically that part dealing with himself, had soured the day. He felt cantankerous and dissatisfied, and in no mood for any of his usual activities... Not but what his ordinary routines hadn't already been disturbed. Ronald sighed and growled. He just couldn't let those twerps interfere with his activities. He rose from the couch and put himself through a lackadaisical set of exercises, though nowadays he dared no jogging unless everyone was gone from the house.

As always, exercising gave him an appetite. For his dinner, Ronald opened a can of beans which he ate with the last of his soda crackers smeared with peanut butter, a rather bland meal which left Ronald's appetite unappeased, especially when, for Sunday dinner, Mrs. Wood served mushroom soup, avocado salad, a beautiful pineapple-glazed ham with sweet potatoes and fresh green broccoli. Ronald glumly watched through the peephole as the five Woods devoured their dinner. Everyone was cheerful; the interior of the house was now completely painted except for trim around the doors and windows, which would require enamel. As Marcia Wood had originally prophesied, fresh paint had gone far to enliven the old house, and everyone enjoyed the spaciousness of the big old Victorian rooms.

"If we added on some turrets and balconies, and bought a few marble urns, we could call the place a mansion," said Ellen.

"A Gothic mansion," said Althea. "That's what they're called in the horror movies."

"The remark is too close for comfort," said Barbara. "The last people to live here were definitely spooky. I doubt if they left any ghosts, however. At least I hope not."

"I share your hope," said Ben Wood. "Because down would go the market value."

"Maybe that's why the house was sold so cheap."

"We could always advertise in spiritualist magazines," said Althea. "A good dependable ghost might be valuable."

"What good is money," asked Barbara, "if we're all found dead in our beds with horrible expressions on our faces?"

"Barbara, you're being absurd, as usual."

Ellen grimaced. "I wouldn't take you seriously, except that the house *does* have an uncanny feeling about it."

"Bah," said Marcia Wood. "That's just ridiculous."

"Sometimes I hear funny noises," said Barbara. "I suppose it's rats."

"All old houses are full of funny noises," said Ben Wood.

"If you say so, Daddy."

Ronald was displeased by the tenor of the conversation. Certain of the remarks verged on the personal, and why in the world couldn't they stop harping about that old subject? They really had no right to criticize when they only knew Duane's side of the story... Well, it didn't make all that much difference. Of more immediate interest was that lovely ham and the platter of sweet potatoes. Ronald was hungry all over again. The lair had its advantages and also disadvantages, such as watching other people devouring savory meals to which he had not been invited.

For dessert Mrs. Wood served a magnificent lemon meringue pie, and Ronald became almost sick with longing. After this he wouldn't watch the Woods at their meals; he only tortured himself... Ha! Ronald dismissed the idea immediately; it was quite unrealistic.

The girls discussed colors and interior decorating. Ellen had painted her room white, with pale green and lavender trim. Althea had used gray, pale blue and dark blue with accents of white. Barbara had ranged the length and breadth of the sample chip rack in the paint store, to achieve what she called 'drama'. "I want lots of excitement in my room!" she declared, and Ronald muttered under his breath, "I'll give you excitement in your room, no fear of that!" Barbara, the youngest of the girls, impressed Ronald as the sexiest, because of her provocative antics, her flirtatious pouts and poses. He had never seen anyone so boy-crazy! Barbara had painted her room white, yellow, chalky blue and pistachio green, with accents of firehouse red and dark blue, and somehow, after arranging her possessions and hanging her posters, she achieved exactly that atmosphere of exuberant frivolity she intended.

HALFWAY THROUGH AUGUST PROJECT Redecoration at 572 Orchard Street came to an end, somewhat to the bewilderment of the Woods, who had started to think of scouring, sanding, and painting as a permanent way of life.

Every room in the house had been refurbished. The living room, originally salmon-beige with dark varnished woodwork, had become off-white with a pale blue ceiling. The woodwork was enameled white, as were the bricks of the fireplace, and a bright-blue rug covered the floor.

Ronald disapproved of the changes. The house had previously seemed adequate; the zeal expended by the Wood family represented a not-too-subtle derogation of himself and his mother. The Woods were just plain finicky, thought Ronald, and pretentious to boot. A chandelier in the front hall! Art prints all the way up the stairs! The eccentric new clock on the kitchen wall with hands three feet long! The Mexican *ollas* planted with geraniums on the front porch! All vanity and ostentation! Still—it made no great difference, one way or the other. The place no longer meant anything to him; they could turn it into a Chinese joss house for all he cared.

Ronald's food supplies had dwindled to the danger point; and he had started to derive items of sustenance from the Woods' refrigerator, bread box and fruit bowl. In the small hours of the night he would sally forth for his meal: a morsel here, a bite there, an apple or an orange, perhaps a slice of bread, a lump of cheese, a swallow or two of wonderful nonsynthetic milk! And occasionally when there was an ample leftover dessert, Ronald would treat himself to an inconspicuous portion, and never had food tasted so good!

Always he waited until the house was dark and still. Then out the secret door, through the pantry, into the kitchen: silent as a wraith, so that not even the floor creaked! Then across to the refrigerator, to ease open the door and there! glowing in the pale light like gems on black velvet, the delicious fragments of food from the meal to which he had been a witness some six hours previously. He knew he must be extremely discreet, but sometimes oh! what an effort to restrain himself from gobbling the contents of the refrigerator. And once he heard Mrs. Wood call out in puzzlement, "How strange! I would have sworn I put away seven of those deviled eggs. Now there's only five. Did one of you girls get at them?"

"Not I." "Not I." "Not I."

"I'm going crazy then," said Mrs. Wood. "I remember so distinctly… Maybe your father ate them last night."

The mystery of the missing deviled eggs slipped from her mind, and she did not think to question Ben Wood when he arrived home from work. But that evening, when Ellen placed half a deviled egg on each salad plate, Babs said to her father, "Mom thinks she's going crazy, unless you ate two deviled eggs last night."

Ben Wood stared blankly, then said, "I'll agree to anything if it means preserving your mother's sanity."

"Oho!" cried Babs. "So you're the guilty egg-eater!"

"Will your mother go insane if I deny it?"

"Not quite," said Marcia Wood. "It's just that I thought I put seven eggs away, and this morning I could find only five."

"Rats," said Babs.

"Or ants," suggested Ellen.

"Or ghosts," Althea murmured.

"Now you're being silly," said Marcia Wood. "Obviously I counted wrong." A sudden thought struck her. She looked at Ellen. "Wasn't Duane here last night?"

"No. The night before last."

"My mind really is going," said Marcia Wood. "He's in and out so often that I can't keep track of him."

Ben Wood hated to think of his girls growing up. He spoke in a grumbling voice, "That's the price we pay for all this pulchritude: we have to feed every good-time daddy in town. Sometimes I wonder whether it's love or hunger which brings them around."

"Now Daddy, that's not fair," said Ellen. "Duane has worked very hard around here. Don't forget who carted away all the rubbish, and also who brought over all that venison and the catfish and the apricots, and who pushed the car to get it started, and who put the flashing around the chimney, and who..."

"Stop, stop!" cried Ben Wood. "Duane is the best of the lot, in fact he's indispensable. In fact I better go and let Duane move in."

"Where would he sleep?" asked Barbara innocently. "With Mom?"

"He's an extremely nice boy," said Marcia Wood. "If only he weren't so intense! It makes me nervous sometimes just to be in the same room with him."

"You'd be intense too if a fiend murdered your little sister," declared Babs, and behind the peephole Ronald pursed his lips.

"I'm glad it's Ellen who's got the fiend's bedroom and not me," said Althea.

Ellen made a wry face. "I think I'll trade with Babs."

"Oh no you don't. I've got my room just the way I want it."

"The house is very old," said Ben Wood. "Dozens of fiends may have lived here and slept in all the bedrooms."

"I don't think I'll watch any more horror films," said Babs. "I'm starting to believe all those things."

"Nonsense," scoffed Mrs. Wood. "The film people just rig up those effects to scare silly little girls."

"Oh I know that, but where do they get the ideas to begin with? Nobody invents things out of thin air."

"I'll believe the supernatural when I see it," said Ben Wood. "Weird things always happen to other people."

"I'm not so sure about that," said Althea. "What could be more weird than the missing deviled eggs?"

In his lair Ronald made a set of wincing grimaces. He disliked all allusions to himself or to his activities. "I hate to explode your mystery," said Mrs. Wood, "but it's all coming back to me: there were only five eggs after all."

Ronald grinned to himself. The eggs had been extremely tasty. But never should he take articles of food which might have been counted.

———•———

THE FLURRY OVER THE missing eggs disturbed Ronald to such an extent that he kept to his lair for two nights. When at last he came forth he took only two slices of bread, a small quantity of butter, a slice off a meat loaf, two cherry tomatoes, and a sprig of parsley. The fruit bowl held four ripening avocados: how he loved avocados! Forbidden fruit! He passed them by with only a longing glance.

Back in his lair he ate the sandwich and the meager salad, and gulped down a glass of reconstituted milk. Everything tasted so good that he wanted to go out for a second helping, and perhaps select the ripest of the avocados. Chances were no one would notice... Remember the deviled eggs? He must learn to control his appetite. All very well, but he also must contrive a way to secure food, because his stocks were just about depleted. Well, he knew what he'd have to do: simply change his method of operations. Heretofore he had taken morsels left over from the evening meal, and he would continue to do so when conditions warranted, but to minimize risk, he must henceforth procure mostly raw materials: a potato, an onion, a cupful of flour, an egg, a slice or two of bacon. If he implemented his plan with judgment and discretion, he should be able to maintain himself adequately and with no one the wiser: a triumph of cool resourcefulness over adversity! For best efficiency he must forage to a definite schedule, that he might not take so much of any one item that its absence would be noticed. A good idea to maintain a record of his acquisitions, or even better, to plot the flow on a chart. Ronald nodded with thoughtful approval. He began to feel that he had achieved a certain self-sufficiency. His mother had often emphasized that planning and foresight distinguished successful men from failures. Ronald now understood the wisdom of her remarks.

First Ronald made sketches to determine the scale and scope of his chart, then drafted it neatly on a large sheet of drawing paper. He would employ different colored inks for the various components of his diet and thus provide instant and accurate information as to what might be called his 'income'. A corollary of this idea occurred to him: he could prepare a second chart to record his consumption, or 'expenditure', and even a third chart to show the level of supplies on hand, or 'inventory'. These charts would then provide a great deal of interesting information, and rationalize what was otherwise a hit-and-miss sort of procedure; he was sure his mother would have approved his methods.

———◆———

RONALD'S NEW SYSTEM PROVED fairly successful. At a glance he could determine his supply of any commodity, and how recently he had commandeered a quantity of this substance; the charts were time-consuming of course, but any worthwhile achievement entailed hard work, which was another of his mother's dictums. The charts helped him formulate a number of guidelines or precepts, the most important of which were:

Never take food from a full or nearly full or a nearly empty container.

Take very small quantities of expensive items.

Take no canned goods unless they have been pushed to the back of the shelves and forgotten.

Ronald's new way of life entailed more effort than the old. He was now obliged to cook: soups, stews, pancakes which he flavored with cheese, jelly, or peanut butter, and cooking was also more of a problem, since he must be careful with cooking odors, and prepare his meals only when any vagrant whiff of this or that would not be noticed: after the Woods had all gone to bed, or while Mrs. Wood herself was cooking. Ronald hung the charts in a neat row on the wall behind the toilet, just under the living room peephole: the only area of wall space not yet dedicated to Atranta. They made an imposing array, and testified to his remarkable and dispassionate logic toward problems which might have confounded an ordinary person. It was clear, thought Ronald, that he combined within himself a pair (at least) of contrasting yet compatible temperaments. To a philosopher's rationality he melded the artist's powers of synthesis; very few people enjoyed this capability!

Perhaps in connection with the Wood family, he should use a more scholarly approach: a spirit of research, so to speak. His situation afforded him a splendid vantage from which to study the activities of a typical contemporary family. He could observe them in a most intimate and detailed manner, like a scientist peering into a terrarium. He could investigate the Woods as an anthropologist examines an exotic tribe; he could codify their activities, the phases of their behavior, their inter-relationships and eccentricities. Someday he might even write a book—a perceptive treatise to amaze the layman and the professional sociologist alike! And how deliriously amusing if the Woods someday should chance upon this book (to be entitled *The Watcher Within*, or *Out of the Secret Place*, or *An Intimate Investigation*, by Ronald Norbert), and marvel to recognize themselves!

Ronald decided to initiate his study at once. Every trifle of knowledge must be organized, every word noted, every gesture analyzed for its symbolic content. He would chart moods and relationships; he would explore hidden currents of pride and envy; he would uncover secrets of which not even other members of the family were aware! The three girls: exuberant Babs, dreamy Althea, luminous Ellen, were the principal topics to which he would address himself. He would learn their likes and dislikes, their foibles and prejudices, their fears and sensitivities; he would know them better than they knew themselves, through his keen and impersonal analysis! Well, not altogether 'impersonal'. Research was all very well, but even better would be a personal study of any or all of the three: separately, all at once, upside-down, or any other way. And Ronald uttered a lewd chuckle, a soft *heh-heh-heh*. Yes, indeed! Yes, sir, indeed!

Chapter XII

RONALD'S new project occupied his thoughts the whole of the following day, a Saturday, but a factor he had overlooked came to complicate the situation. On Sunday the summer vacation ended; on Monday the schools opened and all three girls would be spending half their waking hours away from home: a situation which aroused Ronald's bitter resentment. All summer they had given their time to the house and, by some incalculable transference, to Ronald himself; now they would be off and away, living, laughing, feeling, adventuring, far beyond his ken; and to compound the offense, they looked forward to the prospect with anticipation. On Sunday night Ronald wept for self-pity and rage. The girls, so callous, so pitiless, were the agents of his anguish; they must be held to account, and they must suffer as he now suffered: a retribution, perhaps irrational, but Ronald did not care; nothing else could ever allay his hurt. Ronald lay in the dark musing. Which of the girls appealed to him the most? Babs, for her gaiety, for her possibly innocent provocations? Althea, a trifle strange and exotic, who would certainly be entranced with the Atranta saga? Or Ellen, for her glowing beauty?

Gloomy Monday, the first day of school. Ronald sulked all day in the unnaturally quiet house. When the girls returned late in the afternoon, Ronald was so put out that he refused to go to his peepholes. Let them do as they wished! It was all the same to him; he would remove himself into a mood of austere dignity and withdraw his attention, and maybe not even continue his researches.

But at dinner time his hurt feelings succumbed to curiosity, and he applied his eye to the peephole. After apprising himself of the day's events he felt somewhat better, because none of the girls liked their new schools. Barbara found her classmates uninteresting; the girls were either drab, weird, or stuck-up, and the boys were just children. Althea described her teachers as dreary old educational hacks. Ellen expressed a more temperate version of Barbara's views.

Ben and Marcia listened with amusement rather than concern. "You'll soon find people you like," said Ben. "I didn't notice any lack of boys around the house during the summer."

"Yes, but what kind of boys?" grumbled Barbara. "That little jerk Jeff...Fat Peter...Steve Mullins..."

"I thought you liked Steve," said Ben Wood.

Barbara shrugged. "I can get along without him."

"Well, I wouldn't worry too much," said Marcia Wood. "None of you have ever lacked for friends before. I doubt if you will now."

Ellen gave a wry laugh. "I heard one of the girls say, 'They're living in the old Wilby house'...as if that was something to be ashamed of."

"I wouldn't let that kind of nonsense worry me."

"We're certainly not going to move," said Ben Wood. "You can depend on that."

"That's just like the people in this town!" Barbara declared indignantly. "This is our house now, our very own, and we don't care what anybody thinks!"

"If only the house were less, well, 'Gothic'," Althea mused. "It's not really a pretty house."

"Oh come now," said Ben Wood, almost sharply. "It's a very pleasant old house. When it gets a coat of 'Hunter Green' and the trees grow and the garden blooms, it'll be a showplace."

"Allie is far too sensitive to atmospheres," said Ellen.

"If she doesn't look out, she's going to grow up to be a psychiatrist," said Barbara, who often held this particular trade up to scorn.

"I can't help it," said Althea. "Sometimes the house seems alive. Haven't you noticed, when you're coming up the street, how the windows seem to watch you?"

"All houses have faces," said Barbara. "I've seen crying houses and laughing houses, and houses squinting cockeyed, like they're angry—"

"As if they're angry," said Marcia Wood.

"—and remember the old Ettinger house with the cypresses in front? It always looked like, I mean, as if it were praying."

"That's because the Ettingers were Holy Rollers," said Ellen. "A house always begins to look like the people who live there."

"So long as people don't begin to look like their houses," said Althea.

Barbara giggled. "Imagine Daddy with front steps on his stomach and Ellen with gray shingles instead of hair."

"And you painted dark green, as this house is going to be painted next year!"

Marcia Wood changed the subject. "What about activities? Have any of you signed up for anything?"

"No sign-ups till Thursday," said Ellen, "but I don't think I'm interested. It may seem strange, but I'm already thinking about college."

"Oh no!" cried Barbara. "You'll be going away, probably to Berkeley, where there's nothing but hippies and maybe you'll marry one and go off to Turkey or India."

"Not likely," said Ellen. "I might not go to Berkeley. I'd like to go to India though."

"Berkeley's closer," said Althea. "We'd see you more often."

"We should never separate," said Barbara. "Let's promise never to move, but always live with Daddy and Mom. If anybody wants to marry us they've got to move in too."

"Ho ho!" exclaimed Ben Wood. "I hate to think of the grocery bills. I'd have to take two extra jobs."

"Just the same," said Marcia, "it's a lovely idea. I wish we could have it that way... Speaking of extra jobs, I'm tempted to work part-time at the hospital."

"Oh! we don't want you off working!"

"It would just be part-time—maybe mornings, or afternoons, or a day or two a week, to bring a little extra money into the house. Our grocery bills just won't stop, and I refuse to serve spaghetti five nights a week and hamburger the next two. We're just lucky none of you girls have ever needed orthodontia."

"For heaven's sake," said Ben Wood, "please don't anyone do anything that's going to cost money!"

Ronald, grinning to himself, thought, "I'd like to get them all pregnant. Then old Wood could yell about expense!"

But how could the project be accomplished?

MRS. WOOD WORKED TUESDAY and Thursday, and sometimes Wednesday as well. On these days Ronald was alone in the house. The girls' dislike for their schools relieved Ronald's hurt feelings, and he went about his research with gusto.

Not until Thursday, the third day of Mrs. Wood's employment, did Ronald dare to venture from his lair. Cautiously he peered through his secret door and listened, then crawled out into the pantry and rose to his feet. He stepped forth into the kitchen and sniffed the air, detecting new paint, waxed vinyl, freshly laundered curtains, oranges and bananas in the fruit bowl. New curtains of red and green chintz hung at the windows, obscuring Mrs. Schumacher's view. A decided improvement, thought Ronald.

Ronald stood motionless for two minutes, listening and looking all about him, and thrilling to the sense of adventure. He went to the refrigerator and eased it open just to check on what might be there. He decided that he deserved a nice snack. Bringing out milk and ice cream, he mixed a generous quantity of both into a bowl, added sugar, a sliced banana, and a great mound of pressurized whipped cream. With the refined discrimination of an epicure, he devoured his mid-morning snack, sighing in gratification. When he had finished, he washed the bowl and spoons, disposed of the banana peel, and made sure all was as before, though in this easy, generous house no one seemed to take much notice of trifles.

Ronald went to the dining room. Mrs. Schumacher had come out to change the sprinkler on her lawn, but new curtains again protected him from her curiosity.

Many times Ronald had studied the dining room through his peephole, but to walk in and stand by his old place at the table was a strange experience. In a matrix of familiarity, so much was new. The old dark paneling had been enameled a pale tan, or bisque; the table and chairs were pale wood, of modern light construction, but very charming with the bowl of marigolds on the table.

Three soft steps took him into the front hall. The stairs to the second floor sucked at his gaze, drew his attention up the new red stair runner toward the second floor and the girls' bedrooms. Ronald looked dubiously toward the front door, through which any of five people might unexpectedly return home.

Ronald hesitated. He wanted to explore the living room, even more he wished to visit the second floor. But the front door exhaled sheer menace, as if it only waited until he committed himself before bursting open wide. Ronald drew back and retreated into the kitchen. Here he paused to settle himself. His trepidation was by no means sheer foolishness; it was never wise to ignore a hunch. And there was always the chance that someone might come home when they weren't expected; sooner or later it was sure to happen. If ever he risked the second floor, he must decide upon a place to hide, in case of emergency—such as under a bed. The prospect was not unattractive. If only he dared.

Not today. The front door had given him qualms; he would risk no more adventures. In compensation, he made himself a fine peanut butter and jelly sandwich, and gulped down another cupful of milk. To minimize his depredations, he poured a cupful of water back into the carton, and then he returned to his lair.

——— ✦ ———

FRIDAY PASSED, THEN THE weekend. On Tuesday Mrs. Wood went off to work and Ronald was again left alone in the house.

At nine o'clock precisely he emerged from his lair, to stand a few minutes in the kitchen listening. No sound. He turned his attention to the refrigerator which yielded a nice dish of applesauce, a good helping of cottage cheese, and a mouthful or two of cold string beans, which he ate for his health's sake. For dessert he raided the cookie jar for three gingersnaps and he allowed himself two swallows of milk. More would be risky, and last Thursday evening the condition of the ice-cream carton had prompted Mrs. Wood to remark, "I thought sure we had more ice cream. It's something we're just not able to keep in this house. A wonder you're not all little chubbies."

With a good breakfast tucked away, Ronald wandered through the dining room and into the front hall. Unlike his mother, the Woods never locked up when they left the house. Burglary was unknown in Oakmead, and the Woods were trusting by nature. Ronald cleverly protected himself from surprise by locking the door. He was now safe from an unexpected incursion; if anyone tried the door Ronald could hear and be warned. Almost boldly he walked on past the door and into the living room.

He amused himself almost an hour, investigating whatever seemed of interest: the drawer in the desk where Mrs. Wood kept household accounts, canceled checks and letters not yet answered. The photograph album was a fascinating volume. Ronald studied the Wood family in all its stages. Before his eyes the girls grew from babies into toddlers, from tomboys into pretty teenagers. He saw them at picnics and birthday parties, at the beach and in the mountains. He gazed into faces he failed to recognize: relatives, neighbors, family friends; he saw their old house in Los Gatos and their old school, and a number of school pictures.

Ronald finally put away the album and made a last survey of the living room. By sheer chance he happened to glance out the front window and notice a car halting in front of the house: Ben Wood's gray Chevrolet. With heart pounding Ronald loped to the front door, snapped back the latch, and raced through the dining room to his lair. Even as he closed his secret door Ben Wood came into the house. He ran upstairs to his bedroom where he remained only a minute or so, apparently to find some object or document he had forgotten. Then he descended to the ground floor and departed.

Ronald sat hunched on his cot, listening to the footsteps. A close call? Close enough for alarm. The locked door probably would have protected him in any case. Still, the incident went to show that a person couldn't be too careful.

During the afternoon Ronald worked on his nutrition charts. He had lost interest in his projected study of the Wood family; the task now seemed over-complicated and tedious. The fact of the matter was that Ronald had become preoccupied with the upstairs bedrooms. A simple matter to secrete himself under a bed. No one would notice and he could see everything that went on. The idea always brought its own rebuttal. No matter how appealing the project, caution must remain his watchword! So many things might go wrong, and all would mean big trouble. And yet, and yet... Ronald vacillated between conflicting urges. The thought of supple young bodies and the fascinating things which might be accomplished urged him to gallant enterprise. But too much risk, too much risk! What would he do if he were to lose his sanctum? He had no money, no place to go...

On Saturday night Duane Mathews and Ellen went to the movies, thereby incurring Ronald's displeasure. In many ways he found Ellen the most attractive of the girls; he wanted no one fondling her but himself. Ronald watched and listened all evening until, shortly before midnight, Duane brought Ellen home. Ronald heard the car stop, he heard them mount the steps and stand on the porch, and he knew they were kissing.

Ronald grimaced and showed his teeth. He totally disapproved of this sort of thing, and it must be stopped.

On Sunday all three girls went off on a swimming party with Duane and two other boys, and Ronald was left moping and disconsolate all afternoon.

For dinner Mrs. Wood roasted a pair of chickens, the odor of which tantalized Ronald. She also made two beautiful coconut-cream pies. Duane stayed for dinner, and Ronald watched with indignation as he devoured great quantities of everything, which would only mean a near-absence of those leftovers which Ronald had come to count on. But what could he do? Nothing except watch and fight back his rage while Duane wolfed down portion after portion of the food Ronald regarded as his own.

Dinner was over at last and eventually Duane went home. Everyone went to bed and the house became quiet.

Ronald was out of his lair almost at once. As he had feared, the chicken was totally gone. Not a single piece left for him! And nothing else that was any good, except half of one pie. Ronald angrily cut himself a large piece, and it was the most delicious pie he had ever eaten, and he had to have another small helping; after all no one would notice.

But in the morning Mrs. Wood did indeed notice and made a marveling remark to Ellen as to the scope of Duane's appetite. Ellen said in wonder, "He didn't eat any more pie!"

"He must have," said Mrs. Wood. "There was at least half a pie left when I put it away, and your father didn't eat it."

Ellen shook her head in perplexity. "I'm sure it wasn't Duane."

"It doesn't make any difference, of course," said Mrs. Wood. "He's welcome to as much as he can eat. It just seems strange."

Ronald saw Ellen's clear-eyed face take on an unusually doleful expression. Ronald snorted softly. Maybe now she wouldn't think so highly of Duane, who had just earned himself a reputation for gluttony.

Chapter XIII

WITHIN range of Ronald's knowledge, neither Marcia nor Ben Wood seemed ever to discipline their daughters—not only by virtue of their own tolerance, but because the girls gave no provocation for punishment. Barbara occasionally left her room in a mess; Althea tended to question established doctrine on general principle; Ellen was not always punctual, but such delinquencies incurred at worst a pained outcry from Ben or a crisp suggestion from Marcia.

In regard to boys and dating, the senior Woods were reasonable and flexible. The girls knew what was expected of them and the hours they were allowed to keep, and seldom transgressed, and always with explanations and apologies. In general the Woods trusted their daughters' intelligence and mutual reinforcement to keep them out of trouble. Ben gave no lectures in regard to venereal disease; Marcia never stressed the trauma of early marriage or unwanted pregnancy. Between themselves the girls occasionally spoke of sex and its weird variations, and sometimes marveled at the extent to which it permeated the psychological atmosphere.

On very few occasions did the Woods question the judgment of any of their daughters, and that daughter was always Barbara, the most daring and adventurous of the girls. Ellen and Althea despised hippies and the so-called 'counter-culture'; Barbara conceived hippies to be quaint and wild, like gypsies. At Hallowe'en Barbara was invited to a weekend party at Lake Tahoe, but Ben and Marcia for once put their two feet down. Barbara explained that Tamlyn's parents would chaperone; that Lake Tahoe was a place she'd always wanted to visit; that the boys and girls who already had accepted the invitation were in the main respectable. She failed to persuade either Ben or Marcia.

"Too many things could happen, all of them bad," said Ben. "I don't know the Rudnicks; he might be a drunken driver, or a Democrat. Maybe they'd decide to go off and gamble and leave the kids to raise hell on their own. One of the boys might spike the punch with LSD."

"Daddy! You're just being silly."

"Not at all. I'm being mathematical. Look at the odds. Two out of every five drivers on the highway have been drinking and one out of twenty is dead drunk. Three in every ten teenagers smokes marijuana and one out of ten is hooked on LSD or goof-balls or some other stuff. One out of every hundred men is a thug, a rape artist or a con man. At Lake Tahoe the percentage is higher. Five out of every hundred women..."

"Daddy! You're just making this all up!"

"It's close enough to the truth. I'd put the odds at nine out of ten that you'd arrive home in one piece, and that's not good enough."

"Mmfp. I'm just as liable to fall into the bathtub or eat a can of poisoned tuna. I've read that home is the most dangerous place you can be."

"Yes, but at home we've got Band-Aids and stomach pumps and fathers and mothers and sisters. Lake Tahoe is out."

———— • ————

MONDAY AND FRIDAY WERE the dullest days of the week. Mrs. Wood remained home to curtail Ronald's explorations, and the girls were at school until late afternoon. Junior high let out forty-five minutes earlier than high school; Barbara was usually first to arrive home, though she tended to dally along the way, teasing the boys or gossiping with the girls. Such occasions put Ronald into a mood of nervous irritation. He considered Barbara spoiled, inconsiderate, capricious and utterly adorable. She was rather more aware of her charms than either Althea or Ellen, which made her all the more desirable. Ronald loved her and detested her at the same time— much the emotion he had felt for Laurel Hansen.

On Tuesday Mrs. Wood developed a cold, or an allergic reaction, she wasn't sure which, and stayed home from work. The indisposition persisted during Wednesday, and Ronald was obliged to remain secluded for two extra days. On Thursday Mrs. Wood returned to work, and almost with the closing of the front door Ronald defiantly crawled forth from his lair. He stood listening no more than ten or fifteen seconds, then marched to the refrigerator, where he found only a dish of cold mashed potatoes and a few brussels sprouts. Dared he fry up a pan of bacon and eggs? For three hungry minutes Ronald wavered back and forth. But the bacon was a new unopened package and only four eggs remained on the rack: the missing food would surely be noticed. Ronald ate a peanut butter sandwich and an orange and reluctantly decided against a drink of milk from a nearly empty carton.

His plans for today had already been formed. He went into the living room, looked out into the street, then turned and climbed the stairs.

He barely recognized the upper floor. The hall was painted fresh bright white; on the walls hung a row of gay floral prints, and instead of the old green runner and brown-painted boards, there was now Turkey-red carpeting.

Ronald stood a full two minutes at the head of the stairs; he enjoyed listening to the silence. A car passed along Orchard Street; Ronald froze until the sound diminished and died. If anyone returned unexpectedly he could hide under a bed, but this might be both inconvenient and dangerous.

Ronald moved across the hall. He glanced into the bedroom where his mother had once slept and gave a snort of contempt for the new furnishings. Ellen's room was opposite; to the rear of the house, past the bathroom and the hall closet, were Althea's and Barbara's rooms. Where to start? Perhaps a quick look into all three.

Ellen's room was mostly white, with a lavender ceiling and a pale green rug. This had been his old room! Never in a million years would he have recognized it! He chanced to look in the mirror, and there he saw a face equally different from the old Ronald. The discord between new and old gave him an eerie feeling, as if he were the victim of amnesia or soul-transfer.

On the dresser stood a photograph of Duane Mathews. Ronald scowled down at the bleak bony face and felt a strong temptation to destroy it, or at least blotch out the features with lipstick... Inadvisable. He turned away to the wardrobe. Ellen's clothes hung in a neat array. Ronald reached forth, stroked the charmed garments which had sheathed that wonderful body! Electric thrills ran up and down his arm. He went back to the dresser and, opening a drawer, inspected her underwear. What intimacy he was now enjoying!

Presently he closed the drawer and stood quietly, breathing slowly and deeply, letting the ambience of the room seep into his skin. Everywhere he could feel Ellen. This mirror had reflected her nudity; here in this chair she had brushed her shining hair; this bed had known the warmth of her body and the scintillating flux of her dreams.

Ronald went to the dressing table. In the top drawer he found a flask of perfume: a soft fruity scent with a hint of violet and just a tang of verbena. He touched a few drops of the perfume to the back of his hand; the bottle slipped and before he could snatch it up, half the liquid had spilled.

Ronald stared in shock. He grabbed a facial tissue and mopped at the tabletop. What to do now? He capped the flask and placed it in the drawer on its side. Ellen would think the perfume had spilled. He took the tissue into the bathroom and flushed it down the toilet. In the hall the scent of perfume still lingered. Oh well, by the time anyone came home, the odor would have dissipated.

Ronald felt uneasy and irritated; the magic was gone from his venture. He returned downstairs and out of sheer disgust stalked into the living room and plumped into one of the easy chairs, where he sat in angry reverie.

He was exposed, he was vulnerable! The front door was not even locked! Guiltily Ronald jumped to his feet and trotted with an elastic bent-kneed gait to safety.

Once more secure in his lair, Ronald lay on the cot. He became aware of the scent of Ellen's perfume, and now it was a nuisance. He went to the washbasin and scrubbed his wrist, and effaced most of the smell. When he regarded the face in the mirror the eerie sense of alienation he had known in Ellen's room was gone; here he was normal ordinary Ronald...

Ronald lay dozing until one o'clock, then cooked himself a lunch of tuna and fried onion pancakes. He decided that his health required one of the Woods' tomatoes, which he fetched from the refrigerator, drinking a gulp of milk from the carton as he did so.

Once again he drowsed until the creak of the front door and light elastic footsteps aroused him. Somewhat lethargically he went to the peephole, but Barbara—he recognized the footsteps—had run directly upstairs.

Ronald stood thinking. Upstairs Barbara; downstairs, himself. The situation had occurred several times previously, but the disadvantages of any sort of action were oppressive. Ronald went back to sit on his cot, and tried to read one of his books... Again footsteps on the front porch. The door opened; Ellen and Althea were home from school. They tossed their books down upon the table in the hall and ran upstairs. Barbara called out a cheery greeting. For a period Ronald heard muffled conversation, which came to a rather abrupt end.

Mrs. Wood returned home and presently Ben Wood. Mrs. Wood served a quick and easy dinner of hamburger sandwiches.

There was an atmosphere at the dinner table. The girls sat silently; evidently they had quarreled. Ben Wood finally asked, "Well, what's happened? Is it a private fight or can we all join in?"

"It's no fight at all," said Ellen. "Just a misunderstanding."

"It's not either a misunderstanding!" Barbara declared. "Ellen thinks I spilled her perfume, and I didn't touch it. I wasn't in her room at all."

Mrs. Wood said, "If you say you didn't do it, you didn't do it. Ellen knows that as well as I do."

"She doesn't believe me."

"Of course I believe you, Bobby!" said Ellen. "It's just all so strange! I could swear someone had been in my room. I don't really care a bit, but the perfume *was* spilled and you can even smell it in the bathroom. I know it wasn't Bobby, but who could it be? It wasn't spilled this morning."

"Odd things happen," said Ben Wood. "There might have been an earthquake, or maybe you closed the drawer too hard. There's a dozen explanations."

Ellen nodded dubiously.

"She still thinks I did it," sulked Barbara. "Deep down she does, and I wasn't even near her room."

"Come now, Babs!" snapped her mother. "Please don't be difficult. Ellen knows you wouldn't lie about such a silly matter, any more than she'd lie to you! It's all so ridiculous!"

"Absolutely, Bobby," said Ellen. "Heavens, I know you better than that! If anything, you're too honest!"

Barbara began to cry, and rising from the table, went into the living room. Ellen went after her and petted her and consoled her.

Ben Wood said, "That's Babs for you. Underneath the foolishness she's the most sensitive of all three."

Althea laughed. "People think I'm sensitive, but I just don't care about things. Ellen cares, but she's so secure! Poor little Babs!"

"The situation is certainly strange," said Ben Wood.

"We might have a poltergeist," said Althea. "They come to houses where young people live. That's well known."

Marcia Wood gave a skeptical snort. "So far I haven't seen objects hurtling through the air, and I don't want to either. I'm not all that interested."

"Oh, I'm interested!" said Althea. "I'd love to experience something strange. Everything happens to other people, never to me."

Ellen and Barbara quietly returned to the dining room and finished their dinner.

Althea said brightly, "We've solved the mystery. It's a poltergeist!"

"No," said Ellen, "I remember now what happened. I closed the drawer very hard this morning and I must have knocked the bottle over."

"Oh! I wanted us to have a poltergeist!"

Ellen smiled and for a flickering instant seemed as mischievous as Barbara at her most outrageous. "Can't we still have him, or her, or it, whatever they are? You know what Duane says."

Mrs. Wood said, "How strange that a boy like Duane, apparently so practical, is superstitious."

"He gets it from his mother," said Ellen. "After Carol was killed, she went to a spiritualist to see if she could talk to Carol's soul, or ghost, or whatever it is."

Mrs. Wood was interested in spite of herself. "What happened?"

"Duane isn't quite sure. His mother thinks she had a message, but Duane says it might have applied to anyone. He wants her to go back and ask questions that only Carol could answer, and maybe find out where the murderer is now. What was his name?"

"Roderick Wilson, something like that."

"Ronald Wilby," said Barbara.

"And is she going to ask those questions?"

"When she gets around to going. The spiritualist lives in Stockton."

"Don't scoff!" said Ben Wood. "I've heard of spiritualists helping the police many times! There's a Dutchman, I can't think of his name, who solved a half-dozen murders in Holland. These cases are a matter of record."

Ronald hissed between his teeth. Wouldn't people ever stop chewing over that old business? He wanted to hear no more about it. If he hadn't been so foolish and careless, and left the bicycle in the street and his jacket on a bush, no one would know to this day what had happened. Except himself. And Carol's soul, or spirit, or ghost.

FRIDAY: ONE OF THE dull days, but Ronald was content to lie quiet in his lair. On Saturday he felt somewhat better, but to his disappointment the girls went off to a football game, returning at five o'clock, only to shower and change and go off again to a party. Ronald sat brooding, his mood rank and bitter as sludge. The girls had flitted off like butterflies, gay and callous, and he was left alone in dreary solitude. He longed to punish them, to even the score. He had felt somewhat the same way about Laurel Hansen until the Carol Mathews business, which in some indirect fashion had wiped clean the slate.

On Sunday Mrs. Wood and the girls drove to San Jose to visit relatives. Mr. Wood stayed home to catch up on paperwork and to watch a football game on television. Another drab day for Ronald. He spent the early part of the afternoon exercising, an activity he had neglected for some time, and the raucous outcry of the sports announcer overwhelmed whatever small sounds he might have made. The day was warm. Ronald discovered himself sweating profusely. He removed his clothes and lay down to rest and drowsed until Mrs. Wood and the girls came home.

They went directly upstairs to bed; Ronald not too enthusiastically busied himself with Atranta.

On Monday Mrs. Wood went shopping. Ronald emerged from his lair to check the refrigerator, but found nothing he cared to eat. In disgust he helped himself to nuts from the fruit bowl and a handful of caramels from a paper bag, then went out into the hall and looked longingly up the stairs. The perfume episode had dwindled in importance; after this he'd naturally take pains to leave no traces. The upstairs tugged at him, but Mrs. Wood might return at any time, and he couldn't risk being caught away from his lair. Even now a car came up Orchard Street, and Ronald hastened back to safety.

The afternoon passed. Ronald waited fretfully for the girls to come home, but Mrs. Wood met Barbara at school and took her to the dentist. Ellen and Althea stayed late to play tennis, so that all arrived home together about six o'clock.

On Tuesday Mrs. Wood went to work. As soon as the front door closed, Ronald crawled out through his own door. He stood in the pantry to listen; it was always wise to be cautious.

No sound save a fly buzzing at the kitchen window. Ronald crossed to the refrigerator where he discovered a package of sliced salami, a bowl of tuna salad, green onions: sufficient material for two excellent sandwiches, which he washed down with a generous helping of milk. By and large, a good breakfast.

Now what? The day lay ahead of him. Ronald went boldly into the living room and peered up and down Orchard Street. The coast was clear. He climbed the stairs to the second floor. Who should it be today: Althea or Barbara? He decided upon Althea.

The room was quite different from Ellen's. On the walls hung Art Nouveau posters, and the shelves supported books with titles unfamiliar to Ronald, among them several volumes of fantasy and others of science fiction. Of the three girls, only Althea's perceptivity even remotely matched his own. She'd be enthralled to know that here, in this very same house, the Atranta sagas had been formulated. Ronald toyed with the idea of writing Althea a letter. There'd be difficulty mailing such a letter, unless he slipped out in the dead of night to the mailbox at the corner. He'd have to commandeer an envelope and a stamp from the desk in the living room... Well, perhaps he wouldn't bother.

He investigated the drawers of her desk and this time took extra care not to handle anything which might spill or leak... What was this? Ronald brought forth a book bound in green simulated leather, with a locked flap across the edge. On the front, in gold leaf, was stamped the word *Diary.*

Ronald turned the book this way and that. He tugged gently at the strap, but the lock held the book shut.

Ronald put down the book and searched for the key; Althea would certainly not carry it on her person. He inspected the underside of all the drawers, ran his finger along the picture molding, checked the contents of the jewelry box, investigated the structural members of bed and chairs. No key. Baffled, Ronald picked up the diary, which breathed a soundless music whose purport he could not even guess. Where was the dratted key? He searched the bedside table, the Mexican pottery piggy bank, the pencil cup on the windowsill. No key. Ronald scrutinized the book. He worked the strap back and forth, trying to disengage the clasp. He bent a paper clip, fitted it into the lock, twisted. Something seemed to move. Ronald twisted more vigorously and the end of the paper clip broke off in the lock. Ronald muttered a curse. The broken end could not be dislodged. Inside the keyhole he could see the shine of metal, but no effort would dislodge it.

Well then, what to do? He knew himself to be resourceful and keen; now was the time to demonstrate his craft. Perhaps he could take the lock apart and repair it. Only rivets secured the lock to the simulated leather... Impractical; he had no tools. Perhaps he should simply remove the diary and hide it. Althea after all was an absentminded girl: so everyone in the family, including Althea, pretended to believe. She might not notice its loss for months.

The idea was unsound. A diary, by definition, was used daily. By squinting into the pages Ronald could see that Althea wrote regularly in the book.

A real problem. If he had another similar diary he might attempt to transfer the covers. Then, of course, Althea's key wouldn't fit— unless one key fit all such diaries. In any event, he had access to no such duplicate diary.

In a dispirited mood Ronald tried to disengage the piece of broken wire with a nail file, but only succeeded in scratching the nickel-plating on the housing, and bending the lip of the keyhole. Now sweating, Ronald tried to repair the damage. Althea probably wouldn't notice; none of the girls were particularly observant or critical... But how he wished he could remove that dratted bit of broken wire! Perhaps if he pried up the cover plate—but he could never replace it. He took the paper clip and furiously worried the bit of broken wire: prodding, poking, prying—all to no effect.

Ronald quietly put the diary where he had found it. He was disgusted with the whole thing. Althea might be puzzled, but she wasn't a girl to fret over trifles; she might not even notice. Probably when she put the key in the lock the wire would come loose. Ronald smoothed the bed where he had sat on it, closed all the drawers, and returned gloomily downstairs.

The time was now about noon. Ronald helped himself to a nice chunk of hamburger, two slices of bread and butter, half an onion and a tomato. Sliding into the lair, he cooked the meat in his pan and contrived a very tasty sandwich indeed. In fact, he could easily consume another of the same. Alas, too risky. He contented himself with a good helping of ice cream topped with strawberry jam and a squirt of synthetic cream.

The afternoon lay before him. He went into the living room and sat where he could watch the street. Today Barbara might well be home early. If he went upstairs and hid in her bedroom closet he could watch her changing clothes. When she went to hang up her dress, there he'd be... It wouldn't be so bad if he could spend a whole day or even half a day with her. He'd pretend to be an intruder, and she'd never recognize him as Ronald Wilby. Hmm. The idea was not all that impractical. He could tie her to the bed, go downstairs, slam the front door, then hasten back to his lair. What a hullabaloo there'd be! He'd enjoy every minute of it. Then in a month or so, he'd do the same thing again! Ellen and Althea coming home so soon made the project impossible. Too bad, because otherwise the exploit would be perfectly safe and Barbara, sexy little scamp that she was, wouldn't be all that reluctant. And if she were, so what?

Two o'clock. He'd better be getting back in his lair. Perhaps some day Barbara would be home by herself. Or Althea. Or Ellen.

He lay on his cot, deep in reflection. Since he'd started exploring upstairs he'd neglected everything—charts, exercise, Atranta. He especially wanted to get back to Atranta, where an enormous amount of work remained to be done.

Shortly before four Barbara arrived home, and ran directly upstairs to change from her school clothes. Almost at once the telephone rang and Barbara came flying back downstairs wearing only brassiere and underpants. Ronald, with his eye to the peephole, ecstatically sucked in his breath; never had he seen so enchanting a sight—save one time before. He was hard put to control himself; he made soft moaning sounds under his breath and moved his head back and forth to obtain a better view. If only he had time and opportunity! He'd take his chances with the consequences!

Barbara chatted on the phone for twenty minutes. First she sat on the arm of the sofa, then slumped backwards down upon the cushion, with her knees hooked over the arm. She raised one leg, pointed her toes toward the ceiling. Ronald gasped and sighed. She swung around and sat with one leg curled under herself, then sprawled back with both legs stretched out to the floor, and Ronald bit his lips to muffle a hoarse whisper... Had she heard him! She looked up suddenly with an odd expression, but it was only for a passing car. She rose to her feet and with her back to Ronald, still holding the telephone to her ear, looked out into the street. The conversation came to an end; Barbara hung up the receiver and trotted back upstairs. Ronald stood clenching and unclenching his fists. He sat down on his couch, feeling faint.

The front door opened to admit Ellen and Althea.

"Hello!" cried Ellen. "Who's home? Anybody?"

From upstairs came Barbara's voice, "Just me. But I'm enough."

Ellen went into the kitchen. "I'm starving. I wonder if any cookies are left... A few." She opened the refrigerator, and there was a moment of silence. Then Ronald heard her call in a hushed voice, "Althea, would you look at this!"

Althea came into the kitchen. "Isn't that awful! We ought to make a complaint!"

"Uk," said Ellen. "Let's just throw it out."

"Better not waste it," said Althea. "If I cut it off about here, it'll be OK. After all the hair just caught on the top of the carton."

"I guess we can't sue anyone. Things like that are so disgusting."

"Every loaf of bread is one-half of one percent rat dirt, or some such amount. We shouldn't be all that finicky, because it's useless to start with."

"Think of that!" said Ellen. "For ten loaves of bread we pay almost four dollars. One-half of one percent—that's two cents. Every time we buy ten loaves of bread, we get two cents worth of rat dirt."

"That's no bargain."

The girls went back into the dining room.

"I think I'll do my French right now," said Althea, "and have it all finished before dinner."

"I promised Mom I'd water the lawn. We've got to keep up with the Schumachers. I'm going to change clothes first."

The girls went upstairs where their voices became an unintelligible babble.

Then there was silence. After a few minutes Ellen came downstairs and went out to water the lawn.

Marcia Wood arrived home and then Ben Wood. Mrs. Wood started to prepare dinner. Ben Wood took a glass of sherry into the living room and read the newspaper.

At six-thirty Mrs. Wood served dinner. The table was very quiet; and the usual chatter was conspicuous by its absence. Ben Wood spoke in a fretful voice, "What's the trouble tonight? Why all the long faces?"

"No trouble whatever," said Althea. "We're all busy eating."

"I love tacos," said Ellen. "Tonight I want at least a dozen."

"Oh come now," said Ben Wood. "I can tell something is wrong. Maybe I shouldn't ask?"

"I'll tell you what's wrong," declared Barbara in a voice filled with emotion. "Allie thinks I tried to get into her diary."

"I didn't say anything of the sort," Althea replied in a tight voice. "I said somebody had been trying to open my diary, and that's all I said."

"But you meant me, because you said it was all right last night and now the lock's broken, and I was home before you were, so you were accusing me, and I didn't do it, and I'm sick of being blamed for everything. I'll run away and join the hippies unless people stop acting like I'm a sneak—"

"*As if* I'm a sneak," said Ellen.

"—because I'm not. I'm not interested in your diary, and even if I were I wouldn't touch it, and I didn't touch Ellen's perfume either. I don't care what you think, but I'm just not going to sit here and have everybody calling me a sneak!"

"Come now, come now!" declared Ben Wood. "Less tantrum and more fact!"

"I really don't want to talk about it," said Althea with dignity. "I'm sorry I ever mentioned it."

"You see?" cried Barbara. "She thinks I looked in her diary!"

"No I don't. Nobody looked in the diary. Somebody *tried* to look in it!"

Ellen spoke in a hushed, only half-humorous, voice, "Maybe we do have a poltergeist!"

Mrs. Wood said, "It couldn't be neighborhood children. There aren't any on the block. Mrs. Schumacher would certainly notice if anyone walked into our house."

"Unless it's Mrs. Schumacher herself," suggested Ben Wood. "Old women often get a bit strange."

"With her sore hip and Mr. Schumacher sick?" demanded Marcia Wood. "It's just not reasonable."

"Oh well," said Ellen, then lapsed into silence, and dinner proceeded in an atmosphere of strain.

Ronald meanwhile sat on his cot, head cradled in his hands, elbows on knees. Althea had noticed after all, and once again Barbara had been blamed... As good a solution to the problem as any. Barbara, proud spoiled Babs, flouncing around, always performing and swinging her rump as if she were some big-time sexpot, it was good to see her taken down a peg. It was no big thing, anyway. There'd be puzzlement for a day or two, then everybody would forget the matter... Barbara! He couldn't get her out of his mind. Babs, in her skimpy underpants! Enough to turn a strong man's bones to jelly, and that's the way he felt right now: perturbed, hectic, limp, tired.

———•———

WEDNESDAY MORNING AND THE atmosphere at breakfast was cool. Ellen was pensive; Althea, remote; Barbara, silent and sulky. Marcia and Ben Wood tried to enliven the occasion; they spoke of Ben's imminent promotion to Classification 15-E, qualifying him for division management; they discussed the possibility of a weekend trip into the mountains, but the conversation was stiff and uneasy, and the girls contributed nothing.

The night before, in the privacy of their bedroom, Ben and Marcia had talked over the affair, and had decided that maybe Barbara, notoriously emotional and famous for pranks and tricks, had attempted some sort of strange adolescent joke which had misfired and now couldn't bring herself to admit it. Both agreed that Barbara, no matter what, was emphatically not sly; never would she try to peek into Althea's diary; if she wanted to know something, she'd merely ask Althea, who no doubt would tell her as a matter of course. The whole affair was grotesque, completely out of character.

In their own ways, Ellen and Althea had both arrived at the same conclusion. Still, if not Barbara, who? Ellen thought it might be Joel Watkins, a boy currently pursuing Althea with rather unwelcome attentions. Joel was known to be both brash and irresponsible, but would he dare enter their house and try to read Althea's diary? Unlikely. Also, Joel had been at school all day Tuesday and couldn't possibly have visited the Wood house.

So then: who?

Her father and mother? Absurd. But the whole affair was absurd—and not a little frightening! The person who suffered most was Bobby, who carried on existence in a most uncharacteristic silence. She was the most obvious suspect, and knew it, and resented the situation intensely.

Thursday morning, on the way to school, Ellen had a chance to say a few words to Barbara, "I know you're brooding about that silly diary, but don't. Everybody knows you wouldn't do a thing like that."

"Everybody doesn't know it," said Barbara. "Whenever the subject comes up, nobody looks at me. I'd give anything to know what happened."

ON THURSDAY MORNING RONALD felt taut and edgy, for a reason which hovered just past the brink of his consciousness, but conveniently at hand in case he really wanted to know. He even felt a bit queasy, like an athlete before competition. Imminence hung in the air.

When Mrs. Wood left for work, he did not immediately sally forth into the kitchen, but remained sitting on the edge of his cot, staring down at the floor. With a somewhat pedantic assiduity he took note of his symptoms: a twitching of the skin, delicacy at the front of the stomach, a slight sense of dimensional displacement, or vertigo: sensations odd but not unpleasant.

Ronald heaved a mournful sigh and tried to arrange his thoughts. Nothing came. Those thoughts he sought to grapple fled like thieves; others skulked off in the region of the subconscious. All right then, said Ronald, if that's the way it was, let the subconscious do all the thinking and let the acting take care of itself.

Ronald pursed out his lips at this idea. Very sound. History crawled thick with ditherers. Ronald heaved another sigh, exhaling all his doubts and qualms. It was really so easy. What must be, must be. How blissful was this thought. Destiny flowed like a mighty river. He, Ronald, was another such inexorable surge. If he and destiny tried to flow in opposite directions, the result was turmoil, just a lot of thrashing around. Either destiny must join his direction, or he must swerve to join with destiny. It saved a lot of time and discussion if he, Ronald, were the flexible one, and this was how things were. He rode with destiny, buoyant and free, ignoring trivial distractions, without regard for past or future. A single time existed; that time was now. There was nothing else; there never would be anything else. Time and destiny and Ronald Arden Wilby, three elemental vectors converging to a focus like the Mercedes-Benz insignia. The three were one; the one was three, and this was the way it must be.

Ronald rose to his feet, tingling with power. He opened his secret door, crawled out into the kitchen, and gnawed on a piece of cold chicken. Then he went into the living room and sat where he could watch the street. The front door was locked and the key was hidden under the steps. Today Ben Wood was having new keys to the front door cut; hereafter the house would always be locked.

The prospect meant nothing to Ronald. His mother had always locked up... His mother! He had not thought of her recently. Dear old Mother! The denizen of a far age, like Queen Victoria.

The hours went by slowly. Ronald was not impatient. He felt calm yet highly sentient, as if he had been taking a time-dilating drug. Images flickered through his mind: Barbara in her flimsy little briefs. How she loved to pose and twist and thrust out her breasts! To own such beauty and flaunt it the way she did was inexcusable provocation. So be it, so be it. A girl like that simply demanded to be taken care of. So be it.

The mantle clock chimed twelve noon. Ronald strolled into the kitchen, assembled and consumed a peanut butter, mayonnaise and banana sandwich. He felt quite cool; he was pleased to notice that his movements were exact and deliberate. The result, possibly, of entering what might be called 'phase three'. For he was now truly independent, self-sufficient, alone: himself against the world! So be it! He feared nothing; his lair was an impenetrable bastion, so long as he made no noise... In a way, he felt as if he were really someone new, or, more accurately, his basic self: a person unhampered, unshackled, indomitable! Once a person became one with—'Destiny' wasn't quite the right word. Fate? Cosmos? Oh well, no great matter. Whenever a person merged with this massive force—whatever it was—anything became possible, whatever the mind could imagine! Within reason of course. He couldn't very well fly through the air, or run a mile in thirty seconds, but any ordinary feat was possible.

Craft and foresight of course were the indispensable adjuncts to boldness. Ronald carefully replaced the bread in the bread box, took the margarine and the jar of peanut butter to the refrigerator, rinsed and dried the knife, and put it in the drawer.

The time was one o'clock. Ronald returned to his lair and lay on the cot, tingling to his new vitality... The charts on the wall distracted him. They looked stale and tiresome; they belonged to a different time of his life. He roused himself from the cot and took them down. Better, much better. Exercise? Not just now, he wasn't in the mood. He wanted only to lie on the cot and expand into the new sensations he had discovered.

Three o'clock. His mouth felt somewhat furry; he gave his teeth a good scrubbing. Niceties of this sort were the hallmarks of a gentleman, so his mother had insisted. He frowned down at his fingernails. They probably could use some attention. His mother had also laid much stress upon well-trimmed and clean fingernails. Just now he was not disposed to dwell upon his mother and her precepts. A wonderful woman, of course, if just a bit old-fashioned and conventional. Ronald stretched his arms, scratched his jowls. Should he shave? He allowed the matter to slide from his mind, but he brushed at his hair, which was somewhat untidy. Still, long hair was currently stylish, so it made no great difference.

The time was twenty minutes after three. Ronald crawled out into the kitchen, padded into the living room and stood by the window. The blood sang in his veins; never had he felt so alive, so sure and steady... Of course it was quite possible that Barbara would stay late at school, in which case—a tiresome thought. Anyway there she came now, in a short gray-blue skirt and a dark red pullover. He retreated up the stairs to the landing and waited in the shadows.

The doorknob turned without effect. Barbara had forgotten that the door was locked. She went back for the key.

The door opened. Barbara came into the house, rather less jauntily than usual. She wandered into the dining room, dropped her books on the table, then turned her head, as if an odd odor or unexpected sound had impinged on her consciousness. After a moment she went on into the kitchen and stopped by the refrigerator for an apple and a glass of milk. She decided to sit downstairs for awhile, until Ellen and Althea came home. After those strange things which had been happening upstairs, the old house didn't seem as secure as it had during the summer.

She closed the refrigerator door, turned back toward the dining room, and there stood Ronald, looming in the doorway.

"Hello," said Ronald.

She stared at him.

Ronald smiled a modest kind smile. "You don't know me. But I know you."

Chapter XIV

BARBARA thought, I mustn't get nervous, I mustn't show I'm scared. That only excites people like this. Act as casual as possible. She asked, without hardly a quaver in her voice, "Well then—who are you?"

Ronald chuckled. "My name could be anything. Norbert, the Duke of Kastifax, for instance."

"That's an odd name. What are you doing in our house? You'd better leave, and quick, unless you want my father to catch you."

"He won't be home for two hours. Drink your milk."

"Drink my milk?" Barbara looked in puzzlement down at the glass. Perhaps she could throw it at him and run out the back door. He came two steps closer. Barbara shrank back against the sink. To keep him away she raised the glass and forced two or three gulps down her throat. Ronald, smiling pleasantly, reached for the glass. Barbara moved it indignantly back beyond his reach. "I'm not finished!" Anything to gain time, even a few minutes. She raised the glass again and sipped, but Ronald was not about to be flimflammed by a ruse so transparent. He took the glass, poured what was left down the sink, rinsed it and put it back on the shelf. "Come along," he said.

Barbara shook her head. "I've got homework to do." Her voice still was fairly firm. "Why don't you have some ice cream? Then you can help me with my math."

"This way," said Ronald.

"I don't want to," said Barbara, and now the quaver was evident. She suddenly tried to run into the dining room, but Ronald caught her arm and swung her smartly back. The contact between their bodies worked an abrupt change upon Ronald. His smile vanished; she felt him quivering and straining, and now she could no longer control herself. She screamed. Ronald instantly clapped his hand over her mouth. For a moment they stood tense and poised, motionless except for the glances Ronald darted out the window... He exhaled, relaxed. There was no one to hear. He turned his attention back to Barbara.

"Listen!" said Ronald in a husky voice. "Listen carefully! Because you'll be sorry if you don't. Do you hear?" He gave her a shake. "Do you hear?"

Barbara nodded, her throat too full for words.

Ronald took his hand from her mouth. "You do exactly what I tell you! Exactly! Otherwise—well, I won't say. Do you understand?"

"Yes," mumbled Barbara.

"Come along then. Into the pantry."

"No, no," wailed Barbara. The idea was absurd. "Why into the pantry?"

"Just do what you're told. Don't ask questions. Get down on your hands and knees."

"Oh, no, no! Please don't!"

Ronald cuffed the side of her face; Barbara gasped in terror. At last she understood the dimensions of her predicament. Here was a situation against which her cleverness and charm were useless. Yes, yes; she'd do anything, to keep herself from—the word wouldn't surface into her mind. She dropped to her hands and knees and crawled into the pantry, to freeze in sheer amazement to see the secret doorway, with the light shining forth from the lair.

"Go on in," said the dark shape behind her. She winced at the tremble of excitement in his voice. She slid through the door into the lair.

"Sit down on the cot," said Ronald. He gave her paper and a ball-point pen, and put a book on her knees. "Write exactly what I tell you."

He dictated and Barbara, blinking through tears, wrote.

Ronald read the finished product. "That's good enough. Now sit here, and don't move until I get back." He crouched to leave by the secret door, then turned to look back at Barbara. "I don't want to scare you, but I want to make sure you understand. Do exactly as I tell you, or we'll have trouble."

Barbara nodded mournfully, the tears now streaming down her face.

Ronald hesitated, then rose once more to his feet. "I better not take any chances," he muttered. "You just might try something crazy. Lie down."

"What are you going to do?" cried Barbara, her voice quavering in and out of hysteria.

Ronald pushed her down on the cot; Barbara lost control of herself. She fought and kicked. Ronald cuffed her twice, on each side of the face, the way tough guys did it in the movies. Barbara gasped and drew in her breath to scream. Ronald ominously drew back his hand; Barbara held her breath in terror. For ten seconds they stared into each other's faces, then Ronald slowly lowered his hand. Barbara lay quiet, as if mesmerized.

Ronald lashed her ankles to the bottom of the cot, tied her wrists together and gagged her with a rag. "Maybe this is unnecessary," he said in a gruff voice, "but I can't take chances on anything."

He dropped to his hands and knees and slid through the secret door with the note. Barbara strained at the cords, but they held securely. She looked desperately around the lair. How weird and colorful, with every square inch covered with drawings, maps, portraits... Ronald returned. He closed and fastened the secret door. Barbara did not dare to look at him. She knew who he was: Ronald Wilby, the murderer, and she knew who had spilled Ellen's perfume, and who had broken Althea's diary.

He dropped to his knees beside her and took the gag from her mouth. Barbara lay quiet, breathing shallowly. For ten or fifteen seconds Ronald searched her face. Then in a soft voice he said, "If you make a sound or try to attract attention—do you know what I'll do?"

She whispered, "You'll kill me."

Ronald nodded gravely and began to untie her. "I'd have to. I don't want to. I'd just have to. When anybody is in the house, you lie on the cot and be quiet! Not a sound. Because you'd never make another... I don't want to scare you, but you've got to know what the situation is."

"Whether you want to scare me or not," said Barbara, "I'm scared! I don't want to be in here! What are you going to do with me?"

Ronald, once more urbane, grinned at her. "Don't you know?"

"No!"

"Come now," said Ronald in a playful voice. "Don't be difficult." He considered a minute. "This was my old secret lair, from when I was a little boy. I came back here just a few days ago, to see what had happened to the house. In a few days I'm going away again, and then you can do whatever you please—come with me, if you want to. Maybe we'll like each other by then."

Barbara bit her lower lip, to hold back a shriek of hysterical laughter.

"We can only talk for a few minutes," said Ronald, "because your sisters will be home, and then we'll have to be quiet. Take off your clothes."

This was the time she had been dreading. Still, measured against the other circumstances, it wasn't all that much worse... A nightmare! Oh please, Barbara, wake up, wake up! The faces in the portraits; the grotesque castles; the dark red, purple, black and green rooms: unreal, unreal, unreal!

"Take off your clothes!" said Ronald gently. "You're so beautiful!... I'll help you."

Barbara's fingers were numb. Clumsily, as slowly as possible, she undressed. She could not bring herself to remove her underthings; Ronald pulled them off, hissing through his teeth while she kept her eyes squeezed shut.

Ronald slipped out of his own soiled garments. He glanced at the clock. Ten minutes, maybe fifteen, before anyone came home. He loomed upon her, stroked her body, kissed her. Barbara gasped. "Remember!" Ronald warned her, "not a sound!"

ELLEN AND ALTHEA CAME home. "Hello!" called Ellen. "Who's here? Anyone?"

"Barbara!" Althea yelled, and then to Ellen, "She's not home yet."

"She's probably at the tennis court, the little wretch. Barbara?" No reply. They went into the dining room and there on the table lay a sheet of paper. Ellen picked it up and read. "Oh, no!"

"What is it?"

Ellen showed her the note. Althea read, and the two girls looked at each other in consternation.

"Why, it's fantastic!" cried Althea. "Of course we trusted her! Poor little Babs!"

"We'd better telephone Daddy."

They ran into the living room. With quick fingers Ellen twisted the telephone dial. "Mr. Wood, please... Daddy? This is Ellen. We just got home, Althea and I. Barbara isn't here. She left a note. Listen, this is what she says,

"'Dear Everybody:
Nobody trusts me and I can't stand it anymore. I've gone off to join the hippies. I'll be back after a while. Don't worry about me, I'll be all right.
Barbara.'"

From the telephone came only the hum of the wire. Ellen cried out, "Daddy? Did you hear?"

Ben Wood spoke in a harsh voice, "Is this some kind of a joke?"

"She's not home," declared Ellen. "You know that she's been acting strangely. I hope it's a joke."

"I'm coming right home. Have you called your mother?"

"Not yet."

"Call her, then notify the police. I'll be right there."

Five minutes later Ben Wood raced up the steps and into the house. Ellen and Althea had further information for him. "She didn't take any of her clothes!" "And she left all the money in her piggy bank!" "She didn't take anything!"

Marcia Wood came running into the house, and for a few moments there was confusion with everyone talking at once. Then

Ben Wood telephoned the police department once more and was notified that a bulletin had been passed on to the Highway Patrol. Marcia Wood decided to visit the bus station. She took a photograph of Barbara to show the ticket-sellers and departed. Ellen and Althea telephoned Barbara's friends and asked if they knew anything of her whereabouts. Ben Wood went out in his car and drove to all the likely hitchhiking places at the edge of town and questioned anyone who might have seen Barbara.

At eight o'clock Ben and Marcia had returned home, without news of any kind. Ellen warmed some canned tomato soup, made toast, and insisted that her mother and father eat.

The makeshift dinner was a grim occasion. Everyone was edgy and spoke in strained high-pitched voices. What demon of perversity had prompted gay little Barbara to such a desperate act? The situation was incredible, and no one could really believe it had happened. Still, the evidence was stark and simple: Barbara was gone.

"She's a temperamental person," said Ellen. "But she's not crazy. I just can't believe she'd do a thing like this. She doesn't like hippies any more than we do."

Marcia Wood looked up in consternation. "You think she didn't go off of her own free will?"

"It's a possibility."

Ben Wood said dubiously, "There wasn't any sign of a struggle."

"There was an apple on the kitchen floor," said Althea. "I picked it up. It had teeth-marks in it."

Ben Wood went into the living room and once more called the police. He returned to the dining table muttering curses under his breath. "They take the matter so damn casually. I can't believe they're doing anything!"

Marcia Wood smiled bitterly. "They're used to runaways. It happens every day or so, and no doubt every family tells them the same thing."

"But our family is different!" cried Ellen. "If they don't believe it, I'll go down and tell them!"

"Don't bother," growled Ben Wood. "It wouldn't do any good."

"I've got a better idea," said Althea. "If she went off by herself, she probably headed for Berkeley. I'd like to go there too and walk up and down Telegraph Avenue. I bet I'd find her sooner or later!"

Her mother vetoed the idea.

"We've got to do something!" Althea cried. "We can't just sit here!"

"If I could think of something to do," said Ben Wood, "I'd do it."

The doorbell rang; Ellen ran into the hall and opened the door. She returned with Duane, to whom she had already communicated the news. "I don't know if there's anything I can do," said Duane, "but if there is, just tell me."

"Thanks, Duane," said Marcia. "We know that already."

"We're just sitting here gnawing our nails," said Althea. "If only we had some sort of clue, or knew somebody she might have gone with, or gone to—there's just nothing."

"What about Los Gatos? Would she want to go back there?"

"I can't imagine why," said Ben Wood. "Nothing is sensible to begin with. Los Gatos is as good a guess as any."

"I can't understand it," said Duane. "Babs sometimes acted foolish, but she was really a sensible kid. She wouldn't run away from home like this!"

Ben Wood leaned wearily back in his chair. "I've heard of a wildness, or a psychosis, that comes over adolescents and makes them do all manner of strange things. Maybe this is what happened to Babs."

Duane shook his head. "She isn't any crazier than I am—and I'm not crazy. There's something very strange going on."

"I wish I knew what." Ben Wood rose to his feet and stood indecisively. "We're all worn out. Probably we should go to bed and try to get some rest."

"I couldn't sleep," Althea declared. "I'd just be thinking about Babs... We should be out looking for her! Daddy, Mom, why don't we drive into Berkeley? There's a chance in a million we might find her!"

Ben Wood shook his head gloomily. "The chances of getting killed on the freeway are better than that."

The talk went on. Inside the lair Ronald and Barbara listened, the first indifferently, the second in anguish. Ronald had taken steps to forestall even an involuntary outcry. He had fixed a gag to her mouth, and also had looped a cord around her neck with a single overhand knot under her chin. One end of the cord he tied to a stud in the wall beside the cot, the other he held in his hand. If Barbara so much as squeaked, he could jerk the noose tight, to cut off her breath. To prevent any noisy thrashing about he had lashed her ankles to the cot.

He sat with his ear to the wall. Inasmuch as the light was on, he had covered over the peephole. Why didn't they all go to bed? And Duane Mathews: he had no business around here. His offers of help were just so much malarky; Duane only wanted a chance to get next to Ellen!

The Woods finally trooped upstairs to bed. Ellen and Duane stood talking on the front porch for a few minutes, then she too went up to her room.

Ronald removed the gag from Barbara's mouth and untied her ankles. She watched with dull apprehension. Ronald sat on the cot beside her. He said, "You can't imagine how long I've wanted to do this."

Barbara spoke in a strained whisper, "I thought you said you'd just come back."

Ronald gave a patient little laugh. "I come and go. But this is my home. In fact, it's my world, my very own! What you see on the walls I've created!"

Barbara gazed incuriously at the pictures. "What does it mean?"

"It's the magic land of Atranta!" said Ronald in a rich, if muted, voice. "See the map? It shows the six duchies and Zulamber the City of Blue-green Pearls. These are portraits of the dukes, and this is Norbert, from Vordling, who defeated Duke Urken. I know them as well as I know myself. They're as real to me as you are. Would you like to hear the history of Atranta?"

Barbara closed her eyes. The more energy expended in talk, the less remained for lust. Maybe he'd get excited, and somebody would hear him. Maybe he'd relax and forget to tie the noose around her neck. "Yes," she said. "Tell me about it."

"After awhile," said Ronald craftily. "Right now I'm more interested in you. I just love to look at you. You've got the most beautiful body I've ever seen. I never thought anything could be so wonderful."

Barbara licked her lips. He was crazy, or so she supposed. Or maybe he wasn't. Certainly she didn't dare antagonize him. The lovemaking she could tolerate, but if she ever got free—when she got free—she'd wash and wash and wash; she'd never get enough of it: baths, showers, douches, gargling. Even then she knew she'd never feel quite clean again. Somehow she'd have to use her wits. But not now: Ronald was intent on lovemaking.

*   *   *

RONALD LAY BESIDE HER, lethargic and lax. She hated the feel of his body; the skin felt sticky and greasy, and he exuded an odd musky odor like wax crayons or cows mixed with codfish and the pine boxes in which codfish came packed, and more than a taint of the stable or the outhouse. She wondered how often Ronald bathed. Was he dozing? She dared make no move to ease her own cramped position lest he awake and become amorous again, although now it didn't make all that much difference; it was even a break in the monotony. She wondered what Ronald really intended to do with her. He couldn't keep her in the lair forever; there wouldn't be enough food. Certainly he wouldn't just let her go free. Somehow, of course, she'd escape or be rescued—impossible to imagine anything else with her father and mother so close! Still, if ever in her life she needed strength and resource, the time was now!

So long as she pleased him and obeyed his orders, she could expect to escape serious harm... How could she signal her parents without arousing Ronald's suspicions?... There might be a way.

"Ronald," she said softly.

He was instantly awake, or perhaps he had never been asleep. "Yeah?"

"How long are we going to stay in here?"

Ronald chuckled. "Don't you like it?"

"It's a little cramped."

"It doesn't seem cramped to me. Look at those pictures and the map: right away you're in Atranta. I'm Norbert and you're Fansetta. In the Great History she sent out a troop of black-and-yellow trolls, and they trapped him with a song that doesn't have any end. When you start singing it you can't find the place to stop. They carried him along this path here—" Ronald reached over to touch the map "—around the Three Crags to Glimmis. That's a castle here on Misty Moor. When he wouldn't marry her she chained him to an old statue of black copper and lashed him with a whip woven of scorpion tails."

"I don't want to be Fansetta then, because I wouldn't do a thing like that. Isn't there someone nicer I could be?"

Ronald deliberated. "Mersilde is a cloud-witch. She's cruel but very beautiful. Then there's Darrue, a girl half-fairy and half-ghowan…"

"What's a 'ghowan'?"

"It's a kind of a cave-elf, very pale and mysteriously beautiful. A ghowan has hair like white silk, his eyes are like glass balls with little glinting stars in them. Darrue loves Norbert, but she doesn't dare show herself to him, because when a ghowan kisses a mortal, it takes a fever and dies, and Darrue doesn't know whether she's mostly fairy or mostly ghowan."

"I'd just as soon be someone beautiful who doesn't need to worry so much."

"Hmm. I don't know about that." Ronald was now fully awake, and aware of the girl's body beside him. He began to fondle her, and Barbara lay submissive.

He paused in his exertions to look down at her. He said in a husky voice, "I like this. Do you?"

Barbara groped for words, and came up with one of her insane frivolities. "Well—it's free." She realized that this wasn't quite positive enough. Above all, she must soothe Ronald's vanity and keep his antagonism in check. "And—well, exciting."

"You can't imagine how much I've wanted to do this," Ronald panted, "with you… And now…"

Barbara closed her eyes and turned her head, to keep Ronald's hair out of her face, and presently Ronald spent himself.

A moment or so later he asked, "Like it?"

Unwilling to trust her voice, Barbara nodded.

"What's it like?" asked Ronald.

"I don't know," said Barbara, desperately damming back hysteria, which could only affect Ronald adversely. "It's just—exciting."

"What do you think of me now?"

Ronald tried to sound casual and worldly. Before Barbara could frame a reply, he said, "I realize that we met in a kind of unusual way, and I had to act as I did to get you in here—but now that we've made love together—well, you must have some sort of feelings about me."

"I wish I had met you in the usual way," said Barbara cautiously.

"But then we'd never have gotten this far, lying together like this, without our clothes on."

Barbara wondered as to the exact level of Ronald's credulity. "You never can tell. In fact it would be nice if we could go somewhere where there's more room, up into the mountains, maybe where we could camp, under the trees."

Ronald raised up on an elbow. She could feel his instant suspicion. "Lovely. But we don't have any money. At least I don't. Do you?"

"Just what's in my bank—about twelve dollars."

"That wouldn't take us very far."

Barbara became silent. The outlook was grim. She stirred. Ronald was instantly alert. "What are you doing?"

"I want to use the toilet."

"OK. But don't flush it. We've got to wait until somebody upstairs uses the bathroom."

"Oh."

"And make sure you're quiet... I won't look."

Barbara found Ronald's delicacy intensely droll. But she dared not laugh. She might not be able to stop.

The night passed. Ronald insisted that Barbara sleep on the inside of the cot, against the wall, where she felt stifled and cramped. Somehow she slept, fitfully and without comfort.

For breakfast Ronald served boiled eggs and toast with margarine and jam. Barbara politely forebore to discuss the source of Ronald's supplies.

Her family came downstairs and Ronald again made her lie on the cot, with the noose around her neck. "I don't like to do this," Ronald whispered, "but there's no other way. You might just take a crazy notion to yell."

Oh, for the chance! If he'd be careless a single instant—oh, how she'd yell, so her father could hear, and she'd do her best to fight off

Ronald... Except that her father might not be able to find his way into the lair in time to save her.

Ronald watched the Woods eat breakfast. Barbara lay tense and sweating, thinking of the days and weeks and months she had lived careless and free with Ronald's avid gaze on her. Althea had often complained of the atmosphere which pervaded the old house. How they had joked about ghosts and hauntings!

Marcia Wood stayed home from work, to be on hand in case the telephone rang. Althea and Ellen reluctantly went off to school, and Ben Wood drove to the police station, to make inquiries and to learn what he might do to help find his missing daughter.

Marcia Wood's presence in the house annoyed Ronald, creating as it did the need for continual vigilance. His mood was somewhat surly to begin with, since, like Barbara, he had not slept well.

After Ben Wood and the two girls had departed, Ronald closed off the peephole and turned on the light. He stood looking down at Barbara. What, really, did she think of him? She wasn't half as difficult as he had expected, and she actually seemed to enjoy the lovemaking. At least she said she did, and what could she gain by lying? Her notion of going off somewhere else was theoretically reasonable—but here was Atranta! And he might not like somewhere else, especially now that he had this delightful girl here for his very own... He bent down over the cot and kissed her. She could not bring herself to respond; she hated the feel of his facial hair. Ronald noticed and looked down in frowning suspicion. "What's the matter?" he whispered. "Is something wrong?"

"I don't like the rope around my neck," Barbara muttered.

"It's a necessary precaution. But I'll take it off. You've got to promise to be quiet."

"I'll be quiet."

Ronald untied the rope, which in any event got in the way of the lovemaking. "Is that better?"

Barbara rubbed her neck and nodded. Ronald bent forward and kissed her again. With her stomach jerking in anger and revulsion, Barbara forced herself to respond. Ronald's kissing became wet and passionate. Barbara let herself go limp, and Ronald proceeded with his lovemaking.

BAD RONALD

Meanwhile Barbara's mother washed the breakfast dishes, then went upstairs and made the beds.

At noon Ben Wood returned with a dark stocky man of forty-five: Sergeant Howard Shank from the County Sheriff's Office, whose voice was soft and polite in contrast to his expression of dyspeptic cynicism. Ronald instantly threw the loop around Barbara's neck and held the loose end wrapped around his hand; with a single jerk he could close off her windpipe. Barbara tried to protest, but Ronald refused to listen. "Maybe you wouldn't yell—but I can't be all that sure. I can't take any chances whatever!" He turned out the light and pressed his eye to the peephole.

"...unreasonable," Ben Wood was saying. "We're a close-knit family. It just doesn't make sense to any of us."

"That may be," said Shank. "Still, as you know, it happens all the time."

"Please don't make up your mind before you listen to us!" Marcia Wood declared. "We know Barbara! She was a sensible girl, a good girl!"

Shank gave a quizzical shrug. "What do you think happened?"

"I think someone drugged her, or frightened her, or threatened her—forced her to write that note—and then took her away."

"The handwriting is definitely hers?"

"Yes. Definitely."

Shank nodded dubiously. "I suppose such things happen. I haven't seen it myself. On the other hand, I've chased maybe five hundred girls who left home of their own free will. Sometimes a boy talks them into it. Sometimes they're bored, or their feelings are hurt. In fact, the note makes reference to a lack of trust. What's that all about?"

Ben and Marcia both compressed their lips: the same grimace at the same time. Shank thought that they even looked alike: both tall and spare with well-shaped if undistinguished features. Both were what he considered 'the salt of the earth'—and something about this 'lack of trust' phrase disturbed them.

Ben Wood said, "Some rather odd incidents occurred. We still can't explain them. A bottle of Ellen's perfume was spilled. Ellen is the oldest girl. Althea—she's the second one—keeps a diary which

505

was broken into. The only person who might have been responsible is Barbara. She denied touching either the perfume or the diary—very vigorously, and of course we believed her, but there just wasn't anyone else to blame. So she felt we didn't trust her, which was nonsense... Since then, incidentally, we've taken to locking our house."

"I see," said Shank. "Barbara has a steady boyfriend?"

"No."

"Is she, well, boy-crazy?"

"I wouldn't say so. She likes attention, and because she's pretty she usually gets it. Basically she's a sensible girl."

"Does she smoke?"

"Never."

"No evidence of drugs?"

"Absolutely not."

"And she took nothing with her?"

"She left all her money and she went away—or was taken away—in her school clothes."

"I see." Shank rose to his feet. "Any recent photographs?"

"We've already given them to the local police, but they don't seem very interested."

"To be perfectly frank, there isn't much they can do. They've sent a bulletin out over the teletype, but once a kid gets to Berkeley or San Francisco, the ground swallows him up, and that's how it is unless he gets in trouble or decides to call home. It's a big problem for us, and I can't offer you too much encouragement."

Marcia Wood cried, "But we don't believe she ran away! We think she was kidnapped!"

Shank shrugged. "I'll make inquiries at her school. It's just possible she confided in one of her friends."

"We've already checked," said Ben Wood hollowly. "Nobody knows anything. In fact, she made plans to play tennis today."

Shank was impressed in spite of himself. With rather more vigor he said, "I'll do all I can to get a line on her. But I can't hold out too much hope."

Shank departed. Ben and Marcia Wood drank coffee in gloomy silence. Every idea, every theory had already been verbalized a dozen times.

IN THE LAIR BARBARA lay taut with frustration. A half-dozen times she drew in her breath to scream and each time Ronald sensed her intent and gave the cord a menacing twitch. His amiability had disappeared.

He put his face close to her ear. "I know what you're thinking," he muttered. "Don't do it. You wouldn't live long enough to regret it. I don't have any worries. I've got a way to get out of here that you don't know about. If anybody broke in here they'd only find you, not me."

Barbara's throat was thick with woe; she could talk only with an effort. "Please don't hurt me, Ronald."

"You promised not to make any noise, and about five times you started to yell."

"No, no! I was just catching my breath. This rope is too tight!"

"It's tight on purpose. One good jerk is all it takes."

"Don't talk that way!" croaked Barbara.

"Sh! Not so loud!"

Barbara spoke in a husky whisper. "I thought we were going to be friends."

"I can't trust anybody."

"You could trust me! If you let me go, I could come in here every night! I could bring you ice cream and all kinds of good things. We could have lots of fun! Isn't that better than having me tied up like this?"

Ronald grinned. "No."

"But why not? Everything would be nicer, more exciting!"

"I wouldn't have you for myself. Now you're all mine."

"Then let's go off together. Let's go to Berkeley and live like the hippies do! No one would ever find us."

"No money."

"I could get money—some way. I'd work! Or even steal! Anything would be better than this little room."

"I don't know about that. This is Atranta."

"I'll bet if you wrote a book about Atranta you could sell it and make lots of money. You'd be famous, and I'd be proud of you!"

Ronald gave a ponderous nod. "I've considered that."

Barbara thought to discern a softening in his attitude. "I wouldn't mind leaving home. I'd like to—with you. You know how it's been around here—everybody accusing me of things I didn't do. And my parents are too strict. They don't let me do things I want to do. You and I could have such fun—but not here."

"I'm having fun now," said Ronald. "Aren't you?"

"Not always. I don't like that rope. It makes me nervous."

Ronald grinned. "That's the way I want it."

"Another thing—we don't have all that much food. And we don't have any way of getting more. Just think of the nice things we might have if we went somewhere else. Steaks and barbecued spare-ribs and hot dogs with mustard and fried chicken and french fries and milk shakes."

Ronald licked his lips. "It all takes money."

"We could go up to Lake Tahoe, and work at one of the hotels, or you could get a job at a service station."

"I don't like that kind of work."

"What kind of work do you like?"

"I don't know. I've never thought much about it. I'd like to be an artist, I guess."

"You certainly have the ability. Maybe there's an art school at Lake Tahoe. There must be lots of them in Berkeley."

"It all takes money."

Barbara said no more. Maybe one or another of these absurd ideas might seem sensible to Ronald, maybe she could lure him out into the open world. And then—how she'd run! Naked or clothed, it made no difference; she'd run down the street, through the middle of town—anywhere, so long as she was free!

She heard the telephone ring. Her mother answered. Barbara could not quite hear the conversation, but it seemed that someone at school had called. Her mother made a few polite but terse explanations, and ended the conversation as swiftly as possible.

Barbara meanwhile had a brilliant idea. "Ronald!"

"Sh! Not so loud! Don't talk like that again!"

Barbara pitched her voice at a lower level. "I just had a wonderful idea."

Ronald spoke in an austere whisper. "What kind of idea?"

"Well, you said we didn't have any money. I know how we can fix that problem."

"How?" Ronald's tone was indulgent, if skeptical.

"Suppose we hitchhiked, say, to Lake Tahoe, or Berkeley. I could telephone home and say I needed money for an emergency. I know my father and mother would send it to me." Barbara waited for Ronald's reaction. He said nothing. Barbara whispered eagerly, "Then we'd have enough money to live on."

Ronald whispered huskily, "I don't want to leave here."

"But why not? Think how nice the outside world is!"

Ronald grinned. "It's not real. Atranta is real. And Atranta is here."

"No, Ronald! Atranta is inside you! You'd take it with you, and be able to write beautiful stories, like the Oz books."

"They're for children," said Ronald disdainfully.

"No! Everybody reads them. And they made the author rich. You could be rich too. All you need to do is write about Atranta and draw beautiful illustrations. And I'd help you! I'd like to be rich too."

Ronald made a sound, half-sniff, half-snort. "What would you do?"

"Type. Keep house. Lots of things."

"Huh!" snorted Ronald. "Do you know something? I don't trust you."

Barbara was silent a moment. "Nothing I say seems to make any difference. I'd like to go live in Berkeley myself, or Mexico."

"They wouldn't let us past the border without passports."

"Arizona is another pretty place. My grandmother lives near Scottsdale. In fact—do you know something? We could go live with her. She's got a beautiful house, and she'd be glad to see us."

Ronald was superciliously amused, as if at the antics of a puppy. "She'd telephone your folks as soon as we arrived."

"I don't think she would, if I asked her not to. And suppose she called—so what? I'd tell my folks that I didn't want to come home for awhile."

"Hmmf. Then what?"

"I don't know. Maybe Grandmother would help you get into an art school, if I asked her."

"Is she rich?" Ronald's interest was piqued.

"Oh yes, she's got lots of money."

Ronald turned away and lay staring up at the map on the ceiling.

Barbara held her breath. But Ronald said nothing. Barbara began to tremble. What would she do if Ronald saw through her pitiful artifices? Oh, what would she do? Something, somehow— but what? He was always too close upon her, always too suspicious. With a crawling stomach she twisted her face into an arch smile. "Aren't you hungry? I'd love a cheeseburger with french fries."

"Sh! Not so loud!"

"I think my mother's gone out."

"I didn't hear the door slam." Ronald listened. The house seemed silent, for a fact. He went to peer through his peepholes. During the few seconds his attention was distracted Barbara might have screamed, but if her mother actually had gone out who'd be there to hear? Even if her mother were home, before she figured out where the screaming came from, Ronald could do any dire deed he had in mind.

Ronald turned away from the dining room peephole. "She's writing a letter."

"To Grandmother probably."

Ronald had no great interest in the matter. He came back to sit on the cot, and began to touch Barbara—here, there, everywhere, rapt and marveling, as if even now he could hardly believe his wonderful good fortune. Barbara lay with a frozen face, then forced herself to relax; Ronald's distrust would feed upon any display of revulsion.

———•—•———

AT FOUR O'CLOCK ELLEN and Althea came home, and Marcia had to tell them that Barbara was still lost.

Dinner was silent and gloomy. The girls washed dishes, then did homework on the dining-room table. Ben and Marcia apathetically watched television.

About nine-thirty Ellen and Althea went upstairs to bed. An hour later Ben and Marcia followed. Ronald almost immediately opened the secret door and peered out into the pantry. He looked back at Barbara, and she could almost read his thoughts. He closed the door and said gruffly, "I'm going out for a minute or two, but first I'd better make things secure." He tied Barbara's ankles and wrists to the cot, and gagged her. Barbara lay rigid, chilled by the bleak conviction that Ronald was far too distrustful ever to venture forth from his lair, not to Berkeley, not to Tahoe: nowhere. All her coaxing and fawning had gone for naught. He might have given her proposals a languid theoretical consideration, but never would he risk the open world. Never.

Ronald went forth into the kitchen and returned with an onion, two slices of cold meat loaf, bread and butter, a cup of milk, two stalks of celery, a carrot, and a fair-sized serving of ice cream. This was more than his usual requisition, but now there were two mouths to feed, for a while, at least.

He untied Barbara, and sensed her despondency. It made no great difference one way or the other, but he spoke with brassy jocularity. "Look. Food! Yum-yum. Eat your ice cream first, before it gets cold."

"I'm not too hungry."

"Well, eat the carrot and some celery. Good for the complexion, you know."

"I don't care about my complexion." Tears began trickling down Barbara's face. "Ronald, please let me go. I don't want to stay in here any more. I feel all cramped and stuffy. Please let me go!"

Ronald, eating the ice cream, stared at her in astonishment. "You want to go? When we're having so much fun? It doesn't make sense!"

"I still want to go. Don't you want me to be happy?"

"Sure. I know how to make you happy."

"Then can I go? I'll tell my family that I decided to come home. I promise I won't tell about you being here. Really, Ronald. Please!"

Ronald frowned. "This doesn't make me feel very good. I thought we were starting to get along. You were full of ideas about Berkeley and Lake Tahoe and your grandmother. And now you want to leave."

"I just don't want to stay in here anymore. If you let me go, it would be better for both of us."

"Hah," said Ronald. "You'd tell your parents first thing."

"No, Ronald, I promise I wouldn't. And we can still be friends."

Ronald finished the ice cream. "You're so pretty—especially when you're all worked up. And you've got such a beautiful figure. You're cute all over."

"I appreciate the compliments, Ronald. But..."

"No more buts. Kiss me."

Barbara put her head on his shoulder. "After we do it, can I go?"

Ronald smilingly shook his head. "I enjoy your company too much."

"I'd see you every day, Ronald! After school I'm always home early!"

"Let's not talk."

Barbara sighed and drew a deep breath, fighting the almost overpowering pressure of hysteria. Ronald became busy and she lay inert, tears rolling down her cheeks.

Ronald at last removed his bulk. Barbara slid to the outside of the cot, disliking the constricted space between Ronald and the wall. Ronald made no protest, but sat watching her with heavy-lidded intensity. After awhile he became drowsy, and his interest waned. His eyelids drooped. Barbara closed her own eyes, feigning sleep.

Ronald began to breathe in heavy regular gusts. Barbara slowly turned her head and looked toward the secret door. Twist the latch, raise the door, and slip through. She listened to Ronald's breathing. He was asleep.

Softly and carefully she moved: first one leg to the floor, then an arm. Ronald lay placid. Barbara eased off the cot: slowly, carefully. She took a step to the secret door; she bent and turned the latch. She lifted the door, and the hinges gave a little squeak. She froze for a half-second, then raised it high, and crawled through. A hand grasped her ankle. She heard Ronald's voice: a hissing guttural sound like nothing she had ever heard before. "You treacherous little bitch!"

UPSTAIRS BEN WOOD SAT up in his bed. Marcia said, "Did you hear something?"

"I'd have sworn it was a scream."

"I heard it too. Or I thought I heard it. I was half-asleep."

"Do you know, it sounded like Babs."

Marcia said dubiously, "It was probably Ellen or Althea having a nightmare."

Ben jumped out of bed. He crossed to Ellen's room, opened the door. "Ellen? Are you all right?"

"Huh? What?"

"It's all right. Go back to sleep."

He checked Althea with the same result. He went to the head of the stairs, where he stood listening.

Silence.

He returned to the bedroom. "The girls were asleep... It must have been our imagination."

"It really *was* like Babs," said Marcia. "The sound rings in my ears."

Ben stood indecisive, wondering what he ought to do. Slowly he returned to bed. "For a fact it sounded like Babs... I suppose because she's so much in our minds... Some day she'll come back to us."

Marcia was crying. Ben put his arm around her and drew her close. Marcia said, "Wherever she is I hope she's not lonely or frightened."

Chapter XV

SATURDAY morning was dull and damp. At nine o'clock rain began to fall. Ben and Marcia and the two girls sat late at the breakfast table. No one had slept well, and Althea complained of nightmares, which she couldn't quite remember. "I was off somewhere on a strange landscape. I couldn't see very well through the dark, but it seemed all stone and rock with the cold wind blowing—nowhere I've ever been. For some reason I had to walk along a trail and I didn't want to, but I had to… I remember the wind and voices calling from a far distance. And there was something before that, some terribly sad music, or maybe this was the wind." Althea shook her head. "I don't remember. It's so mixed up, but all so strange and sad."

Ben said, "It might have been…" then he stopped. "I looked in at you about midnight, and you seemed peaceful enough."

"Dreams are so strange," Ellen mused. "The psychologists say they represent fears and secret wishes. But I think they must be more than that."

"Primitive people think dreams are real," said Marcia. "They believe that the soul leaves the body."

Ben was not sympathetic to this point of view. "That's why they think that way: because they're primitive."

"Still, in things like that they know as much as we do."

"Maybe a lot more," said Althea.

Ben shook his head. "Not necessarily. For instance, a computer is much less complicated than a human brain, and computers get their circuits mixed up all the time. Savages don't know anything about computers or buggered circuits. All they know is what they see and feel, and they work out explanations based on what they know."

"Maybe our brains aren't computers," said Ellen softly. "Maybe they act like computers just often enough to fool the scientists."

"Hmmf," said Ben. "An awful lot of 'maybes'."

"I know that I've got at least two minds working all the time," said Althea. "Sometimes I relax the one on top just to see what the other one will do, and very interesting things happen. It's a lovely game to play when you've nothing better to do."

"That's how a lot of modern artists paint pictures," said Ben. "Unfortunately I'm not interested in their souls, any more than they're interested in mine."

"What is a 'soul'?" Ellen asked in an earnest voice. "Is there any such thing?"

Ben shrugged. "Some say 'yes', some say 'no'."

"So many odd things happen," said Althea. "Things no one can explain."

Marcia sighed, and changed the subject. "Is there a football game today? It'll be miserable in all this wet."

"The game's at Barnett," said Ellen. "I don't want to go. Especially not in the rain."

"Where's all the school spirit?" asked Ben with a wan attempt at facetiousness.

Ellen smiled her half-rueful smile. "I'm a refugee from Los Gatos High. I'm just attending classes here to get my diploma."

"I'm not going to the game either," said Althea. "I plan to stay home and read *Titus Groan*."

"You're going to read *what*?" asked Ben Wood.

"*Titus Groan*. It's a book about a strange old castle and the people who live there. I'm rather like Fuchsia, I think. She's a beautiful solitary girl who likes to brood in the attic where the Groans keep all their old junk."

"You and Fuchsia would make a good pair," said Ben. "Both oddballs."

"Sulky-sweet Fuchsia."

"What happens to her?" asked Ellen.

"I don't know. I'm only halfway through the book."

"During Christmas vacation I'm going to read *Remembrance of Things Past*," said Ellen. "I absolutely intend to do so, no matter who laughs at me."

Ben Wood gave a sad chuckle, but made no remark. Everyone knew where his thoughts had been wandering. Two weeks previously the family had made tentative plans to visit Arizona during the Christmas vacation. Now, with Barbara gone, the trip was unthinkable.

At noon Ben and Marcia went out to shop for groceries. Duane Mathews telephoned and half an hour later arrived in person. Ellen made grilled-cheese sandwiches and hot chocolate, and the three ate lunch at the dining-room table. Duane had quit his job at the service station and was at loose ends. He spoke rather despondently of the pressures being put on him by his family. "Dad wants me to work at the bar. He'll put in a pizza oven if I'm willing to take charge of it. I'd make lots of money, and get the whole business when Dad retires. My mother wants me to go to college and learn something. And me—I don't know what I want to do. I'm not anxious to be a pizza cook—still I suppose it's just work."

"I thought you wanted to be a veterinarian," said Althea, subtly seeming to suggest that between the crafts of fabricating pizzas and ministering to sick dogs there was little choice.

"That's my mother's idea. My Uncle Ed's a veterinarian in Lodi. He's got a big house with a swimming pool and a Lincoln Continental. He and my aunt fly to Europe every year. There's lots of money in that racket for sure."

"What about you?" asked Ellen. "You must have a preference."

Duane drummed his fingers on the tabletop. "Oh yes. No question about that. I want to be a criminologist."

"A criminologist?" Althea raised her eyebrows. "Whatever for?"

"The field is obviously wide open. When Ronald Wilby could murder my sister and get away scot-free, somewhere there's a lack."

"What exactly did the police do?" asked Ellen.

"Routine. They put out an alert and asked Mrs. Wilby a few questions. They checked the bus station and asked if anyone had seen Ronald hitchhiking, and that was about the end of it."

"What else could they do?" Althea asked. "For instance, what would you have done?"

"His mother knew where Ronald went. She wasn't the type not to know, and Ronald wasn't the type to go off without mama giving him a lot of help. She must have sent him money. That's the angle I would have worked on. I'd have watched her mail, and I'd have checked on what she did with her money, because she worked herself to death, no question about it, and why? To get money for Ronald."

"That's just suspicion," said Ellen. "How could you prove it?"

"I don't know." Duane reflected a moment, then said almost grudgingly, "It doesn't make too much difference now anyway, because the woman is dead. If I'd been a police detective I'd have nailed her. Sure as anything, she helped Ronald get away!"

Althea said in a musing voice, "Still, you've got to feel sorry for her. She probably suffered as much as your own mother. Maybe more."

Duane gave a bleak nod. "That's what Mom said herself. I don't doubt it. Still, what's right is right, and she should have turned Ronald over to the police."

Ellen reflected a moment. "Would you protect your son if he committed a crime?"

"I'd turn him in," said Duane. "I wouldn't like it, but that's what I'd do. Mrs. Wilby was a silly, selfish woman. She was all wrapped up in that horrible Ronald, and it killed her when he went wrong."

Ellen and Althea sat in silence for a moment or two. The telephone rang. Ellen ran into the living room and picked up the receiver. "Hello... Yes, he's still here... Art's Service Station. I'll ask him." She came back to the dining room. "Mom and Dad need a lift. The fuel pump has gone out on the station wagon."

Duane rose to his feet. "I know where Art's is. Tell 'em we'll be right there."

Ellen and Duane departed. Althea went to sprawl on the sofa with her book.

BAD RONALD

The house seemed very silent. Althea put her book down and lay listening to the rain. She began to wish she'd gone with Duane and Ellen, but no one would be in the house in case Barbara telephoned. How wonderful it would be if Barbara actually did call, from Berkeley, or San Francisco, to say that she wanted to come home. How happy everyone would be! Althea concentrated upon a thought: *Come home, Babs, come home!... At least telephone, let us know where you are!... Babs, Babs, Babs! Where are you?*

She lay passive, receptive, hoping for connection... Nothing. At least, nothing very much. She felt dampness and heard sighing winds: a residue, so she decided, of last night's nightmare. *Babs! Babs!* thought Althea. *Come home, come home! We love you and miss you!* And Althea lay with her eyes closed, holding her mind blank.

"I can't."

Althea opened her eyes with a startled jerk. The words had come in small crystalline vibrations, and it seemed like Barbara's voice.

Babs! Babs! thought Althea. *Do you hear me? Is that you? Why can't you come home?*

Silence, except the rain, the ticking of the clock, a creaking of woodwork from the direction of the kitchen. In Althea's mind: nothing but darkness, the blowing of the dream-wind, a slow seep of the most melancholy desolation imaginable.

Althea's concentration had frayed; she relaxed her attention. Suddenly the old house seemed full of strange noises. Althea became uneasy. Irrational, she told herself with a contemptuous little laugh for her own foolishness. But she sat up on the sofa, then rose to her feet, and went to the front door. Strange, the sounds in the old house!

Althea went out to stand on the porch.

The rain came quietly down; the air was soft and cool. Althea felt more at ease. The air inside had been oppressive. Perhaps someone had set the thermostat too high. She shivered. The air was somewhat too cool. Perhaps the house would now feel less warm. She tried the door to discover that she had locked herself out, and so she had to wait five minutes until her parents arrived home in Duane's car.

519

Days went by. The Woods settled into a new and rather despondent way of life. No one spoke of Barbara, though every mealtime her empty place brought recollection. On Saturday Ben and Marcia drove into Berkeley. They gave no explanation, but Ellen and Althea understood that they intended to look for Barbara, and that they would leave messages at the various agencies which helped strays and runaways.

Duane Mathews dropped by the house at eleven o'clock with a package of pork chops and a loaf of French bread. "Instead of you feeding me," he told the girls, "I'm going to cook lunch for you."

"Pork chops for lunch?" asked Althea.

"Nope. Barbecued-pork sandwiches. I should have brought some potato salad."

"Let's make some," said Ellen. "It won't take long."

"You two can be in charge of the potato salad. Then this afternoon maybe we'll drive over to Steamboat Slough. There's a boat at Pete's Landing I want to look at."

"I can't come," said Althea. "I promised to help Bernice with her costume."

"I can't come either," said Ellen. "I've got a report to write. 'The Reasons for Hamlet's Indecisiveness'."

"It's been done," said Duane.

"Not the way I'm doing it. I've got a new approach. If Hamlet is decisive the play only goes three scenes."

"It's original scholarship, but you might not get much of a grade."

"I don't care all that much. I'm so bored with school. The hell with the report, I'd rather go to Steamboat Slough."

"First the potato salad," said Althea. "I'll peel potatoes. You can chop the onions."

"Thanks."

"I'll chop onions," said Duane. "I need some for the barbecue sauce."

Ellen went into the pantry. "How many?"

"Just one, and whatever you need for the salad."

"There's only three left," said Ellen. "Somebody around here likes onions. Mom just bought a big bag last week. We'll need potatoes—they're almost gone too! I guess there's enough. Just barely... We're out of everything, as usual."

Duane browned the pork chops and simmered them at low heat in barbecue sauce; meanwhile the potatoes boiled.

"What would go well with this meal is beer," said Duane. "In fact, I've got a six-pack out in the car."

"Bring it in," said Ellen. "I love beer!"

"Well—I don't want your parents to think I'm corrupting their daughters."

"That's locking the barn door after the horses are gone," said Althea.

"I can't remember not being corrupt," said Ellen.

"Well, all right, if you're sure they won't be upset."

"Not a chance."

The three had departed. The house was silent.

The pantry sounded to a barely audible scrape. In the shadows a bulky shape stood erect. Ronald came slowly out into the kitchen. His nose drew him to the stove. Duane had cooked generously; in the pan remained a quantity of barbecued pork and ample sauce.

Detesting Duane as he did, Ronald stood glowering a moment or two, then tearing off a chunk of French bread, he smeared it thick with margarine and got to work on the pork. He remembered the potato salad, and opening the refrigerator, served himself a great mound: the girls wouldn't remember whether a gallon had been left or a cupful. It was the best meal he'd had in days! He finished it off with a portion of vanilla ice cream swimming in chocolate sauce, topped with a sliced banana, chopped nuts and a huge squirt of synthetic whipped cream. Delicious beyond words, thought Ronald. Regretfully he decided against a second helping, and cleaned up the evidence of his repast. Then he went into the living room and stood by the window.

BERNICE AND WALLACE THURSTON were the daughter and son of the Methodist minister. Althea suspected that the old adage about clergymen's children held true. Nothing too outrageous had ever occurred in her presence; nevertheless, they generated an atmosphere of excitement and mischief which made for interesting company. Althea found Wallace attractive, and he seemed to like her too, and she was hoping he'd ask for a date. Today she'd flirt as well as she knew how, and try not to scare him off with her intelligence.

Today luck was against her. Bernice's piano teacher had switched schedules and Bernice had a three o'clock lesson. Mrs. Thurston did not care to leave Wallace and Althea alone in the house so on the way to the piano lesson she dropped Althea off at home.

Althea, somewhat miffed at Mrs. Thurston's fastidious propriety, hoped that Wallace would telephone; she had even hinted as much. In the meantime she'd fix her fingernails and do some reading for her English class.

The key was in its usual place. She opened the door and went into the house.

At five o'clock Duane and Ellen returned from Steamboat Slough. The house seemed empty. On the dining-room table Ellen found a note.

> Dear Everybody:
> While you were gone I heard from Barbara, and I'm going to talk to her. I promised I wouldn't tell where she is, so I can't divulge any details.
> Don't worry about me; I'll be fine.
> Love, Althea

Chapter XVI

"I don't believe it," said Ellen. "I just don't believe it!"

Duane snatched up the letter and glared at it, as if to compel further information from the cryptic sentences. "If Althea learned where Barbara was, would she keep the news a secret—no matter what she promised? Would you?"

"No," said Ellen. "I don't think I would. I don't think she did either."

"Oh? Why do you say that?"

"Notice the handwriting."

"What about it? Isn't it Althea's?"

"Oh it's Althea's handwriting all right. But it's backhand. She doesn't write like that."

Duane again inspected the note. "What time will your folks be home?"

"I don't know. I expect they'll make a day of it."

"You'd better call the police."

Ellen telephoned the Oakmead Police Department and reported Althea's disappearance. She told Duane, "They're not too pleased."

"I imagine not. They haven't even found the other one yet. Who lives next door?"

"The Schumachers and Boltons."

"Let's go talk to them."

RONALD TURNED AWAY FROM the wall and directed a haughty glance down at Althea. "So—you tried to trick me. You disguised your handwriting."

Althea said nothing.

Ronald opened his mouth to say something sarcastic, then thought better of it; why bother? None of these girls could be trusted; they said one thing and meant another. Still, he had not expected any such cheap treachery from Althea; he thought somehow she might be different. But she was far more cold and tense than Barbara, and she hadn't so much as mentioned the Atranta pictures.

Well, so be it. If she wasn't nice to him, he wasn't going to be nice to her. That was the way the world went, and she might as well find it out sooner than later. He spoke in an important voice, combining exactly the proper degrees of dignity and silken menace, "Please don't try to play any more tricks on me."

NEITHER THE SCHUMACHERS NOR the Boltons had so much as noticed Althea's arrival home.

Ellen telephoned the Thurston house. Wallace answered. "Althea? She left for home about three with Mother and Bernice. Isn't she there now?"

"I guess she went downtown." Ellen hung up and turned back to Duane. "She left the Thurston's about three."

"So now it's five. She could be anywhere by now... I know that message isn't right. But just on the off chance it is, we ought to go out to the highway and look for her. If she's hitchhiking she might still be there."

"Althea wouldn't hitchhike. She wouldn't ride ten feet with a stranger. Just a minute." She ran upstairs and into Althea's room, then returned downstairs rather more slowly. "Her money is still there."

"Just like Barbara's money."

The police arrived. They examined the note and listened to everything Ellen had to tell them. "So you don't think the note is genuine?"

"I know it isn't genuine. The handwriting is backwards and it doesn't sound like Althea. It's not the way she talks or thinks."

The police officer gave a skeptical nod. "Well, I'll put the word out over the wire. Where are your folks?"

"They went to Berkeley to look for Barbara."

"And while they're gone, another one disappears. Great." The officer examined the letter. "I suppose you've had your hands all over this?"

"Well—yes. We didn't think of fingerprints."

"Hmmf. Ordinary typing paper."

Duane had became restive. He asked, "Isn't there something you can do, instead of just standing here asking questions?"

"Sonny, if I could figure out something to do, I'd do it. All I can think of is that the first girl went off to one of those hippie communes along the river, and the other girl went to keep her company. I can check these places out, and, as I say, we'll put a bulletin out on the wire."

"That's just wasted effort! Somebody kidnapped her, just like they kidnapped Barbara!"

"Well, I suppose that's possible, and I'll take it up with Captain Davis. We'll sure do our best."

The police departed. The house seemed bleak and cold and silent. Ellen began to sob. Duane put his arm around her and patted her hand. "Oh Duane, what are we going to do? I can't bear to tell Mom and Daddy!"

"Let's go out and look for her," Duane growled. "It's better than standing here doing nothing. Leave a note. Tell them we'll be back as soon as we can."

Ellen scribbled a note and left it on the dining-room table along with Althea's message; the two of them ran out the front door and the house was again silent.

RONALD RELAXED THE NOOSE around Althea's neck. "We can talk now, but quietly. First of all, don't be so scared. I'm not going to bite you. All you have to do is obey orders! And that means no noise! no rumpus! no yelling! Do you understand?" Ronald raised his voice a menacing degree or two. "I said, do you understand?"

Althea nodded. In a husky whisper she asked, "Where is Barbara?"

Ronald smiled: a lordly condescending smile. "She was here until she got bored. One night when you were all asleep she ran away. She said she was going to Lake Tahoe. She wanted to play around a bit before coming home."

"What about me?" Althea quavered. "What are you going to do with me?"

"Don't worry about that," said Ronald. "After awhile you can leave—if you promise to keep my secret."

"Then let me go now! Please!"

Ronald smilingly shook his head. "We've got lots of things to talk about. Barbara wasn't much of a talker."

Althea stared at him numbly. She blurted, "Who are you?" But even as she asked, knowledge burst into her brain. This was Ronald Wilby. Ronald Wilby the murderer!

Ronald replied in a gentle, almost mincing, voice, "My name is beside the point. Just call me Norbert." He made a gesture around the walls. "What do you think of the atmosphere in here?"

Althea gave the decorations an uncomprehending glance. "Won't you let me go? Please! I don't want to stay here!"

Ronald's eyebrows lowered into a majestic frown. Althea saw that she had taken the wrong line.

"You'll stay here until I see fit to let you go," said Ronald. "And let's get one thing understood. You'd better behave yourself. I'm good-natured, but I can't take chances. One squeak out of you when anyone is in the house, and I'd have to jerk that noose... Watch!" Ronald tugged on the loose end of the rope. The noose became an overhand knot, barely large enough to push a finger through. Althea stared aghast.

Barbara had been more tractable, more quickly comprehending, thought Ronald. She also had shown less obstinacy and, well, call it nervousness, even though she was younger. Althea was still fully dressed. It would be fun taking off her clothes, one piece at a time. But first, he must make absolutely sure she knew what was required of her. In an easy conversational tone he asked, "So now do you understand what will happen if you make any noise?"

Althea only stared at him, like a person bereft of reason.

Ronald spoke a bit more meaningfully. "Please, tell me that you understand what I'm talking about."

Althea managed a nod. Ronald relaxed. "Actually, I want to be friends with you," he said. "We'll be living here together until you decide you want to leave—"

"I want to leave now!"

"—and I decide to let you go."

Althea whispered, "Tell me where Barbara is."

"I already told you. She's gone up to Lake Tahoe. At least that's where she said she was going. She promised she wouldn't tell about me, and I guess she kept her promise. You'll have to do the same thing."

Althea began to cry. "I'll promise not to tell. But let me go now! Please be kind to me! I don't want to stay in here!"

"Too bad," said Ronald with a grim smirk. "You'll like it after awhile."

Althea shook her head. "Don't you realize you'll be in bad trouble when the police catch you?"

"*If* the police catch me—which is not likely. I've been here for—well, it's been a long time. I've been writing the history of Atranta. Aren't you interested?"

"I don't know anything about it."

"It's a magical country. Those men," Ronald pointed, "they're the six dukes, and those are their castles. The girl is Fansetta. I didn't do the best job with her. Maybe you'll pose for me. She's supposed to look about like you." Ronald improvised the last remark, but it was quite true. Barbara never had quite fit the image;

she was too fresh-faced and alert. Althea had more of a thoughtful fairy-quality to her; she was obviously more sensitive and imaginative, and perhaps more passionate. Barbara's reactions hadn't been all that exciting; she had just laid there. Ronald cocked his head. "Someone's coming." He tied the noose around her neck, with one end made fast to the stud, and the other wrapped around his hand. "Remember! Not a single sound. Or you won't like what happens."

Althea closed her eyes, and let the tears well out from under the lids. Barbara at Lake Tahoe? If only it were true! She shivered, and Ronald threw her a monitory glance. "Quiet," he hissed.

BEN AND MARCIA WOOD came into the house, hungry, haggard, tired, and out of sorts. They read the two notes and stared at each other in despair. Ben stalked into the living room and telephoned the police, who assured him that all possible steps were being taken. Ben wanted to rave and threaten and bluster, but could think of nothing sensible to say.

Ellen and Duane presently returned, Ellen sagging with discouragement, Duane seething with quiet rage. Far into the night they all sat at the dining-room table, forming bewildered hypotheses. Duane went home at half-past eleven; Ellen went with him out on the porch. Duane kissed her and held her close for a moment, and Ellen, who had never encouraged Duane to be demonstrative, relaxed and allowed herself to be comforted. Duane whispered fiercely, "Promise me one thing! That no matter what, you won't go off looking for Barbara or Althea without telling me."

"I promise," said Ellen.

"No matter what!"

"No matter what."

"There's something awfully strange going on," Duane muttered. "If I had any brains I'd be able to figure it out. After all, I'm the one who wants to be a criminologist."

Ellen stirred. "I'd better go back inside—or Mom and Dad will start worrying about me."

The next day was Sunday. Ben Wood telephoned the Sheriff's office. Howard Shank had the day off and Ben Wood left a message. An hour later Shank returned the call and Ben reported Althea's disappearance. "We find it simply incredible," Ben declared. "Althea definitely and positively would not have gone off alone. Even less than Barbara."

"Even if Barbara had telephoned and asked her to come?"

"She'd certainly have given us more facts."

"Read the note again."

Ben Wood did so. Shank asked, "I suppose everybody in the house has handled the letter?"

"I'm afraid so."

"And she left her money behind?"

"She took nothing whatever, except the clothes she wore to her friend's house."

"Hmm. This is an unusual situation, I agree... Well, I'd better drive on out."

Ben Wood gave a shaky laugh. "I know how you must value your time off, but we're at wit's end."

"I'll get the time back."

———•———

HOWARD SHANK ARRIVED. HE looked into Althea's room; he walked around the house seeking traces and clues; he drove to the Reverend Thurston's house and put inquiries to both Wallace and Bernice. Next he visited the Schumachers and the Boltons, and then Kathy Schmidt and Ernestine Long: girls with whom Althea was friendly. Everywhere he encountered a vacuum of information. Everyone presented about the same picture of Althea: a quietly happy girl, if over-imaginative and somewhat dreamy. No one considered her either adventurous or particularly decisive, and no one could take seriously the proposition that Althea would voluntarily leave her home unless forced to do so by some awful emergency—which neither the text of her letter nor its tone suggested.

"On these premises," Shank told the Woods, "we've got to assume that she's been kidnapped."

"That's what I told you when Barbara went!" Ben Wood rasped in a suddenly harsh voice. "The same thing has happened to both of them!"

Shank said stonily, "Perhaps you were right. We never discounted the idea either. But the fact remains that we had no leads. Without straw we can't make bricks. I can't search every house, barn, shed, church, garage, and motel in San Joaquin County."

"What about sex offenders?" Marcia asked.

"We've checked our list," said Shank. "Oakmead's pretty clean. The only sex criminal of recent years was Ronald Wilby, and he lived in this very house."

"And you've never caught him."

Shank shook his head. "Like Barbara and Althea, he simply disappeared."

"I wonder if there could be some connection."

Shank considered the proposition. "Well—nothing's impossible. That's one thing you learn in this business. Still, is it reasonable that Ronald Wilby should come back to Oakmead, where almost certainly he'd be recognized? It doesn't make much sense. There's nothing here for him now with his mother dead."

"Maybe so. But I just don't believe in coincidences."

"They happen all the time."

Marcia suggested, "Why don't we ask the newspapers to print pictures of the girls? And we'd offer a reward for information."

"It won't do any harm," said Shank. "Let me make the arrangements. I can get faster action."

"I keep coming back to this Ronald Wilby," said Ben Wood. "Does he have any friends or relatives in the area who might hide him?"

"No friends we were ever able to locate. None of his relatives are local people, and they all disown him."

Marcia gave a quavering cry of frustration and beat her fists on the table. "It's the same old story. No one knows anything, no one does anything. And meanwhile what's happening to our girls? It's enough to drive me absolutely crazy."

"I sympathize with you, Mrs. Wood. Please believe we'll do everything possible. Let me look at those notes again."

Marcia brought them forth, and Shank studied them for several minutes, then said, "The notes are either genuine—or they're not. If they're genuine, we've got to look for two silly wayward girls."

"They're not silly, and they're not wayward."

Shank nodded. "If the notes are not genuine, if the girls were forced to write them as you suspect, then we've got a very ugly situation on our hands. But—I won't try to fool you—I just don't see any starting point to the case. We've got to hope for some kind of break. Meanwhile, we'll make inquiries everywhere feasible. The city police have suggested that we look into the communes along the river, which is a long shot at best. Still, who knows?" Shank rose to his feet. He studied the notes one last time. "I'll take these along with me, if you don't mind."

Ben Wood made a weary gesture. "Go ahead. We know them by heart."

———◆———

RONALD LISTENED ATTENTIVELY TO the conversation. As always, he deeply resented the terms 'sex offender', 'deviate', 'murderer' when used in connection with himself. Such words simply didn't fit the case; they implied a vulgar ordinary criminality which Ronald was far above and beyond.

So far neither Barbara nor Althea had correctly fulfilled their roles. Barbara had suggested going off to more spacious quarters in Berkeley or at Lake Tahoe; she had naturally been trying to hoodwink him, and obviously had never accepted the ambience of magic Atranta. Ronald had expected more subtlety and awareness of Althea. During the night he had spoken at length of Atranta. He had recounted its history and described the landscapes; he had limned the persons of each of the six dukes and taken her room by room through each of the six castles. He told of bewitching Fansetta and her marvelous adventures, of Mersilde and the halfling Darrue, and he kept watching her covertly, hoping to discern a gleam of interest. But Althea lay apathetic, and indeed the only time she evinced any sort of emotion was when Ronald proposed a session of lovemaking, whereupon she winced and shuddered and withdrew into numbness like a hermit crab into a shell. Barbara had been braver, more matter-of-fact; Althea seemed to regard each coition as a new and separate outrage: a fact which began to stimulate in Ronald a darker, more intricate, pleasure. Althea could not be aroused to passion, but she could be shocked and revolted, and Ronald began to plan a series of variations by which he could constantly stimulate her to awareness, the hard way.

Althea had nothing to say. She lay either silently staring, or torpid and dazed. Ronald became exasperated. He wanted her attention, her wonder, her awe; after all, she was Althea, who loved fantasies! He had opened before her the wonderful vistas of Atranta, and she lay like a half-wit!

On several occasions Althea aroused herself to plead with Ronald. She offered him inducements to let her go free. She swore never to reveal his secret; she undertook to give him money, if only he'd let her go. Ronald listened with a pursy noncommittal smile. When she asked how long he intended to keep her, he said, "Heavens, we've only got started!" And another time, "Time to talk about that when we're bored with each other. I find you entrancing. You have more feeling than Barbara. She was a practical girl."

"'Was'?" asked Althea in a throaty whisper.

Ronald made an easy response. "While she was here. I guess she's still the same, wherever she is."

"But why did she go?" Althea insisted, trying to keep the quaver from her voice. "Why didn't she just come back to the family?"

Ronald's reply was glib and unconcerned. "Because I made her promise not to tell about me. She thought that if she went to Lake Tahoe she could call home and no one would suspect she'd been in the house all that time."

Althea tried to trace the thread of the argument, and discerned a certain weird rationality. Still, why would Barbara delay so long? Althea thought better of putting the question to Ronald.

As for the lovemaking, she recognized that he enjoyed making her squirm, but unlike Barbara, who had borne Ronald's exertions with stoicism, she could not conceal her repugnance. Her refuge was the feigned torpor which Ronald found so irksome.

Meanwhile through half-closed lids she studied every detail of the lair and its contents. No question but what Ronald had a real flair for mood and grotesque detail; under different circumstances she might even have become interested in his contrivings. But now her preoccupation was escape, and she calculated a dozen schemes to this end.

Ronald was wary. With anyone downstairs he gagged her and tightened the noose so she could barely breathe, and she recognized that never could she call for help—unless Ronald became careless.

She studied the layout of the lair and saw how the old doorway had been sheathed with plasterboard. Given five seconds she might be able to hurl herself at this plasterboard and break through into the hall—but more likely she'd find her strength unequal to the task. Even while Ronald slept he seemed alert. Once or twice she stirred and tried to sit up; instantly he was awake and suspicious.

The trapdoor to the crawl-space she noticed but failed to identify. She saw no opportunity to escape.

Could she incapacitate Ronald? Could she poison him, or stun him, or stab him?

For poison, she saw only the watercolors, which probably weren't toxic. She searched in vain for a sharp object which might serve as a weapon. Ronald's two knives were both ordinary tableware, and the forks were equally useless. In all the lair she noted but one object which might be used as a weapon: the porcelain lid to the tank behind the toilet. Such objects, in her experience, were hard to lift free without producing a sepulchral clanking sound. Still, with great care it was surely possible.

When she went to the toilet she took careful note of how Ronald disposed himself. If anyone were in the house he usually sat on the edge of the cot, somewhat turned away from her; when the house was empty or late at night he often remained sprawled on the cot.

Yes, thought Althea; the deed was possible. Quite possible. She began to rehearse the procedure; she accomplished the act over and over in her mind. She'd need all her strength, all her courage, all her decisiveness—because she'd only have one chance.

Success probably depended upon two circumstances. No, three. Could she lift the cover silently? Would Ronald divine her intentions before she could strike the blow? Did she possess sufficient strength to do the job properly?

She thought 'yes' for the first and third situations, and she hoped 'no' for the second.

———•———

ON TUESDAY, PICTURES OF Barbara and Althea Wood appeared in newspapers all over the state. The captions typically read,

> Have you seen either of these two girls? $1,000 reward is offered for information as to their whereabouts. Mr. Ben Wood of Oakmead, in San Joaquin County, believes his two daughters have been kidnapped. Both have disappeared under mysterious circumstances. Please communicate any information directly to the police. Barbara is 13, with blonde hair of medium length and blue eyes. She was last seen wearing a gray skirt and a dark-red turtleneck blouse. Althea is 16, with light brown hair, gray eyes, and was last seen wearing blue jeans and a green sweater.

Duane Mathews sat in the living room with Ellen. The photographs, so they agreed, were good likenesses and might well produce results—if the girls had appeared anywhere in public.

Duane was pessimistic. "I don't think there's a chance. I hate to say this, but..." He could not bring himself to continue.

Ellen failed to notice; her thoughts ran concurrently with his.

"Somehow we should be able to figure something out," said Duane. "These things can't just happen without leaving a trace—but where's the trace?"

Ellen gave her head a weary shake. "We've been over it and over it. There's nothing but the notes."

"Could it be that somewhere in the notes is information we haven't understood? A hidden clue?"

Ellen gave a sad laugh. "You're letting your criminological instincts run away with you."

"Still," said Duane, "let's consider the notes and try to think like Sherlock Holmes."

"Sergeant Shank has the notes," said Ellen. "But I know them word for word."

She went to the desk and, bringing out two sheets of paper, wrote the two messages.

Dear Everybody:
Nobody trusts me and I can't stand it anymore. I've gone off to join the hippies. I'll be back after awhile. Don't worry about me. I'll be all right.
Barbara

Dear Everybody:
While you were gone I heard from Barbara, and I'm going to talk to her. I promised I wouldn't tell where she is, so I can't divulge any details.
Don't worry about me; I'll be fine.
Love, Althea

Sitting side by side on the couch, Duane and Ellen scrutinized the two messages.

"First of all," said Duane, "both notes are short, and both start off 'Dear Everybody'. Would you expect that?"

"I suppose so. It seems natural."

"Barbara's note mentions 'trust'—which refers to your private quarrels." Duane sat frowning at the word. "It occurs to me that's significant! No outsider would have known anything about that."

Ellen nodded slowly. "Well—I suppose you could argue that way."

"It's obvious! Would she have discussed the quarrel, or misunderstanding, whatever it was, with anybody you can think of?"

"No. But there's something else which makes an outsider certain."

"Oh? What?"

"The paper."

"The paper? There wasn't anything strange about the paper."

"I know. It was ordinary cheap typing paper. Just now I thought about it. Feel this paper here. It's good quality paper, telephone company paper. Daddy brings it home from his office. Larcenous Daddy. We never buy typing paper. That other paper was brought into the house—by an outsider."

Duane inspected the paper with scowling intensity. "Are you absolutely sure?"

"Absolutely. I'll show you." Ellen led him to the desk and displayed the contents. "Whenever we want a sheet of paper this is where we come. I don't have any such paper in my room. Let's go check the other bedrooms—just to make sure."

As Ellen had affirmed, no paper similar to that of the notes could be found in the house.

Duane said, "This is absolutely fascinating. Barbara's message almost guarantees that no outsider dictated it, but neither Barbara nor Althea would have had that paper to write on, unless an outsider gave it to them."

"But there's no outsider who knew of our quarrel with Barbara, except maybe you."

Duane laughed weakly. "I didn't do it."

"I think we ought to tell Sergeant Shank about the letters," said Ellen. "It's something I'm sure he hasn't thought of."

"Call him."

Ellen found Howard Shank at his desk, and explained the paradox she and Duane had discovered. Shank agreed that the contradiction was most perplexing. "It certainly bears out the idea that the girls didn't go off by themselves. Who could have known of the quarrel, other than members of the family?"

"Well—Duane might have known. But when Althea disappeared he was with me. I know Duane isn't responsible."

"I see. And he's there with you now?"

"Yes, he is. He's had innumerable opportunities to kidnap me but he doesn't seem to want to."

"Don't take the pitcher to the well too often," said Shank. "Have you told your parents about these letters?"

"No. Mom's shopping and Dad's at work. They'll be home any time now. I'll tell them when they come in. Have you had any results from the photographs?"

"Nothing definite. I'll keep you informed."

BAD RONALD

RONALD STOOD WITH HIS eye to the peephole. The detestable Duane! Never had he hated anyone with such virulence, not even Jim Neale. Duane wouldn't let anything rest; he kept nagging at things. What business was it of his about those notes? For the first time Ronald felt a trifle insecure. Because the only possible synthesis of ideas to explain the paradox of the letters would be this: an outsider, situated where he could overhear the quarrel, had provided the paper and kidnapped the girls. The next question would be: where was this outsider situated? That detestable rotten Duane!

Ronald sat on the cot. Althea turned away her head. Ronald frowned. Something was on her mind. She was brooding. Let her brood. He reached out, fondled her body. She was about an inch taller than Barbara and just a bit more slender and flexible. Her hips were more boyish than Barbara's, but she was probably more enticing, because of her sensitivity. Ronald rather liked doing things to revolt her... She had beautiful eyes, not blue like Barbara's, but gray like storm clouds, large and transparent. She had a beautiful mouth, and he liked to kiss her, because she always pulled her wrist across her mouth afterwards. Once a hair from his beard got caught in her teeth.

The evening passed. Ronald listened to the dinner-table discussion, which he found uninteresting. He'd heard it all before.

For dinner the Woods had brought home a paper bucket of fried chicken with french fries and coleslaw, and a frozen coconut custard pie. Everything looked most appetizing and Ronald hoped there'd be leftovers. Unfortunately, with the gluttonous Duane on hand, the chicken and french fries were totally consumed, and Ronald knew that tonight his mouth had watered in vain. There would be quite a bit of pie left, however: dessert for himself and Althea.

Duane went home at ten o'clock, and a half-hour later the three Woods went upstairs to bed. Ronald stood by the toilet, ready to flush it as soon as someone upstairs did so. Now! Perfect synchronization, as usual.

He came back to the cot. Althea closed her eyes and turned to lie facing away from him. Ronald refused to take the hint, and busied himself.

The first event of the evening accomplished, Ronald sat up. Now for supper. Althea lay limp, humiliated. She'd perk up with a nice piece of pie and a cup of coffee and whatever else he could find. Ronald went briskly to the secret door. He hesitated, looked back. He had neglected to tie and gag Althea—but she'd hardly dare make a sound. He was really hungry and impatient to get to the refrigerator. He'd chance it this once.

He got down on his hands and knees, then chanced to look back over his shoulder. Althea was watching him with a peculiarly alert expression… Ronald drew back, slowly rose to his feet. He'd better not take any chances; no telling what kind of mischief Althea had worked up. She was cunning and merciless and she hated him; this he knew. All of which made for excitement and stimulation and lots of novel schemes, but he could never think of her as trustworthy.

"Sorry," said Ronald with a rather unctuous smirk, "but I think I'd better make all secure before I leave."

———◆———

ALTHEA'S FACE DROOPED. SHE had a plan all worked out; if Ronald ever left her alone for even two minutes, she'd take the toilet lid and break through the plasterboard which covered the old doorway; then, if Ronald tried to come at her through the secret door, she'd hit him on the head.

Ronald, sensing her mood, tied and gagged her with especial care, then ducked out through his secret door and hurried to the refrigerator. As he had feared, nothing much was available except the pie. Hissing in irritation he cut two pieces. Not too much of the pie remained, but the Woods, preoccupied with their problems, would never notice. He poured leftover coffee into a pair of cups and returned into the lair.

Althea, when untied, accepted the coffee, but refused the pie. "I don't feel well."

"Oh? That's too bad," said Ronald. "I'm sorry to hear that." Sitting on the end of the cot he ate both pieces of pie, and regretfully gave over the idea of going back to the refrigerator for what was left. He frowned down at Althea. "What seems to be wrong?"

"I feel sick to my stomach."

Ronald frowned in displeasure. The news put a damper upon his plans for the evening. "Do you want an aspirin?"

"No."

Ronald lay down beside her. Five minutes passed. Ronald raised on an elbow and began to fondle her. So she wasn't feeling up to snuff. A bit of excitement would take her mind off her troubles.

Althea began to make retching sounds; Ronald hastily drew aside. Althea tottered to the toilet and raising the seat stood over the bowl with her two hands resting on the toilet lid. Ronald fastidiously turned his back.

With the utmost care Althea lifted the lid, wedging her fingers under each end. She made more sick noises and looked cautiously toward Ronald. He lay on the couch with his back turned. She lifted the lid high, and took two long steps toward the cot. Ronald turned up a startled glance in time to see the descending porcelain lid and Althea's intent face. Ronald croaked, jerked away his head. The lid struck down with a terrible impact on Ronald's twisted shoulder; it bounced across his neck and the back of his head. He had never felt such pain before! And blood! Look at the blood! And look at the murderous she-devil who had hurt him so terribly and who now stood aghast at her failure to kill him. Ronald lurched forward. Althea opened her mouth to scream, but Ronald swept her legs out from under her and brought her to the floor; her only sound was a gasping squeak as the breath was knocked from her. She fought; she pulled his hair; she opened her mouth to scream, but Ronald knew a very effective method to prevent such betrayal.

Chapter XVII

ON Wednesday morning Ben and Marcia insisted that Ellen return to school. "I know that you feel self-conscious with the pictures in the paper," said Marcia, "but it can't be helped."

"I suppose not," said Ellen glumly. "I still don't like it. Everybody will be staring at me and whispering and wondering what goes on at our house. I'll feel like a leper."

"I'm sorry, dear. It's something we've got to put up with."

"You'll find out who your friends are," said Ben drily.

Ellen shrugged. "I can stand it. But somebody should be home in case there's a call."

"I'll be home," said Marcia. "I'm not going back to work for a while. Not until we get some news."

So Ellen went to school and bore the surreptitious scrutiny with as much composure as she could summon.

Duane Mathews met her after school, and they walked to Curley's for a strawberry sundae. Duane, never voluble, seemed quieter than ever. Ellen, preoccupied with her own troubles, at last took note. "You're gloomy today!"

Duane reflected. "I suppose I am." After a moment he explained. "I don't know if you've ever noticed, but life seems to go in stages. One stage arrives and the stage before is gone, and never returns."

Ellen nodded. "I've thought of that."

"I got a letter this morning. San Jose State is taking me in January. They've got the best criminology department in the state."

Ellen stirred the spoon around in her dish.

Duane went on. "I'd like you to come with me. I want to marry you. In fact I love you, and I can't imagine living the rest of my life without you."

Ellen smiled and tilted her head to the side. "I don't want to get married, Duane. Not right away. Maybe not for years."

"I know this is a terrible time to propose marriage," said Duane hurriedly, "what with all the trouble—in fact, I wasn't going to say anything, but I couldn't help it. When I leave here, this phase in my life is over, and I go into a new phase, and I want you to be part of it."

Ellen rose to her feet. "Let's go home, Duane."

They walked down the street in silence. At last Duane said, "Are you telling me no?"

"I don't know what I'm trying to say. I feel all muddled. Barbara and Althea are on my mind. If they're gone, I couldn't leave Mom and Dad alone. Not just yet... And I'm not sure I ever want to marry."

"You can't stay home forever."

"I know... What I'm trying to say is this. I love Mom and Dad, and they've given me a wonderful home. Ever since Dad got out of the army he's worked for the telephone company. We've never gone hungry or lacked for anything. Every year he gets three weeks with pay and we go to Arizona or Canada or Idaho. We've always had a nice time but I don't think I want that kind of life for myself. I don't want a nice little home and two or three children and a husband with a good job and three weeks off with pay every year, and lot of fringe benefits."

"Do you want a career of your own? Is that it?"

"No, it's not even that. I just want to do something exciting. I definitely don't want to get married and live in an apartment in San Jose while you're going to school... And I am fond of you, Duane. That's the terrible thing."

"But you're afraid I'd give you a comfortable home with a lawn and a patio for Sunday barbecues, and maybe a swimming pool."

Ellen laughed. "That's exactly right."

"Suppose I go to work for Interpol or join the Peace Corps or emigrate to an Australian sheep ranch?"

"I'd be very impressed. But I couldn't marry anyone now. Not while things are in such a state at home."

"I guess I'm just a dull dog," said Duane between his teeth. "I'd make a stupid spy. I don't want to teach the Hindus how to build outhouses. I can't stand sheep. I'm worthless."

Ellen took his arm. "You're not all that bad. You're the best friend I have. And I'm very fond of you."

Duane walked her to the front door of the house. "I've got to go pick up my car," he said. "Would you like to do something tonight—a movie maybe?"

"Not tonight, Duane. I don't want to leave Mom and Dad. The poor things—they're just lost without Babs and Althea."

Duane hesitated on the porch. Then he blurted, "I'm sorry I bothered you with all my plans and proposals at a time like this."

"It doesn't make any real difference." She kissed his cheek. "After all, you're human too." She found the key, opened the door and turned to look back at Duane who stood frowning at her. "What's the matter?"

"Isn't anyone home?"

"I guess Mom's gone to the store."

"If you don't mind, I think I'll come in with you and wait until someone comes home. I don't want you running off in search of Althea and leaving a note."

"Okay. Come in. You can help me with my math."

———◆———

RONALD STOOD WITH HIS eye to the peephole. Detestable Duane and Ellen sat on the couch, Ellen with one leg tucked underneath her and a book on her lap. Ronald appraised her with the keen-eyed discrimination of an expert, trying to gauge her special characteristics. No doubt she'd be like Barbara and Althea in general, and very different in particular. Like Neapolitan ice cream: three flavors. Today his interest was purely theoretical; he was most dreadfully tired and his head and shoulder ached like sin. He hated pain more than anything; in the old days even the most trivial scrapes made him hop and palpitate, but usually his mother had been on hand to soothe him. Now the pain just wouldn't go away; any sudden motion made his head throb dreadfully.

Duane and Ellen talked in low voices: Ronald couldn't make out what they were saying. For a while he watched, then gave a sour grunt and went to lie on his cot, lowering himself with great delicacy.

Marcia Wood came home, then Ben, and Duane went away.

Ronald was in such a gruff mood that he did not even get up to see what the family ate for dinner. Their voices were quieter than usual; once Mrs. Wood said something to disturb Ellen, who spoke rather emphatically in response.

"...he did nothing of the sort!" declared Ellen. "I had a small piece and so did Duane. He doesn't like desserts all that much."

"Hmmf," said Mrs. Wood skeptically. "There wasn't much left this morning."

"Well, don't blame it on Duane. He'd be horrified if he heard what you said."

"He's not likely to hear, because I wouldn't say it to him. Anyway, I like Duane. He's a good-hearted, dependable boy, and you could do a lot worse."

"I expect I could," said Ellen. "I'm afraid that someday I might."

"I don't understand you," said Marcia.

"Today he asked me to marry him."

"My word," said Ben, "marriage at your age? You're not even out of high school."

"I told him no," said Ellen. "I'm afraid I hurt his feelings."

"The idea is ridiculous," snapped Marcia. "Duane is a nice boy, and very responsible for his age—"

"Too damn responsible," Ellen muttered.

"—but you've got college ahead of you."

Ellen changed the subject. "I suppose there's no response from the pictures?"

"Nothing the police take very seriously." Ben spoke in a forlorn voice. With a heavy heart Ellen noticed the changes which the events of the last month had worked in her father. He seemed gaunt and angular, and his skin had taken on a gray undertone. Oh why had they ever moved away from Los Gatos where life had been so easy and happy?

Ben seemed to be thinking along the same lines. "There's going to be an opening in Santa Rosa for my classification, and I'm in line for the job if I want it. We'd have to move again," he added apologetically, "which is hard on all of us."

"I'd just as soon move," said Ellen. "Whatever work we've put into this house has added to its value."

"That's for sure," said Ben, but his voice was lackluster and seemed to trail away.

Marcia clamped her jaw and her eyes glittered. "I don't particularly like Oakmead, and this house has never really been a home for us. But I hate to let it defeat us. I hate to give up and run away."

Ellen looked up in wonder. She never had suspected such complicated eddies of emotion in her nice cheerful mother. She said, "I know what you mean—at least I think I do. But is it worth the trouble?"

"I don't know," said Marcia. "But sometimes when I think of what's happened to us, for no reason at all, I just fall into a black rage." She gave a bitter laugh. "I suppose it's foolish to blame the house, but I can't help it. I do it instinctively."

Ben said uncertainly, "Well, it's something to think about anyway. Naturally we can't do much until we get our girls back, or until...well..." His voice dwindled.

"The police haven't any ideas at all?"

"Apparently not."

———————

A WEEK PASSED. THE days were too long and too lonesome; Marcia finally decided to go back to work. On Tuesday Ellen came home to a quiet house. There was a peculiar rancid odor in the air, which aroused her repugnance; she left the door open and opened the living-room windows for ventilation. She started to go into the kitchen to get herself a glass of milk and an apple when the telephone rang.

Ellen's best friend at school, Mary Maginnis, was at the other end, and the two talked half an hour. Ellen finally hung up and sat musing on the couch. She disliked being alone in the house; it seemed to creak and sigh and give off the most sinister noises. Ellen remembered how Althea had seriously postulated the existence of ghosts. Well, it just might be.

———•·•———

RONALD WATCHED THROUGH THE peephole. His aches had subsided, though for several days he had been very uncomfortable indeed. Like everyone else he found the house over-quiet with the two younger girls gone. Nonetheless he was pleased when Marcia went back to work, and left him the privacy of the house.

Ellen had now become the focus of his interest. He had always marveled at her limpid beauty. She lacked Barbara's antic exuberance and Althea's fairy-world charm, but the peculiar luminosity was hers alone. She had commended herself to him most notably by refusing to marry Duane Mathews. Ronald would have felt savagely hurt if Ellen had done otherwise. He was also rather irritated to hear the family discussing a move to Santa Rosa, to leave him behind, lonely and remote, in his lair. There was no escaping the fact that the association he had enjoyed with the Woods was coming to an end. How wonderful if by some magic he could start all over again! In a sense Barbara and Althea were to blame for the present situation; if only they had met him on his own terms, if they had loved him as fervently as he planned they should! Instead Barbara had tried to deceive him and Althea had hurt him dreadfully, and the subsequent events were nothing but simple justice... He watched Ellen carefully, recalling how Barbara not too long ago had sat telephoning on that selfsame couch, wearing far fewer clothes. He pictured Ellen in a similar costume and the image was fascinating. Ronald considered. Should he chance another foray?... While she spoke into the telephone the project was not feasible. The time was also late; in a very few minutes one or another of the parents would be returning, and Ronald needed at least half an hour, no matter how efficiently he worked.

THE NEXT DAY DUANE again met Ellen after school and took her in his car to Burnham's Creamery, the fanciest ice-cream parlor in town. Today Duane seemed lighter and easier. He had brooded long upon his relationship with Ellen and had recognized wherein lay his lack: he was insufficiently dashing and romantic. He was only good, gruff, earnest, responsible Duane, who eventually would make someone a good husband.

Ellen was thinking along similar lines. If only Duane could manage to be more impractical; if only he wanted to take her on a sailboat to Tahiti or a Landrover to India... Even then, she wasn't sure. Duane never quite thrilled her; he never aroused that delicious spark of primeval female wariness; he was too chivalrous and trustworthy. What a shame that Duane must be penalized for his virtues! And Ellen almost cruelly began to use several of Barbara's flirtatious tricks. And Duane thought that maybe the world was a good place after all.

Ellen said, "Daddy is talking about transferring to Santa Rosa, so maybe we'll be moving from Oakmead. Not right away, of course. We'd stay until we had news one way or another of Babs and Althea."

Duane gave his head a pessimistic shake. "That might be a long time."

Ellen reflected a moment. "I worry about Daddy. He looks terrible, all thin and gray, as if he were sick. He's anxious every minute and keeps it all bottled up inside himself. Mom—she's changing too—just how it's hard to explain. She said something strange the other night, that she didn't want to move and let the house defeat her."

Duane nodded his comprehension. "She hates the house."

"I do too," said Ellen, "but I want to move. You can't defeat a house. Nothing can bring back the old times."

"Remember how dreary it was when you first moved in? For a while it seemed cheerful—but now it's dreary again, in spite of the fresh paint."

"Last summer was fun, but even then we began to have strange notions. Remember how Althea would talk about ghosts and curses?"

"I remember very well. You never took her seriously."

"I do now. It's like there's something shadowy that moves out of sight just when you turn your head: a ghoul or a vampire who plays wicked tricks and steals food and leaves a horrid smell in the house when no one's there."

Duane raised his eyebrows. "Steals food, you say?"

Ellen reflected a moment. "Do you know, I never worried too much about it. I always thought that Mother was forgetful or that Daddy had a late snack, or that Barbara had fed one of her gluttonous cronies—but remember the other night when Mom brought home that coconut cream pie?"

Duane nodded.

"We all had a piece, and half a pie was left. The next morning there was only a quarter of a pie. Mom thought you'd taken it."

"What?" cried the scandalized Duane. "Me? I never did anything of the sort!"

"That's what I told her. I don't think it registered on Mom or Dad. They just brood about—you know what."

"And they still think I'm a pie-stealer."

"Oh no! It's just that when Mom misses something she thinks you've eaten it. It's not that she minds."

Duane rubbed his chin. "How long have you been missing things?"

"Let me think… Almost from the first. Mother is always declaring that she can't keep milk in the house."

"Hmm. Is anything else ever missing?"

"Nothing I know of. My perfume got spilled. And Althea's diary was broken open. Golly, Duane, maybe there really is something there!"

"Have you ever set a trap?"

Ellen shook her head. "No one ever took the matter seriously."

"Do you ever hear anything? Raps, bumps, footsteps, ghost noises?"

"Any old house makes noises. I've never heard footsteps." Ellen frowned. "Or did I? I hardly remember. Just the other day—but I'm not sure. The timbers creak. One night Mom and Dad heard a scream—in fact, they thought it was Babs."

"Indeed. Where did the scream come from?"

"I don't think they noticed. They looked in the street and checked me and Althea. It might have been a cat. But they swore it sounded like Babs."

"This was after Babs went away?"

"Yes. Two or three days, or thereabouts."

"Strange! They both heard it?"

"Both of them."

"Did they tell the police?"

Ellen shook her head. "There really wasn't anything to tell."

"Very very odd," muttered Duane. "Don't forget the paper those notes were written on."

"But Duane—what could it mean?"

"It means something pretty awful, that's my opinion. Let's try an experiment."

"What?" Ellen spoke in a hushed voice. "Oh, Duane, now I'm scared."

"For good reason. Listen now. Don't tell your parents, but tonight after they've gone to bed sprinkle the kitchen floor with talcum, or better, flour which won't leave an odor. Then tomorrow morning get up early, before your father and mother. What time would that be?"

"Seven-thirty. But tomorrow's Saturday. It might be later: eight or eight-thirty."

"Then you get up at seven. Go down to the kitchen, look around and call me right away. I'll get up at seven and sit by the phone. Okay?"

Ellen made a nervous grimace. "I'll do it. But what do you think we'll find?"

"I don't know, but if there *is* anything, we'll find it."

"Duane, I'm scared!"

"I am too. Above all, don't stay alone in the house. That's when Barbara and Althea disappeared—when they were home alone."

"Oh, Duane. It's really awful."

"Yes, indeed."

"Don't you think we should tell Daddy what we're doing?"

Duane shook his head. "I like your father, but sometimes he's a bit impractical."

"I know," said Ellen wanly. "He dithers a bit. He's not very aggressive. I'm not either. I'm a coward."

"But you'll sprinkle the flour? And call me tomorrow morning early?"

"Yes. I'll do that."

<hr>

DUANE WAS AWAKE AT six o'clock. He dressed, made coffee and toast, and went to sit by the telephone. Time dragged past, minute after sluggish minute. Duane sat looking at the telephone, ready to snatch it at the first vibration of sound.

At four minutes to seven the bell sounded. Duane put the receiver to his ear. "Hello?"

"Duane, it's me."

"What did you find?"

"Come over right away. As fast as you can."

"I'll be there in three minutes. Maybe less."

Duane halted in front of the house, switched off the engine, jumped to the ground. On the porch stood Ellen, in white pajamas and a blue bathrobe. Her face was pale, her eyes were wide and bright. She came forward to meet Duane. He joined her on the porch. "Did you find anything?"

"Yes, tracks! Big footprints!" She spoke in a whisper. "I was afraid to tell you over the phone. They lead from the pantry into the kitchen, then back to the pantry again. They don't go to any of the doors! It's eerie!"

"Did you look into the pantry?"

Ellen shook her head. "But there's nothing there—no place to hide: just pantry! How could anyone get into the kitchen without making tracks?"

"I don't know. Let's go look."

They went into the house, through the dining room to stand at the door into the kitchen. Ellen pointed and opened her mouth to speak, but Duane signaled her to silence. A white film covered the floor and the tracks were plain to see. They apparently had been made by large feet in slippers or scuffs, and led from the pantry to the refrigerator, where they made an incomprehensible clutter, then returned into the pantry.

"Make some coffee," said Duane in a matter-of-fact voice. But he made another sign for silence and indicated the floor. Then he fetched a broom from the back porch and swept the kitchen floor.

Ellen made coffee. She asked in a tentative voice, "Are you hungry? Should I scramble some eggs?"

"No thanks," said Duane. He stood contemplating the dining-room wall and its built-in sideboard. Then he went to the front hall and studied the wall opposite the front door.

Ellen brought him a cup of coffee. "What are you looking at?"

Duane made another gesture signifying caution. In a carefully casual voice he said, "You run up and get dressed. I'll wait for you in the car. If your parents are awake, if they want to know why I'm here, tell them—well, tell them that you invited me over for breakfast. But come out to the car as soon as you can."

Ellen nodded acquiescence. Duane thought that she had never looked so beautiful: pale and big-eyed in her blue bathrobe. He pulled her close and kissed her. "Duane, not now," said Ellen breathlessly, and ran upstairs. But as she dressed she still tingled; for almost the first time she had responded to Duane. Grim and practical Duane might be, but he was a man, and when he had kissed her he felt hard and aggressive, by no means a dull dog... She paused to listen at the door to her parents' bedroom but they were not yet astir. Ellen ran back downstairs and out to where Duane stood leaning against his car. A change had come over him; he projected purpose, a peculiar sardonic exultation; it was as if she were meeting a new person.

Duane said, "I know what's been happening." He glanced toward the house, his green eyes gleaming, then looked back to Ellen. "Do you know?"

"Well—yes. I think I do. There must be a trapdoor in the pantry, and somebody uses it to get into our house."

Duane shook his head. "It's better than that—or worse, I should say. What's on the other side of the pantry?"

Ellen frowned. "The outside porch."

"I mean on the other side."

"The living room? The stairs?"

"The stairs, and the space under the stairs."

Ellen blinked and considered. "It's all closed off," she said dubiously.

Duane nodded. "But there's somebody in there, living at the center of the house, like a worm in an apple. And I know who it is."

"Who?" asked Ellen in a faint sick voice.

"Ronald Wilby. Who else? After he murdered Carol he disappeared into thin air. The police never found hide nor hair of him. For a good reason. His mother boxed him in. There must have been a space under the stairs, a closet."

"Or a bathroom."

"Of course! The downstairs bathroom! That's where Ronald's been hiding all this time. And somehow he's able to crawl out into the pantry."

Ellen looked with horrified eyes at the house. Emotion blurred her vision; the house shimmered and pulsed like a stranded jellyfish. "How awful... But it's true, I know it's true! And Babs, and Althea... Oh my God, Duane, how utterly awful. What's happened to them?"

Duane took Ellen by the shoulders. "There's not very much doubt about what's happened to them."

"They're dead... Oh Duane." Her legs felt weak; she crumpled sobbing against Duane's chest. "My poor little sisters."

Mrs. Schumacher, coming forth to get an early start on the sprinkling, glanced at them in sniff-nosed disapproval and pointedly looked the other way. Duane and Ellen ignored her.

Ellen became quiet. After a moment she said, "How can we tell my father and mother? They're still hoping that the girls ran away to Berkeley."

"I guess we just plain tell them. There's no other way... I'd almost rather handle the situation myself."

Ellen drew back a little. "What do you mean, Duane?"

"I mean the police will come and take Ronald away and put him in a nice comfortable institution. In three or four years they'll decide he's as good as new and turn him loose." Duane stared glitter-eyed toward the house. "Myself, I'd like to kill him."

Ellen was awed by the ferocity in Duane's voice. She shuddered. "I couldn't bear to touch him, or even look at him."

"You were probably next on the list."

"Oh Duane." Ellen's breath came shallow and fast as her diaphragm jerked. "I'd go into convulsions..."

"All this time," Duane muttered. "Right under our noses."

They considered the house. Ellen asked in a hushed voice, "Do you think there's any chance that either Babs or Althea is still alive?"

"It seems awful damn remote. There's something I'd better do. You go into the house, cook breakfast, wash some dishes, just keep busy in the kitchen. And turn on the radio in there."

"And what are you going to do?"

"First I'm going to look under the house. Then I want to make sure he can't get away."

"Duane, be careful! He might harm you!"

"There's not much chance of that. In fact, none at all."

Ellen looked dubiously toward the house. "I feel all quivery inside."

"Just act natural. Don't pay any attention to the secret room. If your folks come down try to be casual."

"All right, Duane, I'll try... And please be careful, because I love you too."

Ellen went into the house. Duane took a flashlight from the glove compartment of his car and walked around to the back of the house. From inside came the thump of a cowboy band; Ellen had turned on the kitchen radio.

Duane went to the lattice-work door which opened upon the space under the house. He pulled it gingerly open and dropped to his knees. The opening exhaled a dank sour reek. Duane's nostrils twitched. He shone the flashlight here and there, but with daylight at his back the moth-pale flicker revealed nothing.

Duane drew a deep breath and crawled forward into the dark.

After ten feet he halted and again shone the flashlight around. Details of the substructure were now visible. Duane calculated that he was under the kitchen. To his right a line of piers held up a central girder which supported the floor joists. A foot over his head glinted copper water pipes and a three-inch cast-iron soil pipe. Duane traced the course of the soil pipe. Immediately beside the central girder it joined the main four-inch line from the second floor. Duane crawled to this junction and saw another three-inch soil pipe, coming down from the floor about four feet from the junction. Ronald's hiding place was for a fact the downstairs bathroom. If Ben Wood had ever entered the crawl-space, he had not been curious about his plumbing.

Duane shone the flashlight up at the floor and immediately noticed the trapdoor. He nodded somberly: about as he expected.

His eyes had adapted to the darkness. He crawled to the line of piers and shone his light around the far half of the area. Against the far wall ranged a row of brown paper sacks. One had fallen over, to spill a half-dozen tin cans carefully crushed flat. Here was Ronald's garbage dump, from which issued a stale sour-sweet odor. Duane played the light over the surface of the ground, foot by foot. There: an oblong area with a texture different to that of the surrounding soil, and not too far away another such rectangle of disturbed soil. Duane backed away. Then he halted and stared at the two areas. Someone had to find out. He crawled across the ground and with one of the flattened tin cans scraped into the loose dirt. No need to dig far. Six inches under the surface the tin can encountered something softly solid. Duane turned the flashlight down, though a waft of odor made visual inspection unnecessary. Duane nevertheless made sure.

He refilled the hole he had dug and checked the other oblong area with similar results. With stomach twitching and heart pounding, Duane covered the second hole and returned to the entrance.

He walked around the house. The lattice-work door was the single opening into the crawl-space.

At the back of the lot he found a short two-by-four, which he wedged between the edge of the concrete walk and the lattice door. Ronald's escape route was now blocked off.

Duane replaced the flashlight in his car, and went slowly back to the house. Ellen stood in the doorway. She looked at him questioningly. Duane nodded. "They're down there. Both dead, both buried."

Ellen sighed, and swallowed hard. Nothing now could shock her. Barbara and Althea. Her eyes grew dim. She felt Duane's arms around her and his voice in her ear. "I've got him locked in. He had a trapdoor into the crawl-space."

Ellen sat down on the steps. Duane sat down beside her. "My darling sisters," whispered Ellen. "I loved them so. They're gone, and I'll never see them again."

Duane put his arm around her and they sat quietly for a period. Down the stairs came Marcia Wood, followed by Ben Wood, more gray and haggard than ever.

Duane and Ellen rose to their feet. Duane went to the doorway. "Good morning."

"Good morning, Duane," said Ben Wood.

Marcia stood stiffly, looking back and forth between Duane and Ellen. "What's wrong?"

Duane said, "I wonder if you and Mr. Wood would step out here for a minute."

Ben and Marcia came slowly out on the porch. "You've had news?"

Duane nodded somberly. "Not good news."

"Oh," cried Marcia in a soft melodious voice. Ben's color became even more leaden. "Go on."

"There's no use trying to soften things," Duane muttered. "I can't make facts any better by talking around the subject. You've got to prepare yourselves for a shock."

"Go on," said Ben Wood hollowly.

"Barbara and Althea are dead. Ronald Wilby killed them."

"How do you know?" asked Marcia. Her voice had taken on a harsh, keening overtone.

"Yesterday Ellen told me about the food you've been missing. I told her to sprinkle flour on the kitchen floor. This morning we found tracks."

"Go on."

Duane paused a moment. "You know what Ronald Wilby did to my sister. Afterwards he disappeared. You know that too. Well, his mother hid him in what was then the downstairs bathroom, and he's been there ever since."

"There is no downstairs bathroom!" declared Marcia, her voice metallic.

"It's in the space under the stairs. The tracks we found led into the pantry, and nowhere else. I looked, and I could see where he'd got a way in and out under the bottom shelf."

Ben shook his head in awe. He said huskily, "This is absolutely incredible."

Marcia looked toward the house. "How do you know my girls are dead?"

"I looked under the house." Duane licked his lips. "I found Ronald's trapdoor and I found two graves. That's where they are."

Ben was like a statue carved of oak. Marcia breathed hard through her nose.

Ben finally stirred. "Can he get away?"

"Not by his trapdoor. I've wedged the outside door shut."

"Very well then," said Ben. "We'll go on in the house. I want to look the situation over. Then I'll call the police. You're sure of all this?"

"Yes, Mr. Wood. Absolutely sure."

Marcia spoke to Duane. "You saw the graves?"

"Yes."

"You're certain the girls are there?"

"I'm certain. I dug down until I found them."

Ben lurched droop-shouldered toward the house. Marcia followed, walking like a somnambulist. Ben halted in the front hall and stood staring at the wall. Marcia went through the dining room, into the kitchen and out upon the back porch.

Ben turned to Ellen and Duane. "It's beyond belief," he muttered. "All this time…"

Duane signaled him to caution. Ben sighed and nodded. "Ellen, get that number for me."

On the back porch Marcia poured a gallon of white gasoline into a basin. She carried it into the pantry and set it on a shelf, then went back into the kitchen for a paper towel, which she brought into the pantry. She dipped it into the gasoline and set it aside. Then she kicked at the secret door—once, twice, three times. The latch broke, the door burst inward. Marcia flung the gasoline through the opening. She struck a match, lit the gasoline-drenched paper towel and tossed it through: into the secret lair, into the land of Atranta, and all that

556

magic world, with all its brave castles and evil dukes, its glorious map, and immemorial legends, became a seethe of flame. From within came a fearful scream. The sound startled Ben and Duane and Ellen, already dialing the telephone. Marcia stood in the kitchen, her face stern and calm. In the front hall the wall burst asunder; Ronald stood in the opening, blazing like a fire-demon. The three caught an instant impression of a burly figure dressed in tatters, hair and beard burning and smoking; then Ronald sprang through the front door, out into the open air. He lumbered down the steps, ran back and forth across the yard, flapping his arms, performing the most grotesque capers imaginable. He hurled himself to the ground, pounded at the flames, rolled over and over, bawling and yelling. On the porch stood Marcia and Ben: Marcia impassive, Ben slack-mouthed in wonder at this miraculous creature they had exorcised from their house. Ellen went to the telephone and called the fire department.

Ronald bounded across to the Schumacher's lawn and wallowed in the sprinkler, exuding a rancid steam. Then, as if struck by a sudden thought, he jumped to his feet and started to run. Duane tackled him and threw him to the lawn, then kicked him in the belly and cursed him. Ronald grabbed the hose and swung the sprinkler at Duane like a bolo and knocked him backwards into the Schumacher's privet hedge; then he ran off down Orchard Street and into Honeysuckle Lane.

Sirens howled; a police car appeared, followed by a fire engine. Duane halted the police car, pointed down Honeysuckle Lane, where Ronald could be seen tumbling over the fence into the grounds of the Hastings estate.

The police invaded the dank old garden, probed the thickets, searched the sheds and carriage house, scanned the upper branches of the oaks, cypresses, weeping willows, elms, cedars, and Monterey pines, but Ronald was nowhere to be found.

Five more men, the entire staff of the Oakmead Police Department, arrived to facilitate the search. Inquiries were made at neighborhood houses; pedestrians and passersby were questioned. Among the latter was Laurel Hansen, out walking Ignatz, her new poodle puppy. Laurel hastened home and communicated the news to her mother, just returning from the grocery store.

"That's just around the corner!" cried Mrs. Hansen, peering up and down the street. Hurriedly she loaded Laurel with groceries, took the remaining two bags, kicked at Ignatz who persisted in running underfoot, and trotted into the house. "Lock the patio door and the kitchen door too!" she told Laurel. "Check the windows! We're not stirring out of this house until your father gets home."

Laurel obeyed, then rejoined her mother in the kitchen. Mrs. Hansen was at the telephone, insisting that her husband come home "...actually right here in the neighborhood! Yes, Ronald Wilby!... Naturally I've locked the doors... No, Ralph, I want you to come home. Laurel and I are here alone... What could he do? He could break in and murder us both! That's what he could do!... I think that's absolutely beastly of you!... Not as soon as you can. I want you home now!... I'm absolutely serious, Ralph!... Very well then." Mrs. Hansen, jerking with agitation and biting her lips, went to look out the kitchen window. Usually so petite and poised and cool, Mrs. Hansen, in her fright and fury, seemed to give off an acrid blue fume, as of scorching metal.

Laurel asked diffidently, "Is Daddy coming home?"

"In his own good time. He's so damned inconsiderate. Like all men. It would serve him right if we went over to Edith's and left him to stew... Get his own damned dinner... Do something with your dog, he's crying to go outside."

Laurel asked doubtfully, "Do you think I'd better? I'd have to unlock the door."

"Well, make him stop his whimpering, or whatever he's doing."

"Here, Ignatz! Ignatz! Come in here now and behave yourself. No widdling on the rug!"

Mrs. Hansen muttered, "I still don't understand it. The Wilby boy came back to town? Or what?"

"They said something about him hiding somewhere, and that he was loose."

Mrs. Hansen shook her head. "And the very day he killed that little girl he was here, in this house... It's unbelievable."

Laurel excused herself to go to the bathroom. Mrs. Hansen telephoned her sister Edith and reported the sensational events of the day, "Yes, just down the street!... That little alley that runs

behind the Hastings place. He escaped from wherever he was and…
No, Laurel didn't actually see him, but it must have been touch
and go. Naturally that damned Ralph just pooh-poohs. He told
me to lock the doors and take a tranquilizer. One of these days…
Laurel! Excuse me, Edith, that damned dog is whimpering. I guess
he wants to go outside. Hold the line. Ignatz! Ignatz!" Mrs. Hansen
put down the receiver, looked into the living room. She listened,
and traced the sound down the hall to Laurel's room. Now why, she
wondered, would Laurel lock the dog in her room?

She went into Laurel's bedroom, looked on both sides of the
bed. The dog was in the wardrobe; she could hear it crying. Now
why in the world would Laurel do something like that? She slid
open the door and there stood Ronald, reeking of smoke and burnt
flesh and sobbing with pain.

Mrs. Hansen stood frozen. Hissing and groaning, Ronald said,
"Just a minute. It's all right, really… I just happened to walk in… I
don't feel very well…"

On limp legs Mrs. Hansen retreated, her voice no more than a
gargle. She turned and fled down the hall. Ronald blundered after
her. "Wait!" he croaked. "Just a minute! Do you have some salve, or
some aspirin?"

Mrs. Hansen threw open the front door, ran into the street.
Laurel came out of the bathroom. "Hello, Laurel," said Ronald.

"Ronald Wilby," breathed Laurel.

Out in the street Mrs. Hansen babbled frantically to Ralph
Hansen, who had decided to come home.

Ronald thought it best to leave. He lurched across the living
room toward the patio. Ralph Hansen gave chase. The lock baffled
Ronald; he hurled himself through the glass door. Ralph Hansen
roared in outrage. He caught Ronald beside the swimming pool and
punched him on the side of the head. Ronald toppled into the water.
Moaning and crying, he clung to the coping, for the second time in
his life an uninvited guest at the Hansen swimming pool, and here
he remained until the police dragged him out and took him away.

Chapter XVIII

THE house at 572 Orchard Street stood vacant. On the unkempt front lawn a sign read:

FOR SALE
Oakmead Realty Co.
890 Valley Boulevard
Calvin Roscoe Bill Winger
Telephone: 477-5102

Winter rains washed over the house. A few days of early spring sunlight started weeds in the yard. From time to time Mr. Roscoe brought over prospects: young people, old people, couples with children, couples without, and at last one day Mr. Roscoe tacked a 'SOLD' placard over the sign.

A week later the new owners arrived and a van followed close after with their possessions. By sheerest coincidence Duane and Ellen happened to drive past. They halted to watch the new occupants move in: a husband, a wife and three children, two girls and a boy.

"The house looks different," said Duane. "With every new owner the house changes."

Ellen shook her head. "The house is the same. We've changed."

"There's a fine new downstairs bathroom," said Duane. "Of course it doesn't show from the street."

"I almost feel that I should warn them," said Ellen in a low voice.

Duane gave a humorless chuckle. "Warn them of what?"

"I don't know. I suppose it's a silly notion. Let's go on, Duane."

"The kids wonder why we're watching." Duane put his head out the window. "How do you like your new house?"

"Fine," said the oldest girl.

"Our school is only six blocks away," said the second girl. "We won't have to ride the bus."

"We've all got rooms to ourself!" declared the boy. "And we're going to build a big sun porch on the front so we can have porch swings, and maybe there'll be a second-floor balcony on top!"

"We're going to paint the outside green," said the oldest girl. "To match the eucalyptus."

"That sounds pretty," said Ellen. "Maybe we'll come by again when it's finished."

"You can come in and look around," said the second girl. "It's real pretty inside."

"No thanks," said Duane. "We've got to be going. Goodbye."

"Goodbye," said Ellen.

"Goodbye." "Goodbye." "Goodbye."